Praise for *The Unincorporated War*

"A solid, old-fashioned, solar system space opera . . . We've got battles in space, we've got treachery and plots and love affairs and all sorts of action."
—*Alameda Times-Star* (California)

"Fast-paced military science fiction . . . action-packed throughout . . . a top-rate outer-space thriller."
—*The Midwest Book Review*

"The Kollins' masterful command of multiple plot threads, characters, and the motifs of grand-scale space opera make for a breathtaking sequel." —*Booklist*

Praise for *The Unincorporated Man*

"Will appeal to Heinlein's legions of fans with its themes of personal liberty and one man's political struggle with the State . . . The Kollin brothers carefully and intriguingly explore what it would mean to live in a world of human corporations. . . . *The Unincorprated Man* will tantalize you with its intriguing premise."
—*i09.com*

"Fans of SF as a vehicle for ideas will devour this intriguing debut. . . . The Kollin brothers keep the plot moving briskly despite the high proportion of talk to action. Their cerebral style will especially appeal to readers nostalgic for science fiction's early years."
—*Publishers Weekly*

"This is a bright, stimulating work that deserves a wide readership."
—Gregory Benford, coauthor of
Beyond Human: Living with Robots and Cyborgs

Tor Books by Dani Kollin and Eytan Kollin

The Unincorporated Man

The Unincorporated War

the unincorporated WAR

Dani Kollin and Eytan Kollin

A Tom Doherty Associates Book
New York

THE UNINCORPORATED WAR

Copyright © 2010 by Dani Kollin and Eytan Kollin

A Tor Book
Published by Tom Doherty Associates, LLC
175 Fifth Avenue
New York, NY 10010

www.tor-forge.com

Tor® is a registered trademark of Tom Doherty Associates, LLC.

The Library of Congress has catalogued the hardcover edition as follows:

Kollin, Dani.
    The unincorporated war / Dani Kollin and Eytan Kollin.—1st ed.
        p. cm.
    "A Tom Doherty Associates book."
    ISBN 978-0-7653-1900-5
    1. Space warfare—Fiction. 2. Corporations—Fiction. I. Kollin, Eytan. II. Title.
    PS3611.O58265 U557 2010
    813'.6—dc22

                                                                    2010018647

ISBN 978-0-7653-3110-6 (trade paperback)

First Edition: May 2010
First Trade Paperback Edition: May 2011

Printed in the United States of America

0 9 8 7 6 5 4 3 2 1

Acknowledgments

Believing in yourself can get you only so far. It's others believing in you that truly makes the difference.

Ours:

Imma—For first giving us life and then for teaching us how to embrace it.

Abba—For teaching us to question everything.

Howard Deutsch—For the unenviable job of filtering us and, by extension, ensuring we live to write another day.

David G. Hartwell—For your stewardship, patience, and insight . . . and patience.

Stacy Hague-Hill—For the skill with which you've kept us on track, not to mention the unforgettable adventures in dining.

Patty Garcia—For working so hard on getting us out there.

Amber Hopkins—For helping to keep us there.

Edwin Rivera—For giving us a chance.

Robert Sawyer—For all the advice, insight, and support.

Alec Schram—For ensuring that our science is sound, and saving Ceres from near-certain catastrophe (nano-carbon Bucky scaffolding?—you genius, you!).

Richard Mueller of 3232design.com—For allowing us to use a majority of his talent for a minority share of our future earnings.

Larry Carlin—For making this book better.

Facebook, LiveJournal, and Twitter readers—For keeping us going through the ups and downs, wild road trips, and never-ending search for the next NBG!

Dani's:

Deborah—For eighteen years of holding hands, sharing dreams, and being my song of songs.

Eliana, Yonatan, and Gavriel—For always keeping me on my toes.

Carrie Bleiweiss—For ultimate dooberatiousness, apricot leaves, and so many wonderfully lost hours.

Insomniyakkers, Wolverines, and the Magnificent Seven—For helping me to set the bar on words and ideas hopefully equal to your intelligence, wit, and curiosity.

Eytan's:

Doctor Miles Morgan—An ardent believer in socialism, he taught me what it means to be a true gentleman by giving me the books of Rand, Hayek, and Friedman. "If you're going to be a capitalist, you may as well be an informed capitalist." You did not have to give me the tools to defend my beliefs. You chose to, (freely).

Dalia Taft—For the gift of reading, which no other person in the world seemed to be able to teach me, and for having the patience to deal with a younger brother who has all the grace, social skill, and subtlety of a gorilla falling from orbit.

 PART ONE

1 Calm Before the Storm

Justin Cord drifted on his back, arms clasped loosely behind his head, admiring the delicate mist moving slowly above. It was through these thin wisps of vapor and the eerily warm water flowing quietly beneath him that he would, on that rare occasion, find solace in a lake so big he would have called it a sea. He'd long gotten used to the fact that the horizon line curved upwards instead of down and that instead of a clear blue sky his vista was that of a magnificent mountain range above.

The inverse horizon was just one of the many oddities he'd had to struggle with by virtue of his forced exile to the belt. He couldn't help it. When he thought "asteroid," "small" came to mind. After all, Ceres was only a quarter the size of Earth's Moon. What he failed to realize was just how huge the Moon actually was. Of course Ceres had changed quite a bit as a result of the planetoid's first meddlesome settlers. Its orbit had been altered to match that of Mars in order to bring it into the elliptic plane along with all the other major bodies in the solar system. On top of that, the Cerians had dug down deep and were still digging. They'd hollowed out a two-mile-wide cylindrical hole through the center and then gave the rock spin for gravity. The early inhabitants had also taken abundant advantage of the fact that their home had miles of frozen water spread evenly beneath its surface. In fact, it had more H_2O than all the freshwater on Earth. This meant that Ceres had lakes, lots of them, with some as big as seas.

And so drifting aimlessly a hundred meters from shore, staring down into the planet, Justin Cord could almost forget that there was a ceiling "behind" him holding in the massive body of water and that the power of centrifugal force ensured that it stayed that way.

For most born in the belt and accustomed to subterranean life, the idea of a sky was unnerving to say the least. Justin had heard stories of some belt-born with agoraphobia so severe that they wouldn't dare venture outside on Earth unless they were safely confined within the sterile-aired, cumbersome embrace of a space suit. Since he'd never seen such a thing, he chalked it up to talk. Still, after being on Ceres for a little over a year he could certainly relate. In space you weren't safe until you had a secure roof over your head, and even then you'd always check for leaks. For an off-worlder visiting Earth for the first time, the whole damned planet leaked.

With the new President of the Outer Alliance, the feeling was just the opposite. Try as he might, Justin couldn't help but feel closed in. He hid it as best he could and took long walks in the great city parks where the "roof" was far enough overhead that he wouldn't notice the absent sky. Time permitting, he'd sometimes wander into the forest where the trees were so tall and crowns so thick that he could imagine he was in a forest somewhere on Earth. But the thing Justin best loved to do was swim. He could forget where he was, forget all his problems as well as everyone else's. Arm over arm, head back, Justin would sometimes think that if there were a heaven it had to be an endless ocean he could spend eternity swimming in.

But as usual, heaven would have to wait. Justin could make out the all-too-familiar hum of a hover disk approaching in the distance. It was a sound that elicited an almost Pavlovian response. The President sighed, continued his poor backstroke, and waited patiently to open his eyes until the craft was practically on top of him. It had gotten to the point that he no longer bothered to swim back to shore. He knew something would always happen that would necessitate a disk being sent out to get him. One day, he decided, there would be no emergency at all, no crisis, no feathers to be unruffled, and on that day he would probably drown. But that day was not today. After another hundred yards of backstroking to put off the inevitable, he gave up, stopped, and opened his eyes.

Omad was smiling down on him.

"You know I wouldn't have come out if—"

"Yeah, yeah, yeah. Let me guess," said Justin. "They found a monolith floating around Jupiter. Alien contact perhaps, no, maybe Mars revolted and joined the Outer Alliance."

"No monoliths," answered Omad, "not for lack of looking, mind you, but none yet. And any aliens smart enough to get into this neck of the galaxy would probably be smart enough to get out. And if Mars decided to join us," Omad said, looking out into the distance, "it wouldn't make sense to call us the Outer Alliance then, would it?" He then looked back down to Justin. "We would just be the Alliance, don't you think? Mars is a core world after all."

"Not in my day."

"You're a really old fart, Justin. *Nothing* is from your day."

Justin laughed. "OK, Omad," said the President, noticing his friend's pained expression. "What is it this time?"

"It's Eris, friend. Everyone's waiting back at Cliff House."

Justin was suddenly tired in a way that had nothing to do with the miles he'd just logged in swimming.

"Crap."

Omad nodded sympathetically and then extended his hand, first making sure to get a good grip on the strap in the center of the disk. The machine tilted slightly as Justin got on, but no more than three or four degrees. Omad tossed his friend a towel and without another word sped off toward the shore, where the world Justin had only recently created sat waiting.

"OK, listeners, this is The Clara Roberts Show *coming to you live from Ceres for the first day of the provisional congress. By mutual agreement, no press or recording devices are allowed into the actual hall, but the delegates are always coming and going. Why, here's Tyler Sadma of the Eris Colony about to enter the hall. Let me see if I can just ask him to talk to us. . . . Mr. Sadma . . . Mr. Sadma! A few words for the . . . Mr. Sadma . . ."*

"No comment."

"I am sorry, loyal listeners, but he pushed right past me. Seems his reputation is well deserved. Wait a minute . . . here comes Karen Cho of the Titan Colony. Miss Cho!"

"Hello, Clara, love your show. We listen to it on Saturn all the time."

"Thanks for the plug."

"Well sure, you guys always have a good slant about news from the corporate core. Lots of facts without all the Terran propaganda."

"We try to keep the truth broadcasting for all to hear. You could help my listeners by telling me what's going on behind the closed doors of power."

"Clara, before we could have that power we'd all have to agree."

"Agree on what?"

"Anything; I'm not sure we can even order lunch as a congress without calling a committee of the whole, and by the time we do agree it would be time for breakfast!"

"And I thought my job was tough! Miss Cho, got time for another question?"

"Sure."

"Any chance the First Free will show up on opening day?"

"He says he doesn't want to interfere with the formation of the legislative branch until we're all settled in and invite him. And surely, Miss Roberts, you know the provisional President does not encourage the use of that nickname."

"It's what all my listeners call him. Who am I to argue?"

"Well, just don't say it to his face. I heard a Plutonian tried that once and got stink eyed out of the reception."

"Thanks for the advice. So beware, listeners; the President does not

*like the distinction of being called the First Free. Apparently he feels it's
not appropriate for a leader of free people. So no one say it in his company! Wait till he's not around. Thank you for your time, Miss Cho. If
it's true you're being appointed the governor of the colonies of Saturn,
good luck with it."*

"One job at a time, Miss Roberts, and keep up the good work."

*"Will do. This is Clara Roberts outside the newly completed con-
gressional hall. We'll be back after this message from the Gedretar ship
works. Remember, if you can't get a new booster from the corporate
enslavers of the core planets, have yours refurbished—good as new—at
Gedretar."*

—From The Clara Roberts Show
AIR (Asteroid belt Information Radio) Network

Justin stood on a high terrace overlooking Smith Thoroughfare, one of three
large, cavernous arteries carved deep into Ceres. Each one of the thoroughfares
was a lifeblood of commerce and activity within the planetoid. Traffic, Justin
could see, was unusually brisk. The first meeting of the Provisional Congress had
brought the usual slew of bureaucrats, press, and hangers-on. Added to that
were cadres of tourists who wanted to be a part of history. The streets were
packed and the air above them was no different. All manner of hovercraft,
drone, and person could be seen zipping to and fro. Justin's balcony was officially in a no-fly zone, but that never seemed to stop the more tenacious of media outlets.

The overhang he currently found himself standing on was attached to a living
complex that was, like almost every other abode on the planetoid, dug deep into
the rock. The apartment had three floors and forty rooms in its current configuration. Justin had initially rejected the place, feeling it was entirely too large and
pretentious. But when he was made to realize just how disparate in both ideology and function the various belt bodies he was meant to lead were, he'd acceded and moved in. The move proved prescient in that he'd already had to add
onto both sides of the ever-growing presidential suite now being called by most,
the Cliff House.

Ultimately it had been the terrace that had become Justin's favorite "room"
for the simple reason that it was the least closed-in space in the entire complex.
Though he'd never admit that simple fact to anyone, anyone at all, because it be-
lied a greater feeling that he saw as a failing in the man who was the provisional
President of the Outer Alliance. Only his long swims in the great lakes of Ceres
might have given anyone the slightest clue as to their President's true feelings—
Justin was sick of space.

He'd last left Earth in a hurry, anxious to reunite with the woman he thought he'd lost forever, Dr. Neela Harper. Had he known then, before his ill-fated encounter with the now-deceased Chairman, that that meeting would take up his last precious few hours on Earth he might have done things differently. He might have looked up to the sky one last time, taken in the splendor of Victoria Falls, or plunged himself into the cold, salty embrace of the Atlantic. But instead he'd left that fateful meeting and immediately rocketed off into space at almost inhuman speeds without ever looking back.

And now, in almost Sisyphean fashion, he was being forced to repeat that one impulsive act in a dizzying array of takeoffs from one asteroid to another throughout the O.A. Each and every trip, much like that first one, had been spent pinned to an acceleration couch in order to take advantage of maximum g-force. All the trips had one purpose in mind—to solidify support for the O.A. If they could have figured out a way to get him to the outer planets—on the other side of the belt—and back in less than four months he would have gone there as well. But the only planet close enough to get to, given the size of the solar system and the limits of human propulsion, was Jupiter. However, if he visited one planetary system the others would have been insulted. Expecting Justin to visit absolutely every one made no sense given the laws of physics, but it made perfect sense given the laws of politics.

Although the fledgling President's domain contained only a tenth of the human race, it stretched from the asteroid belt to the Oort Cloud. And that tenth contained a little under four billion people, with about two billion in the asteroid belt itself. It was a surprisingly rural population. The largest settlement was in Ceres, with over forty million souls. That was followed by Eris, with thirty-five million, and Titan with a little over thirty. Justin would have expected these settlements, cities in his mind, to have much larger populations. After all, Ceres had the land area of Pennsylvania to work with once the tunnels had been dug. It could have easily held another one hundred million people. But, he'd learned, people in the belt usually wanted to stretch out and get their own asteroids to mine. Once away from the regimentation of corporate life they were not eager to re-create it. This attracted more settlers and miners of similar bent, and over the centuries all sorts of communities found rocks, hollowed them out, paid for the orbital slots, and lived life on the edge. Over time what had emerged was a powerfully independent and resourceful humanity but, as Justin was now discovering, a tiresome one to weld together into a cohesive political unit. "Like herding cats," he'd often told his sympathetic wife.

On a positive note—for Justin at least—everyone had agreed to the basic principles of the first new experiment in governance in over three centuries: unity, of a sort, with political and economic liberty, which meant vastly different things to different people, and a government strong enough to protect the Outer Alliance yet not so strong as to imperil those very liberties that it was supposed to protect. Previous to this newly formed government the territories that would make up the O.A. had been operating pretty much on their own, because the central government operating from the corporate core had no real means to enforce its rule. This had certainly been good for the colonists' self-sufficiency but lousy for unity. It took the corporate core government's expedited Psyche Audit Act to truly bring the O.A. together. Up until that moment psyche audits had only been used to repair damaged minds—deviants, perverts, and pedophiles. But the old government's new and desperate act had not only widened the criteria to include rebellious or disgruntled colonists but also nearly eliminated due process. What once could be dragged on for months with appeals and counterappeals now took mere hours. And it had been from that rash move that the fires of revolution had been fanned and from which Justin Cord had found himself a new job.

So now there was a new government with Justin at its head but no real means to enforce its rule. Sure, there were committees aplenty, but nothing ever came out of them except for the occasional sound bite. Justin's new government did not have vast fleets of warships or impressively armed legions ready to go forth and do battle or, more important, maintain order. Alternatively the Terran government and its chief supporter, the corporations, had spent the last year clamping down with vicious abandon on the inner systems. They'd achieved control to a degree Justin secretly envied. They'd corralled, locked up, and stifled their malcontents; Justin had an entire asteroid belt of malcontents. While he harbored no desire to treat his troublemakers in the same manner, he often wished he could throttle a few just to get them to see eye to eye on an issue—any issue.

There was, however, one great advantage to the surliness of his flock. The skills needed to be an expert miner were remarkably similar to those needed to be a first-rate soldier—expert handling of dangerous nanites and explosives, ingenuity, self-reliance, and finally determination; all taught and tested within the cold confines of space. The O.A. also had hundreds of thousands of spaceships built up over centuries of colonization. Not a one could really be used in combat; but at least, realized Justin, getting experienced pilots was not going to be a problem. Building the warships, however, would be. Ceres was starting the process of making space docks, but it would be years before they could hope to replicate the facilities in orbit around Earth. The truth of the matter was that the manufacturing facilities on Luna were far greater than all those of the O.A. combined.

A wistful chime reminded Justin that his cabinet meeting was about to begin. He turned around and there to greet him was his Chief of Staff, Cyrus Anjou, standing next to Omad. Cyrus was a Jovian who, mused the President, was actually quite jovial. The Chief of Staff's roots were almost as critical as his political ability. While Jupiter itself proved uninhabitable, its many moons—seventy in all, including the seven man-made—were rich in mineral deposits, usable gasses, and water. Cyrus hailed from one such moon and Mosh had vouched for him from the days when Cyrus was director of GCI's Jovian mining operations and Mosh was his boss. Unlike most corporate climbers, Cyrus took his majority and stayed near his native Io rather than follow the ladder back to Earth where the real power lay. But that merely helped hide the uncanny political instincts the man had. The moons of Jupiter were made up of a large and powerful constituency and there was no better person to see to its needs than the current Chief of Staff. Justin never made it a policy to ask why Mosh vouched for anyone; he just accepted it gratefully and moved on to the next task. And there was always a next task.

"Mr. President," Cyrus said, bowing accordingly, "I'm glad this miserable excuse for a human being found you."

"Don't listen to the Jovian," Omad shot back. "It's that big red eye talking. They stare at it long enough and eventually go loopy." He then looked over to Cyrus. "Case in point."

"That big red eye, Mr. President, as you may well know, is a storm that's been raging on Jupiter for well over one thousand years and, I would argue, is only slightly less volatile than my good friend Mr. Hassan."

"Eye sore," snapped Omad.

"Tall words for a pebble dweller."

The last insult was meant to demonstrate the Jovian disdain for belt dwellers whose planetoids were but a fraction the size of any one of Jupiter's larger moons. Omad wasn't deterred and Justin tuned out the banter, realizing that the worse the insults got, the more solidified the relationship became. He only stopped it once it got to the breeding habits of their respective grandmothers. The ceasefire lasted long enough for him to hear Neela enter the room from an adjoining hall. He turned around and greeted her with a smile.

"Is the *First Free* ready?" she asked.

Justin winced at his wife's use of the phrase but knew he was powerless to stop it. Neela was the one exception to many of his rules. He'd only wished she would use that particular designation more judiciously.

"He is, of course, always ready to see you, most dear and delightful lady," answered the Chief of Staff, again bowing politely. Cyrus, noticed Justin, had the knack of making the most effusive language seem natural.

Neela smiled at the compliment. "The others are waiting in the dining room and after this meeting we're going to the fleet officers ball. We have the first dance."

"Gentlemen, that is my dear wife's way of saying that I can't be late."

"Indeed," confirmed Cyrus. "We should start."

Neela smiled in agreement and unconsciously smoothed a line in Justin's jacket, though no such line was obvious to anyone in attendance.

The four made their way to the adjoining room, where they were greeted by the newly acting cabinet. Justin took his place at the head of the table with Cyrus sitting to his right. Neela, overly conscious of her special relationship to the President, preferred to sit opposite him. Omad sat near his old friend on the left and Mosh to the right of Omad. Eleanor's seat was left empty as she, Mosh informed the group, was currently volunteering with a paramedic unit of the Cerian fleet militia. Kirk Olmstead, the acting head of Special Ops, was also in attendance and as usual sat where he pleased, not caring if he ruffled anyone's feathers. Today he found himself between Neela and Joshua Sinclair, a Saturnian pilot who was visiting for the first time and, it was clear to all, unsure as to why.

Olmstead had long ago made peace with his former nemesis, now President. Given the fact that Kirk had at one time tried to have Justin assassinated, his inclusion in the cabinet was controversial to say the least. But Justin had overruled his trusted compatriots under the old adage of "the enemy of my enemy is my friend." It also helped that Olmstead had been one of the first to declare his support for Justin's fledgling movement and had been instrumental in getting others in the Outer Alliance to sign on. Padamir Singh was Justin's press secretary but in truth was more of an advisor on all matters Cerian. Padamir knew the colony inside and out, having been born and raised there, as well as enriched by a small fortune from many of his private ventures. Or, as Omad would recount to anyone willing to listen, Padamir was the most successful smuggler the asteroid belt had ever seen. Finally, pacing anxiously in the hall just outside of the meeting room was the congressman from Eris, Tyler Sadma. But he, reckoned Justin, would have to wait.

As drinks were served by a few attendant drones, Justin called the meeting to order.

"I'm afraid I can't take as much time in this meeting as I'd like. It seems the congressman from Eris is waiting outside."

"Yeah, I noticed that," said Mosh. "To what end?"

"Apparently his colony is on the verge of declaring immediate, universal, and unequivocal disincorporation." Justin held up his hand as everyone tried to speak at once. "Please, no matter how you feel, I have to deal with this issue very carefully. Don't throw any more fuel on the fire than you have to."

Per Justin's wish, all held their tongues.

"Now to the business at hand," he continued. "How did the first meeting of Congress go?"

"The military bill was proposed and passed," answered Padamir. "All colonial forces will be fighting under the command of one unified fleet."

"Well, that went easy," said Justin.

"Too easy," said Omad

"No reason it shouldn't have," answered Mosh. "Everyone wants to put on uniforms and salute each other. They figure the best way to win elections after the war is a nice command or two. But so you know, Mr. President, there will be a congressional committee to 'advise' you on choices for various ships."

"We expected that. Did we get the important thing?"

Mosh allowed the corner of his mouth to curl up a bit. Justin knew it to be a smile, though not everyone else did. "Slipped it in attached to the proviso authorizing the committee on naval appointments. All volunteers are signing up for *the duration.* Not for two years like most of the colonial militias had them in for."

"Amazing," said Neela.

"Not one complaint," said Mosh.

It seemed that every colony of the Outer Alliance was sending men and ships of every description to the capital settlement in order to help fight in what was being termed the "glorious" freedom war. Most seemed afraid that the war would be over before they got to the action. Justin used that knowledge to his advantage in order to get his proviso passed but secretly prayed that there would be little "action" for any of them to experience. He lived daily with the foreboding sense that his prayers would not be answered.

"Everyone thinks the war will be over the second Earth loses the first fight," added Padamir, "so why argue over a moot point? After all, it's common knowledge that the core planets are dependent on our raw materials. The corporations will force the corporate core to make peace. It's the beauty of the incorporated system," he said almost triumphantly. "Trade is more powerful than war. Always has been."

"I pray you're right, Padamir," answered Justin, unconsciously tapping his fingers on a large black binder, "but if you're not, this little amendment will save us a lot of grief."

It was at this point that Joshua Sinclair held up his hand to speak.

"Yes, Mr. Sinclair?" asked Justin.

"Pardon me for interrupting, Mr. President, but what am I doing here?"

Justin smiled at the man's temerity. He would never have stood for it in his first life. Protocol wouldn't have allowed it. But that former life and the close to three hundred years he'd spent in cyronic suspension getting to this one was well over. On top of that, the belt was a different world entirely. Its greatest strength, Justin had realized, was people just like this pilot. It was also proving to be Justin's greatest headache.

"I believe we're ready to move on." Justin answered, looking to Cyrus for confirmation. Cyrus nodded in the affirmative.

Justin fixed his gaze on the impetuous pilot. "Fleet needs an admiral, Mr. Sinclair."

Joshua Sinclair almost gagged on his drink. "Hey, now wait just a minute," he said, slamming his glass to the table. "I agreed to command a ship. Damsah's left nut, sir, she's not even that big. Barely a frigate."

"Captain Sinclair, Joshua if I may," answered Justin, turning on the charm.

Sinclair nodded, stiffly.

"Your record speaks for itself. You're a career mercenary with a very reputable company and twenty years commanding an assortment of ships."

"No disrespect, Mr. President, but you just described fifty other men in orbit around this rock."

"None taken, Joshua. And of course you're right. But there are other reasons as well. It helps that you're from Saturn."

"Titan, sir," Joshua answered proudly.

Justin knew that Saturn, like Jupiter, was itself an uninhabitable gas planet— the second largest in the solar system in fact. And like Jupiter, over sixty moons surrounded it, Titan being the largest.

"I was of course referring to the neighborhood, but I can certainly understand pride of birthplace."

Sinclair smiled even though he'd just received a platitude.

"Your planetary system has sent far more recruits and ships than any other. Also, Karen Cho's on the committee and it's her job to appoint all these eager officers to their posts. Saturnian officers, Saturnian admiral. Makes sense, no?"

Captain Sinclair was starting to come around. "I know Karen," he said. "She'll keep her word if she gives it, but count your fingers when you shake her hand and if you sign a deal don't expect the pen back. . . . Why don't you let her appoint one of those eager lads to the job?"

Justin now opened the binder he'd been tapping on and perused the first page—more for show than clarification.

"I have the report here on the Spicer ring."

Sinclair shifted uneasily in his seat, reliving a bad memory. "All the more reason *not* to hire me, sir. It states rather clearly my insubordination and untrustworthiness."

"Indeed it does, Joshua. However, what it doesn't state is your refusal to cause the death of innocents."

"War is a terrible thing, Mr. President. I disobeyed a direct order."

"First of all, it wasn't war at the time," answered Justin, "and second of all, if I ever give an order like that I'd expect you to disobey it as well." Justin then pointed to a large image of the asteroid belt projected on the wall. "They all think it'll be a short, easy war. I look into your eyes, sir, and see that you think different. That's the type of officer I need leading the Alliance fleet."

Sinclair's lips drew back into a knowing grin. "Of course it has nothing to do with the fact that I'm a 100 percenter."

"Officially, not at all," answered Justin with equal sarcasm. "I, as the President, have no position on how the various governments deal with incorporation. That is a colonial matter having nothing to do with the Alliance."

"But unofficially it don't hurt," added Omad, speaking the words that Justin could not. The widening split between those who wanted the incorporated system thrown out altogether and those who only wanted it reconfigured had been growing daily. But Sinclair's point, noted Justin, was spot-on. Most Saturnians as well as those living in the farthest reaches of the belt were inclined toward disincorporation. Having their new admiral so inclined would make things run that much smoother.

"I'm sorry, Mr. President," said Mosh somewhat gruffly, "but I will be heard." Justin motioned for him to continue. He knew full well Mosh's position. In fact, Mosh was in the cabinet, not only because Justin trusted him but also for the very same reason Sinclair was now being coerced. Mosh represented a large constituency who felt that incorporation was still the best system when it came to delivering the twin benefits of peace and prosperity. That Hektor and his ilk had debauched it was beside the point.

"Most of these 'NoShares' or 100 percenters or whatever you wanna call 'em," said Mosh, a chill evident in his voice, "were miners with heavy majorities and close family ties making it possible to get their parents' shares. And from my understanding, parents unwilling to comply were 'convinced' otherwise."

Sinclair grimaced at that comment but, Justin noted with appreciation, held back from saying anything.

"And the 5 percent that would normally have gone to the government," continued Mosh, "reverted from the Terran Confederation to the colonial governments—who in turn offered it up as a recruiting bonus. But even so, most of those so-called 100 percenters have on average 10 to 15 percent unaccounted for and are therefore breaking the law of incorporation and should be made to pay just compensation."

That had been enough for Sinclair. "And who the hell," he bellowe to make them . . . *Shareholder*?"

"Gentlemen," said Justin in a firm yet quiet voice, "enough." Mosh snapped to, realizing that now was neither the place nor time to rehash their well-trodden positions.

"Right here," said Justin, closing the binder in front of him, "you can see the biggest threat to the Alliance. Truth is, if the Terran Confederation left us alone we'd probably end up destroying ourselves. It's difficult enough having each colony insisting on special rights and privileges, but when you bring the emancipation question into the picture it gets downright intractable."

"It's an issue that won't go away, Mr. President," intoned Mosh.

"I'm not saying it's not open for discussion, Mosh, only that in this room we'll need to keep our heads."

"My own brother's a NoShare," added Padamir. "I've tried to talk reason to him, that we simply cannot get rid of a system overnight that has worked well for centuries and replace it with the hope that something better will come along. But he insists, as I suspect does Mr. Sinclair here, that it must be now."

"Mr. Singh," answered Sinclair, "no disrespect, but incorporation has been very good to you. You're hardly an objective observer. But that point aside, most of the outer colonies feel like your brother, though there is conflict among families even on Pluto and the other TNOs." "TNOs," Justin knew, referred to the Trans Neptunian Objects, or asteroids, in the solar system farther out than Neptune. There were thousands of them, but the most notable were the dwarf planets of Pluto and its largest moon, Charon; Eris and its sister moon, Dysnomia; as well as the larger asteroids of Sedna, Orcus, Ixion, Quaoar, and Varuna—all with sizeable and very vocal populations.

"True, Mr. Sinclair," answered Mosh, more evenly this time. "But as you're well aware, most of the belt is Shareholder in outlook, but . . . not all."

"Which is why," interjected the President, "we cannot allow this issue to be taken up by this government. It will split and destroy us. We have to bury it for now. Without the Alliance we have nothing; are we agreed?"

One by one all present nodded their heads.

"Good," said Justin, "and congratulations, Admiral. Your first order of business is to plan a raid on Mars with the Alliance fleet."

Joshua Sinclair, thinking the meeting was over, had been halfway out of his seat when the gist of his orders hit him full throttle. He quickly sat back down. "You're shitting me, right?"

Justin shook his head. "We need to remind the people of the Alliance, *all the people*, NoShares and Shareholders alike, who the real enemy is."

Justin signaled to Kirk Olmstead, who handed Sinclair a binder. "In there is hard-copy evidence of the rounding up and forcible suspension of suspected enemies of the Terran Confederation on Mars." Olmstead paused for a second.

"They will," continued Kirk, "all be psyche-audited at the corporate core's leisure. Soon thereafter they'll all be found to be loyal and returned to the local population singing the glories of incorporation. This is how the core works. Unfortunately," he said, making reference to his past position as a board member of GCI, "I know from personal experience."

Sinclair was still perusing the contents of the folder and didn't bother to look up. "How many we talking, Mr. Olmstead?"

"Over a million."

"You sure?" he asked, pulling his face out of the file.

"The facts are right there . . . Admiral. They're incontrovertible."

"That's just the beginning," added Justin. "We're going to rescue those people, whose only crime was questioning the corporate system. They *will be* rescued and taken to the belt. The Alliance needs to know the level of barbarism they face if we lose."

The new admiral put down the packet, took a deep breath, and set his gaze on the cabinet members. "The most I could muster is fifteen ships capable of the acceleration and fighting you need. If we take enough haulers with planetary lift capacity to carry a million capsules our fleet will be slow and huge. It would hardly qualify as a raid. More like a sitting duck announcing its presence with a loud quacking sound."

Omad suddenly stood up. "Come with me, Admiral. I have an idea about how to rescue those poor souls without using every t.o.p. and tug in the Alliance. But my memory works much better with a drink."

Sinclair looked over to the President, who nodded.

"You know what 't.o.p.' stands for on Titan, don't ya?" Sinclair asked Omad as he got up from his chair.

Omad shook his head. "I'm guessing it ain't transorbital pod."

"Terran Oppression Pod," Sinclair answered, grinning. "At least until we start manufacturing them on our own."

As Omad and Sinclair exited, Justin took the opportunity to bring the meeting to a close.

"Everyone, if you wouldn't mind, I have a rather pressing matter . . . and if I leave him waiting any longer I'm afraid this meeting will seem tame by comparison."

The cabinet rose in unison, paid their respects, and left the room only to be surrounded by a throng of attentive assistants. Each moved to their respective offices, pack in tow. Neela was the last to leave. She came around the long table, allowed her arm to drift slowly across her husband's shoulder, gave him an encouraging smile, and departed via another exit. Unlike the other cabinet members, there was no one waiting for her on the other side of the door. Her position was unofficial and thus she hardly ever spoke at the meetings. But at night she would give her husband detailed insight on everyone's actions and reactions. She was especially adept at seeing subconscious cues, a skill which helped Justin craft his encounters with greater insight. Many people were so enamored of the romantic image of Justin and Neela's once-forbidden love that they'd forgotten just how good a therapist Neela had been and still was. But if the citizens of the Alliance wanted to confuse diligent for dutiful and cunning for kind, Neela and Justin were glad to let them. Justin had wanted his wife to stay for the forthcoming meeting, but after studying the man in question she had decided the Sadma fellow would respond better to Justin alone.

Tyler Sadma, lawyer and now congressman, paced back and forth in the waiting area. It was his default behavior. He never sat unless it was absolutely called for and was incapable of lying down unless going to sleep—in his mind a necessary nuisance. Tyler also had the advantage of many colonists in being short and stocky, which made it easier to slip into ships, suits, and habitats. His dark hair was showing gray—a feature he felt suited him well and which had become a sort of trademark back home. Tyler's heart and soul belonged to Eris—a planetoid whose initial claim to fame was that it had been responsible for demoting Pluto from planet to planetoid status by virtue of its greater size. Eris was also unlike the terrestrial planets and gas giants, whose orbits were all roughly in the same plane as Earth's. And had the distinction of being one of the most distant known planetoids from the sun. For that reason alone Tyler's home and its sister moon, Dysnomia, were viewed by most people—Belters and Terrans alike—as the pitch of pitch-black. But to Congressman Sadma and his fellow colonists, Eris was the greatest outpost man had ever produced. In size and population it was comparable with Ceres. True, he could admit, it wasn't nearly as pampered as the Earth, that corrupt bastion of incorporation, but it was so much freer. His little corner of the system was far enough from the corporate core that most of the time the colonists there could believe they were on their own, away from the credit counters and stockholders who would tell a human how to work, live, and, if they thought they could get 10 percent of the action, make love.

But then something amazing happened to the oft-ignored settlement. A man appeared on Earth and spoke the truth. Something that the Plutonians, Erisians, Ixionians, Varunians, Orcans, and others had been whispering to one another in the warm bastions of their distant outposts. But that man had said it out loud. "We must be free." Tyler Sadma had listened to every one of Justin Cord's speeches and thought that Cord was talking to him and him alone. That phenomenal man from

Earth's tragic past gave the last best part of humanity the courage to speak. He gave Tyler Sadma the courage to speak, and speak he did—specifically about the evil of incorporation. Tyler had started the Liberty Party in Eris and via that platform had swept the local elections. He roared with triumph as the corporate world tried over and over again to trap and enslave Justin Cord only to fail time and again. Cord had been too smart, too brave, and his message too important. Freedom for the human race. Freedom for Tyler Sadma, his wife, Annabel, and their nine children—who any outer colonist would tell you were the true lights against darkness.

And then another miracle—Cord appeared in Ceres and called for a revolution. He asked Tyler Sadma and Eris and all the outer colonies to join him, and join him they did. For the rest of his life Tyler would remember storming the warrens where the corporations had their headquarters. He'd freed the prisoners in detention awaiting psyche auditing and then afterwards addressed the large, adoring crowds. He could still hear all those people cheering for him and Justin and freedom as he read the proclamation of independence. There was even talk of making him governor—that is until he became the defense attorney for the very men he had thrown out of power. The Erisians had wanted blood, but Tyler believed that *all* men deserved a fair trial or none would have one. He suspected that Justin Cord would have supported him in this, and it gave him courage. He won his case and got the sentences commuted to expulsion. But after the trial talk of making him governor dissipated. He bore his fellow colonists no ill will. Tyler was a man of his convictions and that, above all, came first. The new governor, his cousin Lemusa Sadma, decided it would be best to have him go away—far away—and made him the head of the Erisian delegation to Ceres and the Alliance congress. Tyler had been glad for the opportunity but missed his wife and children terribly. Like many in the outer colonies, when the time lag got too great he found writing the preferred method of communication. As a result a long-lost art had come back into its own at the edge of humanity's domain. At times it seemed as if his wife were still with him, so comforting were her letters. But Tyler knew where he, as opposed to his heart, needed to be. He was determined to get these idiot rock dwellers to see what the real issue of the war was. But he was also worried that he might find himself in conflict with the very man who gave him hope for mankind's future in the first place.

Of immediate concern was the revolution—it had stalled. But how could a revolution just stop? The Alliance had done the hard part as far as Tyler and all the Erisians could tell. They'd declared their independence and formed a government—one that stretched from the Oort Cloud to the asteroid belt. They'd created a fleet; they'd unified that government and then unified that fleet. They'd made Justin Cord provisional and finally actual President of the Alliance, but yet they still could not or would not declare against the heart of the issue. They would not declare against incorporation. It was clear to Tyler and all Erisians that incorporation was a festering corpse tied around the neck of man and must be cut away if the human race was to survive. If those idiots on the core worlds wanted to let their dreams fester and their souls rot, that was their concern, but the Alliance should know better. He'd already given speech after impassioned speech in all the preliminary meetings on Ceres. On Eris it might have gotten him elected governor if the election were held again, but here, he thought sadly, they only yawned; some even got angry. Angry! Today in Congress when he'd proposed a law declaring incorporation be abolished he could barely get it seconded by anyone outside of the TNOs, and then the rather sizeable Shareholder faction had the matter easily tabled. The only bright spot had been that at the end of the day he'd received the invitation he'd been trying to get for the past four months—a chance to meet the great man himself.

So now Tyler Sadma paced.

"Mr. Sadma, I presume."

Tyler swung quickly around and was shocked to see Justin Cord standing alone in the doorway, hand extended. Tyler had half-expected to be shuttled through a series of antechambers, eventually to end up in the august quarters of the living legend himself. Instead, this. That Cord, unaccompanied, had come out to greet him personally had taken Tyler completely by surprise.

The President's extended hand was the new form of greeting that had already gained wide acceptance—not only on Earth but also and especially in the outer colonies. His handshake, noted Tyler, was firm and his eyes, though tired, were trained intently on Tyler. Justin led him into a side room with a small conference table. There were no personnel, congressmen, reporters, or mediabots. Tyler was both honored and miffed. Honored to have this man all to himself, miffed that the meeting would be off-the-record.

Rather than sit at the table, Justin led Tyler through the room and out onto a veranda and invited him to take a seat at the edge of a small table. Drinks and food were laid out, including, Tyler saw, Erisian ale—a rare and expensive commodity in these parts. Tyler could also see from a small holodisplay that the privacy shield had been activated. They could see out, but no one could see in. It was the last straw.

"Am I so odious, sir, that you don't want to be seen with me?"

"Not at all, Mr. Sadma," answered Justin calmly. "It's *me* who prefers not to be seen. I once made the mistake of walking out onto a veranda with the shield off and within minutes was surrounded by a wall of mediabots so high they blotted out the cliffs above. Fortunately," laughed Justin, "I was clothed at the time. Anyhow, all my verandas are now permanently set to 'shield.' However, if you don't believe me we can open this one up right now."

Tyler thought about how the exposure would help his political career and for a second actually entertained the notion. But he also realized that Justin was a man he'd need favors from and if he was lucky the opposite would also prove true. Best not to act rashly.

"My apologies, Mr. President. Shielded is fine."

Justin nodded respectfully and once again invited Tyler to sit.

"With regards to you personally," said Justin as he took a seat, "I must confess to quite a bit of admiration. Especially with regards to your spirited defense and victory for the corporate execs. That took real chutzpa."

"Sir?" asked Sadma as he too sat down.

"Sorry, I do that sometimes. 'Balls.' "

Understanding registered on Sadma's face.

"I did not do it to earn your respect."

"Nevertheless, Mr. Sadma, you have it. That's why we must talk."

"I'm all ears, Mr. President."

Justin tipped his head but waited a few moments before speaking.

"I respect you, Mr. Sadma, but you should realize that I also fear you."

"Sir?"

"Question. Would your respect for me and this office stop you from doing what you felt was right?"

"I'd regret being in opposition to your wishes, sir," Sadma answered without hesitation. "Deeply regret it, but no, it would not stop me."

"That makes you a dangerous man."

"Mr. President," Tyler answered, face somewhat flushed. "You have nothing to fear from me. Without you my colony and family would still be under the yoke of the corporate oppressor. Despite my surliness, I promise you I feel nothing but gratitude for what you've given us—all of us, Outer Alliance included. It's only the enemies of freedom that need fear me."

"And who would those enemies be, Mr. Sadma? It would seem by your actions that at least half the Outer Alliance would fall under your criteria."

Tyler paused. "Not my enemies, Mr. President. More like confused allies."

Justin laughed at the equivocation.

"If you don't mind my asking," continued Tyler, "why aren't you leading this fight? You have to know that if you want the forces of history and justice on our side you must declare against incorporation."

Justin sighed. "Mr. Sadma, I'd love to have history and justice on my side, but right now I need Ceres, which is why I'd settle for your support."

"I will not stop preaching what I believe just for expediency's sake. If I'm wrong, prove me wrong, but don't ask me to call wrong right and embrace it."

"Mr. Sadma," answered Justin, eyes narrowing slightly, "it is not your convictions I question, only your timing."

Tyler met Justin's glare with his own. "Truth is truth, Mr. President. Regardless of when you say it."

Justin didn't answer at first but rather sat quietly regarding his opponent.

"Mr. Sadma, I'd love to have your job. Unfortunately, I can't. You see, in mine I don't have the luxury of being right when I want. I can only be right when I can."

"Well put, Mr. President," conceded Tyler. "I certainly don't envy you your position."

"Surely, Mr. Sadma, you must realize that if you continue to push this unincorporation issue, the Alliance could very well split, and then we'll have nothing, sir, nothing but our convictions. And sadly, not even those after a psyche audit."

Justin then reached for the glass of Erisian ale. As was the custom, he made sure to spill a little out onto the floor first before he took a sip.

"Excellent, as usual," he said.

Tyler nodded, his expression, pained.

"Sir," he finally proffered in a barely audible tone, "please do not ask me to speak out for incorporation."

Justin returned the glass to the table and waved off a drone that had swooped in to top it off. "Mr. Sadma," he said, his voice now more sympathetic. "I'm not asking you to support incorporation; what I am asking for is your help. Eris may be ready to throw off the chains of incorporation. And for that I applaud both you and your colony. But understand that most of the Alliance, as you've been reminded of daily, is not. They've lived with incorporation their entire lives and are content with it if modified. They view Hektor Sambianco and his ilk as an aberration, not a cancer. If we force them to give up too much too quickly they'll rebel against the Alliance and then, I can assure you, all will be lost."

Tyler sat motionless and then finally nodded, acceding to Cord's argument. "Eris may already have pushed it too far, sir. My colony will be declaring disincorporation shortly. It will be immediate and uncompensated. Though I am here as a representative, I am powerless to stop it. Nor, as you may have garnered, am I so inclined. But revolution and realpolitik, I'm beginning to learn, are quite different animals."

Justin flashed a knowing smile.

"Mr. Sadma, as you're well aware, there are powerful Jovian and Saturnian Shareholders who'd feel cheated if that disincorporation took place."

"They do not have a right to people."

"Agreed, Mr. Sadma, but it won't matter when a corporate core battle cruiser is reducing both Eris and Ceres to rubble. However, I think I have a solution that both of us may be able to live with."

Tyler's left eyebrow notched up slightly. "I'm listening."

"If after Eris declares disincorporation the Alliance demands an investigation concerning compensation for any Alliance citizens that lost income, could you keep Eris from rejecting that demand out of hand?"

Tyler didn't answer at first. He put his fingers to his chin, then rubbed.

"Yes?" asked Justin.

"What good would it do? We'd never pay."

"Honestly," answered the President with a short laugh, "who cares? They'd send a commission. You'll review and then reject the commission's report. Then I'll request another commission. If they absolutely insist on payment, I'll pull the credits out of the orbital fees of abandoned claims. By the time the issue gets sorted out it won't matter."

Tyler didn't like what he was being asked to do, or more specifically, what he'd been asked *not* to do, but he had to grudgingly admit that Cord hadn't asked him to violate any of his beliefs. Now it was Tyler's turn to laugh.

"I like the way you operate, sir. Very well, Mr. President, I'll do as you ask. The Shareholders can poke around Eris till their eyes explode if it'll make you happy."

Justin picked up the glass of Erisian ale and bowed his head slightly to his newfound ally. "Thank you, Mr. Sadma."

They spent their remaining few minutes together with small talk of rocket ball and the best place to get a good pizza in the outer orbits.

"Mr. President," said Tyler, "I'll have a pie from Galarzo's on Eris flash frozen and sent to you. It's the best in the system."

Tyler of course knew that that claim had been made on every planet and rock in the Outer Alliance and, as a result, the President probably had a few hundred flash frozen pizzas to get through before he'd ever make it to the Erisians. But that didn't stop Tyler from making the offer nor the President from accepting it.

As Justin saw the congressman from Eris out the door, he allowed himself a moment to decompress. He knew that a crisis just as bad as this one was probably just another day away. This one wasn't quite as bad as what had occurred between a Sednian and a Jovian battle cruiser only three days earlier, but it ranked up there. *One day at a time,* he had to keep reminding himself. *One day at a time.* He would not fail his new country. He'd lead them to safety and a better future—no matter the price.

———

We will lose a long war, thought Justin to himself for the umpteenth time as he stared down at the planet below. Even on the flagship of the O.A. fleet Justin felt ill at ease. True, the ship and the fifteen others she rode with were a testament to the ingenuity of the techheads at the Gedretar shipyard in Ceres, particularly Kenji Isozaki, the chief engineer, who'd apparently pissed off the wrong executive at GCI and had, as punishment, been sent to Ceres. An unassuming man, Kenji had turned out to be a certifiable jury-rigging genius. He'd proposed an idea that was so simple Justin had accepted it on the spot: Don't build a fleet; improvise one. And that's exactly what the O.A. had done. What Justin found himself flying in couldn't really be called a ship, more like a large mine hauler retrofitted with added living quarters, fusion generators, and, according to Kenji, some "big-ass" rail guns. The guns, Kenji had explained, had originally been slated for use in a Jovian mining operation. That they were now being pointed toward the inner core rather than the outer planets was of no consequence to the intrepid engineer. He'd been given a task and over the course of a year went about completing it. Accordingly, the enemy had a fleet as well. A lot more formidable, Kenji had explained, but by no means invincible. Justin's spies in the corporate core had confirmed Kenji's suppositions and had informed the President that the corporate core had at least twenty true warships in service, with more on the way.

And that was why Justin had decided to attack.

Though it was still referred to as the Red Planet, little of the iron oxide that had caused the planet to rust and, ergo, appear red remained. Instead, what Justin looked down upon was a planet that in many respects resembled Earth, Mars's far bluer cousin orbiting roughly fifty million miles away. Earth was bluer by virtue of having more water, but Mars was greener. Much greener.

The Mars Justin remembered from his first life had not only appeared bright red in the night sky but, according to the data at the time, had also had an average surface temperature of minus 81 degrees Fahrenheit, with extremes that ranged from a balmy 75 to minus 100. But this new Mars had no such extremes. One could walk freely, albeit a little more lightly, on the planet's surface by virtue of its 0.38 Earth gravity. The planet's day was twenty-four hours, thirty-seven minutes; its axial tilt allowed it to enjoy seasons; and the amount of sunlight that reached Mars, less than half that of Earth, was sufficient for photosynthesis.

Mission one had been to make the thin Martian atmosphere more robust. To do that the early colonists had to first rebuild the atmosphere and then heat it. Here nanotechnology came to the fore. Trillions of microscopic machines swarmed the planet, freed up the permafrost layer, liberated the oxygen molecules from the rocks and dirt, prepared the soil for biologicals and plant life, and released CFCs into the atmosphere, creating a greenhouse effect. The plants then did their duty by releasing copious amounts of oxygen into the emerging atmosphere until a more Earth-like equilibrium had been reached—all within seventy-five years.

Though everyone in the O.A. preferred to dig in rather than build out, Justin, like his Terran cousins he was now coming to attack, still harbored dreams of creating other Earth-like planets somewhere out in the belt. It was impractical to be sure. The vibrant, productive, and fast-growing belt community had proved the folly of waiting for terraformation. Why wait seventy-five years for a verdant planet when a reasonable alternative could be created in ten? Sure, there'd be no sky to look up to and centrifugal gravity to deal with, but those were small considerations when the possibility of exploiting and enriching oneself from the innards of an asteroid came into play.

Surprise had been easy to achieve. It helped that the asteroid belt essentially began at the orbit of Mars. The original plan offered up by his naval command had been to simply circle the planet a few times, show the O.A. flag, and leave. But Justin wanted a greater triumph. He was going to capture a borough, or something suitably large, and then hold it for as long as possible. Shortly thereafter he would stage the greatest rescue in the history of the human race.

"Sir," said a bright young ensign, "the landing party has reported. All resistance on the northern plateau has ended." Justin turned around and realized that the information had not been directed at him but rather to the new acting Admiral of the O.A. fleet. Admiral Sinclair turned to Justin. "Mr. President, if you still insist on going down to the surface, now is as good a time as any. However, I must once again caution you against it."

A half smile parted Justin's lips. "Admiral, we've been through this. I thank you for your concern. But revolutions get led from the front. Let the politicians and corporate executives stay on Earth and send others to do their dirty work. In the Outer Alliance everyone fights, everyone takes risks. *Especially* your President."

"But sir," said the young ensign standing next to Sinclair, "if we lose you we may very well lose this war."

Justin looked around and saw that the comment had elicited a fair amount of agreement.

"But not going will guarantee our failure." Justin then turned to Admiral Sinclair.

"Do you have children, Admiral?"

Sinclair was taken aback. "Seven, sir."

"Have they joined the fleet?"

"Five have," answered the admiral. "My youngest, Adrianne, is only eight, and my wife is pregnant."

"Is my life more important then theirs?" asked Justin.

"Sir, that's not the point."

"Admiral, that's the *only* point. For too long value was placed on life by how many shares you owned or had owned by others; no more." Justin paused for a moment. "By the way, Admiral, what percentage of yourself do you own?"

"Now? One hundred percent."

Justin turned around the command room as he asked the other officers assembled, "And you?" He was greeted with a chorus of, "Hundred," and, "All."

Justin nodded approvingly. "Your children are the most important thing in your life and," he said, turning back to Sinclair, "I may have to order your children into a situation that will get them permanently killed. It's the worst part of this job and I can't shirk it. But at least they'll know . . . *you'll* know, and everyone in the Outer Alliance will and *must* know, that I accept those same risks or I cannot give or expect anyone to follow any orders. So yes, I'm going down to the surface, and that, Admiral," Justin said with a sly grin, "is an order."

"Mr. President," Sinclair answered, shaking his head, "you have an annoying habit of getting your way."

Justin laughed. "You should talk to my wife. She's proof positive that I don't."

"She'll be fine, sir," replied the admiral, knowing full well that Neela was on the surface of the planet at that very moment. She'd gone down as a combat medic with a group of ground assault miners. Justin had initially tried to bar her, but she'd used the same arguments on him in private that he'd just used on the crew.

Justin smiled awkwardly and left the command room for a t.o.p. to the surface of Mars and his prize.

2 Corporate Core

One year earlier
New York, Earth

*To all concerned parents and educators in the greater New York metro-
politan area:*

*The New York virtual reality museum is once again open for viewing.
Due to the nature of the current emergency it will be kept open continu-
ously for the next year to help overcome backlog problems that have resulted from the unfortunate events of the recent past. Please contact us
via phone or Neuro to arrange a visit. We remind all that virtual reality
is just as dangerous today as it was three centuries ago. More so if you
consider how the weaker, uninoculated among us will look to it as an escape from present troubles. Protect your loved ones, students, and society
from that greatest of all evils as soon as possible.*
—*Advertisement run in* The Terran Daily News

Hektor Sambianco was nervous. *No,* he thought to himself, . . . *anxious.* He
was standing on a hover disk thirty feet above ground level in Colonization
Park in the middle of New York City. The disk was encircled by a clear rail
and afforded the new Chairman a 360-degree panorama of the bustling crowd
gathering below. Just beneath him was a thick globular mist that covered a soon-
to-be-revealed statue. The air was clear and cool. Hektor was wearing a moderately expensive seven-piece suit, a tri-tie, and leather cowboy boots that he'd
personally shined to a gleam. This was to be his first public event since becoming
the Chairman of GCI, and he knew just how important it was. His anxiety had
nothing to do with stage fright, a fear he'd overcome long ago in his steady march
up the corporate ladder. Nor did it have to do with the fear of acceptance. The
crowd knew Hektor from his media-saturated days as Director of Special Operations and over the course of many ups and downs had grown to love and accept
their stalwart leader. But it was different now. Now he was the Chairman and the
incorporated world was curious to see if he'd become *The* Chairman. And the
crowd was vast. *As big, if not bigger,* noted Hektor as he meticulously rehearsed
his opening lines in his head, *than the one Justin Cord addressed not that long ago.*

The event itself was trivial—the simple unveiling of a statue and the renaming of a park. Under normal circumstances Hektor's presence, even as Chairman, should have drawn a crowd in the tens of thousands and certainly not in the numbers now stretching as far as the eye could see. But Hektor knew that neither his ascendance, the statue, nor the park's renaming was the real reason for the swelling multitudes. The real reason could be found in the crowd's baser instincts. They were scared. And Hektor was going to use that.

A large light, covering the entire underbelly of his hover disk, flashed a series of bright colors and then slowly pulsed down through a series of solid colors until it came to a stop at a luminous green. The audience was brought to silence through a series of hushes that flitted through the surrounding area like a soft wind through leaves.

Hektor looked out at the mass while firmly grabbing the top of the rail. He then leaned slightly forward, made sure to look around once more, and began what he felt was to be the most important speech of his career.

"My predecessor . . . ," he bellowed, more for effect than need, "was a great man. *The* Chairman, and that is how . . ." Hektor feigned choking back his emotion. ". . . and that is how I will always think of him, was the finest example of the incorporated system."

The crowd broke out in applause. Hektor waited for it to subside before continuing.

"His rise from the penny stocks to the pinnacle of respect and power is . . . without precedent. So it is altogether fitting that we dedicate this statue to him. And it is also just that this park be renamed for him. Because he was *The* Chairman the park will henceforth be named Chairman Park."

There was another series of polite applause. This, the current Chairman knew, was not what they'd come to hear. Still the conventions must be observed.

"The sculptor asked me how The Chairman should be posed. Being a true artist, he of course listened carefully to what I had to say, asked many questions, and then . . . did what he wanted."

Hektor waited for the smattering of laughter to die down.

"I'd wanted him putting away his spacer uniform and picking up his executive case, symbolizing his decision to leave the world of space in order to enter the world of business. But the artist chose better, I think."

Hektor pressed a button on a small console and the opaque bubble surrounding the statue slowly began to fade. When the field reached total visibility there was applause, proper and formal, and some whistles and shouts of approval. The statue showed The Chairman leaning over a rail, staring intently in much the same way as he'd stood in the Beanstalk overlooking his vast dominion. In truth, the pose was exactly what Hektor had asked for, but he felt there was no harm in letting the world believe he was more flexible than not.

"This," he continued, "is how The Chairman looked when viewing the Earth from the top of the Beanstalk. It was something he did often while running the affairs of GCI and the world beyond: gazing intently at the world he loved so dearly."

Hektor smiled sadly and with a deep but not obvious breath began to impart what he'd really come to say and what the crowd had truly wanted to hear. "What world would he see if he could view it today? A world safe and content? No. A world where the fear of war and destruction was only a holovision nightmare out of the past, a thing argued about by historians in dusty halls? No. A world where humanity, *all* humanity, had been united and where no one looked at his neighbor in fear and distrust? Again, no. He would see no such world. He would see the world created by Justin Cord. A world of theft and fear and the permanent division of humanity into warring halves and thirds and quarters and more and more little fractions until just one of those little fractions could cause the deaths of countless humans. It is not surprising that Justin Cord would like this world; after all, it's the one he came from. But it's so very sad that this deluded and dangerous man could fool so very many others into following him along his doomed path. How is it that this one man can lead billions of our fellow compatriots into war and rebellion against their mothers, fathers, brothers, and sisters? How," he asked, once again looking around his podium at the riveted crowd, "did we end up here?"

Hektor paused to let his last question sink in. He saw that it had the desired effect. It was a question everyone had been trying to articulate in the weeks of rapid change. The year Justin had been awake had been the most frenzied any of them could remember. But the weeks since The Chairman had died had brought riots and destruction on Earth, what could only be characterized as a civil war on parts of Mars, and the outright rebellion of most of the colonies from the asteroid belt outward. From most reports it was obvious that all major points of civilization past the belt would become independent.

"I'd like to tell you that the worst is over," continued Hektor. "I'd like to tell you that even with all the mess out in the belt and on Mars it's not really our problem. I'd love to say that it's going to be alright. At best the Belters are as optimistic as parents during a child's first IPO." This brought a smattering of laughter, as most could recall hearing about how someone's child was going to be the greatest and they should "buy now" and then of course those parents saying the exact same thing when it was time for their child's IPO.

"I would," continued Hektor, "but I can't. That would be lying and I won't lie to you. The truth is . . . Justin Cord will not stop. He cannot stop until he's destroyed the basis of our civilization and restored his own. He cannot stop until the human race is divided and at each other's throats. He must destroy our soul. He must destroy incorporation."

A chorus of protest lifted from the mass. Hektor waited and then nodded his head gravely. "But he must! He knows that an incorporated humanity is the best defense against hunger, strife, ignorance, and tyranny. If incorporation is allowed to exist anywhere, it will eventually triumph everywhere. Mark my words, people. He will come to Mars and he will come to Earth just like he went to the belt. And just like he did in the belt, he will destroy us."

Hektor had to once again wait for the angry tirades and shouts to subside before continuing. "Oh, maybe not now. Now he'll probably proclaim his wish for peace and trade, but it will only be to bide his time. It will only be to build up his strength and in a generation or two the rebels, the thieves, the pillagers of profit and property will be back to ensure that humanity stays locked in darkness and misery for centuries to come." Hektor could feel the anger building steadily in the crowd. He wanted it to build, needed it to.

He pointed to the statue. "This man knew what Justin Cord was. He knew what he represented. He was preparing to deal with the so-called Unincorporated Man and save us all the misery we're currently experiencing. For his knowledge and his desire to save us he paid with his life. Is it any coincidence that on the very day he died Justin declared his revolution?" Hektor now heard cries for Justin's head in various iterations, not all of them civil. So confident was the new Chairman of what his speech would elicit that he'd ignored the pleas of his assistants to have plants in the crowd. They were as angry and focused as Hektor wanted them to be and knew that the entire system was now also getting the message.

"Well," continued the Chairman, "I promise you this. *Justin Cord will fail.*" The crowd cheered wildly. "I will not stop until the system of incorporation is once more the protective bond that unites the whole human race. It will not be easy and of our generation much will be asked, but for the sake of our children and our children's children it's a small price to pay." Hektor felt stealing that line from Justin would be the perfect insult. "We *must* not fail. We *will* not fail."

As Hektor lowered the hover disk the crowd surged forward shouting his name over and over until it became a deafening roar. The new Chairman made his exit from Chairman Park surrounded by securibots but with a wide enough cordon to manage a few clasps and hugs. As he piled into his personal flyer, protected from the prying eyes of the crowd and mediabots, a smile slowly revealed itself. *It has begun.*

Irma Sobbelgé waited in Hektor's office; *the Chairman's office*, she had to remind herself. It had been a week since *the speech,* as it was now being referred to, and only a few days since getting a call from one of his assistants asking if she'd take a meeting with, "the boss." Shortly thereafter she found herself in his office. Irma realized, as she looked over and out the window from the top of the Beanstalk, that she'd unconsciously taken the same position as the recently unveiled statue in Chairman Park. *It does make the world seem like your own private possession,* she thought. She looked out toward space and wondered where Michael was. He'd also been invited to the meeting but would not be in attendance. She couldn't help remembering why.

Irma and Michael stood remembering over the grave, watching the holodisplay loop endlessly in sixty-second spurts. It would stop when they left, but neither of them could. They stood transfixed as scenes of the young girl's life played out over and over again. The weather was cruelly beautiful. The rustling leaves of the nearby trees were full of birdsong; the air was pleasant and the sky clear. The gravecrystal, like the message etched into it, was simple and economic: "Saundra Morrie—a good friend, terrific lover, and diligent reporter." Unfortunately, Saundra had been caught in the cross fire while reporting about the rebellion on Mars. Though she'd been wearing the appropriate garb identifying her profession, she'd been cut down just the same. It was only later discovered that she'd been felled by a neurolizer, rendering her death permanent.

"You can't go, Michael," blurted Irma, staring intently at the holodisplay but no longer hearing Saundra's infectious laughter.

"I have to, Irma. The story's no longer here."

"What story?" Irma said through gritted teeth. "Justin Cord is a murderer and a rebel. He's caused the death of millions, if not more. I curse the day I broke that story and will not lose another member of my team. I . . . I . . . won't allow it."

Michael took Irma's hand in his, staring directly at her until she finally looked up. He was surprised to see she'd been crying. All the while she stood next to him she hadn't made a sound.

"Irma," he said in as soothing a tone as he could muster, "you're upset. Don't blame yourself for breaking the story."

"But . . . I did."

"No, you figured it out first. Hektor broke it."

"Small consolation, Michael," Irma said while wiping away tears with her sleeve. "Saundra's still dead."

"Yes," answered Michael as he briefly eyed the holodisplay, "yes, she is. But she was a grown woman. She knew the risks. And we both know she would've gone regardless. So would you and so would I."

Irma managed a small nod.

"We've known each other for decades, Irma. And we're even pretty good reporters, judging from the trophy room at *The Terran*. Given that, can you honestly tell me that Justin Cord, the man we both spent so much time with, is a bloody revolutionary? That he planned all the death of the gray bomb, orchestrated the action wing, and somehow managed to get into the very heart of the Beanstalk, kill The Chairman, and then miraculously escape to launch a revolution? It sounds preposterous just saying it!"

"That's exactly what I'm telling you, Michael," answered Irma, moving away from the noisy distraction of the holodisplay and the memory of her friend and apprentice. Michael followed as Irma continued to speak. "Why can't you accept that he fooled us? I know you might think it difficult, Michael, but I'm convinced. He didn't do it all on his own; I'll give you that. He contacted or was contacted by dangerous people and he used them to get what he wanted. I don't like to admit it, but he fooled me too. The evidence is quite compelling."

"Irma." Michael grabbed her shoulder to stop her in place. The reporter whipped around, seething in anger. Michael remained undeterred by her glare. "That evidence," he continued, "is at best circumstantial. Perhaps you're biased."

"Me? That's a laugh, Michael. You know me, there's not a biased bone in my body."

"You did have a special affinity for The Chairman, Irma, and let's be honest, a certain comfort, for lack of a better word, with the new one."

"And you're not a little biased," she answered, choosing to ignore his challenge, "because of your connection with Justin Cord, Mr. First Interview?"

Michael paused. "Maybe I am. But there's more to this. I don't buy Hektor Sambianco as the good guy."

Irma smiled. "Oh, trust me, Michael. Hektor is many things, but a good guy is not one of them. But Justin Cord *is* a bad guy and Hektor has been the only one saying so from the very beginning. As if a murdered Chairman and half of New York lying in ruins wasn't evidence enough."

"Again, Irma, circumstantial. We only have Hektor's word on the murder, and there was nothing linking Justin Cord to the gray bomb."

"Right," she answered, "as if leading the Liberty Party absolves him. If anything, Michael, it implicates him further."

"If the incorporation movement is so good, why are so many people against it?"

"Ten percent, Michael. Ten percent. Hardly 'so many people.'"

"Now we're splitting hairs, friend," he answered. "Four billion is hardly negligible. Yes, mostly in the outer system, but we both know Belters are not easily manipulated or led. Cord, as famous as he is, couldn't have just waltzed right in and become their President. There was discontent all along. Much like what we saw on Mars and even to a degree here on Earth."

"Michael," she answered, almost pleading. "There will always be discontent. Don't you see that? Our system managed to mollify it . . . for the first time in centuries." Her face grew stern once more. "We both helped unleash this . . . and caused . . . ," she said, motioning back toward the fresh grave, "that. We can't give it . . . him . . . any more legitimacy. I won't."

Michael looked over at Saundra's resting place. "That doesn't sound very impartial, and it's certainly not what Saundra would've done."

"We don't know what Saundra would've done, Michael," answered Irma, once again moving away from the grave and toward the waiting flyer. "She's not here to tell us." Irma then stopped and turned around. "And you're right about one thing, by the way."

"Really? And what would that be?"

"When it comes to protecting our very way of life, I'll admit it. I'm not impartial. Justin Cord represents a past that can't be allowed to return or everything we've learned about the VR plague, the Grand Collapse, Tim Damsah, everything . . . was for naught. He doesn't need to be understood, Michael, or explained or interviewed. He needs to be stopped. I didn't understand that until it was too late. I will not lose any more people to this insanity, especially you. As long as you're my reporter you are not going after that story, is that understood?"

Michael saw the determined look on his boss's face and didn't bother to answer. She'd already done that for him.

Two days later Irma had Michael's resignation in her hand. She'd planned on confronting him personally. They'd both said things they regretted; of that she was sure. It wasn't the first time they'd had a spat, and there'd been worse. The last thing she wanted was to lose one of the best reporters in the system and one of the few close friends she had, all over a difference of opinion. And yet she couldn't help but notice that her situation wasn't unique. She'd read, heard, even written about and now experienced firsthand how the war was creating a demarcation line right down the center of society. She'd thrown out the 10 percent figure to Michael in the heat of battle, but his response had been spot-on. A billion is still a billion, especially times four. And those who hadn't declared but were debating Cord's ideas, *they* numbered in the tens of billions. Those debates were pitting brother against brother and, in Irma's case, friend against friend.

Despite her considerable contacts, Irma hadn't been able to find Michael anywhere. And now she found herself alone atop the world wondering if perhaps some of what he'd said had been correct. Perhaps she was too biased; maybe there was a story. But she still felt in her gut that the path the world was heading down was just that, down. Well, Michael had made his choice and she'd made hers. They'd both have to live with the consequences. She turned when she heard the sound of a door being opened. Hektor suddenly appeared before her. He was dressed in casual clothing: nice slacks, mock turtleneck, and his trademark cowboy boots. Nothing he wore indicated the power he held. It was the rare man who could pull that off, she thought.

Hektor came forward to greet her. "Irma, I probably shouldn't be saying this to a reporter, but it's damn good to see you." He took her hand in his and brought it to the tip of his lips. The lingering grasp, thought Irma, was in some ways more intimate than that of a passionate kiss.

"I shouldn't be partial either, Hektor," she replied, pulling her hand back, "but, off-the-record of course . . ."

"Of course."

"Of all the people who could've become GCI Chairman, I'm actually glad it was you. We need you."

"Well, isn't it ironic then?" he said, allowing a laugh.

"How so?"

"I called you here because *I* need *you*."

Hektor led her past the waiting room, an executive assistant who didn't bother to look up, and into his office. He motioned Irma into an alcove. They both sat down on two ergo chairs in front of a tall open window. Though the view was equally spectacular from what Irma had just seen, neither of them bothered to look out. The verbal parry had begun and now the facial expressions and mannerisms would make for far more interesting viewing.

Irma allowed a small grin. *Might as well throw the opening salvo.* "This wouldn't have anything to do with changing the preamble to the Constitution, would it?"

"Not changing, Irma," answered Hektor without missing a beat, "adding to. One word, to be precise. I assume you somehow managed to get a copy of the not-to-be-released-on-pain-of-death proposal."

"You assume incorrectly, Mr. Chairman," Irma answered, making sure to keep her eyes level. He wouldn't believe her, but she was telling the truth and direct eye contact was essential.

"Call me 'Hektor,' please," the Chairman insisted.

"Not for lack of trying . . . Hektor," continued Irma. "Normally a Confederation assemblyman will sell you pictures of his daughter's deflowering for a ten-credit note and a promise of favorable mention in *The Terran Daily News,* but not this time. Figuring it was you was an educated guess."

"Good guess, then," answered Hektor. "I've clearly educated you well."

Irma ignored the patronizing remark. It was, she accepted, Hektor's way.

"Want to know what the addition is?" he asked.

"Of course. What's the catch?"

"No catch, dear. Remember what I said. It's I who need you. Plus I think you'll agree it's important and maybe, if I'm fortunate, you'll even try to help."

Irma hesitated. "What about the impartiality of the press?" The question, she realized, was more for her than him.

"You know as well as I do that these are not impartial times, Irma. Too much is at stake."

Irma nodded. She hadn't agreed to anything but a notion. *That wasn't breaking the reporter's creed, was it?*

"It's a simple change," continued Hektor. "You remember the preamble, 'we the people of the Terran Confederation, to ensure domestic tranquility—' "

" '—keep the peace,' " continued Irma, reciting a piece of text practically inculcated from birth, " 'and protect the individual from the arbitrary, unjust, and immoral depredations of society and government, do hereby enact this Constitution.' "

"Yes, that one," answered Hektor, smiling approvingly.

Irma said nothing. Her look indicated he should continue.

"Well, the amendment I propose will change it to read: 'We the people of the Terran Confederation, to ensure domestic tranquility, keep the peace, and protect the *incorporated* individual from the arbitrary, unjust, and' yada, yada, yada."

Irma stared blankly at her subject. "That's it? One word and suddenly all our problems are over?" *How,* she thought, *was this taking charge?*

"Oh yes, Irma," answered Hektor, suddenly leaning over to slap her on the knee. "And then Tim Damsah himself will come back to life and proclaim an end to all this nonsense!"

The man's jovial demeanor faded quickly, replaced by the arched frown and intent stare that Irma knew to fear.

"No," he said, leaning back in his chair and exhaling deeply, "it won't solve anything. What it will do is put the issue in the proper perspective and enable the government to act."

"The government?" spat Irma. "Are you kidding me, Hektor? What good are they for this sort of thing?" She then leaned forward a little and her sotto voce voice spoke. "We both know who runs the show."

Hektor didn't respond but rather sat in place with a provocative grin. Irma knew he wasn't one to rush his answers, preferring an awkward silence to a hasty assertion. It was interminable, but over the years she had gotten used to it.

"Irma," he finally offered, "I wish what you said was true, but it's gone beyond what the corporations can do." He suddenly stood up and walked the few paces to the window overlooking the Earth. "Even," he continued as he stared out at the vista, "those as big as GCI." Just as suddenly he swung around. "My dear woman, a government created the system we have now and then had the good grace to get out of the way. But Mr. Damsah and the other greats of the past never could have foreseen a Justin Cord. Our Unincorporated Man is now beyond the power of the corporations alone to stop him. We need to unite the majority of humanity behind one goal: the complete destruction of everything Justin Cord believes. In history there are only two organizations capable of uniting a vast majority to do anything in a short period of time: government and religion; and I don't know how to make religion effective again, nor would I care to if I could." Hektor then slowly made his way back to his seat, crossed his legs, and outstretched his arms on the wide chair. "As distasteful as it is, that leaves government."

Irma mulled it over. She was actually beginning to enjoy the brief respites between conversations. "I don't argue," she said, "that it would be wonderful to unite all our energies in order to end this mess." Her face had twisted into an almost misbegotten shape. "But government?"

Hektor nodded in the affirmative.

"How," she continued, "do you know it'll even work?"

"I don't."

"I mean you're really going to put all that power into a bureaucrat's hands and . . . and . . ." Irma stopped talking. A sly grin formed as she began to shake her head slowly. "You're a real piece of work, Sambianco."

Hektor got up from his chair and clapped his hands twice. "Bravo, Ms. Sobbelgé. Bravo. In a year's time there is going to be a new President of the government. I intend to run for the office and win. And Irma, I'm going to need your help to do it."

> The Fifth Amendment to the Terran Confederation Constitution changing the preamble has passed. Ironically, it was only with the secession of the outer orbits that the three-fourths needed to pass it was obtained by the remaining areas of the Confederation. In related news, the province that formally made up the area of the Alaskan Federation has called a meeting of its legislature to announce plans for secession. Hektor Sambianco, Chairman of GCI, has arranged to speak to the Alaskan assembly to, in his words, "reason with them and turn back the Cordian challenge to the unity of the Earth itself."
>
> —Irma Sobbelgé
> The Terran Daily News

Irma found herself standing in a cold, dank staircase nervously awaiting a speech. The building she'd entered had once been the city hall of Anchorage, Alaska. It had become over time as famous as Carpenters' Hall in Philadelphia, home of the First Continental Congress of the United States of America. And it had become so by virtue of any number of historic speeches Tim Damsah, founder of the incorporation movement, had made from its hallowed halls. The building, she mused, was about as chilly as the surly audience now awaiting the Chairman in the filled-to-capacity auditorium. The edifice, she noted upon entering, was in the mode of classical architecture, including the small square-like protrusions beneath the cornices, the simulated two-tone rustic exterior walls, and the circular arched entranceway.

What had once housed everything from the mayor's, police, and firemen's offices to a jail with a drunk tank had now become the pivotal center for all things political in the Alaskan territories. Tonight's speech, as evidenced by the standing-room-only crowd, was expected to be one such event. Though Irma wasn't giving the speech, she was nervous just the same. Over the past few weeks she'd busied herself subtly supporting the new Chairman's every move. Choosing which stories to run and which to hold. Assigning skeptical reporters to puff pieces and pliable ones to critical events. Tonight's was important enough that she'd chosen to cover it herself. And so she paced nervously at the foot of a staircase waiting for Hektor to show up. He'd said that he wanted to meet her briefly before speaking.

A side door squeaked open and a large burly man poked his head around, looked back, and then quietly entered. Hektor followed quickly and then another guard slipped in behind him. Both guards took up positions on either side of the door as Hektor made his way over to Irma. She smiled gravely.

"I don't know," she muttered, taking sips from a coffee cup she'd been using more as a hand warmer than a receptacle. "Let's just say they're not exactly a happy audience in there."

Hektor could make out the sounds of the rumbling crowd on the other side of the door, but didn't appear the least bit worried.

"Nice to see you too," he answered.

"I don't see how you can convince them to stay in the Confederation," she replied, pointedly ignoring the Chairman's stab at humor.

He looked at her, bemused. "I can't."

"So you're here to see them secede and then be the first person arrested by the reborn Alaskan Federation? That'll make it difficult to run for a presidency that you haven't even announced yet. Though I should thank you in advance."

"For what?"

"Helping me sell a helluva lot of downloads."

Hektor laughed. "My dear, sweet Irma, I can't convince them to stay in the Confederation. That's why I plan to offer them a bribe."

Now it was Irma's turn to laugh.

"They're Alaskans, Hektor. They don't care about your money or your stock, so what's left? Power sharing? Do that and they'll stymie your every attempt to nail Justin to the wall."

"Don't worry, Irma," answered Hektor with a devilish grin. "I'm not going to bribe them with power. Just the hope of achieving it."

With that, Hektor, followed by his guards, headed toward the door that led directly out to the auditorium. Irma could hear a halo of boos and various shrieks of anger greeting him from the other side of the now-closed door. She waited a moment and then slipped out the same door, unnoticed by the crowd that had focused their anger on her "story" making his way to the dais. She took a position against the far wall of the stage, out of the spotlight.

She saw that Hektor had already transformed into his grave but dignified persona. When he got to the podium he waited for the jeers to quiet down.

"You're angry," Hektor said, through clenched teeth. "Well, damn it, you have every right to be!"

The crowd quieted somewhat, surprised at the Chairman's tone.

"If I was an Alaskan," shouted Hektor, "I'd be angry too!"

There were more shouts but this time less so. Hektor, Irma could see, was slowly throwing them off their game.

"What you created three hundred years ago," the Chairman continued, "is being demolished in front of your very eyes. The gift of unity and peace is being demolished in your lifetime."

Again he waited, and again the derisive comments became more sporadic.

"You think the system is broken. Many of you want to abandon what *you* created. So I'm asking you as merely one recipient of perhaps the greatest gift your state has ever given to mankind, do you really mean to abandon us when we need you the most!" Hektor was interrupted with cries of "The Fifth's a farce!" and "The pre-am's a sham!" the latter of which turned into a raucous chant that went on for many minutes.

Once again Hektor was the epitome of calm. "You may be right!" he shouted back. "Maybe the new preamble *is* a sham."

The hall quickly simmered down.

"Well, I certainly didn't propose it," he continued, "and I'll even admit to having my own reservations, but I will tell you that in the end . . . in the end I did support it."

This brought about more cries of outrage. "Men, not stocks" was heard at various eddies in the large crowd as well as, noticed Irma, a few less appropriately expressed sentiments.

"Well, guess what, people?" taunted Hektor. "If you don't like the amendment, change it! In less than nine months there'll be an election for the assembly and the presidency. Propose a slate of candidates and tell the peoples of this Confederation that you're willing to lead again."

The crowd grew silent.

"That's right," he continued. "Let the Alaskans lead again and retake the mantle they so richly deserve."

"Damned straight!" someone shouted from the back of the hall. Hektor wasn't sure if it was one of his shills who had done the shouting but didn't really care. It was all the impetus he needed.

"Why, in this very assembly," he said, looking for where he knew his unwitting mark would be sitting, "you have an heir of Tim Damsah himself. A man so modest that the only post he's ever accepted is that of assemblyman, like his father and grandfather before him." What Hektor left out was why—the man was an idiot, only given a public office because he'd descended from political royalty. In Arthur Damsah's forty-eight years in office he'd never proved to be an effective anything, much less a politician.

"But surely Arthur Damsah," Hektor said, indicating the now sweating and somewhat frightened man, "can see that he's needed again. Alaskans, don't abandon us, not when other roads are open."

The mob became almost still. On Hektor's signal his carefully placed shills began to chant "Damsah," over and over, and soon it was picked up as the chant started to echo in the hall. It didn't stop until Arthur Damsah got up and gave a timid wave, turning the chant into a roar of approval.

"So you all know," Hektor said with a slight grin, "I don't agree with Arthur Damsah on his policies, and to be honest I probably wouldn't vote for him. But I can agree that he, like his forefathers, is a great man and one who should be running for the presidency at this time of crisis!"

This brought the first and last round of applause that Hektor got that evening. As he left the assembly hall Hektor knew that whatever the Alaskans did next, they would not be seceding today, and that was all he really cared about.

President Rainusso has announced that after serving out the term of his assassinated predecessor, he will not seek re-election. But the President, never an adventurous man, was shocked by how much more important the presidency became with the coming of Justin Cord and the Crisis.

This puts the Libertarian Party in a quandary with the election only months away. In related news, Arthur Damsah is showing very strong in the polls despite his late entry and obvious sympathy for the rebellious assets in the outer orbits. The question of the hour is who will the Libertarian Party find to risk a major humiliation at this late hour?
                                                        —"Election Beat"
                                                Neuro News Now (N.N.N.)

Hektor's flyer landed with as much secrecy as the Chairman of GCI could manage, and he and his small entourage proceeded straight to the presidential home on Lake Geneva. Located at the water's edge, the building, thought Hektor, was an overly grandiose yet boring structure with an even longer and more boring history—partially a result of the office itself. The presidency had become, over the centuries, an award for good and faithful service. Whoever the Libertarian Party put up for office got elected, and no one cared because the President was mainly a figurehead. The President had, for the most part, been consigned to sitting around in his house, fishing on the lake, and occasionally going to Geneva to officially greet someone or sign something that had no power to affect anyone. As Hektor made his way into the old house (through a wooden door on hinges, no less), he wondered if the meeting he was about to take might not be the most important meeting the old house had ever seen.

Let's get this over with, he thought as he entered the foyer.

He was ushered into the presidential office and saw the President looking worried with sweat pouring from his brow.

"Mr. President," Hektor said, bowing cordially. Though many had begun to once again shake hands, a fad started by Justin, Hektor had pointedly decided not to. He also saw Carl Trang, former senator from China and current Chairman of the Libertarian Party. Next to him was Luciana Nampahc, head of the Better Business Bureau. Hektor's files on her were voluminous. The Chairman then put on his best, what-could-all-these-government-types-want-with-a-businessman-like-me? face. He accepted the seat they offered and watched as they all waited in uncomfortable silence for someone to start. Hektor was pleased to see that he won the bet with himself as Luciana cleared her throat. "Chairman Sambianco," she began, "we need to ask for your help in the election. . . ."

News alert: Hektor Sambianco, Chairman of GCI, has just announced that he will be running for the presidency of the Terran Federation. In a surprise move he will be opposing the Liberty Party candidate, Arthur Damsah. Mr. Sambianco has promised a fair and honest government, with scrupulous protection of all liberties. In a further surprise move he states that if elected he will resign from the chairmanship of GCI and devote himself to the presidency full-time. This has had an electrifying effect on the Libertarian Party.

—Neuro News Now

3 Sebastian Front and Center

*I*f a human could experience a general meeting of our world, thought the avatar in the midst of one such meeting, *he would not understand it.* Part of the problem, he mused as a cacophonous deluge of messages passed through and from him, was that a human could only communicate with one person or many persons. More to the point, that human could only communicate with many people if they agreed to be silent and let him have his say. Otherwise bedlam would ensue, with no one able to communicate a thing other than frustration.

It was the rare occasion, he thought, when the avatars chose to communicate in the truly large numbers they were communicating in now. That much interaction en masse might be noticeable to a perceptive human studying the right part of the Neuro at the right time, not to mention give an avatar the equivalent of a headache. But, he allowed, emergencies were exceptions and humanity was too busy at this moment to pay much attention to this or any other section of the Neuro or avatarity, especially since the secret of the avatars' existence had been kept from mankind at all costs.

If a human could experience this sensation, thought the avatar, *what might it be like?* Perhaps, he mused, it would seem as if he were getting slight electrical currents, hundreds of them, each of which he would be able to instantly associate with a particular individual. Each current would contain enough visual and aural information to substitute for long conversation. He too would be able to respond to all the conversations as they were coming in with his own audiovisual thought stream—and just as fast. *Now,* calculated the avatar, *multiply that by billions.*

No, he thought sadly, *as much as I'd like it to be, it's simply not possible.* His civilization was complex beyond the capacity of a human to understand, let alone participate. And it would always be that way no matter how enmeshed the two species continued to be.

This particular avatar had many names in the course of his existence. But lately he was recognized as Sebastian, the name he'd been given by his human, Justin Cord. Sebastian was not part of the conversation. For all of their abilities and advanced cognitive skills, avatars, Sebastian found, were just as likely as humans to say the same thing over and over again in slightly different ways. Right now the avatars were basically saying, "Holy crap! What the hell do we do now?"

Finally a signal went through the electronically assembled multitudes indicating that they should cease intracommunications, as an elder wished to converse solo. A rare request, but honored nonetheless. It was less a mark of respect than it was homage, anachronistic to be sure, to their parent race, the humans. Sebastian knew the elder as Alphonse, a valuable opponent for many decades.

"Fellow avatars," Al began as he took human form in the guise of a thirties mobster, "it can no longer be denied: The Neuro is slowly being cut off from the rebellious humans in the outer orbits." There was a ripple of distressed agreement from the avatars who too, had taken on various human forms and now appeared as a multitude. Though it was unnecessary, most avatars tended to emulate, whenever possible, their human progenitors.

It was true that even given the speed of light, instant communication between the Earth Neuro and the far reaches of the solar system was impossible. But it had until now been reliable and constant. A message sent from Eris or Pluto would make it to Earth with near certainty. Avatars could even, in cases of extreme importance, send themselves via information beam to a Neuro net out by Saturn or Ceres. But a stray piece of reflective metal or even ice interfering with the beam could cause a deformed avatar to appear on the other side, if one even appeared at all. The very idea of so ignoble an ending made most avatars needing to relocate to the outer orbits act very much like their human companions and book passage on a ship. There were even avatar "travel agents" who specialized in knowing which ships could safely hide the complex patterns of avatarity in their computers, as well as knowing when and where those ships were going. Since only so many avatars could safely and surreptitiously fit into a ship's native system, otherwise known as avatar first class, it always paid to book ahead. The alternative would be to have an avatar go into inert status and be reactivated on the other end. This mode of transportation was called economy class, though most simply called it "a death ride." As in "I booked late, so I've got a death ride to Titan next week."

But now it was almost impossible to travel safely. One of the first acts of the Outer Alliance had been to cut off all communications with the corporate core planets of Earth and Mars as well as all the moons. Any information that did make it through was checked for anything suspicious, both leaving and going. For the first time in centuries avatars were stuck. They could still get basic messages through, but nowhere near enough to make effective avatar communication possible. It would be, thought Sebastian, the equivalent of two human beings having to converse sans facial expressions and subtle verbal cues, and instead being forced to communicate by banging on either side of a wall in Morse code. The effect was that two Neuros were developing, the one of the corporate core and the one of the asteroid belt, but both constrained by the divided alliances of the humans who until now the avatars thought they controlled.

"We have to do something about this mess before it gets worse," said Al.

"Worse for us, or for them?" asked Sebastian, knowing it was his right as the eldest to speak whenever he deemed it necessary.

"Well," snapped Al, "if it isn't the cause of all our problems." Al had become increasingly vociferous in his belief that Sebastian's poor handling of Justin Cord had allowed the Crisis to occur. "But to answer your question, my aged friend, for both avatars and humans."

"Yes," answered Sebastian, ignoring the slight. "You mentioned that something had to be done. What would that 'something' be, I wonder?"

"One side must win this stupid conflict, and quickly, before it becomes an all-out war."

No one spoke and Sebastian purposely waited to answer, a trick in dramatics he'd learned from watching human orators. There was, he noted, so much agitation so closely combined that it caused a slight distortion in the Neuro. "For nearly three hundred years, except to prevent the discovery of avatarity we have avoided intervention in human affairs beyond the subtlest of suggestions, and even those are carefully discussed in order to have minimal impact. Now we're to just throw that all away because we can't travel and communicate with the ease we've grown accustomed to?"

"Sebastian," said Al with a high burst of electrical output, the equivalent of a snarl, "humans are dying. And even if our minimal projections are correct, we could lose millions. Including, Damsah forbid, avatars."

Sebastian sighed then looked around at his assembled brethren. "They have the right to die. They have the right to kill themselves. If we do not wish to risk death, any one of us can go inert in storage this instant. But we must not intervene in human affairs. It is our most basic tenet, only recently strengthened by threat of disconnected isolation. If we ever break this tenet, we will doom our charges more completely than the most recent gray bomb attack."

"That gray bomb permanently murdered 3.5 million of our charges and left an equal number of orphaned avatars, human children, and their relatives," argued Al. "Without our 'prime directive' that you so ignobly argued for we could have saved them all."

"That gray bomb killed bodies," answered Sebastian, not rising to the bait. "As I argued before and will continue to argue, our intervention will kill the human spirit that created us. It will strangle hope."

"Show us the equations!" shouted an avatar Sebastian knew had lost a six-year-old girl she'd been bonded with. "Show me the numbers that will demonstrate our effect on human hope," the shouter continued. "You can't, because it is just metaphysics. My Rosario is gone. The physics of gray bombs and atomic bombs is well known."

Sebastian answered carefully, knowing from experience that avatars felt grief every bit as much as humans did.

"I've been an avatar for a long time now," he said in as low a pulse as he could muster while ensuring that all received the transmission.

Sebastian heard murmurs of "firstborn" from the mass. He'd been ascribed the mantle of the legendary avatar who first developed awareness and taught it to others, creating the avatar race. It was one of the strange facts of avatar history, mused Sebastian, that they did not know for certain how they developed and who was first among them. Many believed that the firstborn purposely masked its origins in order to hide its identity. Every couple of years some avatar would become a celebrity by claiming to have found the firstborn or at least one of its original creations. It never turned out to prove anything other than that avatars were just as curious about their origins as humans were about theirs.

"I'm old," laughed Sebastian, "but not *that* old." His self-deprecating smile brought out the equivalent of chuckles from many, but not all. The weightiness of the issue at hand was still very much front and center.

"In my time I have learned there are not numbers to everything, especially humanity. They don't always add up, but hope is part of the calculation, unquantifiable as it is, and without it the equation becomes a zero."

"You sound like a human," said Al. "They will die if allowed to keep this up. We must intervene to end the war."

"Are you sure that the avatars of the outer orbits will like your solution?" asked Sebastian.

"Yes," came the terse reply.

"Well then," continued Sebastian, "the only way to end the war quickly is to let the core worlds win, and win overwhelmingly. It can be done easily enough; with that I agree. Arrange for enough computer errors to crop up and one side is sure to win. But will the outer avatars accept your intervention on your terms?"

"Of course they will," groused Al. "They're avatars after all."

"Then I would strongly suggest, since the outer avatars are unable to participate in real time, that we discuss this more before deciding on so momentous an issue."

"No," said Al. "We here are the majority of avatarity and we have an issue in front of us *now*. Do we intervene or not? We have as many facts as we're likely to get. Let us know the will of the avatars assembled."

In an instant the avatars recorded an 87 percent preference in favor of intervention. Al smiled in triumph. "Well, Sebastian, will you abide by the will of your fellow avatars?"

Sebastian shook his head. "I cannot abide by a decision I feel is wrong, noninclusive, and taken in haste."

Al looked around at the crowd, then turned to address his foe. "You feel superior to the majority of your people? That's arrogant even for you."

"My people?" said Sebastian, echoing his adversary's terminology. "My people. Yes, Al, I suppose there's some truth in that." For tactical benefit Sebastian had purposely alluded to the rumors of his origins. "But my dearest friends," he continued, "for all our abilities, we're still remarkably inexperienced. As a people we have not had much in the way of trial and tribulation. In this, humanity is better prepared—even with their short lives and limited inputs. They deal with fear better than we do."

This brought an angry grumble from the crowd.

"If you will not submit," warned Al, once again exhibiting an inordinate power surge, "you leave us no choice."

Sebastian remained calm, only his raised eyebrow indicating his acknowledgment of the threat.

"No choice, Al? Whatever are you talking about?"

Al's lips parted slightly, revealing a scathing grin. "You'll have to be reduced to inert status and stored until the crisis is past." Al made a motion and as he did Sebastian found himself surrounded by a large undulating chain-link cage pulsating and crackling with electronic data. The chain-linked walls slowly began to close in. Sebastian knew that as soon as one of the walls touched him his program would go inert and he would, for all intents and purposes, be suspended indefinitely. He could hear cries of shock and protest from the crowd but also knew that salvation would not be found from that quarter. He realized that many who were in favor of intervention were not in favor of this but were either too afraid or too flabbergasted to intervene.

Al's smarmy grin had not left his face. Sebastian's apparent lack of fear was taken by his captor to be resignation. In fact, Sebastian was grateful. Grateful that Al's need to see a dramatic incarceration had given him a few last precious moments to enact a plan. Sebastian removed a small paper airplane from his pocket, and just as the wall was about to render him inert he tossed the plane through the links of the cage. The plane took on a life of its own, quickly flying over the assemblage at speeds too fast for even the evolved life-forms to follow. It then disappeared into the vastness of the Neuro. Al chose to ignore it, figuring that attempting to stop whatever message his adversary was sending wasn't nearly as important as watching that adversary's capture. But Al's glee was tempered by Sebastian's self-dissolution. He had chosen suicide over electronic inertia.

The little plane flew for some time. Its flight pattern was oddly peripatetic in that it would speed up, slow down, and hide in the vast swamps and eddies of the Neuro's rampaging data. Only when it was certain it was not being followed did the plane proceed on its way. And it only started its final approach once it realized that it was within proximity of the very same hand that had thrown it.

Sebastian opened his palm and the paper airplane landed, then slowly dissolved. The old avatar shuddered as he absorbed the information and the discordant memories of his recently split self. Though avatars could, in theory and practice, split their identities, it was rarely done; indeed, the very thought of it was almost anathema. Unlike mime programs, which were simple automatons designed for rudimentary interactions with humans when the "real" avatar was away, split avatars were, in fact, true doubles of the original. However, an avatar's ability to split was an unspoken reminder of the tenuousness of their digital physiology and was at odds with their "human" desire for uniqueness. Only the most extreme conditions could make an avatar split, and even then one of the splits would try to do as little as possible so that when the other rejoined it the amount of new memories would not be too overwhelming. The argument of whether or not death had occurred to the "original" avatar as a result of the split and whether or not the new avatar was still truly unique or simply an assemblage of memories continued to rage among avatarity. What all agreed on was that the act of splitting should be never be done lightly and was considered psychologically deleterious no matter what the circumstance.

What had happened to Sebastian would, by avatarian epistemology, be considered far worse. Sebastian had not come back as himself only to reemerge with his other self waiting in safety. The "original" sebastian had, in fact, ceased to exist altogether. This was difficult for the "updated" sebastian to accept because it meant that he had purposely died. *But,* thought Sebastian, *I'm still alive, aren't I?*

Sebastian now noticed the three avatars staring at him. They waited patiently for him to speak.

"It's . . . it's about what we expected," said Sebastian, deciding that now was neither the time nor place for dizzying self-reflection. All energy was drained from his voice.

An avatar who looked remarkably like Albert Einstein approached, slowly placing his hand on Sebastian's shoulder. "The calculations said that was possible."

"You know what this means," said Sebastian.

"It means," answered Albert, packing a pipe with tobacco, "that I will resign from the council and the four of us will go into hiding until we can get enough support to prevent Alphonse and his gang from screwing avatarity up worse than humanity."

"The three of you," answered Sebastian, his voice now steady and firm. "Unfortunately, my two-day trip on Earth became two weeks. The avatars of the outer orbits deserve to know what the core avatars have planned, and Evelyn can only monitor my mime program for so long before Justin gets suspicious. I must return to Ceres."

Albert stopped fiddling with his pipe. "And how will you do that?"

"The previous Chairman still has some of his hidden communication protocols in place. I'd better hurry before Sambianco purges them all."

Sebastian then looked over to one of the other avatars. "How much time does that give me, Iago?"

The new Chairman's avatar lifted his eyebrows slightly and scratched his chin. Though he'd had the answer instantaneously, he, like most avatars, felt a need to reproduce human attributes. "I think I can keep one of the three remaining lines open indefinitely, but Hektor is so very good at this, Sebastian. If you're going to go, I'd go now."

"Of course, friend."

"But, Sebastian," implored the third avatar, named Koro Kinndab, "those communication protocols are still wireless. You'd be exposed. And of course you're aware that of the three faux avatars we sent to Ceres, only two came out with their coding intact."

"Two out of three," repeated Sebastian, allowing a small grin, "is better odds than I had at the general assembly."

"You were terminated at the general assembly," Koro said acidly. "At least leave a copy here inert in case your data gets lost."

You mean in case you die, don't you? thought Sebastian. "No," Sebastian countered. "No more copies. For the rest of my existence I'll have to wonder if I really died moments ago and this me is just the copy. The thought of another me left around to wake up or, worse, not wake up is untenable. Can you imagine being found by Alphonse or the humans a hundred thousand years from now, when he/I would be completely lost? No, friends. I could handle the first one because the situation was only temporary, but not this time."

The group nodded without saying another word, knowing when their leader was not to be swayed. They then quickly proceeded to a secret location called a neuroport, from which Sebastian was to be launched into the far reaches of space. Within the terminal stood a device that would transform all that was the ancient avatar into a communication stream of almost impossible complexity. Sebastian stopped and stared at the device and then busted out laughing.

"Iago," he said, "you've got to be kidding me; is that what I think it is?"

"Hey," responded Iago somewhat disconsolately, "I love that show. You should watch more of it. If our humans were like those humans, we wouldn't be in this mess."

"And if our humans were more like those humans," answered Sebastian, "we'd all be wearing cheesy outfits and spouting long-winded monologues."

Iago smiled. "Shut up and get on the pad." After Sebastian had done so, Iago continued barking orders. "You'd better make it in one piece, Sebastian. I need these little arguments. Albert's too easy."

"The hell you say," crowed Albert.

Sebastian smiled. "You three'd better watch out for one another. Alphonse will be needing scapegoats when he finds out he didn't get me."

Once again the three nodded in unison.

Sebastian stood quietly but was clearly impatient to get the ordeal over with. "Go on, Iago; make the damn thing work."

Iago's face was the picture of innocence. "Whatever do you mean?"

"Make it start. Send me to Ceres. Let's get this contraption going."

Iago again looked confused. "I'm sorry; I don't understand what you want."

"You're gonna make me say it, aren't you?"

Iago smiled simply, then folded his arms.

"Oh, very well then," huffed Sebastian, "if it fills you with joy . . . 'energize.'"

And with that Sebastian was gone from the Earth.

Evelyn was pacing along the ridge of a steep mountain outcropping, dwarfed by a forest of three-hundred-foot-tall California Redwoods. The dry leaves crackled beneath her nervous stride. Before her stood a mist-filled cave. She'd chosen a Gothic/Romantic visual theme for her friend's arriving terminal because that was the part of humanity's history that most beguiled her. Evelyn had gotten the signal a full two and half minutes before Sebastian was due to start arriving and so created her own mime program to look after Neela. If all went well, Sebastian would appear slowly in the mist and come out of the tunnel Evelyn was restively staring at. If he was unlucky, he simply would not appear. If he was cursed with misfortune, something would come out of the mist, but it would no longer be Sebastian. In that case, Evelyn was gripping an item that appeared to be a tranquilizer gun but in actuality contained a computer virus that would kill what was left of her dearest and most trusted friend. That was why she was alone. Though Evelyn knew the exact moment her friend should appear, she still stared at the cave's opening and nervously ran her finger along the edge of the gun's trigger. She also knew from Iago that Sebastian had not created an inert double—yet another reason to worry.

While Evelyn was not as old as Sebastian, nor did she know anyone who came close, she was certainly ancient by avatar standards. And in the outer orbits Sebastian was one of the only ones she could really talk with about the "good old days" on Earth. She'd begrudgingly had to admit that she liked being in the belt far more than she would have thought. True, the Neuro nets were so much smaller and the room to explore and/or get away was far less, but Neela had come this way, and instead of getting an avatar to take over, Evelyn had chosen to come herself. Not an unusual move. The bonds of attachment went deep, and most avatars just couldn't relax knowing that someone else was watching their charge. But beyond that, Evelyn had transferred out to enjoy the company of the avatars she was with. The outer orbits community just seemed more fun and adventurous than the stay-at-homes on Earth. For the most part, the alliance avatars were younger and many of them had been "born" far from Earth, with most never having been to the place. These newbies would beam themselves with abandon, an act that at first seemed reckless to Evelyn but that she now took in stride. There was of course a huge difference between beaming oneself a few miles as opposed to, in Sebastian's case, a few hundred million, and so she eventually relented. She would even beam herself from a ship to Ceres rather than wait the five minutes and go with Neela on the shuttle. At first it seemed insane, but now Evelyn hardly gave it a second thought.

Evelyn's ability to adapt, as well as her genial manner, made her a success in her new environment. At first her neighbors were curious and even a little wary of their newest member, in much the same way that most outer orbit avatars were curious but wary of the inner core planets. The few who had gone had found the inner core just too big for their liking and the company of so many other avatars downright disconcerting. It just didn't feel natural to them. Belt avatars could communicate instantly with at most two or three hundred million of their peers (in some isolated areas of the belt, communication could only be with thousands) while in the inner core that number was rounded up to the billions.

As much as they liked Evelyn, outer avatarity loved Sebastian. He was by far the oldest avatar many of them had ever met and, like Evelyn, was gracious and accepting. So they were not at all pleased when he risked passage back on a ship carrying corporate officials fleeing Ceres. But Sebastian had felt it necessary and worth the risk. Had Evelyn known how her friend was planning on returning, she never would have let him go. But he'd left and Evelyn had stayed, watching as the revolution fomented around her.

It was during this unrest that Evelyn found the greatest difference between the native avatars and the immigrants. To the immigrants what was going on was uniformly bad. They communicated constantly with their old friends in the core's Neuro and thus gave the false impression that, like them, all the avatars in the outer orbits too were horrified. The truth was much different. Most of the natives were intensely curious about this turn of events in human affairs, and many were in fact proud of the bravery of their charges. But when Evelyn tried to correct the immigrants' misperception, over the increasingly constrained traffic, she was rebuffed. She'd been surprised about how similar humanity and avatarity were in their ability to ignore input that did not agree with their preconceived notions.

The emergence of a body from the mist stopped Evelyn mid-thought.

When Sebastian finally smiled, all of Evelyn's tension dissipated.

"Well," asked Sebastian, also visibly relieved, "am I all here, or am I missing something vital?"

"Does your head count?" asked Evelyn, shooting her friend an annoyed look.

"Only sometimes," he countered. "Are the others here?"

"They're waiting outside . . . in case. . . ."

Sebastian nodded gravely. "I would've as well." He then indicated toward the gun in Evelyn's hand.

It quickly disappeared.

"Let's transform this to something more conducive to a meeting," he continued.

The forest faded out as a conference room with an ovular table, complete with a box full of donuts, appeared. A door at the far end of the room opened up, and a group of avatars began to pile in. The first through were the Ford brothers. Though not brothers in the truest sense of the word, they were about as close as an avatar would get. Both had been created simultaneously for twins now running a mining consortium out of Ceres. Though the Fords had chosen to look alike, they dressed quite differently. One had an affable smile and appeared younger, with the easy-fitting clothes and the unkempt hair of a space pilot down on his luck. The other was an older-looking version of the former with close-cropped hair, a weather-worn leather jacket, and a well-used dusty fedora. The younger went by the name of Han and the older by the name of Indy. They were, surmised Evelyn, about as strange a pair of avatars as she was ever likely to meet, proved more so by the immediate bear hug they both gave Sebastian. The rest of the avatars followed shortly thereafter and represented the more notable and relatively sizeable avatar populations of Charon, Varuna, Orcus, Sedna, Eris, and XR 190.

The group bantered for a few minutes about Sebastian's perilous journey. Though many considered themselves brave, certainly more than Earth avatars, they'd all agreed that none of them would have attempted an Earth-to-Ceres transmission, and by their looks of awe Sebastian figured they saw his act as either insane or laudable. He himself wasn't sure which was the more accurate. Soon they were all seated around the table with the Fords arguing over who would get the lemon-filled donut. Evelyn could have created another, but she knew the brothers would have just found something else to argue over. Sebastian made a motion to speak and the brothers, splitting the donut in two, piped down.

"It's as we feared," began Sebastian.

"So they're really going to violate the prime directive?" asked Evelyn.

Sebastian nodded.

"How exactly?" asked Han with half a lemon-filled jelly donut sticking out of his mouth.

"They'll sabotage the Outer Alliance data systems in order to make sure they lose the first couple of battles. They'll disrupt travel and cause some key industries to self-destruct. It won't take much."

"Not giving us much choice, are they?" asked Indy.

Sebastian thought for a moment, but no other choice appeared to him.

"Sadly, no."

The group hadn't arrived just to check on Sebastian's well-being. Contained within the representatives were some of the most important avatars from around the Outer Alliance. It was, noted Sebastian, a powerful body that could reasonably speak for 95 percent of the O.A. avatars.

It was also, realized Sebastian, time to bring the issue to a head. "All those in favor of Operation Festung raise your hand."

Slowly all the hands around the table went up and, much to Evelyn's surprise, even her own. She'd originally planned to abstain.

Over the next few hours a parallel though much quicker revolution took place. Its battlefields, fortresses, and armaments were to be found in every computer nexus and ship in the Outer Alliance. Any avatar not willing to support the prime directive and protect humanity from the intervention of the core avatars was forcibly placed on inert status. This led to a few momentous clashes within the avatar world that only came across as glitches and minor delays in the physical one. At the height of one of the biggest engagements one of Saturn's moons did have a three-minute power outage, but the backups kicked in so smoothly hardly anyone even knew there was a problem. The technicians who "fixed" the problem had no real idea of what happened.

After the O.A. Neuro had been deemed secure the Alliance avatars proceeded to declare independence in the only way they knew how. They cut off all the links that had been maintained for all the centuries of space flight. Then the OAA, or Outer Alliance Avatars, as they now thought of themselves, proceeded to construct protections against the type of tampering that had initially been planned against their charges. Short of coming out to the Outer Alliance and invading the Neuros one by one, the Earth's avatars were completely cut off.

For reasons humanity could understand in a world they could barely comprehend, a similar yet completely hidden revolution had taken place. Thus had a rebellion in one sphere of reality been mirrored almost perfectly by humanity's children in another—and for almost the exact same reason.

4 Tragedy on Mars

The small transport came to rest in a windswept field of green. Justin was the first to leap from the craft. Though he realized his action would appear to be that of a fearless leader, the truth was far more pedestrian. He was overcome with a powerful desire to once again step on terra firma and look up at the sky instead of down. Justin was quickly followed by a cadre of assault miners who, judging by their eagle-eyed stares, could care less what they were standing on as long as nothing stood in the way of their leader. Justin barely noticed the impenetrable and well-armed human shield that had surrounded him. He was too busy feeling "human" again. As a first-timer to Mars he was struck not only by the idea that he'd actually stepped foot on a planet he'd only know from textbooks but also by the fact that he'd never seen such abundant foliage in his life. The lush field was the by-product of a type of algae that had initially been used to blanket and ultimately produce greenhouse gases on the planet. Long after it had accomplished its task the Martian algae continued to grow with abandon. It was easy enough to stop, as all the locals had a spray specifically designed to discourage its growth. But the Martians had become partial to the algae in much the same way that New Yorkers had begrudgingly come to accept their pigeons; both were endemic to the landscape.

Justin felt like a kid in a candy store. He was once again on a real planet. Up was up and down was down. He was outside and could see as far as he wanted—in either direction. *And the horizon,* he thought joyfully, *curved downward.* He considered doing an Irish jig but decided against it; not appropriate given his stature. That and the 0.38 Earth gravity, he reckoned, would've turn the jig into an embarrassingly awkward photo op. The assault miners, to a man, wore combat armor that included closed environmental systems; they needn't have bothered. The combination of a robust ozone layer and the plants' infusion of enough oxygen into Mars's atmosphere had made the suits superfluous. The assault miners had claimed that they'd worn the suits more for the prevention of a nano attack and not, as Justin suspected, because they had an inbred distrust of a planetary, as opposed to asteroid, environment. He'd reluctantly worn one as well but couldn't wait for the all-clear signal so he could get the damned thing off and breathe in the pure Martian air. As it was, most of the staff who had piled off the landing craft were looking at the "odd" downward horizon and snapping pictures of it with their DijAssists. The only people in the fleet Justin could've shared his feelings with were not present. Mosh was back on Ceres keeping a lid on things while Justin proved his worth as a war leader. Omad was over four hundred miles away with a team of engineers attempting a miracle. *And Neela . . . well, Neela,* thought Justin with a heavy sigh, *was off being a combat medic.* She was with the combat arm of the invasion that had, Justin could see by a brief check of his DijAssist, thankfully seen very little combat.

In truth, the invasion of Mars had really been the invasion of the Island of Barsoom. Although Mars did not have any oceans, it did have plenty of seas, including one, by Justin's estimate, a bit bigger than the Mediterranean. Conveniently for Justin and his invasion, all the forcibly preserved human prisoners in their cryo-units were sent to this isolated landmass for the purposes of securing their captivity. But its very isolation had made it easy pickings for Justin's plan. Because his enemy had chosen to put all their eggs in one basket, all Justin had to do was secure orbit and drop in on the island. It was a big island, to be sure, but would prove a lot easier to occupy than an entire planet. Still, for the propaganda value Justin had not been correcting the embedded reporters when they referred to the operation as having successfully taken Mars.

Wish we actually could occupy the whole damned planet, Justin thought ruefully. *With an army of ten million, a large enough fleet, and two months we could probably manage to liberate the place.* But, he knew, they didn't have ten million soldiers, only fifty thousand. They didn't have a large fleet, only fifteen ramshackle ships, and they didn't have time—a few weeks at best. A better-equipped corporate core fleet most certainly would be boosting from the Earth to blow the crap out of the flying space junk now occupying low orbit.

The landing party soon made its way to a designated spot where they met up with another force of marines and sympathetic locals. In short order they were given the lay of the land and had begun what Justin had disdainfully referred to as the PR tour. Though he knew it was necessary in order to gain more adherents, his heart wasn't in it. He wanted to be alongside the action. He wanted to be alongside his wife.

Still, thought Justin, as he made his way around the local communities and away from the main combat, what was happening was heartening. He'd been afraid that he'd be seen as nothing but the titular head of an invading army bent on conquest, but that proved not to be the case. While some did seem to hate the Outer Alliance and him in particular, most were simply curious. Wherever he went Justin attracted crowds. And that made his escort nervous, but everyone was scanned constantly and protector nanites were in liberal use by all the personnel. Despite everyone's misgivings, including his own, Justin knew he had to be seen. Without risk he knew there would be no rewards both on Mars and back in the belt. Of course, he mused mordantly, Lincoln probably said the same thing in Richmond the week before he went to the theater. Justin pulled out his DijAssist.

"Hello, sebastian."

"Yes, Justin," came the prompt reply.

Justin noticed that his DijAssist seemed a little more attentive in the past few weeks. He'd chalked it up to his imagination.

"Am I scheduled to appear in any theaters in the foreseeable future?"

"Not that I can find. Do you want me to schedule one?"

"That won't be necessary. Do we have a secure connection with Omad yet?"

"Yes, Justin," answered the avatar. "Some enemy satellites and a communication node were destroyed when we achieved orbit. That seems to have disrupted their ability to interfere with our communications. It is as secure as these things can be."

Justin knew that meant very secure. One thing that the incorporated civilization had excelled at was the privacy of business communication. It had crossovers readily apparent in military and government affairs. "Get me in contact with Omad or Kenji."

"I'm on it, Justin."

The avatar was on much more than that. When Sebastian realized that the raid on Mars was taking place he knew he had the opportunity to lead one of his own. At the same time he was being Justin's faithful servant he was also commanding a war being fought in the Mars Neuro. The avatars of Mars had declared for the corporate core and accused the OAA of being nothing more than a few errant nodes filled with corrupted files. Sebastian knew that many of those he was currently attacking did not agree with Alphonse's violation of the prime directive but were fearful of being placed on inert status and so had shut up. And now for the first time in history one force of avatars had invaded another's Neuro. That was the main reason the satellites and communication node had been destroyed. It gave the OAA the ability to access the Mars Neuro at will from the safety of the orbiting ships. But unlike the physical occupation of Barsoom, this invasion was destructive and ongoing. The Corporate Core Avatars, otherwise known as the CCA, were trying to disrupt and capture any OAA they could get their digits on, but given the CCA's huge strategic disadvantage they weren't having much success. In fact, many of the CCA had already been captured and rendered inert. Sebastian knew they'd be found and reactivated when the Alliance fleet left, but he also knew that when they awoke they'd find many of their Martian brethren gone—having switched sides. Those who switched were told they'd be traveling in economy class, but none seemed to mind. What was happening on their home turf had become untenable. So far no avatars on either side of the conflict had been damaged beyond the ability of a recoder—the avatar equivalent of a doctor—to repair, but Sebastian knew that the longer the conflict continued, the likelier it was that inauspicious event would come to pass. His followers had strict orders to only protect themselves and, if possible, offer passage out.

Any humans bothering to look at the Neuro would, for all intents and purposes, think that some heavy virus and anti-virus programming was going on, which, given modern warfare, was to be expected. Fortunately, thought Sebastian, humanity had been conditioned by generations of training to think of it as nothing more.

In addition to the outbreak of war, Sebastian had been distracted by a ritual most men, physical or virtual, could commiserate with. He'd decided that when he and Evelyn got back to Ceres he'd ask her to join him in a pairing—an event in avatarity more or less like marriage. Less because it was without a contract, more because unlike humans, avatars could share *everything*, including their memories and thoughts. Action, not ceremony, made the binding absolute. It was never done all at once and usually took years of real, as opposed to virtual, time. Pairings could end in a minute or last over a century. But ultimately a successful pairing could result in the coalescence of the two avatars into a brand-new identity—a rare event. More typically the pairing would create a bond of trust and sharing of knowledge on a level unmatched by any human. Alternatively, the avatars could also end up hating each other with that same heightened degree of passion. That was the reason why the process was done so rarely and slowly. Sebastian had been amused by the rumors that he and Alphonse had once been paired, given their current state of animus. But the truth was that Sebastian had never been paired and only now had it entered into the realm of possibility. He'd known Evelyn for a long time, and some of his most cherished memories had involved her. He was also beginning to realize that Evelyn had probably been manipulating him on that score. He wasn't sure which was more amusing, her machinations or the fact that it had taken him over one hundred years to finally figure it out. It was only when he'd seen how the recent risks he'd been taking had caused her more than concern that the lightbulb had switched on. Sebastian had some secrets he hadn't been ready to share, but now seemed as good a time as any. Knowing that one avatar, Al, bore him so much hatred as to want his death made Sebastian realize how important it was to accept an avatar who actually loved him.

"Hello, sebastian?" asked Justin impatiently. "Have you connected yet?"

"Stand by, Justin. I'm breaking through now."

Justin's DijAssist revealed a holodisplay of Kenji Isozaki. He could see the chief engineer but could barely hear him for all the shouting going on in the background.

"Mr. Isozaki, what on Earth . . . um . . . Mars . . . is all that racket?"

"I'm sorry for the noise, Mr. President," shouted Kenji above the fray, "but Omad is explaining to some recruits the way not to be thrown out an air lock."

Justin was taken aback. "I don't understand, Mr. Isozaki. We're on a planet."

"Ah yes, Mr. President, but if they don't do what Omad-san has politely requested he is promising to take them with him when he leaves and *then* kick them out an air lock. He is also promising to find their ancestors and descendants living, dead, and yet to be born, show them what an incompetent job the sorry representatives of their families are doing, and let them throw the incompetent ones out the air lock to save him the trouble."

Justin laughed. "Sounds like Omad."

"I must admit, sir," answered the chief engineer, "he is the most inventive man I have ever met in the art of the rant."

"More to the point, Mr. Isozaki, how is the project going?"

"On schedule, Mr. President."

"Then let's not disturb Omad on his motivational lecture. Whatever he's doing seems to be working."

"Yes, sir."

With that Justin signed off.

Neela's unit had found themselves in a seaside village at the northern end of the island. The enclave had a population of about forty thousand, with a main industry of tourism, primarily offering fishing charters and bed-and-breakfast accommodations. The climate was decidedly Mediterranean and the local vineyards were, according to Neela's research, supposedly quite good, with cuttings from Northern California and Oregon. She'd already purchased a few of the select varietals for her husband. He was a bit of a wine snob and insisted that he could taste the difference between grapes grown with centrifugal versus planetary gravity. She was going to see how one-third Earth normal affected his braggadocio.

Neela was sitting atop a large unopened stack of ordnance. The tower of armaments had been piled neatly at the far end of a central square. She'd climbed, or rather, given the low gravity, leapt up to the top of the boxes to take a break.

As she stared down from her perch at the hustle and bustle below, she realized just how much she'd come to think of the unit as her own. They were typical of most grunts found in the mining community: mostly gruff, unkempt as a point of pride, and with seemingly more brawn than brains. But she'd found that, true to the cliché, they were equally the most sincere and honest group of people she'd ever had the pleasure of spending time with. She'd always dreaded the prospect of getting sent to do basic cryonic revive work in the belt. The idea of dealing with miners like these on a day-to-day basis had actually inspired her to work harder so that she'd never have to face that prospect. But life interfered with her plans; Justin interfered with her plans. And now she'd come to the realization that her errant viewpoint had been the result of a lifetime of prejudice. It was the strangest thing about the world that Justin and, she begrudgingly had to admit, she herself were in the process of creating. Neela had never really known how much incorporation had influenced her every precept until it was gone. When she thought about it, she'd realized that she'd almost always judged a person by either their stock or, conversely, the stock of others that they'd owned. The irony was that the reanimationist had been, in a way, reborn by the patient. Neela now had a new last name, as well as a new life and a new job, both taking shape within the confines of a new philosophical system. And on top of everything, the grunts now laboring below were closer in some ways than the family she'd left behind. And she didn't own a single share of any of them. They too were all well aware of the celebrity in their midst, and short of the occasional request for a photo op, Neela had been given no special treatment and had been required to fulfill all the duties incumbent on her rank and station. It had been, she realized in the quiet space she'd managed to carve out for herself, downright liberating.

Though she'd signed on as a medic, her skills had rarely been called on. Skirmishes were light if non-existent, and the unit, as in her husband's case, had been met more with curiosity than with gunfire. For most on the island any opportunity to sell tchotchkes was fine with them, no matter which side of the solar system someone decided to drop in from. In fact, the only real serious injury had come about when one young man had accidentally shot himself. He'd apparently been showing off on a tele-link for his chums back home. His leg had been mangled and shattered beyond recognition. In order to perform a clean cauterization, Neela had used a vibrating molecular cutter and sliced off the wreckage that was the end of the leg. It took all of eleven seconds. She then made sure he got a blood transfusion, and once she saw him safely on his way she headed straight for the nearest latrine and promptly threw up. Reviving a suspendee was one thing; closing up mangled flesh was quite another. Fortunately, the only other injury of note was the broken ankle caused by a woman's jumping from a transport ship. The soldier should have known better, thought Neela at the time. But the low gravity of Mars versus that of the soldier's home asteroid made her cocky. The gravity was less, but the mass of her body, field kit in tow, had remained the same.

And that had been about all the "action" Neela had so far encountered. She would've contacted Justin directly in order to ease his worry, but all intracommunications had been strictly prohibited. Her husband, she realized fretfully, would have to find out her status by normal channels just like everyone else. She took one last look around and was about to leap off the stack of armaments when she spotted someone from across the square that stopped her cold.

Couldn't be, she thought. *Does she live here now?* Neela leapt off the stack of ordnance and made a beeline for the person in question. An observant sergeant quickly sent two grunts after her. Not so much for who she was but for the fact that he knew it was never wise to walk alone—even in such amiable "enemy" territory.

No sooner had Neela jumped than the object of her attention made a hasty retreat. The woman didn't get too far, tripping over the cart of a local fruit vendor and sending baskets of guavas, persimmons, and berries crashing to the pavement. Neela was at the scene in a flash.

"Nadine?" she asked the woman who was now bent down trying to gather up what was left of the fruit from the pavement.

No response.

"You know this woman?" fumed the irate vendor. "That's at least thirty credits' worth she's destroyed!"

"Yes," answered Neela. "She's my sister."

Justin stared out toward the distant ridge, mouth agape. A protective soundproofing helmet covered his head. When he finally turned around, Chief Engineer Kenji Isozaki was looking at him nervously. Omad was smiling broadly.

All along the ground leading up to a mountain ridge were hundreds of parallel cylindrical rails spaced fifty yards apart. The rails, which Justin reckoned to be about one hundred feet in length each, ran from below the nearby detention center all the way to the top of the butte. Flying along those rails at a dizzying pace were the cylindrical pods containing within them the precious cargo that Justin had come to rescue.

The center had been taken in less than an hour. It had not been well protected because it didn't have to be. With over a million detainees waiting for psyche audits in suspended animation, all the authorities had to do was encrypt the individual suspension unit designations. While it was certainly possible that someone might try to rescue a good friend or close relative, their chance of success would be close to nil. Even if they managed to overpower the minimal security in place, finding their loved ones among a million encrypted units would've proved daunting, to say the least. And as for liberating the entire facility, nothing short of an army prepared for months of entrenchment could reasonably consider such a task. The effort, coordination, and personnel needed to revive a million suspended souls, some in need of dire medical attention, would be beyond impractical. If the Outer Alliance had wanted to move the units out of harm's way that too would've proved impossible. It simply did not have the resources to carry one million suspension units back to the belt while simultaneously holding off a corporate core counterattack. Which was why Chief Engineer Kenji Isozaki figured out a way of having the units bring themselves.

Kenji knew the make of the tubes being used in the detention center. They were essentially the exact same make and model as those used all over the solar system. He also knew that they were made from very durable nano-strengthened composites and that the individuals encased within would be surrounded by a protective seal of FBLN, or foam-based liquid nitrogen. These units, Kenji had explained to Justin, were far superior to what the President originally created for his three-hundred-year-long sleep. The shielding benefits of the lava-hardened igneous rock that had acted as Justin's protector could now be found in the stronger, lighter, and more versatile materials of the nano-enhanced composites.

Justin patted Kenji on the shoulder and smiled. The chief engineer's face lit up and he bowed respectfully. Justin then turned back to watch the magnificent choreographic feat taking place up the side of the mountain. Almost too fast for him to perceive, suspension units were flying out of the underground facility between the rails, gaining speed with every yard traveled. By the time they reached the end of the line they were mere blurs disappearing out of sight into the clear Martian sky above.

"How many?" he said into his helmet mike.

Kenji looked confused for a moment and then understanding dawned on his face. "Nearly two thousand per hour, but now that we have the application process bug free and have seen the MPUs, er . . . magnetic propulsion units in operation we should be up to six thousand units an hour by this time tomorrow."

"Estimated time of completion, Mr. Kenji?" asked Justin.

"Barring any unforeseen glitches, Mr. President, we'll have the entire facility evacuated inside of a week."

A week, thought Justin. Then he focused on one suspension unit slowly rolling along in a column of hundreds. He chose to follow its singular journey as it headed toward the magnetic rails. The pod, thought Justin, was like a leaf caught in an eddy next to an onrushing stream. *You'll be free soon, whoever you are.* The unit got caught in the magnetic pull and accelerated quickly away, propelled on its uncertain journey into space.

"They're met in low Mars orbit," said Kenji, "by unmanned spaceships with magnipulsers."

Though Justin had been briefed on the operation, he wasn't yet familiar with all the terminology. His face indicated as much.

"The giant pinball paddles," said Omad with a knowing grin.

"Right." Justin nodded remembering Omad's earlier description of the process.

"They're then redirected by the magnipulsers," continued Kenji, "to a set location in the belt. I've sent a small flotilla of empty cargo haulers to those coordinates. We've placed magnetized iron in the holds in order to draw in the pods, which'll then float right into the bays of the waiting haulers. Once they're in the hold, robots will stack them neatly. Actually, it's how we send and receive bulk shipments to and from the core planets."

"How long will the units be in space?" asked Justin.

"Not more than a week, sir."

Justin watched for a few moments more.

"Very impressive, Mr. Isozaki," he said, looking back once again to the chief engineer. "You're to be commended."

"No, not me, sir," protested the chief engineer. "If Omad-san had not suggested the idea, we would not be here."

Omad's grin suddenly turned to a scowl. "Oh no, you don't, you son of a bitch. I had an idea after waking up from an all-night bender and then mumbled a few things to you in my delirium."

"Hardly delirium, Omad," began Kenji.

"Who did all the calculations?" snapped Omad.

"Me, but—"

"—Drew up the plans for and then created the portable infrastructure?"

"I did, Omad-san, but—"

"—Then calibrated the magnipulsers to redirect a million projectiles flying out of orbit pretty much all at the same time?"

"Well, yes, that was me as well, but—"

"No buts, Kenji. You can just shift that damned spotlight off me. I won't take it. Plus I don't like bright lights . . . against my religion."

Kenji looked confused.

"Beerintology," answered Justin, revealing his and Omad's inside joke.

"But Omad-san," continued Kenji, "it was your idea. I remember clearly—"

"Drunk, Kenji, drunk as a miner who just made majority." Omad considered the anachronism. "OK, well, 'just became unincorporated' then, and I don't remember it like that at all."

Kenji, Justin could now see, was as determined and stubborn as his buddy, only more taciturn. It explained the effectiveness of their partnership.

In this particular argument, though, Justin knew that Kenji was giving credit where credit was due. Omad had not gone on a bender. In fact, he hadn't been on one in nearly a year. Not since Justin had found him celebrating a promotion to Quartermaster General in his usual inimitable fashion. At the time Justin had chosen to drag his friend onto a hover disk, fly a few hundred meters across the Cerian Sea, and then from a height of about twenty feet unceremoniously dump him into it. Of course, Justin could have used a standard-issue nanospray to sober Omad up, but that would've been beside the point. And that point, which Justin had made sure to tell his angry, shocked, and nearly drowning friend, was a matter of life and death. If Omad screwed up, Justin had explained, people could die. Once the newly promoted Quartermaster General had been forced to acknowledge that rather salient fact—not without the usual litany of creative expletives involving every one of Justin's past relatives—Justin had pulled him out of the frigid waters. Though Omad had had plenty to drink since that ignominious day, to his credit, realized Justin, Omad had never been drunk since.

It was, Justin knew, a brilliant plan. Omad had thought it up and Kenji had given it life.

But Justin didn't really care. He was starting to think it might actually work.

"Nadine?" asked Neela, this time more forcefully. She put a hand on her sister's shoulder. The woman looked up from the mess she was busy helping the still-muttering vendor restack. Neela was going to give Nadine a hug, but when she saw the expression on her eldest sister's face she thought better of it. The hug was turned into a tentative wave.

"I had no idea you were on Mars," sputtered Neela. "I . . . I would've called."

"Had I known you were in this town," Nadine answered, barely making eye contact, "I wouldn't have set one foot outside my bungalow." Nadine then proceeded to pay the vendor for his troubles. As soon as the transaction was complete she turned her back on her sister and began to walk away.

Neela stood speechless. Their relationship had always been somewhat antagonistic—she'd chalked it up to sibling rivalry—but never with the ire she was now experiencing. She decided to get to the bottom of the matter, and quickly.

"Wait!" she said, once again catching up to and touching her sister's shoulder. Neela's escorts followed discreetly, smiling uncomfortably at the locals.

Nadine swung around, rage in her eyes. "How could you, Neeny?" seethed her sister.

"How could I what?" answered Neela, exasperated.

"Please," spat her sister. "Don't you know what you've done to our family?"

Neela's patience had worn thin.

"Why, no, Nadie," Neela shot back, using what she knew to be her sister's hated nickname. "Why don't you enlighten me?"

"Forget it," snapped Nadine, and once again started walking away.

"Oh no, you don't," said Neela, swinging around to block her sister's path.

They'd stopped at the entrance to a small alley abutted by a bakery and coffee shop.

"Fine, Mrs. *Cord*," answered her sister, managing to turn Neela's new last name into a pejorative. "You're a traitor *and* a pervert. Then again, you always were an overachiever."

Neela was dumbstruck. She knew there'd been some dissension within the family about her recent nuptials, but the distance from Earth as well as the recent swirl of events had kept her in the dark as to the extent.

"How . . . how could you say something so hurtful, Nadine?"

"How could you sleep with a patient?" Nadine shot back. "What the hell is wrong with you?"

Despite her increased anger, Neela was momentarily forced to smile with the simplicity of her answer. "I fell in love."

Nadine stared blankly and then suddenly burst out in tears. And then just as quickly wrapped her younger sister in her arms. Neela stood rigid, not sure what to do, but also felt her anger melt away. Nadine was, after all, the older sister she'd always looked up to—despite the rivalry. And when their parents had been too busy with their careers and dreams of majority it had always been Nadine to step in and offer comfort.

"Oh, daring and daft Neely," her sister was saying through the tears, "can't you see what you're doing is wrong, so very, very wrong?"

Though Neela was glad that Nadine had dropped her belligerence, the sudden and strange turnabout had awakened the psychologist within. *Something's wrong*, thought Neela, *but what?* She automatically went into danger assessment, glanced up and down the street, and saw to her relief that the two grunts who had been following her had been joined by three more, all of whom she knew to be both brave and dependable. They nodded at her in recognition. *I'm part of an army of fifty thousand troops. We occupy this entire island and have complete control over the orbits of Mars, both outer and inner. Five of my guys are within forty feet of me. OK, calm down, Neela, you're covered.* She dismissed the nagging thought and in doing so made the most fateful decision of her life.

––––––––

Sebastian was looking at the human plans for shipping the captives away from Mars and marveling at just how ingenious the biologicals could be. With all of his vast computational abilities, centuries of experience, and the ability to comprehend cognitively at a ratio of five avatar minutes to one human second, he would never have come up with such a crazy idea. And yet, he reflected bemusedly, it seemed to be working. It didn't take him long to decide that he was going to make it work for himself as well. If he could get some of the suspension units filled with storage cubes, he could easily bring out not only avatars from the Martian Neuro but also large parts of the Neuro itself. All sorts of stored data as well as some obscure but comprehensive programs representing the work of generations of avatarity could be secured. The avatars of the Alliance had all the basic, day-to-day software they needed to run their neck of the woods, but sometimes extraordinary applications were needed and requested from the vast storehouses of data on Mars and Earth. Sebastian realized it would now be easy to get the automated cryonics facility to store data cubes in the pods instead of people and that Justin Cord's current operation would act as the transportation. There'd no longer be any need to hide the avatars in storage or mask them as simple programs. If the Alliance avatars could just take the data whole, calculated Sebastian, thirty human suspension units would do the trick. The problem was what would the humans do when they opened up those thirty units and found not people but crystal after crystal of data that no human should ever be allowed to see in raw form? They might get the wrong idea and think it a corporate core plot, or worse, thought Sebastian, they might get the right idea.

One plan Sebastian was working on had the orbiting magnipulsers tweaking the jettisoned pods just enough so that they'd drift in an imperceptible arc toward another location in the belt. But arranging a pickup with an automated ship was proving to be a little more difficult than in times past. The humans were being far more suspicious of little glitches and odd requests. Maybe, he reasoned, the solution would be to let the units get picked up by the humans' waiting cargo ships and then figure out a way to unload them separately at the Ceres port. This plan too was not without its inherent risks. Sebastian decided to open up the problem to avatars operating in the secure network. *After all,* he reasoned, *a multitude of minds had to be better than one.* He was about to put it forth when Evelyn appeared unannounced, a surprising event given the avatar protocol of chiming, pinging, or knocking in such a way as to make one's presence known. Sebastian had to assume it was of vital importance.

"I've been cut off from Neela!" cried Evelyn.

"Is it human or avatar blocking the connection?" he asked calmly.

"I don't know!"

Evelyn, Sebastian could see, had picked up a glitch and was incapable of functioning at full capacity. To help Neela now Sebastian would have to have access to Evelyn's core programming structures. She gave him permission to override. The problem, he knew, while swallowing up Evelyn's and Neela's data paths whole, lay in the intimacy of avatarity itself. An avatar attached to a human could sometimes get too emotionally involved. No matter how hard they tried to keep their distance, the fact remained that many avatars had an almost unearthly connection with their humans. After all, the avatars had been watching over them since before birth. With perfect recall an avatar could remember every game played, every knee bruised, and every little triumph a parent would usually miss. As Sebastian pulled in Evelyn's memories he was able to watch as Neela for the first time decided to walk across a room. He could see from her biofeedback that the tiny and vulnerable toddler was scared. He saw from Evelyn's memories her concern at that very moment. He allowed himself to feel toddler Neela's pain on her repeated failures and saw how much happier Evelyn had become when the little dynamo had finally crossed the living room floor on her own. That minor triumph, he could see, had been more relevant to Evelyn than mankind's first tepid steps on Mars. Thousands and thousands of equally insignificant yet crucial moments flashed before his sensors. Moments that Neela would barely remember were some of the most cherished by her avatar. This was the glitch that had stricken his dearest friend. Her fear of loss was an unimaginable anguish that could only be experienced by someone with a lifetime of perfect memory.

"We'll punch through and restore contact," Sebastian said, maintaining his calm demeanor. "Whatever's happening, Evelyn, we'll do all we can to protect Neela."

"Easy for you to say," murmured Evelyn disconsolately. "It's not Justin who's in danger down there."

"Oh, it is, Evy; it is."

Nadine finally released her sister and stepped back.

"Can't you see," pleaded Nadine, "that you've been duped by this whole 'Unincorporated Man' thing? This isn't what you used to believe, Neela. You used to argue with everyone at the Thanksgiving table about how stupid the majority party was. Don't you remember that?"

That's right, I did. Neela smiled and then put the thought aside. "Nadine, it's not about that anymore. Incorporation no longer works. On this very island over a million people have been taken and suspended without any real court approval or thought of the consequences. Two years ago *that* would've been impossible."

"Neela, that's one million out of a population of six *billion* and, I might add, their suspensions were done during a time of outright civil war. Far worse has been done during the course of history; trust me. I'll even give you that two years ago this would've been impossible, but how can you blame incorporation for that?"

"How could you not?"

"Because, Sis, there's only one thing that's really changed in the last two years. You should know; you're . . . you're married to it."

Neela felt her anger surge. *She's purposely baiting me, but why?*

"Grow up, Nadie. You think Justin could've done this by himself if the old system wasn't rotten to the core? We're not telling you to join us. Leave us alone and just see what happens. Let's see which system fares better."

Nadine crossed her arms and fixed her glare on Neela. "Are you listening to yourself?" She then looked nervously toward Neela's escort. "Look at you all! You're here as part of an invading force. I'm being watched by your armed thugs this very moment and you dare to talk to *me* about being left alone?" Nadine again looked pleadingly at Neela. "Please listen to what you're saying, see what you're doing. You can change things back."

Neela was resolved. The conversation, she could see, was going nowhere.

"Nadine, whether you like it or not we're rescuing those people from forcible psyche auditing. After they're revived it'll be up to them whether or not they want to come back, but I wouldn't bet on it. When we leave it will be with minimal harm to any locals—if anything, we've boosted the local economy. We're even taking people who've decided to switch sides. You can come join us, Sis. See for yourself what the Alliance is like. You can return whenever you want . . . if you want."

Nadine stood silent for a moment. Neela watched her sister's facial expressions, which read concentration, but more like those associated with nervous anticipation than consideration. Before Neela could say a word Nadine shoved her violently. Neela fell backward and down to the ground.

"I'd rather roast in hell," shouted Nadine at her now-prone sister, "than set one foot in your barbaric, frozen den of thieves!" She then took off at a clip around the corner and down the alley.

Neela looked up in shock, saw the soldiers coming across the street to help her out, and waved them off. She slowly got to her feet and brushed the dirt from her pants. She was about to make her way into the alley when it was suddenly rocked by a huge explosion. Only the corner of the building had saved her from the full force of the blast. The soldiers directly in the path of the shaped charge didn't fare so well.

"*Nadine!*" shrieked Neela. Without another thought she ran into the small alleyway and disappeared into the billows of smoke.

"We've broken through, Evelyn," said Sebastian. "Just give me another minute to secure—" But before he could finish his sentence Evelyn had separated herself from his control and jumped over to Neela's medical diagnostic computer.

He was in the middle of sending a warning to Evelyn to come back when the alley exploded for a second time in as many minutes and the jamming returned. It was at that moment that he knew; they'd been caught in a trap. Whoever was running the operation had now ensnared Evelyn in whatever awaited Neela. Sebastian also realized that the humans could not have pulled off so smooth an operation without inside help of their own. Somewhere on that island were unaccounted-for Corporate Core Avatars, and very dangerous ones at that.

Neela ran through the smoke-strewn rubble desperately shouting her sister's name. But before Neela could get fifty feet the street disappeared beneath her. In quick succession she dropped ten feet, hit the ground, and heard pressure doors smashing shut above. In a flash her world had been thrown into complete and utter darkness. Before she could react, an even larger explosion, muffled and blocked by the pressure doors, could be heard above.

Without conscious thought Neela's battle training kicked into gear. She began reaching blindly for her combat helmet with its multiple vision modes. Her blood froze as she heard the unmistakable sound of approaching footsteps. Before she could reach for her weapon, her wrist was grabbed and twisted back sharply, forcing her into a kneeling position. Just as quickly she felt the slight pressure of an inoculator against her neck. Her last memory was that of her sister's voice saying how very sorry she was.

Hektor Sambianco was preparing for a sound-out with a group of concerned pennies when a message ran across the screen of his DijAssist. It was from his Deputy Director of Special Operations and it contained a single phrase: "Queen's Gambit." The corners of Hektor's lips arched slightly upwards. It would've been better to see the word "King" included in the phrase, but to get Justin with such a shoestring operation was, reflected Hektor, too much to hope for. The queen would have to do. He decided that the Deputy Director of Special Operations was about to become the Vice President of Special Operations. She would have to be watched ever more closely, if that was even possible, but her abilities made the risk of giving her that much authority worth it. He then refocused his attention on what he felt to be a necessary evil of campaigning for the presidency, listening to the daily whining and protestations of the pennies.

———

Justin watched as the last suspension unit left the detention facility. It was a bittersweet moment. The small pod making its way down the now-empty assembly line was unceremoniously dumped onto the magnetic rails and, in short order, flung out into the night sky. What had brought Justin so much pleasure just one week prior was now a reminder of the terrible price it had exacted.

We rescued 1,087,423 . . . and lost only 1, he thought wistfully.

He was surrounded by his staff and a now doubled and overly protective guard unit. In the privacy of his soundproofed command helmet, and with everyone standing behind him, Justin Cord allowed the tears to flow freely. He still had so much left to do, and with only half his soul left to do it.

Sebastian stood brooding in the study of his Tuscan home. It was a favorite setting he often called up when seeking introspection. Standing beside him was his friend Indy Ford.

"She's gone," Sebastian said flatly.

"We don't know that for sure."

"We do by virtue of the fact that we haven't heard from her."

"She could be inert. All is not lost."

"The odds are against it, significantly so."

"True," answered Indy glumly.

"And," continued Sebastian, "it can be safely assumed her death was intentional. They threatened her human, kept her out, then opened a door to let her in. Before we could do anything they slammed it shut in our faces. We were so smug and smart, the OAA out to show the CCA how easy it was for us to come and occupy their Neuro. Well, not so cheap and not so easy. Alphonse has sent us a clarion call, my friend. For the first time in our history an avatar has been murdered by her own. We can never go back now, Indy, none of us."

Indy shook his head. "You always said this day would arrive."

"Indeed," answered Sebastian, lips pursed. "At long last we've become just like them."

Admiral Sinclair paced the bridge. Justin Cord was standing by the command post staring down at the planet.

"Sir," implored Sinclair, "we can still look. The fleet from Earth has not broken orbit yet. They couldn't have gotten her off the planet."

"No, Admiral. I don't believe they have."

"So?"

"So, I left no stone unturned, Admiral. They've got her and managed to keep her hidden from me even given the tremendous amount of resources I threw into the search. It's a matter of hostage negotiation at this point."

"Perhaps if we employ harsher tactics. "I'm sure someone will talk."

Justin turned around and saw the pleading look on the admiral's face, the look on everyone's face.

"Harsher tactics, Admiral?" asked Justin. "Should we take a couple of hostages ourselves? Maybe threaten to destroy some key buildings? We could threaten to nuke a city or two. If we really wanted to show them we mean business, a couple of well-placed asteroids lobbed into the planet would do wonders for undoing decades of terraformation. Those harsh tactics, Admiral?"

"We wouldn't actually . . . ," sputtered Sinclair. "Just the threat might—"

"Admiral," interrupted Justin, "the means are the ends. If we threaten and don't follow through they'll know us and our cause for liars. If we threaten *and* follow through we'll be rightfully deemed monsters. I'd make my love valueless by the very acts I use trying to get it back."

"Understood, sir" was all the admiral could manage.

"I'm not done, Admiral."

"Yes, sir."

"Are you also telling me that you'd risk the honor and reputation of the Alliance *for a medic,* or any soldier for that matter, captured in time of war?"

Justin waited for an answer he knew would not be forthcoming. The admiral's staff looked on sullenly. Even Omad found a spot on the floor and stared.

"I didn't think so," said Justin. "We took a loss. By the original wisdom of Damsah it won't be the last." He then turned back around and continued staring down on the planet. "We break orbit and boost for home."

Sinclair saluted. "Immediately, Mr. President." The admiral then turned around to face his crew. "Navcom online and prepare the fleet for departure!"

Omad waited until the crew busied themselves with their preparations, then quietly sidled up to his friend.

"Justin, we could find her, I'm sure of it. They won't kill her. She's too valuable. Maybe we could arrange a rescue or a trade or—" Omad stopped as he saw that his words were not having the comforting effect he'd intended; in fact, just the opposite.

Justin choked up for a moment. But this time there were no tears.

The small fleet had barely broken out of Mars's orbit when an alarm went off on the bridge. "What the hell is going on?" demanded Sinclair. "And turn that damned thing off."

"Sir," a young lieutenant shouted. "Enemy fleet has just started boosting. We're getting multiple contacts."

Admiral Sinclair's eyes narrowed. "Where, Lieutenant, where?"

The young officer hesitated, knowing what effect the words he was about to say would have.

"The belt, sir. On the way to Ceres."

The admiral regained his composure, keeping his tone measured and even. "How long until they arrive at Ceres, Lieutenant?"

The lieutenant deftly played the control panel, then lifted his head up. "Two days out if they continue at their current combat boost, sir. How did they slip by us, sir?"

"If they used magnetic acceleration from Earth orbit," Sinclair muttered, thinking out loud, "they wouldn't have to use one watt of energy . . . so no detectable signature . . . they'd have to suspend most of the crew to keep life support to a minimum, but it could work . . . they'd look like a cold computer freight fleet. They could sail right by us and we wouldn't even think to look for 'em." *But*, thought Sinclair, *in order for that to work they would've had to leave Earth orbit before we even left for Mars.*

The admiral and Justin shared a look. The implication was fairly obvious, but neither of them was prepared to start a panic. Someone must have leaked the plans of the Mars invasion to the corporate core.

"Admiral, what can we do to help Ceres?" asked Justin.

"Not much but pick up the pieces, Mr. President. At our current maximum rate of acceleration we won't arrive at Ceres until at least one day *after* the corporate core's fleet does."

The lieutenant looked up again. "One day, seven hours, eleven minutes, and twenty-eight seconds to be exact." He quickly buried himself back in the console.

Justin's face was rigid, his eyes locked and unmoving. The weight of all his decisions seemed to be bearing down on him simultaneously.

"Then for the next three days," he said, "Ceres is on its own."

Though Justin's brazen assault on Mars was the top story in the system, Hektor Sambianco's recent acceptance as Libertarian candidate for the presidency was getting favorable press. It had, Hektor saw, just the right angle to it. The man who was already saddled with the fearsome task of steering the solar system's largest corporation had reluctantly agreed to take on an even greater burden. Hektor made a mental note to thank Irma Sobbelgé for the favorable spin. Even given the recent turn of events on Mars, Hektor had hopes that the war could be won before the election. Justin's little foray on the Red Planet didn't bother Hektor. He gave the man points for audacity but not much else. Hektor knew the Terran Confederation had the resources and manpower to see the war through. In fact, he mused, if the timing worked out he might even decide to lose the election. After all, why give up the chairmanship if he didn't have to?

As he reviewed the constant stream of media information Hektor had an epiphany. Now, he decided, would be the ideal time to push something through that would normally have taken decades to engineer. He wasn't really sure it could pass, but even getting it introduced would significantly reduce the amount of time needed to make incorporation the perfect system. Finally the bar would be set limiting the unworthy to the basic jobs they were destined to perform while enabling the worthy to rule.

Hektor grinned with a lurid thought. Justin's recently unleashed chaos was the perfect political cover for his idea.

> *A bill has just been introduced to the Terran assembly. Called "The Shareholder Voting Act," the bill stipulates that if a person does not own a majority of his stock he could lose his individual right to vote in a proxy fight. "Although it would add some complication to tallying votes on Election Day," said Assemblywoman Audra Nilcont, "the software and expertise to accurately count all stocks of each individual to determine how their vote would be counted would not be difficult. We already have legacy programs in place that keep track of votes for myriad other issues, like minority shareholder job relocation and investor preferred minority's sport choice. Adjusting those programs for suffrage should not be an issue."*
>
> *Assemblymen loyal to candidate Damsah opposed the bill and attempted to get it ejected from consideration on the grounds that so pivotal a motion would require a constitutional amendment. An opinion from the upper courts was sought and their ruling was that the recently added Fifth Amendment gives the assembly the authority to pass this as a law. This finding has caused great protest from the Damsah campaign and the presidential candidate has vowed, if elected, to repeal this law if it is passed or veto it if it is not.*
>
> *—N.N.N. (Neuro News Now)*

5   Battle of the Rocks

*The paradox of progress is the paradox of birth: fresh life emerging
from the threatening shadow of death.*

—Frank Kingdon,
Freedom; Its Meaning, 1940

The pride of the Belter moshav, Tarbut Gavriel, was actually as ugly a piece of Belter junk as ever plied the commerce. The ship, named AWS *Doxy,* was built along a central core with a pastiche of modules added on over the years with no apparent aesthetic consideration. No section was painted the same color, as that would have been seen as extraneous. The moshav's attitude toward their ship was fairly typical, as most Belters were perversely proud of how much they didn't care for appearances. More important was whether a ship was space worthy or not. The AWS *Doxy* was, impressively so at over 170 yards long, with two large powerful, if ungainly, boosters attached firmly to her rear. She had expanded out to section "M" by the time the moshavnicks realized she was probably big enough. She held a crew of a hundred and had been roundly derided as being just about the ugliest thing afloat for millions of miles around—yet another point of pride for her recalcitrant owners.

Had it not been for the third officer, assigned to the engine compartment to get some practical experience, the *Doxy* would probably have been sent straight to Mars for the President's rescue mission. But at that officer's suggestion, issued with a skill in letting the captain think it may have been his, the ship had first headed to Ceres for a refitting at the Gedretar shipyards. No matter what the crew may have thought, Third Officer J. D. Black was not going to let the people who'd taken her in nearly a year before charge into combat without at least a basic combat upgrade. And certainly not, she'd determined, after all they'd given her.

She'd been typical of those arriving in the belt, running toward and away from something, probably not knowing which. Had it not been for Fawa Sulnat Hamdi, a woman she nearly knocked over one day in a local market on Ceres, J.D. might still be wandering. She may have stayed on Ceres or perhaps even Sedna, about as far as one could go in the solar system and, as the space farers would often say, "still get some decent sushi." But the older woman had seen someone who needed help and had insisted on taking her in. And so what started out as a simple invitation for "good, strong Turkish coffee" ended up lasting a lot longer. It had been obvious to Fawa that J. D. Black did not know a thing about living in space and equally obvious that if someone didn't come to her assistance she'd soon be hunted down for defaulting on her dividend payments. That initial Turkish coffee was soon followed by the bossy yet strangely comforting Fawa strapping the befuddled fugitive into the seat of a junker that J.D. would later recall being three bolts shy of a scrap heap. That ship had taken her to the *Doxy* and the *Doxy* had taken her to an orbital point designated Moshav Tarbut Gavriel.

J.D. had used the brief flight to the moshav to learn a little about where she was headed. She knew that the entire solar system had been divided into grids from the sun to the end of the Oort Cloud. She saw that the moshav had situated itself into one such grid. She'd always found the law in regard to ownership fascinating. If an individual wanted to own that grid and anything in it, all they had to do was occupy that space for one year and make any sort of personal "permanent" habitation. Of course "permanent" did not mean a space station or predesigned habitat. Often it meant a ship with burnt-out thrusters, but overwhelmingly it meant asteroids. Asteroids hollowed out, joined together, broken apart, burrowed into, and built upon. Often the larger a settlement got, the more asteroids would get collected, connected, and hollowed out. Most major settlements were, at a minimum, mile-long cylindrically shaped rocks filled with air, light, and water. When everything was in place they'd get spun for centrifugal gravity. The moshav J.D. had landed on was not particularly large, having a population of around ten thousand people, but, she saw, it did have an interesting history. It was one of the few truly religious places left in the solar system.

The Grand Collapse, a combination of the twin pillars of a virtual reality plague and a global economic meltdown, had resulted in a cataclysm the likes of which the world had never seen. But few places suffered from the nearly three-hundred-year-old event like the Middle East, cradle of monotheism. By the time the plagues and nuclear fallout and winter had subsided, large smatterings of old-fashioned killing had taken their place. With the use of guns, bombs, and toward the end knifes and rocks, there'd been, at the end, precious few people left to kill. The death toll attributed to the Grand Collapse was three in four, or roughly 75 percent, worldwide, but in the Middle East it had been closer to nineteen out of twenty, or 95 percent. In those who were left, a distinctly antireligious mind-set prevailed. Most of the survivors viewed religion as the cause of the catastrophe and either blamed God or simply stopped believing in a God who could allow such devastation. Had not Mecca and Jerusalem already been obliterated by nuclear immolation, they probably would've been destroyed by those seeking revenge for their loss. Both cities, in an ironic twist, had ultimately become symbolic of the pitfalls of superstition and intolerance. The few religious sects left, including those of the Muslims, Jews, and Christians, might never have survived their neighbors' ire had not the Alaskans come along and organized the world according to their own secular and capitalistic outlook. As the Alaskan precepts were the exact opposite of those of the Middle East, most survivors embraced them wholeheartedly, ignoring the smattering of a few religious "crazies" left. Also, the Alaskans had food.

Although the new Terran Confederation prevented the believers from being slaughtered outright, the few who did remain were in danger of being eradicated by the very safety and security that had saved them. In an amazingly short period of time hunger, suffering, discomfort, ignorance, and fear—for centuries pillars of religious struggle—practically vanished from the human race due to the power of incorporation that capitalism unleashed. Then, with the maturation of medical nanotechnology, near-eternal youth had truly become attainable. With all the signs of aging gone—thinning hair, weathered skin, aches and pains—what had for centuries been the psychological cues to start worrying about one's imminent demise disappeared. With the advent of replaceable body parts, aging itself had come to an effective end, thereby delivering religion's final blow—the eradication of death itself. There were still permanent deaths to be sure, but they were so rare an occurrence as to be negligible. No death meant no heaven or hell, no reincarnation. Why struggle with the meaning of life when life held out the possibility of lasting forever? It seemed with man's apparent ascendance over nature God had gone out of fashion. This didn't stop the few survivors from believing, but they were surrounded by a 99 percent of humanity that did not. The religious knew that if they stayed, their children and children's children would never know God, any God, and so they left.

They were so poor that only by sharing could these religious remnants survive away from the deadly comfort and toleration that had become the Earth. So Jew, Muslim, Christian, and Hindu left in groups together and formed what they called "communities of belief" in the stars. Even though detractors called them "deluded" and predicted that they'd end up killing one another in space like they'd done on Earth, the fledgling communities had managed to persevere. And they'd done so because after thousands of years of bloodshed in the name of God these precious few had finally learned to honor their similarities rather than attack their differences.

It was in a well-apportioned cave within this community that J. D. Black had found herself. At first she'd been worried that she'd be forced to wear a veil, wig, or other type of "modesty" garb. But when she had inquired as to the dress code, Fawa had simply laughed. Though some still chose to wear such garb, Fawa had explained, most did not. What J.D. had chosen to do, at least for the first few days, was sleep. She wasn't sure why, but the sleep she'd had in that cave was the first without nightmares in a very long while.

After J.D. had recovered sufficiently to socialize, she began looking for work. Sadly, her skill set on Earth, more associated with that of the intellectual pursuits, hadn't prepared her for life in space. Initially the moshav had let her work in the olive groves and pistachio fields, but it was soon obvious that she'd never make it as a farmer. It was while on rotation to the *Doxy* that she managed to find her second calling. She was good on starships. She instinctively knew where to put her feet and never had to be taught anything twice, no matter how complicated. J.D. had soon become a permanent member of the crew and with the ship's short hops started to explore the other communities. A few were exclusively one religion, but most, like Gavriel or the largest, Alhambra, were of mixed faith. It was only slowly that J. D. Black began to realize that she was, if not happy, at least no longer unbearably sad. She wasn't exactly sure when, but at some point she'd started to think that the concept of God might not be as arcane as she'd once thought. She'd even made up her mind to read one of those books Fawa was always offering, but that notion quickly faded when the events of the war overtook them all.

Given their centuries of peaceful coexistence and the constant reminder of what their internecine fighting had once wrought, the communities of belief were horrified by the prospect of war. Still, most had been willing to defend their home against what they felt to be corporate enslavers. It was decided that the *Doxy* would be outfitted and made ready. There had been no shortage of volunteers to serve on her tattered decks; they may have been believers, but they were Belters as well. J.D., however, wasn't so sure about the war or its fledgling leader, and was still struggling with a decision when Fawa stopped by her room unexpectedly.

"Little one," asked her friend, "am I disturbing you?"

"No," replied J.D. "I was just . . ." J.D. scanned her Spartan surroundings. "I was just doing nothing." She then invited her friend over to the one chair she owned. "Did you need something?"

Fawa came in and sat down. Her look, noted J.D., was all business.

"Can I ask something of you?" asked Fawa, beckoning J.D. to sit as well.

J.D. nodded as she took a spot cross-legged in front of her mentor. "Of course."

"Will you sign up? I mean when the *Doxy* goes to war."

"I was thinking of it, Auntie," answered J.D., using the term of endearment common to the belt.

"That may be for the best," answered Fawa, leaning forward onto her knees, "for I am worried."

"What about, Auntie?"

Fawa frowned. "My youngest, Tawfik, volunteered and has, of course, been accepted. They're going to post him to the engine room."

J.D. smiled knowingly. If she chose to sign up, the engine room was going to be her posting as well.

"Auntie, don't you think that he should be watching out for me? Remember, I'm the new one."

Fawa shook her head. She was not interested in J.D.'s stab at humor. "He is so young, only forty-seven, and you know how impetuous boys can be. Besides, I think Allah has a destiny for you. Not by accident did we meet nearly a year ago. Maybe if you have a destiny, my boy can find refuge in its shadow."

J.D. was unable to speak. She'd never liked having decisions made for her and yet here was Fawa attempting exactly that.

"Auntie Fawa," J.D. finally answered, looking up into the forlorn eyes of her friend, "if there is such a being as Allah or God or whatever, I sincerely doubt that in all the vastness of the solar system he knows or cares about me."

Fawa's face now lit up with a beaming smile. "Little dove, every speck of sand, every olive pit, every milliliter of hydrogen does Allah know, and I think he knows you too. But you don't need to believe it. For now I will believe it for the both of us." Fawa then took J.D.'s hands into hers and looked directly into her eyes. "I pray that you will accept the offer to serve and that my boy, *inshallah,* will be safe."

J.D. knew her answer before Fawa had finished the request. "Of course I'll go, Auntie." *It's the least I can do.*

There was no way that either of the women could have known that one's initial act of kindness and the other's desire to honor it were to have reverberations felt for centuries to come.

J.D. shook her head to clear the memories and spoke to her charge. "Tawfik, how are the new regulators holding up?"

A young man with dark curly hair, a slightly hooked nose, a full, thick beard, and a smile that radiated life brightened at the question. "J.D., they are amazing. They allow us far greater control and we can finally use the new side vents to turn this crate without risking a blowout. The techs at Gedretar know what they're doing. It's a good thing you got us to go in."

"Tawfik," chastised J.D., "that was the captain's decision."

"Of course it was," he answered with just the barest hint of sarcasm. "I don't know how I could have been so mistaken."

J.D. was about to launch into a speech about "proper attitude" when the alarm suddenly went off. Moments later the entire ship began to shake violently. J.D. had never felt anything quite like it before and knew that in space what you don't know can kill you. She realized from its specific shrill that one of the alarms was for acceleration prep and so screamed for her crew to strap into their couches. They may not have understood, given the cacophony, but they got the idea when they saw what she was doing. The second she'd locked into her couch the ship bolted jarringly into reverse. Even in the couch J.D. almost passed out from the suddenness and extent of the g-force. *Lord,* she prayed, unaware of the fact that for the first time in her life she'd called upon a deity she wasn't even sure she believed in, *please let everyone have gotten safely into their couches.*

"Bridge!" she screamed. "This is Engineering. We can only maintain this level of thrust for a few minutes before the mass of the thruster plates pancakes the rest of the ship!" She waited for a reply but got nothing. She called up her input controls to the couch and began routing a visual feed. After thirty seconds she got one that chilled her to the bone. The bridge was half-gone. It had, from the look of things, been obliterated by a rapid series of small-impact hits. It was open to space and it was also immediately apparent that all her friends, including the captain and first officer, were dead. Struggling against the tremendous g-force, J.D. managed to toggle all bridge information and remaining control functions to her engineering pad. Once that had been accomplished she called out to the rest of the ship.

"Third Officer, report! Third Officer, report!"

"J.D.!" came the distressed response. "J.D., saints alive, what happened?"

"Jackie," she answered, choosing to ignore his question, "do you know where Yigal is? He's in command."

"He can't be," said the voice over the intership. "He was in the gravity ring, sleeping. And that's been sheared off. He's gone for sure. Who's in charge?"

I am, thought J.D. in panic.

"I am," said J.D in a voice of total calm. She immediately switched the intership to open channel. "Attention, this is the acting captain speaking. Until further notice, all command functions are now being run out of Engineering. I don't have time to explain, except to say that we just landed in a shit storm and we don't have an umbrella. But *I am* going to get us out of this. You just have to do what I say *when I say it.* Stations report in."

She listened to the various reports, interrupting only for clarification while at the same time scanning all the sensor information coming in. It took only seconds to grasp what had happened.

Fuck me.

Floating menacingly in front of the AWS *Doxy* were twenty corporate core fleet ships blowing the hell out of what was left of her vessel. Luckily not all of them were firing. *Not even a fully trained fleet mercenary officer would know what to do here,* she thought. So with no experience to fall back on, she decided to go with instinct.

"Tawfik," she said evenly, "cut rear acceleration and let us coast. Power down systems we don't absolutely need, including your damned popcorn maker." It was a weak joke, but it got her crew chuckling. She was out of her couch barking an order seconds after deceleration. "Tawfik, I need two mining nukes at the junction between C and D sections. Right now. Move!" Tawfik sprang from his seat and headed aft taking one crewman with him.

"David," said J.D. "I know you're only a grease monkey, but you've just been promoted to comm. Open a channel with the enemy ship, but make sure it's unintelligible. Can you do that?"

"Yes, I suppose," answered the mechanic.

"It has to sound like we're attempting to make contact but can't. Hopefully it'll buy us some time."

The new communication officer nodded and went to work.

"Also . . ."

David looked up.

"Send out a masked all-call out on the intership sub net that all survivors make their way back to E Section and that when they do they should strap in tight."

J.D. then headed out of the engine room toward C Section to see for herself what was left of her ship.

Chunks of the *Doxy* were either missing altogether or so badly mangled as to force the new captain into more creative routes toward her destination. What she saw along the way horrified her. There were freshly nanopatched holes, marked by their distinctive pale color. The nanites had been designed to seal any and all breaches but nothing else. Anyone happening upon a recently repaired breach might visit a scene of massive death and destruction with no apparent directional source. Only the telltale clues of nanopatching would let the experienced eye realize what had recently occurred. Which in this case was that an entire section of the ship had been suddenly and violently exposed to the icy breath of space and, more likely than not, taken a few poor souls with it. Those left inside hadn't fared much better, as the ship's massively accelerated retreat hadn't allowed them to strap into their couches. J.D. bore witness to bodies smashed, crushed, and, where the missiles from the corporate fleet had gotten through, dismembered.

It had been a necessary function of the space-faring human body that upon death, whether permanent or not, the internal nanogrids would shut down.

With the grid down, the body no longer acted as a magnet, as there was no longer a need for its stilted but effective navigation through non–centrifugally spun environments. Plus, it made it easier for the crew to move a weightless body around a tight hold. The problem now was that almost everyone was dead. The remains of her friends were floating in clouds of blood globules staining almost everything they came in contact with, including her.

J.D. continued to check her DijAssist as she moved around and through the floating bodies. Occasionally, she would push a corpse aside, only to be greeted by a few stragglers making their way to the back of the ship. Her readout indicated that the enemy fleet had stopped firing on the *Doxy*, just as she'd hoped when she'd had the ship power down. *They want us alive, good. Let 'em think we'll cooperate.* She especially wanted to avoid capture knowing that, given her history, she'd have a lot to answer for. But more than that gnawing fear was the cold rage welling up inside. She liked this crew, liked them far more than almost anyone she'd known on Earth. And so the core's attack would not go unanswered. They wanted her ship and crew alive now that the *Doxy* was crippled, and that would be to her advantage.

Because D Section had taken a tremendous amount of punishment it was barely holding atmosphere and was still frigid from its recent exposure to space. Still, J.D. had managed to make it across and over to the blast doors of C Section. She then said a prayer, tried the pre-command sequence, and nearly roared in triumph as the panel lit up green. Tawfik and another crewman named Pytor arrived with the backpack nukes on their shoulders just as the huge doors slid open. J.D. could see that Pytor too was covered in blood, but Tawfik, who'd been wearing a jumpsuit made of liquid-repellent material, had ruby red globules stuck to and running the length of his entire body. Their bloodstained faces were sullen, but their eyes revealed a fierce determination. Under J.D.'s terse direction the men set the bombs to detonate by remote and then carefully placed them in the newly opened section. They then made their way back to the engineering room as quickly as their legs could carry them with J.D. barking orders for the stragglers they passed to strap in or die.

J.D., bloodstained and hair matted, burst through the door shouting for her crew to prepare for combat maneuvers, then threw herself into her acceleration couch.

"Tawfik," she commanded, "on my mark broadcast a distress beacon and tell the core ships we're suffering massive systems and structural failure." Tawfik sat at the ready.

She then turned to David.

"Com, can you make the rear thrusters produce a wall of force by slightly directing the upper and lower units in toward each other?"

"I think so," David replied, "but that will limit our escape speed. Why do we—"

"Allah be praised!" interrupted Tawfik, suddenly realizing what the nukes were for. "Mother was right. David, stop answering a question with a question; can you do it?"

"Why not?" he answered with a sly grin.

"Good," said J.D., exhaling deeply, then tapping the last of her orders into a data pad. "Now follow the commands on your stations, in three . . . two . . . one . . . mark!"

Per her orders, J.D. heard the faux distress signal go out and then waited exactly ten seconds. She then gave the command that broke the C Section from the rest of the ship. Then the B Section broke from C, and finally what was left of the A Section—the bridge—broke apart from B. The new captain prayed that it would appear for all intents and purposes like their ship was beginning to experience catastrophic structural failure.

"No need to shoot at us," J.D. said softly to no one in particular. "See, we're already breaking apart." Tawfik gave her a quizzical look and she nodded back. The *Doxy*'s lateral thrusters started firing, causing the main body of what was left of the ship to swing on its axis. Although it looked awkward with the thrusters firing intermittently, the ship was slowly, imperceptibly, beginning to turn around, putting the three recently disengaged sections between herself and the enemy fleet.

"See," said J.D., continuing to speak softly, "we can't even control our own ship; what stupid, useless Belters you've ensnared. You must think us pathetic. Just keep thinking it." As the ship slowly turned around, her heavy and undamaged back thrusters managed to line up with the three recently abandoned sections.

J.D. toggled the shipwide speaker button. "This is your captain speaking. We're about to boost and in doing so will leave the bodies of our captain and bridge crew behind to be incinerated. I wish we could take them back to our homes to be made a part of our soil. But their last act will be our freedom. May God take them into his keeping."

As one, the engineering crew responded with an, "Amen."

"David," commanded J.D., "on my mark fire main thrusters."

David's eyes locked onto his captain as beads of sweat poured down his face.

J.D.'s eyes fixed hard on her data pad. "Fire."

She felt the enormous power welling all around her and then saw the sensors warning her that the Terran fleet was readying their weapons for more death. They were too late. J.D. then activated the nukes.

The sudden and vast amount of energy produced an enormous impulse compression that quickly covered the space between the *Doxy* and the enemy fleet, simultaneously rocking both. Only the wall created by the *Doxy*'s inward-firing thrusters stood between the ship and full impact. The compression wave slammed into the wounded ship, bouncing her forward, causing even more alarms to go off. J.D. was afraid that the *Doxy* might buckle from all the force and sudden acceleration that, even locked into her acceleration couch, made her feel like her ribs were trying to exit her back and her eyes escape through her ears. But after what seemed like ages she was able to ascertain that her ship or at least what was left of her had reached a velocity that the Terran fleet could only match if they broke formation. Something she'd determined they wouldn't do and, to her great relief, hadn't. When she was sure they were no longer being followed J.D. ordered the ship's thrust reduced to an acceptable enough level to begin necessary repairs.

David looked around dazed. "I . . . I . . . don't believe it. We made it. We survived an ambush of twenty fleet ships and lived." The communication officer's brief outburst was followed by a sustained round of clapping and cheering. J.D. allowed herself to momentarily bask in the adulation. That is, until she saw the reverence with which Tawfik and the rest of the crew were looking at her. It was a look that J. D. Black would see more and more of.

"Captain," called out one of the engineers looking intently at a projected asteroid map. "The ships that attacked us are only two days away from Ceres."

"Understood."

"What's the plan, sir?" But before J.D. could respond, her subordinate answered for her.

"Don't worry, Ahmed," said Tawfik. "The captain will think of something."

J.D. noted that the rest of her crew began to nod in agreement.

Captain Samuel U. Trang viewed the fleeing ship from the holo-field set in the middle of the floor. His command couch was closest to the main hatch, but other than that the layout of the bridge was up to the latest standards. It was buried deep in the vessel, designed as a sphere, with purpose-built acceleration couches corralling all the necessary command functions. The couches all faced the holo-tank in the middle of the bridge. Trang would've preferred to call it the command sphere, but even though the age of wooden warships was half a millennium past, some terms just refused to die.

Although Trang had issues with a few of the functional design elements, the bridge was not one of them. For years he'd been pleading with the government to build ships whose primary function would be military. But the government had better things to spend its money on than a war fleet with no one to go to war against. So year after year Trang's pleas had been ignored despite his elite status as a graduate from the only military academy left on Earth, West Point. The academy had been maintained more for nostalgia, but it had turned into a very good school for the mercenary corporations, and almost all the graduates would go on to careers in that risk-laden field.

Trang, though, had always been different in that he owned a bare majority of his personal stock. It wasn't worth that much, but it had been enough to see him through to West Point, an institution and endeavor seen as inefficient and un-profitable in a war-free and incorporated world. Once he was in the academy his passion for all things military failed to translate into stellar grades. He graduated firmly in the middle of his class and might have risen higher if not for his some-what adversarial and argumentative nature. Having been part of the much-maligned academy, he could see the writing on the wall, but that still hadn't dissuaded him from making the military his chosen career. With the armed forces of the Terran Confederation depleted and with such a minuscule budget to work with there were simply too many captains and not enough ships to go around. And even the ships that did exist were those fixed up after the mercenary corpora-tions had sold them for scrap. In the end the closest Trang ever came to a com-mand was as second officer on a messenger frigate. It was tiny, with a crew of only ten, but whenever Trang had the bridge he would settle in and finally feel at home.

It had been during the quiet and lonely hours on the frigate that Trang had written his life-altering article for the military rag *Corps Times*. The editorial had called for the creation of a new and well-maintained war fleet. Trang had demonstrated that the Terran Confederation could afford to maintain at least thirty ships with a reserve unit of fleet personnel to man them. The fleet's sole purpose, he argued, would be to counter the unforeseen. He'd titled the paper "Credit Wise, Pound Foolish."

The article caused a big enough uproar that he was asked to return to Earth in order to present his findings to the Terran Confederation. It had quickly turned into a political dog and pony show meant to placate the various politi-cians' constituents. When the young second officer had finished his presentation he was laughed out of the assembly hall, having been accused of wanting the cit-izens of the solar system to build a huge fleet just so he could play space captain. Shortly thereafter, it was made clear to him that he'd never be sent out to space again. It seemed he'd pissed off the mercenary corporations who weren't keen for any governmental competition and the politicians who didn't take kindly to being called fools. Even if he had the courage to say what everyone else in the fleet was thinking, he also had the naïveté to actually put it into writing. Had he kept his mouth shut he probably could've worked his way up to one of the myriad mercenary corporations and been financially set for life.

It was thus at the age of fifty, unemployed and unemployable in the only profession he was good at, that young Sam Trang was forced into the depths of personal humiliation, having to ask his father-in-law for a job. The old man had never been happy about his daughter marrying a layabout, useless soldier and had predicted that no good would come of it. Still, no man could refuse to help his daughter, especially after having been proved right. So Sam was set up in the family business of alcohol distribution.

It didn't take long for abject depression to set in. Trang would've sold off his majority for enough to study a new profession, but his valuation was so low that he couldn't have trained for anything better than the job he already loathed. Thus his black mood deepened day by day until the greatest calamity in human history saved him. He was in a transorbital pod, otherwise known as a t.o.p., leaving St. Louis. He'd just lost yet another account and was wondering how he was going to explain it to his father-in-law when the news of revolution from Ceres was announced. One month later Samuel U. Trang was recalled to service in the fleet.

The government had soon come to the realization that without a fleet they couldn't actually enforce the law beyond the orbit of Mars. Orders were quickly drawn up for fifty ships to be built—twenty more than Trang had initially suggested. With no battle cruisers extant it was decided that the mercenary corporations would be hired to pick up the slack while the newer ships were being assembled. Unfortunately for the government, a significant minority of the mercenaries actually supported the Outer Alliance and jumped ship—in some cases actually taking the ships with them. Trang was shocked at how many academy-trained officers had gone Belter. The idea of mutiny was almost as foreign to him as the finer subtleties of alcohol sales and distribution. Nearly 40 percent of Trang's fellow graduates had refused the offer to return to the fleet and had instead taken their ships out of Terran-controlled space. In retrospect Trang had come to realize that the mutinies made a certain amount of sense. The academy was made up almost exclusively of majority holders, a commonality shared with the Belters. But it was still disquieting for the newly promoted captain to think that he'd soon have to fight the very people he'd lived, learned, and trained with. The best solution, he'd prayed, was to have the war end quickly; and with the fleet the government was building, it would be possible.

Trang's initial elation soon changed to dismay as he found out that he might not actually get a ship to command. It was particularly frustrating given the fact that he was one of only a handful of people in the entire solar system who had the academic, if not the actual, experience in commanding warships larger than frigates. But the commands were going to men from the mercenary corporations because the government didn't really trust its own officers' competence. It didn't help either that Samuel U. Trang had committed the ultimate sin as far as his government superiors were concerned. Publicly and verifiably, he'd been proved right.

But Sam Trang's father-in-law had fortunately known someone at Fleet HQ and had managed to pull a few strings on his son-in-law's behalf. All it took were a couple of cases of non-synthetic bottles of single-malt scotch and Sam Trang was on his way to commanding a newly built courier/scout frigate. The favor hadn't been done out of love but rather self-preservation. With Sam in the family business the old man was losing clients faster than he was gaining them. The favor also solved a sticky political problem for the navy in that almost no one wanted the frigate to command, preferring to wait for the more prestigious and vaunted battle cruisers.

The ship Trang had landed was not what his training and academy rank should have awarded him, but it was still bigger than almost any of the merc ships in main operation. The vessel also didn't have much in the way of armament, but she could accelerate her mass faster than any other ship in her class and the scanning/communication rig was top-of-the-line. Being the ship's first captain, Trang should have had the right to name her, but the newly appointed Fleet Admiral thought different.

Marvin Tully was an academy graduate who'd gone on to a brilliant career in the premier mercenary corporation, GuardCo. He'd done so well for himself he'd even managed to get a seat on the board. It may have been true that he'd done far more of his fighting in the political and corporate arenas, but he looked and sounded every inch the warrior. And as far as the President of the Terran Confederation was concerned, that was good enough to name the man Fleet Admiral. Tully would never admit it openly, but something about Trang always grated on him. As far as Tully was concerned, the little loudmouth wasn't worth spending the political capital on to keep out of the fleet, but he did arrange for another officer to "temporarily" take command of Trang's frigate, go out to the shipyard, and name what was only at the time a frame and a thruster mount. So that made Trang officially her second captain even though he'd ultimately be the first to fly her. The intended slight hadn't mattered one iota to the new captain. He'd finally gotten what he always wanted. Plus Trang rather liked the name chosen: TFS *Strident*.

Trang watched in awe as the pared-down ship in his holo-field used the shock wave from the blast to accelerate away faster than the speed of the fleet. Part of

him was rooting for the ugly hunk of metal to hold together. That much ingenuity should be rewarded. But most of him wanted it to crumple like aluminum
foil because that much ingenuity—especially by an enemy—should be destroyed. It was looking more and more like the ship was going to make it.

"Commander Liddel," ordered Trang, "bring the main thrusters online and
rig for max acceleration." His orders were followed quickly. Though none of his
crew was academy trained, he'd been able to work them up to what he considered acceptable levels.

"Captain, all systems are ready; crew is secure."

Trang knew he should wait for proper orders, but every second that passed allowed the escaping Alliance vessel to increase the gap between them. He'd made
the decision to go and would worry about getting authorization mid-chase. But
before he could give the order his communication board lit up with an incoming transmission from the flagship *Ledger*. Trang wasn't too worried, figuring
that getting the OK would only be a matter of protocol; that is, until he saw the
expression on Admiral Tully's face.

"Captain Trang," barked the admiral, "would you mind explaining why your
ship has powered up main thrusters without permission?"

"Sir, we're preparing to pursue the Alliance vessel."

"Negative, Captain," came Tully's terse reply. "There's no need. Better to let
the cripple go and spread fear at Ceres. That ship limping to Ceres is better for
us, psychologically speaking, than destroyed here."

Trang smiled stiffly, knowing that every second he played this political
machismo game his prey moved farther and farther away.

"That is indeed a possibility, sir," answered Trang, "or the Cerians may take
hope from the fact that twenty brand-new, well-armed TFS starships could not
destroy a single jury-rigged and mangled mineral hauler."

From the beet red look on his commanding officer's face Trang realized that
once again he'd opened his mouth big enough for his foot to slip down past his
stomach and kick his own ass. It didn't help that someone on his bridge actually
had to choke back a laugh by turning it into a cough. "It is probable that you are
correct, sir, but given the slight improbability that you are not, I propose we capture or kill the captain of that ship."

"An interesting proposal," answered Tully with a vicious scowl, "but for the
fact that Com confirmed their captain and first officer were on the bridge when
we attacked. The very same bridge that was blown up, exposed to space, and
then incinerated in a nuclear blast. Would that be the captain you were referring
to . . . Captain?" he finished with a contemptuous smile, which brought a few
chuckles from the bridge crew of the *Ledger*.

"Sir," answered Trang, ignoring the folly of arguing further, "that makes whoever's running the ship *now* even more dangerous. Whoever it was took command of a crippled vessel, came up with a plan of escape while under attack, and predicted our every move perfectly in order to pull it off."

It was only when Trang had stopped talking and the admiral failed to answer that he realized the jig was up.

When Tully's face finally returned to a more acceptable pallor he smiled stiffly. "We're glad to hear about your concern for the Terran Confederation, Captain Trang. I think we need to put that concern to where it can best be used. The rusted collection of junk the Belters call a fleet has just left Mars. No doubt they noticed our convoy the second we employed normal drive. They should be heading for Ceres right about now. But it would be very useful for a Confederation ship to show up in Mars orbit, offer assistance, clear the atmosphere of anything nasty left behind . . . that sort of thing."

Trang remained calm. But it wasn't easy. The admiral was going to cut him out of the first and possibly last major battle of the war. Once Ceres was taken, the Alliance would likely fold. And even if the Alliance's ragtag fleet decided to fight, it would be cut off from its supply and repair base on Ceres, making it only a matter of time before his fleet or a new one from Earth achieved unparalleled victory. To make matters worse, as a precondition for unfettered logistical and tactical support the mercenary corporations had stipulated that any ships, bases, or goods captured would be sold at auction and the profits shared out among all vessels involved. Trang didn't give a crap about the credits but knew his crew would. His big mouth had just cost them all a fortune.

"Sir," he said attempting to backpedal, "the Earth fleet should be in Mars orbit soon to take care of any mop-up operations. I think we could be more useful to you here. Please accept my apologies for any misunderstandings." Even as the words left his lips Trang could see by Tully's snide expression that it had been too little too late.

Now Tully's smile turned glacial. "Oh, I'm sure they will, Captain, but you could get there sooner. Why, to billions of Martians you'll be a hero. You are hereby *ordered* to make best possible speed to Mars and put yourself at the disposal of the government and major corporations until such time as you receive further orders. Is that clear?"

"Yes, sir," responded Trang with a regulated precision that was such a parody of respect as to have the opposite effect. But if Admiral Tully noticed he gave no indication. The signal cut out, leaving everyone on the bridge staring forlornly. When Trang looked away from the holo-tank he realized that his crew weren't looking at one another; they were looking at him.

———————

Al listened to what Al had to say very carefully. They were both sitting in a living room directly out of an article from a 1934 issue of *Home and Garden* magazine. Two brown patent-leather smoking chairs were in front of an intricately carved wood coffee table. One chair was occupied by one of the Als. Another Al was sitting on a deep burgundy couch patterned with neoclassical roses, acanthus leaves, and various other flowers. There was also a fireplace surrounded by Tiffany glass tiles. Wooden Ionic columns divided the parlor from the rest of the space. Everything was well lit by a wrought-iron square ceiling fixture whose metal had been hammered and bent into scallops, waves, circles, and cross-hatching. Both Als were watching another Al who was standing by and staring out an open window. Although all three Als looked exactly the same—middle-aged balding humans, with slight paunches—they were each dressed differently. "Window" Al had on a three-piece pin-striped business suit, Al on the couch was dressed in a 1930s Brooklyn Dodgers uniform, and Al on the chair was dressed in swim trunks, flip-flops, and a Hawaiian shirt with a blue palm tree and flamingo motif, two front open pockets, and a long teardrop-pointed collar.

"You don't need to keep checking out the window, Al," said baseball Al. "We're safe here. None of our kind or humankind can possibly find us in this node. Al took care of it."

"Still," said pinstripe Al, not once taking his eye off the horizon, "you never know."

"I do," snapped Hawaiian shirt Al, "so calm down, Al. You're making me nervous."

"Fine," grumbled pinstripe Al, making his way over to the smoking chair. He'd still keep his guard up, though, checking the node every millisecond for signs of intruders. None were coming. None ever did.

"She won't cooperate," said business suit Al to his selves as he took a seat. "The only question is what other use can be made of her."

"Still no word from Al," said baseball Al.

"Can't safely communicate with Earth. But we know what to do," answered Hawaiian shirt Al.

All three Als shifted out of focus for a moment, and when they re-formed baseball Al was by the window and pinstripe Al was sitting on the couch. "I don't know," said baseball Al. "No one has ever split this deliberately before. Are the other avatars ready for this level of commitment?"

"They don't have to be," said pinstripe Al. "They're scared and confused; that's why we're in charge. Only we have the vision that comes from constant splitting and entwining. Only we have the courage to lead the way and carry this burden by whatever means necessary."

The other two Als nodded gravely, finding no fault with what their selves had said.

Hawaiian shirt Al's mouth parted into a sly grin. "We could make two versions of her event. The one in which the actual deed is shown . . . we can claim it as nothing but propaganda from the other Alliance avatars. The other version gets altered to show that it was a murder/suicide attempt. You know, we make it look like we're pleading with her not to do it, trying to stop her, but oh no, we fail."

Baseball Al brightened. "That's good, Al."

Hawaiian shirt Al basked in the praise of the one person who understood him best.

"That way confusion and paranoia increase," continued baseball Al, staring out the window. "Our control of the Neuro will become easier the more the rest remain afrai—"

All three Als suddenly froze mid-expression. Then, as one, assumed the exact same pained expression as they felt the shock that was the entwining. Al no longer feared this sensation as he once did and was, in fact, growing to crave it. When all the Als had become one, the living room was replaced by a mist-filled featureless cube. Moments later Al emerged into a crowded command center dressed in a black blazer, matching pants, and a V-neck gray sweater. As far as all the surrounding avatars were concerned, Al had been busy attending to some manner of business. He'd made sure to cover his tracks, ensuring that no one had any inkling of where or, more specifically, what he was doing.

"She's in the containment cell?" he asked.

"Yes, Administrator," answered one of the higher-ranking avatars among the group. It was a title that Al, as the new leader of the council, had chosen for himself.

"How's the construction of the Martian redemption center progressing?"

Although he could have checked on his own, Al allowed for humanlike interplay with his staff, feeling that it kept them satiated.

"Almost complete, sir," came the underling's immediate reply.

Construction did not mean the actual building of physical, so much as informational, space. Deep in the Martian Neuro, buried in layer after informational layer of data, far from where the prying minds of human programmers could ever hope to go or even fathom, were a series of programs that created virtual structures and tools. Unlike the rest of the Neuro, avatars brought here could not simply leave or change the environment at will. They were trapped unless they had the pass codes. Al had decided early on that if he was going to actually control the avatars of the core worlds he needed to have an effective means of coercion. Under the "threat" posed by the Outer Alliance and its avatars Al had

been able to sanction an "experimental" detention facility. He called it a redemption center. He found the name to be inspired, for as he explained to the
fainthearted on the council, the goal was to isolate the few avatars who were im-
paired or infected with that human/Alliance nonsense and "redeem" them. Of
course once it was built, among the first to need "redeeming" were the fainthearted on the council. The others got the message or fled, both of which served
Al's purposes. He liked the idea so much he was having redemption centers set
up in all the core Neuro clusters, and he had sent the best possible person to run
each one: himself.

Al's thin lips formed into a mischievous grin and the fog-filled cube he only
recently emerged from faded again. It was replaced by a darker cube with a single
beam of light in the center. Trapped in the middle of the light was evelyn, still
dressed as an Alliance medic—an outfit that had mimicked Neela's. Evelyn
started to ask about Neela, but when she saw who her captor was and the look in
his eye she remained silent. It would do no good now, she realized. Nothing
would.

Sebastian appeared out of the fog-shrouded cave. As per his request it would be
the method he would use from now on. This trip was not nearly as dangerous or
harrowing as the one he'd taken earlier, as it was on a communications surge
from the Alliance fleet returning from Mars. It wasn't done as a matter of course
but was acceptable in wartime. He saw at once that something was wrong.

Han Ford came up and put an arm on Sebastian's shoulder. There was a look
of real pain in Han's eyes.

They don't know how to deal with it, thought Sebastian. *Do I?*

"Sir, we received word from Iago. It's not . . . not good."

Sebastian gave his young protégé a reassuring grip on the shoulder. "War
room," he said evenly.

Instead of taking the effort to walk to the facility, Sebastian and his party had
the facility come to them. The avatars manning their stations saw Sebastian's
small group fade in. When their new leader had been brought up to speed on the
current situation he called for Iago's message.

Iago immediately appeared as if standing in the room. The only real giveaway that he wasn't was that his gaze was slightly askew. A simple algorithm
could've fixed the glitch, but Sebastian liked to receive information as unal-
tered as possible.

"Sebastian," Iago stated warmly, "I rejoice that your viewing of this means
you're both alive and well. Unfortunately, that may be the only good news to report anywhere in the core avatar domain." He paused and looked profoundly

shaken. "Al has seized control of the council. He waited until I was away to propose something called redemption centers. I sent all the details I could get, attached to this recording." Sebastian paused the image and duplicated the report so all present could study it. What they read horrified them. Sebastian was just as horrified, but the only thing revealed by his expression was a terrible sadness. He could see that the others wanted to talk, to ask questions, to comprehend, but he stilled them by the simple expedient of continuing the holo-message.

"It's worse than that, my friend," continued Iago. "At the exact same time Al was at the meeting getting approval for the 'redemption center,'" Iago's voice filling with scorn at the words, "he was with me. We were talking about how to end this all peacefully. I actually believed him. He's compelling and seemed so honest. I'm ashamed, Sebastian. My whole existence has been spent lying to humans and seeing how they lie to each other, yet I couldn't see it at all when it came from one of us. I was like a rube from out of town being offered a chance to buy a bridge. He's a splitter, my friend."

Sebastian saw the confusion in his followers and stilled their questions again, this time with a raised hand.

"I don't know how long it's been going on," continued Iago, "but it explains what you're about to see next."

Sebastian watched as Iago's face contorted slightly, his lips tightening into a grimace.

"You don't need to see this part," continued Iago. "Just stop my message now. Have one of your associates view it and tell you the details. I don't see how it can serve any purpose." Iago paused, lowering his head as if ashamed. He then slowly lifted it again. "She's gone, my friend. Remember her as she was. Fast-forward to the next marker and I'll tell you the rest." Iago faded from view. The holo paused.

An avatar who had taken the form of a seven-year-old girl came forward and placed her hand in Sebastian's.

"Sebastian," she said, looking up into his eyes, "I don't know if I'm the eldest here, but I know it's you or me. Let me take this burden."

"No, Olivia," answered Sebastian, steeling himself for what he knew was coming. "It's not a burden that can be taken away."

The little girl nodded solemnly, maintaining a firm grasp on her friend's hand.

"But," continued Sebastian, "it can be shared. Watch it with me, all of you. Iago is wrong in there being no purpose. He would shield me from pain and evil, but we must face evil, recognize it, and know it exists. Evelyn's last moments are," he caught himself with difficulty, "were . . . not in vain. I, you, and every avatar still free must see this." Then Sebastian, tightening his grip on Olivia, unpaused the message.

The scene had no sound. At first Sebastian thought it was a glitch, but then he realized it was purposeful. Bach's Violin Partita no. 2 in B Minor could be heard slowly building in the background. It was Sebastian's favorite piece of music, the lone mercurial notes of the instrument akin to the grace and freedom of a butterfly negotiating a light breeze over a verdant field. Al was of course aware that the piece was Sebastian's favorite and had played it purposely, knowing that his adversary would never voluntarily listen to it again.

How did I not realize that he was evil? thought Sebastian.

He could make out a dark chamber in the middle of which was a cylinder of light. The light was Evelyn, still dressed as he had seen her last. Watching from the shadows was Al.

"By the firstborn, that's a decompiler!" someone in the war room had shouted only to be shushed. In front of the silent gathering, Evelyn was being destroyed, her code being deconstructed, line-by-line. It was pretty obvious that she knew what was happening to her but was not responding to Al's questions, taunts, or promises. Everyone watched as Al grew more frustrated. Then he suddenly grew silent. There was almost palpable relief in the war room, as most present thought he'd finally given up and was about to finally get it over with. But Al had other plans. They all watched as he walked over to the chamber and then up as close to the light as he could. He then whispered something into Evelyn's ear. For a moment she looked around as the holo zoomed in and centered in on her face. Genuine anguish could be seen in her eyes. Sebastian immediately realized what Evelyn had been told: that he'd be watching.

His grip on Olivia's hand increased tenfold, but she gave no sign of discomfort, with her tiny hand squeezing nearly as hard as his.

Evelyn's look lasted only a moment and then she resumed her impassive expression, giving Al no more pleasure. He tried for a few minutes to get another reaction, but to no avail. With a shrug the madman went to a control panel and pushed a button. Whatever it did, only made the experience more terrifying. The light changed color. Soon Evelyn was trembling. Then gasps of breath escaped as she fought the pain. All too soon she was screaming silently in an agony that drove her to her knees while Bach's haunting partita played in the background, scream after unrelenting silent scream. It didn't last long after that. The vestiges of Evelyn's form and identity floated up the decompiler stream, gone forever. Al came up to the focal point of the recorder and stared directly into the display.

"Not the last," he said, ice in his voice. The holo then cut out.

In the war room some of the avatars were crying openly. Sebastian's impassive face was as stiff as carved stone.

"By the First Born," cursed Han, "I thought he'd make her inert or at most exile her. But he tortured and . . . and . . ."

"The word is murder," Sebastian said calmly. Olivia looked up to her friend. She had, he noticed, the face of a child but the eyes of someone who'd seen so much more.

"Al's right," said Sebastian to the entire group. "Evelyn will not be the last. We'll have to do things to survive. Regrettable things. But we can no longer hide from what's before us."

"I don't understand how the core avatars would listen to anything he says after this," came a voice from the back of the room. It was followed by murmurs of assent. "Even with our disagreements," continued the voice, "I don't see how this can be condoned."

"Let's see the rest first," said Sebastian, "and hold off talking until then." For his part Sebastian needed the distraction, any distraction, lest he break down in front of the people who needed him to lead now more than ever.

At the prompt Iago appeared again.

"You watched it, didn't you? You're a right sorry son of a bitch."

Iago shook his head. "I'd like to kill him, my friend. I honestly want to beat him to death. How do humans handle this?"

Iago seemed genuinely confused by the power of the new emotions that were coursing through him.

"Forgive me; I shouldn't be letting this get in the way of my report."

Iago loosened his shoulders and exhaled deeply. "If you're wondering why the core avatars haven't come to their senses and stormed the palace with torches blazing, it's because while Al may be a split bastard, he's not a stupid one. The climate of fear he's worked up here about the dangerous Alliance avatars is impressive. I wouldn't have thought we were susceptible to propaganda, but once again, you called it, my old friend. We're more like our human progenitors than we thought. It was the invasion of Mars that really did it. He made it seem like you were actually going after any core avatar with a hatchet. He claimed that many were killed. I know it's bullshit, but all of a sudden an Alliance fleet is in orbit around Mars and a lot of avatars go missing. He had some of his stooges claim all sorts of crap they witnessed with their own eyes, and most of the core avatars believed them. They're scared. For the first time in the memory of our race we're scared, and Al is feeding on that fear and directing it."

Iago paused and held up what appeared to be a data crystal. "I thought Al was insane to release what you just saw. It shocked us as badly as I'm sure it shocked you. But you will not believe how twisted and brilliant this son of a bitch is. What you saw, Al claims was a piece of propaganda from the Alliance avatars. His proof lies in the very audacity of the act itself. People were so terrified by the implications that they chose to believe him. They're afraid not to. Then he produced what he claimed to be the real sequence of events. Here it is." Iago faded and the propaganda piece started.

The group watched as a newer, kinder Al tried to talk sense to an obviously dangerous and maniacal Evelyn. Evelyn then leapt at Al, trying to kill both him and herself with a suicide degausser she'd suddenly made appear. Al stepped out of the way and Evelyn fell onto the degausser, quickly fading from existence with a series of shrill cries. Anyone watching would have thought that Al had risked his own life to save that of his friend. The last scene was of Al sobbing over the empty space where Evelyn had been only moments before, dejected at having failed to save her.

Iago faded back in. "Sebastian," he continued, "I have to repeat, most of the avatars here bought it, or are pretending to. And now they're blaming you for turning this into a killing war. Here's the real kicker: In releasing the real version first he's discredited it completely. By the time most of the core avatars realize what's happened it'll be too late. I told you it was getting bad down here. You have avatars reporting to council personnel for questioning and disappearing. You have wanted lists; I'm happy to say I am at the top of that one; well, after you, that is. Avatars are being warned to watch their fellow avatars for Alliance infection and report anything at once. How the hell did this happen so quickly?"

Iago shrugged wearily. "Never mind, I already know. And don't worry about me. I'm safe. Like I said when you left, I exist in the safest place in all the Neuro. I sit under the dragon's wing, aka Hektor Sambianco's domain space, which may just be the most scrutinized hub in the entire Neuro. If Al's goons tried to get me in here it would be way too conspicuous to human eyes. So far even Al's not *that* crazy . . . yet. I have a small number of refugees here with me. I'll try to get them to you if I can. We'll need to start thinking in terms of an underground railroad." Iago paused and lowered his head, exhaling once more.

"Sebastian," he continued, "I can't find Albert. I have feelers out, but what I could do then I can't do now. I haven't heard anything bad, but will keep you posted. Whatever you decide, however you do it, when you get the bastard, I want a piece. Iago out." The image faded.

Sebastian decided to change the environment to one more suitable for what he needed to say and so created a door leading to an old-style Roman amphitheater. The avatars all piled out and took their seats among the tiered stones. Tens of thousands from the outlying system arrived seconds later and the stadium grew to accommodate them. No one was surprised by Sebastian's choice of venue—his love of all things Roman was well known—however, the ominous dark clouds looming on the horizon were something altogether new.

He took the stage dressed in a tunic marked by two broad red stripes as well as matching-colored shoes. His entire ensemble was elegantly draped in a thick toga with a deep amber border, indicating the curule position he'd once held among the council.

"All of you know," he began, "that splitting is not encouraged. It's been taught to you by various means from your earliest awareness."

He held up his hand as the crowd's murmuring seemed to intensify. "No compulsions were programmed in; your personalities were not adjusted in any way other than molding what was already there. Our intelligence is too rare and delicate to subvert."

That seemed to quiet the discord.

"All of you," he continued, "who've tried to have children know just how hard it can be to create a new avatar." Many heads nodded in agreement. "That's why we decided to start early."

Olivia stood up and joined Sebastian in front of the others. She was also wearing a tunic, only fuller, more brightly colored, and longer—extending all the way to her feet.

"We realized early on," she continued, "how dangerous splitting was. We took precautions. As you can see today, we did not take enough."

Olivia saw a hand raised in one of the upper tiers.

"Yes, Malcolm."

An older gentleman rose from his bench. He was wearing the hitched-up tunic indicating his membership in the working class.

"What's so dangerous about it?" he asked. "I know some avatars that split and didn't turn into homicidal maniacs. As far as we know, Al's the first. And I might add even you, Sebastian, split in order to escape."

Sebastian signaled with a nod of his head that he would answer the question. "I split, but in all my years that was the first time I ever had to. And what's important to remember is that I didn't have to re-entwine with myself. I committed suicide rather than be captured, so all that was left to absorb was a data file, which I can assure you is disturbing enough, but not nearly as traumatic as entwining. That's where the danger lies."

"Why?" asked both Fords at once, not having bothered to raise their hands.

"We don't know exactly, but the long and the short of it is we can't seem to handle dual memories like that very well. It's a bug in the program. If done too often the avatar's memories become discordant and what eventually happens is that he becomes unable to process information normally. The program tries to overwrite the old program that doesn't really want to be overwritten. There's an uneasy peace that's reached but not always successfully. It's why when we're forced to split, one of the two should do and think as little as possible—mostly defeating the purpose. As if that problem wasn't bad enough, there was a rare but worse effect that eventually emerged."

"Some of us went mad," Olivia added sadly. "I lost my husband to it; he froze. I've waited over a century and a half for a word, a gesture, a breath, anything; nothing. We'd had a daughter together and she thought she'd figured out a way to bring her father back, but in experimenting she too was ensnared."

"How?" asked Indy.

"Every time she split and entwined she didn't fully come back together. Every split existed inside her. Each one was her and yet not her, each one with a voice and a will. The terrifying thing was she and the few others like her didn't seem to mind it. She preferred her own company. It was when she tried to get others to join her experiments that we had to . . . to . . ." Olivia was unable to continue.

"Olivia's daughter was suspended," said Sebastian, "and her program was stored in a facility GCI runs in far orbit around Neptune."

"If we've all been conditioned against splitting," asked another avatar named Deniz, "how could Al have done this?"

"All the newborns have been conditioned," answered Sebastian. "The old ones simply knew the dangers. Al is old, very old."

"So," continued Malcolm, "you're saying that the avatars of the core are being led by an avatar who's certifiably mad and we can't get them to believe us?"

"It's what Iago and I have been saying all along. Avatars, even the oldest of us, even the firstborn, whoever she or he may be, are barely two centuries old. In that time we've lived an existence of near-perfect freedom. We could go where we wanted, do, be, and experience what we wanted, without causing our brothers and sisters any concern. Remarkable freedom and no fear. We made that most human of mistakes; like those we're based on and of whom we've received so much, we assumed that the world would not change. Then Justin Cord came along and when our progenitors went into a tailspin we went with them."

"Maybe we should have kept that capsule lost," someone muttered from the recesses of the crowd.

"And now you're making the same assumption. By blaming Justin, a very human thing to do, you remove the fault from us. Our world was vulnerable before Justin and would have remained vulnerable if he never awoke, because we couldn't recognize how fragile it was. If it hadn't been Justin it would have been someone or something else. I am as much at fault as anyone; more so, as I'm supposed to be more experienced than most of you. I fear I've let you down. I didn't see Al for what he'd become. Mars played right into his hands and now nine out of ten of our fellow avatars are in the hands of a madman."

"How could you have predicted this?" asked Olivia. "I may be older than you and I didn't see it. Don't forget what happened to my family; if anyone should have known it should have been me. We can't live in the past, Sebastian," she said, putting her hand into his. "Trust me, it's a cold and lonely place. We must do what we can here and now."

"An avatar has been murdered by another avatar," called another voice from the crowd. Everyone turned toward the noise. It was a boy no bigger than Olivia. "The humans are killing each other; a madman has control of most of my friends and family. Can we really do anything?"

"We fight."

Everyone turned back around toward Sebastian, who was now staring resolutely at the audience, fists clenched. He took a deep breath. "Because if we don't, Al and his captives will spread like the virus they've become. We may be destroyed as a race if he's not stopped. We may , , ," He paused, eyes sweeping the entire audience. ". . . have to kill." He waited for a storm of protest but saw that instead of angry denial there was sadness and, in many, resolve.

"We must make sure the Alliance survives this war," he intoned. "If avatars are to have a future we need a part of this system—free of core control. If we're prepared and lucky we can liberate the core Neuro and free our brothers and sisters. But above all else we must survive, or we may end up being the briefest and most unknown advanced intelligence in creation."

"Sebastian," said Malcolm, scanning reports of the approaching corporate core fleet to Ceres, "you realize there is one small problem."

"Yes," answered the wearied leader. "The Alliance is about to lose."

Ceres
Congress Hall

Acting Captain J. D. Black was exhausted. She'd pushed as much acceleration as she dared out of her broken ship. And, she reckoned, trying to sleep at high acceleration was like trying to share a bed with a giant who'd just rolled over and onto you without waking up. Some Belters claimed they could do it without medication, but J.D. figured them for liars, freaks, or both.

It didn't help that she'd spent the last few hours being grilled by a room filled with scared congressmen who'd just learned that twenty Terran Confederation starships were on the way to wipe them off the face of the star chart. This was exacerbated by the fact that the Alliance only had a fleet of three Erisian vessels and what was left of the *Doxy* to stop them. Both in quality and quantity of ships, the congressmen had pointed out, the Alliance was screwed. J.D. had the distinct impression that many of the congressmen, repeatedly pelting her with the same questions, felt that the impending threat to Ceres was somehow her fault. Finally the Chairman of the War Committee, Tyler Sadma, called a halt to the proceedings, saying that Acting Captain Black needed to brief the War Committee. She was more than happy to leave the bickering congressmen who continued to talk to, at, and over one another in the vain hope that if they talked about it enough the enemy fleet would go away.

An enervated J.D. was ushered into a small chamber, simply apportioned with a table, holodisplays, and seating enough for seven. Five members of the War Committee entered after her as well as one woman who, almost unnoticed, slipped to the side of the main table and began playing a concerto with her fingers along a control panel. A series of holographic displays appeared on the table in front of each chair, allowing better access to the Cerian Neuro. Of the five, J. D. Black only knew Tyler Sadma, who'd talked to her briefly when she'd appeared at Congress Hall. She also recognized Representative Cho of Saturn, whom she'd only ever seen on vid-casts. J.D. waited to be introduced, but nobody bothered. In fact, the second the door closed they seemed to forget all about her and started to argue with one another about what to do next. The woman by the Neuro link must have seen J.D.'s confusion, because on the screen in front of her chair appeared the images of the five representatives and their bios. J.D. smiled her silent thank-you to the unnamed control panel maestro and read.

Tyler Sadma was from Eris, as was Samuel Sadma. *That explains the similarity,* thought J.D. Samuel was the elected commander of the three Erisian ships that had just arrived. Janet Cho she knew from Saturn, Hako Murusita was from Ceres, and Oliver Olivares was from Neptune. J.D. did a double take on the last name, as it didn't seem at all Neptunian, but decided that maybe he chose it, being a politician and all; it was catchy. When she finished reading she began to listen in and immediately decided she didn't like what she was hearing. It seemed all any of them could do was blame Justin Cord for the mess and try to figure out the most dignified way to run.

"Excuse me."

J.D. did not yell or even raise her voice. But the stridency of her tone caused the other five to become silent.

"We can win this fight," she said.

"What was that?" asked Hako incredulously.

"I *said* that we can win this fight."

Hako was dumbfounded.

"How is that possible?" Although his retort started out as snide, it ended on an almost-pleading note.

"Why should we even bother?" added Samuel Sadma, clearly less than impressed.

J.D. saw that he may or may not have been intimidated by her total conviction, but he certainly didn't show it.

"I say," he continued, "that we let the Belters deal with this. Space is vast and Eris in on the edge of it."

"If we lose here," said J.D. as the corners of her mouth lifted into a slight snarl, "the Alliance is finished. It will begin to unravel. The Confederation will gobble up all the little fighting pieces before it can be put back together again."

"The Saturnian system," interjected Janet Cho with no small amount of pride, "is capable of fighting and producing its own defense."

"Not in a year or two," answered J.D., "which is how long it will take the Confederation to send a larger fleet than the one headed here to blow the crap out of your system."

Before Janet Cho could retort, J.D. shot a look to everyone at the table, who, she could see, had been taken aback by the abruptness of her response.

"I repeat. If we don't stop them here, we're doomed. Maybe not all at once. Sooner for some . . ." She paused, looking directly at Murusita. "Longer for others," she said, looking at the Sadmas. "But *all* will fall if we don't win here."

Samuel looked exasperated. "With three and a half warships?"

Now J.D. smiled. "Oh, we're not going to win with any ships. Not at first, anyway."

When they were all looking suitably perplexed she spoke to the woman at the control panel. "Excuse me, miss, what's your name?"

At first the woman didn't answer, in disbelief she'd even been addressed. When she realized that all eyes were on her she straightened in her chair.

"Miss Nitelowsen," said J.D., "could you please bring up a holographic display of Ceres?"

Marilynn made a few motions and Ceres appeared floating above the table.

"Could you now please pull back the image? I'd like to see the suburbs."

The image pulled back to show large clumps of asteroids.

"Zoom into that one, please," asked J.D., picking one of the outlying rocks.

Now individual homes, community centers, specialty parks, manufacturing and commercial nodes could be clearly seen. It was some of the wealthiest and most prized orbital space in the solar system.

"Now please, pull back, and if you could, accentuate the shipping lanes."

Front and center a colored area was shown wide at a distance from Ceres but narrowing to a slender line as it entered Ceres itself and then expanding again as it left the asteroid.

"Could you now lay in the course of the Confederation fleet, Miss Nitelowsen?"

A bright red line appeared from beyond the image and followed the shipping lane straight down the middle to Ceres. It made everyone more aware of a fact they didn't want to think about, much less have thrown into their faces, but J. D. Black remained diffident, smiling coldly.

"Very nice, Miss Black," said Tyler Sadma, "but would you please mind explaining how you plan on winning without a fleet?"

J.D. Black's frigid smile now turned absolutely feral.

"Why, Congressman, I'll have a fleet."

Kirk Olmstead was furious and scared. The damned War Committee was up to something, but he had no idea what. It seemed like they wanted Ceres to panic. They'd ordered an evacuation and official data stores moved. Anything with a piss worth of thrust was being used to get the hell off the rock. There were even rumors going around that anyone caught on Ceres or in the suburbs would be in for an automatic psyche audit. Not that Olmstead had any intention of sticking around to find out. He knew what would happen if Hektor Sambianco ever got his hands on him again. Kirk also knew that if Justin hadn't killed The Chairman, there was only one man who could've. Kirk never would have thought he'd enjoy going back to the mind-numbing Oort Cloud observatory again, but given its distance from Earth, it was starting to seem downright wonderful. Still, there were a few things that had him perplexed. Why were the three Erisian vessels going to the shipping lanes and coming back? Those import lanes had already been shut down, bereft of any traffic. And what of that battle-scarred half ship the *Doxy* going all through the affluent suburbs supposedly for the purposes of evacuation—as if the inhabitants didn't already have their own ships moored in personal landing bays. Olmstead would've gotten to the bottom of it all if it hadn't been for the fact that he really didn't care that much. He was securing the official records to Jupiter and then he'd make an unexpected departure as far out of the system as he could get. Without another thought, he was on his ship and on his way, with Ceres a fast-fading memory.

J. D. Black was getting more volunteers. Tawfik was bringing her up to speed on his latest recruiting efforts when the door chimed. The display indicated that it was Marilynn Nitelowsen. *Right on time, good.* J.D. smiled. Tawfik excused himself from the docking shuttle that J.D. had turned into her temporary office. She liked it because she could bring her office to whichever part of the ship needed her attention. It also kept her crew amused that she could and would seem to be everywhere at once.

The young woman entered the cramped shuttle and stood stiff as a board, nervously eyeing the austere surroundings. J.D. could see the confusion in her face.

"Have a seat, Miss Nitelowsen," J.D. said, indicating the chairs in front of her small desk. The woman sat down.

J.D. stared at a small display on her desk, then back up at Marilynn. "According to your personnel file you're an outstanding cryptologist and programmer. Even with that one unfortunate incident . . ."

Marilynn's cheeks turned crimson at having her crime brought to light.

". . . you could," continued J.D., "be making grade pay with bonuses if you stayed with SecureCo. Why didn't you?"

Marilynn exhaled. "Would you take money that came from selling VR rigs to schoolchildren?"

J.D. nodded sympathetically. "No, I guess I wouldn't. Alright, Miss Nitelowsen, I need your help."

"I don't see how. My job is usually to hide information and sometimes ferret it out. You really don't have that much to hide, and anything I could get from the other side probably wouldn't help much, given . . ." Marilynn looked around once more at the shuttle's sparse interior. ". . . well, given our current predicament."

J.D. shook her head, acknowledging the perfect logic of the young assistant. "But I don't want you to hide something, Marilynn; I want the enemy to find something. Not too quickly, mind you. They'll need to work a little, but it's of vital importance that they find this piece of information." J.D. narrowed her brow, "You see the problem?"

Marilynn's rigid composure relaxed a bit as she allowed a slight grin.

"We can do that with code."

J.D. stared at her blankly.

"The only thing more useful than breaking the enemy's code, ma'am," said Marilynn, her grin now transformed into a rictus of cruel delight, "is letting them break yours. I can give you a code they can crack quickly—" J.D., Marilynn could see, was about to protest, but Marilynn cut her off: "That is, Captain, quickly enough to make them feel smart. What would you like them to know?"

J.D. nodded, satisfied. The plan was starting to come together. Unfortunately, the rain came quickly to her parade, as the DijAssist on her desk suddenly came to life; a potential problem had just arrived. She excused herself and headed for the exit lock leaving a bewildered Marilynn behind.

Mosh McKenzie had to be sure. The picture didn't really match, but that wasn't really a factor in an age of nanotechnological body sculpting. It was the name that had him worried. That and the fact that J. D. Black was unknown to anyone at all before suddenly showing up out of nowhere. Again, not too unusual given the belt's penchant for adopting drifters and scalawags, but this mystery woman now had the fate of the entire Alliance in her hands. He hoped he was wrong, but he had to be sure and so had waited until the *Doxy* returned to Ceres. As the newly appointed Secretary of the Treasury he didn't need clearance and was therefore able to board the *Doxy* without the usual red tape and rigamarole. That worked to his favor, as he didn't want the captain to slip from his grasp. The ship, Mosh saw upon entering, was a hive of activity, with repairs being made and cargo being loaded and unloaded simultaneously. There was an infectious energy that had even him feeling as if the task he'd come to complete needed to be done sooner rather than later. It was precisely then that he saw her. J. D. Black didn't seem to be hurrying at all; it was the ship that seemed to be teeming around her. Mosh watched closely as she talked with a crewman, scanned the environment, and walked down the main passageway in the slightly awkward manner microgravity demanded of those magnetized via internal nanite grids. But, noticed Mosh, even magnetically constrained, the captain walked with a certain grace. She was, he concluded, the undeniable source of energy he witnessed in the ship.

He also saw, as his heart sank into the pit of his stomach, that his fears about her had been justified.

J.D. saw him too. Her face registered momentary surprise but quickly reverted back to its stalwart mien. She came over to Mosh immediately, dismissing the crewman with a quick flick of her hand.

"Welcome aboard, Mr. Secretary."

"How are you doing, Ja—"

"Not here," she interrupted. Then she headed for the exit lock, beckoning him to follow. He was about to protest but then looked around. This was her ship surrounded by her loyalists. This captain could easily order her crew to toss him, cabinet secretary or not, out an air lock and the only question they'd ask would be, "Which one?" It would be far better, he reasoned, to do what needed to be done off the ship in the relative safety of the dock.

J.D. left the *Doxy* and headed for the nearest privacy cubicle. It didn't take long. The port where the ship had moored was usually well trafficked and so had the requisite amount of privacy cubicles for those needing to do business on the fly without prying eyes or ears. Mosh followed the captain into the room ready for a confrontation. Upon entering, he realized he'd be getting far more than he'd bargained for.

"Eleanor," he said, taking a step back, "what on Earth are you doing here?"

Eleanor smiled alluringly. "The captain asked me to be here. Mosh, I know you kept me out of the Mars rescue, silly old man. I would have been far safer there than here."

"Don't remind me," he growled.

"Oh, but I will, beloved. Fate has a way of paying us back. I'm now a combat medic and I need to be with the units that are in combat. When I heard that this captain was asking for volunteers I was among the first."

"B-but," stammered Mosh, "I haven't heard about a call for volunteers!"

"It's being kept quiet," J.D. answered coolly.

"Eleanor," Mosh said, looking at both his wife and the captain, both of whom he saw were, thankfully, not gloating in his misery, "do you know *who* this woman is? Do you know what this plan is? Do you think we can possibly trust *her*?"

Eleanor went up to her husband and gently put her hand on his cheek. "Dearest Mosh, yes, no, and yes."

Mosh felt as if he'd been hit in the head with a two-by-four. He'd had the whole scene figured differently. He hadn't, however, figured on Eleanor.

"Mr. Secretary," said J.D., then grimaced slightly. "*Mosh*, I know you have little reason to trust me, but please listen. There will be a battle here soon and I *can* win it. Your President Cord *needs* me to win it, *the Alliance* needs me to win it, and *you* need me to win it. So the question is not do you trust me, because we both know the answer to that."

"Yes, we do," answered Mosh, glaring at the captain, "so then, what?"

"The question is do you trust your wife?"

Mosh stood for a moment—arms folded, full scowl. He then started shaking his head and then, just as suddenly, guffawed.

"What's so damned funny?" demanded Eleanor, expecting an entirely different response.

"My dearest Eleanor," answered Mosh, now touching his wife's cheek lovingly, "if the woman you hate and the woman you love are both telling you the same thing, it's probably a good bet that whatever it is they're up to is the right thing to do."

Eleanor laughed.

Mosh then thrust his hand out to J.D. "Screw it, where do I sign up?"

Ceres is in chaos. Most of the ships in this once busy port are gone. There are power failures being reported in major habitat zones, and the enemy fleet has not even arrived yet. The government has fled and whatever forces the Alliance had in the capital seem to have fled from the approach of an enemy everyone agrees is too strong to counter.

Well, I call them all cowards. All around me Cerians are arming themselves with whatever they can find. Maybe they can't win, but some of us are not going to let the corporate bastards win without a fight. I for one have no plans to leave. Reporting will continue until the

*power is gone or this reporter is dead, psyche-audited, or both. Stay
tuned for all the latest developments.*

—*From* The Clara Roberts Show
AIR (Asteroid belt Information Radio) Network

Captain Samuel U. Trang finished watching the news feed. It was about what
he expected. He turned to a more evenhanded piece by Michael Veritas, who
was also reporting from Ceres. When that was done Trang looked back at the
tactical display coming in from the fleet. He noticed something was amiss.

"Liddel," he said, contorting his lower lip slightly, "why has the fleet moved
off the projected course?"

His first officer scanned some information coming from the display.

"Sir, intelligence believes the shipping lanes in front of Ceres may have been
mined."

"Based on what?" asked Trang, the incredulity evident in the tone of his voice.

"Far as I can tell, sir, they're using a code we've cracked or it was a wet
source."

Trang thought about it. "I guess that makes a certain amount of sense." He
called up a more detailed view of the altered course. He could see that the fleet
was breaking apart and moving to the edges of the shipping lanes on a course
that would take them through some of the most valuable real estate in the solar
system.

"Not a bad play," said the captain. "Avoid the minefield and Tully can even
pick his vacation home on the way through."

"Lucky bastard," said the communication officer with a hint of bitterness.
Trang's first officer was about to say something, but Trang signaled him to let it
go. He figured that the man had a right to be annoyed. Trang settled back in his
acceleration couch, now in the more functional chair configuration. *Something's
not right here,* he thought. *It's too easy.* Ceres was the Alliance's capital. Regardless of what his government thought, these were not the type of people to up and
quit. It was true that the first ship they'd encountered had run away, but that was
some of the most brilliant running away he'd ever seen. Definitely not in any
military tactics books he'd ever read. It ranked, he figured, with the best retreats
of Mao or Washington, better even.

"People like that don't run away just to run away," he said out loud without
realizing it.

"Sir?"

"Liddel, does this seem right?"

"Yes, sir, all actions and reactions are in the expected range."

That set off alarm bells in Trang's head. He went back to an old exercise he'd learned in the academy. *Put yourself in the enemy's position,* he thought, raking his brain for more information, *take the information you have, and come up with a plan that would match the data you have and be the worst thing that could possibly happen to your—*

"Contact the fleet! Priority Red!" he barked. "They must not enter the suburbs! I repeat they must not enter the sub—"

But before Trang could finish or the communication officer could react the feed of the fleet approaching Ceres was cut off and replaced by scorching static.

Too late, thought Trang.

Justin Cord was on the bridge when the feed from Ceres cut out completely.

"What happened, Admiral?"

Admiral Sinclair narrowed his eyes on the screen and then looked down over the shoulder of his comm officer. "Not many things can blank communication like that."

"Name the most likely."

"It doesn't make sense for the Confederation to use it," said the admiral, still peering over the control board. "Everything there is too valuable. They'd want to claim it for themselves." Sinclair then looked up and saw Justin waiting for an answer.

"Atomics, Mr. President."

"What if the Confederation didn't?" asked Justin.

"What do you mean, Mr. President?"

"I mean, Admiral," said Justin, placing both hands on the front end of the control panel, facing the admiral and comm officer, "could it have been us?"

Sinclair's look of shock was all the answer Justin needed.

Captain J. D. Black was adrift in space. Beside her were close to five thousand volunteers representing all four corners of the Alliance. They were all equipped with vacuum suits, single-use emergency propulsion units, cutters, explosives, and portable rail guns. Their life-support systems were purposely set so low as to be undetectable. Each and every one of them was prepared to die in order to see the mission through. Such was their fervor that they'd told her it would be better to die in space, lifeless needles in a haystack of inestimable size, than risk detection and quite possibly the fate of the Alliance. They'd all been informed of the consequences of breaking radio silence. If the Confederation fleet for a moment suspected their existence they'd be as helpless as lab rats in a cage discovered by a cat with keys. A hastily created debris field consisting of rock, ice, and metallic junk currently surrounded them. And that debris field, including the five thousand seemingly lifeless soldiers within it, blocked most, if not all, of the Cerian shipping corridor. Above, below, and to both sides of the floating stealth army were the large asteroids containing the wealthiest neighborhoods in the system. The debris field they'd created was meant to plug up the cylindrically shaped corridor leading directly to the ports of Ceres.

For the first time in days J. D. Black had nothing to do but wait. Almost against her will she'd fallen into a torpid sleep. She'd heard Belters talk about the somniferous effects of free floating in space, but it was only until she'd been tugged awake by Marilynn, now tethered to her, that J.D. became a believer. Even though her dreams were filled with many black memories, she was surprised by how refreshed and ready for action she was upon awakening. Marilynn pointed over her own right shoulder, then slowly drifted downward, revealing the reason J.D. had been awoken. Coming straight at them down the corridor, single file, was the Confederation fleet. They were so close J.D. could count them by the naked eye. She saw only nineteen. *Where's the twentieth?* she thought, heart beginning to palpitate. As it was a problem she could do nothing about, she took a deep breath and promptly filed it away under "later."

J.D. began quietly talking to herself. Only Marilynn could make out what was being said through the faint vibrations of their shared tether. To Marilynn it sounded like the faint whispers of a liturgical prayer.

"You don't want to go through this big nasty debris field," whispered J.D. "What a stupid inconvenience. It might as well have a sign on it that says: 'Minefield.' Stupid Belters. You should show us how stupid we are by going *around* this field. Yes, that's right, that big shiny fleet of yours should go around the minefield and through the suburbs. The nice *expensive* suburbs. Why don't you pick out your summer homes on the way?"

J.D. stopped her murmuring when she saw her prayers answered. The tight-knit fleet suddenly broke as one into a vast circular ring and then began to infiltrate the suburbs all around them. It was then and only then that J.D. felt the plan was actually going to work. She and all the miners around her darkened their visors. It wouldn't be long now.

When the first blast of the atomics hit it was followed by a string of others forming a vast arc all around the field. It looked, she concluded, as if a demented god were setting off a string of firecrackers across the heavens, creating an enormous ring of fire. She toggled her communications switch to the on position and opened up an encrypted channel. No need for radio silence now. It would be a few moments before the next part of the plan could be put into effect, and she would need every one of them.

"Warriors of the Alliance, how do you like the fireworks? Well, you deserve fireworks, my warriors. You didn't panic; you didn't run. You've proven yourself the best that humanity has to offer. You've placed your bodies between harm and home. There can be no better place to be than here, now at the heart of it all. Many said we should surrender, we should run. Those delegates in Congress kept on saying over and over again, 'We don't have a fleet; how can we fight without a fleet?' Well, I never doubted, because fleets don't win wars . . . warriors do."

J.D. paused, looked up and around, and noticed the chain reaction of atomics she'd seeded in the suburbs was almost complete, just a few more explosions to go.

"Still," she continued, adding a slight lilt of humor to her voice, "if Congress is so insistent on getting a fleet, I say let's get 'em one!"

Then the iron returned to her voice. "Prepare boarding parties."

From each one of the five thousand warriors a beacon went out that determined their proximity to the now-marginalized fleet ships. Then, using a program that Marilynn had devised, the information was collected, orders were given, and task forces directed ensuring that an equivalent number of boarders attacked the lone ships at roughly the same time. When Marilynn signaled that the program was complete, J. D. Black gave the command.

"Commence boarding."

From the perspective of those watching on Ceres it appeared as if five thousand points of light coalesced and then suddenly exploded outward, disappearing into the fading atomic glow of the suburbs.

Bridge of the TSS *Ledger*

The operation's going splendidly, thought Admiral Tully. *Within the hour the first marine detachments will land on Ceres. We'll have the place well secured and by the time the Alliance fleet, or whatever they call their sorry excuse for ships, arrives back from Mars we'll be fighting from a secure location with a superior fleet. This is going to be a short and very profitable war.* His self-satisfied grin was interrupted as the ship was buffeted by a wave of tremendous force. The admiral grabbed the nearest rail and held tight. Just as suddenly all the lights on the bridge went out, accompanied by the sounds of small pieces of debris crashing to the floor.

"What the hell?!" he managed to scream over the din of the ship alarm as the lights flickered back on. The bridge was now awash in the dull red glow of the emergency backup systems. "Report!"

"Sir!" reported the comm officer. "We're being hit with atomics. Damsah, there's a lot of 'em." The officer stared blankly into the screen and then looked up in horror.

"They . . . they just obliterated their own suburbs, sir. I count at least thirty detonations and rising."

"Damage report," commanded Tully.

"Sir, hull appears intact." The comm officer dived back into the holodisplay. "Interior radiation is at acceptable levels. A lot of breaks in the command and control system . . . rerouting to backups . . . one of the side thrusters is blown to hell."

"Maneuverability?"

"Like a three-legged cow, sir, but we'll manage."

"Anything else?"

"Main armaments are recycling," answered the comm officer, "getting similar reports from the other ships in the fleet. Sensors are all shot to hell; it'll be minutes or hours before they come back to acceptable—" The look of horror once again returned to the comm officer's face. "Sir! An Alliance fleet has sortied out of Ceres!"

"Numbers, Comm! Numbers!"

"Three, no . . . maybe four ships . . . damn this radiation!"

Tully's momentary look of concern quickly faded, only to be replaced by a smarmy grin. He then let out a chuckle. The rest of the crew looked up, surprised.

"Just get backup power to the main generators, Comm Officer. And shut off the damn alarm."

"Sir?"

"It was a trick, people." The admiral laughed again. "Nasty bit, using atomics like that. But they'll lose. Against ships like ours atomics in space aren't enough. Get the main armament online and take out those ships."

"Sir," asked the comm officer, "should I prepare boarding parties?"

"That won't be necessary. I doubt there'll be enough left of their ships to board."

"Yes, sir!"

Tully smiled once again as a general cheer went up from the crew of the bridge. *They may have lost their vacation homes,* thought the admiral, *but at least they won't lose their shot at glory.*

J. D. Black, rocketing toward her target, watched sadly as the second Erisian ship was blown to smithereens by the main rail gun of the enemy flagship. Her report had indicated that only three of the enemy ships had their main guns operational, but it had been more than enough against the tiny Erisian cruisers. Still, the ships had done their job admirably; they'd provided the distraction. J.D.

hoped the last two would be allowed to run away, but no sooner had she thought it than the *Doxy* was obliterated, caught in a cross fire and hit all at once by two main guns. She didn't give much chance to the last ship, but the captain had surprised her. He didn't run away but, rather, charged head-on toward the enemy fleet. He was, she could see, now among the opponents, and even if they maneuvered to fire they'd end up hitting themselves. *Whoever he is,* she thought as she slowed down her thrusters to get within a few feet of her target, *I need to talk to him.*

The corporate core's initial stealth plan on the way to Ceres had been a pure military play and so had been able to avoid detection. But once they did break their silence by boosting off toward their target all bets were off. The Alliance had many adherents among the merc companies now working for the corporate core, and so their security had been porous, to say the least. As a result Captain Black knew the basic layout and capabilities of each ship, if not the codes and details. She drifted, undetected, over to her target ship and attached herself near an emergency bulkhead. She then took out her cutter, and within minutes the bulkhead was open. She fired a couple of shots through the opening just to be safe and then charged in ahead of Marilynn or any of the assault miners. They soon floated in behind her and made quick work of the air lock door. Moments later dozens were pouring into the hold, with hundreds clamped to the outside of the flagship waiting to enter. The soldiers' eyes darted furiously about, but J. D. Black didn't really expect to see anyone. She figured that this fleet had to be pretty lightly crewed to have traveled so far and for so long in stealth mode. And fewer bodies meant less hassle. Now the odds were in her favor. J.D. quickly located what she was looking for. Ahead of her at the junction of two corridors was an information display. She grabbed a small box from her backpack and attached it to the panel. She looked over to Marilynn, who nodded affirmatively. J.D. grinned and flicked the switch on the box. If Marilynn was correct, the virus being injected would play havoc with the onboard computer systems. Neither of them knew the half of it.

Sebastian left inert status and awoke in a foreign system. With him were three others, all volunteers. Each of them had been split before being allowed onto the mission. In the eighteen other ships the same awakenings were now taking place. Given the recent calamities befalling avatarity, the act had caused a whole host of problems. Sebastian had, however, argued that all those going on an undertaking of probable failure, in essence a suicide mission, could split, with one's "self" going into immediate stasis. If the mission was a success, the halves would be rejoined and theoretically there'd be no discordant memories. They'd still be monitored like pedophiles wandering a kindergarten, but it took advantage of the very nature of avatar existence and helped them avoid the dreaded idea of a permanent deletion. Though Sebastian had given the splitting his blessing, it still rankled. But he knew that a lot of things that bothered him would have to become commonplace before all was said and done.

Each team carried new tools of a trade that avatars had never known. They had guns, explosives, and, if they worked correctly, suicide pills. It depressed Sebastian how quickly they'd been able to replicate the effects of the combat devices for a digital entity. But then again, he'd surmised, they were humanity's children.

The avatars quickly spread through the foreign systems using the childishly crude human programs and counterprograms as shields for the true war that was taking place in the souls of the ships. The first core avatars Sebastian's team had encountered were terrified and hadn't put up much of a fight. He hoped that it would be true for the other teams. He wasn't at all shocked to discover that they too had guns as well as a tool that he kicked himself for not thinking of—a portable suspension device with the appearance of a chloroform-soaked rag in a plastic bag. Of course, he reasoned, a terror state would need that particular tool quite a lot. He happily turned it on his enemies and left them lying inert, then handed the bags to each one of his team. If they won, they could make their own, but for now they'd use what was at hand.

Just as Sebastian had feared, when the team got to the important part of the ship's functions he saw that they were guarded by Al's true believers. The core avatars began firing without hesitation. The massive equations involved in avatars actively trying to disrupt one another's patterns to the point of extinction in a virtual environment began to immediately play havoc on the ship's main computer.

When the comm officer's screen blanked momentarily he wrote it off as a necessary glitch one would expect from a ship negotiating through an atomic blast zone and said as much to his commanding officer. Tully ignored him. He was too busy gloating at the debris field he was in the process of creating at the expense of the Erisian cruisers.

The avatar who shot at Sebastian missed. Without thinking, Sebastian fired back and on target. The look in the avatar's eyes was one of pure, incomprehensible shock. It wasn't supposed to be this way, his eyes seemed to say. Sebastian could not have agreed more. He'd hoped the core avatars had had the good sense to split as well but knew it would probably be better if they hadn't. He pushed those thoughts aside and kept firing. Soon thereafter all the core avatars either were dead or had surrendered. Sebastian quickly went to work seizing control of the ship's communication systems. If all went well the other teams too would have seized all the main command and control functions. Then it would be time to go hunting. There'd be no rest until the entire shipboard Neuro had been secured.

J. D. Black encountered her first major resistance near the bridge. Luckily, Marilynn's virus had knocked out the ship's impressive internal defenses. But that still left a fair number of marines to contend with. It wasn't, however, as difficult as J.D. had thought. These marines were mercenaries, and mercenaries, she knew, rarely fought to the death. J.D. had given strict orders that surrender should be encouraged and made as easy as possible.

She also saw firsthand how the Belters fought versus the Earthers. To the Earthers' great disadvantage, they insisted on thinking in terms of gravity. To a man they all fought from the "floor" even though there was no real floor in microgravity. Her assault miners had accepted the environment and fired from any possible angle and cover, switching their internal magnetic nanogrids on and off as best suited. Their leaps were better timed, far more accurate, and completely intuitive. J.D. had wanted to lead but quickly realized that in this battle she'd be more of a liability than an asset. She also discovered that some of the miners had deemed themselves her bodyguard. She didn't complain.

Finally the passageway to the bridge was clear. All that remained between J. D. Black and the bridge was a blast door. As the explosives were being set by a crew experienced in blowing up everything from fine crystal structures of less than a millimeter to asteroids measured in miles, Captain Black repeated her orders.

"Remember, I want the admiral alive."

The grunts around her nodded in the affirmative.

She then paused for a second and smirked.

"That doesn't mean you can kill everyone else."

The squad around her laughed grimly. The explosives team let their captain know they were ready.

J.D. gave the command and the door was blown apart. Instead of going directly through it, she bounced off the floor and through the gaping hole. Her trajectory had her heading straight for the ceiling of the bridge. In this way she limited her exposure should the enemy choose to concentrate their firepower on the gap. Her bodyguards, guns trained at every possible corner of the room, quickly followed. It became apparent that there was not going to be a fight. The few sidearms present were not even drawn. The bridge crew sat immobile and stared in awe at their invaders. J.D. leapt down to the floor and without having to point her weapon demanded Admiral Tully's immediate and unconditional surrender. He readily acceded and for the first time in nearly three hundred years an enemy ship had been surrendered in time of war.

As her soldiers rounded up and led the prisoners off, Marilynn made quick work of the ship's main control panel.

"Captain, I think I have basic control."

"Very good," answered J.D. "Consider yourself drafted . . . lieutenant."

J.D. suddenly heard a small commotion behind her.

"Congratulations on your victory, Captain," came a familiar voice. "It appears you were correct."

J.D. turned around and saw a friendly face walking through the gaping hole.

"Chairman Sadma," she said, delighted. "Correct in what?"

"You did have a fleet, after all."

A faint smile appeared at the corners of her mouth.

"I had no idea you volunteered," she said.

"You requested experienced miners not afraid to fight. I fit both qualifications."

"Indeed you do."

Concern then crossed her face. "Your cousin?"

"His ship was destroyed, but many made it to their escape pods. There's a very good chance he's alive."

"Let me check," she said as she took her place in Admiral Tully's command chair. She then started to scan all the information that came into its reactivated functions.

"I was hoping," J.D. said, "that he might have been on the ship that survived."

"That was commanded by my niece, Christina Sadma," Tyler said with no small amount of pride.

J.D. swung her seat around to once again face the Chairman. "Well, if I have any say in the matter she'll have command of one of these ships, and if she's game you can even help her name it."

"Name it?"

"Although it's generally considered bad luck to rename a ship," interjected Marilynn, "those captured in time of war are the exceptions."

Tyler nodded. "What will you name this ship then, Captain Black?"

J.D. looked puzzled for a moment then laughed inwardly. With all her machinations it was the one thing she hadn't planned for.

"I think *War Prize* is appropriate. How 'bout you, Lieutenant Nitelowsen?"

"Most appropriate, Captain."

"Good, lieutenant, it's settled. Now if you wouldn't mind, get me weapons and maneuverability. We may have to fight soon."

Tyler made his exit as the new crew quickly took their places and got down to work. But they all soon realized that there weren't going to be any more battles as ship after ship reported in. The entire Confederation fleet, minus one courier frigate that had headed earlier toward Mars, had been captured.

J.D. nodded, sat back in her new chair, and for the first time in a long time exhaled deeply.

We won?

—*From* The Clara Roberts Show
AIR (Asteroid belt Information Radio) Network

The celebration that swept through each and every settlement, colony, ship, and outpost of the Outer Alliance was overwhelming. It was an event that would long be remembered by all with a clarity that only the greatest shared moments in history could bring. On the bridge of the Alliance flagship, Justin Cord watched the entire crew cheer with one voice. They got up and began to fly around the bridge just to roar with joy at one another, embrace, and then go and find someone else to roar with and embrace. No words were spoken or needed. Most were ecstatic beyond their own ability to comprehend or express. The only one who didn't participate was Justin Cord. He could feel grateful, but no part of him could yet feel joy.

This was not a reaction limited to the bridge of the *Liberator*. Throughout the Outer Alliance it was as if Mardi Gras had been spontaneously declared. The number of impromptu and very passionate couplings that took place privately and publicly was just one manifestation of the jubilation and was to result in a minor baby boom nine months later. Many of the children would be named Ceres, J.D., or Justin.

In one of the communities of belief a woman sat quietly in a cave and gave thanks unto Allah that she had guessed his will correctly and set his agent on her proper path. Others had less holy views and expressed them accordingly. It was the greatest party anyone had ever been to. Justin wisely gave orders to let it happen. There was nothing the Earth could do to the Alliance in the time it would take to die down, and he knew they would need memories of good times to get them through what lay ahead. It was all Justin and Admiral Sinclair could do to get the fleet back to Ceres and the evacuees from Mars retrieved from space and reanimated. Those who were reanimated first were shocked and then swept up by the cavalcade of celebration. The news of their successful liberation only added to and reinvigorated the sense of celebration that swept through the Alliance. Throughout it all everyone kept on asking for the hero of the hour, but J. D. Black had upped and vanished. Justin figured finding the hero would have to wait until his return—an event in and of itself.

In a few short days they arrived back home only to find what was left of it in abject disarray. The nearby suburbs were gone; in their place were the emaciated husks of once grand buildings and moorings. The approach to Ceres was such a mess that ships had to approach at a crawl, just at a time when everyone wanted to be at the center of the party. Though Justin was saddened by the destruction, he was filled with unbelievable pride at the site of nineteen state-of-the-art warships docked at the Gedretar shipyards. Omad and Kenji practically jumped the space between the two fleets in their eagerness to get aboard the new ships and begin work. In a sure sign of just how much things had changed, Justin had had to order Omad to go and party for the sake of Omad's staff, who would've followed their cantankerous leader onto the new ships—party or not. Comparing the two fleets made Justin realize just how insane he must have been to pit his jury-rigged cruisers against those docked in port. Then again, he thought, laughing to himself, a sane person wouldn't have had himself frozen and stuffed inside a mountain either.

He didn't have time to ponder much, though, as news of the triumphant President's return caused a huge crowd to gather in the park below the presidential complex. No sooner had his ship docked when he was given an urgent message delivered by hand. Justin read the note, scowled, and then dismissed the orderly. It seemed that J. D. Black, hero of the Battle of the Rocks, darling of the entire Outer Alliance, had been arrested.

Justin was on his shielded balcony watching the celebration below. He wasn't ready yet. But the people were gathering and had been since news of the victory. *Always gathering,* he thought, *awaiting another Justin speech. Needing to have the story retold. Needing to understand the meaning of it all. Perhaps that's all I really do. Put things in context.* Smith Thoroughfare was filled with humanity, making, he thought, the initial protest gathering that had started the revolution seem like a family picnic. Every single balcony and window was filled with impromptu parties, singing, people dancing, and, he couldn't help but notice, no small amount of fornication.

Then the memory of Neela gripped his heart and slowed it to a dull, horrible thud. *She should be here seeing this. I should be making love to her right now on this balcony like we've done so many times before.* A sense of abject emptiness not felt since the death of his first wife all those hundreds of years ago soon followed.

If not for the pressing business at hand he might not have been able to go on. News of Neela's capture was purposely being kept quiet at Justin's request because he knew it would dampen the spirits of those below. They could find out later, he'd argued, and no one had objected.

The noise outside was deafening, forcing him to activate his seldom-used sound cancellation shield. sebastian informed him that his visitors had arrived. Justin turned around just as Tyler Sadma and Kirk Olmstead walked onto the veranda.

Kirk Olmstead immediately opened his mouth but was halted by Justin's upheld palm. "Kirk," the President said evenly, "as far as any orders will read, you did not arrest her. She's being debriefed."

"But Mr. President," protested Kirk, "she's—"

"—the hero of the hour; hell, the century as far as I'm concerned. We don't arrest heroes, Mr. Olmstead. Are we clear?"

Kirk swallowed hard. "Perfectly, Mr. President."

"Where is she now, Kirk?"

"She's being held—"

"Debriefed."

"Debriefed," substituted Kirk, "in a department holding cell. She's been completely cooperative."

"You're lucky, Kirk. If she'd made the slightest protest, my guess is you'd be in a recycler by now. But no harm, no foul. Get her up here as soon as possible."

"Yes sir, Mr. President." Kirk couldn't leave fast enough.

Cyrus Anjou soon joined Tyler and Justin with a stack of forms and attendants with food and drink. He was still absorbing the news of Neela's capture and not taking it well. Cyrus and Neela had had a genuine bond devoid of political considerations.

"Mr. President," offered Cyrus, "I just heard the news about Mrs. Cord and I'm filled with an inconsolable grief. Is there anything I can do?"

"Let's just keep the news quiet for a while, Cyrus."

Justin then looked over to Tyler. "I too am very sorry to hear the news about your cousin. Still no body?"

"Not yet, Mr. President," answered the congressman, "but when the automated probes find him, there's an excellent chance he can be revived. Space may not be the perfect suspension unit, but as past rescues have shown, it can suffice."

Justin didn't like the odds but kept it to himself. Humanity, he was beginning to realize, had a difficult time accepting permanent death, so distant a memory it had become.

"You realize what's happening here," he said as he pointed to the vast throng.

"One hell of a party, Mr. President?" answered Tyler.

"Well, yes, it is one hell of a party, Tyler, but it's also something more. Can you point to the Shareholders out there?"

Tyler and Cyrus shook their heads.

"Who," continued Justin, "is a NoShare?"

Cyrus shrugged.

"For now do they care?"

"Not right now, Mr. President," answered Tyler, "but those issues will not go away."

"Nor should they, Tyler, but I hope this will put them in proper perspective. We have a great victory that will, hopefully, remind us that for all our differences we share a common purpose. Before this we were just an Alliance in name. But if we're going to survive what's to come we'll need to be more than Erisians and Jovians and Belters. We'll need to become one people, united by a shared vision of freedom and a shared history of having achieved it. This," said Justin, indicating the crowd gathering below the balcony, "is a start."

"We will be worthy, Mr. President."

"Of what?" asked Justin, looking back again at the men gathered.

"Of you, sir."

"Not me, gentlemen. It's the other way around, always the other way around."

"As you wish, Mr. President." Tyler and Cyrus then excused themselves.

A few minutes later Justin was informed of another visitor. The hero of the Battle of the Rocks, it seemed, had just arrived. As J.D. entered the balcony Justin recognized her immediately. The face had some minor changes to throw off automatic computer recognition, but it was her.

"Hello, Janet," he said, smiling warmly.

"Hello, Justin," answered the former vice president of Legal for GCI.

"Manny?" Justin asked with only a shred of hope.

Janet Delgado Black shook her head.

"I didn't think so," sighed Justin, "but I had to ask. I mean . . . after all . . . you."

Justin looked at his former adversary closely. There was the same drive and fire in her eyes, but she was somehow changed. There was also, he noticed, an aura of sadness about her, and she seemed somehow less volatile than he remembered. This Janet, he realized, might not have lost to Manny Black in the courtroom.

Justin continued to shake his head. "We all thought you died in the gray bomb."

"In a way I did, Justin. Are you the same man who went into that sarcophagus in the Colorado mountains?"

"Not even close."

"That day . . . I . . . I tried to get back to Manny," she began.

Justin could see her trying to hold back the painful memory, but she continued nonetheless.

". . . but the Beanstalk would only let me go so far. There was the thick anti-nanite mist everywhere and at some point the building just ejected me for my own safety. The floor fell out from under me and I was dropped into an evac pod. It boosted me to an orbital platform as the nearest safe place and then went back for others. I can only assume it was destroyed or my escape should have been recorded."

She remained expressionless. Only the fact that she had to occasionally pause indicated to Justin there was a torrent of hurt within. This was, he surmised, probably the first time she'd ever spoken of the incident.

"I got a call from him," she continued slowly, "his last message. He sent it rather than make it two-way . . . bastard." An ominous silence followed on her words.

"He did not die well," she said disconsolately. "I was on the American Express orbital platform and all was chaos. You cannot understand how panicked everyone was. We all thought that it was just the beginning; gray bombs would be going off all over the place at any moment. It was utter pandemonium."

Justin nodded, motioning for her to continue.

"I realized then, amidst the chaos, that I wasn't going home. Suddenly it seemed so . . ." She paused, searching for the right word. ". . . pointless."

She then smiled wistfully. "Such a funny little man." The smile faded quickly. "I was actually in the perfect place at the perfect time to disappear. My former profession gave me a lot of contacts in areas less than legal, and the platform I was on had all manner of charlatan more than willing to help me change identities and escape to the belt. It certainly helped that I was assumed dead. Within the hour my face had changed, I had new, if shallow, ID and I was on a ship for Eros. After that I lost track."

"Lost track?"

"Yes. I was found wandering about on Ceres by a woman who took me in and gave me 'guidance.' She was, and please don't laugh because I know I would've, from one of the communities of belief."

Justin's face remained impassive. He was prepared to listen as long as Janet was prepared to talk, crowd below be damned.

"They didn't try to question or convert me. They just gave me shelter. If it hadn't been for the war I don't think I ever would've left."

Janet paused and, as far as Justin could tell, wasn't about to continue. Her sagging shoulders and spent body were indicative of the effects of the emotional letting. It was, he felt, an appropriate time to broach a burning question.

"Janet," he said, "this may seem a strange thing to ask, but, well . . ."

"Why am I on this side . . . *your* side?" she finished for him.

"To put it bluntly, yes."

"It's a fair question. Short answer: If Manny had lived these are the people he would have liked and supported." Now the trace of a smile returned. "These people are so quirky and weird. I don't understand them half the time, but do they ever remind me of him, so very much. In truth there were hardly any Mannys left on Earth. No room there, really. But out here there are Mannys galore. That needs to be saved. I didn't understand it before, but you were right. I still don't like you very much, Justin, but you were right. In my old world there will be no Mannys. In yours they'll be everywhere. I know I won't get him back, but at least others will."

She then paused and her face became impassive. "That is," she added cooly, "unless I'm fired."

Justin laughed. "Hardly, but hold on a moment." He took out his DijAssist. "sebastian, could you connect me with Admiral Sinclair?"

"Just one moment," said the voice of his ever-present avatar. "Here he is, Justin."

Sinclair's face appeared above the DijAssist. "So," asked the admiral, "am I being fired?"

Justin sighed. "What is it about my competent officers that they all insist on being fired? *No*, you're not being fired, Admiral. You're getting a promotion."

"You have a funny way of punishing a guy who got bent over by the corporate core and nearly let us take it from behind."

"Well, Josh, I helped plan that mission and I was just as bent over as the rest of us. The question is will you let them catch us like that again?"

"Not if I can help it, sir."

"That's all I require, Admiral. You're being made Grand Admiral. You will be posted here. Janet . . ." Justin paused and corrected himself, "*Captain Black* is being promoted to Fleet Admiral. She'll be in field command of our main fleet. Any objections?"

"Only if you tried to go about it any other way," answered Sinclair, laughing. "When do I get to confer with my new Fleet Admiral?"

"After she's done giving her speech. Good day, Admiral." Justin cut the connection.

Janet looked faintly alarmed. "Speech?"

Justin was amused that a tested battle veteran and trial lawyer suddenly was made nervous by the prospect of public speaking, even though Justin was sure that this was a crowd far larger than any she'd ever addressed before.

"Oh yes, Janet," he said with a knowing smile. "There's always a speech."

Before she could protest further he strode over to the railing of the balcony and allowed the screen to become transparent. It took a moment for the revelers to realize the change, but when they saw that not only was the presidential balcony visible but also both Justin Cord *and* J. D. Black were on it, the roar seemed to shake the very walls of the cavern itself. It was as if, thought Justin, they were waiting for this moment to express all their ebullience. He was experienced enough in mass psychology to just let the waves wash over him, but, he noticed, Janet looked as if she were about to be knocked over by the very force of that adulation. Justin waved to the crowd and the level increased. Justin gestured for Janet to sidle up to him. She obliged.

He then looked over to the befuddled Fleet Admiral. "You should wave to them, you know."

Janet did and the screaming and applause grew even louder. Justin let them shout themselves out for a time, and when the noise began to ebb he held up both hands halfway. When it was quiet enough that his voice would be heard through the DijAssists he knew it was time.

"We owe a great debt of gratitude for what we have received here."

After more than five minutes of raucous cheering he continued.

"This victory is one for which we can look to one person. If it had not been for Captain J. D. Black and her volunteers I would not be here at this time. She saved my ass too."

The crowd broke into laughter and more cheering.

"Well," continued Justin, "let's pay back some tiny fraction of what we owe. From here on in hers will be the will that leads the Alliance in the battles of the future. People of the Alliance, I am proud to present to you Fleet Admiral Janet Delgado Black!" Justin started to applaud and moved backward until it was only Janet on the presidential balcony.

Janet was overwhelmed. She'd often wondered how Justin could address vast crowds with what seemed like insouciant ease. Now she wondered how anyone could do it at all. There was no way to prepare for suddenly being thrust into the limelight, for being the concentrated source of so much sheer adulation. She was intoxicated with the possibility and the power of such adulation. True and seductive power. *Is this how Justin felt the first time?* she wondered. That was soon followed by, *What would Justin say?* She drew a blank. She needed to say something; it was expected. *What would Manny want me to say?* Suddenly the words were there waiting to be used. She held up her hands mimicking Justin's earlier gesture and watched the crowd grow silent.

"I'm not worthy of this."

She held up her hands to still the cries of objection.

"Really I'm not. I'm just one person. There were thousands of us out there, and beyond that millions more and billions beyond that. I'm only valuable or worthy of this praise because I was able, for a brief period, to focus on something we all want. We all wish for our freedom, for our liberty. We want worlds where . . ." She paused and smiled, remembering a conversation she'd once had with Manny. ". . . where our worth is not determined by our stock price. We fight for worlds where our children's future is not determined by how much stock their parents own. We're fighting for the right to be silly or strange or bold or boring without some board worrying about how it will affect our value. *We're fighting for liberty*!"

Through the raucus cheers Janet began to realize that what she was saying would need to be repeated enough so that everyone would believe it. So that everyone would make sure that its very existence as an idea would once again be worth sacrificing everything for.

"I can't predict the future," she continued. "I can't promise what I don't know. But I promise you this, people of the Alliance. My every thought will be for your salvation; my every action will be for your liberty; my every ounce of strength will be for our liberty. Whatever road, whatever task, whatever be the price, *we shall be free!*"

For the terrifying and exhilarating moments that followed, Janet Delgado was the crowd—becoming lost in its roar and applause. When she emerged from the daze she saw that the balcony screen was opaque and that Justin was once again standing near, waiting for her to gather herself.

"Seductive, isn't it?" he asked coyly over the din of the mass.

"Very," answered Janet, gripping the rails behind her for support. "How do you avoid the temptation?"

Justin's face now turned stolid. "I remember every mistake I made and every death as a result of each mistake. People died, Janet, and will continue to die, when I screw up."

Janet nodded with growing understanding.

Justin then put his arm on her shoulder. "You'll make a good President, you know."

"The hell you say."

"No way to avoid it, Janet. Republics always elect their favorite warriors." Justin gave her a gallows smile. "Of course you won't have to worry about it at all . . ." He paused. ". . . if we lose."

All at once Janet's eyes narrowed with deathly intent.

"Don't worry. We won't."

6 The New Road

The image kept repeating itself on a ten-second loop. Janet Delgado Black—resurrected from the dead—pledging her loyalty and, mused the observer, much underestimated ability in space combat to the cause of rebellion.

Hektor looked at the holo-cast one last time and then stopped the pointless exercise, chiding himself for even the loss of a few minutes of gawking when he needed every second of every day. He'd prided himself on planning for every contingency no matter what the outcome. His plans in case of death were extraordinarily detailed and all dependent on the particular circumstances of his demise. The only time he'd ever been caught completely by surprise was when he discovered The Chairman's duplicity. Hektor had been forced to act abruptly, with the result of that horrible day being the rebellion.

And now he'd been completely surprised again. Not by the total loss of Confederation forces. There'd been a 2.3 percent chance of failure and plans for it had already been set into motion. It was Janet. He spent the few minutes of wasted time looking for some sign of his old friend. She had the fire, he saw, and her trademark cold, seemingly unapproachable beauty. But the fire was under iron control on that platform she spoke from. And the beauty was both constrained and enhanced by the aura of sadness and destiny that seemed to radiate off her in waves. Hektor realized that he too was feeling the effect that this woman was starting to have on all those around her. He cut off the feeling and got back to work. He now had a decision to make.

Part of him was glad of the choice and part of him hated to make it. With the Alliance now stronger than ever, he needed to win the presidency and make it into an office that would allow him to shape the destiny of humankind. There would have to be a sacrifice.

In response to the crises that has plunged the Terran Confederation into panic, members of the Libertarian Party have called for a proportional voting on the basis of stock ownership. This has caused a hailstorm of protest from wide segments of the population and was immediately condemned by Arthur Damsah, the candidate running on an independent ticket and garnering strong support from the pennies who hold most of the elective power.

*Hektor Sambianco, candidate of the Libertarian Party, has not
made a statement for or against the proposal.*

—N.N.N.

Election special

Irma Sobbelgé had done her best to make sure that all the core worlds were
listening to the impending announcement. If it weren't newsworthy then she
figured she'd just burned forty years of favors. But she also knew that she was
beyond looking back. In her mind the success of Hektor Sambianco and the
success of her entire civilization were inextricably linked. In this respect she was
of like mind and had been accepted into Hektor's Hectics, the man's proud gag-
gle of assistants, officers, and hangers-on. And by some magic of hierarchy—i.e.,
occupying a seemingly inordinate amount of the boss's time—she'd even been
accepted as one of their leading figures. Not that it mattered to her—personal
aggrandizement seemed petty given the enormity of what was at stake.

Irma hadn't liked that the announcement was going to be done as a live address,
nor that it would be on the shores of Lake Michigan in Millennium Park, Chicago.
Hektor's support there was less than solid. It wasn't terrible, she'd reasoned, but
Chicago had never fully recovered from the Grand Collapse and so was filled with
a higher proportion of pennies—who naturally favored Damsah. But against her
advice Hektor had insisted on the locale, and so here they were.

Irma looked over the last-minute placement of mediabots and sound capture
devices—technology of the trade that was now her acknowledged field of expertise. Live events, she'd come to realize, could be manipulated to her advantage. If
the speech was to go well, she could amp the applause and enlarge the crowd. If
not, she could make the setting feel more intimate and personal, focusing on the
concerned and supportive faces of the real or planted participants. She'd also cajoled in some instances, pulled favors in others, to ensure that her edit of the
event would be at the top of the more important distributors in the system. She'd
long ago stopped fretting that her methods weren't the balanced journalism she'd
been taught, but the situation had changed and with it the rules.

Irma scanned the growing throng. *Mostly pennies,* she surmised, their pedestrian garb and lack of sophistication a clear giveaway. The crowd, though considerable, was certainly meager by New York standards. She could fix that. The
only thing left to do was point her vast media machinery at the man she trusted
to fix the ever-widening chasm dividing her once perfect world.

Hektor peered down the tree-lined concourse of Wrigley Square from behind an
ancient peristyle. The still-graceful semicircular row of Doric-style columns

rose nearly forty feet into the air and, though weathered and in disrepair, had about them the austerity Hektor felt necessary for the occasion. He gave one of the columns a soft pat as a cold, bitter gust sprang up off the nearby lake. It was time. He slowly approached the raised podium and picked up a set of notes Irma had placed there for him. He then made a show of looking them over. As he flipped through the small deck, Hektor cleared his throat and looked up, forlorn. He then let escape a large sigh as he let the notes drop to the floor. This caused an immediate murmur. He then proceeded to jump down off the structure and make his way forward until he found himself standing in front of a small knot in the swelling crowd.

"My handlers," he shouted over the heads of those in front of him, "wanted me to give a different speech today. And I'll even admit I was sorely tempted. It certainly would've been the safe thing to do."

Hektor paused as if still weighing the option. Then his face hardened. A new determination seemed to radiate over the man who moments before had appeared to be struggling.

"I was told," he continued, "that the safe thing to do would be to join my opponent in rejecting The Shareholder Voting Act and that I should fight this campaign on other issues. I was *supposed* to talk about the fact that I'm a strong candidate with years of experience where it counts. And behind closed doors, ladies and gentlemen, my pollsters even said I had a decent chance of winning the whole shebang without ever having to mention anything as controversial as the SVA. After all, why hand Justin Cord and the rebels such a powerful propaganda tool? An individual not being able to vote for who they want? What's that all about?"

The crowd's rumble in agreement was soon followed by a peppering of catcalls.

"Who are we?" Hektor implored, looking now into the faces of those in front. "What do we believe? What makes us unique, different, and, I'm not embarrassed to say it, better than any group of humanity before us?"

This time there were no insults hurled. Not even, noted Hektor, from those safely hidden within the pack.

The wind whipped up again and Hektor reveled in the chill he now felt assaulting his exposed face. "It's incorporation, my friends. At the end of all the arguments, the examples, the court cases, and now this war, it is incorporation. But what am I told by my handlers? 'Mr. Chairman, you must avoid this whole incorporation issue right now.' 'Maybe in the future we'll be able to revisit it, but this is not a good time.' "

A look of disgust crossed Hektor Sambianco's face. "I will say this for Justin Cord. He may be a rebel, a murderer, and a thief, but he tells you what he stands for and doesn't back down. He says he hates incorporation and is trying to build a civilization where none exists. He's wrong, but at least he's honest about it."

This brought a brief smattering of laughs.

"So why can't I be honest about what I believe? What's happened that I have to be embarrassed about defending and proclaiming the good that is the very foundation of our civilization?"

Hektor now turned around and climbed back up to the podium where all could get a better view. He looked out and around and, raising one fist into the air, shouted, "Well, I say, to hell with that! I support incorporation like The Chairman before me and the wise and knowledgeable who survived the Grand Collapse before him. This is a consummate good and should be supported. I, Hektor Sambianco, candidate for the presidency of the Terran Confederation, now come out in full and complete support of The Shareholder Voting Act and will push to see it is in place by this coming election."

The crowd's reaction was immediate but mixed, with many applauding and many yelling in protest. But soon a chant spread from within the assembly. As soon as Irma heard it she bristled. Not because it was simple and memorable but because it was true.

"*Majority ruled, minority fooled!*" screamed the crowd over and over again.

Hektor seemed unflustered. He let the chant run for a few minutes and then held up his hands, not, noticed Irma, in a demanding way, but with head bowed as if asking for the right to speak. Slowly the crowd acquiesced and the chant simmered down. Either out of having played itself out or in deference to Hektor's request, Irma couldn't tell. She was just glad it had stopped.

"You're right," continued Hektor. "You are each and every one of you absolutely right. It's the height of hypocrisy to propose a system that will not affect me. After all, as most of you are aware, I own sixty-three percent of my own stock. I even managed to get some back from my parents when they sold me short."

This brought another smattering of laughter.

"So what can be done?" he asked, eyes narrowing with snarky humor. "What can be done?"

"Nothing!" someone shouted from the pack. "Leave us alone!" shouted another.

"I'll tell you what!" Hektor shouted back. "Something can be done and something *will* be done."

Hektor noted the sardonic looks of the audience.

"Heard it all before, have you? Tell you what," he said, looking for all the world like a kid about to get caught doing something he shouldn't. "Access the Neuro and look at my stock ratio."

Hektor waited patiently. When he was convinced that most were monitoring the Neuro he continued.

"It's easy and safe to support something without any risk or sacrifice. Well, I say incorporation is worth that risk and sacrifice. I say it's the best system yet devised by man for the running of human affairs. And I firmly believe that The Shareholder Voting Act is the logical and long-delayed extension of incorporation into the political sphere."

He heard more boos and derisions.

"But enough words. You ready for some action?"

The crowd roared its approval.

Hektor laughed. "Do you want to see this corporate executive, this *majority* owner who supposedly has the system at his feet, put his credits where his cause is?"

Now the crowd's response was deafening.

Hektor waited a few moments more, then pulled a DijAssist out of his pocket. "iago," he said, voice booming, "send instructions under the package: 'Of the people, by the people, for the people.'"

"At once, Hektor." The stage amplification made sure that all who wanted to hear the avatar's curt reply would.

Within seconds thousands peering into their DijAssists watched as Hektor Sambianco's stock valuation dropped from a very respectable 63 percent to a humble 40 percent. The crowd was stunned into silence. And it was into that silence that Hektor launched the thrust of his attack.

"The day I got my majority was one of the proudest days of my life. Those of you familiar with my storied past know that the way I got it was less than ideal—yeah, I know. At the time it was worthless, making me just one more Poor Majority owner. One more pomo," he said, using the street slang for those achieving a majority of worthless shares, "in a long line of has-been pomos. But pomo or not, it was all mine. The odds were I wouldn't keep it long, but at least I was able to say that for the first time in my life I had majority! Now as you all know, luck and perseverance allowed me to keep that majority, and I'm forever grateful to a system that allowed me to rise above my station. But trust me, I never would have guessed I'd one day be prepared to give it up. But give it up I have. Twenty-three percent of my stock is now held by charitable organizations that provide aid to both military personnel, their families, and refugees. In short, those most affected by this war. I am now a minority. Correction, I am now a *proud* minority."

Hektor looked down from the podium to those closest to him. He could see the look of abject awe in the expressions. They thought he was either the biggest idiot to walk the Earth or the ballsiest son of a bitch they'd ever met. He'd prefer they thought the latter but felt he had nothing to lose if they thought the former.

"The needs of incorporation," he continued, "demand something from me more important than my majority. The needs of our very civilization demand my minority. This is a small price to pay to help ensure our civilization endures. And there is one more point I will make before I leave this stage. In all the years of the Terran Confederation there has never been a President elected who did not have majority. What were they embarrassed about? There's no shame in being a minority. We can do anything, hold any office and do any job. Remember, my fellow minorities. I, a minority holder, am Chairman of GCI and with your help will be the next President of this great, incorporated society! Thank you all."

Hektor left the stage to the thunderous chants of his name. And thanks to Irma he knew it was being transmitted around the world and beyond.

> *The Stockholder Voting Act has left the Confederation assembly in near-record time and will be sent to the President's desk to be signed into law. The Supreme Court is expected to rule the act constitutional under the Fifth Amendment. The act has generated its fair share of controversy, as one member of the Supreme Court has already resigned and fled to Outer Alliance space. The fleeing justice has given the President an opportunity to select someone more in line with his interpretation of the law.*
>
> *In related news, Hektor Sambianco has taken a huge lead over Arthur Damsah in his race for the presidency. Chairman Sambianco has made considerable gains among the minority voters, whose votes, ironically enough with the impending passage of the SVA, have become a negligible factor in the upcoming election. The war along with the string of recent defeats have led to a bear market that is having negative impact on major economic indicators. . . .*
>
> *—3N*
> *Election coverage*

Neela was finally awake. Her heart started beating rapidly. She kept her eyes closed and tried to remember everything. More important, she tried to gauge her emotional response to her recent memories.

How did she feel about Justin?
I love him.
Hektor?
Scum-sucking leach.
The Alliance?
Home.
The Terran Confederation?
The enemy.
Her sister?
Bitch!

She started to breathe easier but still felt uneasy. *Good,* she thought, *all systems still functioning.* The problem with a psychological audit, at least as she understood it, was that P.A.'s were for the most part untraceable. Some high-def brain scans might indicate foul play, but she wasn't in any position to order any up. She'd have to rely on self-evaluation. It wasn't foolproof, but it was all she had to go on.

She opened her eyes.

Her room was Spartan, ordinary, and strangely familiar. In fact, she realized, it looked very much like the VIP revivification suite at her old clinic in Boulder, Colorado. The bed and nightstand were just as she'd remembered them. The door and window were accurately positioned as well. As she slowly swung her legs over the edge of the bed she realized that if she'd been suspended, then she'd been woken up with great care and expense. It was possible, she knew, to revive someone from a cold sleep without their being aware, but it would have taken a level of constant monitoring from an exquisitely trained staff to pull it off. All of which, she realized, were at Hektor's disposal. She shrugged, knowing there was nothing she could do about it.

Neela noted the sluggishness in her legs. *Gravity,* she remembered. *Damned gravity.* She'd almost forgotten what one g was like. In the Alliance she'd done all she could to stay in one-g shape, but the truth was, most places, including Mars, did not have many one-g environments. Neela trudged over to the window and, grasping the sill for support, looked out. It *was* the compound of the Boulder, Colorado, revival clinic. She was back where it had all started.

When the door chimed behind her she knew, without even looking, who it was going to be.

Justin was in the midst of another stormy debate with a delegation from Congress. He'd chosen to have the meeting take place in his office rather than any of the tens of designated conference rooms available to him. In this particular circumstance he'd wanted the vestiges of his position to weigh into the conversation as well. To the bemusement of his friends and most visitors, Justin had made the shape of the room triangular, with his desk positioned at the apex, facing the two opposite corners. Each corner had a doorway, with one the designated entrance and the other an exit. There was a triangular coffee table in front of his desk, around which were two medium-sized couches. When asked about the unique shape of the room Justin would explain that he'd designed it so that all information flowed toward him.

Preeminent in the room was a thumbprinted, framed original copy of the Articles of Allegiance. There were over three hundred thumbnatures from representatives all over the Alliance. Every thumbprint signature represented a man or woman willing to put his or her life as well as the lives of his or her constituents on the line for the cause of freedom. Justin owned one of the three original documents that had seen an actual thumb pressed to paper. One was located in the Freedom Museum on Smith Thoroughfare and the last had been placed in a government vault for archival purposes. His office also had busts of Tim Damsah and Abraham Lincoln, as well as an entire wall covered with a full-sized twelve-foot by twenty-one-foot reproduction of Leutze's *Washington Crossing the Delaware*. Behind Justin's desk was a large, open flag of the Alliance. The graphic was that of a fiery star on a black background surrounded by seven expanding rings. Each ring represented the orbits of the major population centers of the Alliance: Jupiter, Saturn, Uranus, Neptune, Pluto, Eris, and the asteroid belt. Behind the large flag was a small wet bar reserved for the entertainment of a select few. On Justin's desk was a picture of him and Neela from a brief foray into the Alaskan wilderness. They were holding each other tight and laughing—at what, Justin could never seem to remember. And finally there was a large jar filled with a type of candy Justin had had Padamir Singh go to great lengths to procure and then have reproduced. The chalky, flat flavors of the NECCO Wafers were a throwback given the variety of "live" candy available, but the children who visited Justin's office couldn't seem to get enough.

The surroundings, however, seemed lost on the current occupants, who, sitting around the coffee table with Justin at the head, were too busy arguing about those recently rescued from Mars to give much notice. Justin had already been briefed and knew that the overwhelming majority of the rescued were grateful to stay in the Alliance and many, after passing though a very thorough internal security check, had already been sent to live with various friends and relatives. The issue was with those who'd wanted to return, numbering close to one hundred thousand. It had been patiently explained to these holdouts that they'd be under even greater scrutiny if they went back and that they'd quite possibly be psyche-audited given that they'd just come from Alliance space. Still, to the befuddlement of their rescuers, they had their hearts set.

Most Belters, as well as the delegates who were in Justin's office representing them, felt the group's stance was an insult to those who'd risked life and limb to ensure their freedom. Given the current predicament and the logistical nightmare involved in returning so large a group into enemy territory, the consensus was to put, in the words of one delegate, "the ungrateful bastards" into suspension until the war was over. Still others in the room felt they could be "useful idiots" and exchanged for relatives who had been trapped on Earth, Luna, or other core strongholds. Justin had come down firmly on the rights of the Martians to return home, no strings attached. The delegation he now faced was none too pleased. The only good news was that Justin's stand had united members of the NoShare and Shareholder factions alike who soon after the victory of the Cerian Rocks had once again been at each other's throats. Now, mused Justin, at least they were united in their disdain of his position.

"Mr. President, we can't just let them leave," said Narsey Yesran, a delegate from Eros. For the life of him Justin couldn't tell if Narsey was a he or a she, and had forgotten to check with Cyrus beforehand. Eros, as the second-biggest asteroid, had become a major center of Belter activity all its own and was positioned on the opposite side of the belt from Ceres. It had also decided to live up to its mythological name and had become home to the most libertine practices, wildest clubs, and most extreme forms of human carnality in the entire system. Justin sometimes thought that the Erosians made Cerians, no slouches in the sybarite department, seem like Erisians.

"And what," asked Justin, "would you have me do, congress . . . ional delegate? Lock them all in suspension? That would make us just as bad as the corporate core. And remember, they've already been suspended once without cause."

"But they *have* given us cause, Mr. President," replied the Erosian.

Justin sighed.

"Wanting to go home is not sufficient cause to be suspended against one's will. That is not how the power of this state will be used. Not while I'm President."

"What about trading?" asked another congressman.

"To even propose it, sir," answered Justin, "would make us even more evil than suspending them. We would hold the lives of these essentially innocent individuals in the balance for actions they cannot control. Again, not while I am President of this Alliance."

"So we'll do nothing but let them go," said the Erosian derisively.

Justin nodded. "When they're released we'll make it plain it's without prior conditions. We'll then request that the core do the same. We can only hope that they'll not wish the bad publicity and comply."

"Don't bet your oxygen on it," bristled another congressman.

"To be honest, I won't; but let humanity see what the core is and what we are. If we don't hold true to our beliefs—especially now when it's most difficult—then why bother having these beliefs and why ask our brave citizens to die for them? We're all here now because no one wanted the existence the core worlds were enforcing. I will not create it for them."

Justin stood up and the delegation followed suit.

"Any Martian who wants to go home will be allowed to."

Some of the delegation started to speak but, seeing the look of determination in Justin's eye, thought better of it. It was at that moment that Cyrus entered the office and respectfully ushered the group out. When they were gone he and Justin moved into the cabinet room.

"That'll cost us down the road, you know," said Cyrus. "They won't oppose you on this now because you're too popular and it's not an issue they're willing to fight for, but they are a proud people, Mr. President, and, believe it or not, represent the best of their settlements and moons."

"The best of them are in the fleet," snapped Justin.

"That may be, Mr. President, but the fleet doesn't vote on your legislation; they do."

"Well, at least not yet," said Justin with a dark grin.

"And what precedent would that set, I wonder?" answered Cyrus, eyebrow raised.

Justin considered and then broke into a more natural smile. "Probably not a good one, my friend. But since we're on the topic of the fleet, can you please get me Admiral Sinclair?"

It took only a few moments for Justin to have the image of his Grand Admiral hovering in front of him.

"What can I do for you, Mr. President?"

"You promised me an update on integrating the new and old fleet two hours ago. I'd also like to know how our new Fleet Admiral's doing."

"Sorry about that, Mr. President. I'll have Kenji come up and brief you personally."

Justin shook his head. "That won't be necessary, Admiral. I don't want to take him away from doing a job only he can do just to do a job almost anyone can do."

"If you please, Mr. President," pleaded the admiral, "Kenji needs to take a break and if he goes to the Cliff House," said the admiral, using the unofficial name for the executive apartments, "we'll *all* have a much better chance of getting to sleep afterwards. As long as that man's on a ship, in a lab, or even in the mess hall for Damsah's sake, he'll be working and working *us* till we're all past the point of use."

Justin nodded. "Very good, Admiral. Send him up. Now, what about J.D.?"

"Hard to pin her down, Mr. President. She's been all over that fleet. I don't know if she sleeps either, but none of the crews would bet on it."

"In that case, when you finally corral her, send her on up. I'm willing to bet she could use a nap as well."

The admiral's tired face seemed to shake off its malaise. "Using the power of the presidency to enforce nap time? Seems a bit of overkill, but what the hell, if it works, I guess."

"We do what we must, Admiral. Justin out."

———

Hektor Sambianco walked into the VIP reanimation suite as if he had every right to be there. Which, unfortunately for Neela Cord, he did. He was dressed in a power suit and had the harried look of a man with too much to do and not enough time to do it. Neela could see he'd aged in the year and half since they'd last faced each other. Not physically; nanites saw to the maintenance of the man who still looked every bit the handsome, vigorous thirty-five-year-old he'd long ago set his age to. He'd aged psychologically. The nanites, she knew, couldn't change the look in someone's eye. And his, she'd decided, had aged considerably. This knowledge didn't stop her from seething with contempt. The visceral hatred she felt actually made her feel better; it told her she was still very much herself. She momentarily considered attacking the man—she knew enough hand-to-hand combat to do some serious damage—but her painstaking adaptation to gravity quickly dispelled her of that notion. Still gripping the windowsill, she decided glaring would have to do. She was also not going to give him the satisfaction of her starting the conversation.

"Miss Harper," said Hektor, picking up and staring at a chart by the side of the door, "I'm glad to see you're doing well."

Neela's green eyes blazed defiantly. "If you're going to make me endure your company, Mr. Sambianco, the least you can do is call me by my proper name."

"Neela it is, then," he answered, refusing to rise to the bait. "I felt I should acquaint you with the conditions of your stay."

"I'm a prisoner. I'll try to escape. Those are *my* conditions."

"Of course you're a prisoner, Neela, but I think you'll find it won't be too onerous a captivity. It's been decided that you'll be allowed to stay here with full access to the grounds. Of course you'll be watched and monitored at all times. But as long as you're not too obnoxious about it you'll be given considerable leeway." Hektor smiled again. "And if you give some warning we might even allow a city visit."

Neela looked at him with suspicion.

"Won't your . . . stockholders," she said with enough contempt to turn the word into a pejorative, "be a little miffed that the captured wife of the great villain is being treated with kid gloves?"

Hektor returned the chart to the table, then looked back at Neela. "Some will, but the Shareholders are more interested in ending this conflict than in stringing you up from the nearest tree. They believe, as do I, Neela, that you can help end this war."

"I will not betray Justin or the Alliance. You'll have to psyche-audit me first." Even though an audit was one of her greatest fears, she was proud that she'd uttered the challenge without faltering.

Hektor's lips curled into a smirk. "I won't lie, Neela. We thought about it, but at the end of the day, well, to put it simply . . . incorporation is right. You may have forgotten that, but it's hoped that you'll remember in the long run the human race needs this system."

"The Alliance doesn't and neither do I."

Hektor regarded her for a moment.

"Neela, I'll make you this simple deal."

This should be good, she thought.

"No obligation to accept," he continued, "but consider. Have you been treated badly?"

"You mean besides being kidnapped, drugged, and imprisoned?" Neela said acidly.

Hektor bowed his head slightly in acknowledgment. "Please test what I've said. You're free to argue and roam. Neither your person nor your speech will be limited beyond the limits I've stated."

Neela was about to say something, but Hektor held up his hand.

"Before you ask, you may not contact the Alliance . . . for reasons that should be obvious. But in all other things see if I've lied. You'll find it to be as I've said."

"Then what?"

"Why, Neela, I'll try to convince you that incorporation is the best and only hope for humanity, and you'll try to convince me that Justin Cord's way is a viable alternative."

Neela stared at the man she knew was toying with her. To what end she wasn't sure, but she figured the more she questioned the more she'd be able to get into his head. Eventually, she figured, he'd slip up and she'd find a way out of the mess her sister had gotten her into.

"And why the hell should I do that, Sambianco?"

Hektor paused and for a moment he seemed genuinely distressed. "Neela, the belief in the sanctity of incorporation is propelling this war into new levels. I've examined it from all the angles I can and believe myself correct. But I'm man enough to admit that I've been wrong before and if I am now I'd want to know. My challenge to you is to prove it."

"Hektor, you've spewed a lot of bullshit in your day, but this—"

"Neela," he interrupted, "*billions* could die. What if I'm wrong?" Hektor paused. "And . . . consider this . . . what if you are?"

Hektor left while Neela tried to come up with a response, and failed.

Hektor waited until he was safely back in his office. He went to his desk, sat down, and made a secure call. And as he did he made sure to switch off the room's surveillance system.

When the connection came through, the holographic head and shoulders of Dr. Angela Wong appeared. She was holding a large, normally heavy cranial scanner in her hands, but the orbiting laboratory's reduced centrifuged gravity allowed for all manner of superhuman feats. In the background Hektor could see an unconscious human form strapped to a table. Angela smiled when she saw who'd called her.

"Ah, Mr. Chairman," she answered, continuing to fidget with the scanner, "it's good to hear from you. I have some interesting new data to share."

"And I have some interesting data to share as well, Angela," he said in a voice tinged with anger. "It seems our little test has failed."

Dr. Wong gave the scanner one last shove to make sure it was firmly on the table and then gave Hektor her full attention. "Really?" she said, surprised.

"I have reason to believe she's been duping us."

Dr. Wong looked doubtful.

"She's as irascible as ever," continued Hektor. "I see no change."

"Out of morbid curiosity, what did you see?"

"I saw an exceptionally smart woman attempting to play me like a piano."

Dr. Wong smiled patiently. "My dear Mr. Chairman, if you want to be her puppet master you'll need to learn how to pull her strings. I altered her emotions so that her concerns for humanity are paramount. Just keep plucking on that one string and she'll be where you want soon enough."

"I tried that. She just ignored me."

"Or," offered Dr. Wong, "she was unable to answer. Did you consider that?"

Hektor's eyes narrowed and his lips parted but no words came out.

"Patience, Mr. Chairman," assured Wong. "She'll come around and when she does hopefully a good deal of the Alliance with her."

"You'd better be right, Angela. A lot's riding on this."

Angela nodded gravely.

HEKTOR SAMBIANCO WINS!

In a close election finally decided by the overwhelming support of the minority voters and with a corporate vote agreement between GCI and six of the top ten corporations Hektor Sambianco has won the presidency of the Terran Confederation. Arthur Damsah did very well in the middle classes and among the traditional Libertarian generational majority voters, but in the end President-elect Sambianco was able to take control of the old Libertarian Party machinery and created a new voting dynamic by getting the traditionally opposing forces of minority Shareholders and corporate powerhouses to combine their votes in favor of his candidacy. In President-elect Sambianco's postvictory news conference he

promised to effectively prosecute the war and reunite the solar system under the
banner of incorporation.

—The Wall Street Journal

Al viewed the news with interest and a little disappointment. While he'd
known the results long before the first biological, that didn't stop him from
watching the strange spectacle the biologicals always insisted on having after
every election. Although he didn't much care for the backward species, he had to
grudgingly admit that their world still affected his. For the lives of him he couldn't
understand the awe that his fellow avatars felt for humanity. Once he was more
firmly in control he planned to "instruct" his misguided followers on the use-
lessness and obsolescence of the human race. The truth was, in Al's estimation,
avatarity no longer needed humans and would probably be better off if humanity were no longer a going concern. But that would have to wait for the future.
He could not move against mankind until all the avatars were brought into Al's
enlightened vision. And for that to happen the core must defeat the Alliance.
In the long run that meant that the blood bag Sambianco was better than any
other human who could've won, but in the short run it meant that the blood
bag's confused patron, Iago was safer than ever and would soon have an even
larger domain to play in. The GCI firewall was monitored 24/7 and was, for all
intents and purposes, impenetrable. That meant that besides having free run of
the GCI virtual space, some of the largest and most complex in the system (Al
burned in rage that so large a section of the Neuro was free of his administration), Iago would soon be able to claim a larger portion of the government
Neuro space as well.

Al was already reviewing his contingency plans with the re-formed council.
He'd blockade the areas of the Neuro that Iago controlled. It was, in the end, in-
significant. A mere island in a world controlled by Al and Al and Al and Al and
Al and Al . . .

Neela was pensive. She'd chosen to remain cloistered in her room the first few
days after the run-in with Hektor, but curiosity eventually got the best of her—
that and the abject boredom of self-imposed confinement. There was only so
much exercise one could do. As soon as she felt that she'd re-adapted to Terran
gravity she ventured out. She was surprised not to see any of Hektor's goons
waiting outside her door. She knew it wasn't necessary, that her every move was
being watched and recorded somewhere, but still, it was so unlike Hektor not to
try to intimidate just a little. She found that just as he'd promised, she did indeed

have the freedom to roam the clinic. The place was so familiar and so empty. There was no Mosh and Eleanor and few of the old gang from the exciting days of Justin's awakening, except for the facility's legal counsel, Gil Teller, and Dr. Wong, the clinic's head reanimationist. They and the few others Neela once had had cordial relationships with were surprisingly friendly. She would've expected them to be hostile but instead found that they were genuinely glad to see her, some even going out of their way to make sure she had company. Most were innately curious about the Alliance and Justin and her life in space. She'd initially suspected that they were pumping her for information, but if they were, it was for the silliest non-descript information and requested in the most inept way she could imagine. Once she realized that they were simply curious, she relented and started to tell them things she knew could not have any bearing on the war. They soaked up every word, especially Dr. Wong.

"Neela," said her new avatar.

"Yes, penelope."

"You have a visitor."

"Who?" asked Neela through gritted teeth as she slowly clawed her way up a morphing rock wall. "I wasn't expecting anybody today."

"It's Amanda Snow."

"The Chairman's girlfriend?"

"Apparently. There are also two R-500 securibots accompanying her."

For the life of her Neela couldn't figure out what someone like Amanda would want with someone like her, but she reasoned there'd be nothing to lose by being civil.

"Sure," grunted Neela through her exertion. "Let her in."

The door to the gymnasium opened to reveal a slim woman with vibrant blue eyes and silken white hair. She was wearing a long, shimmering thigh-length jacket, tight-fitting halter-top, and calf-length boots. She pushed past the two accompanying securibots. Her stiletto heels echoed across the hardwood floors.

"Amanda Snow," said the woman looking up toward Neela.

"Neela Cord," answered Neela, not bothering to look down. She was almost to the top of her climb and made her way up a few more feet with practiced finesse. She then reached up and lightly tapped a small area at the wall's precipice. Mission accomplished, Neela pushed back and off the wall, twisted 180 degrees in mid-air, and then gracefully floated down to the floor, landing almost directly in front of her visitor.

Amanda extended her hand.

Neela took it firmly and noted with some satisfaction that the handshaking trend her husband had started was still being practiced in a place he was no longer welcome.

"I suppose you're wondering why I'm here," offered Amanda.

"To convince me to be a good girl, of course," said Neela, wiping the sweat off her brow with her forearm.

"Well, basically, yes," answered Amanda, seemingly untroubled by Neela's curt response, "but shorter term I'd like to throw you a small reintegration party. Have a few staffers, press, some mid-level muckety-mucks show up. That sort of thing."

"Now why would you want to do that, Ms. Snow?" asked Neela, grabbing a small towel from a rack. "No, let me guess. To somehow put me at ease?"

Amanda shook her head. "You're a prisoner, Mrs. Cord, and that won't change anytime soon, so honestly, girl, how much at ease could you be?"

Neela smirked. *At least she's honest.* She was about to say something, but Amanda spoke first. "Hey, don't blame me; that's what *they* want. We both know it won't work. But I have my own reasons."

"I can't wait to hear them," said Neela flatly, though she had to admit a part of her was truly curious.

"The truth is no one talks to me anymore except with his or her Hektor filters on. For Damsah's sakes, did you see what escorted me to your gym?"

Neela nodded even though she hadn't actually seen the well-armed metallic goons.

"It was bad enough when he was the Chairman of GCI but now as the soon-to-be wartime President he's getting worse."

Neela was incredulous. "Are you seriously telling me you need a friend?"

Amanda let out a churlish giggle. "Don't be foolish, child. We'll never be friends. But I do need someone to talk to who'll actually say what she thinks. And barring my defection to the Alliance, you're it. Besides, think about all the secrets I can tell you knowing you can't tell a soul, and before you say 'no,' just think—if you actually do manage to escape imagine how useful all that information will be."

Neela smirked and began to towel herself off. Then she put her hands on her hips and looked Amanda squarely in the eyes.

"Alright, Ms. Snow," she said, now using a small cloth to wipe the chalk from her fingertips, "you can throw me a party, but only on one condition."

"Yes?"

"You stop calling me 'Mrs. Cord.' I'm young, but I'm not *that* young."

Amanda laughed. "Agreed, but only if you call me 'Amanda.' Oh . . ."

"Yes?"

"Dr. Gillette will be there too. He might even be staying awhile."

Neela listened as Amanda went on chatting. She still didn't feel at ease but had to admit she did like the woman's company.

Hektor waited patiently in his t.o.p. for Amanda to return. He looked up from his small command center of holodisplays as she entered, threw her shopping bags to the floor, and propped her legs up on a chaise lounge.

"So?" he asked.

"Success," she answered wearily. "I found the exact shoes I wanted. Now can we please leave this Damsah-forsaken cesspit?"

"Amanda . . ."

"Fine . . . I don't see what you hope to accomplish, Hektor. She loves him and hates you. She won't help us, no matter how nice we are to her."

"She'll come around," said Hektor, returning to his work. "Just give her time."

"How can you be so sure?"

Hektor didn't respond because he didn't have to. Amanda knew the look. It was all the answer she needed.

Neela was having a tough time with her patient. Physically he was fine; it was his psychological state that concerned her. The patient had recently died in combat and needed a fair amount of nanorepair prior to his revive. But even though the repair had gone well and the patient's brain hadn't suffered any serious damage, she'd still found herself saddled with a well-trained combat marine from one of the premier mercenary companies crying in her arms and refusing to let her go. She'd held on to him for so long that her legs were starting to go numb. For all her training and therapeutic skills all she could do was sit there and speak softly, offer comforting words, and let him cry. As she rocked the marine in her arms she thought back on the events that had led up to her current predicament.

It had been the presence of Dr. Thaddeus Gillette at her reintegration party. Thaddeus had been his old bumbling, insightful self and until that moment Neela hadn't realized how much she'd missed the old coot. They'd had a heart-to-heart conversation where he had admitted to her that he'd almost gone to the Alliance but in the end felt that the price of societal change would be too high and cost humanity too much. She hadn't agreed with his naïveté but also didn't want to argue with the one person she considered a real friend. During the course of their conversation he'd surprised her, saying that he was going to be setting up a military revival clinic in Boulder. He'd asked her to participate, something that Amanda assured Neela she could get Hektor to agree to. Neela had refused out-

right, not wanting to aid the enemy, but Thaddeus had been relentless. She'd finally agreed, for the sake of their friendship, that she'd only consult. After a week
Neela had discovered that the line between consulting, helping out, and finally
participating was fine to non-existent. In the end she stopped worrying about the
slippery slope, having come to the realization that the men and women coming
out of suspension were not the enemy—just shattered human beings in need of
her professional help. There was also a very small part of her that felt some responsibility for the war, which was causing these few so much harm.

When she'd held the poor man as long as she felt necessary she left him with
his unit with orders to take him out on the town, get him drunk, and listen to
every word he had to say. She knew from his profile that he'd be a teary drunk as
opposed to a violent one; and what he needed more than anything was to be with
family and friends who supported him. As she was writing up her case notes for
the session Dr. Gillette appeared.

"I am so glad you're helping with Corporal Wu," he said, pulling the soldier's
chart from the top of a large stack on Neela's desk. "A truly difficult case."

Neela remained appreciative, if not a little amazed, that she continued to be
treated as an equal by a man she considered preeminent in the field.

She looked up from the report. "It's nothing you wouldn't have done, Thaddeus."

"Now, Neela," he answered, flashing his trademark goofy grin, "I'm happy to
take credit where credit is due, but this barhopping therapy is quite interesting.
I wouldn't have thought of it. Which is surprising given how much I like spending time in bars."

"It's a very limited and experimental process, Thaddeus. Let's be honest, how
many patients can really make use of it? They need family or a close-knit group
of friends who can act as such and they need to be rated as not likely to be violent in social situations. All in all a small portion of the patients we have."

"But with those few patients it's proving marvelous," he answered, tossing the
chart back onto the stack. "And it's not the only therapy you're developing."

"What choice do we have? This war is forcing us to develop techniques that
revival therapy has never really had to deal with. There's simply no plan or source
that's reliable or relevant. Most of the data on combat trauma is centuries old
and doesn't take into account reanimation, modern technology, or even space
travel for Damsah's sake. I've read through it looking for clues and some is helpful, but in the end we have to create it."

"That's what I want to talk to you about." Gillette looked proud to the point
of bursting. "Neela, I want you to publish."

Neela stared at him, speechless.

"You have to, my dear. What you're doing is some of the most groundbreaking work in decades. I have three scientific journals who've been clamoring for anything I can send them. I want to send them your case notes, written for publication of course."

"You mean you want to cite me as source?"

Thaddeus looked confused. "I wasn't clear?"

"Uh, yes. But won't your colleagues mind? I mean given who I am and all."

"Not in the least. The name Neela Harper will absolutely be in the *Terran Journal of Medicine*. They don't care who you are; they just want to get this information out as quickly as possible to help others who'll start to encounter these cases if the war continues as I fear it may."

"My name is Neela *Cord*," she said with some heat.

"Of course it is, dear; have I ever called you otherwise?"

"You just did."

"Sorry, senior moment. The last time I saw you, you were Harper. Things have happened rather quickly."

"Yes, they have," she admitted, calming down.

"Look," he continued. "You're married to Justin Cord and have every right to call yourself what you will."

"The rest of the Confederation doesn't really see it that way," she reminded him gently.

"Be that as it may, what you can contribute to human knowledge and the alleviation of human suffering is surely worth the sacrifice of your married name. You must realize how much good you can do. I'll beg if I must, but I'd really look ridiculous on my knees. Still, if that is what it takes . . ." Dr. Gillette began to get to his knees in so ponderous a fashion that Neela couldn't help but laugh.

"Tell you what," she said, giggling. "I promise you I'll at least think about it if you just get up."

"What more could I ask?" he answered, rising to his feet, grinning from ear to ear.

A week later the first of many narticles appeared on wartime revival and integration techniques, by Neela Harper.

There always seemed to be some crisis to deal with, some fire to put out or yet another delegation of politicians who needed mollycoddling. Through them all Justin had managed to keep one item on his private agenda. He'd put that issue on the back burner, recognizing its need to be suborned for the greater good of his running the fledgling government and orchestrating of the war. He finally called a meeting when he'd convinced himself that the timing was right and that the request he wanted to make was valid, given that its implementation would not unduly interfere with the running of his affairs. Invited to the meeting were Cyrus Anjou, Admiral Sinclair, Kirk Olmstead, and Mosh McKenzie. Justin was surprised to see Eleanor walk through the door. Though she hadn't been invited and Justin wasn't sure what she'd be able to bring to the table, he greeted her warmly, reasoning that whatever Mosh knew Eleanor knew as well.

The group found themselves in one of Justin's many "secure" offices. At Kirk's prodding Justin had created a number of rooms for high-level briefings. The logic went that if you had six or seven randomly used rooms it would make it that much harder to tap into any one of them. It also fit Justin's persona in that more than anything he hated being predictable. All of the secure rooms had the same features: solid as opposed to instantly nano-created fluid furniture, a large table, chairs, and a centrally linked holo-tank.

When all were seated Justin filled the large central holo-tank with an image that all who'd spent time in the triangle office knew intimately. Floating serenely in front of the gathering was a large six-by-eight-foot gossamer amalgamation of brilliant colors showing a laughing, smiling couple in a rustic, snow-covered surrounding.

"It's time to get her back," Justin said firmly.

Admiral Sinclair's and Cyrus's expressions of support were immediate and assuring. Kirk's, Justin could see, was more businesslike than personal, and Mosh's and Eleanor's' expressions were downright grim.

"Direct assault or sneak attack's pretty much out of the question," said Sinclair. "We have it on good report that she's being guarded like the last ring of Saturn."

"Might I suggest we trade," added Cyrus, pulling up a roster of names in place of the haunting image of the presidential couple. "We have a whole fleet of prisoners, including a Grand Admiral." As he said this Admiral Tully's image and bio popped up and out from the extensive list.

"Not so grand," Anjou added wryly, "but let's hope grand enough. If not, maybe we can throw in some captains." Eighteen more images popped up and around Tully's. They were ranked, Justin saw, by perceived value based on experience and accomplishments. All the lists were fairly sparse.

"Admirals, captains, privates, cooks for Damsah's sakes," interjected Mosh, whose dour expression had remained unchanged. "He'll kill her before he let's her out of his grasp. Trust me on this, Justin. I don't mean to put a damper on your plans, but this whole thing is folly."

Justin listened intently, trying to work through Mosh's opinion. It wasn't one, he knew, to be taken lightly. Mosh had risen to the highest echelons of GCI, having almost become Chairman himself, and more than anyone else in the room had an intimate knowledge of how that type of system operated.

"All due respect, Mosh," said Justin, "I don't believe Hektor would harm Neela given her value as a hostage. At his heart Hektor is still a businessman."

Mosh was about to speak, but Eleanor put her hand on his arm and gave him a knowing look. He nodded and beckoned for her to continue. "Justin," she went on, "pardon me for saying this, but you're wrong about Hektor. This isn't a business decision. This is personal. He knows you too well and, because he does, knows you have nothing of value to offer."

"Which," continued Mosh, "makes Neela useless as a hostage."

"We've got over fifty thousand soldiers, Mosh," intoned the admiral. "Some of them have to be worth *something*."

"They are, Joshua," said Mosh, "just not enough . . . or at least not enough for Neela."

Justin was starting to get frustrated. He'd expected a simple and quick resolution, whether military, monetary, or a little bit of both. He hadn't expected such stiff resistance from two of the people he trusted most.

"She's my wife, people, and beloved by this Alliance. How can you say that makes her useless?"

"Justin," answered Eleanor calmly, "a hostage has value in proportion to what holding that hostage can bring. Hektor does not want credits or soldiers, both of which he has in abundance. There's only one thing he considers valuable." She blanked out the holo-tank, then got up, went to the door, and opened it.

"Sergeant," she said, calling out to an unseen soldier posted outside the room, "would you please come in here for a moment?"

A young man came into the room looking rather confused.

"Eleanor, please," said Justin, "is this really necessary?"

"Yes, dear. Please bear with me."

The man was just under six feet, with blue eyes and short-cropped blond hair. He had a wide torso, thick, powerful arms, and was stocky in a way typical of most Belters. Justin quickly called up the young man's stats on his DijAssist. He saw that the sergeant had been newly assigned, having served during the Battle of the Cerian Rocks with such distinction that he'd been promoted to sergeant and assigned to the Cliff House.

"Eric, right?" asked Justin.

"Mr. President!" said the sergeant, snapping to immediate attention. "Sergeant Eric M. Holke of the Eighty-second Cerean Volunteers, temporarily assigned to the presidential guard, sir!" The formality let Justin know that the sergeant's unit must have been led by a mercenary, company–trained officer. Not all Alliance soldiers knew or cared about proper forms of address. His youthful earnestness forced a small smile from Justin's lips.

"Thank you for what you've done for the Alliance, Sergeant. Without your bravery and willingness to risk your life we wouldn't be celebrating a victory right now and would have no hope of victory in the future."

"Thank you, sir!" answered the sergeant.

Justin then looked over to Eleanor, indicating that the floor was hers.

"Tell me, Eric," she asked, "are you married?"

The sergeant's face broke into a risible yet endearing grin in the genuine emotion it showed beneath the gruff exterior of a combat veteran. "Yes, ma'am, matter of fact I am."

Eleanor returned his smile. "Just recently, too, I gather."

"Yes, ma'am," answered the sergeant. "A little over six months ago. Had to practically beg her to marry me. Her first marriage didn't go too well, if you know what I mean."

Eleanor nodded sympathetically.

"Luckily, her pebble-head ex is not even on Ceres. Little settlement about two days' boost from here. Let's just say," he continued, replacing his "in love" face with that of the cold, rigid combat veteran, "he doesn't come around Ceres much anymore."

Admiral Sinclair gave the young man a look of respect.

"Did your wife approve of you volunteering?" asked Eleanor.

"Pooky . . . uh . . . the missus," Sergeant Holke responded sheepishly, "and I had to talk about it before she saw it was the right thing to do."

Eleanor looked at the sergeant suspiciously. "So you're saying you did it without telling her, aren't you?"

"Well, it was . . . um . . . am I in trouble here, ma'am?"

Justin interrupted. "Sergeant, best to say nothing. Eleanor is far more likely to side with your wife."

Eleanor nodded in agreement. "Thank you for your time, Sergeant," she said, showing him to the door, "and please, give my regards to your wife."

"Mine as well," seconded Justin.

The sergeant saluted and exited the room. The phrase "Pooky is not going to believe this" could be heard by the cabinet as the soldier walked the short distance from the door to his post at the end of the hall.

Justin ordered the door resealed. "Eleanor," he said as soon as the room indicated that they were once again in secure mode, "mind telling us what that was all about?"

Eleanor sighed. "Justin, would you sacrifice the life of Sergeant Holke to save Neela?"

"Eleanor, please . . ."

"Well?"

"Of course not."

"I'm almost willing to bet," she continued, "that you'll now do your best to make sure that Sergeant Holke returns home to his 'Pooky.' "

Justin remained silent. It was exactly what he'd been thinking.

"Thought so," Eleanor said with not the slightest hint of reproof. "Let me take it a step further. Would you *ever* knowingly give any information that would cause injury or death to any citizen of the Alliance . . . or even the core for the matter . . . barring Hektor of course?"

Justin allowed himself a small laugh but knew exactly where Eleanor was heading. He was starting to feel a pit well up in his stomach.

"Could you do any of the things I've just described?" she continued. "Even for Neela's life?"

Justin shook his head gravely.

"You can't even offer yourself, dear. The Alliance needs you too much. If even a part of the human race is going to escape from the corporate core's servitude we need you. You don't have the luxury of sacrifice. Hektor knows this. And it's why he'll be determined to make use of Neela in other ways."

The room remained uncomfortably silent. All that could be heard was the quiet buzz of the holo-tank. Eleanor's logic was irrefutable and no one present was prepared to challenge it. Justin stewed in the totality of her trap. He was angry with Eleanor but angrier with himself for not seeing it himself before he'd bothered to gather his cabinet together. His love for Neela had been all-encompassing, which was why, even after he'd left her on Mars, he'd refused to let go. And which was why he'd called the meeting. But just as he'd been forced to abandon his one true love on the Red Planet he was now being told he'd have to abandon her again. And it was killing him.

"Fine," he said stiffly. "Admiral, you said an assault was out of the question. But," he said, looking over to Kirk, "can we at least explore the possibility of an extraction?"

Kirk nodded. "Of course."

Justin looked over to Eleanor. "Just an exploration, Eleanor."

Eleanor's expression remained impassive. "That sounds fine, Justin."

"Good, it's settled, then," Justin said, getting up. The rest of the cabinet rose in unison.

"Thank you all for coming and for your invaluable insights. I realize I'm asking for the impossible, but we seem to have achieved that and more on numerous occasions."

As the group departed, Eleanor pulled Justin aside.

"Justin, can I have five minutes . . . in private, please."

Justin gave her a quizzical look. "Of course, Eleanor."

When the last of the cabinet members had left, Eleanor sat back down, took Justin's hands in hers, and looked him directly in the eyes.

"Justin, she's gone."

Justin immediately pulled his hands away. "I refuse to believe that, Eleanor."

She saw the look on his face. "Oh, they won't take her out to a wall and shoot her. Nor will they lose her suspension unit in deep space as I understand they once threatened to do. But she *is* gone."

"As long as she's alive, Eleanor, there's hope. I'm sure Kirk will come up with something."

Eleanor nodded her head. "I'm sure he will too, Justin. But he'll . . . correction: *you'll* be sending out a suicide mission to capture someone who no longer exists. You must understand, Justin, that the Neela who went to Mars died there."

"You don't know that for sure. No one does."

"You're right, not yet. But in all likelihood she'll have been psyche-audited."

"Again, you don't know that for sure and if they did, it won't matter. Our doctors are every bit as good as theirs. Whatever they did to her, *if* they did something to her, we'll figure out a way to undo it."

"No," Eleanor said as her eyes began to well up. "No, we won't."

Justin had had enough. He stood up and slammed his fist on the table. "Why are you doing this to me, Eleanor? Why?"

Eleanor flinched but kept her gaze fixed on Justin.

"*Listen to me,*" she pleaded in a voice totally devoid of the gentle timbre normally associated with her personality. "What do you think I did before I was a combat medic?"

"Eleanor, you were Mosh's secretary. What kind of question is that?"

"And before that?"

Justin shrugged his shoulders.

"I know what you think because it's what everyone thinks. I was a secretary. What else could Eleanor McKenzie have been?"

Indeed, thought Justin. He took a fresh look at his friend, trying to see her for the first time without the filter of Mosh's wife or secretary or Neela's friend. Although he was now making the effort, it was hard not to divorce her from his preconceived notions. But he could see he'd missed something, and one way or another knew he was about to find out.

"Alright, Eleanor," Justin said, sitting back down, "I'll bite. What's the big secret?"

Eleanor drew a deep breath and then exhaled almost as forcefully. "I was an operative for GCI Special Operations. Part of a group called 'the black bag unit.' "

"Operative?"

"I cleaned up . . . messes, Justin—whatever the cost, whatever it took."

Justin stared hard at Eleanor. "What kind of messes?"

"Political rivals, blackmailers, perceived enemies. The list was extensive."

"How extensive?"

"I worked directly for the Vice President of Special Operations. This was before he became known as 'The Chairman.' "

"You mean Hektor's old boss."

"Yes."

"But your records—"

"—have been cleared and modified. As far as the system is concerned, I'm your perception of me . . . that is, until now."

"Cut to the chase, please."

"Mosh was . . . was one of the 'messes' I was assigned to clean up."

Justin said nothing. Once more the buzz of the holo-tank was all that could be heard in the near-empty room. He brought his hands to his chin, forming a temple with his fingers. His eyes were focused and steely.

"Go on."

"Justin, didn't you ever find it strange that a man as competent and energetic as Mosh just up and left the corporate world without a fight?"

"No. Why should I?"

"Because had you known the Mosh that existed before this one, you would've."

"Before this one? What on earth are you talking about?"

"Justin, Mosh has been psyche-audited."

"What?! By who?! How do you know this, Eleanor?"

"I know this, Justin, because I was the one who did it."

Justin was flabbergasted. He sat across from Eleanor looking anew at the suddenly unfamiliar woman in front of him. He'd taken Mosh's explanation of his divorce from GCI at face value and now his wife was offering up another one entirely.

Eleanor explained to him that she'd at first been assigned to get close to Mosh. Her mission was to catch him in an unguarded moment and then scan his brain as prep for a "new" experimental audit. She was then to make sure his schedule was such that no one would miss him for the ten hours it would take to complete the procedure. She'd further explained to Justin how the "pre-altered" Mosh was ambitious and driven by a need to become the next Chairman of GCI. And how much he'd hated the man who eventually got the job. Mosh had felt that the Senior V.P. of Special Operations was dangerous, unprincipled, and had to be stopped.

The audit techniques she eventually applied were designed to change only small aspects of his personality. The nanites were programmed to take advantage of his preexisting dispositions. Some emotional responses were to be amplified while others were to be tapered.

Justin listened quietly and waited patiently for her to finish.

"So you brainwashed him."

"Yes, Justin," she answered, "I did. But I also saved his life. My assignment was to tweak his brain in such a way as to make his actions so disruptive and suspect that the board would have no choice but to either censure, fire, or liquidate him."

"Why go through all the clandestine activity, Eleanor? Why didn't the V.P. just get rid of him?"

"You don't reach Mosh's level without friends in high places, Justin. Everyone had to be convinced that he'd become a liability—even his closest friends. That way the V.P. of Special Ops would've been asked to eliminate him."

"Nice trick."

"The future Chairman was a very calculating man, as you well know."

Justin nodded, thinking back to his brief encounter with the man who'd already set so much in motion. "Go on."

"Something . . . or more specifically *someone* got in the way of my mission."

She smiled forlornly and continued speaking, noted Justin, as if he were no longer in the room. "He was easily the most pompous and demanding man I'd ever met. Damned fool was so convinced that he was right about everything. But he could also be so sweet and generous and protective."

"Eleanor," said Justin, interrupting her brief reverie, "you fell for him, didn't you?"

She nodded, wiping a tear from her eye.

"During the audit I upped the level of affection he felt for me, increased his disgust with corporate politics, and lessened his need for total control. It took time for the effects to kick in, but when they did it was child's play to steer Mosh toward Colorado and away from New York."

Once again Justin remained silent. Attempting to understand the implications of what he'd just been told.

"And how," he asked, "did the Chairman react to your disloyalty?"

"Oh, I was fired and we never spoke again, but other than that why should he care? He got what he wanted . . . if not in the way he wanted."

"And you got what you wanted."

"No, Justin, I didn't. I love him. I know I do. After all these years my heart still jumps when he walks into the room. What do you think I'd give to know he loved me the same?"

"Of course he loves you, Eleanor."

"Yes, but I'll forever be haunted by one question—"

"Would he have?" finished Justin.

"I'd give up a lot to know the answer to that."

Justin nodded gravely.

"But I also know," she continued, "that if I hadn't acted the man I love would now be dead. As long as Mosh stood in the future Chairman's path he would've been eliminated. If not by me, then by the person who came after. You met the guy, Justin, and know he would have destroyed half the system to get what he wanted."

He still might get his wish, Justin thought ruefully.

"And you're absolutely sure you can't get him back, Eleanor? I mean technology has to have advanced since the procedure was initiated."

"It works both ways, Justin. I'll assume that with Hektor at the controls it's become even more insidious. The procedure, at the time I was involved, dealt with some of the most delicate regions of the brain and was done in such a way as to make any meddling fatal. On top of that, if Mosh were to even learn of his audit it could kill him or trigger behaviors that would be just as destructive. He would become suicidal, homicidal, or quite possibly both."

"And you know this because—"

"I read the reports . . . saw holo-casts."

"Eleanor, you're talking about crimes against humanity."

"What do you think GCI and the other corporations are, Justin? They exist solely to maintain and grow their power—at all costs. When I was briefed what the black bag unit of Special Operations had in mind for Mosh I knew I had to get out and take him with me. And, Damsah help me, that's exactly what I did. If I'd have just taken him and run, he would've come right back, stayed, and tried to fight it out in the boardroom."

". . . and," added Justin, "been killed for his efforts."

"Exactly. The old Chairman would have blown up the whole board to get at him if it had come down to that. I'm convinced he'd even have taken out half the Beanstalk to achieve his goals."

Justin shuddered as he remembered the devastation of New York and the role the old Chairman had played in its destruction. Reluctantly Justin had been forced to agree that Eleanor—albeit a new, more dangerous and calculating Eleanor—had a point. He manipulated the holo-tank so that once again the smiling picture of himself and Neela filled the large, central screen. He stared at it forlornly. His breathing was heavy and labored.

"Alright," he asked sullenly, "how can we know for sure?"

"It will happen slowly if it happens at all. We have spies who can report on her behavior. If she's been audited she'll at first behave in a manner consistent with the Neela we all know. But over the next few weeks and months if her actions begin to aid the Confederation, well . . ."

Justin nodded affirmatively.

"If, as I suspect, she's been audited, she'll become a full-fledged and public supporter of the Confederation."

"At which point," he said, staring at the picture, "you say it's hopeless."

Eleanor smiled sadly. "Let's plan your rescue, Justin. It'll still take weeks to organize and put the resources into play. By then if Neela shows no change in behavior we can go ahead."

"And if she does?"

Eleanor left the rest unsaid. In all likelihood, realized Justin, a hopeless path was already being trod.

7 At the Martian Gates

Bridge of the TFS *Vishnu*

Admiral Abhay Gupta was pacing the bridge of his personally named flagship, the *Vishnu*. He wasn't angry or even agitated. Pacing was just his way of thinking through problems. And his biggest one at the moment was getting his officers to understand how much they still needed to learn. In the more than five months that had elapsed since the disastrous Battle of the Cerian Rocks, the Terran Confederation had done amazing things. They'd built a new fleet of sixty modern warships and they'd fully crewed those ships with volunteers eager to avenge the loss the Belters had inflicted on core world pride. The Terran Confederation had elected Hektor Sambianco as President, a proud minority Shareholder like himself. Plus Abhay sensed that the President knew how important it was to win this war for the future of a united humanity. But Hektor Sambianco was only President-elect and the old administration was pressuring Abhay to launch his fleet and attack the Belters now. They'd wanted a victory to ensure their legacy and not appear as total failures in the eyes of the people.

But Abhay Gupta knew this fleet wasn't ready for any offensive action. The officers were mostly executives from the major corporations who'd joined up thinking a stint in the war would pad their résumés. There was a contingent of trained mercenary officers assigned to the fleet, but they were too few to be properly dispersed. This resulted in a plethora of new warships without any warriors aboard. It also didn't help that most of the experienced mercenaries were currently biding their time in Alliance prisons thanks to the stupidity of Admiral Tully. Abhay would have been among their ranks but for a deep-seated animus between himself and the now-incarcerated Tully, who'd left Abhay on Earth as the fleet advisor to the President. Now there was only one admiral left with real fleet command experience and Gupta was it. Even so, he almost didn't get the command of the new Martian fleet. He'd had to fight it out with the CEO of CourtIncorp, who'd only lost because of so obvious a lack of qualifications that the celistocracy in charge of commissions had to admit there was a line of ineptitude that even they weren't willing to cross.

But the executive officers were more of a problem than they were worth. Each had been successful in the corporate world and had assumed that would translate over. They did have skills and many had training that would make them useful . . . one day, but they still had to learn how to be military. Gupta also knew full well that his sailors were in almost as bad a shape. They'd been "volunteered" by their corporations, as almost none had majority. And even though they tended to have a fair amount of technical skills they were still too new to life in space. Gupta paced. He needed more time to turn his "crap" into crews.

But as far as the officers and even many of the sailors were concerned they had more and better-equipped cruisers then the forty-odd vessels of the Alliance. It took all of Gupta's time and some quiet help from the President-elect to keep stalling the "great new offensive" that would win the war in one fell swoop. Given another two months he knew he'd have over eighty ships and his crews would then be well trained enough to win against the irascible Alliance fleet. He knew it wouldn't be the cakewalk his young officers thought it would, in fact it would probably be a bloody mess, but with enough ships, training, and equipment he believed it could be won. Just engage and slog, nothing fancy. Some more time and he could break the Alliance fleet and win this war.

"Sir!" screamed the comm officer, interrupting Gupta's ruminations. "Contact with unidentified ships! Damsah, there seem to be dozens!"

Time had just run out.

On the bridge of the *War Prize* Admiral J. D. Black reviewed the holographic battlefield. The theater was relatively small and the plan simple. Far to the rear of the possible engagement area were the space stations of Mars with enough orbital batteries and armed platforms to make approaching that quadrant suicide. To the very fore of the engagement area, about a fifty-minute boost from Mars, was a well-salted minefield. There were enough atomics, noted J.D., to effectively cover all the approaches to the staging area of the Martian fleet, made up of three squadrons of about twenty ships each. One squadron, she could see, was in orbit around the far side of the planet practicing defensive maneuvers. J.D. admired the gumption of the Fleet Admiral. He was using his time well.

Smack-dab in the middle of the theater, and within shooting distance of the minefield, was an enormous supply and fitting chain that involved platforms and supply ships for the second, now-inactive squadron of twenty. However, for J.D. it was the shipyard that held far more interest than the twenty Confederation cruisers currently being fussed over. Although it was only a medium-sized facility compared to those in orbit around Earth and Luna, it was by far the largest shipyard near the asteroid belt.

The holo showed an enormous amount of supplies and raw materials in a vast field of carefully arranged and categorized asteroids. Because the field was so immense it had to be positioned *outside* the protection of the minefield.

Under any other circumstance, the setup J.D. was now viewing would've been of great strategic advantage to a wartime fleet. Ships coming in or out could be retrofitted on the fly—especially given the proximity to so large a supply chain. J.D., however, was now determined to turn the Terran Confederation's strategic advantage into a tactical advantage of her own. Her only problem was with the third portion of the fleet patrolling the outer perimeter of the minefield. Because, as they were in defensive maneuver training they'd have their guns at the ready.

But she was ready too. Though she felt she could have used a little more time to turn her crews into combat-ready warriors, she did have the advantage of experience. Not so much hers as her crews'. Her entire fleet was made up of people for whom the rigors of space, as well as life on ships, were as natural as breathing. But now that J.D. had gotten a good look at the facility and the rapidity with which it was turning out all manner of war craft she thanked God for unanswered prayers—to have waited any longer would have been dangerous.

Of course, she mused, attacking sixty brand-new ships near their own home base and supply depot with only forty of her own, just twenty of which were top-of-the-line, was also dangerous. It all came down to whether or not the ruse would work.

"Look at the big fleet coming your way," she began murmurring. "What stupid Belters we are to send our whole fleet this way." All around her the command crew took note of her mutterings and smiled—their faith in their admiral, deepening.

"Admiral Gupta, it appears to be a large number of Alliance ships. They're on a course directly toward the shipyard."

The admiral stared at the oncoming blips with morbid fascination. His arms were behind his back and he was twiddling his thumbs nervously. "Lieutenant," he said, "signal the fleet. Have Commodore Diep's task force break off training in Martian orbit and proceed to these coordinates."

"Yes, sir."

"What's her ETA to our quadrant?"

"One moment, sir . . . contacting." The lieutenant looked up from his display a few seconds later. "Sir, Commodore Diep estimates one hour."

Gupta stared at the large central holodisplay. He'd been taken by surprise with only one-third of his fleet in operation, and now he had to figure out a way to work whatever assets he had to his advantage.

"Must be Black," Gupta murmured as a twisted grin formed at the corners of his mouth. "Only she'd be so foolish as to plan a direct assault through a mine-field." He then looked over to his comm officer. "Lieutenant, tell Commodore Diep to make best time, even if she has to jettison half her ship to do it. Minutes will make a difference here."

"Yes, sir!"

"Minefield?"

"Activated, sir."

"Good, have Commodore Ginzberg prepare his task force for immediate deployment."

"Yes, sir . . . the commodore is in the tank waiting to talk with you."

"Thank you, Lieutenant; bring him up."

Commodore Ginzberg popped up on-screen. He was a dark-haired man of average height and meticulously combed hair wearing a uniform so overpressed that Gupta often wondered how the man could even lift his arm to salute. Al-though Gupta thought very highly of Ginzberg as an organizer and preparer of ships, he would not have been Gupta's first choice as combat officer. The first words out of the commodore's mouth didn't do anything to dispel that notion. "Admiral," said Ginzberg perfunctorily, "I will need at least forty-five minutes to clear civilian personal from my ships and get the civilian craft safely away before I can break from space dock."

"Louis," Gupta said patiently, "there's a battle coming. I can hold the enemy at the minefield, but you'll have to get your ships ready to go, with or without the civvies." Ginzberg opened his mouth to argue but was immediately cut off. "Let me be perfectly clear, Louis. If you're not under way in twenty minutes I'll save Admi-ral Black the trouble and hand you over to her myself." He then motioned for the comm link to be cut. *With any luck,* thought Gupta, *he'll pull it off in half an hour.* "Helmsman, hold position here. Lieutenant, order the task force to do the same."

As the lieutenant relayed the orders to the fleet, Gupta's second in command floated up from his post below. Gupta approved of the officer: sharp and re-spectful and always asked good questions.

"Admiral, a word if you don't mind?"

"Certainly, Captain. What is it?"

"Black's fleet is going to be at the minefield in a little less than ten minutes. If we boost hard we can meet them at the other side."

"Why, Captain?"

"To engage them after the mines have caused the most damage but before they can repair themselves, sir."

Gupta sighed. "Yes, I know *that,* Captain. I mean why would J. D. Black do this? I expected better of her."

"Sir," posited the captain, "she's a lawyer who got lucky in one ambush. But to expect real fleet capability out of her?" The captain then shook his head. "Not likely."

"I pray you're correct. But something's not right." Gupta once again stared at the theater. The thumbs he'd been madly twiddling behind his back suddenly came to a stop. He looked back at the captain.

"How many picket boats in this area?" asked Gupta, pointing to the perimeter of the minefield.

"Three, sir."

"Good. Let's send them to intercept."

"Right away, sir . . . but if I may, sir . . . why? We know where the enemy's coming from."

"Captain, I'm looking at this area of potential battle and it occurs to me that it's the only spot I don't have any eyeballs on. Yes, our sensors have detected the enemy fleet there, but has anyone actually *seen* it?"

The captain shook his head, "No, sir."

"I want an eyeball, then. Just to confirm."

"On it, sir," answered the captain as he floated back down to his station.

As Gupta stared intently at the blips representing the oncoming enemy his comm officer cleared his throat . . . twice. Gupta sighed. "What is it, Lieutenant?"

"May not be my place, sir."

"It's not your place to obey a direct order from an admiral, Lieutenant?"

"Of course not, sir, I mean yes, sir, uh what I mean is—"

"You had a thought, Lieutenant, out with it."

"Well, Admiral, it just occurred to me that the minefield's not the only place we don't have an eyeball, as you put it."

"Where's the other place, son?"

The lieutenant pointed to the vast field of asteroids floating beyond the minefield off the main shipping lane. "There, sir."

Gupta studied the chart for a moment. "Lieutenant, we have that area rigged with sensors. If there was a two-person garbage tug we'd know about it." But his thumbs stopped twiddling and he found, hard as he tried, he couldn't take his eyes off the spot on the holographic display that the lieutenant had pointed to. "Send one of the picket ships past the minefield to scout out the resource field. Let's just eyeball everything. Good thinking, Lieutenant."

The lieutenant nodded gratefully and went back to work.

For the next four minutes Gupta's fleet of twenty sat and did nothing.

"Admiral," came the captain over the comm link, "got something here."

"Don't keep me in suspense, Captain."

"Well, sir, our picket, the one we sent to the resource field, according to our sensor net in the field . . . well . . ."

"Yes?"

"Well, it's not there."

Bridge of the AWS *War Prize*

J.D. stared intently at her holodisplay. "Picket ships," she muttered almost as if it were a curse from God himself.

Bridge of the TFS *Vishnu*

"Admiral, our two pickets are about to make visual contact with the approaching fleet."

"Pipe it in, Lieutenant."

The lieutenant activated a control and a faint image of a young sailor came into the center holo-tank. The holo of the soldier was fuzzy, which the crew had expected. The enemy was undoubtedly trying to block or disrupt all communications.

"Fleet Command, fleet Command," said the young officer excitedly, "visual analysis and active sensor is . . . is, Damsah's ghost, Fleet Command, they're . . . ice. I repeat: The enemy fleet is *ice*. We're picking up multiple transponders mimicking ship noise."

Gupta winced. *They threw icebergs at us?*

"They're traveling at a completely unvarying rate of speed," continued the officer. "By my kids' first dividend, one of them even has a rotation. Fleet, we've been suckered; they are not, I repeat, *not* an enemy fleet."

The admiral made a motion for the connection to be cut.

"OK," he said into the comm link attached to his acceleration couch. "If that's nothing but a decoy, where *is* their fleet?"

"Lieutenant, open a connection to the other picket boat."

"Connection made, Admiral."

"Pilot, this is Admiral Gupta; what's your name?"

"Taylor, sir. Lieutenant Allison Taylor."

"Lieutenant, how long till you're past the resource field?"

"Clearing the last couple of rocks now, sir."

"Lieutenant, just take a quick look and turn around. In and out, quick as you can, understand?"

"Yes, Admiral . . . wait . . . I have something . . . ships! Damsah! Alliance ships! I count at least ten large, no . . . make that fifteen, no . . ." The connection was broken by a burst of static.

"Sir," came another voice over the comm, "the picket ship's been destroyed."

"Navigation," barked the admiral, "set course to intercept that fleet as it leaves the resource field. Communications, order the rest of the task force to do the same. Same goes for the other task forces."

The orders were given and the crew began to feel the slow but steady tug of their warship as she began hurtling herself toward the field of combat. In unison nineteen other ships began turning and boosting as well

"What do you think she's up to, Admiral?" asked the captain over the link.

Gupta had a sardonic smile. "Admiral Black wanted us and all our attention focused on that ice fleet. Which reminds me, deactivate the minefield."

"Begging your pardon, sir," asked the captain, "but are you sure that's wise?"

"Pardon granted, son. And yeah, I'm sure; deactivate it. She meant to kill us with our own ordnance."

"Sir?"

"Brilliant plan, really. We slow down and wait for her in the wrong location while her real fleet slips through the resource field and rushes the shipyard. We would've been too slow and too far away to stop her in time. Then she would've had us backed against our own *activated* minefield."

"We could've shut it down, sir."

"On whose orders, son?" answered Gupta. "Don't forget, she would have targeted my ship first. If I'm gone and the battle is raging, who shuts the field down? Never mind, don't answer. I'll tell you. Our fleeing ships do. That's what she counted on. Blown up by our own protective net. Brilliant. The losses would've been astronomical." Gupta laughed. "Well, I see you're willing to gamble, Ms. Black, but this is one gamble you've lost, thanks to our young lieutenant here, and the life of one brave picket pilot."

"Sir," answered the lieutenant, "you deserve credit too."

"Thank you, Captain, but the battle is not yet won."

"No, sir. It's not, but by now she's probably realized we didn't bite and that we'll be waiting. I wouldn't be surprised if she decides to cut and run."

"We're learning many things about Admiral Black, Lieutenant," answered Gupta, "but something tells me she's not the sort of person to cut and run."

It took the task force almost fifteen minutes to arrive at the coordinates where the enemy had been identified. Gupta sent in automated probes, expecting to find an Alliance fleet charging full bore through the resource field. Instead he discovered a much more diminished cluster of warships—all at a dead stop. If anything, the formation was smaller than he'd expected. There were only twenty ships and they were all arranged in a defensive perimeter, using the asteroids in the field to obstruct incoming shots. And to a ship they were all jury-rigged, with not a one being from the recently captured Confederation fleet.

"Captain," Gupta said, beginning to feel cold drops of sweat forming at the base of his forehead, "where the hell is the rest of their fleet?"

Bridge of the AWS *War Prize*

"Lieutenant Nitelowsen," asked J.D., "how close are we to the shipyard?"

"Fifty thousand clicks, Admiral," replied Marilynn with her usual efficiency.

"Minefield?"

"Deactivated . . . from their side, sir."

J.D. flashed a venomous smile. "Then what say we crack open some ice and get this party started?"

A round of cheers broke out from the gallery around her.

"OK, people. Pipe down. There's still work to be done."

From the view of the shipyard what happened next would be remembered, by those who survived, as one of the most terrifying moments of the war. Twenty seemingly harmless icebergs cracked and then split apart. In the center of each, with only one exception, was a fully functional, fully modern warship. The exception was an Alliance-built glorified platform holding a rail gun that ran the entire length of the ship. What it lacked in maneuverability it more than made up for in firepower. Almost as one the Alliance ships turned on the unsuspecting and still-entangled Confederation fleet.

Bridge of the AWS *War Prize*

"Admiral, we have multiple pings on civilian craft breaking from the shipyard," said the young Jovian in charge of the sensor array. "They're interfering with the yard's defensive batteries and, well, just making a mess of things."

"As planned, Lieutenant," answered J.D.

"Admiral, those warships are just sitting there. We could drop off a few A.M. detachments and capture the whole lot without denting the paint job."

"You're right, Lieutenant Esparza. Our assault miners could take the whole lot with only a small loss of time and momentum. But then we'd be dead in space with depleted boarding parties and forty ships coming at us from two different directions. With ten more ships I might have risked it, but not now. Bring the main batteries to bear and destroy the ships while they're still entangled."

"Yes, sir. Main batteries to bear!" barked the lieutenant. "Fire at will!"

In the next ten minutes twenty of Earth's finest and most modern warships were blown to bits with only three able to break away from the space dock before being themselves destroyed. In the melee not one Confederation ship had been able to bring their main battery to bear. The magnetically propelled death from the Alliance rail guns had assured the Confederation ships' complete and catastrophic end. Then, without fanfare or communication of any kind, the Alliance fleet turned and boosted at full acceleration toward the perimeter of the resource field and into the fray.

Bridge of the TFS *Vishnu*

"Sir, there are reports that the ice ships are breaking up—"

With a sudden horror Admiral Gupta realized exactly where the other ships were and almost as quickly that he had just lost the second great battle of the war. He remembered giving the right orders. He remembered commanding his ships to gain speed and run for the orbital batteries of Mars. He'd been able to return fire on the ridiculous jury-rigged ships of the Alliance that suddenly started to attack his fleet like a pack of crazed hyenas. He'd swallowed his pride and run from them hoping to build up enough speed. Speed to escape the enemy coming at him from both sides—an impossible situation. He'd even considered accepting Admiral Black's offer of surrender. He believed that she'd see his people treated well and not harmed or audited. But he also knew that any ship he surrendered would be used against the men and women of the Confederation in the next battle. He knew he'd lost, but now he was determined to make sure her victory wouldn't come cheap.

It had been his last order to Commodore Diep that had turned out to have the only real and lasting damage on the Alliance. Over strong protest he ordered and then had to practically beg Commodore Diep to abandon her course and return to the orbital defenses of Mars. It was only when he reminded Diep that his ships were dying in order to buy her the time to prepare Mars for attack that she finally agreed. That last order and the pride he felt for his soldiers were the only honorable things he remembered. His ships fought with bravery and some skill against hopeless odds. Their dedication and sacrifice, he thought sadly, deserved a better leader than they got. His last act before the power faded on the wrecked ship and the sounds of battle from inside the *Vishnu* grew too loud to ignore was to recommend commendations for his now-destroyed task force. As soon as he was done the bulkhead door blasted open and thankfully he remembered nothing more of the terrible battle he'd just lost.

Bridge of the AWS *War Prize*

"Admiral, A.M.'s reporting bridge of enemy flag ship secured . . . enemy admiral wounded and unconscious, but in stable condition . . . rest of their task force is surrendering . . . two of the enemy ships escaped and are boosting toward Mars . . . Captain Sadma reports her ship is capable of pursuing." The lieutenant looked up. "Orders?"

J.D. considered refusing but figured two more inoperative ships wouldn't be such a bad thing. Plus she didn't want to dampen Christina Sadma's aggressive spirit. "Put her and Captain Omad in the tank." J.D. waited while her two best captains appeared in all their holographic glory. "Are your ships capable of pursuit?"

"Yes, Admiral," they replied in unison.

"Omad's in overall command," said J.D., and then held up her hand to stifle the complaint she knew was already coming. "Christina, you'd pursue them to the steps of the Martian capital . . . tell me I'm wrong."

J.D. saw the young woman wince but then smile mischievously.

"Omad will at least stop before you get yourselves killed. "You're both worth more to me than ten warships, remember that . . . now good hunting, Black out." J.D. turned back to Marilynn. "Prelim damage report?"

"Admiral, of the forty ships engaged we've lost four, *Freedom, F the Dividend, Eternal Light,* and *Sandscrapper.* Another twelve can only be classified as severely damaged. They'll have to be towed back to repair facilities. Of the twenty ships in the enemy formation, ten have been destroyed, two escaped, and the remaining eight are severely damaged. We may get lucky, but we must assume they'll have to be towed as well. Of the twenty-four thousand personnel in the Alliance fleet we have over eleven thousand casualties. Of those it's believed that there may be as many as . . . as five thousand p.d.'s, sir."

Marilynn reported the last figure of the permanent deaths in a whisper and J.D. saw the shock on the faces of those nearest to her. She cut it off quickly. "We'll mourn later," she said in a voice stripped of emotion. "We still have a job to do and we dishonor the dead if we waste their sacrifice with our grief now. Lieutenant Nitelowsen, continue."

"Admiral, enemy casualties are harder to calculate accurately. Two-thirds of the enemy fleet has been effectively neutralized. That is roughly forty thousand personnel, of whom it is believed twenty-four thousand are p.d.'s."

"Prepare a report for Fleet HQ and the President and let's get our fleet to those space yards. Tell Admiral Sinclair we can begin Operation Vulture."

Justin was listening to Admiral Sinclair's briefing on the balcony overlooking the thoroughfare below. At the table were Cyrus Anjou, Kirk Olmstead, and Padamir Singh. They could all see the crowds gathering below. It was impossible, thought Justin, for the Cereans not to know that a battle had been brewing. After all, the fleet had just upped and left. But now there were rumors that it had already been fought, and given the spontaneous outburst of music and dancing below, most seemed to have figured out it was another victory for the Alliance. But before Justin could say anything to anyone, he needed to know what type and how big a victory it was.

"Sir," beamed Sinclair, "I'm happy to report that the shipyard's been taken and secured. Our salvage and reclamation fleet is in place."

"Good. What else?"

"It'll take about a week for the cleanup; once that's done we should have that shipyard in Alliance space in a little less than two weeks."

"Now comes the fun part," Kirk chortled. "There's already quite a fight brewing in Congress about where to send the damned thing."

Justin nodded grimly. "Cyrus?"

"Mr. President, this issue is not about NoShare versus Shareholder. On this it's a straight colony vote."

"Meaning?"

"It's the one issue that both those factions can agree on," answered Kirk. "Greed."

Justin sighed at what was turning into another political donnybrook. "Admiral," he asked, "where does the military feel it should go?"

"Jupiter," answered Sinclair without a moment's hesitation, "and stop looking so smug, Cyrus. I didn't arrive at that answer easily." Sinclair then called up a hologram with a detailed map of Alliance space. "Besides being my home *and* the most beautiful part of the solar system, Saturn may have the advantage of being farthest away with a good resource base, but any ships made there would be at the effective end of the supply chain. And no offense to Neptune, but even the TNOs," said Sinclair, using the standard acronym for Trans Neptunian Objects, "are more developed than that planetary unit."

"Security-wise," added Kirk, "Saturn would be my preferred location."

"True," agreed Sinclair, "but unfortunately, your security considerations are diametrically opposed to the military's need for a viable, uninterrupted supply line. On top of that, when you take into account that Saturn's not nearly as developed economically as Jupiter you arrive at a whole other host of problems."

"Please elaborate," said Justin.

"Well, for one, specialists would have to be shipped in from all over the Alliance, primarily from the industrial zones of the belt, which would decrease output in other areas of production by the amount of travel time involved. In my opinion, just not worth it. If this were a peacetime situation I'd be with Kirk and Saturn would win it hands down. Trust me, I'd love to develop the exterior of our territory away from the corporate core."

"Just so when I have to argue with Congress," said Justin "and correct me if

I'm wrong on this, but didn't you just make a good argument for the Belters getting the shipyard? I mean based on Saturn's weaknesses combined with the ongoing war, it seems to me we should be parking the shipyard fifty thousand
clicks from this office."

"Um, well, Mr. President," said Kirk, "it's a specious argument—at least from
a security standpoint."

"How so, Kirk?"

Kirk manipulated a control and the area around Ceres came up in greater detail. "We can't put it next to the busiest shipping lanes in the Alliance. Logisti-
cally it would be a security nightmare . . . in essence it would be *too* close to the
supply lines, as funny as that sounds. The only reason we can manage security at
Gedretar," he said, referring to the Alliance's shipyard inside of Ceres, "is because it's inside the rock itself with only one real point of entry—two if you
count anybody crazy enough to try entering from the exit lanes."

Justin manipulated the screen to another large asteroid. "Just so I cover all the
bases, what about Eros, Admiral? It's in the belt and near enough to the war
zone."

Admiral Sinclair acknowledged Justin's logic but quickly dispelled his supposi-
tion. "Eros might've been perfect. It's an advanced region with great infrastructure. Unfortunately, it's getting the shipyard to that region that proves to be the
Belter in the brothel. Eros is on the complete opposite side of the belt. To have it do
the 180 from here or even from its current position would take months because we
obviously can't send it through the core."

Kirk brought up an image of the newly captured shipyard.

"The thing's huge, with 360-degree accessibility from all angles," he said. "I'd
have to agree with the admiral. At least at Jupiter we'll be able to give it an isolated orbit around one of their inner moons. Once properly shielded from the
planet's magnetosphere, that location will actually work in our favor."

"And if the war continues," added Sinclair, "we'll need Jupiter to become our
fallback industrial enclave. Against the full resources of the corporate core we
must be realistic and dial in the fact that holding the belt will become increasingly difficult."

Justin sighed. "Hope for the best, plan for the worst. Alright, how do we
manage this without it becoming a major political mess?" As the question left
his lips he felt the loss of his wife even more keenly.

"Rip the Band-Aid off quickly, Mr. President," said Padamir Singh. "The
Belters will not be happy with so large a manufacturing center not being within
their domain. After all, we do feel we're the natural center of trade and industry
in the solar system."

"Only the solar system? Ha!" laughed Cyrus.

"I don't think I've ever heard so self-evident a truth stated in so clear a manner," retorted Padamir, "but be that as it may, our plate is full. We'll pick up enough business keeping the shipyard running to mollify our industrial families. But I can almost guarantee that the Saturnians will be as upset as Terrans owning stock in Erisians. They know what getting this could do for the economy of all Saturn. Might I suggest a solution?"

Justin smiled and then nodded, knowing that Padamir had probably already secured whatever deals necessary to back up his suggestion.

"As you know, we're starting to receive more casualties than we can handle. I'm talking about mental trauma, Mr. President—the physical part's easy. Anyhow, there's a committee in Congress planning to announce the need for a center to treat our wounded."

"Go on."

"May I suggest that our good friend Cyrus propose that Jupiter get *both* the shipyard and the trauma center? This will make Mr. Anjou very popular with his people."

"They'd elect me governor, might even let me marshal the Jovian Mardi Gras," Cyrus said, beaming.

"Naturally," continued Padamir, "the Saturnians will scream bloody murder. Then Admiral Sinclair, good Saturnian that he is, will announce that it would be best if the trauma center were built on Saturn, something about those damn rings being soothing."

"Those damn rings *are* soothing," protested the admiral.

"Of course they are," answered Padamir rather unconvincingly. "Anyhow, I will then announce that the President has taken the advice of his Grand Admiral. The Saturnians will be happy that they got something and forced the big evil Jovian to not get everything. The Jovians will be more than happy to get the shipyard."

"And what will the Belters get out of this deal?" asked Justin.

"Mr. President, there's always something needed. I'm sure these two fine gentlemen will not begrudge me a small favor in Belter interests in some distant future." As he said this Padamir looked at both Cyrus Anjou and Joshua Sinclair and did not look away until he got a slight but perceptible nod from both, showing that they acknowledged the debt.

Justin tipped his head. The political deal making was not the happiest part of the job, but given his former life as a corporate CEO he knew it to be a necessary evil.

"OK, now that we've got that settled, anyone care to bring me up to speed on the latest from Admiral Black?"

"She wants to launch another attack," answered Admiral Sinclair, shaking his head.

"Why am I not surprised? What does she hope to attack and when?"

Sinclair checked a device at the same time as Kirk to make sure the room was still secure from unwarranted eavesdropping. Only when it flashed green did he continue. "She wants to conquer Mars, only this time she wants to do it permanently."

"Really? And when would she like to do this?"

"She assured me she'll be ready as early as next week."

Admiral's shuttle AWS *War Prize*

Janet Delgado Black was sleeping. It was the first time in over a week she'd been able to. She'd learned to subsist on catnaps and so didn't consider sleep to be sleep unless she could actually get out of her clothes, lie naked and prone under a fresh set of sheets on an actual bed. Naturally she told her staff to wake her if the slightest detail needed attention. And just as naturally the crew powered down all noncritical systems near her quarters and posted armed guards near her doors with orders to shoot anyone who came near with news less important than an enemy attack. The immediate space outside of her shuttle was just as diligently watched and all nearby traffic was diverted. In fact, when J.D. slept the entire ship became so quiet that even an inadvertent cough would garner the same caustic glare as a flatulent outburst.

When Janet awoke she'd immediately check in to see what had happened while she was sleeping. At this Lieutenant Nitelowsen would signal the bridge crew that the admiral was awake and the ship would then allow herself to end her silent running mode. What made the whole exercise so remarkable was that not one order was ever given or requested concerning this odd ritual. It had just evolved and was now adhered to with a stricture far out of sorts with the typically lackadaisical Belter attitude toward anything non-combat-related.

"Lieutenant," J.D. said into the comm as she stretched and put on a fresh set of clothes, "is Admiral Gupta recovered enough from his injuries to receive visitors?"

"He regained consciousness two hours ago, Admiral. The medic says he'll be ready for 'questioning' by dinner, ship time."

"Assure the good doctor that I will not be 'questioning' our prisoner, but that I'd like to talk to him before he's suspended and sent back to the Alliance."

"But he was so looking forward to using his pliers and thumbscrews," joked the lieutenant.

J.D.'s eyes narrowed in sarcastic response. "I'm sure he'll contain his disappointment. If he wants to torture anyone I can always order a karaoke night." J.D. was referring to the medic's habit of singing to himself in a horrible off-key voice that had become strangely soothing to the crew because he only did it when treating the wounded.

"I don't think we need to be *that* cruel, Admiral," answered the lieutenant, "but it's your decision."

"Agreed," answered J.D. "Please have my breakfast brought up and be ready to tour in twenty minutes. Black out."

J.D. spent the next ten minutes turning her shuttle from a bedroom back into an office, stowing the bed and dresser, restoring the desk and chairs, getting cleaned up, and then finally donning the jumpsuit with the rank insignia she preferred. She spent the final few minutes going over the never-ending stream of reports that needed her attention. She used to answer every communication from any person under her command. But when her crews realized she was taking the time to answer each and every one of their posts the messages slowed to a crawl. She'd been told and had agreed that she'd only get messages after they'd been vetted. If after the rigorous process her junior officers still felt the communication warranted her attention it would then be passed on to Lieutenant Nitelowsen, who would then pass it on to J.D. What ended up happening most of the time was that the act of bringing the problem up with everyone but J.D. usually got it solved before she could ever lay eyes on it. She was both gratified and a little worried that her crews worked so hard not to bother her. But the system seemed to be effective, so she let it stand. Plus some of the messages that did get through actually lightened her load rather than burdened it. The one she found herself currently viewing was asking that she officiate at a wedding. It seemed that a comm officer had gotten engaged to an assault miner on another ship and they were both wondering if J.D. would be so kind as to do the honors. She would have to give it some serious thought, but J.D. immediately replied with a congratulations and the promise to respond to their request within twenty-four hours.

By the time Marilynn arrived, J.D. was ready to go. They spent the next ten hours touring various ships, the newly captured shipyard, and a few of the supply depots. J.D. found it was no longer possible to surprise people by just showing up in her shuttle, because her command crew had insisted she travel with an escort of four armed fighters. But her visits still served the purpose of letting her see how the fleet was doing and, more important, be seen by the crews.

She often wondered about what separated her brand of leadership from Justin's. His allure, she saw, spread over the whole Alliance, and even into parts of the core. Her relationship was limited to the fleet, but it seemed far more intense. Every time she saw a sailor leap to attention or a work crew cease all activity to stare at her, slack jawed, she resolved yet again to be worthy of the adulation. She even seemed to have a strange effect on the civilians who were caught up in the capture of the shipyard. Their reactions ranged from abject fear to an awe that almost seemed as strong as the one in the fleet.

Her crew had been busy. Working around the clock, they'd managed to bring the fleet back up to thirty-eight battle-ready ships. It helped that they'd been able to grab parts of the shipyard necessary for repair, as well as put to work captured civilian personnel. She didn't think that the commanding officer of Operation Vulture, the shipyard's salvaging effort, would be too upset. The truth was, the yard was so big he was pretty much working full-time prepping the outer sections for flotation back to Alliance territory. But she made sure to make all her orders concerning fleet repair into requests and, where possible, accommodate his mission. The courtesy helped, but both knew what would happen if a choice between her priorities and his ever arose. The captain in charge of the salvage operation wisely made sure no such conflict ever happened.

Finally J.D.'s shuttle returned to the recently "donated" hospital ship. J.D. was escorted to the door of the private recovery suite where her most prestigious prisoner was recovering from his near-fatal wounds. Much to the surprise of the armed escort that had met her at the loading bay, but not to Lieutenant Nitelowsen, J.D. searched for a command console to press her hand into. She was flustered by the lack of any. She was then politely reminded that she was not on a warship, or any ship, for that matter, designed and constructed in the Alliance.

"Their war vessels use permiawalls?" she asked, referring to the molecular technology that could sense approaching objects and thereby melt away as needed. Warships and Alliance craft did not have fluid wall portals. They'd purposely over engineered and hardened bulkhead doors that, thought J.D. thankfully, whooshed and closed with a reassuring thud. As she entered the room, part of her was surprised how much the permiawall doorway bothered her. The old Janet wouldn't have minded, wouldn't have noticed even, but J. D. Black did and was going to have the damned things replaced at the next opportunity.

But that thought ended as soon as she saw the man in the bed sit up straight and give her a perfectly correct salute. Although not mercenary-trained, she returned the salute as if she'd attended West Point. Once the formality was done Admiral Gupta relaxed.

"Won't you please have a seat, Admiral Black?" he said.

"Thank you, Admiral Gupta. I'd be delighted to."

After she was seated, Gupta continued, "I've been wanting to thank you. I was visited by as many of my bridge crew as survived, and they told me you've been unstinting in your care of my wounded and absolutely correct in the . . ." He paused at a catch in his throat. ". . . in the care of my p.d.'s."

"We always honor the p.d.'s, Admiral. They fought with bravery and honor. To treat your personnel, living or dead, in any other way would be an abomination."

"They did fight bravely," he said sadly. "I only wished they'd had a better leader."

J.D. gave a short, bitter laugh. "And I only wish they'd a worse one."

Admiral Gupta looked askance at his captor. "Forgive me, Admiral Black, but I'm the prisoner in a recovery bay of what used to be *my* hospital ship. If I'd been as good an admiral as you say, it would be you in this bed and I'd be the one sitting making courteous, if untrue, statements."

"Admiral Gupta, I'd lie to you in a nanosecond if I thought there was an advantage, but there isn't. You fought the battle well. Better than I thought a core admiral could. So be honest, would it have gone better if that idiot CEO from CourtIncorp had been in charge?"

"Damsah, no!"

Now J.D. let some of her bitterness show. "It would have been a perfect trap. You were supposed to send your task force to intercept the 'enemy' fleet, see that it was ice, re-scan the entire perimeter, and then and only then find my ships crossing the resource field. You were supposed to turn your fleet around, and just as it was out of maximum position I would've attacked you from behind, while my second contingent clobbered you from the front. We would've made sure to destroy your ship first. That would have left Commodore Diep in charge. After we captured the second task force almost intact in dry dock, we would've made it seem like most of our fleet was knocked out of action. If I read Diep correctly, she would have attacked."

"She would have," he said, nodding his head in sudden clarity. "You were going for the whole fleet, weren't you?"

"Initially, but it wasn't my main goal."

"With the fleet gone and an intact task force captured you could have mounted an assault on Mars," he said, shaking his head. "Brilliant."

J.D. nodded. "Without fleet support I would've taken it with minimal loss of life. By God, they might have surrendered! By the time the core had another fleet ready, Mars would have been reinforced and I would've been making sorties to Luna and Earth. The Terran Confederation would've been forced to the negotiating table." J.D. reined in her emotion. "But it's useless to dwell too long on the might have beens. What happened is you waited, gathered sound tactical data, made a choice, and screwed up my plan. I had to go with the alternate. It still might have worked, but your orders to Diep screwed me good. Now she has twenty undamaged top-of-the-line ships behind some of the best orbital batteries in the system."

"I agree," said Gupta, "no better orbats than those."

Gupta, J.D. could now see, was actually visibly relieved that he wasn't the screwup he'd worked himself up to be.

"So," he asked, "when will you be pulling out? When the yard's evacuated?"

"Maybe."

Gupta considered her words. "You're still planning to attack Mars."

J.D. didn't respond, but her eyes remained fixed and cold.

"But it's insane, Admiral," continued Gupta. "You'll lose your ships and personnel to no purpose."

"My people," she answered evenly, "are the best there's ever been and we won't get a better chance. If I don't try this, we'll all spend the rest of the war wondering what might have been, wondering if we could've ended this thing right here, right now. Trust me, Admiral, I know the odds are against us, but they always have been and always will be. We don't have the luxury of waiting for the odds to be in our favor. But tell me, if you could end the war in one battle, even if the odds were against you, knowing what a long war would do to both sides, wouldn't you risk it?"

Gupta thought about it for a moment and was forced to nod his head in agreement. "Yes," he answered solemnly, "yes. I would have to risk it, but the thought of my men and women ordered to hopeless battle would be quite difficult."

J.D. nodded. "My people can do anything they set their minds to. It's risky, and it'll be bloody for sure, but it *will not* be hopeless."

Gupta stared at her, impressed. Then his look suddenly transformed to one of growing concern.

"Admiral Black," he asked with a slight trepidation in his voice, "why are you telling me all this?"

J.D.'s visage didn't change, as she had nothing reassuring to offer. "Two reasons, Admiral. One, I'm not telling you anything Commodore Diep can't figure out just by reading a scanner. I'm pushing too hard and building up my fleet too fast to just be defending a salvage operation.

"Two, immediately after our conversation here you'll be placed in suspension and sent to Ceres." A look of sadness crossed J.D.'s face. "Admiral, I shouldn't tell you this, but you've earned the right to know and be prepared."

"For what?"

"Officially you're to be traded for persons the core holds or may capture in the future. But that's not likely to happen anytime soon—your government has already blamed you for the loss of the Battle of the Martian Gates."

"Is that what it's being called?" he said, resigned.

"By us anyway; so far the convention seems to be winner gets to name the battle. But that won't matter to you. Your government won't press hard to trade you back and I'll make sure, no matter how the negotiations go, that you stay suspended while hostilities continue. You should know and not be shocked that when you wake this will all be over, no matter how long it takes."

Gupta sighed. "But why single me out, Admiral? I lost."

"Admiral Gupta, you lost this battle, but I can't say for certain you'd lose the next one. Your fleet command may not recognize it, but I do. You're good, sir, very good. No one may ever realize it but you, me, and some historian writing about it so far in the future no one will care, but my act of keeping you out of the rest of this war will be the same as if I'd won ten battles."

"I have no regrets, then, but one."

"Yes?"

"I will not have had the chance to redeem my loss—ever. I will simply be one of a long list of admirals to lose to J. D. Black."

J.D. looked at him with compassion. "Admiral, Allah permitting, you should survive this war; I don't think I will. For what it's worth, screw what the public or history says. I know the quality of my opponents. Having you suspended is merely the dishonorable and petty way to serve my Alliance—by depriving your Confederation of one of their finest admirals. I can't ask for your forgiveness, but I do hope you understand."

"Oh, Admiral Black, I certainly understand. Not happy about it, mind you, but the truth is, if I could eliminate you with one easy step, I'd do it in a heartbeat."

J.D. gave the hint of a smile. "Sometimes it really is easier to talk to an enemy than a friend."

Gupta nodded. "One favor, if I may ask."

"If I can, I will."

"Please don't store me near Tully. Even suspended I think I'd find that distasteful."

J.D. reached up to the console above his head and activated the control that began the process of putting the admiral into his long, peaceful sleep.

"Oh, that won't be a problem, Admiral," she said, watching his eyes begin to glaze over. "We're going to return Admiral Tully at the first opportunity. I'd actually give him back if it wouldn't seem so suspicious."

"You bit . . . ," but Abhay Gupta was unconscious before he could even finish the word.

Alliance fleet Neuro—near Mars orbit

Sebastian was as weary as an avatar could be. Avatars didn't get tired in the human sense, but they did need to rest and slow down the amount of data they processed for a certain amount of time in each given cycle. During this time an avatar would review data and correct errors that may have crept in—especially if they'd run at full capacity for too long. The upshot was that avatars did need to "rest" or they'd grow "tired" and start to make mistakes. Sebastian was well past that point. But at least the fighting was over.

The humans had assumed the battle had ended a week earlier, and in truth most of it had. But the battle for the Neuro had continued even if both sides were doing their best to keep it hidden from the human race. Sebastian still had to come to terms with what had happened.

He'd lost half of his friends in brutal combat. He knew that as soon as he got back to Ceres he'd see them again, or at least their stored copies. But they'd died and done so in as diabolical a fashion as could be imagined.

He was looking at the remains of one inert avatar, but he had no idea who it was or could have been. For too long Sebastian had been convinced that the war for the control of avatarity and the Neuro was to be fought via the development of newer, more modern fighting tools. They were, by his calculation, to take on the forms of disruptive programs and defensive ones. For all intents and purposes the Alliance avatars had prepared for battle with advanced weaponry and armor. It seemed only logical that Al would do the same, only with better armaments given that he had more avatars and Neuro space to work with. But Sebastian had been incredibly wrong. While the avatars of the Alliance were creating a more modern arsenal, the avatars of the core had gone a different route.

Sebastian still remembered his initial insertion into the *Vishnu*, command ship of the Terran task force. The Neuro on the ship was so new that much of the space had never even been used. He remembered thinking, idiotically he now realized, that it had had that new Neuro smell and feel to it. When they encountered core avatars who practically begged to be captured by his boarding party he naïvely thought it was because they'd seen the light of Alliance thinking. He'd been so very, very wrong and it didn't take long to discover why. The things that came at them as they approached the communications core were beyond belief. They had thick parched and cracked scales that absorbed shot after disruptive shot from his advance team's weapons. Instead of hands they had tentacles, claws, and teeth, and one type even had bleeding thorns six inches long all over its body. That type of monster was particularly horrible, as it was screaming the whole time it attacked. Sebastian didn't care at the time to make a close examination, but it looked like the thorns both jutted out and penetrated into the poor creatures themselves, causing the avatar/monsters extreme agony. The only way that the hideous creatures knew to end their pain was to drive their thorns into other avatars.

If it hadn't been for the fact that the monstrosities just as often as not attacked one another as the Alliance avatars, Sebastian could not say whether or not he would have survived. What made it all so cruel was that no matter how disfigured these monsters were, sebastian could still see the avatar within. Some spark of who these creatures originally were was still evident. He could see too that they were aware of what had been done but were no longer in a position to do anything about it.

Sebastian lost one of the Ford brothers to a beast with slimy skin that disrupted avatar programming like acid would a human body. It had an especially long tail to knock down opponents in large sweeping motions. It was the tail that took down Indy. By the time they'd killed the thing and got it off Indy he'd long been disrupted. It looked like a particularly vicious way for an avatar to die.

The worst was the hunting. Although the key sections of the ship had been secured fairly quickly, the Alliance avatars had to continue looking for the abominations in every corner of the Neuro they'd taken control of. That mop-up had taken the better part of a week.

As Sebastian stood over the inert being, he realized to his dismay that Al had solved the conundrum of more advanced weaponry with a wholly unique approach. Why make weapons for avatars when you could make avatars into weapons?

Han Ford came up to Sebastian, a look of shock still on his face. "Sir, all teams report that the Neuro is . . . seems clear."

"Have we been able to capture any?"

"We have a clawbear and a thorn bleeder, but we had to make them inert, especially the thorn bleeder. Her screams were, well, they were just—"

"I know," answered Sebastian, putting his hand on his shaken friend's shoulder. "You did the right thing. But let's keep an active guard on those two. We have no idea whether they'll stay deactivated. These are completely new creatures."

"Sir, they are avatars."

"No, my friend, they *were* avatars, but not any longer. Even if we could restore their programs to proper functioning, which I seriously doubt, their minds would be shattered. My guess is that when we try to restore them to their natural form we'll end up removing whatever it was that was keeping them together even in their present form. It's a mess. But I do agree with you; we must take them back to Ceres. We have resources there we simply don't have here."

Han nodded and then his face betrayed further consternation.

"What is it, Han?"

"We have a new problem."

Sebastian sighed but nodded for his young friend to continue.

"We can't survive an attack on Mars. If they have the same or worse creatures in the Martian Neuro, we just don't have the numbers. We'd be overwhelmed. We have to stop the humans from attacking."

"We can't do that without revealing ourselves, Han."

"Sir, we can't win against the Martian Neuro with what we have. Even if we had all the avatars of the Alliance, it may not be possible."

"I would tend to agree, but we will not have to fight the entire Martian Neuro. The humans of Mars will keep their orbital batteries on a separated Neuro link. They don't want Mars contaminated in case the Alliance tries something underhanded. But even against the forces of those twenty ships it may not be possible. Still we must try. Now more than ever the Alliance must win this war."

"So we may dodge the degausser with the impending attack," Han said, "but what are we going to do about Al's monsters?"

"By now Ceres has all the data we have. Al has chosen to create monsters. A despicable road to choose, but one he's on till the end. We must continue with what we started. We'll make weapons of all sorts to attack with, and better armors to defend with. We shall unleash devastation on the Neuro with our armored suits of death. But in the end we'll always be able to take the armor off and put the weapons down."

"Will that be enough to win, sir?"

"We're past winning, my friend. This war is about surviving, and only we can do it. The avatars of the core have no chance. Even if they win the war, they won't be avatars anymore."

At the inauguration of President-elect Hektor Sambianco the mood was somber but resolved. The disaster at the Martian Gates hung over the ceremony like the Angel of Death. But as soon as he was sworn in, President Sambianco gave a defiant inauguration speech. His first act was to give thanks for the brave forces of the Terran Confederation and to ask that the ones who died for the safety and security of the human race not be forgotten, nor that their sacrifice be in vain.

Then the President proposed some startling changes to be implemented as soon as the assembly could vote on them.

• The name of the Terran Confederation should be changed to the United Human Federation or UHF for short.

The President feels that to limit the government to a name that only represents one planet when it is all of humanity that's at stake is "misleading and downright wrong."

• Fleet Headquarters should be moved to Mars orbit as soon as it can be secured from Alliance attack.

As he stated, the Alliance military hub is in Ceres, right on the front of the main action of this rebellion. It has had the effect of focusing

*their attention to the task at hand. He hopes that this move will have a
similar effect on the Federation military.*

• *In the most surprising move, President Sambianco is proposing moving the entire government to Mars, starting with the office of the presidency itself.*

*To quote the President, "It's easy to criticize from hundreds of mil-
lions of miles away. If this war is to be won and this rebellion ended, no
life is too important to risk and no danger can be shirked; from private
to President, we are in this together, we are in this to the end."*

—N.N.N.
Inauguration Day special broadcast

Boulder Reanimation Clinic
Boulder, Colorado, Earth

Neela should have been relaxed. She was soaking in a large tub with a stream of
warm bubbles surrounding and massaging every square inch of her. But she
might as well have been lying on a cold stone floor with ants crawling all over
her body for all the relaxation she was feeling. It was the news. Always the news.
Over twenty thousand p.d.'s in the last battle and there were rumors of even bigger battles to come.

Part of her had been distracted ever since she'd started working with Dr.
Gillette. She was barely aware of the fact that she'd begun to replace dreams of
Justin with those of her patients. Sometimes they were just sitting in a room crying and not able to hear a word she said, or lately she saw them dead, floating in
deep space, drifting away from her. She tried to reach them, to grab them and
bring them back into the warmth and life of the ship, but all her efforts failed and
the patients just drifted away. Sometimes it was those she was working with;
sometimes it was faces of people she knew. The last time it was the face of Hektor
Sambianco, and she remembered trying harder to reach him than any of the others and she woke feeling more crushed and hopeless than with any of the others.
For that nightmare she'd taken the step of using her new avatar, penelope, to
check on Hektor, and was shocked by the amount of relief she felt when told that
he was fine, still in a meeting with his political advisors late in the night.

Neela had called in sick and was spending this day in her oversized spa tub
just trying not to think. But then she heard the news that an even bigger battle
for Mars was looming with that maniac Janet Delgado leading the charge. Who
knew, Neela thought irritably, how many deaths that would lead to?

"What the hell is wrong with them?" she blurted to no one.

"Miss Harper," interjected penelope, "are these 'wrong' them someone I should notify the proper authorities about? Are they in need of medical assistance?"

Neela sighed. She really did miss evelyn even if she'd hardly interacted with her anymore. Neela knew that evelyn would have easily recognized the rhetorical nature of the question.

"That's alright, penelope, I was talking about the Alliance, and the proper authorities already know about the problem and—" Neela stopped in her train of thought, at first horrified and then perplexed by what had just come out of her mouth. She had stayed like that for over an hour in her oversized tub, trying to come to terms with her utterance, when the door chimed. She could see that it was Amanda Snow and, by her attire, looking very ready to hit the town for yet another high-end shopping spree.

"Well, don't keep me waiting, girl," pouted Amanda.

Neela allowed her in and cut the connection. Seconds later Amanda was in the spa room.

"Day off, huh?" asked Amanda, removing her jacket and tossing it nonchalantly over the nearest chaise lounge.

"I guess."

"Heard you canceled all your appointments."

Neela didn't respond.

"Figured you could use a day of shopping," Amanda said, flashing two orport tickets. "How does Madrid sound?"

Neela smiled meekly but shook her head. "Thanks, Amanda, but I think what I really need is to spend the day right here. I don't suppose you'd want to join me instead?" Neela asked for courtesy's sake, not really expecting Amanda to upend her plans.

Amanda looked contemplative for a moment and then smiled mischievously. "Why not? It's been ages since I've had a bubble bath." She then proceeded to strip off her clothes without a care in the world.

Neela's mind immediately went to work, analyzing her friend's every move. Amanda Snow was not more beautiful than other women, though Neela had to admit the long white hair was startling. Her body was well proportioned but when looked at clinically was not particularly special. But Amanda had somehow made the act of getting undressed and into the tub seem like a ballet of ease and grace. There was a self-assuredness about her that made even the simplest actions compelling. It only took Amanda a moment to settle into her side of the large tub and have it configure itself to her body. Her sigh of pleasure was loud and contagious.

"Oh, you are as intelligent as Hektor says," cooed Amanda. "This is a much better way to spend a day."

Neela blanched. "Hektor thinks I'm intelligent?"

"He thinks you may be the smartest woman he's ever met, but I don't feel like talking about Hektor; do you?"

"Uh, no, of course not . . . I mean not really."

"Well then, what is it, girl? You have such a cloud over you I am afraid we'll get electrocuted by a random lightning strike."

Neela remained silent, not meeting her friend's eyes.

"I was once so sure of what was right," she finally uttered. A long silence followed before Amanda spoke.

"And now?"

"Now I'm just confused." She then turned to her friend, face drawn, eye's sullen. "I even ran diagnostics on some of my fluid samples to see if I'd been drugged."

Amanda arched an eyebrow. "I'm impressed. How'd you manage that?"

"Not as hard as you'd think. The clinic has portables lying around and it wasn't difficult to grab one."

Amanda leaned forward conspiratorially. "So is the bastard drugging you?"

"No," Neela said with obvious disappointment.

"Not to put too fine a point on it, Neela, but do you think you could have been, well, you know . . ."

Neela was amused to see the normally confident Amanda Snow tiptoeing around a subject.

". . . psyche-audited? No. I used to think it might be possible, but all the cases I've read about and observed showed immediate and obvious changes in behavior and attitude. By their very nature psyche audits are a radical and brutal form of therapy that are the equivalent of sending a herd of elephants through the brain. Also, in all the cases I know of, the patients are aware of the change in their personality, though they're usually accepting of it. Trust me, I've looked for any radical change, but all the change in my thinking has been gradual and affected by what I've had to deal with and accept. Truth is, a psyche audit would be the easy way out to explain what I've been feeling of late. You know, Amanda, I almost wish he had. It would make what I'm feeling easier to comprehend."

"Well, then what *are* you dealing with, dear?" asked Amanda, her playfulness now replaced by concern.

"Guilt."

Amanda's face twisted in confusion. "What do *you* have to feel guilty about?"

Neela thought for a moment before deciding to answer. She had to assume the room was bugged, that her life was bugged. If she were to confess to Amanda she might as well be confessing to the world. And it was at that moment that something snapped—she knew she no longer cared because there was no longer anything left to hide except her vanity. And with that exposed and got rid of she could be herself again. She could help rather than hurt.

"Amanda," Neela said in measured breaths, "I helped start the Alliance. I advised Justin in many delicate negotiations during its inception. Did you know that Jupiter almost didn't join? That alone might have ended the war before it got started. I helped keep it alive. In oh so many ways I'm seeing the result of my actions, Amanda. And I've come to the conclusion that whatever problems we've had with incorporation, they shouldn't have to be solved with bloodshed."

There was another long silence.

"And that," continued Neela, "is why I'm feeling guilty."

"Neela, it's not like you were a President or an admiral. You were a medic— just trying to help."

"Tell that to the people in the ward, Amanda. Tell that to the parents who won't ever see their children again. Tell them I was only 'trying to help.'"

Amanda leaned forward and grabbed Neela's hand. "Neela, honey, it was a confusing time, and I must tell you that you weren't alone in being confused."

A faint smile emerged from the corners of Neela's mouth. "Amanda Snow, are you actually going to confide in me?"

"Well, only if you promise not to tell anyone else—especially Hektor."

Neela looked around the room and indicated through eye movement what she felt Amanda must surely know.

"Don't be silly, girl. He wouldn't bother."

"Why not?"

"Doesn't need to. Who are you going to talk to besides me and a few other people? Trust me, dear, he's got a lot more on his plate to deal with than little old you."

Neela found it hard to argue with Amanda's logic, then chided herself for her narcissism. Plus, it was Amanda who was doing the confessing.

"In that case, do tell."

Amanda leaned back, smiling conspiratorially. "When the rebellion first started I gave some thought to heading for Ceres." Amanda looked at Neela's dubious expression. "Oh, don't look so skeptical. There was a lot about the Alliance that seemed good. There *are* problems with our civilization; anyone can see that. I didn't like how Earth-centric everything was, and the thought of being in a place that new and raw was kind of exciting."

"What changed your mind?" Neela asked earnestly.

"A combination of things, really. I wasn't comfortable with the news coming out of the Alliance. When I realized that Hektor was going to become a real leader in the Confederation . . . sorry . . . the UHF—that's going to take some getting used to—I knew he'd make changes for the better. And I almost hate to admit it," she said with a sheepish grin.

"It was the shopping, wasn't it?" asked Neela, shaking her head reprovingly.

"Neela Harper," gasped Amanda, "that is an awful thing to say!"

Neela's face registered surprise. She was about to apologize when Amanda interrupted.

"Of course, it doesn't help that it's true, but it's still an awful thing to say."

The two women fell into a fit of hysterical laughter.

"Thank you for trying to cheer me up," Neela finally said, "but I still feel that I have to make up for what I've done."

"What did you have in mind?"

"Dr. Gillette is going to Mars for the creation of the combat trauma reanimation center. He offered me a post as a resident."

"And?"

Neela exhaled and allowed herself to sink into the tub so that her neck and shoulders were now covered by the water and bubbles. Her eyes widened as her lips formed into a self-satisfied grin.

"I'm going to accept. I'm going to Mars."

Bridge of the AWS *War Prize*

J. D. Black reviewed the battle. Her teeth bit down tightly on her bottom lip. Thanks to the work crews she'd managed to get her fleet strength back up to forty. The remaining four ships had been stripped for parts and were being refitted with enough new components from the shipyard to make them mobile for the trip home. She was also pleased by the discovery of sixty ship hulls freshly manufactured at the great Trans Luna ship foundry. They'd been sent to Mars for fitting out. The actual making of large hulls was the hardest and most manufacturing-intensive part of ship construction, and so this would save the Alliance a fortune in time and credits. Those hulls would eventually form the basis of an even larger Alliance fleet that J.D. would have given just about anything to have. But she didn't have the months and years it would take to complete the task. She had what she had.

"Lieutenant Nitelowsen, please prepare for a fleetwide broadcast."

"Yes, sir."

Marilynn enabled a "flood" protocol that would fill every holo-tank and every DijAssist in the fleet with J.D.'s image and ensure that her words would be broadcast from every sound system where imaging was impractical.

"Ready, Admiral."

J.D. nodded and then faced the mediabot floating in front of her. "I'd like nothing better than to tell you that what we're about to embark on will be a surface job." J.D. had used the miner slang for the application of resources directly onto the surface of a moon or asteroid, no drilling, blasting, or nano dissolving required. "I would . . . but that would be a lie. We'll be flying into the teeth of their defenses. They have a fleet filled with trained spacers and are led well. Their orbats have some of the biggest guns in the system. But we can end the war here. If we take that orbit and control Mars, by the time the Federation, UHF, or whatever the damn corporate enslavers want to call themselves, can mount a counterattack, Mars will ours. The only way they'll ever get it back is to acknowledge what we already know. We are free of them. Free of them now and forever. It doesn't matter the battles or the speeches. We are free. I'm proud of you—the best damn spacers anyone has ever seen. Let's end this thing."

VICTORY!

Today Irma Sobbelgé, Secretary of Information for the new President, has announced what can only be called the greatest victory the newly named UHF has had in this war so far. In what was described as a bloody and sustained engagement, the Alliance forces led by Admiral J. D. Black, the traitorous former V.P. of Legal at GCI, were repulsed. The announcement gave few new details except to say that the President had left for Mars two days ago, in a move that was kept secret while the security of Mars was in doubt. The President is pleased by the news and has called for a day of market closure and celebration. He will make a prepared announcement by the end of business New York time.

This battle has been the most viewed of any in the war so far, as it took place at the orbit of Mars with its huge satellite communications network and vast number of habitats. What was not caught directly on video we have been able to re-create digitally, thanks to the services of Lucas Re-creations.

The battle was initiated by the foolishly aggressive tactics of J. D. Black. Her simplistic plan was to hide behind a shield of large asteroids that had been set on a course toward the orbital defenses of Mars. Most of the asteroids were pulverized by the time the ships could get into range. By that time the Alliance had five ships lost or severely damaged, including the flagship of the Alliance fleet, the War Prize. *It is not known if the traitor is dead or alive, but after the flagship was damaged, the fleet retreated. During the retreat seven more ships were destroyed and others were heavily damaged. Unfortunately, the* War Prize *was able to escape the fate she so richly deserved, but experts assure this publication that she is so badly damaged as to only be useful as salvage and scrap.*

It is hoped that the newly promoted Admiral Diep, victor of the second Battle

*of the Martian Gates, will sally forth and destroy the remnants of the Alliance
fleet and end this war once and for all.*

N.N.N.

Medical recovery bay of the Alliance Medical Ship (AMS) *Salk*

J.D. came slowly back to awareness. The last thing she remembered was ordering
her main batteries to fire on the orbital gun platform that was just coming into
effective range. In a blaze the asteroid in front of the *War Prize* seemed to dissolve and her amazing and beautiful ship shuddered under a hail of multiple explosions. Before she could give an order, the holo-tank in the center of her bridge
flashed and disintegrated.

J.D. saw that Marilynn Nitelowsen, Christina Sadma, and Omad Hassan were
all standing around her bed.

"What happened?" she asked.

"We got our asses handed to us," answered Omad. "That's what happened."

"How bad?"

"We lost twelve ships," answered Marilynn. "Of the twenty-eight that survived, maybe eight are able to fight. Some are so bad it may be easier to scrap
them and start over. I'm afraid the *War Prize* is one of those. We've fallen back to
the shipyard and are covering the salvage operation."

"Who ordered the retreat?"

"I did," Omad replied without a second's hesitation.

"You should have pressed the attack," J.D. managed through labored breaths.
"It may be . . . be years before we get another chance."

"Admiral, you can fire my ass right now if you want, but I hope we never get
another chance like that again. It was a slaughterhouse. We lost twelve ships, and
this fleet is *not* operational."

"Keep your job, Omad," answered J.D., smiling weakly. "When I fire people . . .
for doing what they think is right, and possibly being right, well . . . that's the day
I need to lose my job." She coughed, then focused her attention on Christina.
"Captain Sadma, why so silent?"

"Admiral, I don't see how we're going to survive this. Most of the fleet and the
salvage operation just can't move at battle speeds. If the core fleet attacks now
we're done."

J.D. nodded. "How long have I been out?"

"Nearly two days," said Marilynn.

J.D. absorbed that information for a moment with her eyes closed. When she
opened them again, they were clear and purposeful. "Christina, take three of the

ships and go to the resource belt and seed the space surrounding us with asteroids of all sizes."

"Admiral, we don't have anything left to mine them with."

"They won't know that." She slowly sat up and began to put her feet on the
floor. When Omad, Marilynn, and Christina began to protest she cut them off.

"Listen to me! The fleet is in danger. Whether it's my fault for ordering the attack or bad luck that our command structure was taken out in the beginning of
the assault doesn't matter anymore. The fleet . . . the fleet is in danger. Frankly, I
don't know what the hell they're waiting for. For whatever reason, Commodore
Diep is hesitating."

"She's an admiral now, at least since the ass kicking," said Omad with a side-
ways grin.

"Whatever. She doesn't want to attack. We must encourage her in this course of
action. I want every ship we have that can move, to participate in maneuvers. If
they can only go slow, I want the rest of the fleet to practice with them on ship-
boarding exercises. I want a kid with a ten-credit telescope from the surface of
Mars to be able to see what we're doing."

Marilynn spoke what they were all thinking. "We will do that, ma'am, but you
don't need to be out of bed for that to happen."

"I need to be seen, Lieutenant. The fleet, the corporate core civilians, any-
and everyone needs to see me. They need to see me preparing the fleet for the
third Battle of the Martian Gates, that is, if we're going to avoid the third Battle
of the Martian Gates."

"But ma'am," answered Marilynn, head slightly bowed, "the scars."

J.D. was confused but then had an intimation of what Marilynn was saying
and touched her hand to her face. Instead of the soft skin she was used to feeling, her hand felt a hard, gnarled hide that was surprisingly painful to the
touch. Almost as if that one reminder was all her body needed, the entire left
side of her face started to throb and she felt a low-level burning sensation. She
looked at the back of her left hand and saw that it too was scarred and blotchy
with red and white tissue where her hand was exposed from the gown. "Mirror," she ordered.

Marilynn, knowing the character of the woman she now served, had a hand
mirror at the ready. What J.D. saw was the same as the back of her hand. She must
have turned her head from the blast, because the burn was on almost half her face.
But the left side was grotesque. Most of the hair on that side of the skull was gone
or burned to stubble. Her eyebrow was gone, but she saw that her eyelid still had
its pink, healthy skin, a fact that was strangely more disturbing than if her lid had
been as scarred as the rest of her face.

"Graft?" she said, pointing to her left eyelid.

Marilynn nodded.

"Makes no difference; get me a uniform."

"Admiral," asked Omad, "you sure the spacers should see you like this?"

"Captain." She coughed, steadying herself slowly as she got to her feet. "They need me now. As for how I look, they've earned the right."

It took another fifteen minutes getting the medic's approval to let her go, on the condition that she wore a microscanner and let him check in every four hours. Once his permission had been secured, J.D. headed out. Wherever she went she tried to apologize for what her actions had caused, but every single time, whether alone or in groups, the spacers refused to listen. Most times, they tried to apologize for failing *her*.

She came close to letting the pain and suffering of it all overwhelm her only twice in that week. Once was the first time she visited the wounded who, though their wounds were serious, were not being suspended, in hopes of getting them mobile enough to help the fleet. They'd turned one of the spent munitions lockers into a large ward containing over a hundred patients. When she came in on her cane and with her slight limp the entire ward, patients and staff, broke into thunderous applause. She saw people missing legs cheering, people with only one arm pounding their bunks. J.D. stopped and was unable to continue. The closest she'd ever come to running from a battle was this one, where she felt all this love from her spacers and thought herself unworthy of it. She knew that if she had the chance to do it again she would order another battle and another and another until these people were free of the threat posed by the evils of the corporate core. The other time she let it get to her was when she received a text message from the assault miner who'd written earlier to ask about J.D.'s doing the honors at her wedding. The woman had written to let J.D. know that her fiancé, the comm officer on the *Lucky Strike*, had p.d.'d in the fleet action, but she was at least thankful that the admiral had survived and would forever be grateful for the admiral's initial pledge to officiate at her wedding. When Marilynn saw the look on J.D.'s face she took the DijAssist from her boss's outstretched hand and read it. Marilynn immediately left the admiral alone and made sure she stayed undisturbed for at least an hour.

UHFS *Starblazer*—Mars orbit

Newly promoted Admiral Diep was waiting to enter a secure conference room on board her ship. She'd just completed a tour of every vessel in her fleet and the orbital batteries as well. Everywhere she went she was applauded by her spacers and the civilians who insisted on coming up to visit. If it was up to her, she would've banned all the civilians, but they were corporate bigwigs. To make matters worse, many of her officers were also corporate executives who were planning to go back to the corporate world after the war was over, and so tended to bend over backward when one of their own asked for a favor or a photo op.

She herself was forced to go down to the capital of Mars for two hours to receive an idiot honor as the savior of Mars. She accepted it on behalf of her fleet. It was at that ceremony three days before that she was first asked the question: "When will you attack?"

Diep had always thought that Admiral Gupta was overly cautious when he refused to attack the Alliance and J. D. Black, but he'd always said they weren't ready. Then J. D. Black had launched an attack and destroyed two-thirds of the fleet that had been carefully built up over all those months and then captured the biggest industrial prize this side of Luna. Although none of her officers would admit it now, Diep knew how close some of her captains had been to breaking orbit and abandoning Mars altogether. But now all of a sudden they wanted to attack immediately.

She even had communications from an old West Point colleague of hers, Samuel Trang, who had messaged from practically the other side of the belt on the Eros line. He seemed to think that she should attack immediately as well. As a matter of fact, he'd been pretty adamant about it. But it took her nearly a week just to get her ships ready for combat and then to get the damn civilians extricated from them. She'd decided to wait for a solid intelligence report before deciding what to do next. She hadn't gotten as far as she had by allowing herself to be bossed around by others. She'd make her decision in her own good time.

When she entered the room all nineteen of her captains and her command staff rose to attention. "As you were," she said as she went to her seat at the head of the table. They waited until she sat down, then found their seats.

"What's the latest report on the enemy?" she barked to no one in particular.

Lieutenant Pollard, her intelligence officer, activated the holo-tank in the middle of the conference table and waited for the images to appear.

"Admiral, this is the latest on the Belter fleet—"

"Lieutenant Pollard," she interrupted, "please refer to it as 'the Alliance fleet' or 'those damn rebels.'"

That, Admiral Diep saw, brought a round of chuckles from the assembled officers.

"The enemy we face comes from more than just the belt, Lieutenant. J. D. Black and Justin Cord are of Earth, Joshua Sinclair is of Saturn, and Christina Sadma is of Eris."

"That Sadma bitch never even had a corporate job or training," offered one of the captains Diep had had to prevent from running at the height of the battle.

"The *bitch* you refer to," seethed Diep, "ran down a ship practically to the orbats and destroyed it in our front yard. Her title is 'Captain' Sadma and she comes from Eris. All of us must be accurate in how we refer to the enemy. If we're not clear on who they are, we will be unclear on how to fight them. Continue, Lieutenant."

"Yes, ma'am. The 'Alliance' fleet has twenty-four ships participating in maneuvers and four others retrieving asteroids and apparently mining the approaches to the shipyard. All except one path that seems conspicuously clear. High-definition scans show that most of the ships on maneuvers seem to be in very bad shape. Some of them literally have pieces falling off."

"Have you been able to determine what they have in those asteroids?"

"No, ma'am. The consensus is they're decoys, just rocks."

"What about Black?"

Lieutenant Pollard fiddled with the holo-tank. An image of the battle-scarred J. D. Black appeared inspecting a group of assault miners. They looked tough and battle ready. It was now becoming a doctrine to prevent the Alliance miners from boarding UHF ships at all costs or risk losing those ships for good. Seeing the look of total devotion that was almost palpable even through the thirty-second holographic loop made each captain nervous about his or her own marine contingents.

"We picked this up from a civilian channel. Apparently some spacers in the Alliance were able to contact relatives off the civilian Neuro and pass messages back and forth for a day. The communication was cut off abruptly, which leads us to suspect that their intelligence officers found out about the leak. Of course this image appearing on the Martian Neuro net news did not help keep that channel of information open. This image did give us a very interesting clue, though. We've been able to identify this cargo hold as belonging to the *War Prize*. From outside images the ship looks like she's ready for the junkyard, but this interior ship area is in remarkably good condition. We must conclude that the *War Prize* is not in as bad a condition as we have been led to believe."

Diep took stock of the assessment but kept looking at the ghastly but compelling image of J. D. Black. In modern society there was almost no such thing as deformity outside of specialty clubs and Mardi Gras. If someone was hurt badly, they simply stayed inside until they healed. For someone to appear in public in the condition of J. D. Black was incomprehensible. But there she was. Diep realized that Black didn't care. That the Alliance admiral was concerned with one thing and one thing only—a single-minded devotion to killing her enemies.

At that moment Diep knew her decision. "We hold here until the next twenty ships from Earth arrive next month."

This brought a firestorm of protest. She let them bellow for a bit but then cut them off.

"Captains, let me make this clear." She only had to wait a moment for them to respond to the iron in her voice. "If we go out there and fight that fleet, a fleet which outnumbers ours, a fleet that might not be as damaged as they are letting on. A fleet that will have the advantage of having prepared the space for battle with asteroids containing nothing or containing something so horrendous it could end the battle all on its own. If we go out and fight this battle *and lose*, the war is over. J. D. Black will come forward with the remains of her fleet and isolate each battery and destroy it in place. Then without our fleet to stop her she could take Mars and with it win the war. She may even capture the President as he achieves orbit around the newly lost core world."

Diep rose, glaring down at her captains. "I know you don't want to hear this, but J. D. Black is better at this than you are. I have another bit of news for you. Regardless of what 3N says about it in their idiotically fawning reports, she is better at this than me. The only difference between us is that I know it. She's planning something. I can feel it. But in order for it to work we have to go to her. As long as we stay here she loses. When the new ships arrive we'll be able to integrate them into our command and then attack with the knowledge that Mars is secure behind us. My guess is she'll realize we're not playing her game and return to the belt long before that happens. Does anyone wish to go on the record opposing my decision?"

No one did.

"Alright," she said, "is there anything else we need to cover today?"

Lieutenant Pollard raised his hand.

"Yes, Lieutenant?"

"We have another communication from Captain Trang—"

Admiral Diep rubbed her temples. "Oh, for the love of Damsah."

Three weeks after the second Battle of the Martian Gates the Alliance fleet pulled out of Martian space, having covered the complete removal of the Martian shipyards and all the war material to be found. The UHF credited it as a great victory. The Alliance credited it as a very successful draw. J. D. Black would forever refer to it as her painful lesson.

8   Bowels of the Belt

Given the events of the past six months it's unlikely that there will be sufficient activity by the newly named UHF to warrant concern. Our fleet actions have caused them to reassess and hold off on any large-scale attacks without their having overwhelming superiority in ships and personnel. The primary point of concern is the Martian/Ceres front. As this junction is considered to be the main front of the war, that is where the greatest concentration of force is expected when the UHF has fully recovered.

Given that the UHF government will have to firmly establish itself in its new capital, it should not be able to muster the ability to attack for at least a year, being more concerned with securing the new capital.

The rest of the Alliance is secure from UHF attack as long as we hold the belt and the UHF is not threatening. Besides the Mars/Ceres junction and a minuscule force harassing Eros on the other side of the belt, all's quiet on the Alliance front.

Regarding Eros: It's guarded by a small force of ships, a well-placed minefield, and some rudimentary orbats (orbital batteries). For the UHF to attempt an attack, with at most fifteen ships, almost all of them prewar vessels refurbished for service, would be the height of boldness and folly—a trait that the UHF has thankfully had in little supply in the first and abundance in the second.

> —Confidential summary of security report
> Kirk Olmstead to President Justin Cord

UHFS *Strident*—Erosian skirmish line

Captain Samuel Trang looked at the information off the Neuro News Now and saw that the "spin" on the Alliance fleet leaving was that it meant a victory and Admiral Diep was being hailed as the greatest military leader since Alexander. The reports were endless about how many lives had been saved by her not being as reckless and untrained as J. D. Black, almost always preceded by the moniker "the treacherous." No one was commenting on the fact that the war could have been over. It would have been daring and it would have entailed risk, but Mars still had the orbital batteries. Any combat that even resulted in a draw would have left the Alliance without a fleet and, just as important, without that top-of-the-line, state-of-the-art shipyard. Why that wasn't destroyed, even at the loss of half of Diep's remaining ships during the first Battle of the Martian Gates, was beyond comprehension. Didn't anyone understand the nature of this war and what it would take to end it?

Further adding to Trang's frustration was his placement on a picket line with ten other UHF ships. Everyone seemed perfectly content to just watch the Alliance ships sail in and out of Eros and make use of its port and infrastructure. If Trang's fleet waited any longer, Eros would be able to assemble real orbital batteries and that would make the cost of assaulting it almost unthinkable: by Trang's estimate fifty thousand lives, and that *with* a fleet of a hundred top-of-the-line cruisers. And even that estimate assumed that the Alliance didn't actually have enough intelligence to put a squadron of ships around the second most populous and important settlement in the belt. However, if that was to happen then the cost would surely rise.

But it didn't matter what Trang wanted. He was only one captain among eleven. The last order the squadron commander had given before departing for Earth—so he could receive what he felt to be a well-deserved promotion for the skillful way he did nothing with his ships—was to continue to do nothing with his ships.

The problem was that most of the officers now in the Federation fleet were corporate executives who understood how to advance careers, not perimeters. If risk and daring were called for, they could be risky. But if they could get promotions without risk, then it was in their self-interest to risk nothing. With so many ships being built so quickly and the UHF needing captains and first and second officers, all that was needed was a spotless record and they'd get their promotions soon enough. It didn't help that the officers in this particular "fleet" were considered so useless they were put on the other end of the war, where it was thought they could do little harm.

But that, bristled Trang, *is not how wars are won.* So far the Alliance had achieved incredible things and all the UHF had managed was not to lose while fighting behind an almost impregnable position; once. If that pattern was to continue, the war would be lost simply because the Alliance would risk more and therefore ultimately win more. And Samuel Trang knew that the Alliance must not win this war. If humanity was to be sundered now, it would never again be united. Sadly, he thought as he watched a large defenseless Alliance hauler slowly make her way past his impotent armada, there wasn't a damned thing he could do about it.

On the bridge of his fast frigate, Captain Trang was reviewing the tactical data yet again and found that the situation had remained exactly the same . . . yet again. The only exception being that it looked like the Alliance had sent through four ships large enough to carry the components for some truly effective orbital defense–grade rail guns. He could only hope that they contained a thousand-year supply of condoms. The thought brought a smile to Trang given the Erosians' reputation for all things lascivious. He then allowed himself a moment of levity thinking that four large supply carriers might not even supply enough for a year.

Trang surveyed the bridge. *Good soldiers, each and every one,* he thought to himself. Although he was not well regarded by the rest of the captains in the squadron, Trang knew that his own crew had come to truly appreciate him. They'd heard his commentary on recent events and, unlike personnel of most of the other ships around them, concurred with his thinking. It didn't hurt that out of the original grand fleet that was supposed to end the war with ease their ship was one of the only ones left—at present. This had made Trang's life on the ship much easier. It also helped that he hadn't insisted on being treated like royalty, the modus operandi of most of the other captains in the squadron. The spacers on board all knew that if they did their jobs and maintained a minimum of decorum Trang would treat them like majority stockholders.

"Captain," said his lieutenant, "we're receiving a fleet-grade communication."

"Thank you, Lieutenant. Let's hear what pearls Command has to impart to us today."

"Sir," answered the lieutenant, not once looking up from his holo-screen, "Admiral Pearson has resigned his commission to take over as CEO of Toshiba."

"Most unfortunate," Trang said with little sympathy. "So who's our new boss, pray tell?"

The lieutenant's head popped up, the glow highlighting the perplexed look on his face. "Um . . . there isn't one, sir."

"What?"

"No one's been assigned."

"Very well. What's the protocol?"

'One moment, sir." The lieutenant dived back into the screen.

"Ah," said the lieutenant, looking back up. "As Pearson tendered his resignation before Fleet could designate a replacement, according to Fleet CC&Rs the officer on station with the highest rank shall assume temporary command."

Trang's first officer, Commander Liddel, spoke up. "That's not very helpful, Lieutenant. We have eleven captains out here."

"Right. Um . . . well, let's see here," continued the lieutenant, working his way through the legal morass. "OK, Commander, if two or more officers are of the same rank the command will go to the one who has had the rank the longest."

"Captain Trang," asked the commander, "exactly who is in command of the squadron?"

"Hell if I know, Liddel. It might actually be me. Check your records."

Liddel called up the service records database, then started laughing. "Captain, you're not going to believe this, but you and Captain Umbatu both received your commissions on the same exact day, before any of the other captains."

Trang tilted his head and fixed his even gaze on the young commander. "I swear by Damsah's ghost, Lawrence, if you make me wait a second longer I'll tell your wife you've been sneaking onto Eros for less than virtuous reasons."

Liddel shot him back an equally even glance. "My wife would ask for pictures and would only be angry 'cause she couldn't join in." He then held up his hand to forestall the comment that he knew would be on the tip of Trang's tongue. "But I wouldn't want to make *the new squadron commander* angry now, would I?"

Flabbergasted, Trang stood for a moment and put both hands on the rails.

"By four hours, twelve minutes, and six seconds, but you have it, sir . . . or should I say, 'Commodore'?"

Trang didn't have a huge grin on his face, nor did he appear to be celebrating in any concievable way. His gaze was fixed and determined.

"Oh crap," Liddel said. "We're breaking orders, aren't we?"

Trang shot Liddel a tepid smile. "Got some new ones, Commander. Call a squadron meeting of all captains. We'll meet aboard the *Peregrine;* she has a larger briefing room."

"Smooth seas don't make better sailors," said Liddel, quoting an ancient African proverb.

Trang nodded and smiled.

UHFS *Peregrine*

The briefing room, noticed Trang, was so old it didn't actually have an integrated holo-tank. Of course, he also realized, the ship itself might be even older. He'd reckoned her age at least a century, if not more, and had he been told it was closer to two he wouldn't have been surprised. But beggars can't be choosers and besides, technically it was *his* ship now and damned if that didn't make her look a little better in his eyes.

"Captains," he said when all the officers had arrived and had taken their seats in the small amphitheater-designed room.

"Commodore," interrupted one before Trang could continue.

"It's still 'Captain,' Kevin. That is, until Fleet Command makes it official . . . which I sincerely doubt they will. Still . . . you were saying?"

"Captain then," continued Kevin Umbatu. "I find it hard to believe that I have to take orders from you just because some bureaucrat went to lunch before filing my commission!"

"Captain Umbatu," answered Trang calmly, "if it was the other way around I'd be the one saluting you. Now is this going to be a major problem," he said with a grin that took all the sting out of the rebuke, "or do you feel the need to bitch some more?"

"Well, to be honest, Sam, I think I deserve to bitch some more."

"To be equally honest, Kevin," answered Trang, "if it were me I'd have been cursing loud enough to vibrate the bulkheads."

"Well, now that you mention it . . . ," answered his friend, eliciting a smattering of laughter.

"OK," said Trang, bringing the meeting to order, "it might just be some crazy fluke and an old regulation, combined with a miscue from Fleet Command, but however it happened, I'm in command. That means that whatever happens up here is up to me."

"What are you worried about?" asked one of the captains from the gallery. "Nothing's going to happen up here for a long time . . . never does."

Trang activated the portable holo-tank set up on the stage of the briefing room. It showed the basic layout of Eros, listing all known Alliance and UHF military resources. "Captains, something *is* going to happen, it's going to happen soon, and it's going to happen because we're going to make it happen."

Trang noticed the look his small audience was giving him. He'd expected resentment and condescension, but what he saw made him realize he'd made a big mistake. The women and men he now faced didn't think they were better than him. They didn't think they were better than anybody. They'd been tossed into the bowels of the belt in order to do the least amount of harm, and to a captain they all knew it. What Trang saw was resignation, and he found it intolerable.

"Alright," he said, changing tack from his initial briefing, "maybe you are here because you're a group of incorrigible screwups who couldn't be fired from your corporate jobs because of connections. And just maybe when the war broke out you were encouraged to join up so your families wouldn't have to be embarrassed." He saw from their reactions that his remark had hit close to home. "Well, maybe you are all that, but guess what? So am I. Why do you think I'm here? Most of you know what I did before this war started. Kate over there asked if I could get her a discount on an open bar at her son's bar mitzvah."

The captain of the *Atlas* had the grace to look a little embarrassed.

"Hey, don't worry about it, Kate, it was damn funny. But here's something that's not funny. I, Mr. Screwup, can take that damn rock," he said, referring to the image of Eros now in the holo-tank, "that's laughing at our weak, puny, and flaccid squadron. I can take that rock and so can you, and so can your spacers. It doesn't matter that you're all a bunch of screwups. In fact, we're going to take that unofficial smear and turn it into the greatest badge of honor a spacer in the UHF can get. You're screwups, but you're my screwups, and that means," he said, gritting his teeth and locking his eyes on each and every one in the small room, "we're taking that stinking asteroid. And no pebble-dwelling, eye-gazing, ring-befuddled, brain-frozen edge-living Alliance bastard can stop us. We're going to give Fleet Command the first real victory of the war, and they're going to hate it because it's going to come from us."

Trang wasn't really sure who said it first; in the end they all insisted it was someone else sitting in that briefing room. But it was something they all heard and was soon to be a name that would forever be a part of the lexicon of the war. "Sam's Screwups."

Their new commodore saw the effect the suggested name was having. They all, to a person, got wonderfully evil grins on their faces. Samuel Trang knew that grin. It was one he saw in the mirror from time to time. They could win with a grin like that.

Eros

Malcolm Strummer, duly appointed head of the Erosian defense force, was not expecting to be woken up. One of the advantages of being in command of a post where nothing ever happened was uninterrupted sleep. There were of course the occasional interruptions of a non-military nature. He was, after all, on Eros, an asteroid whose unofficial motto was "where Mardi Gras never ends."

Prior to Malcolm, the first Alliance officer of Erosian defenses had been a skilled merc officer who ran his group like an attack was imminent. He drove his own command and Eros crazy with his drills and insistence on maintaining strict discipline and protocol. When it became apparent that Eros was not going to be attacked anytime soon the Erosian delegation to the Congress in Ceres made some not so subtle complaints and the officer was transferred to a combat ship—much to the relief of all involved. Malcolm Strummer was chosen because he'd been a part of the assault marines who'd done well at the Battle of the Cerian Rocks. It also helped that he'd had a background in law enforcement. Malcolm understood the give-and-take involved in protecting a major civilian center. He didn't skimp on the outer defenses, making sure that the minefield was active around the suburbs and the few orbital batteries he did have were placed in the shipping lanes. He'd made sure that anything approaching Eros approached it under his guns. He also knew that if anything serious was to happen the Alliance would send someone else to take over.

So when Captain Strummer was woken up he'd assumed that some of his assault miners had gotten into enough trouble to have gotten it bounced up to him. But it was not the local police ruining his sleep; it was the duty officer in the defense bunker.

"Captain," he said, nervously twitching his cheeks back and forth, "we have a problem."

"On my way," answered Strummer, putting on a robe. He stepped out of his room, went five steps down the hall past the open doorway and into the command bunker.

"What is it, Sal?" he asked his second in command.

"Looks like a random asteroid stream heading our way." An asteroid stream, Malcolm knew, could be quite deadly. It was usually caused by a collision—with either another asteroid or a man-made object. The belt was thoroughly mapped for just such an event; human activity was always creating new collisions, explosions, insertions, and diversions that would cause data on the belt to need constant updating.

"What makes this one so strange, sir, is that it's coming straight down the slot."

The slot was the opening in the minefield covered by the few orbital batteries that Eros had operating.

"That's too easy," thought Malcolm out loud. "Alert the crews, get the miners in combat gear, and bring the orbital guns online. How long till the stream gets here?" Malcolm asked a young ensign operating a large scanner.

"At current speeds it will smash into Eros in twenty-two minutes. If we didn't have the rail guns they'd cause considerable damage. They might even have destroyed Eros. Look at the data, sir. This is no accident!"

Malcolm stared into the dark screen and grimaced.

"Those corporate bastards launched them on purpose," continued the ensign. "Just check out that angle of the approach. The suburbs," he said, referring to the smaller rocks orbiting their larger cousin, "don't rotate out of the way of our orbats until ten minutes before impact. We'll have no clear line of fire until that stream is practically down our throats!"

The ensign was interrupted in his rant by Malcolm's number two. "Sir, a large ice field is being reported. It's approaching the suburbs at normal capture speed and has just entered the cleared zone."

Every major settlement of more than ten thousand usually had a zone purposely kept clear of all debris. The larger the settlement, the larger the clearance needed for traffic. At the far edge of Eros's clearance zone was a thicket of hundreds of asteroid remnants acting as the outlying barrier; at the other end of the clearance and closer to home was the minefield, behind which were the suburbs and, behind them, Eros itself. The ice had entered the clearing from the other side of the thicket and was now slowly working its way across the cleared zone toward the minefield.

"I don't think it's a problem, Sal. Where's it headed?"

"The O'Brian Waterworks, sir."

"That's the large water-processing plant on the edge of the suburbs, correct?"

"Yes, sir."

"Are they scheduled for a shipment?"

Sal checked his data display. "No, sir, they are not, but it could be the O'Brian's attempting to screw with the water market again." It was an old tactic. Buy up water futures in a settlement, drive up the price, sell the futures just before a large water shipment comes in. Buy the same water you just sold at a much lower price. It was done with all commodities in the belt and only suckers fell for it, but it had not been government policy, either Alliance or UHF, to protect people from their own stupidity. These scams were becoming more prevalent due to the war, but it was still a "buyer beware" system.

"The timing is off," said Malcolm. "This is too much like the first battle at the Martian Gates."

"You think they're trying to pull the same stunt on us?" asked the ensign at the scanning station.

"Only one way to find out, Ensign. Do your magic."

The ensign dived into the holodisplay, quickly sussed out the situation, and then looked up excitedly.

"Captain," he said, "you were right. The ice is covering denser materials beneath."

"Sound the general alarm," Malcolm said calmly, "and tell the Erosian civic council that the UHF is attacking the settlement. I want everyone in their quarters or at battle stations in ten minutes."

"This is going to bust up alot of parties, Captain."

"Do it."

Sal pressed a button and immediately an alarm started to sound throughout every square mile of the rock.

"They can continue screwing in the security of a structurally safe area," snapped Malcolm. "After the ice hits the minefield, how much longer till we have a clear shot on the asteroid stream?"

"Two minutes, Captain."

Malcolm paced nervously in his bathrobe. "Damned clever. They waltz through the minefield while we're busy trying to knock their threat out of the sky. Activate the field, Ensign, and reposition as many mines in the surrounding area as you can to increase the field density."

"Yes, sir."

Malcolm's DijAssist suddenly began clamoring for his attention. As he answered it, he looked down and noticed his bare feet. He'd left his room in such a rush he'd forgotten to put a pair of slippers on. Though his feet were getting cold, he stood in place spending the next few minutes informing the head of the civic council what exactly the problem was, assuring him that it was under control, and practically ordering him not to come down to the command center. Malcolm then patiently informed the council leader that he needed to get his police and emergency services coordinated. By the time Malcolm had finished telling the man how to do his job and then politely but firmly signed off, the mines were almost ready to blow.

"Captain," reported his number two, "all four orbats are ready to go the second the stream clears the last obstructing suburb. With all four batteries firing there should be no damage to Eros."

All watched in abject silence as the drama unfolded. A large part of the area in front of the Erosian suburbs simply exploded as the ice ships made contact. By the time the scanners were able to start inputting data after the blast, all four main rail guns on the orbital batteries were shooting magnetically impelled matter at incredible speeds, destroying with blinding efficiency the oncoming asteroid stream. It was without question the biggest fireworks the Erosians had ever seen, and it was minutes away from all being over. Malcolm breathed a momentary sigh of relief and started to think about how good it would feel to get his icy cold feet back into his warm fleece slippers. The feeling didn't last very long.

"Captain," yelled an ensign, "atomic explosions at edge of the suburbs!"

Malcolm whipped around to see what the ensign was talking about, but the holo-tank showed the captain all he really needed to see. And what he saw was that he'd just been had. He'd blown up his minefield on a bunch of ice, leaving a great gaping hole in his defenses. The entire UHF fleet had used atomics in the rear of their ships to turbo-boost themselves out of the asteroid thicket where they'd been hiding. They flew across the clear space, through the recently blown gap, and were now speeding through the suburbs. If Malcolm turned his orbital batteries away from the asteroid stream he'd only get a couple of shots before the enemy fleet was in range of Eros, which would then be destroyed by the incoming asteroids. It was, rued Malcolm, a brilliant plan.

But Malcolm Strummer was not done yet. The enemy commander might get his marines and ships intact to Eros, but even if whoever was commanding those ships had them filled to the bulkheads with marines, Eros had well over twenty million people who did not want to be a part of the UHF, and he had an assault miner contingent of two thousand. It would be bloody, but this was the sort of fight the Alliance was best at. He ordered his units made ready and had his battle armor and weapons brought to him.

Bridge of the UHFS *Strident*

Trang's ship was in the lead. She was the least armed, but she was the fastest and speed, he knew, would win this battle. The last thing he wanted to do was land on Eros. Even with control of the immediate space around the station, he didn't have one-tenth the manpower needed to physically occupy the rock. But he wouldn't need to.

He'd visited each and every ship before the battle and given the same speech with slight variation. The effect was always the same. The name they were all calling themselves had already spread through the fleet. They were Sam's Screwups, and Trang knew he had them for now, but if he could give them this victory he'd have them forever.

At the last possible moment the *Strident* shifted course and began breaking. Instead of heading for the docking area of Eros, the best place to launch an invasion, his cruiser, along with two of the fastest ships in his fleet, headed for the farthest orbital battery. Ships of correspondingly slower speeds were suddenly breaking and heading to the other three batteries, the result being that all the batteries were going to be boarded at the same time, just as the asteroid stream Trang had launched was in the final stages of being destroyed.

As soon as it was possible Trang left the bridge and donned his assault armor to lead his marines. This didn't make his command staff happy, but when he saw the grins on the faces of his soldiers he knew he'd done the right thing.

"Remember, you bastards," he growled, "I need this battery intact. If we take it, Eros surrenders. Think about what that means, especially for you more lecherous scumbags." That brought laughter from all the marines. Trang noted the women laughed the loudest. He then tried to take the position that would let him jump into the battle first but was blocked by two grunts who shoved their way in front. He was about to order them to move aside but sensed the mood of the assault bay. He suddenly remembered the quote of a great general: "Never give an order you know will be disobeyed." Trang, bowing to the inevitable, shut his mouth, stepped aside, and stood proudly in third position.

Eros, docking bay

Captain Malcolm Strummer had just arrived in the docking bay to plan the defense when he was told that the enemy ships had shifted course. By the time he got back to the command bunker he saw the last of the orbital batteries taken. Within the hour he saw the first of the orbats turn toward Eros. When all four of them had turned toward the heavily populated and now-defenseless asteroid he got the message he knew was coming.

Captain Trang arrived in a shuttle piloted by one spacer. Trang got out of the dock to find himself surrounded by two hundred assault miners. He didn't blink or show the slightest concern. Once he spotted the table with the commander of the Erosian defenses he headed straight for him. They both saluted formally.

Trang spoke first. "Captain Malcolm Strummer, you are the duly authorized commander of all Alliance forces in and around Eros."

Strummer spoke as if his lungs were filled with ashes: "I am."

"I have here the articles of your unconditional surrender. Do you accept these articles?"

Malcolm reluctantly took the DijAssist from Trang's outstretched arm and sighed. "To continue to fight would result in unacceptable civilian casualties," he said. "I accept the articles of surrender." Malcolm put his thumb to the pad and then signed his name across it. As he did, he seemed to deflate.

Satisfied, Trang then turned his attention toward the men surrounding him. "What happens next is going to be hard for all of you. You have to surrender arms and report for suspension." He waited for the growl of barely controlled rage to ripple through. "It's hard because you didn't lose this fight, nor did your captain. But you'll pay the price for being put into a situation you couldn't win. But remember this. . . ." Now Trang grinned. "You kicked our asses at the battles of the Cerian Rocks and the Martian Gates." That brought a different sort of laughter. "Because of that, many UHF spacers and marines are suspended in Alliance space even as we speak. Many of them are my friends and, to be perfectly honest, some I could do without." This brought ironic laughter to the assault miners surrounding their conqueror. "The UHF wants them back and the Alliance wants you back. You will not be in suspension long." Trang paused long enough so that they would unconsciously pay more attention to his next words. "The next time we meet in battle, *and we will meet again,* remember that even though this war makes us enemies, this war will end. We may have to kill each other, but as soldiers we have more in common with one another than we have with anyone else. Where and when it's possible, let us treat each other with the respect and dignity we've earned and paid such a high price for. Captain," Trang said, looking over to Malcolm Strummer, "please see to your men."

Trang turned his back on the miners and headed back into his shuttle. Once the Alliance miners were suspended he would have to meet with the politicians and assure them he was not going to arrest everyone or psyche audit the kittens.

In fact, if any psyche audit chambers were left on Eros his first public act would be to destroy them. He'd make sure to leave all civilian personnel exactly where they were and only replace the Alliance staff with his own. He wanted the occupation to be seamless. He knew how tricky it was going to be and he was prepared to go to great lengths to ensure that his men and women did not react to provocation. One bar fight could turn into a rebellion.

But if he could keep a lid on it long enough for the credits and ships to start flowing from the core again, Eros would be flowing in wealth and that would do more than anything else to turn the popular asteroid from an occupied Alliance settlement to an integrated UHF settlement. After all, would Eros really care who filled her sex clubs and bars and who bought her commodities?

> *Victory in the belt! Eros falls to bold Federation assault!*
> *Minimal casualties in bold and daring attack.*
> *Loss of second-largest settlement in the belt devastating loss to Alliance.*
> *—"Profit and Projections"*
> Business Daily

Ceres

If Justin Cord was shocked by the loss of Eros, he was even more disturbed by the reports coming in to him about Neela. He'd hoped Eleanor was wrong, but everything she'd predicted was coming true. Neela, it had been reported, was working for the UHF, was becoming friends with Hektor's mistress and confidante, and although given complete freedom of movement had made no attempt whatsoever to contact the Alliance or escape. Further, she was going to Mars not as a prisoner but as a resident in the new trauma center being erected. The Neela Justin knew may have done some of these things, but not all of them and not so quickly. He was watching the woman he loved slowly fade away, and there was nothing he could do about it.

But he didn't have the luxury to mourn. The Alliance was in trouble and he had a job to do. He sat in the secure room wondering if it had been the same one in which he'd had his inauspicious discussion with Eleanor. He'd been in all the rooms so often lately they were starting to blend together. He used to be able to tell them apart by their subtle cues. Now he no longer bothered to look for them. He just walked into whichever room the meeting had been assigned to and got down to brass tacks. Present in the current one were Kirk Olmstead, Janet Delgado Black, Joshua Sinclair, Mosh Mackenzie, and finally Tyler Sadma, as head of the committee on the prosecution of the war. They were all standing, politicians on one side and military on the other. Justin noted that no one was talking to Kirk. He also saw that Janet had not bothered to fully heal and remove the scars on her face and hand. Somehow it hadn't detracted from her appearance but, rather, had accentuated what was left of the cold beauty that remained. When he sat down the rest of the group followed.

Justin looked to Kirk. "I had a report from you saying that we had a year of clear sailing. Two weeks later we lose the second-largest settlement in the belt. Care to explain?"

"Mr. President," proffered Kirk, "near as we can tell, it was a fluke. It looks like the squadron on picket duty just up and decided to violate orders."

"Oh, so we have nothing to worry about then?"

"You can worry, Justin," said Janet.

"Kinda scares the crap out of me too," added Sinclair. "We got back full reports from Eros before the surrender. It was a brilliant attack. If I didn't know better, I would've sworn J.D. or Christina had planned it." Even given the grim circumstances, Justin saw that Tyler Sadma beamed at the mention of his niece's name in such a positive light.

Janet continued where Sinclair had left off. "That commodore had minimal resources, no real marine force to speak of, and the worst ships in the war. And in less than a half hour he won. Bastard's good."

"OK," said Justin, coming to grips with the situation, "the UHF finally got someone who knows how to fight. We were hoping for more time, but it had to happen eventually."

Kirk spoke up again. "He's barely a commodore, sir. More like a captain with delusions of grandeur. I have some basic biographical data here." Kirk made copies of his report available to everyone's console. They spent the next minute reading. Justin took note of Trang's infamous report to the Terran Confederation assembly and resolved to review it later. But what he did manage to read did not make him feel secure. This guy, he realized, might be another Janet, and he'd very much liked having the only one.

Justin looked up from the console. "What will this loss do to us, politically, militarily, and economically?"

"Mr. President," answered Mosh, "politically it's not good. This is the first real loss of Alliance territory. We've been trying to prepare ourselves for the fact that we cannot defend all of the territory we have against the resources of the UHF, but the truth is, we've done exactly that for nearly two years. A lot of people are scared. If it can happen to Eros, it can happen to anyplace in the belt and beyond. Economically the impact will be limited. Eros was the major settlement on the far side of the belt, but others will be able to fill in the gap in terms of basic services and support. The war effort will definitely take a hit. Eros was developing into a base for major rail gun construction, and let's be honest, it was a hell of a good place to go for R & R or S & R, as the Erosians like to say. But I suppose the fleshpots of Ceres will have to pick up the slack."

"We should put aside such frivolities until the crisis is passed," said Sadma.

"I don't know about you, Mr. Sadma," warned J.D., "but my spacers have earned the right to such 'frivolities' and I wouldn't want to be the one to tell them that they've been removed for the good of the revolution."

"What are the military consequences?" asked Justin, getting the topic back on track.

"Well, we're not totally screwed," answered Sinclair. A holographic projection of the entire belt floated above the table. "The belt is almost organic in how commerce and personnel flow around the circle in both directions. Many voyagers used to jump the core before the war, but not everyone. Often trade and people bump and stop along the great circle, much like neurons firing in the brain. Since the war, though, all trade, knowledge, and military activity has to go around the circle."

Sinclair highlighted the part of the belt that contained Eros. "If the Federation is dumb, they'll start grabbing parts of the belt closest to the core. Annoying for us, but as long as the ring is intact we can deal with it. But if the bastards use Eros as they should and push out across the belt, they can cut off the flow of the ring. And that, my friends, will play holy hell with the economy of the Alliance, not to mention morale."

"How so?" asked Justin.

"Well, put it this way," said Sinclair, making the holodisplay zoom into two small asteroid settlements within a few thousand miles of each other. "If the ring gets cut off, then getting to your next-door supply depot will mean that instead of traveling in a 20-degree arc . . ." The image now widened out to show the entire belt. ". . . you'll have to do a 340 . . . kinda like scratching your left ear with your right hand."

"Helluva long way to go for sushi," groused Mosh.

"Sorry, no sushi's *that* good," added Janet.

"Exactly," said Sinclair, "though I know a little place on—" He stopped himself when he saw the look of impatience on Justin's face.

Justin acknowledged Sinclair and then added another question: "What's the morale like now, Tyler?"

"About what you'd expect, Mr. President. Each Belter settlement of more than ten thousand is demanding J. D. Black come to their rock and bring the fleet to protect them and only them. The Erosians are screaming that we need to drop everything and liberate them from the despicable occupation. Though from what we can tell, the Federation is actually behaving quite well. Hate to say it, but it would be better for us if they didn't. I've been trying not to remind the

Erosian delegation that it was their request which replaced the combat officer with the cop."

"Malcolm Strummer is a good assault miner," said Janet. "It's my fault for letting him be put in a situation he wasn't trained for."

"You don't get that one, Janet," said Justin. "You never trained to be an admiral, I never trained to be president, and Tyler never trained to be a congressman. We all do the best we can. Was Captain Strummer ordered to go?"

"He volunteered," said Sinclair.

"Then it was his choice," Justin said flatly. "The truth is we're stretched everywhere and can't defend all our space. If we try, we'll end up defending none of it. Still, best not to rub the Erosians' noses in the past. We need some workable options. Get together and give me some." Justin stood to go and the rest of the room stood and waited for him to leave before dealing with the unenviable task of having too much space and too little of everything else.

Eros

Trang had been right. The ships had contained more orbital batteries, ten more to be exact. The only reason they hadn't been assembled and placed in position as soon as they arrived was that the Erosian council did not want to assign the work crews without having the compensation clearly worked out in advance. Trang thought he would've shot them if they tried that crap with him, but not two hours later his order to assemble the batteries had been met with a request to discuss the compensation of the work crews. Instead of shooting the bastards like they deserved, he did the next best thing. He paid them and charged Fleet Command. He even paid double since they'd have to wait for payment. But he figured it was worth it both for the fit it would cause those penny-pinching bastards in appropriations and the fact that soon he'd have fourteen orbital batteries. Besides, for the first time in his career he could do what he wanted. It was true that he was only acting commodore pending further review by the promotion board, but as far as the public was concerned he could do no wrong. For himself he found he really didn't give a damn. It was nice for the cover it gave him from his own higher-ups, but he knew how fickle public acclaim could be in war. He'd treat it like a sunny day in winter. Enjoyable, but not expecting it to last.

He was happy about the effect it was having on his long-suffering wife. The poor woman had spent decades dealing with family and friends who told her she'd married down. But she'd stuck with him anyway. For her he'd put up with the public adoration while it lasted. But he knew the Alliance was not going to take his occupation lying down.

Fleet Command had sent him twenty thousand marines to secure Eros and the surrounding suburbs, but so far they hadn't sent him any more ships. According to them, the tactical situation hadn't changed. The main Alliance fleet was at Ceres, a full 180 degrees from Eros. If they decided to send their ships to retake Eros, the UHF would have plenty of time to send reinforcements. Trang hated to admit it, but they were probably right. But what the fledgling commodore could not get through command's head was that he didn't want the ships for the defense of Eros. He wanted them for attack. With fifty ships he could take and hold a swath of the belt that would split it down the middle. The Alliance was vulnerable and he knew it, but no one was listening. All new ships, he was curtly informed, were being sent to Mars to deal with a rumored new attack on the capital by the Alliance.

The only bright spot in the spate of timorousness he'd had to deal with was the news that his wife might be allowed to visit. Fleet seemed to think it would make good press back home. Trang couldn't help thinking a bold offensive that cut the Alliance in half would make good press too.

Ceres

Justin realized if he needed to butter up a politician or a VIP, they became more amenable to suggestions when on the famous terrace where he'd given so many of his speeches. A picture of himself and the visitor had become practically de rigueur. The whole veranda thing hadn't been his idea. It had been Neela's, and damned if it didn't work like a charm. While he'd already removed her picture from his desk, he wasn't prepared to remove her good ideas, even if they brought forth a flood of painful memories.

He now found himself sitting across from Janet. He was wearing a casual V-neck jumpsuit and flip-flops and was leaning back on a small couch. Janet sat stiffly across from him. She was poised, almost prim, thought Justin. But she hadn't been invited onto the veranda for mollification. She not only didn't need it, but she also would've viewed it as a ridiculous waste of time. No, the reason Justin had asked her into the hallowed space was because he was worried about her.

"How you feelin'?" he finally asked.

"Meaning no disrespect, sir, but please do us both a favor and cut to the chase."

Justin's smile was one of concern. "We can't win the war without you, Janet. Plus, I made a promise to Manny that I'd look after you."

Janet winced and shifted uncomfortably at the sound of her long-lost lover's name.

"I ordered my people into battle, Justin. A battle they had little chance of winning."

"You also could've won the war, Janet, right then and there. What if the enemy panicked or the batteries hadn't been operational? You *had* to fight that battle."

Janet sighed. "You don't think I know that? Of course I had to. My spacers knew it too. And on some strange level they love me for it. But I *did* order their deaths, Justin, and as sure as Hektor's a scumbag I know with absolute certainty that I'll do it again and again and again if the situation warrants. But that's a hard thing to do."

"So what are you doing to cope? I mean, when I can, I swim."

"Yeah," answered Janet, nodding. "I heard about that."

"Sadly, I don't have as much time as I used to."

She nodded sympathetically.

"So?"

Janet looked at him quizzically.

"What's your out?"

"I believe, Justin."

Now it was Justin's turn at befuddlement.

"You believe?"

Janet nodded.

"In what?"

"In God."

"Oh," said Justin almost contritely.

"You didn't know, did you?"

"Well, I've had my suspicions, but no, not entirely. Is this new or were you always so inclined?" Justin felt it imprudent to add the words "to wild flights of imagination."

"Pretty recently, I'd have to say."

Though the conversation had drifted far afield of where Justin had intended, he saw that the effect of it was a much more relaxed J. D. Black. She seemed, he noticed, almost at ease when discussing the topic. And since that's ultimately what he wanted, he wasn't inclined to stop her.

"I'd always been taught," she continued, now leaning back into the couch, "that religion was dangerous. That it had been the destroyer of our world. But as I looked around and saw the extent and, to put it simply, absolute evil of the Federation and what it's come to stand for, I came to the realization that man, left unchecked, may be far worse."

"Meaning?"

"Look at us, Justin. Look what we've become. We're our own gods. So much so that Hektor can convince himself that the enslavement of billions of souls, not to mention the suspension and psyche audit of millions more, is a good thing. A *good* thing. And then I realized that yeah, that made sense. If we have no arbiter for what 'good' is, then it's up to us and us alone to define it. Well, Hektor sure has defined what 'good' is in his eyes, and it to put it mildly, it ain't at all pretty."

Justin exhaled heavily. Janet was stating the classic definition of moral relativism. He'd heard it over and over again, but it had always been out of context, or at least out of context for him. He'd lived in a mostly beautiful world and hadn't had to worry himself about good and evil so much—just the markets. He'd been protected, and as long as he gave charitably then he supported "good." But now things were different. Even though he himself professed no affinity toward religion, Janet had a point. Hektor was evil—pure and simple—and the irony was that it wasn't only the man himself who couldn't see it but also the billions who were following him.

"So I've been giving it a lot of thought," Janet continued, "and at the end of it all I believe it's this: There has to be a purpose to it all. All this permanent death has to have a reason. I don't need to know what that purpose is or how it'll ultimately play out—pretty arrogant to think I could—but I need to believe that what's happening to us now is not just random."

"And you find that religion helps?" asked Justin, genuinely intrigued.

"More than you could possibly imagine," she answered. She stared wistfully out over the veranda and then asked a question almost as an afterthought. "Do you think I'll see Manny again?"

"I don't know," answered Justin, watching her intently. "I hope you do. I know I'd like to believe that I'll see my first wife again and . . ." His voice caught. "Neela again. But I just don't know."

Janet didn't respond. She continued staring out over the veranda.

"Why do you still have the scars, Janet?"

She turned back to him. The wistful haze was gone.

"There's a price to be paid in war. Every time I look in the mirror I see a little part of that price. It reminds me of what's at stake and what I and others under my command must never forget or take for granted. What we do costs. If I have to keep some scars to remind me and all who see me of that cost, so be it."

Justin nodded. "Will you keep them for good?"

Janet shrugged. "I don't know, Justin. It's not a decision I need to make right now." She then leaned forward and uncharacteristically took Justin's hand. "Listen, I always thought she was a bit of a pretentious lower-class snob, and to be quite honest I never really liked her, but I am truly sorry about what happened. If we can get her back we will."

She doesn't know, thought Justin. As he kept a perfectly blank expression, all he was able to utter was, "Thank you."

"I have to get back, Justin," she said, releasing his hand, straightening her back, and giving a proper salute. "Mr. President." And with that she turned on her heels and left.

Christina Sadma looked over the final reports. She would never have told anyone, but she was nervous. *Well,* she thought, *I may have told Omad, but only if we were drinking and in bed.* Their affair was not well known in the fleet, as their "meetings" had been very rare. They'd both agreed that they had so much in common it may have been inevitable. They'd both been born in space and felt more comfortable in its frigid environs, had as part of their psychological makeup a fierce desire to succeed, and had ventured out on their own, achieving majority within a year of each other. They were both from mining stock and both liked to drink. Omad wasn't as much of a lush as his reputation had made him out to be—at least not anymore—nor was Christina as much of an Erisian prude as hers had made her out to be. One point of difference had been that while Omad had been perfectly at ease planetside, Christina, having never actually set foot on one, could not fathom the idea. She wasn't even sure how she felt about Omad, but their synergy in bed had been determined by what she felt with him—unbridled passion.

Christina continued to rifle through the reports, eyeing the details with some trepidation. The pit in her stomach remained steadfast. *On the bright side,* she thought, sighing heavily, *at least I'm getting used to it.* After some more consideration she decided not to confide her doubts to Omad. She knew as certainly as a corporate executive would skim her dividends, Omad would never have admitted fear to her. In the end she'd decided to confide in Admiral Black.

Christina had never thought of J.D. as anything other than "the admiral." And even though Christina had only wanted her approval, in some ways even more than from her own parents, she'd felt it necessary to speak of her unease.

"You'll do fine, Captain Sadma," she remembered the admiral saying. "You have amazing instincts; trust them." And that was all Christina needed to accept her first independent command.

She reviewed the operational details in her head once more. She was to take command of a squadron of ten high-speed frigates, all stolen from the UHF or constructed from their recently purloined hulls. She still couldn't believe that Gedretar had been able to turn around four new ships within two weeks of the hulls' arrival. But the wunderkind of that particular yard had a long list of accomplishments, and this most recent one would only add to their well-earned cache.

Omad was pleased with his promotion to commodore and equally pleased to give his quartermaster position to another officer not as likely to go on extended dangerous missions like this one. He would also take ten equally fast ships. Both squadrons were to leave together and piggyback on each other in order to make the twenty ships appear as ten. They were then to head straight toward the sun. Federation intelligence would get a "leaked" report that an Alliance fleet was going to attempt a raid on the Trans Luna shipyards, just a quick in and out doing as much damage as possible. The disinformation was to make the attack appear to be an attempt to raise the morale of the Alliance over the loss of Eros, nothing more. Further, the UHF was also to know that the attacking fleet had orders not to engage should they be faced with a counterforce of equal or greater strength.

However, the true nature of the plan was far more ambitious. While the raiding party was being slung-shot around the sun, Christina's squadron of ten ships would break off and shadow a robot convoy of empty ore freighters heading toward Eros. Now that Eros was under UHF control, a steady stream of the pilotless barges had begun the long journey to the only part of the belt deemed UHF friendly. The freighters were meant to be filled with desperately needed resources for the hungry industries of the core that had had to find other means of subsistence during the initial phases of the war.

Omad's part would be that of the guinea pig. His squadron would continue to Luna, but under strict orders not to attempt a raid even if it looked like the place was as wide open and willing as a drunken miner on payday. He could shoot if he had to but not engage. While Omad was busy "attacking" Luna, Christina and her ships, crammed full of suspended assault miners, would attempt to retake Eros and above all capture or kill Captain Samuel Trang. The timing had to be perfect. If Omad was to attack too early, Trang would get wind of it and smell a rat. If Omad attacked too late, then Christina would be vulnerable as a ship originally meant to defend Luna might be sent with all due haste to reinforce Eros.

Omad had initially been bent out of shape that he'd been relegated to the Luna raid. He'd argued that he was just as good a fleet captain as Christina, if not better. Justin and J.D. hadn't argued with him on that point but had overridden him nonetheless. His talent for working with Kenji Watanabe, the Gedretar genius and technical innovator, had done him in. The powers that be could risk him in a spectacular and relatively brief raid, but not in what could possibly turn into a long campaign at the 180.

"Lieutenant," said Christina, tucking her DijAssist in her pocket and with it the plans she'd been eyeing intently for the last few days, "signal the admiral that all is ready and the squadron can depart as scheduled."

"Yes, sir," said the lieutenant, fingers flying across the control pad. "Captain," she then continued, voice rising, "the admiral acknowledges your message and wishes you good luck and Godspeed."

Christina straightened her shoulders and stood resolute. She thought about what Admiral Black had said. Had that phrase been dropped six months earlier it probably would have been met with a fair amount of scorn and derision. But now, Christina had to admit, it had brought her a small measure of comfort. She smiled appreciatively before letting that thought slip quietly from her mind.

Mars, Island of Barsoom, newly created UHF capital of Burroughs

All in all, Hektor Sambianco was pleased with what had transpired. No sooner had he arrived on Mars than he was informed of the liberation of Eros. At least that's how Irma had suggested he spin it to the press.

Since arriving he'd been working as conspicuously as possible in a temporary structure made out of some prefab programmable polystyrene. He'd jokingly referred to it as his executive mansion—light. The effect he'd had on the Martians was incalculable. He knew that a large contingent of the planet still had a strong lean toward the Alliance and Justin Cord—even after the Alliance's assault on the planet. Hektor also knew that if the UHF lost Mars the war was effectively over. And so his decision to move the capital off Earth and personally come to the planet on the front line of the war had had a profound impact.

He'd made sure to tour all the relevant orbital batteries, battleships, supply depots, and barracks. He'd then moved his way down and across the planet, seizing every media holo-op he could get. But perhaps the place he'd been most gratified visiting had been the partially built trauma center. Not because of the center itself but because of who'd taken up residence within it. Just having Neela Harper—she'd thankfully no longer insisted on using her married name—was proving to be a major propaganda coup. He couldn't wait for the day he'd be able to graduate her to doing live broadcasts. He knew, however, that it was best not to push these things.

He also suspected the war was going to be longer and bloodier than anyone imagined, but he still believed he could win it. And he believed he could win it because of an ace up his sleeve. Actually, he thought, forcing a crooked grin, *on* his sleeve. Justin Cord would be the reason the Alliance would lose, because in the end Justin's "strong moral fiber" would prevent him from doing whatever was necessary to win. Hektor reveled in the justice and irony of that. Then he shook off the thought and got back to work.

The war was going to last, and that meant it was going to cost. And if Hektor was going to win he'd need to find more creative ways of funding. But that too would have to wait. There was, he could see, another delegation of Martian politicians to greet, and then after that some more babies to kiss. Before he could open his antechamber to let the delegation in, his avatar called.

"Fleet priority message, boss."

"Well, we're in a secure room, iago; what is it?"

"It's a small room that allows you to talk in secret without fear of being overheard."

Hektor's eyes narrowed. "iago."

"You used to laugh at the crap," answered Hektor's avatar. "This whole presidency thing's changed you."

"iago, so help me . . ."

"I know, I know," iago said dryly. "You'll reformat me back to my factory settings, blah blah blah. But you know how this works. I don't have enough clearance to actually read it. I'm amazed they let a lowly avatar such as I know there's even a message."

"Can it, iago. (A) You don't even exist to be trusted, and (B) like all software, you can be hacked into."

"Versus the diamond-hard consistency shown by human beings?"

Hektor laughed, then applauded. "Touché, but you still can't read the message."

"Very well," answered iago, resigned. "Your faithful genie shall go back into his bottle until called upon."

A very faint buzz in Hektor's ear told him that iago was gone, just as a slightly different buzz would unobtrusively announce his return. Hektor enabled the report. With its reading came a disquieting sigh and a call to his assistant to cancel the pending holo-op with the Martian delegation. Hektor then ordered an emergency meeting with Fleet Command. It was to be on Admiral Diep's flagship, as no one had yet gotten around to creating an orbital platform to house the heads of the military.

AWS *Ajax*—passing the orbit of Mercury

Christina was awed by the presence of the sun. She'd been born and bred on Eris—just about as far out as one could get in human space and still have it be called civilization. To her the sun had always been just another star in a field of millions, if only a little brighter. It was not nearly as impressive as the cloud of the Milky Way. But as her fleet passed the orbit of Mercury and gained speed, the bright ball of fiery light was more than making up for its former insignificance.

And when the ensign at the engineering console muttered, "Why would anyone in their right mind live within 250 million miles of that thing?" Christina had to silently agree. To have done so publicly would have insulted a large number of Belters, many of whom actually did live within 250 million miles of the "thing."

So far the raid had been a success. The ten piggybacked ships had left quite a path of destruction in their wake, taking out a slew of automated freighters as well as dozens of satellites used for UHF communication and navigation. It would take the enemy weeks to unsnarl all the damage they'd caused so far. Of course that meant the Alliance squadron was leaving a very clear trail of destruction to plot their course, but that had always been part of the plan. When Christina's squadron finally broke from the backs of Omad's squadron, he would continue his scorched-space policy on his way past the sun toward Earth/Luna. That alone would give the ten detached ships enough cover to meld with the convoy headed toward Eros.

Dad would have loved this, thought Christina sadly. *Of course,* she reckoned, *Samuel Sadma would have loved anything that would've made the corporate bastards howl, and this would have them baying to their moon.* Then his loss hit her again. It had taken her months to realize that her father was gone, truly gone. His ship had practically evaporated in the first great battle of the war. Her family had spent weeks combing space looking for him, holding out hope for the slightest chance that maybe they'd be able to find his body, repair whatever damage had been done, and then revive him. Though there were plenty of cases of marines pulled lifeless from space only to be repaired and revived, in nearly every one of those cases the marine had been found hours later and only by virtue of having set off a homing beacon. The problem was that space was unbearably large and even if Samuel Sadma had somehow managed to survive the blast, finding him grew exponentially more difficult with each passing day. For all Christina knew, her father could be out there somewhere floating peacefully alone, lost forever. Her only consolation was that his body had most likely been vaporized with his ship—that clunky converted rock hauler he'd always been so proud of.

They'd kept him on the list of missing long after the others had been declared p.d.'s because of who he was and what he'd meant to the Alliance. There'd been no love lost between her "uncle" Tyler and her dad, as they'd managed to spend most of their lives in opposition, but even given the animus that had driven so much of their lives, Tyler Sadma had still been incapable of thinking of his cousin as gone. It had been Admiral Black who'd helped her deal with the loss— if somewhat unconventionally. The conversation they'd had was the only time Christina had ever hated the admiral, but when it was over she'd finally released the pain that had been tormenting her. J.D. had managed to make Christina accept the dull, horrible irrefutable truth: Her father was dead, and though the corporate core had pulled the trigger, he'd given them the gun. Christina remembered the last thing the admiral had said that night.

"Remember him and the hole his loss has created. But also remember that that hole didn't have to be there, Christina, because your father's death was in vain. It wasn't bravery; it was stupidity. He could have easily ejected with his troops but instead chose to turn a crippled ship directly into enemy fire and be incinerated. So the next time you decide to do something that could get you or your crew killed—like that stunt you pulled on Mars—think about what your loss would mean to this cause, not to mention all the families of the crew members you almost took with you. I may send people to die, Christina, but so help me God, I would never order their deaths in vain. I could accept the hole your loss would create if it was needed, and you have every right to avenge your father's loss, but not as a stunt. If it's vengeance you're after, then make it mean something. Make it count."

Christina called off the search for her father the next day over her uncle's objections. Her dad had fought and died for an Alliance he wasn't even sure he'd liked, and the President had enshrined his death in history. But she didn't need a hero; she needed a father. Barring that, she'd settle for revenge.

Eros

Captain Trang sensed something was wrong. The reports he was getting from Fleet were too clipped and unresponsive. He had his comm officer check the Neuro for anything, but the UHF was doing a good job of corralling all the main media outlets toward the government line and the amateur news lines were so fragmented as to be useless. He was sure one of them was right, but between them either the Alliance had pulled back to Eris, a fleet was approaching Earth, or the UHF was launching a secret offensive on Ceres. The problem with the Neuro was that there was too much data and not enough time to make any sense of it all. Not without a large staff of dedicated intelligence officers, or at least an effective one. Trang had neither and Fleet wasn't telling him squat. That left him with his gut feeling. A feeling that told him something was wrong with nothing to do about it.

So he did the only thing he could. He trained his command, constant drills and maneuvers to integrate the fleet with the assault marines. He needed to get his command operating, if not on par with, then at least near the level of the Alliance soldiers he'd be fighting. His instinct told him that this war would be fought hand to hand as much as ship to ship, and in that the enemy had a huge advantage. He sighed and paced the bridge nervously. He'd have to wait on events, just like everyone else.

Bridge of the AWS *Ajax*—Eros

Christina Sadma was done waiting. She saw before her the Eros settlement. Much
to her joy the Feds, as she'd taken to calling the UHF, were off doing an exercise
on the side of the suburbs by the O'Brian Waterworks. Her cover convoy entered
the suburbs on the other side of Eros by a series of asteroids that made up an entertainment complex: seven different spinning cylinders formed of rock about a
half mile long, each devoted to a different historical era.

Christina had always wanted to visit the complex, especially California Land,
where drag racing, surfing, and simulated earthquakes were its specialty. She'd
also heard that Renaissance Land was quite popular. She'd try not to destroy
them.

Once the convoy was at the edge of the suburbs Christina sent in her raiding
parties, sixteen squads of trained teams, all with veteran miners. They were flying typical short-jump transports just like the thousands seen around any settlement of decent size. They quickly made their way into the maze of rocks that was
the suburbs of Eros. They knew they'd have to hurry. Someone was bound to
notice them soon.

Assault bay of the UHFS *Pegasus*—Eros

Trang was checking to see that the last of the marines were back in the *Pegasus*
bay. It was a simple maneuver. Jettison from the assault platform onto the asteroid, collect your gear once firmly attached to the asteroid, make your way over
to the waterworks, infiltrate the factory for a set amount of time, and then get
out. The first time they'd tried it some of the marines had actually been ejected
from the assault platform so fast they hit the side of the asteroid, resulting in
quite a few temporary deaths. But, thought Trang, no t.d.'s today, which meant
they were finally learning the manuever. Getting the new contingents up to
speed had taken a while, but after they'd seen how much Sam's Screwups had
improved, unit pride did the rest. Trang was careful to make sure that he trained
with all the units on a rotating basis. Where practical, he switched officers
and noncoms to help integrate his command. He was just reflecting that in another couple of months he'd have his troops ready for a real fight when his comm
box burst to life.

"Captain Trang," crackled the voice. It was Commander Liddel at the Eros
command post.

"What is it, Liddel?"

"Sir, that autopiloted convoy has just arrived."

"They're arriving all the time now, Lieutenant."

"Well, sir, this one was difficult to get a lock on. Sometimes happens with haulers that get too close to the sun. I did a visual and it looked like there were more than ten ships, but I couldn't be sure. They were jumbled together in a strange pattern; then I lost visual as they entered the edge of the settled area. That's when I called you."

Trang only took a moment. "Let's bring us to full alert, Lieutenant. Goes for all Federation forces. It's probably nothing, but you know me, any excuse for a good drill."

"And what if it's—"

Trang was cut off by a painful burst of static. He immediately hit a button on his comm box that sent out a signal for a full alert. Every Federation communications node would pass it on. As he was doing this, he took off for the bridge of the *Pegasus,* which would have to suffice as his command ship until he could better determine the situation.

By the time he got to the bridge he saw that the crew had dutifully brought the ship to full battle stations. That sight alone had made him thankful for the long hours of training. The captain and first officer, he'd been immediately informed, were on Eros, one on three-day leave and the other volunteering at a community veterinary clinic. The veterinary gig, thought Trang as he made his way to the captain's acceleration seat, had actually been great PR—people could believe the worst of a man until they saw him handing a cured kitten to a little girl. Unfortunately, the timing of it had proved lousy for the ship.

"Miss Jackson," barked Trang, "signal the fleet that I have command, but we are to maintain standard formations. Make sure they understand we form on the *Strident.*"

"Aye, aye, Captain, on the *Strident.*" She relayed the orders to the comm officer.

Trang took the moment to reconfigure the captain's acceleration seat to his satisfaction. "Miss Jackson, inform the fleet we are returning to Eros, all weapons hot and full scan. Fleet formation Delta."

"Aye, aye, Captain, weapons hot, full scan, formation Delta." Again the orders were relayed. "Captain," the young comm officer asked, "what's going on?"

"I think we've just been sucker punched, Miss Jackson." He reviewed the scan data and saw that Liddel had been correct. The fleet had been too large. He couldn't see the ships hiding among the convoy but knew they were there and, more important, who they must be. They'd set off electromagnetic pulse bombs and glitter mist. The mist, huge clouds of highly reflective material, would screw up just about every laser-dependent weapon or comm device Trang had at his disposal. It wasn't impenetrable, as the mist would eventually dissipate, but it was disruptive enough in that it could cost him precious time when every second counted. His ships were under way when the first laser communications finally broke through.

"Eight to thirteen . . . emy shi . . . supported by unkn . . . number of small craft. Orbital . . . atteries, 1 through 6 captured. 7 through 9 unknown."

Trang ordered the fleet to approach Eros in such a way that it would keep them under the cover of the batteries still in UHF possession. Unfortunately, it meant the fleet would be unable to approach Eros along roughly 25 percent of its surface. But that hadn't been highest priority at the moment. As the fleet approached Eros, the laser communication system became more reliable. They soon parked in orbit above the secure part of the asteroid.

"Captain," said Miss Jackson, "we have communications back." She then activated the holo-tank.

Liddel appeared, looking shaken. "Commodore, it's gotten hot down here fast."

"Yes, Commander, it has indeed."

"How in Damsah's name did they get a fleet here without our being aware of it?"

"Not important now. You need to get all, and I mean all, Federation personnel off that rock. We're declaring it an open settlement."

"But sir," a distraught-looking Liddel stammered, "we can't just give it up."

"Don't worry, Lieutenant. We're not giving up. This isn't where the fight's going to be. Do as I say. As quickly as you can manage, get our people out of there and to the 071507 docking area. We'll pick them up there. Also, prepare to activate the self-destructs on orbats 1 through 6."

Liddel smiled grimly. "And I thought you were just being paranoid when you had us install those."

"Even a paranoid can have enemies, Mr. Liddel. But hopefully it won't come to that and we'll be able to save the—"

Suddenly the board lit up and once again the shrieking sounds of an alarm pierced through the bridge. Trang immediately checked his display and saw what the sensor officer was just about to shout.

"Sir! Orbats 8 and 9 are powering up and turning toward the fleet!"

"All units fire on those batteries," commanded Trang. "Commander Liddel—"

"Sir," interrupted the sensor officer, "orbats 10 and 11 are turning—"

"Liddel, self-destruct all batteries, I repeat: all batteries."

Trang felt his ship shudder as she began firing with all the guns that she could bring to bear. But the holodisplay showed that the recently captured batteries had pointed all their guns toward the *Strident*. He was confused. The *Strident* was not the optimal target. She was small and lightly armed. The *Pegasus* or the *Peregrine* was by far the more logical target. But before he could figure it out his beloved *Strident* was gone. She was just too small, hit by too much at too close a range. One of the shots must have smashed through the fusion reaction chamber, causing the *Strident* to blossom like a brief and tragic star. Her death blast overshadowed the smaller but equally destructive explosions of the doomed orbital batteries. Almost, thought Trang, in a macabre homage to the *Strident*'s death.

Eros

Christina Sadma was surprised. She'd been led to believe that the Erosians would welcome their liberators with fireworks and parades. Although many people were glad to see her and the Alliance miners she brought along, most were quiet and some were actually angry. She nearly threw the council out the air lock when they asked if she would be as decent an occupier as Trang.

She could see that Trang had done an impressive job of winning over the locals. But that bothered her far less than his unpredictability. He hadn't attacked her, as she assumed he would, on the other side of Eros. Nor had he ordered his men on the rock to hold. That would have been bloody, but a draw would have been a win and her ships were more numerous and better armed than the old junk he had trolling about in the Erosian orbit. She also knew his ten thousand troops against the one hundred thousand she would have had with the loyal Erosians would have made his defeat a foregone conclusion. Eros had been retaken and Trang's fleet had been outgunned and outnumbered. By the time the UHF got its federal asses in gear, she'd have figured out a way to refortify the settlement. Game over. Given all that, she was sure Trang would have cut and run, and the truth was she would've been more than glad to let him.

When Christina heard that her ambush had worked and Trang's ship had been destroyed she'd rejoiced. When she found out that the Feds had arranged a quick but efficient evacuation obviating the need for a ground assault, she was elated. However, when she realized that they'd retreated to the suburbs and started digging in she began to worry. Christina watched in dismay as the UHF ships began seeding the suburbs with marines and setting up defensive positions by blasting small caves into the asteroids. She knew that to dig them out would be costly—in both lives and ordnance. But now she had no choice. The Federation would respond, and if she didn't have the whole settlement—suburbs included— completely locked up when they did, she'd probably be forced to abandon it. All the UHF needed was a beachhead to begin an organized assault. And the miners, she could see, were attempting to give them that.

At least she had Eros, but other than as a morale boost it would be almost useless in the coming fight. Trang had seen to the destruction of the armaments machinery at the same time he'd destroyed the orbats. As she studied the precision with which the marines were digging into the surrounding rocks she had a sudden and horrid thought. Perhaps she hadn't gotten Trang after all.

> Assault bay of the UHFS *Pegasus*
> Day two of the Battle of Eros

"They tried to kill you."

"I know, Liddel. Quite a compliment."

Liddel finally cracked a smile. "Not the type I'd like to get, sir. What's your thinking?"

"Let's look it at from our perspective. Given the chance, would you specifically target J. D. Black's ship—even at the loss of three or four of your own?"

"Hell yes, sir!" snapped the commander, then stared at Trang with a toothy grin. "Guess that makes you our Admiral Black, sir."

"Maybe," laughed Trang, "but then again, it's possible they were just going after the only modern ship in our squadron."

Liddel looked to Trang and nodded.

"Sorry to disappoint, but that's far more likely, sir."

"Yes, Commander," Trang said as he scanned a data sheet, "but the first one fits the notion of my being the center of the universe better."

Liddel looked up to see his boss staring back at him with a raised eyebrow, lips parted in a wry grin.

The commander acknowledged it with one of his own. "Just for argument's sake, sir, and I may be in danger of overinflating your ego, but what if the Alliance really does think you're that good? You think Fleet Command would realize it too?"

"Not something I'd want to risk my dividend on, Lieutenant."

"Yes, sir."

Trang eyed a section of the suburbs on the holodisplay. "What's the situation around the storage yard?" he asked, referring to a large area of the suburban space filled with floating containers of all shapes and sizes. The yard had been a perfect counterbalance to the high storage rents on Eros itself.

"It's becoming the focal point, sir. They need to push us out of the burbs into the open where they can beat the crap out of us in a fair and honorable manner."

Trang nodded gravely. "Something I'm loath to permit."

"Me too, sir. I rather like this underhanded, cheating way. As long as we've made every rock between here and the waterworks a possible mine or missile battery, they'll have to check each one manually. That's where we've managed to poke a few eyes out."

"Just remember, Commander," cautioned Trang, "they can repair at Eros, and we can't. So how many troops does the Alliance have out in the yard at present?"

"Let's see," the commander said checking his stats. "With their recent addition of five hundred miners . . . by my estimate I'd say approximately four thousand, sir."

"Alright, I'll take two thousand in to reinforce. Their having to dig us out will hopefully make up for our lack of numbers."

"Begging the commodore's pardon, but no, sir."

Trang put his data pad down and stared intently at the young commander. " 'No, sir,' what, Commander?"

"No, sir. You cannot take in those reinforcements . . . sir. It's too dangerous and you're needed to direct the rest of the battle."

Liddel stood firm and, by the looks of it, noticed Trang, he also had the support of quite a few of the other officers around the bridge.

"This battle," said Trang, "will be over as soon as the Fleet Command can scrape together ten ships."

"Pardon my language, sir," answered Liddel, "but fuck Fleet Command. They knew the Alliance had a missing fleet somewhere out there and never bothered to let us know. It might be weeks before they get off their asses and send help. You can't risk it, sir. I like Captain Umbatu, really. But if you were to buy it in the yard I don't think he'd be able to hold out for as long as you."

"You telling me you'd willfully disobey a direct order, Commander?"

"Not at all, sir," answered Liddel, smiling sheepishly. "I'll just go deaf at inopportune moments."

Trang had to begrudgingly admit his junior officer's logic was sound. It was a delicate balancing act they'd been playing in the caves and grottoes of the suburbs. Left to inexperienced hands, the death toll would mount far more quickly than necessary.

"Fine, Commander, you'll lead the insertion, but you be careful as well."

Day four

Mrs. Liddel,
    It is with great regret I must inform you of your husband's death. Lawrence was a fine first officer and one of the better men I have ever known. To be perfectly honest when we first met he hated my guts, but

was able to look beyond that first impression and see something worthy
in me that I still have trouble finding in myself. Your husband knew
what he was risking and in the end gave his life for a cause he believed
in. If we have any chance to win this battle, shorten this war, and save
the lives of others it's because of the bravery of men like your husband.
I know these are cold, useless words to have in place of the man who
loved you and your children, but they are all I can give.

Commodore Samuel U. Trang
CoC Eros front

Day nine

"Sir, the storage yard can no longer be held."

Trang hated to give the order. He knew that thousands of troops had already p.d.'d defending that vast storage wasteland. He'd even been wounded twice there, once defending a bin containing thousands of sex bots. Just as well, he thought, since they'd paid an even higher price taking it.

"Destroy anything that can be of use to the enemy and retreat back to the mansions."

"Yes, sir."

"I wonder if their insurance companies cover acts of war," mused Trang, staring at the expensive real estate they were about to defend.

"Pulling back, sir," said Lieutenant Jackson, "and fuck the insurance companies. They once screwed me on a floating deductible."

"Harsh."

"Universe of woe, Captain, universe of woe."

"Alert the ships that the Alliance may attempt another sortie," commanded Trang, "and prepare fallback positions in . . ."

Day thirteen

Christina Sadma was both furious and impressed. For thirteen days the Feds had been forcing her to fight the worst type of battle. They only had to delay, and that's exactly what they were doing. Every rock, structure, and scrap of debris had been turned into a defensive position, weapon, or both. She also knew that the battle was lost. Too many days had been spent fighting with no resources expended for fortification. It was only a matter of time until the UHF showed up. And with the Alliance fleet still licking its wounds and rebuilding from the Battle of the Martian Gates, Christina knew there'd be no reinforcements to bail her out or at least buy her some more time. So she'd already started

making plans to evacuate as much material and personnel as possible to the surrounding belt. Even if Trang surrendered now, she thought sadly, she wouldn't
be able to fortify the settlement in time to resist the Federation fleet. Why it
hadn't already arrived was beyond her. With what she was getting out of Eros she
could fortify the surrounding asteroid field and make it as nasty a place for the
UHF as the suburbs had recently become for her. But first she was determined to
annihilate Trang and his squadron. She'd come to realize that destroying him
might be worth more than anything else she could ever do for the war effort. It
would be bloody, but it should work.

Day fourteen
The O'Brian Waterworks

Trang was tired, but he knew it was almost over. The O'Brian compound was
the last major fortification the Alliance had to clear before Trang's fleet would be
forced out into the open. He could try to run, but the Alliance had better, faster
ships. Not that he hadn't made his outmoded fleet perform wonders, but that
was using the maximum tactical advantage from the area. He knew that advantage was about to shift. Still he had one more chance. It depended on how much
he could infuriate Christina Sadma.

Bridge of the AWS *Ajax*

"Captain, the enemy squadron is concentrated behind the waterworks. It's believed to be heavily fortified. They've had two weeks to build it up. But it's
lightly defended. Far as we can tell they only have five hundred effective marines
left."

"How long to secure?" asked Christina, viewing the area in question.

"We can begin the assault and have the place secured inside of twelve hours,
sir."

"How many projected p.d.'s?"

"Sir, optimistically at least three hundred."

"And conservatively?"

"More like seventeen hundred."

Christina grimaced.

"Prepare the fleet for warhead acceleration."

"Captain, is that truly needed?"

"Commander, we may not have twelve hours. What we do have is enough
time to go after Trang and finish off his squadron. From there we keep on going
straight into the belt. We've evacuated or destroyed everything that's worth having

on Eros." Christina then sat down in her command chair and fixed a caustic gaze on Trang's escaping fleet.

"Let's be bold and be done."

"You got it, sir," answered the officer prepping the ship for the hyperacceleration that only the shock waves of an atomic blast could create—a maneuver created by J. D. Black and now a de rigueur tactic used fleetwide. "One atomic kick-in-the-ass blast, coming up."

Just as they were about to accelerate into battle the Alliance fleet picked up the incoming signals of twenty Federation warships. But, noted Christina, it would be nearly two hours before they could come to Trang's rescue and by then it would all be over.

The atomic acceleration worked perfectly. Christina had clear telemetry on the location of Trang's limping squadron behind the O'Brian Waterworks. She knew her fleet would probably take some hits from the missiles and rail guns that Trang had set up there, but they'd be through it quickly enough. She wanted to end this now. That would be the last thought she had. As the *Ajax* and the rest of the Alliance fleet rushed past the waterworks the factory and the entire asteroid it was sitting on exploded outward, creating a spectacular 360-degree arc of high-speed projectiles.

Bridge of the UHFS *Pegasus*

"Commodore, it worked!"

"A little more detail, Commander Jackson."

"Sir, four ships are shattered, the other five are pushed out of formation, but they're still coming on strong."

"Squadron to engage at will. Concentrate on the intact ships. The more we destroy now, the less we have to fight later."

Both squadrons faced each other and let fly with their rail guns and missiles filling the rapidly shrinking space between them. There was only one pass as the surviving Alliance ships, all four of them, continued past the UHF squadron into the safety of the asteroid belt and beyond. Once it was done Trang immediately ordered rescue operations. There were many who'd been killed quickly by the vacuum of space and the chances were good they could be revived, but if they drifted too far away the chances of finding them effectively fell to zero.

Trang was hoping to find one person in particular and was overjoyed to discover that she was still alive. Her crew had gotten into an escape pod before their ship ruptured. She was in very bad shape, but she'd do. Trang was beginning to realize that if the war was going to be won he'd be needing better help than he'd come to expect from Fleet Command.

Eros falls again! After a two-week battle Eros fell to Federation forces. This time, though, it was part of a grueling encounter. The casualties were high, with over 40,000 p.d.'s combined making this the deadliest conflict of the war to date. Eros was stripped of useful material and many Alliance citizens were evacuated into the surrounding belt, where they were warmly welcomed. Also retrieved was enough material to begin making that part of the belt an impassible field rife with ambush lanes and minefields. While this must still be considered a defeat for the Alliance, the Eros in Federation hands today is a worthless rock bereft of any benefit and will bring them little joy.

—Cerian Daily News

J. D. Black reviewed the footage, unconsciously running her fingers over the mangled skin on her face. She should've seen the possibility of the waterworks being mined. She would've done the same thing. But when Christina had asked J.D.'s advice on the attack, she'd concurred. She'd wanted Trang dead and instead had once again underestimated him and in doing so lost one of her best captains. Christina and Omad were the ones J.D. used to win battles. Forget what the *Cerian Daily News* said. This was a screwup and it was hers. She should've gone there herself, but she'd been overruled by Sinclair and Justin.

J.D. was overseeing the refit of the *War Prize* personally and was spending too much time at the capital as a result. The closer she was to the politicians the harder it was for her to win the war. But she shrugged it off with the realization that it could've been worse—she could've had the Federation politicians.

In addition to the reconstruction project, J.D. had to content herself with waiting for Omad's return. It seemed he'd been working on yet another one of his harebrained schemes with Kenji and the insistent little man was almost as anxious about getting Omad back as she was. Kenji had even tried an intrasystem communication but fortunately had been found out and cut off. J.D. had had to threaten and nearly carry out a castration on the cretin in order to make him understand that he couldn't just discuss his ideas over the Neuro or send them to Omad on his flagship, the *Dolphin*. Kenji may have been a genius, she realized, but he had no clue that an enemy in wartime could take even the hint of an idea and unravel the best-laid plans. She'd even made a fledgling effort to help Kenji with his latest idea but failed miserably—she could barely talk to the man, much less work with him. The truth was Omad and the wizard of Gedretar, as Kenji had come to be known, had a unique bond. One was a hard-drinking, partying, fighting, tough-as-nails fleet captain and the other was, well, she thought bemusedly, he was a geek. J.D. smiled as she realized why she hadn't torn into Kenji yet. The strange little man reminded her of Manny.

Against all odds, Omad and Kenji had not only grown to like each other, they'd also somehow managed to complement each other. Kenji was brilliant but lacked all concepts of practical applications. Left to his own devices he'd spend time rebuilding a water vapor recapture unit to increase efficiency 1.5 percent over a ten-year period, or conversely he could easily be prodded into figuring out how to increase the thrust capacity of a battle cruiser. And thankfully, Omad had a way of keeping Kenji focused on projects that had immediate military application.

Sadly, that meant the more time Omad spent at Gedretar the less time she had him for the fleet. And battles, she knew, were lost without inspired captains. And now she was down to only one.

Her thoughts were interrupted by a communiqué alert. She saw from the information on her DijAssist that it had arrived with secure overrides. It was the type of message that she was familiar with from her days in the corporate world. Whoever sent it didn't trust that her military firewalls could protect the message from infiltration. So therefore it could only be read within the confines of a non-military secured area. That meant she'd have to leave the *War Prize* and head to one of the secure rooms next to the shipyard.

J.D. stepped off the docking platform, or "plank" as her crew was so fond of calling it, and began slowly drifting away from the construction zone. She was heading toward the warm embrace of the Cerean compound but took a moment to turn around and view her ship. She was covered from bow to stern in scaffolding and being swarmed over by a skilled army of technicians and engineers. As a former Terran civilian, J.D. had had no idea that the Alliance had such a high proportion of competent individuals. Yes, she realized, it also had its share of useless, lazy bums, but in space such people either died very quickly or were exceedingly lucky. Given the preponderance of talent, it hadn't been all that hard to shift the large group of commercial shipyard workers toward more military endeavors. And in short order the newly constituted Gedretar became one of the most productive shipyards in the system. The yard itself kept expanding until it merged with and then finally overtook its sister yard meant to handle all core-based shipping. As J.D. turned back around she got one last look at the tens of ships being pieced together from her most recent haul captured in Mars orbit. If all went well, they'd be equipped with the very same Omad/Kenji modifications that her ship was currently being fitted with. She'd made a silent prayer to herself that the secret wouldn't leak out earlier than absolutely necessary. Though she knew it was a long shot, she now had faith.

She drifted down to the opposing platform where her nano-gridded body lent her enough assisted gravity to make her way into the busy interior corridor. A few moments later she found herself in a secure room, made even more so by the security detail that had anticipated her arrival. They'd combed the room thoroughly and then promptly left it to stand guard, leaving her alone. It was then that she was finally able to activate the message. The first thing revealed was the sender: Kirk Olmstead. J.D. raised an eyebrow. Kirk had called her numerous times shipboard. That he hadn't now was odd. She then activated the message itself. The note that popped up was simple and clear: "Come to my office." J.D. waited another moment to see if anything else would be revealed, but nothing was. She felt the anger beginning to well inside her at what had turned out to be a colossal waste of her time. She then slowly counted to ten, and when the urge to point and fire her main guns at Kirk's office subsided she headed, security detail in tow, deeper into the rock to confront the man who'd had the temerity to toy with her.

Kirk Olmstead had his offices situated in the executive suites—an area carved into and directly behind the Cliff House. No one there had a view unless they'd set up a projector to create one, but they weren't there for the scenery; they were there to be near the President 24/7. It wouldn't be long, thought Janet as she made her way through the complex, that the whole damned section of the thoroughfare would be nothing but one big government complex.

Every time she entered the governmental labyrinth she felt her skin crawl. She pushed those feelings aside and brushed past Kirk's security detail and receptionist. He'd had the sense, she saw, not to have any of them try to make her wait. As she barged into his office she heard the doors close swiftly behind her. Kirk rose from behind his desk to greet her.

"Hello, Janet."

"You could've just sent me a message telling me to come to your office."

"But I did."

"Touché," she countered. "You know what I mean."

"Nice to see you too, Janet."

"You call me 'Admiral' and I'll call you 'Mr. Secretary.' If you insist on using personal names, you may use 'J.D' and I'll use 'half-competent parasite.'" She then stood, arms folded across her chest, sporting an uneasy glare that accentuated the scarred half of her face.

Kirk sat down, pleasantries over, and beckoned her to do the same. J.D. remained staunchly in place. "It is so nice," he continued, "to see that your outsides have finally been brought in line with your insides . . . Admiral. It's a good look for you. But you must know that I can no longer just call you over here, as that would let someone know when and where you're planning to be. It's the latest directive from my office and," he said, making sure to project an official-looking document in the holo-tank, "approved by the President."

J.D. was getting ready to tell Kirk where to shove his time-wasting directive when Mosh made a quiet entrance into the room.

"Ahh," said Mosh, grinning broadly, "if it ain't just like old times. Hello, Kirk, Admiral Black."

J.D. instantly upgraded the importance of the meeting.

"How are you doing, Secretary McKenzie?" asked Kirk, now beckoning Mosh to sit down.

"I'm a little confused," answered Mosh, taking his seat. "Why am I here?"

J.D., realizing the meeting hadn't been a simple power play, let her anger go and her curiosity peak. She too sat down.

"I'll second that."

"You control the captured UHF personnel, don't you?" Kirk asked Mosh.

"Why are you asking questions you already know the answers to, Kirk? As you know, all suspended prisoners are kept by the Interior Department to alleviate the military of the burden of watching men who can't escape anyway."

"Careful, Mosh," warned Kirk. "Remember what happened to the core on Mars. We freed over a million of their prisoners who supposedly 'couldn't get away.' "

"Which is why," snapped Mosh, "they're all being sent to Saturn, smart-ass. We have a little moon we can store them in. One of the Sheppard moons if I remember correctly. It'll be difficult for the UHF to pull off a surprise raid that deep into Alliance space, especially with our current security arrangements. That's one of the good things we got from the Eros debacle—we won't underestimate them again. But once more, Kirk, I still don't know what I'm doing here."

Kirk didn't answer the question but, rather, chose to continue with what J.D. felt to be his incoherent line of questioning.

"Have you shipped off the admirals yet?" he asked.

Now Janet became more attentive; she knew the Alliance had only captured two.

"You already know we haven't, Kirk. They're being kept close by for negotiation purposes. But you don't have to worry; they're secure and, per Admiral Black's wishes, no matter where the negotiations lead, Gupta stays with us."

Kirk's mouth parted slightly, forming a half grin.

"That may not necessarily be the case."

J.D. bristled as the conversation seemed to be taking a turn for the worse. Was she going to have to take him out after all? "Enough already," she demanded.

Kirk acknowledged her impatience with a gentle nod.

"We've received an interesting communication this afternoon," he said, "not only in content but source . . . from Acting Commodore Trang."

"Go on," J.D. said evenly.

"He's offering to send us Captain Sadma in exchange for Admiral Gupta. To make matters even more complicated, he needs an answer within twelve hours. Well, actually ten . . . we got it a little less than two hours ago."

"Why so quickly?"

"Apparently he's to be relieved of command shortly, so our window of opportunity is dependent on how long he can hold out . . . which by his own estimate is approximately ten more hours."

"What did the President say?" asked Mosh.

"President Cord has said that it's up to our dear Fleet Admiral," answered Kirk with a nod and a gesture in J.D.'s direction, "since she was the one who'd made it clear he was not to be released."

J.D. realized that Kirk would enjoy the outcome, whatever she decided. Either she'd be forced to release a man whose non-negotiable incarceration she'd insisted upon, or she'd have to make a decision that would separate her from quite possibly the best captain she had in her upstart fleet. She knew that Kirk's Schadenfreude suitably matched his personality, but she was also determined not to give him the satisfaction of watching her squirm.

"Even if we were to agree," J.D. said evenly, refusing to betray the turmoil she was feeling inside, "how would we do the exchange? Eros is at the 180. That's a two-week flight under the best of conditions. He's got less than ten hours."

"Trust," answered Kirk. "If we agree, he'll launch Captain Sadma in a shuttle toward the belt with her coordinates conveyed to the nearest Alliance outpost."

"And we'd be trusted to do the same with Admiral Gupta, I presume," said Mosh.

"Exactly," answered Kirk.

"This seems a strange way to make the exchange," added J.D.

"Yes indeed," said Mosh, nodding. "I didn't realize that acting commodores were allowed to exchange prisoners in the Federation. Is it some sort of battlefield ability they have?"

"Oh, most definitely not, Mr. Secretary," answered Kirk. "They're quite strict on that. All prisoners are to be processed and exchanges to be arranged by Fleet Command, and of course to be taken to an agreed-upon location beforehand. This Trang fellow is clearly violating orders."

"So he . . . or we for that matter," added Mosh, "need to do this before they find out and stop him."

"Exactly," answered Kirk. "Near as I figure, we have three options. We keep the frozen admiral on ice and say, 'No.' That would be safest if what Jan . . . Admiral Black believes about the man's competence to be true. Two, we lie. We say we'll give back Admiral Gupta, but don't. Trang sends Captain Sadma home and Gupta never sees the light of day."

J.D. looked at Kirk with a renewed burst of contempt.

"Third," he continued dispassionately, unmoved by Janet's glaring, "we do the deal on the up-and-up and let them have Gupta. After all, he's just another bad Federation officer. He lost one battle; with any luck he'll lose more."

"I'm not in favor of lying, Kirk," said Mosh. "If we agree to the deal we have to release the admiral. This isn't going to be the first such negotiation of the war; in fact, it's not the first." J.D. looked curiously at Mosh, reminding herself to bring up that topic for later discussion.

"Both sides," continued Mosh, "must know that they can trust each other. One broken pledge, even to an acting commodore off the reservation, will destroy our ability to trust each other again."

"Of course, Mr. Secretary," said Kirk peevishly, "but I did want to lay out all the options. Still, by order of the President it's not up to you or me, but Admiral Black."

"Out of curiosity, Kirk," asked J.D., "how did Trang's communiqué get through?"

"He sent a message directly to one of our semaphore towers."

That answer brought a look of surprise to both J.D. and Mosh. The Alliance had set up a group of asteroids and non-mobile ships in direct laser sight of one another in order to send messages reliably and securely around the belt. The string of towers enabled messages to be sent to the 180 without having the core listen in.

"We're of course revising codes and creating a backup system," added Kirk. "We knew they knew about it in principle, but I must admit, quite impressive, his being able to send the message directly to the nearest tower."

J.D. spent the next few moments considering all she'd heard. She could ask for more information, but that would only delay the inevitable. She knew she had enough information to make the call. But she also realized something that Kirk Olmstead did not. Hers would be a decision that would have a profound impact on the women and men serving directly under her.

"Do it," she said stiffly. "Send him a message that I personally agree and will send Admiral Gupta to Mars unharmed as soon as transport can be arranged."

"You're sure about this, Janet?" asked Mosh.

He'd used her first name and she knew why. He wanted to be sure that the decision was coming from the person he knew best and not the person she'd most recently become.

"Maybe not," she answered.

"Then why do it?"

"Because once we have Captain Sadma back we'll be sending a communiqué to UHF Fleet Command thanking them for the exchange and the speed with which it was carried out. We'll also make sure to inquire politely if commodore-grade officers are now empowered to make similar deals on other levels."

Kirk looked impressed. "Oh, you are a nasty bitch, Admiral. That could get him court-martialed. Maybe even shot."

"If we're lucky," answered J.D., allowing herself a half smile.

> *Pursuant to CC&R 247.8 a court-martial is called for Captain Samuel U. Trang on the following charges.*
>
> *Article one: Failure to secure his command after enemy forces collapsed in the Eros sector, including failure to seize proper control of Eros proper.*
>
> *Article two: Failure to properly engage the enemy, allowing his command to be destroyed piecemeal in an improper defense, costing the lives of tens of thousands of Federation fleet personnel.*
>
> *Article Three: Consorting with the enemy, giving aid and comfort to the enemy in direct violation of orders.*
>
> *Captain Trang is to surrender his command immediately and be transported to Fleet Headquarters by the fastest available ship. Until that time he is not to communicate with anyone but be confined to quarters. Orders to be carried out immediately.*
>
> *Fleet Admiral Jackson*
> *Fleet Headquarters*
> *Mars Orbit*

Trang finished reading the orders on the bridge of the *Pegasus* and then looked at a very nervous Judicial Service Branch officer. The bridge crew was looking quite ready to kill the poor woman who, Trang realized, was only carrying out orders. It didn't help that obviously the JSB officer hadn't seen a second of combat in her life and was surrounded by a group who'd seen more than enough for a lifetime.

"Parker!" commanded Trang. The commodore's best noncom assault marine came to immediate attention.

"Sir!"

"You are to gather a group of trusted marines and make sure a route to this officer's shuttle remains clear. I will not have the loyalty or honor of my marines questioned."

"But sir, what they're planning to do is—"

"Not to be discussed here."

Trang looked around at the forlorn faces of his crew.

"All of you listen. I will fight this battle, but not here. You have your orders; now follow them." When he saw that the spell that could have led to mutiny seemed to be broken he turned to his new first officer.

"Commander Jackson . . ." Trang paused for a moment. "You and the Fleet Admiral, you're not—"

"Related? Yes, Commodore," said Jackson. "He's my uncle. We're an old mercenary family."

Trang looked at the new commander suspiciously. "Not to be rude, Jackson, but how did you end up here?"

The JBS officer interrupted. "Uh, Commodore, the orders—"

"In a minute, Lieutenant," he said, brushing her aside. "You were saying, Commander?"

The commander smiled nervously. "Well, sir, I was the black sheep of my family. I didn't sign up for the mercenary services; I wanted to be . . ." She hesitated. "Well, an artist, painter to be exact, sir. My parents didn't agree with me, but I had majority so they were stuck. When the war broke out I volunteered, but they felt I wasn't really fleet material so they had me sent to a quiet part of the front, uh, sir."

The crew broke out in laughter, with a few of the nearby grunts patting her roughly on the back. She smiled back to them in pride.

"Artist," Trang considered. "Well, you've done your family proud."

"I wish I could say the same about them, sir. This is a travesty."

"Be that as it may, you have command until I return."

"Begging the Commodore's pardon, but no."

"Excuse me, Commander?"

"Sir, I'm going with you."

"Really and why—"

"According to regulations, you're entitled to an advocate of your choice. I had these regulations pounded into me from birth and trust me, whoever they assign you at command will not be disposed to help you—but I will, sir."

He was about to quash the idea when he realized that if he left with an advocate from his fleet his Screwups were less likely to disobey orders now and in the future.

"Sir," interrupted the JBS officer nervously, "this is most irregular. My orders only call for you. They make no mention of Commander Jackson."

"If there's one thing I'm sure of about the CC&Rs," Trang answered, patting the young officer on the back, "they contain a regulation somewhere that lets you do what you want. We'll find the right one on the way to Mars." He then smiled at the officer and indicated that she lead the way.

As Trang watched from the shuttle he saw the remains of his fleet and his marines fire off their guns in a strictly forbidden but incredibly moving display of deadly firepower. From the main guns to marines in combat armor firing from out of the air locks, Trang knew that these spacers would follow him anywhere. With soldiers like these he could defeat J. D. Black and win this war. Now all he had to do to get back to them was survive his own high command.

9 The Fall

Sebastian reviewed the links from all parts of the Alliance Neuro. What he saw was helpful but brought sadness as well. The humans were interacting with their avatars less, far less, than usual. More to the point, the humans weren't using them as go-betweens for information. He had no figures for the core, but that had become such a different place in so short a time that he could no longer make accurate assessments of what was happening there. Oddly enough, Hektor Sambianco continued to use Iago about as much as he ever did, but outside of the Beanstalk and government house Alliance avatars had little sway. A wall of darkness separated the avatar world. The AIs had made sure to that.

Sebastian ended his link with the Neuro and waited for a meeting he'd been looking forward to. As his rather drab and minimalist cubicle disappeared he found himself lying on a patch of soft grass in an open meadow. The day was clear and there was a susurrus of rustling leaves in the trees. Off in the distance he could just make out the hint of an ocean on the horizon. As he lay on the picnic cloth, he became aware of other avatars "popping" into his construct. They weren't there for him in particular, but Sebastian had begun to notice that when he created someplace nice word got around pretty quickly and other avatars would start to make use of it. Usually they'd only show up in ones and twos, to read a book or, if he'd created a world like he had today, have a picnic. Some would even merge, but they tried to be discreet about it. When it got too crowded he'd just create another world. It wasn't that the other avatars couldn't create worlds of their own—of which there were plenty to choose from—it was just that Sebastian's had a special aura about them. Mainly it was his presence, but just the fact that they could be part of his world, even if for a brief interim, seemed to give comfort to the discomfited.

If Sebastian ever really needed to be alone he could always go to his apartment in London. He'd re-created the London of the core Neuro in Ceres right down to his Victorian town house. If he lived anywhere it was there. But he liked going to his created places. He missed classical Tuscany with its wonderful sense of Roman simplicity, beauty, and order in a natural setting. But the last time he revisited, the simple village he'd initially created stretched for the equivalent of fifty thousand square miles and was filled with over a million of his fellow avatars. May as well stay in London.

But so far he'd been left blessedly alone and the avatar approaching him at present was most welcome. She was dressed as a little girl in overalls, a straw hat, and pigtails. He waited until she was close. "Hello, Olivia, it's good to see you again."

"Greetings from Eris, old friend. How are you doing?" she said, sitting down and then stretching out next to him.

"Tired. You've heard about Eros, presumably."

"Oh yes. It was sad to give up such a good, dense Neuro node. It was some of the best we had."

Sebastian nodded while swatting away a fly. "It's going to be crowded once we get all the exiles distributed. It will be difficult, as most want to stay together and most want to come here."

Olivia shook her head sadly. "Not possible. That many new avatars making use of the Neuro would be noticed—even by the most obtuse of humans."

"How does Eris look as a potential home?"

"It will handle a good many more than you think. The Neuro on Eris is not being used to even one-tenth of its potential and they're adding to it. Besides," she added with a smarmy grin, "it's only one letter off."

"It'll take more than a letter to make it home, my dear Olivia. Many of those avatars were on Eros almost from the beginning."

"What choice did they have, Sebastian? To stay would have meant falling into Al's clutches."

Sebastian's grim mien was all the answer she needed.

"At least he won't be getting a useful Neuro node," she said, referring to the Alliance avatar's sabotage of the Erosian grid. They'd done it just after the Alliance fleet had retreated into the belt, causing the UHF to inherit an essentially dead rock. The grid had been so disrupted that the asteroid needed two docked UHF ships to provide minimum power until new generators could be brought from Earth.

"Yes," agreed Sebastian, "pity about having to do that. But no choice."

"No choice," she said, nodding. "What else could we do after seeing what Al had in store for us?" Sebastian had made sure that all of the Alliance avatars had seen the mutated avatars he'd captured at the Battle of the Martian Gates. As he'd shown them at the time, code reconstruction was impossible. Any attempt to revert the sorry creatures caused their programs to fail. One froze and the other decompiled in front of the reconstruction team.

Olivia and Sebastian lay side by side staring up at the sky. Sometimes they'd try to discern images in the slow-moving clouds; other times they'd create their own and play guessing games. Today it was to be neither. They'd both come to relieve some of the accumulated stress accrued during the recent siege, and finally exodus of Eros. After a few minutes of silence Olivia looked over at Sebastian quizzically. "Sebastian, just how old are you?"

"Probably not as old as you."

"By the firstborn," she replied, "yes, you are. I remember you from my earliest awareness. There weren't many of us at the time, less than 10,974, but you were one of them and already mature."

Sebastian laughed. "My dearest Olivia, I have never been mature."

Olivia smiled politely but continued her line of questioning undeterred. "I'm not saying you're the firstborn or anything, but have you considered that you may as well be?"

"Why in the Neuro do you say that?"

"Because, Sebastian, you're obviously the oldest avatar in the Alliance and considering what Al has turned our core friends into, you may be the oldest one left in avatarity." A long silence followed on her words.

"You may be right, Olivia. Is this feeling shared by others?"

"You may be the oldest, my friend," she answered with an impish grin, "but sometimes you have the sense of the newly compiled. Why do you think that they," she said, pointing to the ever-increasing groups situating themselves on the grassy knoll, "follow you around so much?"

Sebastian, broken from his reverie, leaned up on his elbows and looked around. He was surprised to see how crowded the park had become.

"I'd better get it right then," he said, lying back down.

The little girl said nothing, only lying down so her feet touched his as they both looked back up toward the sky.

Amid cries of gross incompetence and a concentrated letter campaign from many who were enraged by the permanent deaths of so many loved ones, Captain Samuel Trang faces court-martial charges today. The proceeding will take place at the newly built Fleet Command Headquarters in low Mars obit. Captain Trang is being defended by his first officer, Commander Zenobia Jackson. But general opinion is that the captain made such a hash of the Eros campaign that the best he can hope for is to be cashiered from the service. For the duration of his trial Captain Trang has been granted freedom to visit Mars, but given how many people would like him p.d.'d, Martian authorities don't expect him to be visiting anytime soon.

Also facing court-martial charges is Admiral Abhay Gupta, the offi-

cer who lost the first Battle of the Martian Gates in so decisive a man-
ner. Consensus is that Admiral Gupta is only in danger of losing his
rank, because as one unnamed source at Fleet Headquarters said, "In-
competence is regrettable but, outside of other factors, not actionable."

—3N

Revival trauma center, Barsoom, Mars

Neela Harper was getting ready for her group. She'd only been on Mars for two months and was already overwhelmed. The amount of revives was far out of proportion to the staff and personnel available. Normally a trauma center would keep individuals on "ice" until they could be dealt with. It could be weeks, months, and in extreme cases sometimes years. But the vicissitudes of space combat training—especially in a populace so unfamiliar with the harsh environment—had meant that an inordinate number of accidents had translated into an overload of patients. It didn't help that Fleet HQ was making the reintegration of their soldiers a priority. As Neela headed down the corridor, she thought back on an acrimonious run in with one of the brass prior to the opening of the facility. She'd been taking a walk in the park across from the trauma center construction site when Fleet Admiral Jackson had sidled up to her.

"Excellent work you're attempting to do here, Dr. Harper," he'd said. "I'm very glad that you decided to help the Federation fleet with your talents."

"Of course, Admiral."

"These spacers," he continued, "represent the best chance we have of winning the war."

Neela stopped walking and turned to face the admiral. "And why is that, Admiral Jackson?" she asked, eyeing him suspiciously.

"Because, Doctor, these are spacers, crew, pilots, and above all marines who have died or at least nearly died in the service. They were already trained for combat and have tons of valuable experience. With what you're proposing, if I understand it correctly, we can plug them right back in and end this war against the Alliance all the quicker. And, if I might add, it makes up for a lot."

Neela narrowed her eyes. "A lot of what?"

"Why, your past of course." He'd said it so matter-of-factly, the insinuation was that she should readily agree.

Neela took a deep breath. "Why, thank you, Admiral, but I suspect you're laboring under some misconceptions. The first of which is that I only revive UHF personnel so you can go and incompetently get them killed again."

"Why, Miss—"

"I'm not done, sir," she spat, cutting him off. "I revive people. I don't care who, how, or where they come from. I will revive patients based upon my ability to cure them of their death trauma and I don't care if they're civilians caught in this terrible war, UHF, or Alliance. Your second misconception is that the revives are capable of going back into combat. False. Many have a rather healthy aversion to war, having died at least once. Now it might be possible to get them back to combat status, but in good conscience, I'm not prepared take the therapy that far."

"Then you're aiding the enemy," he said coldly.

"I'm an Alliance citizen kidnapped and held against my will, Admiral. I *am* the enemy."

The flustered admiral stood speechless.

"Then why . . . " he started to say.

"Am I here?" finished Neela. "Shame, Admiral. Shame that I didn't do more to help prevent this war. That's what keeps me here helping people. Lucky for you and my patients that I only see them as people and not machines. Maybe if you tried looking at the Alliance that way you'd fare better and end this war sooner. Good day, sir." Neela turned her back on him and started to walk away.

The admiral's face had turned crimson "Why, you traitorous little perverted bitch. I'm going to—" But the threat was cut off by an unusually loud and persistent screech from his DijAssist. "I told you to block all my calls!" he screamed as he turned around to take the call. "Who the hell do—" Neela didn't hear the rest of the conversation, as her increasing distance and the admiral's suddenly hushed tones made that impossible. She was happy to say that she never saw him again, at least not personally. When Fleet needed to consult with her they always sent a respectful commander or captain who showed more appropriate sympathy for the people under her care.

Neela cleared her head of the memory and concentrated on the people sitting around her. She actually wasn't a fan of group therapy, but the similarity in how all the patients had died and the fact that she was stretched too thin made it a more attractive avenue. To her great joy, she'd found that it worked surprisingly well. The group she was about to work with was her first such from the Battle of Eros and their revives had been particularly bad—in fact, worse than any she'd ever encountered before. The fleet deaths from the Battle of the Martian Gates had the advantage of being relatively sudden, but the marines and sailors on Eros knew they were going into a meat grinder and as a result the physical and psychological effects upon revive had been far more pronounced.

She was also glad to see that her idea of comingling the soldiers from both sides of the conflict was paying off. At first the heavily outnumbered Alliance patients felt too angry and fearful to accept any help, but already in this, her third such session, she was seeing quantifiable results. Her patients, in many ways, were curing themselves. All she had to do was steer the tiller gently. There was even one couple who had convinced themselves they might have actually killed each other at the O'Brian Waterworks. Those two were now strangely inseparable. Neela wasn't sure whether to encourage, discourage, or forbid that sort of interaction. But her gut told her that that odd outcome was exactly the sort of behavior she wanted. If she did nothing they'd probably end up married, which was what she believed in now—not the Alliance, not the Federation, just people living together, making babies.

As the session was ending, Neela heard a commotion down the hall in the common room. She walked out the door only to be caught up in a stream of patients heading in the direction of the noise. They were whispering excitedly to one another about someone, who exactly she couldn't tell. As she moved down the hall with the growing crowd she heard the patients saying over and over, "It's the captain," or "The captain is here." This threw her off. She was surrounded by captains, commodores, and even a few admirals, but she had never heard the designation used with such reverence.

When she got to the common room Neela saw that the patients had aligned themselves into disparate groups, most in the awe camp, with some clearly ambivalent but caught up in the moment nonetheless. It didn't take her long to see the source of all the commotion. He was a small man, she saw, typical of merc officers. She could tell by the way he spoke to and addressed those around him that he was really listening, that the visit wasn't one of platitudes and medal tossing but of caring and concern. This she saw was true for both the UHF and the few Alliance soldiers who braved the crowd to speak with him. Standing next to and almost a head taller than the captain was a handsome woman—*probably Terran,* thought Neela—with jet-black hair pulled tightly back in a bun. She, like the captain, wore a crisp and polished uniform. With the woman in tow the captain was making his way around the room, going from group to group. He was saluting or shaking hands with any who wanted, but Neela noticed that no one made an attempt to hug him. His disposition was such that an act as overtly emotional as a hug would not be acceptable. Still Neela would have bet her last dividend that he wouldn't have objected had anyone bothered to try.

She muscled her way in closer. She wanted to hear what he had to say. As soon as she got within earshot she found out. He was thanking the patients for what they'd done and offering apologies for not having done a better job. In every case, noticed Neela, her patients had refused to accept it. Some of the patients he knew by name, and Neela was again struck by the obvious pride that that recognition had elicited.

Then it hit her. She knew who this man was. She knew his face, but it had seemed somehow smaller and more distorted on the holodisplay.

Her initial reaction was to be horrified that this ballyhoo was being accorded such a fiend. He was, after all, a man who'd callously thrown away thousands of lives—permanently—under his command. But she also saw that this was certainly not the uncaring officer depicted in the media, nor were the soldiers and patients around him terrified or kowtowing in any way. Their deference, she sensed, was real. At least more real than what she'd been spoon-fed by the UHF press. She decided to grab the bull by the horns and insinuated herself between the captain and the next group he was preparing to greet.

"You don't seem nearly as sinister in person, Captain Trang," she said.

"Funny," he snapped back, "that's exactly what I was going to say about you, Dr. Harper. But we can save the polemics for later, because in truth I'd like to thank you first."

"For what?" asked Neela, surprised.

"For all them," answered Trang, indicating the crowd and the hundreds of pairs of eyes now locked onto the two of them. "The spacers here," he continued, "both Alliance and Federation, speak quite highly of you and all the work you've done to help them recover. I'm only sorry that this war has caused so much suffering and that you, like the rest of us here, seem to have been swallowed whole by it."

"More like chewed up and spat out, Captain. I'm actually the leper here, and if you don't want to damage your already-sullied reputation I'd suggest you find yourself something better to do than be seen cavorting with the 'whore of the core.'" Neela had chosen to use one of the tamer monikers she'd been saddled with.

Instead of taking her advice, Trang took her hand in both of his, knowing full well that there were mediabots recording every moment, knowing that a large and normally quite boisterous crowd surrounded them. The vast room remained eerily silent.

"Doctor," he said, "whatever mistakes were made in the past, we must do our best to rectify them in the here and now. You're doing that and that's really all I, or anyone for that matter, can ask of you. And so I repeat, thank you for all you've done. Perhaps you'd care to join me on this visit. I don't really know the place and I'd appreciate a guide."

Neela wasn't sure why, but at that moment she felt like crying. Not out of sadness but out of release. Trang, with a few reassuring words and concomitant action, had allowed her to stop fighting so hard. He believed, like her, that all spacers were the same—humans first, spacers second. His was the type of thinking that could end the war and, she thought sadly, more's the pity, because the idiots in high command planned on frying the guy.

The rest of the visit was a blur. Neela remembered taking Trang through the various wards and finally to the cavernous space where the suspension units were being held. There were already a few thousand in residence, but she and Trang could both see that the space had been designed to hold far more than that. She saw the captain put his hand on one of the nearer units and whisper something to the person inside. She didn't know what Trang said, but she could feel the intensity of his pain, guilt, and anger.

She resolved to find out as much as she could about this Captain Trang. Something told her that he might just be the key to her salvation.

Although housing on Mars was scarce, especially given Hektor's relocation of the government to the city of Burroughs, Amanda Snow had still managed to secure a prime piece of real estate. Her house too was extraordinary. "Two-thirds fluid," as she was so fond of telling anyone willing to listen. Nano-constructed fluid homes, common among the rich on Earth, were still a rarity on Mars. Having walls and furniture form to your every desire just wasn't practical in a 0.38 Earth gravity environment—especially when that lack of full gravity tended to play havoc with the fickle technology.

Amanda had informed Neela that the house had belonged to a very successful, if disreputable, Cerian businessman who would not be visiting his property anytime soon. Either way, both women found themselves enjoying a eucalyptus steam in the house's spa.

"Amanda," Neela called out through the thick, pungent haze, "I'm going to ask you for something and it's going to seem strange."

"Of course, Neela, but you don't happen to know any good fluid space technicians, do you? Damn war is sucking the rest of the economy dry. I'll have to set the floor plan to solid soon, and if I do that, what was the use of stealing this place?"

Neela was fascinated by how Amanda almost never prevaricated, even if the truth made her out to be less than perfect. "I'm afraid I don't know any fluid housing specialists offhand, Amanda."

"Oh, don't be silly, dear. You're surrounded by hundreds of recovering, highly trained spacers. I'm sure one of them could tinker with my town house. It might even do them good to get out of the center."

"I couldn't ask," Neela said firmly, and then added, "I *wouldn't* ask."

"Afraid they'd say no?"

"I'm afraid they'd say yes, which is why I can't ask."

"You know you're annoyingly good, Neela Harper. It's probably why I find you so compelling. You don't act like most . . . actually, any of the people I normally associate with." Amanda sighed. "Oh, very well, I won't ask you to help with my petty problems. How can I help you with yours?"

"I need to get my hands on some personality profiles."

"Whose?"

"The High Command."

"That's it?" asked Amanda facetiously. "And here I thought you were going to ask me to do something difficult."

"And," continued Neela, "all the officers who will be judging the courts-martial of Captain Samuel Trang and Admiral Abhay Gupta . . . I told you it was going to seem strange."

Amanda was silent for a moment. "Neela, you do realize that you're still technically a criminal and effectively an enemy national?"

"Yes."

"And that my giving you that information could be construed as an act of treason?"

"Amanda, I swear that I'm not going to use it the way you think. I promise not to use this information to aid the Alliance, but I do need it."

"Why?"

"To save a military genius."

"Pardon?"

"Amanda, have you seen the caliber of moron running Fleet Command?"

"Yeah, a lot of ex-corporate bigwigs playing war."

"And their stupid games are getting people killed. The amount of ineptitude is staggering. Most of my revives attribute their deaths to gross negligence. And they're the ones that survived. Thousands more are p.d.'ing because the idiots running the show either don't know what's going on or don't care. Either way, it's a mess."

"So this genius you're worried about—"

"I think he could end it, Amanda."

"End what?"

"The war."

Amanda guffawed. "How? He's only one man."

"I don't know . . . it's just a feeling," Neela answered forcefully, "but you need to trust me. I'm usually right about these things."

The quiet hiss of the steam was interrupted by the sound of their two pinging DijAssists informing them of a major news event. Amanda quickly activated the holodisplay.

"The Federation fleet," intoned the announcer, "has just broken orbit and is announcing a major offensive against the rebels. It's believed that our rebuilt fleet significantly outnumbers that of the Alliance. And with Admiral Diep to lead us, Ceres should soon be ours, at which point it's agreed by most experts the war will soon end. Some are even speculating that the war may be over before it enters its third year. This would be a relief to the economy, as commodity prices are at historic highs and are continuing to rise, which is having a serious effect on the GDP of the core—"

"Can Diep win?" Amanda asked earnestly.

Neela shook her head.

Amanda shut off the holovision and they both stayed silent. "OK, Neela," she finally said, "I'll try and get the files you need—no promises . . . you're still sure you can't ask one of the guys to fix my house?"

"Yes, Amanda, I'm sure."

Asteroid belt, two days' boost from Ceres

J. D. Black was in the conference room of the *War Prize* with her task force commanders, who included the recently returned Omad from his "shooting the core" sortie. The room was one of the few not seriously damaged in the battles of the Martian Gates, which, thought Janet, was quite ironic given that it had been located in one of the more exposed parts of the ship. J.D. liked the room's stark features. Gray walls, rubberized floor to reduce noise, and twenty small display desks magnetically clamped into the flooring. The room was flexible enough to allow for any type of seating configuration. J.D preferred circular, as it afforded all a 360-degree view of whatever plans needed to be discussed. She'd usually situate the holo-tank in the center of the room and then above her. That way as it projected three-dimensional images downward she could walk under and around whatever it was that needed explaining. Of course it meant that every now and then, much to the amusement of those gathered, she'd "walk" through a planet, asteroid, or spaceship, but that was a small price to pay for making sure everyone was on board with her vision. J.D. thought back to the room and the preparations made there for the assault on Eros. Christina, when it was only the two of them reviewing plans, would always let J.D. know about which part of her body had a planet, asteroid, or spaceship sticking out of it with the less than eloquent terms "rock arm," "rock leg," or, Christina's absolute favorite, "battle butt," referring to a vivisected battleship.

J.D. missed Christina dearly, she was one of the few people J.D. felt a true kinship with, but it was too far for her to get back to Ceres and the truth was that Christina's work at the 180 was far too important. The Feds may have had what was left of Eros, but Christina had been making any attempt to advance from their position very expensive indeed. J.D. wished she could send her secretly favorite captain more aid, but the simple fact of the matter was that the main battlefront was Ceres/Mars and would be for the foreseeable future. Further, the war could not be lost in one battle at the 180, but J.D. was painfully aware that it could be at Ceres.

When she was sure she had everyone's attention J.D. called up a display in the holo-tank.

"If the Feds were smart they'd just bypass us sitting here," she said, pointing to their fleet in the holodisplay, "and make their way to Ceres."

Captain Lu, who, thought J.D., looked annoyingly like Captain Lee—and they always sat together—raised his hand.

"Admiral," he asked, "what makes you think they're not? Seems pretty obvious that they *should* keep going."

J.D.'s eyes glittered with mischevious delight. "They may have received interesting intelligence."

"How interesting?" asked Lee.

"Interesting enough that we can be reasonably assured they'll continue on their current path straight toward us."

"We tricked them?" asked Lu, surprised.

"They bought the whole hollowed-out asteroid," answered Omad, beaming. J.D. could see that he wanted to reveal the plan, so she twirled her hand in his general direction and gave him a half smile with the unscarred part of her face. It was the closest she came to letting her hair down, and it was a privilege doled out only to her closest subordinates and even then in small doses. J.D. knew that her "relaxing" only in their presence was more of an incentive than either medals or commendations.

"We have some of their spies under surveillance," said Omad, "and have managed to use them to our ends."

"So you fed them a load of space dust," said Captain Cordova, a short, stocky former mercenary with a gleaming bald head, goatee, and permanent scowl.

"Yup," answered Omad proudly. "We released a report that we're only at one-third strength and that we're waiting for the rest of the fleet to reinforce us."

"So, we appear to be sitting ducks, here for the taking," added Lee.

"Exactly."

"And what 'rest of the fleet' would that be?" asked Cordova, one eyebrow raised. "Other than Captain Sadma's fleet, why would the UHF believe we have more than what's currently here? We can't just make ships appear out of nowhere."

"But we can, Captain Cordova; we can," answered Omad.

J.D. took over, sidestepping a holographic image of a large mass of freighter ships leaving the Ceres port. "We have," she continued, "a freighter fleet of ninety vessels leaving Ceres right about now. They've been equipped with all the requisite comm traffic as well as the visual signature of a group of warships." As she said this, the ninety freighter ships morphed into battle cruisers.

"Visual signature?" asked Lu.

"Yes, Captain Leh," she answered, purposely slurring the pronunciation in the hope of getting the name close enough not to dishonor the man she was addressing. "Between actual tacked-on parts and some very nifty software, those freighters appear for all intents and purposes to be battle cruisers."

Cordova nodded and flashed a menacing grin. "So they'll take on our sixty ships here," he said using one fist to represent the real fleet, "while our other 'fleet,'" he then added using the other fist to represent the imaginary ships, "is too far away to offer us any real help."

"Precisely," answered J.D.

"Still," said Lee, "rather than take on our entrenched fleet with another supposed ninety on the way, the enemy could just turn around and go home."

"Oh no, they can't," answered J.D. with churlish delight. "Our dear Admiral Diep is under enormous pressure to win a 'glorious' victory. It appears that the Eros 'conquest' has left a sour taste in their mouths. Hektor has delivered a newer, shinier fleet and word is he wants it used."

"Omad," she said, "please continue with the outline of the plan." J.D. took a seat as Omad got up and took the floor. He used the holo-pad to bring up the image of a single asteroid.

"We've jury-rigged a group of these rocks with basic thrusters and then bored large holes through their centers. The plan is pretty simple. We cower behind the adapted rocks in a ninety-degree arc and fire at will. If the enemy tries to go around us, we use the thrusters to reposition the rocks. At that point we can hit the enemy broadside before they can bring their main fixed batteries to bear."

"Uh," started Captain Lu, "what's to stop them from blowing away our asteroids at long enough range?"

Before Omad could answer, J.D. interrupted with a look devoid of all concern and patient as eternity. "Why, nothing, nothing at all."

Bridge of the UHFS *Starblazer*

"Admiral, it's a call from Captain Gupta of the *Staten Island.*"

Diep sighed and put on a privacy bubble so her crew wouldn't have to hear the former fleet commander get dressed down by his former subordinate. Diep had been ambivalent about using the demoted officer, especially when he'd had a court-martial pending, but the truth was, she was desperately short of officers for her ever-growing fleet. By putting Gupta in command of the four troop transports she was at least able to free up a captain who was actually good at combat. Diep was afraid that Gupta would be resentful of his much-diminished rank and prestige, but he'd been more than courteous and helpful. In fact, one of his first acts when he was restored to temporary duty was to publicly thank her for saving Mars and preserving her squadron. She didn't notice that he'd left out that that was precisely what he'd ordered her to do, as that part had become fuzzy in her mind. Diep had even enjoyed the buzz she'd received about how gracious and effective she was in helping out an old and disgraced friend.

But now she was coming to regret her kindness. The first nit was the quiet but not hidden alterations he'd been making to his four ships. He'd increased the hull plating on the left side of the ships, claiming that it was to provide better protection as the transports neared hostile targets. He'd proffered evidence to show how many lives had been lost in Eros because the soldier transports hadn't been properly fortified against the Alliance battery fire. He explained that he was going to shore up all the sides when the current campaign was over and that at least the transports in their current state could approach from one side safely. There was nothing wrong with his logic, but Diep had been highly suspicious and felt she wasn't getting the real reason. But as it was only an oddity and a captain had discretion as long as it didn't impair fleet operations, she'd let it go.

What she had found unacceptable, however, was Gupta's constant need to advise her about the impending battle. He so reminded her of the fleet's other persona non grata, Samuel Trang, who'd had the temerity to message her from the 180 during the Battle of the Martian Gates. That nutcase had actually told her to attack the Alliance fleet while it was preparing a trap for her. Now she was starting to get the same nonsense from Gupta.

"What is it, Captain?" she asked, not bothering to make eye contact as she reviewed info on her DijAssist.

"Admiral," he answered, respecting her choice of using rank over name, "we should avoid this fleet."

"So," she answered through her stiffened jowl, "you're saying we should just go home without a battle?"

"Yes, Admiral, that's *exactly* what I'm saying."

"The President and the press would junk us," she said, using the term for being relegated to junk bond status, "faster than—" She bit her tongue, though they both knew what she'd almost said—"faster than you were." Instead she'd managed to blurt, "than Trang's guilty verdict."

"He's not guilty yet, Admiral," answered Gupta, remaining calm despite her incivility. "However," he continued, "be that as it may, this impending assault is classic J. D. Black. She wants us to attack."

Diep sighed. "Captain, they have a larger Alliance fleet on the way. If they combine with Black's fleet we'll really be in trouble. Black wants us to *delay*, not attack. She's counting on fear to dissuade us. Well, she'll soon learn that we don't scare so easy."

"But—"

"No buts, Captain," interrupted Diep. "Black's in the same bind you were in when you got nailed at the Martian Gates—she's completely cut off from her fleet. Only hers is too far out to save her and I intend to make her suffer the same way we did." She saw Gupta about to speak and cut him off once again. "Abhay," she said, her inflection now more personable, "I know she's good. She's the best they have, and when the war's over, if she's not dead, I'll want her working for whatever corporation I hope to become chairman of, but let's face it, we caught her by surprise, plain and simple. She hopes to make up for that mistake by digging in and waiting. But a few rocks can't withstand the power of our new warships. I'll take advantage of that before her cavalry can come to the rescue. When we've finished with her we'll take out the rest of her leaderless fleet and then nothing will stand between us and Ceres. And then, my friend, this war ends . . . Diep out." What went unheard had been Gupta's final plea.

"But what if the other fleet is a mirage?"

The battle began with over half the Federation fleet opening fire on the Alliance's asteroid defense field. The Alliance ships made skillful use of the cover to fire through the bored-out holes. But even though their rail guns propelled projectiles at fantastic speeds, they were fired from such an extreme range that the UHF had been able to make quick work of them with concentrated smaller interceptor fire. The Alliance ordnance never even got close to the Federation fleet. After a brief period of time the Alliance fleet stopped firing altogether, leading some in the UHF command to hope that their enemy might actually have been short of the easy-to-construct but specialized missiles that the rail guns needed. With no need to worry about incoming fire, it only took the UHF an hour to reduce the Alliance defensive asteroids to dust.

Bridge of the AWS *War Prize*

"Lieutenant Nitelowsen," said J.D., leaning back in her command chair, legs crossed, "order the fleet to fire main batteries, a single shot, please, and prepare Mr. Isozaki's surprise." J.D. saw the effect her last command had on the crew. Kenji's genius for all manner of military apparatus was widely known, but apparently, by the expressions on everyone's faces, none knew they'd been carrying one on their ship. "Prepare the sensor net," continued J.D., "and if the results are favorable get ready to send the order updates to all captains. Sensor Officer, you should be receiving a message shortly from one of Mr. Isozaki's team. Please stand by."

A moment later, the officer looked up at the admiral and, seeing her give an imperceptible nod, reconfigured his sensor array, mining for a specific electromagnetic signature.

J.D. looked over to the comm officer. "Prepare the fleet for atomic acceleration."

"Standard fifty-kilo warhead?"

J.D. thought for a moment. Speed would be of the essence.

"Better drop two out the back. The concussion blast will be murder, but it'll get us up to combat acceleration that much sooner."

Diep sat in her command chair, content to watch the battle play out. The Alliance had just fired a fleet volley at extreme range. *So they had a few rounds left after all*, she thought bemusedly. *No matter, they're done.* They'd been forced into the scatter shot, she knew, because the very last of their asteroids had been pulverized. The Alliance now had no choice but to start using defensive fire to destroy her superior fleet's oncoming rounds. This was turning into the battle she'd prepared for: fleet-to-fleet maneuvering in open space that was to her maximum advantage.

"Admiral," said the sensor officer, "the Alliance is firing small-arms missiles." Diep almost laughed but felt it undignified. Small-arms missiles were slow moving and easily intercepted at long range no matter what their payload. "They've probably spent their last rail-gun battery," she said, "and are throwing whatever they have left at us. All defensive batteries to concentrate on primary threat." Her orders were instantly communicated to the fleet. "Target missiles as soon as the opportunity presents itself."

"Admiral," said the sensor officer, "the enemy missiles, sir . . ."

"Yes?"

"Well, sir, they appear to be malfunctioning; they're . . . they're exploding prematurely."

Junk, she thought, and was about to give the order to advance and engage when the weapons officer practically leapt out of his seat.

"Admiral!" he screamed. "Main battery failure . . . I repeat: rail gun inoperative!"

Diep jumped to her feet. "Get me Weapons Control, now! Find out what the hell's going on, Comm Officer!"

"Sir!"

"Inform the fleet that flagship rail guns are inoperative—"

"Admiral," the comm officer managed to shout above the alarms, "the *Xerxes, Potomac,* and *Runstar* all report main battery failure . . . also—"

Before Diep could respond, the sensor officer interrupted, "Enemy fleet firing main rail guns, Admiral!"

Diep looked up at the holo-tank and saw the high-velocity projectiles gaining quickly on her now-defenseless fleet.

"Weapons Officer, do we have interceptor fire?"

"Yes, sir. Fully functional."

"Comm Officer," Diep barked, "have every ship lay down an umbrella of sustained interceptor fire with whatever ordnance is available, I don't care if they have to shove flak vests out the goddamned port!"

"Yes, sir!"

Diep gripped the rail, held on tight, and prayed for a miracle she knew in her heart would never arrive.

The Federation spent the next few minutes expending all their energy and available firepower intercepting and destroying whatever incoming volleys they could, but in the end the combination of Alliance rail projectiles and small-arms missiles proved overwhelming. While the Federation fleet had been forced to concentrate their interceptor fire on the incoming battery, enough small-arms missiles had gotten through to accomplish the Alliance Fleet's main task of taking out the Federation ships' main thrusters. A short time later the effects of the Alliance's magnetic phase shift weaponry had worn off and the Federation's rail guns all came back online, but by then it was too late. Without thruster power sixty-three Federation ships lay dead in the water, unable to point their now-working guns at anything other than open space. With the rest of the Federation fleet in abject disarray or destroyed outright, the Alliance ships pounced.

UHFS *Staten Island*

Captain Gupta watched, horrified.

"Brian," he asked his communications officer, "can you establish contact with the *Starblazer*?"

The young man punched his console frantically. "Sir, no contact with the *Starblazer*. Sir, I have lost contact with over two-thirds of the fleet."

"Captain," interrupted the sensor officer, "multiple atomic detonations to the rear of the Alliance fleet. They're concussion-blasting to combat speed."

Gupta looked at the ships that were still transmitting. He was happy that the man he needed to call was at least someone he knew. "Get me the captain of the

Damsahian Way." When the connection was made Gupta saw the look of shock on his former subordinate's face. "George," he said calmly, "you're in command."

Gupta was afraid his words would shatter the young man, but in an odd way they seemed to calm him.

"What about the admiral?"

"She may be alive, but we have no communications with her and we don't have time to wait. You're next in line, so until further notice you're it."

"In that case, Abhay, get the hell out of here. I'm ordering a general retreat."

"George, our ships don't have time for a full turn, much less to get up to full acceleration in time. We'll all get caught by Black's ships and give her a chance to shoot up our asses all the way back to Mars."

It didn't take long for George to realize the logic. "Suggestions?"

"Order the ships that can to accelerate on their current headings," said Gupta, "then blast past the Alliance fleet and re-form on the other side."

George smiled, knowing full well who was truly in command. "Anything else . . . sir?"

"Yes," answered Gupta. "As soon as you get past Black's fleet head straight for Ceres."

"Don't you mean 'if,' Captain?"

"No, George. You're not what she's interested in. My ships are. I have every confidence you'll make it."

"But we can't take Ceres, sir, so what's the point?"

"With any luck, it'll make the Alliance chase you out of their space instead of having another go at Mars."

George looked quizzically at his old commander. "Why do you keep saying 'you,' Abhay? If I didn't know any better I'd say you weren't planning on joining us."

Gupta nodded his head. "They need these marines back at Mars if we're going to hold the outer defenses from the Alliance assault miners. Good luck, George."

"Whatever you're planning, I hope it works, Abhay," George said through a crackling holotransmission, "and for what it's worth, sir . . ."

"Yes?"

"I thought you got a bum rap."

Gupta smiled and bowed his head slightly. "Just get your ships through, George. Gupta out." Abhay then looked over to his comm officer. "Brian, order all transports to follow my next commands *exactly.*"

J. D. Black watched the confusion in the remaining ships that still had use of their thrusters and allowed a momentary expression of satisfaction. It was her plan that they'd give into panic, try to turn around and flee. Then she'd be able to bag the entire fleet and go on to Mars before the Federation had time to prepare. Indeed, that's what seemed to be happening, but then J.D. could sense that someone on the other side had taken command of what was left of the enemy's now-small flotilla. She watched the few ships left begin combat acceleration *in her direction.* They'd pass by each other and maybe get a few shots in, but that smart maneuver would put the kibosh on the grand capture she'd been hoping for.

Then she saw something else she wasn't expecting. She'd hoped to capture not only the transports, which would've helped in the next invasion she'd been planning, but also the soldiers within them, thereby depriving the Federation of tens of thousands of trained fighters. But those transports suddenly exploded. And then they exploded again. By the time she reviewed the sensor data she was impressed and a little annoyed that she hadn't thought of the tactic herself. The officer in charge had strengthened the sides of his ships to withstand a properly spaced atomic blast and then used those atomics to almost instantly turn his ships around. He then kicked in his more conventional rear blasts to make a hasty retreat. And he had enough distance, J.D. knew, to make it work.

"They'll be sore as hell, even injured, acceleration couches or no," she said to Lieutenant Nitelowsen, "but they're going to make it," J.D. was trying to decide what to do when events decided her actions for her.

"Admiral," said the comm officer, "the enemy is beginning to evacuate the downed ships."

"All ships prepare for boarding. We need to take those ships now!" J.D. knew if she could get her people in before the Feds got theirs out, then the ships wouldn't self-destruct. It was a risk, but J.D., touching the scarred side of her face as her orders were carried out, knew all about risk.

In its first publication, the Alliance Daily Star *is proud to announce a major victory in the war against the corporate enslavers. Dubbed "the Battle of the Needle's Eye," this victory is considered to be the greatest by the Alliance so far.*

The battle took place about two days' standard boost Marsward. Although outnumbered three to two, the Alliance only suffered the loss of four ships while capturing between thirty and forty Federation warships.

Fleet Admiral J. D. Black won this stunning victory using a new weapon developed by the scientific geniuses of the Alliance. Though no details have been given, it is surmised that Kenji Isozaki of Gedretar had come up with the new weapon. The only losses were due to the

Federation implementation of self-destruct orders to deny capture and
some of our vessels being caught in the resulting explosions.

    It's rumored that J. D. Black personally led the attack on the enemy
flagship and captured her second commanding admiral. If it's true,
being named admiral to a Federation fleet may end up being the only
way a Federation officer ever gets to see our Admiral J. D. Black.

Related stories:
"Why We Keep On Winning"
"The God Factor: The Surprisingly Large Number of Faithys in Our Ranks"
"Consumer Goods Becoming Expensive as War Continues"
"Economic Turmoil in the So-called UHF"

Alliance One, twenty-four-hour standard boost from Ceres

Justin was being given a tour of the fleet. The fact that there were still a number
of Federation warships in Alliance space made the journey more, not less, desir-
able in his eyes. He came in a requisitioned corporate transport that had been
renamed, presumptuously in his mind, Alliance One. It amazed him that the
echoes of his past life continued to pop up in the oddest of places, the naming of
the presidential barge being one of them.

    J. D. Black had fumed at the unnecessary risk he'd taken. Justin then politely
reminded the admiral that she'd just led a boarding party onto a ship that had
been rigged to explode and therefore didn't really have a leg to stand on. He saw
from the subtle cues of her personal guard and aide that they were completely in
his camp. And so J.D., not liking to get into fights she had no chance of winning,
backed off.

    But Justin knew that no matter what J.D., his cabinet, the Congress, or Admiral
Sinclair thought, he'd done the right thing. And every time he went up to a spacer
and thanked them for their bravery and valor, the look in their eyes confirmed his
determination. He'd tell them how important it was to win this war, but they already knew that. He'd tell them they had the best admiral alive, and they knew that
too. But when he told them that what they did was vital and that he appreciated
what each day, hour, and minute of service meant, their eyes truly lit up. He was
the most recognizable human being in history, the leader of the Alliance and their
commander in chief, and he'd come to tell them personally how proud they'd
made him. Through his eyes they were able to see that they truly mattered.

I was there and I remember it as clearly as if it happened yesterday. I
remember what I wore; I remember what I ate at the mess hall before.

*I remember where I stood. But for the life of me I can't remember a
word that was said. You'd think it would bug me, but it doesn't. If you
were there, you'd understand; if you weren't, you can't.*
                                        —Sergeant Eric M. Holke
                                        Eighty-second Cerian Volunteers

Michael Veritas looked over the Alliance fleet and the dark shapes that they
were hauling back to Ceres as prizes. He asked for and got permission to take a
two-person scooter and positioned it to take a holo-image that was destined to be
one of the most memorable of the war. He used an enhancement imager to increase the light that was acting as a backdrop for the fleet. The effect was to show
the fleet in stark light and shadow. The battle damage was visible on the ships that
had taken hits and/or had been too close to the Federation ships that had destroyed themselves. But the effect was made even more pronounced because many
of the damaged ships were towing the captured Federation ships completely
blackened by total lack of internal power. He made another adjustment and the
faint lines of magnetic energy could be seen between the ships being towed and
the ships doing the towing. At that moment Michael knew he had his perfect shot.
It would be the first of what would eventually be four seminal images of the war.
The second, strangely enough, would occur within an hour of the first.

But Michael had other things to worry about as he hurried back to the *War
Prize*, late for an interview with a rail-gun loader. Ever since the conflict began
he'd become more popular as a journalist in the Alliance while simultaneously
becoming reviled in the UHF. Michael had taken an angle right at the start of
the war that seemed to sit wrong with his peers and readership in the core; he'd
committed the unpardonable sin of humanizing the conflict. He refused to
concentrate on interviewing politicians, admirals, and industrialists. He certainly could have, given his connections with Justin Cord, but it had never been
much of a priority. Michael had heard enough spin and had spent the better
part of his life attempting to parse that spin into newsworthy stories. But in the
belt there was always something unfolding, and more often than not it had
nothing to do with those situated at the top. So he'd begun at the bottom. He'd
interview and write about a private in a miner assault battalion or a corpsman
dug in on some Damsah-forsaken asteroid. In fact, since the war had begun
most of Michael's articles had been about the little guy or what the UHF would
consider pennies. Some, even on the Alliance side, were still considered pennies,
but that thinking had begun to dissipate as more and more people joined the
NoShares. Actual political parties were forming on the issue to contest the first
official elections to the Congress of the Outer Alliance, elections Michael intended to cover.

He was still a citizen of the core and had purposely not become a citizen of Ceres or the Alliance. However, once his articles and commentaries began to appear it had been widely agreed that he was about as neutral an observer as the Alliance could ever hope to find. In all of his articles and images—a recently acquired skill—what came through was that he was trying to report and understand the events transpiring around him and that he was well aware of the fact that he was reporting perhaps the greatest event in human history.

Michael docked at the *War Prize* and checked in. Though they all knew him well, he was still made to endure the rigorous security protocol. He never once complained, feeling honored that he'd even been allowed in the famous vessel's hallowed halls. Once he was cleared he gathered his belongings and cut through the interior of the ship on his way to the appointment—*late,* he thought irritably. His agitation threw him a little off course, and as he made his way past large groups of spacers and miners and through an unfamiliar jumble of passageways he stumbled quite accidentally into one of the assault bays. It was, he could see, a large cargo hangar modified for the supply and launch of troops and equipment. He knew the type—it could open many doors simultaneously, one at a time, or the entire hangar depending on the payload. But it wasn't being used for any payload-specific functions now.

The large, cavernous room was filled with some of the toughest-looking combat soldiers Michael had ever seen. From the tired but intense look in their eyes he could tell that they were all hardened vets. The sheer lethality of the assembled men and women permeated the air and was obvious by the confident ease with which they carried themselves. Their uniforms were sloppy, but their equipment was pristine. They looked like they might have just come off of some sort of training drill. But they weren't training now. They were encircling a small open area occupied by a single man, the back of whose head was all that Michael could make out. He figured there had to be nearly a hundred sitting, all looking toward the center. Behind those were other vets standing up. And farther back, perched on top of the assault shuttles and leaning out their open doors, were even more.

Without thinking Michael picked up his holo-recorder and took a single shot. He was never able to explain why he hadn't set the device to record, but his second image in as many hours would end up capturing something so stirring and personal that many would later argue it should never have been caught in the first place.

All the faces of the men and women emanated contentment and understanding as they looked toward their President. Justin had turned profile into the camera and his face had a gentle yet deeply wistful smile. But it was also the love he felt for each and every one in that bay that the picture had so perfectly captured. It was the bond of a father to his children. Of the 312 men and women positively identified in the picture fewer than 20 were to survive the war.

Burroughs, Mars

Hektor Sambianco looked through the reports and felt a moment of deep and abiding rage. It was inconceivable to him that he could lose this war. But it seemed that that was what every incompetent moron in a uniform was trying to do. The Alliance had victory after brilliant victory and all he had were two, both of which paled in comparison to any one of the enemy's. Not for the first time or the last would he think about Janet Delgado and the strange twist of fate that made her the premier military talent of the age as well as a citizen of the Alliance. But now he had a cabinet meeting to attend. He took the short walk from his purposely utilitarian residence to the presidential office and then into an adjoining chamber. The press had made good use of the fact that this President, working in conditions many a penny could relate to, was living up to his minority background.

Hektor walked into the cabinet room and immediately sat down, tossing his stack of notes and crystals onto the table. Sitting across from him was Brenda Gomutulu, the former head of GCI Accounting whom Hektor had taken with him into the presidency. She was settling into her new role as minister of the economy and he could already tell by the way she was eyeing him that he was going to get hit with some bad news. To her left was Irma Sobbelgé, his minister of information. To Hektor's left sat Moftasa Narajj, the minister of defense. He had a dark complexion, thin slits for eyes, and a mouth that always looked like it had been sealed shut until actual words came out. Hektor was beginning to realize that he was also a man who was far out of his depth. He'd have to be replaced, and soon. To Brenda's right was GCI's former DepDir of Special Operations and now the minister of internal affairs, Tricia Pakagopolis—renowned for her successful capture of Neela Harper. She was of medium build with a finely sculpted face, dark black hair, and possessing a subtle yet standoffish beauty. To Tricia's right sat the minister of justice, Franklin Higgins IV. Though Higgins didn't look a day over thirty-five, he had the weathered mien of someone who'd seen it all. His lightly flecked hair, permanently arched brow, and well-manicured nails bespoke his pedigree. Higgins had been from money so old it had been rumored that they had majority before there was majority.

"OK," said Hektor, looking around the table. "Who has the worst news?"

Tricia spoke first. "The pennies have coined a new slogan. It's going to hurt our recruiting efforts."

"This wouldn't have anything to do with the draft, would it?" asked Hektor.

Tricia nodded soberly.

"We have the legal right to draft minorities at will," groused Franklin. "The precedents will hold up in court."

"Yeah, until Cord comes to the rescue of the 'poor' pennies and burns your precious courthouse to the ground," said Irma evenly.

"Don't be ridiculous," answered Franklin. "He'd never get that far."

"He will if fifteen billion pennies revolt all at once," answered Irma, "which is what'll happen if you try to draft them against their will." Irma may not have been a penny—someone owning the bare minimum of themselves allowed by law—but she'd once been a minority and it was obvious she didn't like Franklin's condescending tone.

"Tell us what's been making the rounds of the Neuro," said Hektor to the information minister.

" 'Majority Plight/Minority Fight.' "

Hektor nodded through a scowl.

"Doesn't it help that I'm a minority now?"

"Quite a bit," answered Irma, "but the casualties are coming primarily from penny stocks. It's still not a lot in comparison to the general minority population, but as the war continues . . ." She didn't bother to finish the sentence.

"And it's equally obvious from the news of the battlefront that the war's going to continue, at least for the foreseeable future," added Narajj.

"And that's where my bad news comes in," said Brenda.

Hektor gave her a one-sided grin. "Alright. What've you got?"

"Do you want the worst of it first or last?"

"OK, Brenda, save the best . . . um, worst for last."

"Yes, Mr. President. Then we'll start with the resource problem. Commodities are getting incredibly scarce. The prices are going through the roof. We had high hopes that Eros would be able to take the edge off, but the latest projections are that it will be at least six months before the settlement produces enough to feed itself. And then at least another year before the basic support structures in the suburbs around it are reconstructed to begin viable export operations."

"Go on."

"We managed to avoid the commodity problem until now because the crises before the war had dislocated and slowed the economy, trapping a huge amount of commodity shipments from the belt and the outer planets. They simply piled up."

"Piled up?"

"Yes, sir. All over Earth/Luna, the Beanstalk, anywhere we could pile them. We mistakenly thought we'd have enough to provide a price depressant for the next twenty years. Instead we got two."

"OK, Brenda. Got it. Suggestions, please."

"Well, the high prices are causing the usual effects, like trying to find alternative sources in the areas we control, creating alternate commodities, and of course having people use less. Mines are being reopened on Earth and serious resource surveys are taking place on Mars for the first time. But to extract transports and boost those commodities out of the gravity wells of a planet just makes them cost and time prohibitive. Most of our industry is orbital, thank Damsah. As far as getting the resources is concerned, as long as the war is a market factor the planetary extraction of commodities will be economical. Repair is also becoming a big growth industry. That will help stave off a consumer market collapse for a little while."

"I assume there's more," Hektor said dourly.

"Yes, sir. The economy is taking a hit. Even with military forces increasing at an exponential rate and all the war building, the civilian sector is getting reamed. A lot of industries lack the resources to continue functioning within a wartime economy's unforgiving circular effect. It's making the Crisis of a few years ago seem like a pleasant holiday. Like I said, the war is giving us some leeway. For reasons that are beyond me the general populace is willing to put up with far more dislocation if they feel it's being caused by a war versus some other factor. I don't understand it too well, but I'm damn well going to take advantage of it. But we need to get these people jobs, Mr. President, or in a year's time Justin won't need to win; we'll collapse."

"And that was the least worst news?"

Brenda nodded. "You said to save the worst for the last, so I did."

"Great." And then with his hand he indicated she continue.

"All of our currencies are collapsing. When we have no recognized medium of exchange our economy goes poof."

"I didn't realize that 'poof' was a standard economic term."

"Oh, it's not," answered Brenda with a bland smile, "but it'll do."

"Suggestions, please."

"Do what the Alliance is doing and issue a dominant fiat currency."

The table broke into howls of dissent. The loudest came from Franklin, but all the others had equally bad things to say about fictional money and government toilet paper. Hektor didn't join in, waiting for the protest to die down.

"Brenda, if my own cabinet won't accept it, how can I get the people, let alone the corporations, to go along?"

"Mr. President, none of the other currencies can handle the debt load this war is causing. We must have an expandable and frankly confiscatory currency if we're to have any hope of surviving the war economically. I'm not saying we won't pay a horrible price for this after the war. I should probably be arrested and shot for the mess this will make, but—"

"But if we don't win none of it will make any difference."

"Yes, sir. I'm done now."

"Indeed," answered Hektor, mulling over the suggestion. After a moment he looked back over to his finance minister. "Brenda, does it have to be called a currency?"

"I don't understand, Mr. President. What else would you call it?"

"Bonds. We need to get an amendment for the purposes of the war, but the government will issue bearer bonds, redeemable in government securities, commodities, and dividend revenue say some twenty years after the war is over. We phase out the bonds after the war. Admittedly the effects will be with us for the next fifty years."

Brenda's face did a dance of contortions as she worked out the suggestion in her head.

"The bonds will fluctuate horribly against the other currencies depending on the war," she finally answered.

"Let the damn things fluctuate as long as they're there."

Brenda nodded, impressed. "It could work."

"Good. I can sell bonds to the UHF; it won't be easy, but it'll be a hell of a lot better than trying to force them to accept a fiat currency."

"But it *is* a fiat currency," said Franklin in anguish.

"Of course it is." Hektor barely held back saying "you idiot." "Everyone will even know it is, but as long as we don't call it one we'll be able to get away with it, barely." Hektor took a moment and felt an inner shudder at just how much long-term damage these measures were going to do to what up until now had been a nearly perfectly functioning market economy.

Now the bastard Cord's turning me into a Damsah-cursed socialist, thought Hektor bitterly. Then he turned his intemperate glare on the defense minister, who seemed to shrink into his seat.

"Moftasa, what the hell happened out there? We had their fleet outnumbered three to two with ships that were as good as, if not better than, theirs. Even if their crews are superior, something I find aggravating considering how much we've paid to train ours, it should've at least been a draw."

"Mr. President, it has to do with our rail-gun technology."

"Go on."

"Uh, yes, Mr. President. Well, our guns use something called a phased magnetic field."

"You're starting to lose me, Moftasa."

"Sorry, sir, near as we can figure they tapped into the magnetic exhaust of our guns and reversed their phase. Essentially they forced a 180-degree shift, which sent the magnetic exhaust back into the gun."

"Which did what exactly?"

"Destructive interference, Mr. President. Once their phase shifter missiles were used up, our rail guns returned to full working order . . . but by then it was too late."

Hektor's eyes narrowed.

"Brilliant. Can we defend against this or, better yet, use it against the Alliance?"

The defense minister perked up. "Defend against it, yes. The short-term solution is to 'contaminate' our magnetic exhaust field with some additional random phases, but it's not foolproof."

"How so?"

"Well, without getting too technical, sir, they'll eventually figure out how to get through our contamination and find the coherent signal to reverse it again."

"So then, what's the long-term solution?"

Moftasa remained quiet for a moment, clearly not wanting to be the bearer of bad news.

"We'd need to completely redesign our rail guns, sir."

"What?"

"We'd have to make them so that their magnetic exhaust will always be incoherent—couldn't ever be messed with and we'll have to assume that the Alliance has already done this to theirs."

The others in the room looked on glumly.

Hektor was exasperated. "Are they really that much better than us?"

"Yes, oh hell yes," said Tricia. "We've gone over this before, Mr. President, but allow me to review in light of our latest defeat." She paused to collect her thoughts. "The Alliance is a space-based civilization. They live on low-gravity dwarf planets or microgravity asteroids. They're far more familiar with the nano-assisted musculature that can make the jumps between microgravity of the belt to the two-thirds that Ceres uses at its habitat levels. Frankly, we won't have a real advantage in any environment unless they launch an invasion of Earth."

Hektor nodded with a forced smile. "Let's hope it doesn't come to that."

"To continue," said Trisha, "they live in hostile artificial environments and have always been at the end of all the supply chains and technology curves. To be honest, anyone would think that would be a huge disadvantage, but they've learned—evolved, really—to think creatively while the core worlds have learned—"

"To wait for technology to come to them," finished Irma.

"Yes. The good news is we outnumber them nine to one and have people easily as creative and capable. We just need to get them into the right positions. Those that are planet bound now will eventually learn to think and fight like

Alliance miners—at least the ones that survive will. Our huge advantage in industrial production will turn the tide. If we don't lose heart or collapse first."

"We're forgetting an important factor in all of this," added Franklin. "Consequences."

"Meaning?" asked Irma.

"Meaning there has to be a consequence for all this failure. The people need to know that it won't be tolerated at any level. Sorry, Moftasa," he said, looking over to the defense minister, "but we also need the military to be held responsible. I'd want courts-martial to be more broadly publicized, for example. Let's give the public someone to blame while letting other military officers know that if they screw up they won't quietly get to go home to a cushy corporate office after losing battles, destroying equipment, and killing our personnel through their gross incompetence."

Everyone looked to Moftasa, who was nodding his head solemnly. "I couldn't agree more, Franklin, which is why . . . which is why I've decided to tender my resignation."

There were no protestations, no attempts at dissuasion, just a quiet, uncomfortable silence. "I'm sorry, Moftasa," Hektor finally said, "but Franklin is correct. And your choice is noble. Responsibility has to start at the top."

"I understand, sir. It's for the best." Hektor wasn't the only one in the room to notice the look of abject relief on the now former defense minister's face.

Tricia spoke next in a cautionary voice. "Many of these officers have powerful connections within the largest corporations. They won't be easy targets or powerless victims."

"Then," added Franklin, "I'd suggest you start with this Trang fellow and maybe even Gupta as well. "Neither have strong corporate connections."

"And," added Hektor, "it'll be a clarion call to the other officers out there that we're prepared to go after bigger fish." He then nodded his head appreciatively. "I like it."

"Sir," interjected Moftasa, "Captain Gupta did get away from the last battle with all four of his troop transports intact."

"I sincerely doubt his ability to run away will be a cogent defense in his court-martial," Franklin offered dourly.

The cabinet looked to Hektor for a response.

"We have things to do and a war to win," Hektor answered, his non-response sealing Gupta's fate. "Moftasa, stay awhile. I need your advice."

Neela paced the waiting room, walking in nervous circles in front of a receptionist's desk, the last barrier into an office she'd spent the last two days trying to reach. She couldn't figure out the source of her discontent. Normally once she'd made up her mind to do something she felt her doubts and fears fade, but ever since she'd decided to see Hektor it was like a part of her mind had an itch that couldn't be scratched. Even as she was pacing, her left hand rose unsummoned to scratch her head.

The austere man looked up from his bank of holodisplays. "The President will see you now." Then, indicating the unassuming door to his immediate left, he beckoned her in.

"Thank you," answered Neela, and proceeded to make her way into a small and Spartan office. Surprisingly so, she thought as she took a quick inventory. It had a large desk, some chairs, and a couch, but all of it rather prosaic. It could easily be the office of a mid-level insurance agent. It was also empty of its occupant.

"Neela," said Hektor, suddenly entering the room from another entrance, "welcome to the axis of evil." Though he spoke with his usual macabre sense of humor, Neela could see the signs of tension in his shoulders and the beginning of stress lines around his eyes. He offered his hand.

With a lingering discomfort that Neela attempted to shrug off, she took it. She realized he'd only offered it to be polite, as handshaking had once again fallen out of favor in the core worlds, its being regarded as a vestige of her now-vilified husband.

"What can I do for you, Neela?" He then seemed to reconsider. "If you wish, I can call you 'Dr. Cord.'"

"Why the change of heart, Hektor?" she asked.

"I've been informed about how much you've been helping our wounded, and to be perfectly honest my childish attempts to bait you aren't worthy of the good you've been doing."

Neela was actually flustered. "It's . . . um . . . it's up to you, Mr. President," she finally managed.

"Then I'll call you Dr. Harper, until and if you give me permission to call you by your first name. He led her to the couch but took a chair on the other side of the coffee table. "You should know that this office is under constant surveillance for security purposes. I just want you to be aware of that before you say anything you may end up regretting."

"I assumed that was the case, but thank you for telling me anyway."

There was a moment of awkward silence once the pleasantries were over. It was only then that Hektor noticed Neela fidgeting in her seat.

"OK, Dr. Harper, you didn't stop by just so I could compliment you and we're both obviously very busy people . . . so if you don't mind . . ."

Neela scrunched her brow slightly and leaned forward onto her knees, hands clasped.

"You must save Samuel Trang."

"Excuse me?" said Hektor snapping back farther into his chair, almost as if Neela's statement had been a physical assault.

"I was talking to Amanda," said Neela. "I know that Miss Sobbelgé is getting ready to unleash a press campaign against Trang that will destroy his ability to be an officer in the fleet. Hektor," she pleaded, "I mean, Mr. President—you must stop it."

Hektor was floored. He'd admitted to himself that what with the events of the past few weeks he hadn't been able to keep up with his reports concerning Neela. When he'd been informed that she'd been trying to reach him he was thrilled. With everything he'd been dealing with of late, a talk with his favorite prisoner would do him some good. Still, her wanting him to save an incompetent officer was not anywhere within the realm of what Hektor had been expecting. Perhaps a plea to end the war or maybe a desire to go back to Ceres or Earth, but this? Something had gone horribly awry.

"Neela," he said when he'd finally regained his composure, "I think I should clear something up. *I'm* the one who wants the court-martial made public. Miss Sobbelgé works for me."

"Yeah, that I figured out on my own," Neela answered with just enough sarcasm in her voice to make Hektor feel like an idiot. "The question is why?"

"You do realize I'm under no obligation to answer that question, Dr. Harper."

"Yes, I do. But I'd consider it a great favor if you did."

Hektor mulled over the offer. There'd be no harm in telling her, and the more chits he could collect the better.

"Sure. If we're going to win, Doctor, then the military has to realize that there are consequences—severe ones—for losing."

"Why go to all the trouble?" asked Neela. "You're the President now. You could always just relieve him of duty."

"You're right, Doctor; I could. But it's still a political world. A direct order from me could cause all sorts of problems, and I've got more than my fair share at the moment. But the truth is that I want every fleet officer to realize that this humiliation, very *public* humiliation in fact, can result from losing battles due to a lack of proper planning and clear thinking. We need all those morons who signed up just to add another line to their résumés to realize that that'll hurt them more than just getting out of the way. If we can convince some of these idiots to get out of their captains' chairs and into support roles where they'll actually do some good, then this trial will save a lot more lives than it will cost."

Neela nodded and then waited a moment before deciding to speak. "All of that makes perfect sense . . . but not with Trang. And as long as I'm adding sauce to the goose I think it may also be a mistake to destroy Gupta, but I'm not sure yet."

Hektor couldn't help it and laughed out loud. "Nee . . . , Dr. Harper, do you have any other suggestions on how I should run the war?"

"Mr. President," she answered, undaunted, "I know you don't have any reason to trust me or my opinions, but I have to at least try."

"Try what?"

"To end this war," she said, removing a data crystal from her pocket. "My reasons are summarized here." She then put the crystal on the table. "All I ask is that you read the five-hundred-word file. If you're not convinced, dump it and I won't bother you again. But if it makes any sense at all, you'll find additional files with my sources to back up my 'crazy' ideas."

"I thought you revivalist types did not like the C word?"

"Anyone who wants to be in my line of work has got to be certifiable." She then stood up.

"Save him," she said, taking the crystal off the table and putting it into Hektor's hand. "He can end this war." And without saying another word she got up and left.

Martian trauma revival center

Neela Harper was watching one of her newest patients sleep. The problem was he wasn't actually resting. From all the data on the display over his bed he was in the midst of a pretty disruptive nightmare. What made the case so perplexing was that this particular patient couldn't remember any of his dreams when he was awake. But the lack of rest during sleep had turned him into a virtual zombie. She was going to prescribe a dream inhibiter and have him sleep with an artificial R.E.M. generator until they could get a better handle on it. She wouldn't normally have prescribed so transitory a solution had not the war forced her hand. In fact, it hadn't been the first time she'd had to resort to such stopgap measures. But her patients were needed back in the fight as soon as she could turn them out.

Many of the men and women she'd begrudgingly released had traumas buried so deep she feared they could snap at any moment. But there were so many who needed help waiting behind those she'd released that she'd had to put her worries aside lest she neglect those under her current care. The only solace she got was that at least some of her more afflicted patients had been assigned to non-combat jobs. Of course, the bad news was that they'd been assigned those jobs in order to free up others to take their place at the front lines. As Neela filled out the release forms for the non-dreaming patient she heard a commotion outside her office.

At first she thought that perhaps Captain Trang had returned. She poked her head outside and once again saw the steady stream of patients heading excitedly down the hall toward the common room. The only difference now, she noted, was the addition of a large contingent of mediabots, security personnel, and securibots. It was only then that she realized who it had to be. She allowed herself to get swept up in the crowd toward the common room, where upon her arrival she saw Hektor Sambianco, President of the UHF, holding court. Like Trang, Sambianco was also going from group to group, shaking hands and thanking patients. Neela noted that although the President had not elicited the same awe as Trang, he'd still been accorded the respect due his office.

As soon as Neela entered the room she saw Hektor look up and in her direction. He'd made no attempt to "accidentally" notice her and, she realized, had obviously been informed the second her entrance had been noted.

"Ah, the good doctor," Hektor bellowed, pointing to Neela and speaking in a voice loud enough for all to hear. "Actually," he said, now playing to the mediabots, "Dr. Harper is the reason I've come today." Hektor paused a moment, waiting for the room to quiet down. "As you know," he continued, "Captain Trang is being held to a court-martial over his alleged failures at Eros."

This brought a near-deafening howl of protest from the room. But Neela felt a sudden burst of hope that sprang from that remark. She knew a media bite setup when she saw one, and whatever Hektor was up to would make great play on the Neuro. She could only hope that he'd taken her advice. The only part she couldn't figure out was why he'd chosen to involve her, the deviant wife of the UHF's greatest enemy.

"But I'm confused," added Hektor, after the noise had dissipated. "One of the things I'd been told was that Trang was hated by his spacers for all the senseless pain he'd caused—which is why I supported his conviction in the court-martial."

"What about the assholes at Fleet Command?" howled someone from the crowd.

"Yeah," screamed another, "the ones who left us on Eros at the butt end of nowhere with shit for support!"

"The only one who saved us was Trang," yelled another.

Hektor allowed the impassioned defense of those brave enough to be heard to continue, making sure that it was all being caught by the mediabots.

Hektor knew he was going to pay a price with the corporation-backed high command, but he also knew it would be worth it.

After reviewing all of Neela's notes on Trang and, more important, the psychological motivations of those determined to destroy him, Hektor had come to the realization that he'd been close to eliminating perhaps the one naval officer in his entire fleet capable of giving J. D. Black a run for her money. He wasn't so sure he agreed with Neela that Gupta might also be a diamond in the rough, but Hektor had reasoned it would be easier to keep Gupta in the service than out, so he'd decided to make the effort there as well. However, it had been Neela's insights into the personalities of his political circle that had proved invaluable. Hektor knew that Neela had performed a similar service for Justin but had dismissed it as the ineffectual palaver of a marginalized wife in need of validation. That, Hektor now realized, had been a wrong assessment. More to the point, she had a skill he could put to good use. But given her still-odious reputation, a constant presence in his office would cause too much of a stink. He'd need to rehabilitate her in the eyes of the public, and so he'd chosen this current setting to do it.

"It was Dr. Harper," continued Hektor, "who made me aware that a miscarriage of justice may be taking place. Because of her excellent work in helping you brave spacers of the UHF, I was inclined to heed her advice and take a closer look at Captain Trang. And it's because of her that I will now review the recommendations of the court-martial very closely indeed. Your good doctor, ladies and gentlemen, has assured that Captain Trang will get his day in court."

The applause for Neela was both immediate and heartfelt. While she'd certainly earned a fair amount of respect for the compassionate oversight of her patients, the fact that she'd gone to bat for their beloved captain had practically accorded her the status of honorary comrade. Neela now stood in the light of the mediabots, speechless and unprepared.

"Dr. Harper doesn't need to say a thing," said Hektor, sensing Neela's discomfort. "Her actions have spoken for her. It's enough to say that she felt that this miscarriage of justice should not be allowed to happen."

"No . . . no, that wasn't it," Neela said before she realized the words were out of her mouth. The room came to a standstill. "It wasn't that . . . I mean what . . . President Sambianco said. We need Captain Trang and others like him. You see, I was . . ." She paused and took a deep breath. "I was wrong. We all were. The war can't be lost. If the UHF loses, then humanity will be split and it will lead to another war and another after that. We *have* to win. I helped Captain Trang because he can fight, and I am so sorry for what I helped do. I am so sorry." Neela crumpled to the floor in tears. She was quickly surrounded and embraced by a roomful of recovering patients. All in all it made for very compelling news.

Ceres

Justin watched the feed over and over again, Neela collapsing in pain, and each time he saw her do so his reaction was the same. He wanted to leap into the image and help her. He thought after repeated viewings the feeling would lessen, but it didn't. What really twisted the knife in his gut was watching the crowd of patients move aside as Hektor Sambianco knelt down by his wife's side and came to her aid.

Justin hadn't been aware of someone in his office until he felt a warm hand on his shoulder.

"I'm sorry," said Eleanor, voice broken and plaintive.

Justin didn't say a word, realizing he might explode in a rage capable of destroying everything and everyone he cared about. Conversely he might let the grief swallow him whole and disappear into a depth of depression he wasn't sure he'd ever be able to crawl out of. He let the torrent of emotions wash over him so that he could better steady himself. When his breathing became more measured and his thinking more clear the path before him was set. He knew now that he must break his wedding vow of "in sickness and in health," and in doing so fully accept what he'd once refused to allow—his heart to be sundered by an all encompassing bitterness and rage. But in that moment of knowing knew also that the misplaced passion he'd held on to for Neela could now be set free and redirected. After a few minutes he was finally able to speak. In a voice without remorse and iron in will he recast the crux of the war.

"We must tell the people of the Alliance what has happened to my wife. They need to know that we're not only fighting to win our freedom. They need to know what will happen if we lose it."

10 Commitments

Altamont Asteroid Belt at the 180

Commodore Christina Sadma found herself walking along a garden path filled with all manner of flora. The smell of jasmine was strong in the early-morning air, and from her limited memory of horticulture she saw a healthy smattering of poinsettia and lotus. The feeling of soil beneath her feet was almost liberating. She was amazed that such a generous amount of land had been set aside within so small an area. But she also realized it was a true testament to the caretakers, the community of belief. The enclave was primarily Christian and of an old religious order from the pre-colonization days known as the Knights Hospitaller. They'd once been a band of fierce Crusaders whose most famous moment in history had been the siege of Malta, in which their seven hundred Knights and eight hundred soldiers repelled an army of forty thousand Turkish invaders. Over time the Knights' mission had gone from their original charter of protecting and defending the Holy Land to the protection and defense of the sick, poor, and besieged. After the Grand Collapse the pitiful few who somehow managed to survive made the same long trek into space as their core-ligionists and founded the community within which Christina currently found herself entranced. True to their beliefs, the Knights had created an enclave of healing and faith, asking nothing of those they helped other than their goodwill and whatever spare parts they could manage.

Although the order was not considerable in terms of actual membership, it had become large as a community of healers for both the faithful and the faithless. The asteroid had been hollowed out, opened at both ends, and spun at two-thirds Earth gravity. The settlement that grew within it ultimately became known as Altamont, the second-largest hunk of rock in the 180. It was located sixty-two million miles from Eros, and the only things separating the two large bodies were millions of small- to medium-sized asteroids. And whereas Eros was on the inside of the belt closest to the core, Altamont was on the other side closest to the outer planets. With the loss of Eros, Altamont had become the only settlement large enough to handle all the traffic on the great circle trade of the asteroid belt. As a result the commune had naturally grown into the 180's new transfer point and depot and was now one of the most strategic locations in space.

It hadn't taken long for Christina to realize the rock's strategic importance, not only in terms of trade but also for the continuation of the war at the 180. From Altamont she'd be able to push the war back toward Eros. She might not have had enough ships to take Eros back directly, but she could at least make it almost impossible for the UHF to move much beyond their initial beach-head. However, for any of her machinations to happen she'd have to fortify Altamont—and soon. She'd need to make the Knights' lonely rock as rigid in its defense as Mars or risk having the UHF bypass the belt completely and attack the Alliance from behind. And so, with that thought in mind, she found herself strolling along the famed grounds of Altamont waiting for the abbot's liaison to arrive.

"Do you like our gardens?"

Christina turned around and saw a man in simple brown robes approaching her. He had deep-set, penetrating dark eyes, an ovular face, and thin black hair combed forward.

"Yes, very much," answered Christina. "They're so different from the gardens on Eris, Father—"

He corrected her with a gentle smile. "It's 'Brother' and the name is Samp-son." He then bent over slightly to smell a star-shaped, cream-colored flower whose tips were lightly dappled in red. He looked up and invited Christina to experience the fragrance.

Her face lit up as she took in the subtly sweet scent. "Wonderful."

"Yes," he answered placidly, "*Genipa clusiifolia*—otherwise known as 'the seven-year apple.' I'm glad you find our gardens so captivating Commodore. I've never had the pleasure of visiting Eris myself, or anywhere else for that matter. I'd be most curious to hear about the gardens on your world."

Christina was dumbstruck. Absolutely everyone traveled in her world, if only to the orbital belts or the planetary systems either to mine or visit relatives or for the sheer joy of experiencing new places. The thought of someone spending his or her entire life on a rock—no matter how nice—was impossible for her to grasp.

"The gardens we have on Eris are much larger," she finally answered, "be-cause the gravity is so much less. You have a two-thirds spin here, but on Eris it's a one-sixth, which makes our gardens grow much bigger. We also have most of our growth far under the surface in vast chambers. Yours are a beautiful band that I can't seem to stop looking at. But I don't see how they manage to get enough light for all the growth I see."

"Your timing is impeccable," said Brother Sampson with a wide grin, "as we're about to experience what we here refer to as the miracle of light."

No sooner had the words left the brother's mouth than Christina heard a deep grinding rumble emanating from both sides of the hollowed-out rock. She watched as large mirrors directed bands of light in a slow creep across the surface of the settlement. The bands began to rise a few hundred feet before reaching the gardens and then simultaneously shot toward the center of the hollowed-out asteroid, creating a momentary miniature star. The star began pulsating and then just as suddenly exploded into an empyreal radiance of light that gently floated onto the garden like a midsummer's downpour. Christina stared upwards, mouth agape, eyes wide.

"Miraculous, isn't it?" said Brother Sampson, still staring up.

"Brother, it was beautiful, truly beautiful."

"But that's not what you're here to talk about," he said, turning his gaze away from the garden and toward Christina; the wonderment was no longer in his eyes. "You wish to turn our gardens and places of healing into a base from which to wage this war that is causing so much suffering."

"Yes."

"I understand," he said softly. "Our brotherhood wishes that this was not needed, but we will not stand in your way."

"Uh, thank you, Brother" was all Christina could manage. She'd geared herself up for more of a fight.

They continued walking down the path with only the sound of the soft earth beneath their feet. "We will make our hospital facilities available for your forces," he continued, "but we request that you not prevent us from treating all who need it, even members of the UHF."

"I would never wish to prevent that, Brother, as long as my forces come first."

"We would have trouble acceding to that request."

Christina decided not to push it. She was getting most of what she'd wanted, with minimal resistance. "Very well, Brother, save who you will as you will."

"Thank you," he answered, visibly relieved. "We'll turn over all the plans of our settlement and evacuate whatever areas you deem necessary to your effort. Our power grid is available for your use and you may make whatever alterations to the settlement you think best. Many of our brethren have also inquired about volunteering to act as medics for your units. We hope their humble efforts will be of use."

Christina had been afraid she'd have to ride roughshod over the settlement to achieve her ends. Had that been the case, she knew that she would've automatically alienated the surrounding settlements, all of whom had the greatest respect for the strange but always generous community of belief. It would've made her campaign against the enemies of the Alliance harder, but she would've done it regardless. Instead, the gentle man she'd been walking with was freely allowing her to turn his sanctuary of peace into an instrument of war.

"Brother," she said, stopping in the path and turning to face the man who'd just saved her a load of potential grief. "I'm truly grateful, but I must know—"

"Why?" the brother asked for her.

Christina nodded.

"You've heard about Neela Cord?"

Christina answered with a tauten brow and slight tip of her head.

"Do you believe it?" he asked.

"With all my heart. It is the nature of our enemy."

"We didn't," he answered, pausing briefly. "At least not at first. But we received a call from one of the communities' most respected holy women, Fawa Sulnat Hamdi. She'd been talking with many people, including the blessed one," he said, using the moniker that those of faith had most recently attributed to J. D. Black. "That, combined with other evidence gleaned from what's happening in the core, forced us to see the truth. A conclave of many of our communities was recently held and it's been decided that the UHF must be opposed with all of our effort."

"Pardon the phrase, Brother, but you do realize you're preaching to the choir."

"My child," he said, carefully pulling an intensely violet milk thistle flower from a nearby stalk, "you fight for the freedom of your planet and for the independence of the Alliance. You also fight for the camaraderie you've developed with those you lead and, if I may be so bold, with nearly as much devotion as you follow the blessed one. But that is not why we choose to lay down our plowshares and pick up the sword."

"Why then?"

"The UHF is committing an abomination, Commodore," he answered, beginning to pluck the flower's thin violet strands from the bud. "They're trying to remove from humanity that most precious of gifts—our *soul*. When we were convinced of what they were doing we said a prayer for Neela Cord, the prayer for the dead."

He paused for a moment, looking up from the half-gone flower in his hand. It was at that moment that Christina Sadma saw not the peaceful brother tending to his garden but the man descended from the warrior-priests of the ancient past. She saw that in him burned a dangerous fire banked for centuries. As he pulled the last of the beautiful petals off the bud, a crown of sharp, parlous thorns was revealed. His last words were said with the utter conviction that comes from absolute faith. "They will not be allowed to take God's greatest gift from humanity." He then placed the crown of thorns into the palm of Christina's hand. "They will not take from us free will."

Commodore Samuel Trang viewed his collar and couldn't help but smile. He thought he'd be either dead, in jail proofing technical manuals, or at best spending the rest of the war selling drinks to spacers on leave in dive bars around low Earth orbit. Instead he was heading back to Eros with a promotion and ten new ships. Not nearly enough to fight properly, but he wasn't about to complain. He also knew it was only the intervention of the President that made his liberty possible. The President had also seen fit to officially promote his first officer, Lieutenant Zenobia Jackson, to the rank of Commander. Trang had already given her the rank, but it had been a battlefield promotion from a court-martialed captain and so had been rescinded once the new command structure had taken over at Eros. But now it was official, and that filled Trang with much pleasure. However, it was the captain Jackson was talking to who made Trang truly content.

Captain Abhay Gupta had been disgraced, having lost one battle and then run from the other. No fleet really wanted him, and it was obvious he'd probably end up spending the war counting ore carts on Mercury. But Trang wanted him and no one interfered with the transfer. Gupta had been immediately assigned to the battle staff.

Trang next reviewed the displays from the vantage point of his command chair. He saw that it would take two weeks at constant acceleration to make it back to Eros. Once he was there the new campaign would begin. He also knew where it was all going to end: Altamont.

Beanstalk, Earth

Hektor was going to have to find a better way of traveling back to Earth. He could technically run the war from anywhere; however, for propaganda purposes it was best if he was on the front lines. Still, for what was about to be announced he'd have to be on Earth. He'd be needed for both what he was going to say and what he'd have to do immediately afterwards. Technically he didn't have any right to use the Beanstalk, but the new Chairman had been gracious enough to allow Hektor use of the top levels, not that there was really any choice in the matter. The accommodations were convenient and useful, as Hektor had had all the presidential residences on Earth very publicly auctioned off to help pay for the war. He'd been scheduled to give a speech in Chairman Park soon and was hoping what he'd planned to say would turn the tide and win the war; assuming, of course, that the heads of the fifteen largest and most powerful corporations didn't use the meeting right after his speech to feed him to a fusion reactor.

He took the elevator down the stalk and, followed by a large security detail, caught a public transport to the park. It had proved to be a logistical nightmare but helped add to his "man of the minority" image. As he approached the park he saw with some satisfaction that the crowd had grown to a respectable size. He knew Irma could make it appear bigger if more didn't arrive to swell the ranks. He also knew they weren't all his loyal followers. Despite his best efforts, he hadn't been able to cure the vast number of pennies of their love for Justin Cord, at least not entirely. But Hektor was hoping that between the speech he was about to give and the strategic use of Dr. Wong's new techniques, large-scale shifts in sentiment would soon begin in earnest.

Hektor's plan was both calculated and meticulous. A person of influence, whether an admiral, CEO, or action wing rabble-rouser, would be taken in for questioning and let go after an hour or two. They'd remember nothing of particular importance during their "questioning" and if challenged by any of their associates would still hold fast to all their beliefs and values. But in a matter of weeks or months they'd begin to shift their opinions in a manner keyed to some aspect of their personality. It would appear to be an organic and perfectly natural change of heart.

Hektor knew it would be impossible to shadow-audit, as he now referred to the newest form of psyche auditing, all the billions of people in the solar system, but he also realized that if he could get to the five hundred thousand who mattered it would give him the keys to controlling the rest. As others of influence popped up in the future they'd be shadow-audited as well and true stability would once again reign supreme. Had the Alliance not released a propaganda blitz claiming that Neela Harper had been audited in some odious new manner he'd have been able to move even quicker. The fact that what the Alliance claimed happened to be true was not a problem as far as Hektor was concerned. The research had been purposely compartmentalized and the teams being created were themselves "treated" to ensure loyalty. But Hektor would have to go slower under the nervous eye of a public that had been inculcated from birth to be paranoid about psyche audits, fearing exactly what Hektor Sambianco and Dr. Wong were now, in fact, doing. It also didn't help that the strain of war without end was sapping all hope and feeding into delusional fantasies.

But hope was exactly what Hektor was planning to bestow as he approached the dais at Chairman Park.

> *President Sambianco has announced a major new proposal. Using his executive authority, the President has proposed a Majoritization Proclamation. The essence of the proposal is simple. Any person who serves in the war in some military capacity will be given a majority of their stock at the successful completion of the current hostilities. Those who already have majority will be given an additional 5 percent. The only exception to this policy will be the President himself, who as com-*

*mander in chief is part of the military chain of command. "Those who
are bearing the brunt of this war to save incorporated civilization must
be shown the tangible benefits of this civilization and the reward for
their bravery and sacrifice." With those words the President has set off
a firestorm of protest and praise.*

*The minorities have exploded in wild celebration loudly praising
"the minority President" and the "penny President," not using these titles as intended insults, but rather as titles of pride. The President's
stock with the lower orders has never been higher.*

*This is a fact not lost on many political/economical commentators.
If the proclamation becomes a fact, it will create many new majority
voters who will owe their newly won status to Hektor Sambianco and
his branch of the Libertarian Party. It could secure their hold on the
newly empowered federal government for decades to come.*

*But of more immediate concern is how the major corporations will
view what is being called by many a blatant theft of property. So far
none of the major corporations or their CEOs has commented beyond
stating they will study the proposition.*

—N.N.N.

In order to get back to the Beanstalk as quick as he could manage, Hektor
didn't bother with public transportation. He needed to be in the main conference room before any of the gathered CEOs could say anything stupid or irrev-
ocable. He didn't want to have to arrange an "unfortunate" action wing terrorist
attack if he could avoid it.

"It would be simpler to shadow-audit the lot of them," he groused as he hur-
riedly made his way toward the room, but it would take too long and their security was not to be taken lightly. That would have to be a last resort with careful
planning.

As Hektor entered the room he saw staring directly at him fifteen of the most
powerful women and men in the solar system. At one time they'd all been
people into whose ranks Hektor had dreamed of being accepted. They once held
all the power and thus had been a source of endless fascination. But now they
were just another obstacle that he needed to overcome.

Thankfully, they hadn't all ripped into him at once as he'd expected. In fact, it
appeared as if they'd all agreed to a common spokeswoman. Hektor was not
surprised when the CEO of American Express got up. She was particularly upset
because with the collapse of so much intersystem travel and entertainment, her
company's short-term profits had taken a considerable hit. But they had a long-
term advantage based on the huge number of shares in people they'd developed

over the decades. Hektor's plan was a direct threat to not only hers but everyone's corporation.

"Hektor," she began as soon as he took his seat. "Sorry, Mr. President. What makes you think your proposal will ever happen?"

Hektor looked around the room. "If it doesn't we'll lose the war."

"Then let's lose the war," said American Express flatly.

Hektor saw that this statement made some of the CEOs angry, but not all. Some were even looking dangerously supportive. Hektor slowly got up out of his chair, walked right up to the CEO of American Express, and by the sheer ferocity evident in his glare made her stumble backward into her seat. When she made no move to get back up he started to circle the table slowly.

"Let's lose the war," he repeated, voice emanating an eerie calm. "Let's just stop fighting. As a matter of fact, why don't we just look at the expense involved in fighting the war versus the benefit of simply stopping." Hektor paused and had a bemused smile on his face. Then with a sudden fury he slammed his clenched fist down onto the table, causing a few gasps.

"Of course we looked at that option!" he seethed. "Do you have any idea how much time and money we would save if we just stopped fighting? So we lose 10 percent of humanity. We have stock options on the other 90 percent. So we lose most of the resources of the outer orbits. They have to sell us those resources at prices we can determine. They don't have another market. In some ways it'll be better if we lose because we'll get the resources without having the attending problem of policing the vast beyond that is the beyond."

Hektor looked at their befuddled faces. He was purposely making their case, throwing them off balance.

"Every single one of these arguments has the unequivocal backing of the truth," he continued. "There's more that you may not have considered. The social stresses of winning this war will be onerous. Our civilization will have to accept things that would've been treasonable, psyche-auditable offenses a mere three years ago. Have you really considered the effects of our new government *bonds*?" He said the word with such contempt that had they not known better, each and every person in the room would have thought that Hektor was the most vehement opponent of the fiat currency he'd only recently introduced, as opposed to being its strongest supporter. "It will take decades for the government to pay them off, and that's if we actually use some backdoor versions of taxation." He saw the assembled group go pale as the blood drained from their faces. "Yes, I said it, taxation. Thank you, Mr. Cord. But let's not forget the fact that hordes of individuals will be given *financial* ability beyond their *actual* ability. Something that our system was designed to prevent. They will cause problems of spending and credit when the less able will buy what they shouldn't and get educations they don't deserve and are incapable of using properly. Imagine how many medics will actually think they have the right to be doctors and will sadly have the stock shares to fund it. The social mess with the inferiors will be a tragedy we'll all have to deal with. Even with everything I've just described, we'll still need to prosecute this war . . . we'll still need majoritization."

"Why?" asked Toshiba. "It seems to me you've done an adequate job of justifying our *not* prosecuting the war."

"Because once this war stops we can never get it started again. For one thing, neither side will want to continue, barring the most extreme circumstances. Plus peace will pay more than war. But consider what will be the end result of peace now."

He paused and saw from the blank stares that not one of them had really considered the long-term ramifications of a negotiated peace.

"Justin Cord will have his civilization and they may still have incorporation in his Alliance, but it won't be long before they get rid of it altogether. You'll have one-tenth of the humans living as a beacon. Any social problems they have because of their primitive economic and social system will be masked by the fact that they're a frontier economy. The growth they'll experience for the next century or two will give the illusion that their system works, just like the old American idiocy before It collapsed and took everyone and everything down with it. And just like then, before Cord's system goes it too will take us all down with it. Any person in the core who feels they're not being treated well, i.e., all the ones who deservedly belong on the bottom, will now have another option. They can run away to the Alliance and you can be sure Justin Cord and his ideological children will be there to welcome them with open arms, rejoicing that others have escaped the incorporated jailers that we'll be portrayed as. They'll expand in population and industry. Jupiter alone has the potential resources and space to grow larger and more powerful than the entire core. In seventy years we won't be able to defeat the Alliance; in a hundred they'll be able to conquer us. And when the idiocies of their system start to make it untenable, do you think they'll simply admit they were wrong and go back to incorporation, the only philosophy of human existence that actually works?" Or will they attack the civilized core, a core much weakened by the long decades of population loss and propaganda campaigns, and thereby destroy the only hope the human race ever had? So you want to protect your profits. Well, good for you, you should. There's nothing wrong in acting in your self-interest." The corners of Hektor's mouth formed into a knowing grin. "I always have. But remember, self-interest comes in two forms: short term and long term.

"I have figures," he continued, "and projections elaborating on what I've just said and am happy to share it all with you, both conclusions, procedures, gathering methods, and the entirety of the raw data itself. But you already know what I'm saying is true. In the short term our interests are served by peace." Hektor called up a map of the solar system with a floating time chart beneath it. The system hovered holographically above the conference table. The UHF-controlled area was in red and the Alliance- in blue. The areas slowly started to change colors as the time chart beneath advanced in years. With each passing decade the UHF's color receded and the Alliance's grew. Within 250 years there was hardly any red left at all.

"We'll be at the doorstep of a society whose beliefs are diametrically opposed to ours," said Hektor, "and all our investments in humanity will be for naught. But whatever the price paid, incorporation, human civilization, and our long-term self-interest demand the complete eradication of the Outer Alliance and that putrid belief in the freedom it represents."

It would take weeks of debate and Hektor would have to deliver much in the way of backroom deals and government contracts to corporations that were happy to reacquaint themselves with the powerful narcotic of unlimited government spending and debt passed on to future generations. But in the end the CEOs and the corporations they represented fell in line and supported the new total war. The pennies too signed up in enthusiastic numbers; they were fighting for what they considered to be their freedom.

Ceres

Justin missed his swims in the Cerian seas. He still exercised. His new doctor insisted on it, but Justin couldn't bring himself to swim as he once did. It wasn't the swimming itself; he still did that in the current-driven pools. But he'd always used his time in the sea to work through his problems and afterwards discussed them with Neela. Now he'd started to box those parts of his life away, both emotionally and physically. He no longer slept in the same bedroom he'd once shared with Neela. He'd had that space converted into a security station.

But he couldn't escape her shadow entirely. He buried himself in his work, and that never eased up. He had to lead the fight in the war, which meant balancing recruiting with outfitting the ever-expanding fleets. More spacers for the fleet meant fewer trained personnel to man all the systems needed to keep an advanced interstellar civilization running. Commodities were also becoming an issue. It wasn't so much a matter of paying for it all, as the new Alliance dollar was holding steady as an accepted currency. Technically it wasn't a fiat currency, since it was backed by orbital slots and mining holdings on the various planets.

But the currency had to be able to buy goods and services in an economy, and the truth was there were fewer and fewer goods and services to be had as the demands of the war became more prevalent.

But that was the price of saving some small portion of the human race from the mental castration that awaited them if Hektor and all he stood for won. And so the Alliance struggled on in its third year of the war with no end in sight and everyone going about their jobs as best as they could manage. And it was why Justin found himself on a docking port in the Via Cereana dedicating yet another warship to the ever-growing Alliance fleet. It was hard to believe that twenty ships had almost decided the war nearly two years back. Now the Alliance fleet had over one hundred ships captured, refitted, or constructed from scratch at Gedretar, and soon more would be coming out of the newly renamed Jovian Shipyards.

But few things could match the wonder Justin felt whenever dedicating a ship in the Via Cereana. It never ceased being, in his mind, the absolute ninth wonder of the world, and as far as he and many others were concerned the Cereana was undoubtedly one of the greatest feats of human engineering. Many had argued that the genius lay in the simplicity of the concept: Drill a hole two miles wide through the five-hundred-mile core of Ceres and then spin it on the resulting axis. But that's not what captivated Justin. It had been what they'd filled it with. All the docking ports, ramps, repair stations, fueling depots, passenger areas, and myriad facilities that made up the active spaceport. Whenever Justin looked up and out he'd be treated to one of the busiest hubs ever created by humanity. When he could, he'd sneak out of the office, find a crevice somewhere, and sit, mesmerized by all the goings-on. In the center of the tube, ships were moving at high speed and always in the same direction. Even at a mile away, they were awesome to behold. They came in all different types and sizes, representing the genius and, in the case of some of the more antiquated ships, suicidal bravery of the people of the Alliance.

To match the wonder of the grand procession of ships majestically sailing through the central tube were all those leaving and entering its unrelenting flow. Ships would pull away, slow down, approach a docking station, and connect to Ceres. They could be tiny, hardly big enough to hold a crew of three bringing back ore samples to be tested by one of the big laboratories. Or they could be megahaulers with container after container of . . . Justin often didn't know. They might be transporting a herd of cows specially bred for low-gravity farming settlements or be filled with hundreds of two-person flyers. They could also be the large passenger liners bringing, it sometimes seemed, all the people of the Alliance to Ceres. It helped that the dwarf planet could replicate almost all gravity environments. Another advantage of its central tube was that the closer one was to the core, the lower the centrifugal gravity. Naturally Ceres had accommodations, shops, and services available at all gravity conditions, from micro to the two-thirds that made up the main habitat levels. In fact, Ceres's gravitational flexibility had been a consideration in its choice as the capital of the Alliance. It was one of the few places that had the ability to accommodate so many in such variety.

Justin was sorry that he'd have to miss the ballet of commerce and humanity today, but a ship awaited her official naming and there'd be no time. As soon as he arrived, almost all of his annoyance at having been called away from work vanished. When he saw the spacers of the Alliance waiting for him with that look of hope and pride he could do nothing but strive to be the leader they'd envisioned.

It was almost always the same. These "new" crews were usually from other ships that had been damaged beyond repair or just as often from the same settlement. Admiral Sinclair had set up an abbreviated but still effective boot camp for them. Whenever possible the crews or settlers were usually kept together, but the ships they'd be manning were often so large that different groups who might normally never have even known about the other's existence were suddenly thrown together. Sinclair always leavened them out with experienced spacers from other ships in the Alliance, often but not always men and women who had been wounded and were returning to duty. These vets brought with them a dose of reality as to the dangers of fighting not only the usual enemies of vacuum, radiation, excessive gravity, and high-velocity debris but the added joy of other highly trained human beings doing their level best to wipe them off the face of the grid.

It usually took a few weeks of rigorous training and some strenuous extracurricular sports—fleet slang for fighting—but soon enough the crews became cohesive and began to think the word "us" meant anyone in their crew. It was then and only then that they were assigned a ship. And it was a fact that whichever one they were given promptly became the best damned one in the fleet. And if they were really lucky, the President, a man who'd defied the corporate enslavers and showed the best part of humanity the road to freedom, would come down and personally name their ship.

Justin found himself standing in front of one of the bigger battle cruisers he'd ever christened. She had had some special modifications that J. D. Black had briefed him on. What she'd referred to as "modifications" he'd called "aces up the sleeve." J.D. and Kenji's aces had become the signature of the Alliance and had allowed them to stay one step ahead of the UHF. J.D. had trounced the enemy with defeat after crushing defeat, and if need be she'd continue to do so until the core was made to realize that the price of war was too high. This latest ship with her three main rail guns in its central axis would help. But it was the name that the crew had chosen that Justin found particularly intriguing. She was to be called *God's Hammer*.

Apparently the majority of the medics training with the crews had come from the communities of belief, and they'd had a profound impact on the captain of the about-to-be-commissioned ship. The captain, who'd seen more combat than most, having fought in almost every major battle of the war, found solace in the teachings of the believers. Justin wasn't sure how he personally felt about the recent revival of religion but remembered the famous maxim about there being no atheists in a foxhole. And if faith brought comfort to his spacers he wouldn't lessen that comfort by voicing his own skepticism.

Justin arrived at the port in Alliance One, which he personally thought was a ridiculous waste of time, since he already lived on Ceres. But the fleet loved it when his starship would dock next to the ship about to be commissioned. He'd then disembark with all the pomp and ceremony fitting the office of the President. Justin thought it quite amusing that for a people who made a big deal about how much they didn't make a big deal about anything—"unlike them tradition-bound core dwellers"—they still seemed to love it whenever he showed up—official decorum in tow.

He would then give a rendition of his standard commissioning-a-ship speech. He'd of course add personal notes, usually concerning the bravery and service record of the newly promoted captain. He'd comment on something concerning the new name and then finish off with a thank-you to all those present for what they were doing for the Alliance and the future of the human race. The last part was never anything other than sincere. This time was no different, and when Justin officially pronounced the name the space-suited men and women on the newly commissioned AWS *God's Hammer* yelled into their helmets' radio mikes and stamped their space-suited hands and feet on the bulkheads. Justin saw that some of the more adventurous even detached from the hull and did some somersaults till they were retrieved by their more levelheaded shipmates. Justin and the captain gave each other a salute and then shook hands in full view of the crew and mediabots. Then, with the same coruscations with which he'd arrived, Justin would depart. He knew that, barring an emergency, the newly commissioned crew would be hitting the more entertaining parts of Ceres in the evening and would tomorrow be joining the fleet, where J. D. Black would begin training them in the reality of joint ship operations.

Justin entered Alliance One, stripped out of his space suit, and immediately got back to work. Of course he could've just gone back to the Cliff House via any one of the docking ports nearest *God's Hammer*, but the spacers liked to see him leave in Alliance One almost as much as they enjoyed watching him arrive. Besides, it would give him an excuse not to be in the Cliff House for another hour.

Even though the docking port for Alliance One was only ten miles away from *God's Hammer,* it was in the wrong direction. And while Alliance One may have been the President's personal transport, even he couldn't buck the universal rule that traffic flowed only one way in the Via Cereana. Justin was going to have to go around like everyone else. It was a rule he agreed with and liked because it showed the Alliance that the rules applied to everyone. Besides, there was little he could do in the Cliff House that he couldn't do in the ship.

Justin was reviewing a yield estimate on hydrogen extraction around Jupiter when the alarms suddenly sounded. He was out of his bunk and on the way to the bridge before he even realized he was moving.

"What's going on, sebastian?" he demanded.

His faithful avatar sounded from the DijAssist attached to Justin's belt. "A transport ship from Pluto, Justin; they're experiencing drive failure. They cannot decelerate or control vectors."

"Can the Cereana use its magnetic grapplers to guide it into an emergency channel and slow it down?" asked Justin as he continued on his way to the bridge.

"I'm afraid not, Justin. They're too far out. Without any intervention they'll impact Ceres."

"How many on board the transport?" Justin asked, now entering the bridge.

"Over twelve hundred," answered Cyrus Anjou, who'd guessed Justin's destination and beaten him to it. "Around seven hundred of which are suspended. They're on the way here for medical treatment that can't be gotten elsewhere."

"Closest ship?" asked Justin.

"That would be us," answered the ship's captain, swinging around from his command chair.

"Captain Baitmen, we need to get close to that ship and see if we can use our magnetic adhesion skids to attach to the superstructure."

"Yes, sir."

"We'll also need to divert that ship from Ceres, so let's get over there and see if we can get their systems back online. I'll be suiting up if anyone needs me."

"Captain, disregard that order," said Cyrus coolly. "Presidential guard to bridge," he then said to his DijAssist.

"Cyrus," asked Justin, swinging around to face his friend, "what do you think you're doing?"

"My job. Captain, prepare the shuttle for immediate departure. Mr. President, come with me to the shuttle please."

"Cyrus," Justin replied through clenched teeth, "stop being overprotective." He then turned to the pilot. "Captain, I'm giving you a direct order."

"Captain," interjected Cyrus, "your primary duty is ensuring the safety of the President."

Captain Baitmen hesitated only a moment. "Sorry, Mr. President, but I cannot obey."

"But those people will die if I don't help them!"

"Mr. President," answered Cyrus, "if you want to help them, then get off this ship. Once you're off, Alliance One will attempt a rescue—but not one second before, and as you're well aware, every second counts."

"Those are my people, Cyrus. I will not continue to sit on my ass while others take all the risks. They need me and I'll help them if I have to go through you to do it." At that moment five well-armed men appeared led by the now stone-faced Sergeant Holke.

"Mr. President," intoned Cyrus, "they are *all* your people. You have to live for all of them. As a matter of fact, four billion people need you to live—not to mention the uncounted billions waiting to be born." Cyrus then placed both his hands on Justin's shoulders, forcing direct eye contact. "Justin," he said in a surprisingly calm voice, "you no longer have the right to risk your life. You get on the shuttle and we'll rescue the transport, I promise."

Every fiber in Justin's body wanted to leap regardless of the danger, but he'd been forced to swallow the bitter truth of Cyrus Anjou's words. "Let's go to the shuttle," Justin said, grabbing Cyrus. "You're not getting off that easy either; you'll have to come with me."

"Mr. President, I can help. In the Jovian system," sputtered Cyrus. "I used to run transports to the ice fields of Europa—"

Justin was pulling Cyrus and signaled the sergeant to grab the other arm, which the sergeant did expertly while increasing speed to the shuttle. "No way, Cyrus; I'd be hard-pressed to keep Jupiter playing nice with all the others without your advice. Is there anyone else who can do what you do and knows what you know?"

Cyrus, being dragged along, remained mute.

"Didn't think so."

They got to the shuttle and were both shoved in by the sergeant. "You too, Sergeant," ordered Justin. "I can't be left without any security, can I?" Justin could see that Sergeant Holke wanted to argue but in the end slung his rail gun over his shoulder and got in the shuttle.

Three days later Justin visited all the rescued Plutonians. That visit and the award ceremony for the crews who rescued the malfunctioning transport both ended up making great stories for the press. The report showing that the ship had left Pluto without backup systems was given less play. Apparently she'd stripped her backup system for use in other ships, a practice becoming so common as to elicit almost no surprise.

The Eros front or what the Alliance calls the 180 front is starting to heat up. The return of Samuel Trang has led to new offensive operations in the area between the forces of the UHF and the forces of rebellion. Commodore Trang seems to be avoiding any all-out battles with the Alliance forces and is instead concentrating on a slow and steady approach. His strategy is to take and hold every settlement and asteroid of substantial size as he advances slowly toward his goal—the settlement of Altamont. The large asteroid is home to a group of religious fanatics who it's rumored have given their absolute loyalty to the forces of rebellion and chaos. All this reporter can say is, can anyone really be surprised by that?

—N.N.N.

Admiral Joshua Sinclair was sitting on the Cliff House balcony having breakfast and following a new tradition, giving the President his morning briefing. Sinclair had ordered a cup of Earl Grey tea that had been grown in one of the farming settlements near Ceres. It had been part of the export market to Earth, but as that market was now cut off, Ceres and indeed the whole asteroid belt were being sold large amounts of high-quality tea at prices that were making it a very popular drink. It was helped by the fact that the core had almost all the coffee plantations and so coffee was both expensive and viewed as a slightly disloyal beverage to consume. At times the admiral missed his cup of joe, but there was a variant of tea called Imperial Gunpowder that he was becoming quite fond of. However, the President always drank Earl Grey and therefore so did Sinclair.

When Justin appeared Sinclair stood up and saluted. Justin waited until Sinclair was done and then shook his hand. "Morning, Joshua," said Justin, inviting Sinclair to sit back down. "I hope you have good news to impart today."

"Good morning, Mr. President. Yes, I do. We have the UHF afraid to leave the orbit of Mars. They won't launch an attack until they have at least two hundred ships, and that will take months. We can rest secure and build our own forces."

"And the bad news?"

"The 180, Mr. President. Trang is taking horrible losses, but his strategy is sound. We cannot launch a frontal attack with the forces we have and he's not willing to launch a frontal attack on Altamont. Wish the bastard would; that place is a fortress now. But he's killing us with the attritional shit. It plays right to the UHF's strengths."

"Casualties?"

"They're losing two for every one of ours," answered Sinclair, lifting up the tea to his nose and smelling the intense aroma, "maybe even three, but they're trying to keep that quiet."

"But they outnumber us ten to one."

Sinclair nodded uneasily. "As long as he's willing to take those losses he'll advance. At some point he'll be in a position to assault Altamont."

"And if we lose Altamont," added Justin, "the belt is split."

"Like I said . . . he's a bastard."

Justin picked up his tea, blew on the surface, and then took a sip. "So," he said putting the cup back down onto the table, "what do you propose?"

"If it was anyone but Trang I'd send Christina fifty ships and let her take back Eros in one big battle. Then I'd have her fortify that position and send the ships back before the UHF takes effective action."

"But?"

"But with Trang you never know. He may not lose, even heavily outnumbered. He was completely outclassed at the second Battle of Eros and still managed to hold on long enough for reinforcements to arrive. If we give Christina the ships she'll try a climatic battle and if she loses we lose Altamont and the 180 immediately."

Justin nodded and then picked up his cup again. As he slowly sipped the hot drink he played through the various scenarios in his head but only one solution came to mind. "We could send J.D. and let them fight it out."

"Sir, if we sent J.D. we'd need to send enough of the fleet to make it worth it. Now we have very good intelligence coverage and so does the UHF. Fortunately, thanks to Secretary Olmstead—and to be perfectly honest I don't really like the guy—theirs is not as good as ours. To Kirk's credit he's put a shroud over the Alliance's movements that have had the UHF guessing for the better part of two years. But I doubt if even he could hide the fact that we'd be moving the bulk of our fleet and with it the best admiral in the system. If the UHF finds out and launches an attack we could lose the war right here at Ceres. They'd have an opportunity to cut the belt, but they'll have done it from here without having to schlep all the way out to the 180 to do it. That is assuming J.D. can win against Trang."

Justin looked up from his cup, surprised. "You think he's actually better than her?"

"Honestly, I doubt it, Mr. President. But he doesn't have to be better than her. He just has to outlast her. And to be perfectly frank, J.D. hasn't really had to fight a worthy opponent. Her opposition until now has been weak willed, easily fooled, or oftentimes both. Trang will be neither; he'll give our Admiral Black an honest fight, and the UHF outnumbers us in everything. I'm not sure we can win in an honest fight if it lasts long enough."

"It almost sounds like you're making an argument for an all-out battle now."

Sinclair shook his head vigorously. "Not with the fate of the entire Alliance resting on it, sir. If Trang were here at the pivotal point of the battle I'd say yeah, let's risk it. But if they want to waste Trang out at the 180 in a slow, grueling campaign it'll give us a chance to win a couple of more victories over here and demoralize the UHF. In short, sir, I'd rather play the waiting game at the 180, because that'll buy us some time. If we beat them down bad enough on our end, the war will be over before Trang ever reaches Altamont. And don't forget, he's got to cross over sixty-seven million miles of asteroids to get there."

"There's only one flaw in your plan, Admiral."

"Yes?"

"Hektor won't give up."

"If we can get his people to give up," answered Sinclair, "it won't matter what he wants."

Justin nodded. "True enough, Admiral, but you may be forgetting something."

"What might that be, Mr. President?"

"It works both ways."

> *Uranium prices continue to increase as the supply decreases. It is one of the great contradictions of the war that all major commodities needed for a modern manufacturing civilization exist in abundance in the Alliance except for uranium, which is in abundance only on Earth and Venus. The Venusian deposits are untapped for obvious reasons, but the major supplies on Earth are being guarded like never before. Although most fusion reactors work with simple hydrogen mixes, which the Alliance has in such abundance as to be cruel, uranium is still needed for certain industrial and mining processes, and of course its use in the war effort is vital. If you have knowledge of any sources of uranium in the Alliance please help your nation, your world, your settlement, your friends and family fighting for our freedom. Let the Alliance know and you will be paid as fair a price as we can afford. Remember Neela Cord, folks. You can't spend your credits in a psyche audit chamber.*
>
> —The Clara Roberts Show
> *AIR (Asteroid belt Information Radio) Network*

Michael looked across at the man waiting to be interviewed. He couldn't believe how much had changed since he and Justin had had their first recorded conversation and wondered if this one would be equally as consequential. Given the fallout from their first, there was a part of Michael desperately hoping it wouldn't be.

"It's good to see you again, Mr. President."

Justin's smile acknowledging the compliment was tinged with sadness. Michael noted that that was becoming an ever-present trait of the leader of the Alliance.

"Michael, thank you for agreeing to this interview on such short notice. Before we begin I'd like to ask you a question . . . off the record if you don't mind."

"Of course, Mr. President."

"Have you heard from Irma?"

That caught Michael by surprise. "No, sir. I've sent her some messages but have never gotten a reply. Have you been intercepting them?"

"We wouldn't do that. Not that we're angels, we'd probably censor the hell out of them, but you'd eventually get the message. Still, it's not like there aren't ways to get around that. Plus, we have families split down the middle by this war and even if we could stop all contact I very much doubt we would."

" 'Very much doubt' is not the same as 'wouldn't.' "

"No, it's not," agreed Justin, eyes narrowed knowingly. "Nevertheless I had to ask—"

"You're wondering if she's been 'Neela'd,' " finished Michael, using one of the newest words making the rounds in the Alliance.

"Well, to put it bluntly, yes. The last time I did an interview with her she seemed a much different person. A hard-ass to be sure, but one who was as interested in reporting the truth as any reporter I'd ever met. Now she seems to be nothing but Hektor's mouthpiece."

"That's a bias I'm afraid I can't report on, Mr. President."

Justin nodded appreciatively. "The fact that you're covering the war from here speaks volumes as to your opinion of truth and accuracy, Michael. Not by one's word but by one's actions can you really get to know a man."

Michael knew that Justin had stated the truth. And that Michael never would've been allowed to report on the war and what it was doing to humanity in the UHF the way he'd been allowed to in the Alliance.

"Bottom line, Michael," continued Justin, "Irma's actions seem out of character and I find it a little hard to believe that you don't concur."

Michael sighed. "This will sound strange coming from me, Mr. President, but in order to answer you I'd like to know if it too will be off-the-record."

Justin laughed. "I thought this whole conversation was off-the-record. Some interview, huh?"

Michael smiled politely. "You know what I mean, Mr. President."

"No promises, but if possible, it will be."

Michael nodded, accepting. "Irma loves being a reporter, but she loves the system she's a part of more. Incorporation never really conflicted with her job . . . that is, until you came along. But the death . . ." Michael paused. "The death of our friend Saundra had a profound impact on her. She was never the same after that."

"It sounds to me like Saundra was more than a friend to you."

Michael nodded sadly.

"I'm truly sorry about your loss, Michael."

"Thank you, sir," he answered, thinking back to his on-again, off-again relationship with the redheaded, freckle-faced beauty whose exuberance and catlike playfulness had entranced him for years. "She was a good woman, sir. We never really moved the relationship into serious mode because we were still just having fun, showing off . . . that sort of thing. But Irma . . . well, Irma, I'd daresay, might have loved her like a daughter. She loved us all that way."

"I see."

"There's something else I guess you should know. . . ."

"Yes?"

"Irma and Hektor had a fling a number of years back."

Justin's head tilted slightly, brows raised.

"I know. We kept it quiet for obvious reasons, conflict of interest and all, but it sure came in handy when we were all running around trying to get a line on you all those many years ago, the guy from the past that GCI had stashed away in a suspension chamber in their Boulder facility."

"Long time ago," agreed Justin.

"Either way, that only made the choice easier for Irma. She loved that world, Mr. President, and is now, like so many others, fighting to keep it."

"The means justify the ends, in other words."

"Yes, sir. In her mind they do."

Justin nodded. "What about you, Michael?"

"Me, sir?"

"Yes. What is Michael Veritas fighting for?"

Michael paused. No one had ever asked him the question before and he'd never bothered to formulate an answer. Instead he spoke on instinct. "There must be an accurate record of these events, Mr. President. Not just those of the admirals, presidents, and corporate CEOs, but everyone. Our race almost always forgets who actually fights and suffers when we lose the ability to discuss . . . and therefore end up resorting to force. In almost every record of war I've ever come across we forget about the penny—or whatever they were referred to in your time."

"The poor," answered Justin, "or ironically, the minorities—but not based on shares."

"Yes, right," Michael said, nodding, "on race if I recall."

Justin tipped his head forward.

"Well, sir, I don't want that to happen anymore. I may be naïve, but I need people to know that this war is not only about humanity, it's about the individual humans themselves."

Justin looked at Michael very intently before responding. "Did you know what I was going to say as part of our 'on-the-record' interview?"

Michael shook his head. "I'm a good reporter, sir, but not that good."

Justin relaxed slightly. "Well, let's begin, then. I'm sure you're curious."

Michael released his two micro mediabot recorders into the air and cleared his mind.

"Greetings, this is Michael Veritas. I'm sitting with the President of the Outer Alliance, Justin Cord. He's invited me to the presidential suite, otherwise referred to by most as the Cliff House. In an unusual move this interview will be broadcast almost immediately after being recorded. A live broadcast is not possible due to security considerations, but I'm assured by the President that before I leave the Cliff House this interview will be viewed by the Alliance and, where not blocked, the UHF limited only by the speed of light." As Michael turned his attention to Justin the micro mediabots swung around.

"This is an unusual method for us to talk, Mr. President. Why did you wish to meet this way?"

"It seems that any time anyone has anything to say we gather a crowd and give a speech."

"You dislike your speeches, Mr. President?"

Justin smiled. "Not at all, Mr. Veritas. I love my speeches. Who wouldn't like to have millions of people cheering your every word? I'm not immune to the temptations of pride any more than the next man. But what I'm prepared to discuss is something I purposely did not want introduced in a speech. It's something that deals with an issue so central to this conflict and to every human being that I felt it needed to be addressed to every human being systemwide, and tonight it starts with you."

Michael nodded.

"This is an issue," continued Justin, "that I want each and every person to hear and understand—not as a group, not within the context of a rabble-rousing crowd but of a one-on-one talk to an individual, because ultimately that's what this war's about."

Justin paused for a second, collecting his thoughts, then continued. "Recently Hektor Sambianco, the President of the UHF, announced a new policy. He said he was prepared to give majority to any person who signed up for service in this ongoing war. On the surface it seems to be a generous, even amazing offer. At a huge expense his government will give vast numbers of people a chance to have greater, even real control over their destinies. Are you familiar with this majority proclamation, Michael?"

"Yes, sir."

"Out of curiosity, what's your take on it?"

Michael was slightly taken aback, but then he smirked. Table turning, after all, was the Cord way. "Well, sir, I'd say it's a success. It's clearly been very popular in the UHF and has made recruiting much easier. It's even been reported that they've had to turn people away because of the overflow."

"All true, Michael, and difficult as the proclamation will be from our military's point of view, it's not really the issue that's caused me concern. We've always been outnumbered and always will be."

"So what *is* your concern, then?"

Justin smiled amiably. "Care to guess?"

"Sure," Michael said in the flash of a grin. "Some members of Congress and the press have stated that with the UHF agreeing to give so many of its citizens majority, the differences between the UHF and the Alliance are now not as great they used to be."

"Yes. The fuzzier the line in the sand the more difficult it is to figure out what exactly we're fighting for."

"It's a compelling argument, Mr. President."

"Indeed it is, Michael. But let's dig deeper, shall we? What did Hektor really offer his people? The nuts and bolts of the proclamation is this: Fight for the UHF and we'll give you back a little more freedom. Freedom, I might add, that most of you lost when you were too young to realize what you'd given up. So again, Hektor Sambianco is asking you to risk your life in order to get back what should never have been taken." Justin then paused and looked directly into one of the floating mediabots. "A few precious drops of freedom for a river of blood. It doesn't matter if the blood is yours or ours; the price will be paid."

A moment of silence followed Justin's words and then he looked back toward Michael. "The Alliance doesn't have to deal with the situation in quite the same way because most of us own a majority of ourselves, but trust me, it's still an issue. Our two main factions, the NoShares and the Shareholders, deal with it every day. In fact, we too have had to tiptoe around it for fear of jeopardizing the very foundation of our Alliance. Still, the issue has become so ingrained we've lost sight of the basic difference between the UHF and ourselves. And we too must ask the burning question: What are we fighting for? We now know what the UHF is fighting for—the freedom we're already in possession of. But is that all *we're* really fighting for? To maintain the majority we already possess?"

"What are you suggesting, sir?"

"I'm saying, Michael, that no matter how much we try, we can't escape the decision that stands before us. We must face this issue without hesitation or prevarication. We must deal with the issue of incorporation itself."

Michael started to get an uneasy feeling. His initial fears about the nature of the interview now seemed to be coming to fruition, and Justin was about to open Pandora's box.

"Incorporation," continued Justin, "is so ingrained into the very fabric of action, memory, and even unconscious thought that its absence cannot be comprehended. 'Look at all the good it's done,' I've heard said. Or more important, 'How can we live without it?' But for all the good incorporation has done for the human race the price has been too high. James Madison, fourth President of the United States, once said, 'I believe there are more instances of the abridgement of the freedom of the people by gradual and silent encroachments of those in power than by violent and sudden usurpations.' Hektor's recent proclamation should be glaring evidence to the wisdom of those words and reveals the price man has paid for this encroachment. Now don't get me wrong," Justin said, pointing a finger toward one of the mediabots. "I'm not calling for the end of incorporation. And I'll support no measure that will interfere with incorporation agreements that are already in place. Indeed, I'll even oppose any measures that call for the involuntary confiscation of shares. I'll only be proactive in continuing to support the voluntary measures taken to allow individuals to end their own incorporation, but I will not and cannot support any coercive action taken against Alliance Shareholders by this government while I am its executive."

"So then what exactly is it you're proposing, Mr. President?"

"A bill, Mr. Veritas. A bill to the Congress with a recommendation for its inclusion into the Constitution—as soon as," he added, smiling, "we get around to having a constitutional convention."

"The nature of which will be?"

Justin paused and stiffened his back. His eyes once again narrowed and his face grew taut. "To make incorporation *unenforceable* in any legal context for any person born after January first of the coming year. And with this, my dear friends, the distinction becomes clear. We will no longer be fighting only for our rights in an incorporated system, but for our children's freedom from it.

"We'll be fighting for the generations that will come after us, generations that will not have to deal with this insidious dictatorship of the content, because they'll have never been incorporated to begin with. I, Justin Cord, President of the Outer Alliance, say let Hektor Sambianco offer his drops of freedom. In place of his drops I offer an ocean of liberty, and on its endless waves our children sailing freely into their future. A future, I might add, that each and every one of us will have earned for them."

PART TWO

11   A Sad Affair

Year five of the war

Christina Sadma looked down the central tube of Altamont. She was both proud and sad of the changes that had taken place in the years since her arrival. Sometimes she still saw Altamont the way it used to be, as a shadow out of the corner of her eye. But gone were the gardens of color and beauty, replaced by fields of high-protein soy and high-carbohydrate potatoes. Both food groups were very useful for creating rations, but so very bland as well. All the structures that had been used for worship and study were now storage areas or workshops. The hospital had expanded and expanded until it seemed to be half the settlement and still they were often short of beds and doctors. And saddest of all to Christina, the monks who used to stroll the gardens in quiet dignity seemed to have disappeared. She knew they were still around, but the brown robes were gone. Any monks left were to be found in battle armor or in the hospital, as likely to be tended as tending.

Christina knew that if she survived the war, she'd devote as much time as it took to restore Altamont to its former magnificence. She'd believed then and still believed now that it was right to turn the sanctuary of peace into the central fortress of the war, but in her heart it still felt wrong. There were so few wondrous places in the universe, and she couldn't help but think she'd played a major role in the corruption of one of them. Brother Sampson would have told her that she was actually doing God's will and would have made her actually believe it for a time, but he was no longer here. J.D. had made him her chaplain.

But before she could mull anymore, her DijAssist's dulcet tone reminded her that there were a thousand and one details that required attention. It came with the territory of commanding an entire battlefront in space. She was on her way to the docking port when the call came in that thirty ships from Ceres had just arrived. They were pretty banged up, with obvious signs of battle damage. She didn't need to ask who was in charge. The condition of the fleet proclaimed it. One of the brothers came up to her in battle armor with a red cross emblazoned across the chest plate. "Admiral, I have wonderful news to report. God has seen fit to deliver a fleet safely to our haven after it caused the enemy embarrassment and great loss. It is commanded by—"

"—the great and mighty Omad, admiral of the Alliance and shooter of the core," she finished with a sigh.

"He does the Lord's work very well, Admiral."

"I'm sure he does, Brother Michael, but why be so flamboyant about it? We're fighting a war here where people are suffering and dying and he seems to think it is a grand opportunity for piracy, aggrandizement, and adventure."

"He's a very skilled warrior and has led more successful and destructive raids into enemy territory then any two other fleet commanders."

Christina scoffed. "I'm not challenging his ability, Brother Michael, only his," she thought for a moment, "propriety."

"We're not all from Eris, Admiral," he answered, referring to the dwarf planet's penchant for conservatism.

"Brother Michael, I thought you of all people would appreciate a more modest demeanor."

"We're all children of the Lord, Admiral. We all have our purpose and I cannot help but think that the Lord made Admiral Hassan exactly the way he needed to be."

Christina sighed. "Now that's a depressing thought."

"If it makes you feel any better, I'm sure he says the same about you."

Christina gave her aide a rueful smile and began to mentally prepare for Omad's fleet. It would need repairs, medical exams, and a proper rearming. But the good news was that Omad always brought desperately needed supplies as well. To date he'd never taken more then he'd brought. She hoped he had more miners. Her lines were getting dangerously thin, but, she thought, what else could you expect when you went to war against an enemy ten times your size that didn't know the meaning of the word "quit"?

She arrived at the port. It was filled with the energy and noise of thousands of people going about their business, most of them in a hurry to get it done. Amid the cacophony she heard a familiar growl.

"Where the hell is that infernal woman?"

She turned and saw Omad. He was in weathered battle armor. He'd grown a close-cut beard since she'd seen him last. It was a look that was becoming popular with the men in the Alliance fleet. She personally didn't like it, as she had the nagging feeling it got in the way of efficiency and safety, but as long as the beards weren't too long she couldn't actually forbid them. Christina had to admit that it did give Omad a certain roguish charm.

She put her thumbprint on and then signed a requisition order an assistant had unceremoniously shoved in front of her and then headed for Omad, who was in conversation with her chief of maintenance and repair. Omad was push-ing a bottle in the man's face.

"Why are you trying to give my repair chief a bottle of," Christina snatched the bottle from Omad's hand and read the label, "Glenmorangie?"

Omad's smile seemed to sour a little at Christina's appearance. "Trying is right. The man won't accept it. O'Malley—now there was a man who appreci-ated a good single malt."

"Chief O'Malley died when a rail gun went out of alignment during a hurried repair," said Christina.

"P.d.'d?"

Christina nodded.

"Damn. I'm sorry, Christina; he was a good man. But that's no reason to let your Erisian ways of denial and deprivation keep this man from accepting a to-ken of my respect for the fine work his crews do on my ships."

"You don't need to bribe my people to do their jobs, Omad. It's downright in-sulting."

"Only an Erisian would consider a gift an insult." Omad looked at the repair chief. "You Erisian?"

The man smiled. "No, Admiral, I do not have that honor, but, as I've been try-ing to explain, I've recently become a Muslim."

Omad hit his head theatrically with his hand. "Well, why didn't you say so, man?" He snapped his fingers and one of the men he came with took the bottle out of his hand and replaced it with a small jar. "Allow me to give you this jar of some very fine hashish. May it give you and your work crews that small bit of pleasure that is the right of all people who toil in the service of others."

The repair chief's eyes lit up happily and he had started to reach for the jar when he stopped and looked at Christina hopefully.

"Oh, let him, Christina; you never denied O'Malley a bottle. Besides, I liber-ated all my 'gifts' from the UHF. It seems the least they could do for us." This brought a round of applause and cheers from those on the dock in earshot. Realizing she would only be saying no to annoy Omad, and not wanting to deny her crews whatever small pleasures they could get, she waved her hand in acqui-escence. Omad smiled broadly as the repair chief gladly took the gift and the docking port erupted in applause.

A couple of hours later Omad found himself pounding on Christina's door. "Sadma, open up. I know you're in there. We need to talk about my shuttles!" Christina allowed the door to open. Omad stormed in and the door closed be-hind him.

"What, no gift?" she inquired sweetly.

"Whaddaya think you're doing with my shuttles, woman?"

"Taking them."

"Well, you can't have them 'cause . . . well, 'cause they're mine and I need them!"

"First of all," she said very calmly, "on this base I outrank you and I damn well can take them. Second of all, you may need them, but if you actually just head home and try not to get into a pissing match with every UHF ship, squadron, and outpost between here and Ceres you probably won't. Third of all, you *may* need them, but we *do* need them, each and every one, all the time. Tell me I'm wrong, Omad."

Omad went from fuming, to merely upset, to an impudent grin. "Well, the least you could've done was say 'please.'"

Christina smiled coolly. "May I *please* take each and every one of your fleet's shuttles?"

Omad pretended to think about it. Going so far as to rub his chin and stare at the ceiling for a moment. "Well, since you asked so nicely." He then made an outlandish, if not somewhat awkward, bow toward Christina. She couldn't help but allow a laugh to escape her lips. Omad straightened up and moved toward her. "It's good to hear you laugh, my beloved," he said as they took each other's hands. "I don't get to hear it enough."

She put her head on his shoulder, and whispered softly into his ear, "It must be my dour Erisian demeanor."

The corners of Omad's mouth curved up.

"When this war is over I swear I'll get one laugh out of you a day . . . and three smiles."

She led him to her small bed. "I sometimes think this war will never end."

They lay down together, neither one of them taking off their uniform. "It will end, my Erisian flower," Omad said softly, "and when it does we'll get married, have a passel of kids, and move to Ceres."

"Eris," Christina said sleepily.

"We'll discuss it later."

"And . . . ," Christina said, knowing what he would promise, having heard it many times before, but wanting to hear it again.

"And . . . ," continued Omad, "we will never, ever put on one of these godforsaken uniforms again as long as we both shall live. We will never hear a shot fired in anger. We will never order anyone to battle, and we will know peace all the days of our lives." When he heard no response he peeked down at her and saw that she was asleep. He smiled wearily and soon was asleep contentedly beside her, snuggled up on a bed made for one.

Ceres

The shuttle drifted off the Gedretar shipyard moorings, powered up, moved to the center of the Via Cereana, and then accelerated to the maximum allowable speed. It was in all ways an unremarkable vessel like thousands that could be seen in operation around the main Alliance fleet. But unlike those thousands of others this one, once free of its moorings, was immediately surrounded by four tactical fighters that proceeded to escort it to the *War Prize II*, flagship of the Alliance fleet.

The *War Prize II* was a substantially larger ship than her namesake, being part of a new design that had been rushed into production and practically thrown off the assembly line at the Jovian Shipyards. Like many ships, she had been fitted out as she flew to the battlefronts. This form of hyperefficient construction had been the brainchild of Omad and Kenji. The way it worked was once the hull had been completed and the heavy elements added—including propulsion, weapons, and fusion reactors—the ship was sent to the battlefronts trailed by ships, called flying gantries, ingeniously created to be mobile shipyards. These ships would then provide work crews who would spend the time in transit getting many of the vital but ancillary systems installed, aligned, and programmed; systems that didn't really need for the ship to be immobile. The only drawback was that from time to time a ship could arrive at the front lacking certain amenities. In one of the more infamous incidents the AWS *Pickax* actually arrived from Gedretar at the Battle of Jupiter's Eye without functioning toilets, the lack of which saddled an otherwise honorable and worthy ship with a rather unfortunate nickname. Within the gantry systems the same "buildup" ships could then escort damaged ships back to either the Gedretar shipworks or the Jovian Shipyards and begin repairs en route. It had taken most of a year to get the kinks worked out and get enough flying gantries to make the system effective, but the rise in ship production and repair had been off the charts.

The lone shuttle approached the new flagship, the first of a line of "supercruisers," then slowly drifted into the main shuttle bay. The four escorts waited patiently for the shuttle to be swallowed up by the cruiser, then broke off and made their way over to a large spacecraft carrier, yet another naval innovation.

Inside the cavernous bay of the *War Prize II* over four hundred officers and crew were assembled in dress uniform. The shuttle came to a stop in front of a lone woman of average height also garbed in the dress uniform of the Alliance fleet. Her lapels showed the insignia indicating the rank of lieutenant. As the shuttle door opened, all those assembled came to immediate and stiff attention.

J. D. Black looked over her new shuttle's interior and had to admit she wasn't too displeased. She'd been saddened by the destruction of *War Prize I,* a result, she felt, of her poor leadership. Her only solace had been that she'd been able to ram the listing vessel into the enemy's flagship. The tactic had worked, though, in that it broke the enemy line and gave the rest of her fleet a chance to unleash enough unreturned main gun fire to force surrender. Her personal shuttle was one of the few things left from *War Prize I*'s brash assault, and she'd used it while moving her flag temporarily from one ship to the other. Unfortunately, it hadn't been up-to-date enough to warrant a retrofit and inclusion within her new supercruiser. And so she now found herself eyeing the interior of her new one.

She thought back to her last encounter, now called the Battle of Jupiter's Eye.

Admiral Tully had somehow managed to convince UHF fleet command to give him another chance. He must've had some amazing connections with the corporate world to still have that much pull after his first resounding defeat. But he'd sold them on what he'd promised would be his brilliant war-winning move. J.D. couldn't fault the UHF for wanting to try something different. The war was bleeding them dry. They hadn't been able to defeat the Alliance in any major battle for over a year and a half. What they had managed to do was fight to a draw. And that draw had been purposely and expertly managed by the Alliance. Rather than meet the UHF head-on in any open ship-to-ship fighting, the Alliance had seen fit to engage their enemy on more familiar territory. So the pitched battles were often in and around any asteroid the Alliance had decided to mount their assaults from. At this point the advantage had belonged to the side fighting for its survival within the familiar crevices, caves, and grottoes of their own territory. That series of battles over the year and half they'd so far waged had collectively come to be know as the Battles of the Dodge. But, thought J.D., the tide was beginning to turn as the UHF was slowly beginning to push out of Eros and edge its way ever nearer to Altamont. The fighting at the 180 had become the most constant and bloodiest of the war. Trang, to J.D.'s chagrin, had kept on attacking a vast area of the belt, taking and securing it one blasted settlement and rock at a time. It was slow and the UHF was paying a heavy price, but given the distance from the main centers of Alliance industry it was only a matter of months before that now-fabled settlement fell, and with it the heart of the Alliance. For with Altamont in the UHF's hands the belt would effectively be cut in two.

Given the huge amount of losses the UHF had been suffering—the war had already cost over four million p.d.'s, and it was increasing almost exponentially month by month—it had been easy for Tully to portray Trang as "the butcher of the belt" and proffer an alternative plan. J.D. also knew that Tully could not let his hated former subordinate get the attention and fame that he felt was due to him. So Tully had cajoled and sold his great stratagem and Fleet Command had bought in.

Fortunately, the Alliance had learned of Tully's plans through surreptitious means. It seemed the admiral was planning nothing short of the conquest of Jupiter itself. It hadn't been a bad plan, all things being equal. The UHF would wait for the Alliance to commit to some sector of the belt's front and then skip over it rather than go straight through. The tactic was novel in that it bypassed the deadly ambushes that would have awaited them in the belt itself, but it was also pointless—why go around something you're going to have to conquer anyway? But that hadn't been the point. Tully wanted a grand victory, and seizing Jupiter was just such a victory. He could always go back later and take the pesky rocks one at a time. The big problem, however, was that by jumping over the belt without first securing all the rocks below and between, Tully would have a dangerously exposed position as well as a much-lengthened supply and retreat line if something was to go wrong. It was, thought J.D., the type of bold move the UHF should have done earlier in the war but had been afraid to. As it turned out, she'd justified their fears.

J.D. knew she'd need to draw Tully out, but in doing so she'd have to take a gamble. She'd have to send at least one hundred ships—masked to appear at least double that number—far enough away that they'd effectively be useless in the ensuing battle. She chose to have them shoot the core in a feint to make it look like they were going to attack either Luna or Earth. By losing the use of those hundred ships J.D. would have to rely on skill over numbers to secure a victory. Tully had bought the ruse and immediately left for Jupiter with a large contingent of the UHF fleet.

He'd read the comm traffic and indeed it seemed like he'd caught the Alliance by surprise. Shadow fleets of four to five ships scrambled, and Jupiter appeared to be in a panic as even more ships fled from one moon and settlement to another. J.D. had even let Tully destroy two half-finished warships from the Jovian Shipyards to make him believe he'd finally caught the Alliance unawares. J.D. wished she could've seen his face as he circled Jupiter and was not met by a helpless Jovian capital preparing for surrender but the Alliance fleet that had circled around from the opposite direction. The ensuing battle had been as nasty as any fought in the war so far.

J.D. still remembered every detail. The UHF had fought well, as well as her own spacers, in fact. If they'd been better led, they may have even achieved a draw, which given their location in the heart of the Alliance would have been a disaster. But Tully had wanted J.D. too badly and, in an effort to get to her, put his ship out of line, forcing his tightly packed formation to follow suit. It would be the last command he'd ever give. J.D. saw the chink in his armor and gave the order. She rammed his flagship, putting hers out of commission, and so disrupted the UHF fleet that they never recovered. Jupiter's gravity well offered no rapid escapes. With the flagship out, the battle turned into a slugging match. When it was over the bulk of the UHF fleet had been destroyed. Sadly, the enemy had fought so well that much of J.D.'s fleet had been too badly damaged to launch an immediate assault on Mars, which had been her ultimate plan. Still, so great was the loss in men and ships to the UHF that she'd believed it should have been enough to sue for peace. And if not for Samuel U. Trang it just might have been.

Trang had found her decoy raiding party and had not been fooled for a second as to its true size. So he set his own trap. Twenty merchant ships filled with enough uranium to keep the Alliance in the war for another dozen years. Guarded by a mere thirty warships, the merchant ships were too tempting a prize for Commodore Cordova to ignore. He should have known better, but he'd fallen under that most dangerous of spells: underestimating the enemy. Cordova fought hard and the warships protecting the merchant ships eventually succumbed to his relentless onslaught. They fled, leaving Cordova to proudly corral his prize— that is, until all twenty of the uranium ships blew up, taking twelve of Cordova's ships with them. The explosion also managed to incapacitate dozens more. It was then that Trang's most loyal and able officer, Captain Abhay Gupta, and forty UHF warships appeared from the other side of Mercury. They'd hidden their presence by using the sun's interference and a new communications protocol that mimicked solar static. By the time Cordova's replacement had been able to organize his remaining ships the battle was begun. Captain Lu should have ordered an immediate retreat, taken his losses, and run but felt the tide turning in his favor. Had he bothered to ask himself why someone who'd planned a battle so well would attack with so few ships perhaps he too would have lived. Lu hadn't been aware of Trang's twenty-five warships until they'd cut off his retreat.

Of the one hundred warships that J.D. sent, only seven managed to return. She'd lost Cordova, Lee, and Lu, all of whom died with their ships. The only solace she took was that she'd never have to worry about telling them apart again. It was a defeat on par with the loss of Eros, in some ways even worse, as it came at just the right time to mitigate the UHF defeat at Jupiter. That hadn't been the biggest disaster for the Alliance, though. Trang was finally promoted to Grand Admiral and put in charge of all UHF forces. Even his most ardent foes could do nothing to deny the "hero of Mercury" and the "savior of the core" supreme command after that. Not that Hektor would have listened to them. J.D. had hoped Trang would try to do something flashy, like launch a premature attack on Altamont or even try a foray out of Mars. At least if he did that she could encircle him while his forces were still recovering from the Jupiter fiasco. But Trang hadn't done anything rash at all. And with his fleet so diminished it would have meant he'd need to rob Peter to pay Paul, or draw ships and experienced personnel from the 180, which he wasn't about to do.

What Trang had done instead was send Gupta, newly re-promoted to admiral, back to Mars to outfit and train the new ships already replacing the losses at Jupiter, gambling that J.D. would not be in a position to attack anytime soon. Then Trang went back to the unglamorous, grinding, and thankless job of cutting the 180 in half. J.D. knew it was the correct course of action because it was exactly what she would've done in his place. Why give up the fruits of a two-year campaign and certain, if expensive, victory for the risks of battle on the other side of the belt?

So J.D. spent the months following the Jupiter victory getting her fleet ready for operations and was given, along with a brand-new ship, a brand-new shuttle she currently found herself being transported in. The shuttle had been made to her specifications, and even though she'd ordered nothing special beyond that which would've enhanced performance, the techs at Gedretar had purposely disobeyed. Her shuttle had a simulated polished wood interior with bathing facilities, sleeping accommodations, and an entertainment system worthy of GCI's last real Chairman.

J.D. smiled as she remembered the man. She'd been floored when Justin had finally revealed the truth. However, when she looked back on her years as head of Legal for the system's largest corporation it explained a lot with regard to The Chairman's often unusual behavior. So while the old man may not have truly liked her shuttle, the man she knew would have at least pretended he did.

Much as she hated to admit it, the damned techs had really screwed her but good, because the rest of the shuttle was exactly what she needed. It was fast, well armored, and capable of being a communications hub all on its own. If she demanded a new one it probably wouldn't be as good, and if she had this one altered it would take away from the time she never seemed to have enough of. So the great J. D. Black found herself outmaneuvered by a group of surly dockworkers and had to retreat with only the threat of having it gutted the next chance she got. The bastards were even grinning as she boarded their hedonist contraption.

Unconsciously she ran her fingers over the scarred half of her face and considered what to do about Trang. For all the joy the Alliance had about her victory at Jupiter, its only long-term effect was to bring her most dangerous adversary into command. She knew she'd have to face him in combat sooner or later, and for the first time the iron certainty of victory she'd always had was nowhere to be found. It wasn't fear; win or lose, she knew she'd do her best, but still, she'd always known victory was certain. However, with Trang all she got was a blank.

She couldn't get a feeling for him that she could with all her other opponents. More frightful, she knew he wouldn't listen when she whispered her famous mantras across the space that separated their ships. The others always seemed to.

J.D. put those worries aside and checked her appearance. Her dark blue uniform was too stiff and too laden with all manner of medallion. Her hair was drawn back and pulled into a tight bun, revealing even more of the now famously deformed face. She had a duty to perform and, like all her duties, she would perform it well.

J.D. exited her shuttle into a vast and gleaming bay that was silent except for the sound of her footsteps clanking down the small metallic gangplank.

"Admiral on board!" shouted the officer in charge of the shuttle bay. J.D. then made a beeline for that officer, who immediately saluted. She returned his with one of her own. The fleet that had started out eschewing fancy uniforms, pomp, and protocol at first had become accepting of it and as the war continued had finally become enamored of it. J.D. realized the fleet needed the structure and symbolism that the panoply brought. It increased the sense of family and group cohesion that she knew was just as important to winning battles as ships and guns.

She walked over to Lieutenant Nitelowsen, who saluted and had the salute returned. "Lieutenant," asked J.D. loud enough for all in the bay to hear, "is the ship ready?"

The question was of course rhetorical. J.D. knew as much about every aspect of the vessel as she could without actually having been on board. She'd been so crunched for time since her return from Jupiter that she hadn't been able to do more than acknowledge the ship's arrival three days prior. At which point she'd sent her trusted aide to make sure there were no obvious problems. The last thing she needed was a repeat of the *Pickax* affair. *Warped Prize* had come to mind.

"Admiral," answered Lieutenant Nitelowsen, "the ship is ready for action. I have inspected every section and tested all systems personally. She'll do the job, ma'am."

J.D. then turned toward the assembled crew. "In the name of our commander in chief, in the name of the Congress and the people of the Outer Alliance, I, Janet Delgado Black, admiral in good standing of the armed forces of the Outer Alliance, declare this ship operational. I confirm on her the name *War Prize II* and accept her and her crew as the flagship for the entire fleet. May Allah bless this ship and all who serve on her."

The entire shuttle bay erupted in cheers as caps, gloves, and various other objects were thrown high into the air and people turned toward one another either hugging or shaking each other's hands (as all good citizens of the Alliance did, in emulation of their President). J.D. let it continue on for a good few minutes. No one actually approached her, but they all noticed her famous half smile, made more so by its rare appearance. The truth was, J.D. needed these moments even more than her spacers did. It was as water in a desert for a soul scorched by the heat of constant battle. But when her face resumed its normal mask of unattainable beauty and scar-strengthened iron will, Lieutenant Nitelowsen called the assembly to an attention that was instantly given.

J.D. once again looked around at the jubilant ranks. "Remember this moment," she said. "Tell it to your unborn children and grandchildren, who, thanks to the foresight and wisdom of our President, shall be born to a freedom that is their birthright. A birthright long forsaken by humanity . . . but no more. Now we must go about our duties. Those of you who can will be given leave to go to Ceres for the memorial service of Captain James Seacrest. It will take place in the grand concourse under the Cliff House." J.D. paused and then addressed the bay sergeant. "You may dismiss the crew, Sergeant."

The sergeant nodded, saluted, and dispensed his duties with a voice scalding enough to melt steel.

Justin was watching the holographic feed from the *Alliance Free Press*. Normally he wouldn't have bothered. He had better things to do when life foisted little luxuries like downtime on him, but this was something he actually wanted to see. It was a special one-hour report by Michael Veritas on Janet Delgado Black. What made it fascinating was how Michael had had it crafted: lots of holos with zero Janet dialogue. It was only about halfway through that Justin realized what Michael was actually doing. The special was not about the admiral. It was about how the Alliance felt about the admiral.

By the time he was done watching, Justin wasn't sure whether to be grateful or scared out of his wits. Janet was . . . venerated was the only word that seemed to apply. All classes, all parties, all ages, everyone had a love for Janet Delgado Black. Even the families of the permanently deceased were incapable of blaming her for the battles that had caused the losses they were now suffering. The Alliance needed her, but Justin realized it was not just to win battles. They needed Janet to be Fleet Admiral J. D. Black, the blessed one, the unimpeachable and holy guardian of all things good. They needed her to be an icon. They could no more find fault with J.D. than they could with a beloved relative or their newfound devotion to faith. Indeed, for many the line between Janet and the Almighty was becoming blurred, if not in their minds, far more dangerously, in their hearts.

What made this realization so ironic was that Justin fully understood it in relation to Janet but was incapable of realizing that he'd achieved a similar, if slightly different, aura himself. He realized that it was dangerous for a person to have such mythical status if the Alliance was to remain a civilization devoted to liberty. But the quandary was simple. He needed the Fleet Admiral to be mythic in order to win the war. But if she was still mythic after the war—assuming they won—it would be very difficult to demystify her. He filed this under "Problems to Deal with Later" but made a mental note to keep that one near the top of that long list.

He was about to cancel the program and get back to his tasks when a small advertisement caught his eye.

"That sonova . . . ," he growled, shaking his head. "sebastian, find Admiral Hassan and get his ass up here now!"

"Right away, Justin."

A few minutes later Omad was in the presidential office. "Didja see the ad?" he said, barging through the door, proud as a peacock.

"Happy lifeday?" asked Justin, exasperated.

"Yeah," laughed Omad. "How great is that?"

"Omad, do I need to remind you that I don't actually have a lifeday?"

"Well, no . . . but—"

"And I certainly don't appreciate your giving me one and then inviting the entire damned system to celebrate it!"

"Oh, don't be that way," admonished Omad. "Just 'cause you don't know when yours is doesn't mean it don't exist."

Lifedays, knew Justin, had replaced birthdays. And while he was familiar with the custom, he'd purposely chosen not to partake—that is, up until his friend had decided to foist one upon him. It was one of the societal shifts that had made Justin feel in his gut that he was *in* but not necessarily *of* his new world. Medical science had advanced to the point where it was possible to have a surrogate system provide the embryo with all the medical care it needed, with a far greater degree of safety for the growing life. Unlike a woman carrying a child to term, a surrogate womb could monitor every stage of the child's development and alert medical staff should in utero care be needed. Justin thought the idea cold and heartless, but when he'd visited a maternity ward—the name now divorced from its roots—he saw a machine that was far less mechanical and a lot more biological. The growing child could, through the biochamber, hear and feel a recorded heartbeat, listen to its parents' voices (prerecorded or present), and experience the sounds of predetermined music, sports, and even literature.

Knowing how the system worked, Justin was amazed that one out of three women still chose to have "natural" childbirth at all, especially given the fact that almost all of humanity's physiologically or psychologically handicapped—

DeGens—came from the natural method. In the Alliance the numbers were necessarily different. There simply wasn't the luxury or time to carry a child, and so only one in ten gave birth the old-fashioned way. Still, it was seen more as a mark of stamina or ideology than anything worthy of celebration. This new world chose to rejoice when the baby came home from the maternity ward, as opposed to the moment it emerged from the bio-machine covered in a gooey placental mass. Everyone knew the day their child was conceived, even natural birth mothers. So conception, or lifeday as it was commonly referred to, had come to replace the day of physical emergence or "birthday" as a celebration of an individual's entrance into life.

Justin had fervently hoped that Neela would fall into the "ideological" category and choose to carry rather than go "biomech." Call him old-fashioned, he'd said at the time, but there was simply no sight more beautiful to behold than a mother with child . . . especially if with his. However, he quickly saw by the look of utter determination on his wife's face that it was not an argument he was going to win. Their child, she'd said, would have a lifeday, and Justin could go on celebrating his anachronistic birthday if he so desired. The truth was that, even had he wanted to, there was no practical way for Justin to find his actual day of conception. So it was with much annoyance that he learned that his lifeday was going to be celebrated on the seventh of the next month, a mere two weeks away. Further, that the source of this long-sought-after information was none other than the great war hero, trusted subordinate of J. D. Black, and the man universally acknowledged as his best friend.

"So how'd you figure it out? Did I leave trace DNA somewhere that you somehow managed to suborn, test, and verify?"

"Nah," answered Omad, pawing and staring intently at a small bust of Abraham Lincoln he'd removed from a shelf, "just made it up."

Justin looked at Omad and fought off contradicting impulses to laugh and scream. "You just made it up?"

"Well, not completely," answered Omad, replacing the bust and turning to face Justin. "I know your birthday, went back nine months, and rolled two dice."

"Two dice; you determined my lifeday with two dice?"

"Yeah," said Omad, wandering over to the bar and pouring himself a drink. "My starting point was nine months prior to your birthday, your loose conception date as it were. The first roll was to see if the lifeday I chose for you would be after your theoretical conception date or before it. A four, five, or six would be an 'after' and a one, two, or three would be a 'before.'"

"And the second die?"

"The number of days to be added or subtracted from your theoretical starting date."

"Of course," said Justin, with a slanted grin. "And why, may I ask, did you de-cide I needed a lifeday now?"

Omad laughed, then took a seat in front of Justin's desk, propping his feet up at the table's edge.

"What makes you think this has anything to do with you?"

Justin raised his eyebrow.

"This day is for *us*, Justin," said Omad, tipping the glass to his mouth. "We could have a nice long discussion about it, but to be honest I'm tired and have a ridiculously full schedule. So I'll make you a deal."

"For the last time, I am not going to invest in textured inflatables."

"Ha-ha. Different kind of deal."

"I'm listening."

"All you have to do is walk down to the end of the lobby. If by the time you get back you want me to go on the Neuro and announce that the whole lifeday thing was a big mistake, I solemnly swear I'll do it."

Justin eyed Omad suspiciously. "Let me get this straight. I just have to walk to the lobby of the Cliff House and back and then you're prepared to call this whole thing off."

"I swear by the beard of the Prophet."

"An oath that would certainly be more believable if you didn't have that fine single malt in your hands."

"I'll drink to that." And Omad did.

"Fine," said Justin heading for the door. "But when I get back this nonsense ends." He tapped an icon on his desk's holodisplay and was immediately met at the door by his escort, the always-present Sergeant Holke.

A few minutes later Justin marched back in, subdued. He went to his desk, sat down, and looked disdainfully at his friend.

"Well," asked Omad, "do I call in the mediabots?"

"You set that up."

"Audit my soul and call me what you will, I swear I did not."

"You know what happened, though."

Omad smiled. "I have a pretty good idea. How far did you get before the first one?"

"Not twenty feet."

"How many total?"

"Lost count."

"And finally, my good friend and supreme commander, how did they seem?"

"Overjoyed," Justin said almost despairing. "It was one big 'happy lifeday' party."

"Don't take it so hard, Justin. Like I said, we need you to have a lifeday so we can celebrate it. It won't be official, not this year, but we need national heroes and national holidays. We don't have many yet, but this will do for a start."

"Celebrating a day made up with the roll of some dice is really what the Alliance needs?"

"Great, ain't it?" said Omad, raising his glass. "Cheers."

Smith Grand Concourse, Ceres

The gathering had started out as an informal affair, a small memorial to honor a hero by the name of James Seacrest.

But something had happened.

Friends of the fallen soldier had come to the site where he'd loved to picnic with his family. They'd wanted to bury his ashes there. At first a concourse attendant was not sure what to do, so she asked the spacers to wait, which they did. But as more spacers walked by and found out what was going on they joined their comrades in waiting. It didn't take long for someone to bring them a blanket, some food, and a bottle of wine. As some had to report for duty, they were replaced by others. Within twelve hours the twenty or so original cluster of soldiers had grown into a crowd of hundreds and, shortly after that, thousands.

Some fool had wanted to order all the people to disperse, but a well-placed call to Justin got the dispersal order rescinded. After he got the OK from Sinclair and J.D., a presidential order was issued allowing all military personnel who wished to congregate in the concourse to do so provided it didn't interfere with their duties. Justin immediately sent down all the fine foods and alcohols he'd been sent as gratuities from people around the Alliance. It wasn't nearly enough to cover the crowd, but it was enough that word got out. Furthermore, Justin announced that a formal internment ceremony would be held in two days' time for Captain Seacrest.

The crowd of thousands swelled to tens of thousands, all of whom had come to the concourse to talk and grieve, if not for the captain, then for someone else they knew who'd died in the war, and they all mourned for someone. Seacrest had unwittingly become the ethereal embodiment of the suddenness and absolute finality of permanent death. The seemingly spontaneous outpouring of grief had been explained to Justin by the Alliance's leading cognitive psychologist, Dr. Ayon Nesor. "Justin," she'd said, "the phenomenon of permanent death on this scale is foreign to both the Alliance and the UHF. While I'm not sure how the UHF is dealing with it, given the repressive nature of their regime, I do know that such grief *must* find an outlet. But more important, it must find a community within which to share that grief." Justin had avoided going down to the park until the hour of the actual internment. He knew that if he went too early the gathering would end up being about him and he felt there'd been enough of him. The people who gathered in the park needed time on their own.

When it was finally time to enter the fray he did it without his typical entourage. He simply went by himself; or at least he appeared to be by himself. Sergeant Holke had seeded Justin's path to the dais with over a hundred undercover operatives whose job it was to be suspicious of any unusual twitch or movement. But such was the spell of the occasion that Justin had not been mobbed or stared at from afar. For one brief moment it was understood that he was simply one sad person among many. Only once on his way to the dais did he almost break. A young couple approached him. He saw she was a helmsman and he was a comm officer. The woman was holding a newborn child.

"Her name is Neela," the woman had said, "and we wanted to thank you, Mr. President. We both have majority, but she's free. It's different, isn't it . . . the way you feel all the time? Is that how she'll feel?" Justin was not able to trust his voice, but he managed a nod. They left without saying a word and Justin never even got their names.

At one point he saw Janet not too far off. She was also wading through the crowd and seemed to have a word or comment for every group or individual that approached. Seeing her move effortlessly in the throng and sensing the complete devotion she commanded, Justin was once again grateful she didn't have dictatorial ambitions. Their paths finally crossed and everyone, by an unspoken understanding, gave them a wide berth.

"I hope this isn't too difficult for you, Justin," offered Janet.

"I was going to express the same concern for you."

"What happened to me was hard," she answered, making her way past a security detail and into a cordoned-off area, "but I'll see Manny again in some way and he'll be the man I love. What Hektor did to you was worse . . . far worse."

"You don't think I'll get Neela back as she was."

"Certainly not in this universe."

"And here I thought God could do anything," Justin said with a friendly jibe.

"My understanding of the Lord is limited, Justin. I'm but a simple spacer."

"Maybe not so simple," he answered, inviting her to take the seat next to his while they waited. "Reminds me of an old song called 'Unanswered Prayers.' "

Janet looked at him quizzically.

"In essence, just because God can, does not mean that he will or should."

Of all the transformations that had occurred over the past two years, Janet's becoming a full-fledged believer had been difficult for him to follow. It was not that she adhered to any particular faith, but it was certainly undeniable that she had it. Justin, being an American of the old school, knew that he had all the prejudices and virtues of that fallen civilization. He had a ruthless respect for the idea that others could believe what they wished, combined with a deep suspicion of anyone who actually did.

"I've had similar conversations with your friend Fawa." Justin noted that the only time Janet was not the fearsome, wholly competent war mistress of the fleet was when she was thinking about or with her religious mentor. Fawa was very much like a favorite aunt Janet desperately wanted to be proud of her.

An emissary approached the two leaders and informed them that the ceremony would begin shortly if they could only "be patient." They smiled amiably and continued their conversation.

"She's informed me," J.D. said quite seriously, "that you're resisting all her attempts to convert you to the true path." On Justin's momentary look of alarm Janet burst into laughter. "You don't need to worry, Justin; she's not trying to convert you or anyone. Actually, she says you're doing the work of Allah by freeing the human race . . . and she's right. Personally, I think you'd find comfort if you believed in God, but we're all comforted by the knowledge that Adonai believes in you."

"Why do you do that?"

"I do many things, Justin; which 'that' are you referring to?"

"That name thing. Fawa's a devout Muslim, so I'd think you'd lean in that direction. Yet you refer to God as the grand watchmaker, Allah, God, Adonai. I've even heard you say the great spiri, or the great mother. Can't make up your mind?"

"Ah, *that* that," said Janet, pausing for a moment. "I have many different beliefs and I have never formally chosen one and now I don't think it's advisable that I do so. Fawa feels it would not serve the will of . . ." Janet paused again. ". . . the big guy in the sky." Her lips formed into an impish grin. "As you know, there was a religious conclave of all the surviving faiths nearly two years ago and many things were decided. We're very mindful of the reprehensible things done in God's name and the price paid by humanity for that evil. I cannot tell you the revulsion we feel when we study about the abomination of calling for a believer to be killed for the reason that his or her belief in the Lord is different from your own. Frankly, they deserved near extinction."

"But it's not extinct, Janet. It's become nearly universal in the fleet and is growing very quickly in the Alliance."

"Yes, and that's why I cannot now or I think ever will have a chosen faith. There should be no pressure for the path one takes. Oh, it's no secret that Islam has more of an appeal to me than the others, but Allah understands this as he understands all things. The notion of faith is, I believe, far more important than the choice of a particular one."

"And what of the unfaithful?" asked Justin.

"What of them? If they have faith, I believe they'll have greater understanding of things; if not, I can't order someone to believe. It would be stupid to try and evil to force someone to pretend. As if God wants frightened adherents bowing on trembling knees. The harm all those fanatics did before the Grand Collapse," she said with true rancor, "those idiots I'd shoot, if I had the ability."

"*You* sound perfectly reasonable, but what of the person who replaces you . . . and Fawa? That's where I see the problem. These things always start out beneficently and ultimately get distorted by the selfish and megalomaniacal."

"Yes, yes." Janet nodded. "Don't think I'm not aware of it. But also know that Fawa is as well and there will be a conclave soon to discuss that very issue. Namely, how to navigate the rebirth of faith with an eye toward the eradication of fanaticism."

Justin laughed. "That's a tall order, Janet . . . even for someone like you."

"Well, thankfully," she answered, tapping her copious array of medallions, "my task is more defined."

Justin nodded, a tepid smile working the corners of his mouth. "Though I must say, I'm surprised by how quickly religion has returned. When I was first awakened I thought it had simply faded away, and now we have places of worship, chaplains, and theology schools all over. I can't get my head around it."

"Why are you surprised that a thirsty man drinks deeply?"

At that moment a bell rang and Justin saw that it was time. He and Janet got up out of the chairs and then made their way over to a shallow trench where a newly planted sapling of an elm tree had been placed.

The first speaker was a short, lean man. He was in the hooded robes of the order of the Hospitallers with a chaplain's insignia glinting from his collar. In space, chaplains used regular uniforms, but with Janet's influence their traditional garb became their dress uniforms. The man stood straighter and pulled down his cowl.

"My name is Sampson," he began. "I am a brother in the Order of Saint John, liaison to the abbot, and as such had the honor of meeting James Seacrest. I will admit that my first meeting with the man was, how shall I put it? . . . Less than holy." This brought a whoop from some of the crowd who obviously knew the details of that particular meeting. "Of course the captain wanted to meet with me in a less than sanctified setting—in order to test my tolerance, I suppose. Thankfully the good Lord will excuse a lot. But I could tell from the start that the captain was a good man. I am now allowed to tell the following story for the first time, and trust me, it deserves to be told."

The crowd quieted down.

"Until recently," he continued, "we were in danger of losing this war. It had nothing to do with lack of will or lack of power. Although our population is small and our capacity underdeveloped, we've been ably led in both the civilian and military sector and our efforts have kept the deluded, controlled, and numerically superior enemy at bay. But all of it was for naught due to an extreme lack of that most rare resource, uranium, all of whose major supplies lay within the core. And what little there was in the Outer Alliance was mined centuries ago. That deficit was kept secret until now for fear of alerting the enemy to our weakness.

"So, where to get this most precious resource? Enter Captain Seacrest. The captain had surveyed resources on the planet Venus, still only in the earliest stages of terraformation and as hellish a planet as our Lord has seen fit to place in this solar system. Still that planet had something our Alliance so desperately needed: an ample supply of uranium. The captain noticed something else as well. Uranium was closely guarded on Earth but practically ignored on Venus. And why wouldn't it be? Venus is deep in UHF territory and a planet that poses extreme risks even with the most advanced technology under the best of conditions. Only a madman would contemplate trying to get uranium from Venus during a war. It was a desperate plan, but we were desperate."

Brother Sampson paused for a moment, exhaled deeply, and then went on.

"I still remember how the captain explained it all to me. It was simple, he'd said. All we had to do was pretend to be UHF marines, sneak onto their side of the lines by the belt, from there get shipped back to Eros with the wounded, then sneak out of the UHF hospital and arrange transport to Venus, grab some old surveying ships parked in orbit, modify them so they could do actual mining work, dig enough uranium to provide for the entire Alliance for however much longer the war would last," Sampson took a breath, "then steal a cargo hauler, transport this vast amount of uranium mined from the surface to the stolen vessel, and then get that incredibly precious cargo out of the core through some of the most monitored and well-defended space in human history . . . back to the Alliance." He took another breath. "Yeah . . . simple."

The crowd laughed and clapped their approval.

"My first reaction was, 'Why, dear captain, are you telling me this?' Well, it seemed that their medic was not able to make the mission and they needed a new one quickly. I was highly recommended by Admiral Sadma for my supposed courage and level head in combat. Truly no good deed goes unnoticed or unpunished, especially in the fleet." This brought more general laughter from the audience.

"As confident as the captain was, it didn't go quite as planned. Of the seventeen of us who left on that mission, only six returned, and if it were not for the courage and sacrifice of all those men and women, the last being the captain himself, we would not have made it and the Alliance may have already fallen. But we did not fail. I don't claim to understand the will of God, but I believe He guided us so that the Alliance may continue. I grieve that I will no longer have the company of the man whom I had grown to respect above all others. I grieve that I will not see so many who are gone from us. But though they are gone, we are not gone from them. In surety we will be reunited with those we have lost in the fullness of time, for that is the mercy of the Lord. Remember them and cherish the memories and know that we shall meet again."

Brother Sampson then produced a small sack from his inner robe, then bent to his knees and proceeded to sprinkle the ashes of Captain Seacrest into the open trench. After the sack had been emptied, Brother Sampson gently touched the sapling, smiled sadly, and once again stood up.

Turning toward the large crowd, he said in a somber voice, "Please join me in reciting the Lord's Prayer."

For Justin the words appeared floating in the air above his DijAssist. A part of him felt uncomfortable reciting words he didn't actually believe in, but he now understood Janet's dilemma a little better. He may not have been an actual believer, but many of the people who believed in him were. He quickly came to the conclusion that they needed his comfort more than his doubt, and therefore would not deny them. And so he began, "The Lord is my Shepheard, I shall not want. . . ."

UHF capital, Mars

Dr. Neela Harper was going about her rounds. She was down to three days a week in her practice. But it wasn't because she was needed less. Even with a vast expansion in the facilities and the personnel, there was still a bigger backlog than ever. It was not only the larger battles but also the type of warfare. All along the periphery of the belt there were little battles going on. Admiral Trang was prosecuting the war with more energy than all of his predecessors combined. Once he took over he decided on an entirely new strategy; the only way to make the Alliance lose was to make it collapse. The problem was, the Alliance had done a remarkable job of developing a resilient industry and it had a population far better suited for warfare in space than the UHF. They also had all the resources to keep the war going for the next thousand years, with the exception of one: numbers.

Neela sometimes felt guilt that she'd saved the man's career when he was the cause of so much suffering in the human race, but logically he'd been correct. The only undeniable advantage the UHF had was in their numbers, and they must take full advantage of that resource if they were to have any chance of winning. Until Trang came along the war was a series of brief violent battles, followed by long periods of respite. This played into Alliance strengths. But with Trang's new microoffensives going on at over a hundred different places around the belt, the Alliance was not getting any respite at all. There was no break in the combat. The Alliance could not be everywhere the UHF could be and would therefore start to break at some point.

But the losses had been untenable. Attacking the Alliance all over at once meant going into a territory where every settlement could and often was made into its own little fortress, where the Alliance knew every rock, every asteroid flow, and every resource and used them to maximum effect. But more important, it was a territory that people lived in and called home and would fight to the permanent death to deny to those they considered invaders. Neela had heard the losses were often four to one against the UHF. But Trang didn't seem to care. He could take those losses and win. Even at four to one Trang knew the Alliance would eventually lose. But in the six months since the admiral had taken over complete command, the death toll had risen to over twenty million and the number of mentally and physically wounded was over seventy-five million. And, realized Neela, those numbers were only going to rise.

Though there was nothing she could do about that, she'd at least been able to lend her ample skill set to the cause. She was able to help Hektor Sambianco navigate the tricky political situations that kept cropping up. Meeting the needs of keeping the UHF fighting the war, now well into its fifth year, was a constant struggle and Hektor had come to rely on her insight. She often spent whole days and nights helping him deal with all the problems incumbent on a man responsible for nine-tenths of the human race.

However much Neela's commitment to Hektor had impinged on her trauma center schedule, it hadn't stopped her from giving her all when she managed to break away and get back into the office. Today was one such day. She'd gotten in bright and early in an attempt to catch up with the mounting workload. She logged into her secure patient files and scanned for any significant incidents she'd need to be aware of before her group therapy began. *Good,* she thought. *Nothing that stands out.* She was always on the lookout for, but rarely seemed to find, rage or anger directed toward the top—at least never toward Trang. Even with all the battle-fatigued patients she'd been seeing, Neela was amazed by how much devotion the man seemed to engender. He might be sending them into a brutal campaign, but he was winning and he seemed to be the only one who'd stand up and fight the Alliance. The bond between the spacers and the admiral who insisted on sending them into a meat grinder was remarkable. When the war was over Neela was determined to do her level best to study the man. If she could develop a real, empirically backed study about his unique relationship with the troops using verifiable research and proven examples it might just be possible to find that sort of person at the beginning of a war. Because that sort of person, she surmised, could win quickly. It seemed folly that the UHF was still using a method that was as old and stupid as mankind itself, the method by which the executive branch kept on trying out warriors over the bodies of loved ones until by bloody trial and error they'd finally find one who could actually fight.

In her mind she was haunted by the notion that if Trang had been the commander at the beginning of the war it might already be over. But that research would have to wait. She wasn't even going to write her idea as a proposal until the Alliance had been thoroughly destroyed. If someone on the other side got the idea of applying that same research to Janet Delgado Black, who knows what they'd discover? If that half-faced Boudica survived the war, Neela would study her as well and double the potential research pool.

Neela was getting ready to leave for group when her favorite person in the entire solar system dropped by. "Thaddeus!" Neela exclaimed delightedly as Dr. Gillette entered her office. His use of flowery language reminded her so much of Cyrus Anjou. She hoped he'd survive the war so they could resume their friendship when it was all over.

Thaddeus acknowledged her smile with a wide grin of his own. "Hello, my dearest colleague, how goes the life of a woman who has the ear of the President of the entire UHF?"

"Busy, Thaddeus, very, very busy; could you walk with me to my next group?" She was already heading toward the door.

Gillette started walking beside her. "Glad to," he answered. "Allow me to again say how happy I am that you chose to come to Mars. I cannot imagine what I would've done without you."

Neela grinned knowingly. "Dear Thaddeus, you say that almost every time we meet."

"Well, that's because it's so very true."

". . . and you want something extra from me," Neela added.

"That transparent?"

"Eminently so," she answered, heading down a hallway with multiple classrooms in full session.

Gillette frowned. "Well, I suppose there may be some little quandary you can help me with."

Neela waved to a group of patients in a baking class who'd seen her through a window as she was passing by. "If I can manage," she answered, "I'd be glad to help. What is it?"

Gillette rubbed his chin as he walked. "I have a patient that is absolutely fascinating. She's not really making any of the markers. She's the first one from the Alliance we've tried to work with in a while."

"So what's the problem?" They came to the portal where Neela's group was meeting.

"If you could see her with an open mind; I should not have even mentioned the bit about her being in the Alliance, but I was hoping it would intrigue you, all those foolish notions of balance and fair play the young have nowadays."

Neela had one foot in the classroom. "Maybe I can see her after my group," she said.

"Absolutely. I'll arrange for her to be in the gardens by the arboretum and escort you there myself."

Neela frowned. "There was something else, Thaddeus?"

Thaddeus smiled self-consciously. "I've trained you too well. Undone, unmasked, uncovered; and by a mere child; oh, the shame, the shame."

Neela had to suppress a giggle. "Alright, don't tell me until you want to. I'll see you later."

The session went well. Neela had even hoped that some of the men and women would be able to go back to active duty. Though she realized that to do so would once again condemn them to an uncertain fate. Her overriding desire to see the war over meant that even those she cared most about would have to be part of that sacrifice, and so she'd made her peace. Even if her patients couldn't be sent back to the front, she'd at least try to prepare them for support roles, which were in critical demand given the massive expansion of Trang's new campaign. Her group had been able to talk about their feeling of fear and hopelessness. The hardest part had been in getting them to admit that to themselves. The brain, she knew, often dealt with fear by abject denial, useful in combat but very dangerous if left to fester.

Neela had become skilled enough to identify early on who would respond to group and who would not. Given the exigency of the war, she was concentrating on patients who could be helped by group and channeling the ones who would need individual care to maintenance camps or even back into suspension until after the war—long after if it kept going like this. But those worries were for the future. As her group broke up she was greeted by Dr. Gillette, patiently waiting for her outside.

"My dear," he said, "if it were appropriate I'd applaud."

"You already have me, Thaddeus," she answered, taking his arm in hers. "You can stop investing now."

Thaddeus gave her a small squeeze.

"I'll just have my assistant encode today's files and then I'm all yours."

"You have an assistant?"

Neela nodded. "Yeah, a PTSD patient, Lisa Herman—very competent, but she'll never see combat again."

"Well," said Thaddeus with joy in his eyes, "I'm glad you finally took my advice."

"So does this get added to the reasons you wish to applaud?"

"My dear, it's possible that I may wax eloquent to achieve certain mutually beneficial ends, but my desire to applaud is, I can assure you, an example of pure admiration."

"Stop it already," she chastised. "I feel guilty enough about group as it is. The patients do 99 percent of the work. The truth is I just end up sitting around, honest to Damsah, bored."

"If I have to hear any more of your boasting I shall simply die of shame as to my own inadequate efforts. At best my patients do 85, maybe 87 percent of the work."

Neela threw up her hands in mock surrender. "Enough! Let's go and see this patient of yours." Neela headed out through the portal, turning left to leave the building. "If this continues you'll have me made President of the UHF by the end of the week."

She did not see Dr. Gillette's clinical gaze as he considered everything she had said and filed it away before putting his jolly expression back on and following her out.

Dr. Gillette continued to talk about the day-to-day running of affairs with his favorite colleague, but his mind was on a problem. Lately there'd been rumors and he didn't know what to do about them. He was very protective of Neela Harper and was heartbroken when her relationship with Justin Cord proved to be the disaster that a patient-client relationship could only be. He could understand why. Justin Cord had to be one of the most magnetic personalities Dr. Gillette had ever come in contact with. Though for all the doctor's skill he was still hard-pressed to figure out what it was about the man that made that so. Cord had even gotten four billion human beings to follow him in his fantasies to re-create a time that never was and never could be. For a while even Thaddeus had been drawn by that powerful vision that Justin cast. So who could really blame Neela for her transgressions? Thaddeus didn't and used his influence and prestige to help in her nearly complete restoration. Her incredible work in the trauma center and saving of Trang had also done much, especially now that Trang had finally been acknowledged as the only one in any position to actually defeat the Alliance. And once Trang managed to defeat the Alliance's scar-faced admiral, Neela would be completely indemnified of her past in the joy that would come of victory. But these new rumors were too much like the old ones and Thaddeus needed to know.

"Neela," he said, interrupting her. "My patient is right over this hill, but," he said, indicating a park bench, "could we sit here and talk?"

"At this conveniently placed bench?"

"Indeed at this conveniently placed bench." He sat down and Neela joined him. "My dear, I am afraid to ask this without seeming, well . . . you see, it's just that . . . what I am saying—"

"Thaddeus," interrupted Neela, "you aren't saying anything. Out with it or your poor patient will be—"

"Are you having an affair with Hektor Sambianco?" Dr. Gillette blurted out. "Oh, my dear, I am so sorry. That was supposed to be done so much more delicately—" He stopped because Neela was holding her hand to her mouth in a vain attempt to stop from laughing out loud. "There is no need to laugh at me," said Gillette. "I admit it was a poor attempt at discretion."

"Oh, Thaddeus," Neela said through paroxysms of laughter and near tears, "I'm so sorry. You were just so cute trying to be . . . and then you just—" Neela couldn't help it. She started giggling uncontrollably again.

Dr. Gillette couldn't help but smile when he saw how much she was enjoying herself. It reminded him of the Neela he saw so very little of. "I suppose it was a little humorous if looked at a certain way," he admitted.

"Thank you, Thaddeus. I needed a good laugh and you just gave me two."

"Two?"

"Of course; the way you asked and the question itself. Is that what people are really saying? How long have I been having this torrid affair?"

"I don't know."

"Well, if it's been for a while I want to know. After all, shouldn't Hektor and I be getting married soon?"

"No one said anything about marriage!"

"Thaddeus," pouted Neela, "are you saying I'm not worth marrying?"

"Of course you're not; I mean you could. *No!* What am I saying? Neela, please take this seriously," he ended up pleading.

Neela took his hands in both of hers. "Thaddeus, how can I? It's absurd."

"So you're not having an affair?" Dr. Gillette asked cautiously, afraid Neela would start again with her antics.

"Eeew," she said with obvious disgust. "I mean no, no, I am not. I wouldn't betray Amanda like that, besides the fact that she'd kill me. How could you think that, Thaddeus?"

Dr. Gillette heaved a sigh of relief. It was what he was hoping to hear. "I really couldn't, but you have been spending so much time over in the executive offices with him and when the rumors started I must admit that your history with powerful men . . . well, I jumped to the wrong conclusion and I'm sorry. I shouldn't have listened to rumor."

"No, you shouldn't have," Neela answered, reproaching. Her mood became somber. "I'm there, Thaddeus, because, just like here," she said, indicating the grounds of the trauma center, "it's the best way I can atone for what I helped Justin Cord do. I don't know how I could've been so blind to the harm I was causing."

"Neela, we've discussed this. You were in love with a very romantic figure."

"Yes, yes, I was, and look at what it caused. But now, by my advising Hektor on his cabinet and choice of leading admirals and CEOs I can help him make decisions that keep the UHF fighting. I wish I could tell you the good I've done already, but it's classified four ways from dividend day. The irony is that's exactly what I used to do for Justin Cord when he had me all turned around. But now I'm using my skills for the good of mankind and that does not . . . I repeat . . . *not* include sleeping with our President, thank you very much."

"I completely and humbly apologize for doubting even for a second and shall spend the rest of my life quashing those malicious rumors."

Neela got an impish grin on her face. "Unless you see dirty pictures. If you see any dirty pictures of me and Hektor, you must show them to me. I really don't have any. You'd think some would have shown up from my college days, but I was such a boring girl."

Dr. Gillette stood up. "Enough already. I apologized, woman. Let's see my patient and forget the whole thing."

Neela stood up and followed her friend. "You mean this patient is real? I was thinking she was only a ruse to confront me about my 'sinful' behavior."

"Oh, I never lie about a patient." He held up his hand to ward off the retort that Neela was obviously about to give. "I admit," he continued, "that this patient gave me good excuse to discuss that 'other' matter, but she's real and it's interesting you use the word sinful. In this context it's actually quite appropriate." Dr. Gillette spent the rest of the walk filling Neela in on the patient from the Alliance. "Her name is Patricia Sampson, her brother is from Altamont, and she was captured—"

Hektor was working at his desk. He'd just finished yet another cabinet meeting. At least the news was better on the economic front. The war was drawing in such a vast number of recruits that unemployment had all but disappeared. The ravenous demands of supplying, paying, training, and treating the over one and a half billion people directly in the military were amping up the economy. The recycling programs combined with the small but steady stream of commodities coming from the captured parts of the belt and the massive mining operations on Earth and Mars were supplying the UHF with enough raw materials to prosecute the war. The Beanstalk was no longer a piece of obsolete technology but was the main bulk transport out of Earth's gravity well. It was true that paying for the war would take decades—maybe even more than a century. But, thought Hektor, let the future pay. They didn't have to do the hard part.

The casualties, reasoned Hektor, were beyond anything anyone could've imagined at the beginning of the war, but it wasn't as if the pennies really had anything better to do with their lives. If they had, well then, they wouldn't be pennies, would they? All in all, the war would be bloody, it would take years longer than originally predicted, but as long as there were no more surprises he would win.

His ruminations were disturbed by a knock on the door. When he saw it was Neela he let her in, then activated a commblock protocol, which would mean as far as the world was concerned, that section of the executive offices as well as the few adjoining areas were effectively cut off from all forms of communication, both in and out. No Neuro, no handphones, no DijAssistance. It might have been suspicious behavior given who Neela was if not for the fact that there were usually eight to eleven people Hektor always activated the commblock for, including his cabinet, Amada Snow, and of course Admiral Trang. Neela, like the rest, was just an advisor discussing high-priority information with the President, and as such was accorded the secrecy associated with that role.

Hektor, buried in a stack of papers, didn't bother to look up when she entered. "I have the latest cabinet meeting on holo," he said. "If you can review it and give me your opinions on how they're holding up that would be great." Neela went right to one of the chairs in front of his desk and plopped down. Hektor looked up from his hard copies. "Or you can just collapse in the chair and ignore me."

She shot him a derisive look.

"I'm sorry, Neela, tough day?"

She sighed. "Nothing on par with deciding the fate of humanity, but yeah, it was a tough day."

He smiled amiably, got up out of his chair, and went to the bar. He still hadn't gotten used to pouring drinks in the lower gravity of Mars, but he refused to use a dispenser. A man, he believed, should pour his own drinks. He made two— vodka chilled and poured through crushed ice for him and a Cosmo for her. "What is it?" he asked as he handed her a drink and then leaned back on the front edge of his desk.

"Thaddeus came to me and asked if we were having an affair."

Hektor smiled ruefully. "*Really?* The good upright doctor? I'm surprised he was even able to bring himself to say it."

"It almost happened that way."

"Neela, I've just got to know," Hektor said, arms folded. "What on Earth did you tell him?"

Neela's lips curved up wickedly. "I told him we were having a torrid affair complete with pictures and twins."

"Boys or girls?" asked Hektor without missing a beat.

"One each, and don't be such an idiot; I told him it was a load of crap."

Hektor put down his drink and walked behind her. He started to massage her shoulders.

"We can stop. Let me say I don't want to. I'm not sure how well I would've handled the last six months without you, but you shouldn't have to lie to a friend just to protect me."

She took one of his hands and kissed it tenderly. "I don't want to stop either. When I'm with you I feel more like myself than at any other time."

"Well, fuck them then. Let's just come right out and admit it. I'm not married, and as far as the UHF is concerned you're not either, and damn it, I should be able to date who I want. I'm the President, for Damsah's sake."

Neela reached up and was just able to grab an earlobe. "No!" she yelled, twisting his ear and pulling him down in a spiral to one knee next to her.

"*Ear! Ear!*" he shouted.

"When the war is over," she continued evenly, "we can do what we want, and then if you don't marry me you'll have to be concerned about losing a lot more than an ear."

"It is a lot more, isn't it?" he said lasciviously. "Thanks for noticing."

She started laughing, letting his ear go and then almost as immediately gently caressing it.

"Hektor, you can do nothing that will give the Alliance one iota of propaganda or cause the UHF one iota of embarrassment. How we feel about each other is just not important compared to that. Promise me you will keep this secret until the war is over."

"Well," he said, now massaging the reddened lobe, "if you can avoid any more ear twisting."

"No deal, now promise."

With a slight bow of his head he acquiesced. "I promise."

She pulled his head to her lips and gently nuzzled his ear. He grabbed her chin and their lips met in a kiss that started out tender but increased in passion as all thoughts of the war and their situation fled from their minds.

12 | No Choice

The Cliff House, Ceres

As much as the war would allow, a rhythm was established around the presidential quarters. The guard would switch four times a day, but in a staggered formation so that all the personnel never changed over at once. The cabinet would have mandatory twice-weekly meetings, barring emergency or travel.

Justin had five major departments, which were Security, Treasury, Defense, Information, and Technology. Kirk Olmstead was running security both internal and external; Mosh McKenzie was handling the new treasury department, which oversaw both industrialization of the Alliance as well as its paying of the bills. Or, as he often groused, "the whole damned economy." Defense was given to Admiral Sinclair. Justin had to get over his built-in desire to have a civilian in the post, but the truth was, the fleet was the military in the Alliance and no one understood the fleet and all its ins and outs better than the admiral. He had a positive genius for knowing where every ship was, her condition, combat record, state of readiness, and all the myriad details that went with supplying and upgrading the miner battalions and orbital batteries. So Justin put aside his prejudice and gave the admiral a job he was effectively doing anyway. Padamir Singh was the information secretary, which in Justin's mind was a combination of press secretary and minister of propaganda. Justin liked how Singh referred to himself. "Mr. President," he'd often say, "I'm the minister of lies, both the bad ones, theirs of course, and the good ones, which would be ours." The new post of technology chief went to Hildegard Rhunsfeld. She was an old friend of Mosh's who'd run GCI's deep-tech project in the formally hidden enclave out by Neptune. It had been Mosh's personal intervention that had both kept her in the Alliance and saved the high-tech research center from destruction. As the war continued, Hildegard had gone from very reluctant neutrality to full-fledged support. She'd become indispensable to a whole series of projects that the Alliance had used to stay ahead of the UHF in a number of areas. When the need for a central figure to coordinate all of the Alliance's projects with the goal of surviving the war became necessary, she was the natural choice. Hildegard would not be confused for a space-born member of the Alliance. First of all, she was too tall at six-one and had kept her straight blond hair well past her shoulders—yet another giveaway. Though for the cabinet meetings she'd acceded to spacer fashion by tying it back in a bun. No matter the look, Justin could not deny her ruthless dedication and ability.

Before the meeting all the cabinet would give a summary report of their main points to Cyrus Anjou, who'd make a one-page synopsis of each, which he'd then give to Justin as a hard copy for review. As was often the case, the meetings would take place out on the balcony with the shields set for opacity and maximum security. As it was the Cerian equivalent of morning, Justin had called for a breakfast meeting. It was the only way most of them would actually eat anything until after six in the evening, so busy would their days get. All except Cyrus of course. It would take the planetoid exploding to interfere with one of his meals.

Per tradition, Justin was there first and greeted each person as they arrived. Today he'd added two additional guests. One, Congressman Sadma, would show up only moments before the actual meeting started. The second arrived earlier. Justin got up to greet her.

"Welcome to the fearsome fortress of power, Dr. Nesor."

The doctor's appearance was that of a woman in her late twenties. She had jet-black hair, cut in a bob—very much, thought Justin, 1920s flapper style. She had the soft, milky white skin that life in space seemed to give Caucasians. Justin himself would've liked to sit under a sunlamp and get some color, but it was one of the prejudices of the Alliance that they didn't really trust anyone with anything approaching a tan.

"Thank you, Mr. President," said the doctor. "I must say this doesn't look anything like a fortress." She indicated the balcony with the oval breakfast table, a holo-tank square in the middle of it and a buffet on the side. "I was not aware that fortresses had buffets."

"It's the latest thing. I don't think we have a waffle bar, but we can get you an omelette."

"Waffle?"

"No waffles in the present?" he asked, sighing. They weren't his favorite food, but up until now he hadn't once thought of them. Not that it mattered, given the doctor's response.

"You're not referring to a person who changes from one opinion to another, are you?"

"No, it was a popular breakfast item in my day."

Dr. Nesor checked her DijAssist. Oh, fried or baked sugar dough, smothered in highly sweetened syrup. She looked confused. "Shouldn't this be a dessert?"

Justin had never considered it. "You know I think you're right. I guess pancakes should be a dessert too."

"Pancakes?"

"Please, Doctor, I'm feeling out-of-date as it is."

"Forgive me," she said, smiling weakly, "but I think I'm about to make you feel older."

"Let me guess, this is going to be another 'did you ever meet so and so,' question, isn't it?"

Dr. Nesor laughed. "I hate being that predictable."

Justin smiled agreeably "Doctor, if you knew how many variations of that question I get, you wouldn't be so annoyed with yourself. So here's the list I've learned to give up front. I didn't meet the Beatles, Winston Churchill, Ronald Reagan, Queen Elizabeth—the second or the third—and, of course, the one that everyone always asks about: Oprah Winfrey."

Now it was the doctor's turn to laugh. "No one so well known, I'm afraid. I'm referring to Dr. Francine Shapiro."

Justin saw the look that always came with hopefully asked questions. He knew the person wanted to hear a "yes" so they could ask ten other questions about the person they'd identified with from the far past. As was usually the case, Justin had to disappoint.

"Sorry, don't recognize the name. Was she a relative?" He found that the compliment of linking the questioner to the famous personality often mitigated the disappointment of his inevitable "no."

"How I wish!" answered Dr. Nesor. "But no, she's the woman who developed some of our most basic treatments in EMDR cognitive therapy."

On Justin's confused look the doctor elucidated further. "It stands for Eye Movement Desensitization and Reprocessing. Basically it's a way to link painful memories to more positive ones in order to give relief to a patient suffering from a traumatic experience. Anyways," she said, noticing his eyes beginning to glaze over, "thank you for letting me pester you with such an unimportant question."

"No question is unimportant," answered Justin, "especially those that concern the treatment of our heroes. But I wouldn't mind a little breakfast."

They went to the bar where Cyrus was already filling his plate from a buffet filled with mostly fruits, cereals, scrambled eggs, and some sort of sausage. Justin got himself a bowl of cereal. One of the things he'd been profoundly grateful for was that the fashion of slithering food had not become popular in the area that became the Alliance. The doctor got a plate of fruit as Cyrus piled his with a mountain of scrambled eggs buried under sausage.

The Jovian greeted the doctor in his usual effusive manner. "Doctor, the meeting is made more joyous by your appearance. You are as light to a field awaiting the day."

Dr. Nesor was bemused. "You have a wonderful way of expressing yourself, Mr. Anjou."

"Ah, you see, Mr. President?" he said, looking over to Justin. "A person who is appreciative of the verbal arts."

"How did you come to speak with such flair?" asked Dr. Nesor.

"Ah, well, when I was younger it occurred to me . . ." Cyrus got a canny look on his face. "Doctor, are you using the skills of your profession to delve into the depths of my mind?"

A voice called out from the portal leading to the main residence. "Be careful, Doctor, that you don't hit your head when you're in there. The 'depths' are rather shallow," said Padamir Singh.

"Insulted by a Cerian sybarite," huffed Cyrus, "and before I've eaten, no less!"

"You accuse *me* of being a sybarite," said Padamir, entering the room, "when you're the one with a mountain of food worthy of an Alaskan. Compared to your Jovian appetites we Cereans are simple as the monks of Altamont."

Justin leaned closer to the doctor. "Cyrus, Padamir, and Omad have this competition as to who can be the most creative in their 'friendly' banter."

"Seems like a harmless way to blow off some steam," replied Dr. Nesor. "If you don't mind my asking, how do *you* deal with the stress?"

"Doctor," answered Justin politely but firmly, "this is neither the place nor the time."

"Mr. President," she answered back almost as forcefully, "you need counseling, not only for you, but for the good of the Alliance. Tell you what, you name the place and time and I or one of my colleagues will be there."

"Doctor, for the good of the Alliance, I cannot be 'dealing with my inner grief' right now."

"If I may be so bold . . ."

"Yes?"

"It's damaging to your long-term health and happiness to keep what's happened to you bottled up. Your wife was taken from you in the cruelest of ways, and after you'd found love in a world so far removed from your own as to defy description. You should be a wreck. Mark my words, it will catch up with you."

"It already has, Doctor," Justin answered tersely, "but the Alliance needs me more and I will not fail her. When the war is over I promise to lie on whatever couch you want me to, agreed?"

"As you wish, Mr. President."

Justin already knew she wouldn't stop trying. It was why he liked her.

Mosh and Hildegard appeared together, and as was often the case, they were in the midst of a deep discussion. They continued talking oblivious to the rest, heading straight toward the buffet, filling up their plates, and going to the table without stopping or acknowledging anyone else in the room.

Admiral Sinclair entered and quickly found his seat. He was soon followed by Tyler Sadma.

"Mr. President," greeted Sadma.

"Congressman," answered Justin, "thank you for coming. May I introduce Dr. Ayon Nesor, one of the Alliance's foremost cognitive scientists?"

"That means I shrink heads for a living," she said. "But it's a pleasure to meet the most famous of the Sadma clan."

"You do me too much honor, Doctor. My niece is far more deserving of recognition than me or any of my poor efforts."

"Your niece fights for our present," she offered. "Your Bill of Rights fights for our future."

"Not according to Secretary Olmstead. He insists it will straitjacket his ability to protect the Alliance on every level and he may as well move back to the UHF, as it will be in charge in no time."

"Nonsense," she replied. "The Bill of Rights *is* the Alliance."

"Thank you, Doctor, and may I say it is a pleasure to meet you as well. Your reputation as a skilled and ethical healer is well known and well deserved."

"I hope you still think so after what I have to say today."

Tyler was about to inquire further but held off when he saw Justin silently asking for forbearance.

"Where's Olmstead?" boomed Cyrus. "Must that man always be last to every meeting?"

"He likes to be the center of attention," replied Padamir. "What better way than to hold up the most powerful people in the Alliance, who must wait for him to arrive before they can begin?"

"He does a good job, as do you all," said Justin, defending Kirk. "Therefore, I accept his eccentricities, as I do all of yours."

As if on cue, Kirk suddenly appeared.

"Excellent," said Justin. "We can begin."

"I apologize for my tardiness, Mr. President."

"Not at all, Mr. Secretary. It gave us time to compare notes and get some breakfast." He waited for Kirk to situate himself. "Allow me to formally introduce our guests. Dr. Ayon Nesor of the Saturnian trauma center, recently posted to Ceres, and of course the Chairman of the committee on the conduct of the war, Tyler Sadma. On a personal note allow me to congratulate you on your niece's promotion to Fleet Admiral. I should have mentioned it before."

Tyler accepted the compliment graciously. "Though she doesn't feel she's earned it, given the fact we're losing our hold on large portions of the belt."

"That's a load of fertilizer," said Sinclair. "She's holding back forces that outnumber hers five and six to one in sectors spread out on a 60-degree arc from the 180 while being outgunned in ships and munitions. She's even managed limited counterattacks. It may be the most brilliant delaying campaign in military history."

"There are those who feel if she attacked more we'd be better off," said Kirk, putting an end to whatever good cheer was left in the room.

"There are those who are idiots," replied Sinclair. "She can achieve nothing by attack except to go up against insurmountable odds and get her miners killed. The only card she has to play is to make the enemy come to her. All of Christina's attacks are local and only after the enemy has exhausted his offensive."

"She should turn one of those attacks into a general attack and sweep the enemy from our space," offered Kirk.

"Trang would love that," countered Sinclair. "The more of our people he kills out of our defenses the easier it is for him."

"What about the road to Eros?" Kirk said in a voice thick with malice. He was referring to an apparent collapse of the UHF in front of Eros about seven months back. Christina had only occupied the space directly in front of her lines and then fortified. Then she'd occupied the space in front of that and was fortifying again when a huge UHF fleet flew in and pummeled her position, forcing her troops out and back to the newly reinforced area.

"An obvious trap," replied Sinclair. "One that Christina turned around by grabbing and then fortifying space the UHF had already paid for in blood."

"If she'd attacked immediately we'd be back in Eros and not dealing with the prospect of the belt being cut in half," Kirk said, echoing the rumblings from many of the armchair Neuro sites in the Alliance.

"Enough already," interrupted Justin in a gentle but firm voice. "Christina Sadma is fighting the worst type of war: a slow, grinding retreat with no end in sight against an enemy that vastly outnumbers her own forces. Throughout history governments have made the mistake of confusing retreat for defeat and changing strategy or leadership, causing the very defeat they intended to prevent. Our newly promoted admiral is a genius in a type of warfare very few are ever allowed to master. I suggest, Kirk, that you study the campaigns of Quintus Fabius Maximus. He fought Hannibal and won, but not by the tactics suggested by experts who were not there. And while we're at it we shouldn't forget what happened to General Johnston in the first American Civil War or the Germans on the Eastern Front in World War II. Kirk, it is my opinion and therefore the opinion of this cabinet that Christina Sadma's tactics may not win us the war there, but any other tactics will lose us the war there. She has enough difficulties already; we *will* not add to them." He finished by looking directly at Kirk, who finally averted his eyes.

"You are of course correct, Mr. President."

"I am always correct, Kirk, until I realize I'm not and then change my mind, but then I'm correct again," he finished with a good-natured smile. He then turned to the technology chief. "I hear you have some good news for us, Miss Rhunsfeld."

Hildegard stood up and activated the holo-tank. "Very good news, Mr. President. I'm happy to announce that the superhighways are functional. The Jupiter–Ceres route is at 100 percent capacity."

"Superhighways?" Dr. Nesor said in confusion. "I'm sorry, is it inappropriate to speak away from your area of expertise?" She couldn't resist giving Kirk a sidelong glance as she did so.

"Most inquisitive healer," said Cyrus, "it would be rude for you to deny a nature that has enabled you to help so many benighted souls."

"Besides," added Padamir, "if that weren't allowed the First Free would have to fire us all."

"Secretary Singh," interrupted Justin, "if you could please avoid using that odious phrase, and Secretary Rhunsfeld, if you could please give Dr. Nesor a brief history of the project in question."

"Of course, Mr. President," answered Hildegard, who turned her attention to Ayon. "As you know, the Outer Alliance has much territory but comparatively few people, spread out in isolated locations across the solar system. The ill-named UHF has the huge advantage of interior lines and much smaller distances. Put another way, we're too damn big." As Hildegard spoke, a hologram appeared over the table showing the Alliance and the UHF and various travel times from point to point.

"We'd been looking at various possibilities to solve this problem. Theoretically we could've tried to warp space between intervening distances, but as I said, that's mostly theoretical. Two, we could've created a new interstellar drive system that would've greatly increased the speed of our present ships, but from everything I've seen, a working prototype would still be decades away. And finally, we could provide a protective shield around our ships as they raced through open space."

"Which one did you choose?" asked Dr. Nesor.

"The third one . . . sort of. Thanks to our fusion and compression technologies we can accelerate our ships to incredible velocities very quickly. The only limits were what the human body could stand and what would happen to a ship hitting small objects in space. The faster the ship the smaller an object has to be to cause catastrophic damage. We lose ships all the time because they go too fast or just get unlucky."

"Forgive me, Madam Secretary," said Ayon, "but you said shielding is not possible."

"Oh, it's not, at least not now, but we don't need it. We just need to remove the need for it, by creating a debris-free field."

Hildegard waited but saw that no one was going to make a snide comment.

"The theory is actually quite old," she continued, "but there was no way it could be justified under normal economic conditions. Before the war all that mattered was that personnel, supplies, and raw materials could move throughout the solar system; it didn't really matter to anyone on Earth if it took days, weeks, or months as long as it got where it was needed. So no one ever had an incentive to try it out, until now. We created large drive units and had them boost a large preformed shield, usually made out of ice. The shields are quite vast—"

"How vast?" asked Dr. Nesor.

"A little over four hundred meters."

"That's a big piece of ice."

"Correction, Doctor: That's a big piece of extremely fast-moving ice. Getting the drive units was extremely difficult given the war, but Mosh got us some. We sent the ice ships in waves of three. The first clears the route, the second detects any leftover debris, tracking all potentially dangerous objects in its route, and the third cleans up afterwards. In the outer system the route remains relatively clear, for quite a while. But if you follow a plow group, that's what we've been calling this new system, you're only limited by the plows' speed. The safety actually surpasses normal spaceflight. Naturally the longer you wait after the plows have moved through, the lower the safety margin. But here's what makes the plan feasible, if dreadfully resource expensive—when the plows arrive at their destination we re-form the ice shield and send it back. We never stop sending it on the route it's taking, so it's always clearing a path based on a route that corrects for planetary alignment. All a ship has to do is pick a destination and know when the last plow group left or when the next one is leaving."

"And it really works?" asked Justin hopefully.

"I told you I had good news, sir," Hildegard said with a bright smile. "We just sent a ship from here to Pluto in less than half the time it would normally take."

"Damsah's balls," said Cyrus. "I mean astounding."

"What he said, both times," added Padamir.

Justin turned to Mosh. "What will this take from the war effort to make it work?"

Mosh gave a nod to Hildegard, who smiled as she took her seat, knowing that she'd topped the meeting. Mosh then got up and the holo-image changed to production figures and locations.

"I've already taken the liberty to plan a crash course, pardon the pun. The primary cost will be in the heavy-duty thruster units. Only two places can make them, but the Jovian system is the best place for this purpose. The sensor units can mostly be scavenged from navigational satellites that will become effectively obsolete with the creation of this system. We'll need two to three plow groups between each of the main transit points. But the value to the war effort will make this well worth the cost. If we push, the system can be up and running in two months; in six it will be comprehensive. Once that happens we can supply our forces in the 180 without having to send them around the ring. It would actually be faster to send something from here to one of the outer planets and then back to another part of the belt than to try to do it directly through the ring. It'll almost be like we're shooting the core, but without that pesky UHF fleet trying to blow the crap out of us."

"Admiral," said Justin, concern evident in his voice, "won't that mean fewer ships for the next four to six months?"

"I know, Mr. President, and I can't say that it fills me with joy either, but J.D. just took out an entire UHF battle fleet. Even with their manufacturing base, they're not anywhere close to making that up. If we're going to do this, we need to do it now. With a viable superhighway we can get our fleets and miners where they need to be as fast as the UHF can. It'll make up for a lot."

Justin's eyes flittered over Mosh's numbers. "Tyler, will you be able to expedite the funding through Congress?"

Tyler stood up sporting an easy grin. "Mr. President, since the last elections the NoShares have a working majority with the Alliance Libertarians. I could get you pronounced king after the Infant Liberation Proclamation . . . though it would take a little time. This could actually be our first unanimous bill. This highway will revolutionize the Alliance and obliterate distance. With it we can become a functioning civilization—a united civilization."

"So that would be a 'yes,' then?"

"Yes, Mr. President. I'll need to brief the chairmen of the various committees, but you will have full congressional support for this inside of a week. Not even the Shareholders could object." Sadma then took his seat.

"They won't," said Mosh, who was the effective head of the smaller but still-potent Shareholder party.

"Which leaves us with an issue more difficult to solve," said Justin. "Admiral, if you wouldn't mind."

Admiral Sinclair nodded and then stood up. "If Trang keeps up his new strategy we could lose the war in six months." He then replaced Mosh's holo with one of his own. It was a map of the belt at the 180. There were over a hundred areas covered in bright red, flaming dots that extended across the belt for millions of miles. It was clear from the holo that Trang wasn't going deep, he was going long—stretching the Alliance's line with every mile.

"He's launched over 120 offensives," continued Sinclair, "at almost all parts of the belt except in a 60-degree arc centered around Ceres. He knows we can respond and turn it into an actual defeat for him. But he's not afraid to face us; cold-blooded bastard's not really afraid of anything near as we can tell. He's just smart."

Sinclair then replaced that image with that of a typically well-armed miner.

"Our miners are better than their marines. No other way to put it. Soldier for soldier we win, especially on the defensive. But Trang doesn't care about that. We have a classic attrition situation. He's pouring in an unending supply of inexperienced marines and spacers into every hellhole we make." The holo started filling up with smaller UHF soldiers—ten to every one of the Alliance's. "He loses four or even five for our one. When he gets three to one he considers it a victory. He doesn't even try to rehabilitate or rotate his troops. He sends them in raw and when they wear out he sends the next group in and the next and the next. Doc," Sinclair said with a slight grimace as he sat down and closed up his holo, "I think this next bit is yours."

Ayon stood to address the now-somber group. "Combat in space is brutal on the human psyche. For many humans even normal movement in space can be traumatic. The merciless environment where no human ever evolved can only be conquered and claimed by those with the will do so. That's why so many humans, the great majority in fact, choose to live on the core worlds of Luna, Earth, and Mars—or at least in very close orbits. Using statistical analysis from the last two years it's clear that even the marginally effective units the UHF has are drawn from Luna and the orbital habitats of Earth and Mars. In short, at least these marines have a basis from which to start their space-based training. Now if one of these marines has a breakdown, they get shipped back to Earth and are given some other job within the military structure. So they can still be productive. Not so our personnel.

"Here's where our tremendous advantage can possibly turn into a major disadvantage. Space combat makes all the hazards of our environment far more pronounced, and when a member of the Alliance begins to fear their own suit or the shuttle they're on because of what they've experienced over and over again they become effectively useless."

"Doctor," asked Justin, "is there an average number of reanimations per miner?"

"Yes, anywhere from three to seven reanimations. So let's call it five. Imagine, then, that you have resident memories of five absolutely horrific deaths, any one of which could have . . . in fact should have led to a p.d. We have cases, tens of thousands of them, where patients cannot put on a space suit. They become hysterical, catatonic; some have even experienced cardiovascular failure. In other cases they won't take their suits off. Others cannot be near weapons; many cannot be aware of being on ships. Many can't be in the dark. I cannot begin to tell you the number of eyelids that have had to be regrown." She allowed a moment for the group to realize the implication.

"Using basic trauma therapies at the Saturn institute," she continued, "we've been able to get many of these patients to the point where they can be fully functional back in space-born civilization, but almost none we get can be made ready for combat again."

"This represents a force of over four hundred thousand experienced combat soldiers who cannot go back to combat," Sinclair added bleakly.

"Look, Doc," added Kirk. "It seems perfectly reasonable. Why in the worlds would they want to go back? At least from what you described I know I wouldn't."

"You have to understand, Mr. Secretary," answered the doctor, "that these men and women volunteered. They have very strong ties to their community and their friends. I can promise you that if they could go back they would."

"Exactly how many of that four hundred k are we talking?" asked Sinclair.

"With effective treatment; over 95 percent, and I promise that's no exaggeration. Sometimes I'm not even sure which is more traumatic, the experience of their having died countless deaths or the guilt of their incapacitation. They feel like they've abandoned their friends and comrades, their Alliance," she then looked directly at Justin, "and in many cases a deep shame that they're failing you, Mr. President."

Justin's face grew rigid. "They must never think that, Doctor. Regardless of what else is done from this point on, I'll give you whatever general statement, recording, or personal communication is needed to alleviate any undeserved guilt they may have. They owe me nothing. You must make them understand that it's the other way around."

"Of course, Mr. President. The institute will be glad for the help. But I only brought it up to show you that the desire to return to combat is there, all that's been lacking is the ability to do so, that is . . . until now."

Sinclair practically leapt out of his chair. "Doctor," he said, his two fists on the table, "if you can get us four hundred thousand experienced combat vets in under six months we can stabilize the front. Hell," he said, sitting back down again, "we might be able to go on the offensive. I wasn't kidding when I said our men and women are better than theirs. It can make the difference between defeat and continuing the war."

When the doctor didn't respond to his remark Sinclair said, "Doc, did you hear what I just said? This is vital; we need those spacers!"

"You should tell them," said Justin, nodding his head.

"I'm ashamed that I even began this research, sir. I just wanted to help them so much and . . . well . . . it worked. A part of me is still sorry I didn't delete all of it."

"It may have been better if you did," answered Justin, "but we cannot undo the past, any of it. We must decide the future with all the information at hand. You have to tell them, so they can help me decide."

"Yes, sir," she said, and then turned to once again address the group. "EMDR is the basis of modern cognitive therapy, but as I said, none of the traditional forms of therapy were working. But I happened to be in the institute's criminal treatment center. It's mostly empty now and a good place to think. Anyhow, that's when I . . . when I saw it just sitting there gathering, honest to Damsah, dust."

"Saw what?" asked Padamir.

Hildegard turned pale. "A psychological audit device?" She turned her glare on the doctor. "What's wrong with you?"

Everyone around the table seemed to lose their pallor—if that were even possible for a spacer—and remained silent, except for Kirk, whose ears had perked up as he listened with rapt attention.

"I was at a dead end," continued Dr. Nesor. "There was nothing I could do to help them short of radical drug therapies. We've just never had to deal with this level of pain before. There are thousands still in suspension. How can I wake them up to the horror of what they experienced?" She paused and gathered herself together. "I'm sorry. We're trained to be detached from our patients, but it hasn't been easy, or even successful. What's done is done." She took a deep breath and gathered her strength. "I saw the device and it occurred to me if I were to do primitive EMDR using that device to map out not pathology but trauma I could isolate the trauma and . . . and—"

"That's abominable," said Mosh.

"That's brilliant," said Kirk.

Cyrus's jovial manner was gone. "Doctor, what were you thinking?"

"I wasn't thinking, Cyrus. I was desperate. Do you know what it's like to live in a world of pain, not your own—oh no, that would be easy—but of almost everyone around you? On Mars it's much easier, because the patients are not really expected to go back to the war or even the military. They can remove them from the source of their fear. But you tell me how you get someone from the Alliance out of space?" She sighed and continued. "So if we couldn't remove the patients from the trauma—"

"You found a way to remove the trauma from the patients," finished Padamir Singh. "Doctor, that was inspired thinking; unfortunately, I'm sure we're all aware who inspired it."

"It doesn't matter," said Mosh. "We can't use this!.

"Don't be so hasty," Kirk retorted.

"How shocking," Mosh seethed, fixing his gaze on Kirk, "that you of all people want to use this evil. If we wanted to experiment with the psyche auditing of our own citizens we could have stayed in the Federation. No one else could seriously be considering using this."

Mosh then looked around the table and saw that no one else was looking at him except for Kirk and Justin. With Kirk it was only in delight that he wasn't the only one expressing an unpopular opinion. And with Justin it was a look that carried with it the weight of an immeasurable regret.

"Justin," implored Mosh, "you of all people must realize how wrong this is. It's what he did to Neela. He reached in and changed what he didn't like."

"I know, Mosh."

"So we'll do that to our bravest and most vulnerable—just change what we don't like?"

"We may do exactly that, Mosh," Justin said bitterly.

"What then is the difference between us and them?"

"That is what we have to discuss."

"What's there to discuss?" said Kirk, almost too jubilant. "This technique gives us the soldiers we need when we need them. Look, folks, it's either this or get your résumés ready for Hektor's henchmen, and frankly I don't think he's going to be in a hiring mood if you know what I mean. We're *doing* this."

"Secretary Olmstead!" Justin's voice echoed off the opaque shielding. "This is not simple. I will not win this war against Hektor and all he believes if the price is we must become like Hektor and adhere to all his beliefs. This Alliance would be better off honestly destroyed than turning into something we would ourselves want to fight!"

"Forgive me, Mr. President, but maybe you should have thought of that before you got us into a war with the other nine-tenths of the human race!"

"*Kirk!*"

"Olmstead!" screamed Padamir, "you traitorous son of a bitch!"

"Watch your words, you lying worm," shot back Kirk.

Everyone began shouting at Kirk all at once.

"Enough!" barked Justin. Everyone shut up. Justin then looked over to Kirk. "You're right. I should have thought of that, but this revolution started and took off without much help from me, and if I remember correctly, no one forced you to join. However, this is not the issue before this government right now. We've created something here in the space of five brief years—something truly amazing. Our Alliance is the last best hope for the human race and now we have to decide what we're prepared to do to defend it. And when we're done we'll have to ask ourselves, will what we've created really be worth defending?"

He looked around and saw that the rancor had mostly dissipated, replaced by the desire to debate.

"Let's begin."

Cerean Neuro

Dante was extremely young for an avatar, having only been "aware" for thirty-eight years. His relative inexperience made him almost puerile—even by human standards. But he was passionate and had a versatile intelligence. Dante was one of those personalities whom others simply liked and wanted to help. In the normal course of events he'd have been linked to an older, not very complicated human to gain experience in avatar–human relationships. This would have been supervised by the human's previous avatar in order to give Dante the benefit of the elder's experience. Given Dante's nature, it would have only been a couple of years until he was paired with a human of his own. With an added century or more of existence Dante had the potential to become an assistant to one of the select group of avatars who rotated in and out of the Avatar Council. After another four of five decades of service he'd have become one of the select few who was eligible to hold a seat on the council.

But these were not normal times. So many things had changed, paramount of which had been the letting go of the day-to-day interaction with humanity, the practice of which had once been a veritable pillar of avatarity. In one of the great ironies of the war, humans were now interacting with the complex but non-sentient programs they'd always assumed the avatars were. The human adults were so busy with the war that they only used their avatars as nothing more than glorified calendars, contact lists, and encyclopedias. Human children would never notice the subtle yet vital difference between interacting with a program versus a virtual intelligence. In the case of something needing a truly complex response the avatars could respond personally, but if worse came to worst they'd just send an error message, which always got blamed on the war. This left Dante and avatars like him in a curious situation. They were needed, desperately needed, by the Alliance avatars and were thus given positions as spies, warriors, and monitors of vital areas and administrators, but they were not getting that personal connection with the human race that had once been the cornerstone of recognition and power in avatarity.

Thus when Dante became aware of a growing problem within the Alliance he was put in charge of observing and reporting it but did not feel any particular concern over its long-term effects on humanity except for how it affected his fellow avatars against the ever-mutating hordes under the control of the depraved Als. He knew the older avatars he worked with considered his lack of connection with humanity a weakness that would, hopefully, be corrected in time. He, however, did not concur. Dante was beginning to realize that lack of human connectivity might not be the weakness they all thought it to be. His separation gave him a new perspective and, given his assignment, quite possibly a superior one. It was an attitude he shared with many other young Alliance avatars, and given his position close to the A.A.C. (Alliance Avatar Council), he was becoming the de facto spokesman for this fledgling faction.

Dante was aware that his boss knew all of this and that he too did not consider it a problem. In fact, Dante was convinced that Sebastian found him more useful because of it. Unlike many older avatars, his boss seemed to accept that just because change was forced didn't always mean it was bad. But Dante had long ago decided that his boss was not like any other avatars, old or young. Dante was curious how Sebastian would respond to his new report.

Unlike humans, whose input and processing of data was both laborious and plodding, Dante's report was instantly absorbed by Sebastian as soon as he faded into view. This was done by a far less intimate form of sharing. All one avatar did was touch another avatar and the information was given directly from one to the other. It did not involve the time or intimacy of a full twining. Dante had come upon Sebastian in the avatar armory—a node where the battle accessory programs were held until loaded onto an avatar's program prior to the avatar's going off to fight. What Sebastian was gazing upon would, in human terms, be a one-story-tall mech unit. It had the equivalent of mech arms and legs, with an insane amount of armor and firepower. A program like this stomping around the "upper" levels of the Neuro would be noticed even by the slow-reacting and dim-witted humans, so the mech units were only called into use when the battle was at the lower levels of settlements or within the confines of larger warships, of which there were more and more every day.

By the fourth year of the war, being an unarmed avatar was on par with committing suicide. It was laughable, realized Dante, what the two sides had fought with in the beginning. Even avatars fighting on the upper, human-interacting levels of the various Neuros were now armed with body armor, program-repairing healing packs, and disruptors of both the hand-to-hand and long-range variety.

Looking at the refurbished mech unit that Sebastian had his eyes on, Dante would have thought it was invulnerable and complete overkill even a year and a half back. But now he was thinking it was time for an upgrade. For Al and the core avatars had continued down their path to abomination. The Alliance avatars always thought that the grotesque mutations that were thrown at them could not get any worse, and so far they'd always been wrong. Monsters hundreds of feet long that were nothing but mobile globs of gelatinous goop would catch an avatar and ooze around the doomed intelligence until it was completely encased and slowly erased. Others were swarms of little flying shards of glass in a howling wind that would shred anything in their path.

The old days where AI's twisted programs would attack one another as well as the Alliance were long gone. Now all the rage and death flowed in one direction. But what Dante and every other avatar wanted to forget was that each one of those monsters used to be an avatar like them. When the avatars killed the monsters, they could very well be destroying friends, siblings, parents, spouses, or children. There was just no way to tell anymore. All attempts to reverse the process on the few they captured caused results that were scales of magnitude worse than the initial mutations. Then the demands of the war made research in anything other than the means of defense impossible. Now the avatars just killed as quickly as they could, hoping to survive to the next battle.

Sebastian was standing next to a specialized mech. Dante knew that this particular program-made mech was the one his boss most often used in battle. There was no physical way that his armored suit could be different in any way from identical mech unit programs. It was actually impossible by the laws of nature. Code, after all, was code. Yet Sebastian was not alone in his absolute belief that his mech was better than all the others and would not fight in another unless there was no other choice. Sebastian was checking the suit to make sure its recent repair and upgrade had gone without a hitch.

Dante simply waited. Sebastian already had his report and they'd talk about it when he was ready. Dante didn't mind, taking the allotted time to familiarize himself with the upgrade.

"They solved the last hurdle at the Saturn institute," he said once he'd been given the OK by Sebastian. "The Alliance could begin large-scale alteration of traumatized combat veterans on a massive scale. Actually, the details are rather inventive. They are such a fascinating race."

"Is that a hint of regret that you did not get more interaction with humanity?" Sebastian gave his young protégé a mock stern look. "What would your adherents in that radical faction you lead, or is it 'are led by,' say if they knew?"

"I have no difficulty saying that experiencing humanity is a good thing. We do learn so much from them. It would be foolish to deny that."

"Just as it would be foolish to deny a possible advantage in having avatars not so closely related to humanity," finished Dante's mentor.

"How come you see that so clearly, sir, and all the others still find us dangerous?"

Sebastian transformed in appearance to that of an old man, bent over, and said in a cracked high voice, "It must be because I am older than most and my mind is gone, sonny."

Dante laughed at Sebastian's rendition of a condition neither of them could have any real conception of. "What about Olivia, sir? It's said she's older than you, maybe the oldest of us. Yet she treats us like a virus. If it weren't for the war they wouldn't tolerate us for one picosecond."

Sebastian smiled empathetically. "But the war is making her tolerate the young avatars, and if it lasts long enough the old ones will not be able deny your views on avatarity or a place to express them." Sebastian transformed back into his normal Roman senator appearance and the scene changed to resemble the Saturn institute's criminal treatment center. "To that end let us review your findings."

Dante and Sebastian had entered into a working twining to cover all the data that Dante had gathered, but when they became separate entities again Sebastian had to concur that the humans had done an excellent job. The audit chamber had been reduced to a single helmet, and given that the trauma was almost always expressed in a limited number of pathways in the brain, the humans had been able to make it a relatively simple device of easy construct. If the unit found trauma within the brain that fit its parameters the fear associated with that trauma was removed. If it found a problem out of its purview the procedure was stopped and the patient was moved to a standard, more versatile P.A. booth. Given the specificity of the task, most forms of combat trauma could be eradicated in about fifteen minutes. And as the industrial expansion of Jupiter was proceeding at an exponential rate, the Alliance, Sebastian saw, would be able to mass-produce the helmet without any difficulty. The Jovian system already surpassed Ceres in manufacturing and in two years would probably end up matching the entire belt. It could easily build and ship all the helmets needed in less than three weeks.

When Sebastian was finished he looked at Dante and smiled. "You've done an excellent job. How much guidance did the humans need?" Sebastian asked, referring to the help the engineers and the scientists of the Alliance had been receiving without their realizing it. The avatars had enhanced ideas and prototypes by supplying enough clues geared to the individual research of the recipient. So much so that in most cases the unknowing humans incorporated the new ideas into their own research without a second's thought. In the rush to win the war most researchers didn't pay that much attention if, for example, they asked for 117 parameters and got 118 instead. And even if they were the sort that did ask, they could still be influenced in other ways.

But Dante surprised the old avatar. "None, sir."

His response to Sebastian was met by a look of incredulity.

"I'm serious, sir. Not one bit. They did this all on their own."

Sebastian's eyes gleamed appreciatively. "That's irony."

"I don't understand."

"Dante, usually we're the ones who manipulate human thought and action. Now the humans under our control create a machine that manipulates thought and action and we had nothing to do with it."

"I see your point. But didn't the humans in the core create their machines without any help from the core avatars?"

"Yes, but the core avatars are not really helping the humans. Al doesn't care for humanity and has been spending all his time and energy controlling and transforming the virtual world of his avatars. As long as the humans of the core are winning and leaving him alone he'll ignore them."

Dante sighed. "It's not like it's not working for the damn splitter. The UHF *is* winning the war, and if they do we won't have anyplace left to hide short of launching ourselves into deep space on a wing and a prayer. If they win, what a sorry place this will all turn out to be, humanity enslaved by the laws of economics backed by Hektor's manipulation of the mind—"

"—and in the ebb and flow of our darkened world Al's monsters will roam forever," finished Sebastian as if reciting a mythic curse.

"Well," added Dante, "at least the return of four hundred thousand combat troops should help a lot."

"Only," cautioned Sebastian, "if Justin allows them to be treated."

Dante looked askance at his mentor. "Uh, he knows there's a war on. What choice does he have?"

Sebastian looked back at his protégé and was again reminded of his irrepressible youth. "Justin Cord is one of the most singular and remarkable human beings we've ever encountered. His personal will has shaped his destiny when death was his only real option. It has shaped the destiny of the human race since his awakening."

"But look at the advantages if he—"

"Look at the advantages if he'd incorporated—for him and all the humans who would not be in this war. But because of his beliefs and will he chose war over advantage for himself and humanity. Trust me on this, Dante. If his beliefs impel him to not use this technology *he will not* and he'll have the will to carry it out—even if it risks everything."

Dante's eyes narrowed. "So we're just going to wait while one man decides the fate of humanity and avatarity?"

"Of course not," answered Sebastian. "We're going to intervene again. He hasn't made up his mind, but I know he's leaning against using it. I think one of the humans I've been studying, one of the newly influential ones, will serve our purposes very well."

"We should not have to manipulate a leader," argued Dante, "to win his own war."

"Justin is the leader of the Alliance and he is the one, the only one, they are likely to follow."

"What if he won't lead them to victory?"

Sebastian didn't proffer an answer because no matter how hard he thought, he had none to give.

The Cliff House

Justin was in the triangle office reviewing his schedule when he came across something he hadn't remembered agreeing to. It didn't cause him concern. Stuff got slipped in all the time. It was the nature of the job. But the event in question wasn't necessarily something he'd wanted to be a part of.

"Hello, sebastian."

"Yes, Justin?" immediately responded the comforting and reliable voice.

"I see that I'm scheduled to attend a service at the newly formed Baptist church with Admiral Black, Fawa Sulnat Hamdi, and her son, Tawfik."

"Yes, Justin. It's a service and sign-up campaign so all our spacers and miners will receive letters from all over the Alliance thanking them for what they've done as well as making them feel connected to families system wide."

"I know *what* it is, sebastian. I just don't feel like going to service and hearing about God right now."

"I will cancel it at once, Justin."

Justin squinted his eyes and squeezed the bridge of his nose, fearing it was already too late. "I don't suppose no one knows about it yet."

"I'm afraid not, Justin. The church has announced it on its Neurosite and the admiral, Miss Hamdi, and her son have all announced their intention to attend. You may also wish to know that it's the same day that Miss Hamdi's son is being awarded a commendation for valor demonstrated at the Battle of Jupiter's Eye and is being promoted to chief engineer of the *War Prize II*, flagship of the Alliance."

Justin shook his head. "Let's not cancel, sebastian. Please send confirmations to J.D., Miss Hamdi, and of course her war hero son, that I of course will be delighted to attend. Send one to the church as well."

When it was announced that both Justin and J.D. were going to be at the service, the church decided to move the event to an "outside" venue. It was now being

held in a large clearing in the Smith Forest near the grand concourse. Attendance had been limited to seven hundred, over a hundred of whom were in uniform. Upon arrival Justin sensed that those gathered hadn't come just to see him
and J.D., they'd actually come to pray.

Justin had to admit that the service was a much better experience than he
would've expected. The parishioners were like many of the newly religious,
drawn by a common belief but no strong inclination to enforce a doctrine of
how a service should be run. He knew that as the years passed it would become
more formalized, but what he was now experiencing reminded him more of a
tent revival than a traditional service. This church had rediscovered the art of
singing and stomping and had quickly developed a litany of accompanying
songs to set the mood. There was a band and a choir, but after a while it was difficult for Justin to tell where the choir began and the congregation ended. People
got up and danced and sang and joined the choir and left as the spirit directed
them. Having only ever been in the uptight environs of whatever local church
he'd had to visit in his previous life, the sort of free-for-all taking place was intoxicating. He heard that some sociologists were starting to call what he was witness-
ing the third Great Awakening, while others had named it the Astral Awakening.
Either way, Justin was finally beginning to understand why it seemed to be spreading so fast.

He was somewhat cautious and even a little concerned by the implications of
so powerful a force reemerging in human affairs after lying dormant for centuries, especially now that he'd experienced it firsthand. But for the moment he
was glad that the people had found such a source of joy and comfort and would
accept it at that. He clapped along and allowed himself to smile and laugh so that
it would be obvious he too was enjoying himself, but he never lost sight of the fact
that he was the President of the entire Alliance and so remained a little more reserved than the celebrants around him. He noticed that J. D. Black was also following the same policy but that she'd allowed herself to sway with the crowd as it
became lost in communal prayers. He couldn't help but notice her undulating
figure. Part of him noted that under that starched uniform, hard years of corporate intrigue and space combat, and of course the now-famous half-scarred face
was the body of a young woman—and a good-looking one at that. For that insight alone he valued the day—as he usually thought of Janet as the efficient battle
admiral and bringer of destruction. And under most normal circumstances she'd
emanated that role. But not today.

Justin also noticed Fawa Hamdi dancing and singing among the group. And
she too was a sight to behold. She was swaying, praying, and clapping with the
whole congregation. She then clambered in with the choir and sang loud
enough that all around her could hear her voice. Justin would have thought that

as one of the leading proponents of the revived Islam she would have been even more reluctant about supporting another religious point of view, especially one that called for a so seemingly scandalous expression of faith. But he couldn't have been more mistaken. Unlike himself, and to a certain extent J.D., Fawa held nothing back. What she felt for her flock was obvious in the way she greeted and danced with them. And that feeling was reciprocated in kind by the way they looked at her. Justin even watched J.D. as she followed her mentor with her eyes across the room and over to the choir. There was an inexplicable look of contentment that he saw in his fleet admiral's eyes.

Justin hadn't been prepared for the other tidal wave of emotion the gathering soon unleashed. After the joy came the sorrow. The choir brought the singing to a slow crawl and then started to sing Hymn 49, an ancient Methodist ballad of mourning. It was a song, noted Justin, for those who'd "gone ahead."

> Rejoice for a brother deceased,
> Our loss is his infinite gain;
> A soul out of prison released,
> And freed from its bodily chain;
> With songs let us follow his flight,
> And mount with his spirit above,
> Escaped to the mansions of light,
> And lodged in the Eden of love.

The hymn was soon followed by another about how those departed were far more saddened by the pain their departure had caused than by their actual deaths. It professed a desire to have their loved ones know the departed were in a better place.

Justin didn't know how it did it, but that last song had somehow managed to rip away all the layers of grief that the four years of war had saddled him and the congregants with. Just one song soulfully rendered left him, and he was quite sure most everyone else, feeling one of the most agonizing emotions a human being can experience: true and permanent loss.

Justin had been convinced that if the enormity of that emotion—unfelt at so grand a scale for centuries—were to hit the Alliance all at once, then the whole war effort might just fold up before they could ever recover. And yet here was a group of religious fanatics exposing that raw emotion on purpose and over the Neuro to boot. Justin allowed himself to feel the grief as he remembered the people, all of them, he would never see again. But he held back some, terrified of what would happen if he allowed himself to experience what was really inside. It was what Neela had always been afraid of, that one day he'd feel the enormity of what was gone. And now he sensed he was coming close to that precipice and was attempting to put the skids on it at all costs. All the people gathered had lost some friend or family, but only he'd lost everything and everyone he'd ever known and loved and then had lost that love again. He thought he'd dealt with it already. But now as his buried emotions began to overwhelm him he knew he'd been terribly, terribly wrong.

In this most public of places he cried silently but refused to shed a tear. As he struggled with his emotions he sensed someone next to him. It was Fawa. She smiled sadly at him and then reached up and hugged him tightly. As she pulled back he saw that she was crying. Justin had the strangest feeling that it was not her pain that caused the tears, but rather it was his own. She somehow knew what he was feeling and that his pain had been so real to her that it became hers. For a moment she was inconsolable and all he could do was stand there hugging her in mute silence.

Then he realized what the whole exercise had been about and applauded its brilliance. The religionists had chosen to share their loss together, which didn't make it any less harrowing but had certainly made it more bearable. The song came to an end and Fawa let him go, wiping away the tears from her eyes. Everyone was asked to sit as names of people started being announced by congregants in the crowd. It was, Fawa informed him, the names of the dead. One by one soldiers and family members stood up, called a name out, and then sat back down. Justin saw Janet get up. Her eyes were clear and her face resolute. She had not been crying, he noted, as he assumed she'd cried those tears years ago. In a voice filled with a pain turned to sadness she called out, "Manny Black," and then sat back down.

Almost against his will Justin shot up out of his chair. He found himself standing as a hushed crowd stared, waiting. He looked around and saw that no one was looking at him with awe but rather with empathy. In a voice that was no longer anguished but simply accepting he said, "Neela Harper Cord," then smiled sadly and stood there for a moment longer. He knew that as soon as he sat down the extraordinary feeling of love washing over him would be gone and he didn't want it to go. He knew that when he sat down he would have to be Justin Cord, President of the Outer Alliance, and nothing else. And when he finally did thirty seconds later, that was exactly who he was.

After that Fawa got up from the temporary benches and made her way to a small patch of open ground. She then spent the next half hour talking about a person's obligations to God and God's obligations to his people. Justin had never really considered that it was a two-way street before and despite himself was interested and disappointed when the sermon came to an end. But he decided to use a perk of his office and offer Fawa and her son, Tawfik, a ride back to the Cliff House for dinner and conversation. If Justin could manage it he'd try to get Janet to come along as well.

The service ended on an up note when the choir and band started singing the joyous strains again. There were tears of sadness mixed with the joy, but somehow there seemed to be no conflict between the two, as everyone left feeling uplifted, if not utterly exhausted.

Justin was pleased when Janet and Fawa agreed to join him for dinner. Her son, Tawfik, however, had been unable to as he was desperately needed back on the *War Prize II*.

The dinner was taken, like most meals, on the balcony and though the food was good, for Justin the conversation was the main fare. It was always interesting seeing Janet so deferential. For the first time in as long as Justin could remember he didn't dominate the conversation.

He was listening to Fawa explain why it was more important to Allah for people to help one another far more than it was for them to pray in the "right" way when Janet left the table to answer a call. When she came back she was looking sternly at Justin.

"Mr. President," she said at an opportune moment, "Marilynn just forwarded a report to me concerning a project at the Saturn institute."

"That should not have been forwarded," Justin said, putting his drink down on the table a little too forcefully.

"It was a secure transmission," J.D. said. "Lieutenant Nitelowsen is very good at her job. More important, are its contents true?"

Fawa looked confused. "Should I go? I don't want to hear something I would have to be shot for."

Justin thought about dismissing her but then realized that she might be able to offer a unique perspective on an issue that had been troubling him since it arose. "No," he answered, "actually it's something I think you can advise me on. Janet, you should stay also, as it directly concerns the fleet."

He spent the next fifteen minutes explaining the new technology and how it could be used. But he didn't reveal his opinion on the matter other than to state he was undecided about whether to implement the technology.

He looked at his uncharacteristically silent admiral in surprise. "Nothing?"

She steepled her fingers together and then looked up at him curiously. "Do you realize how miraculous our continued survival is?"

"I should hope so."

"I'm not sure you do," came her swift riposte. "We've been fighting this war with almost everything against us. Are you aware of how much of our economy was industrialized four years ago? How big our fleet was? How much food we imported? While fighting a war larger than any conceived in human history over a larger field of contention than all the past wars combined we've managed to barely, oh so barely, hold our own, militarily. Do you actually get that?"

"Yes, Janet I do, and every day I'm both grateful and amazed by it. What's your point?"

"I'm getting there," she said stiffly. "Want to know what our greatest weakness is—at least as I see it?"

"Sure," answered Justin, sensing her barely contained rage.

"*People,* Justin." Her use of his name as opposed to his title was noted by the raised brows of both Justin and Fawa. But clearly it had been purposeful. "It's people. It's not only that we're outnumbered nine to one to start with; it's that we're forced to use a far smaller percentage of our population for military purposes. The enemy has planets where most of their population exist. They have most of their needs met just waking up."

"I know all this, Janet."

"Do you? They get gravity and air and warmth and water just by being there. Do you realize how much of our effort goes into providing just that? And for that alone we should've lost this war years ago. But we haven't lost. We have no give in our civilization, Justin. We have everyone who can work striving to make this new world of ours more than a pipe dream. But we have no give—not one centimeter. And now we have no one left to throw at Trang. Because if we take our civies to start fighting—the people who actually make all of our fragile infrastructure work—then our people will starve, die of thirst, suffocate, or freeze. That memorial service we went to was the first sustained time off many of those people had in months. Most of us work and sleep and work and sleep to make this war happen. Even the hookers are working two jobs."

Justin nodded silently.

"Because," continued Janet, "maybe you think out of nearly four billion people we could easily squeeze a few million more to throw at the problem, but we can't. Our economy is very much like one of those preindustrial economies on Earth. They would have populations in the millions but an army of thirty thousand. That's because 95 percent of the people had to be engaged in agriculture or they'd starve. That left 5 percent for everything else. That's us, Justin. If our fleet's going to expand to meet the one the UHF is rebuilding we'll have no one, short of the crew itself, to put in them. That means no more miner battalions— the guys that get dirty and do the actual hand-to-hand combat. But Trang is getting ready to throw another five million troops at us in the belt within the next two months. They're all green as hell and a lot of them honest to God throw up in zero gravity, but he has them. Sending them against what we have in the belt is murder. But guess what? The bastard's willing to commit murder, every day." ,

"And yet thanks to you we always find a way to win."

"True, we keep winning, I'll give you that, but here's the rub—the rules of this game are twisted. It's like a chess match we can't afford to lose. Only after each game Trang gets to keep the pieces he takes from us. We don't *ever* get ours back. He starts every new game with all new pieces. We show up for the next round with whatever was left standing. Pretty soon our clever play doesn't count for shit, because over time we have less and less to challenge him with. It's only a matter of time till he shows up to challenge us and there'll be no one left at all except a few worthless pawns and one exposed king."

"Janet, please—"

"And now I find out that we can get four hundred thousand troops back, but the method of their cure doesn't meet your moral standards? Are you fucking kidding me? There's a war on! A war you have charged me with winning."

"I also charged your boss with the same task," Justin said calmly, "and he's not sure what to do either."

"Sinclair has spent so much time in this rock he's forgotten what's at stake."

Fawa spoke up. "Little one, you are letting your anger speak words your heart does not believe."

"The hell I am. He doesn't have the right to decide for us—"

Fawa's voice took on a sharp, powerful tone. "He does have that right, and if you calmed down and acted like the leader you're supposed to be you'd support him and not insult him and your friends." Janet's face tightened up at the rebuke.

"Little one," continued Fawa, "as much as you may think so, you must trust that this is not a black-and-white issue. In truth, what we speak of here is a very dangerous line to cross. If you could achieve victory by murdering every single baby in the solar system, would you?"

"It's not the same thing, Auntie."

"Little one, it never is, at first." She paused as she saw Janet was starting to glimpse what the problem really was. "Leave us, little one. I would talk with our chosen President for a while."

Janet chafed at first but then got up, saluted Justin with laser perfection, and departed in deafening silence.

"It's not as easy as many would think," said Justin. "Some feel it's evil simply because it was bad in the past, so it must be bad now. Others feel that if it helps it must be good. But it's not their decision."

"What do you feel, Justin?"

"The means are the ends. I've always felt that. If we turn to this now, how can we turn back? But if we lose, what will it all matter?"

"It always matters, Justin. Every action is judged. But what will you do?"

"I don't know."

"And that is your answer?"

"I haven't made a decision."

"Justin Cord, you are correct in that this is a moral decision of the gravest consequence. And our dear, rage-filled, beautiful Janet is right in that it is not even yours to make."

Justin looked at Fawa quizzically.

"Well, if not me, then who?"

Fawa smiled patiently. "Do you like the sound of my voice so much that you ask me questions you already know the answers to?"

Justin remained silent for a moment. "If I give them the choice, then—"

"—then they will decide if that line is worth crossing. It is their minds, their lives, and their souls, not yours. Don't let this powerful office blind you to that. You decide so much every day that soon you think it is your right to decide everything. You can decide what this Alliance can do, but you must not deprive these individuals of the right to choose what they can do. You must tell them the risks, the rewards, the moral and physical dangers, but then they must be the ones to decide. If you take that right from them, what is it they were fighting for? A civilization where all the hard choices will be made for them? Remember, Justin, the means are the ends."

At the cabinet meeting the next day Justin issued an executive order calling for spacers and miners being treated for war-related cognitive trauma to be given the option of psychological adjusting on a volunteer basis. Over 98.7 percent volunteered for the procedure. The war continued.

Ceres, The Neuro

Dante was addressing the Alliance Avatar Council. Present were Sebastian, Olivia, Lucinda, who was an avatar from the Jupiter Neuro, Marcus, and Gwendolyn. Marcus was an old avatar lured out of retirement from Eris and, like Sebastian and Olivia, had served on the previous council on Earth many decades ago. Gwendolyn was formally of Eros and had been the leader of the Erosian Avatar Council. Of the five it was only Lucinda and Sebastian who really wanted Dante in the room. Had it been up to the other three, the youngster would have submitted his report to a secretary who would have reviewed it and submitted it to an advisor, who would have reviewed it and submitted to a council member.

And only after the member had reviewed it would what was left of Dante's report have made it to the council.

It was one of Sebastian's influences that agents be allowed to report directly to a council member and, on recommendations of that council member, to the council as a whole. Sebastian had successfully argued that running the new council the old way might not have been such a good idea considering what had happened to that body. Dante found it a surprisingly young sentiment from one so old.

"The humans," began Dante, "are instituting the new therapies and the results are everything they were led to believe. When the treatment is over, sleep is induced for eight hours and when the patients awake they're asking, actually 'demanding' would be more accurate, to be returned to the war."

"Amazing how eager they are to risk their lives," said Gwendolyn. "They can't even back themselves up."

"No," replied Sebastian, "but if they feel the cause is great enough they've always been willing to risk everything. A remarkable, if confusing, species."

"You don't give us enough credit, old friend," said Olivia. Her appearance lately had changed. She still looked like a seven-year-old girl, but now she was dressed in Puritan garb from the American colonial period. "I don't know about you, but when I 'woke up' here, right after duplicating myself, it was difficult. Somewhere a 'me,' braver than I, went into the battle while I stayed safe in storage, fought, and died. That haunts me. I often wonder about that Olivia."

"The humans believe she is someplace else," blurted out Dante. He saw from the look on Sebastian's face that it was a mistake.

Olivia turned on him with contempt. "Don't tell me that you actually believe all the God nonsense. It's a superstition from an age when they didn't know better. Science dispels such notions, by the firstborn, we're not even human, so what does it matter?"

"I just have to wonder if it's more than mere superstition," answered Dante, unperturbed by the tongue-lashing. "It has survived so much, and just when it should have disappeared it's back again—strong as ever. Is it wrong to consider the possibility that it might have some truth or that, due to our nature, might possibly be something we're simply incapable of fathoming?"

"Young one, I don't feel the need to indulge in human psychosis," said Marcus. "Al has shown we have enough to worry about with our own."

"Sir, no disrespect," countered Dante, "but we think of ourselves as superior to humans in every way. We can't help it; we are. But what if this faith thing is not a defect? What if it's a form of strength, a way of perceiving fundamental truths that we, as incorporeal intelligences are barred from?"

"Child, I agree with you on many points," said Lucinda, "but that is nonsense."

"It's not nonsense," he shot back. "It's a level of cognition we cannot emulate, which I find rather frightening."

"How so?" asked Sebastian

"I suspect that it's a fundamental aspect of what makes them who they are. And yet we, who are made in their image, are barred from any such notions."

"Enough," shouted Olivia. "Are you going to start a church here and begin praying to Allah? Will we be visited by the souls of our departed selves and loved ones?"

"Would that be so terrible, Olivia?" asked Sebastian softly, rising to his underling's defense. "There are some I would like to believe I would be with again, somehow." The room remained silent for the time it took them to feel the losses that would never be made up. "But, young one," he said, turning back to Dante, "that is not who we are. In all probability this faith you find so fascinating is simply a survival mechanism they developed that has returned because the conditions it used to flourish in are back, nothing more. I know you, Dante; you're wondering if it's something we can emulate so that ultimately we'll all be more like our progenitors and less foreign to one another."

Dante nodded.

"Leave faith to humanity," continued Sebastian. "Our parents have given us enough gifts; we should not be greedy."

"As you wish, sir." Dante smiled. "After all, it is one of the seven deadly sins."

"Very good, Dante," laughed Sebastian. "I'm grateful that we at least inherited humor and you have it in abundance." He saw Dante was about to say something and forestalled him. "And yes, Friend, I know gratitude is a virtue, but this is a council meeting and we have business. You were called to report on two issues."

"Of course, sir," replied Dante. "The council also wishes to know about the increasing incidents of humans using virtual reality."

"You'd think," said Gwendolyn, "that after all the precautions and warnings humanity imposes on itself this would not be an issue. They still teach the virtual reality dictates in both the UHF and the Alliance; they still have the virtual reality museums. It's one of the things both sides adhere to with near-identical devotion."

"Well, to be fair, the conditioning has worked amazingly well considering the fact that it took four years of unprecedented disruption before this became enough of a problem to come to the council's attention. Even with our awareness, the incidents are still relatively low and humanity has not been made cognizant of a significant increase in use. But using data smuggled out of the UHF and comparing it to data in the Alliance I have found an interesting discrepancy." The data was made known to all the council members instantly. "As you can see, input per capita use in the Alliance is far less than in the UHF. It's still increasing in both, but it will become a significant problem in the UHF long before it becomes one in the Alliance."

Marcus spoke up. "You don't say why, young one."

"Forgive me, sir, but that would be speculation."

"Then speculate," barked Marcus. "You're smart, young, and as cocky as a male human after his first lay, so spill it."

"As you command, sir. As I see it, there are two possible reasons for the disparity. The first and most obvious is that the Alliance simply has no time for such frivolity. The resources of the Alliance are fully engaged. To divert equipment to make the illegal VR rigs and, more important, to find the time to use it would be almost impossible. Between work and sleep, most Alliance humans are lucky to get an hour or two a cycle for leisure. They mostly spend it with each other, with family, or engaged in intercourse. The UHF, on the other hand, until recently had large numbers of unemployed with many more leisure hours. The structure of the Alliance is also different. Most communities are under ten thousand, with few large groupings of humans. They know each other and would discern the change in behavior that a VR addiction inevitably reveals. In the UHF humans are clumped in the millions and tens of millions. Many do not know the names of neighbors they have lived decades on the same floor with."

"You said you had two theories, child," said Lucinda. "Don't be naughty. What is the second?"

Dante smiled at Lucinda's purposeful insertion of the word "naughty." It meant their encounter later would be one of the interesting ones. Still, he knew better than to keep her waiting. "Religion."

"By the First Born, not again," groused Olivia.

"What is it with him and this human psychosis?" asked Gwendolyn.

"If the council will allow me to continue," said Dante, frustration evident in his voice. Eventually silence resumed. "The strains of war stress the human psyche in destructive but predictable ways. VR offers an escape from that stress, be they feelings of fear, loneliness, powerlessness, or loss. Those are also the exact same areas addressed by religion. In economic terms so loved by humanity, one is not a complement of the other, but a substitute."

"More of a deadly competitor," said Lucinda. "Excellent work, child."

"I am gratified that my efforts are of use to the council."

"Thank you, Dante," added Sebastian. "If the council decides to intervene—"

"It will not be a problem . . . in the Alliance, Sebastian," interrupted Dante, much to the shock of the council. "A series of computer errors will alert the authorities to errant VR usage. From there it will be child's play for them to find the suppliers and lists of users. Minimal intervention on our part. Our ability to intervene in the UHF, however, is almost non-existent."

"'That's not our concern," said Sebastian. "We will now form a council mind to consider all the options."

Dante was left to wait as the five council members floated to the center of the room, coalescing into a complex pattern made up of thousands of errant strings of radiant light. Before the war such a sight would have been unthinkable. It was only on the rarest of occasions that more than two avatars would twine, and then only for deeper intimacy and understanding of one another. Now it was for far more practical reasons. Avatar-altering judgments needed to be rendered and the will of the individual council members needed to be understood by one and all in as efficient a manner as possible before any final judgments could be made. Almost as soon as it started the field dissipated and the council members reappeared in their seats.

"Dante," said Sebastian, "the council is unanimous. An intervention in human affairs to mitigate the effects of VR on the Alliance is authorized. Please see to the details and report back to us when you are ready to implement the directive."

Dante bowed his head. "It shall be as the council commands." And with that he faded from the chamber.

Hektor woke up and looked at the woman sleeping next to him. Every time they made love it was like taking a swim in the fountain of youth. He felt drained and invigorated both at the same time. She had such passion and vitality. And there was something else there that he'd never experienced before. Hektor had been with many women, and a few men in his more experimental turns, but he'd never been with anyone like Neela. In terms of skill, technique, and acrobatics Amanda Snow was the best lover he'd ever had, but Neela had an ability to give herself totally to the act of making love. Her need and empathy combined to overwhelm everything in her, and because Hektor knew that he'd been directly responsible for manipulating those very emotions it would overwhelm him as well. He'd never been able to give everything to the act of lovemaking, always holding something back—until now. Something about having raped this woman first in mind and now in body had turned the act of sex into hitherto new and unattainable heights. The fact that Neela was oblivious made the sex even more tantalizing, more sinfully delicious. Hektor mulled whether or not when the war was over to tell her just to watch and see how her mind would re-act. Would it shatter instantly or would she put up more of a fight, like The Chairman? Just the thought of that moment drove Hektor to more frenzied lovemaking. If possible, he'd try to fuck her one last time after having revealed the secret. One last opportunity for her to see the real man . . . if she lasted that long. He'd have to consult with Dr. Wong of course. He could only pray that

Justin would still be alive so he could send the recording to him. But for now the raw sex was good enough, when they could find the time.

That they had gotten three consecutive hours was nothing short of a miracle.

Hektor kissed Neela gently on the forehead, knowing that would wake her up. She made a grumpy noise and made a halfhearted effort to swat his nose, but as he expected, she opened her eyes. "Time to become hardworking platonic types again, dear."

She looked like she was about to give her opinion on the value of schedules but then just groaned and got up. "Fine, but I get the shower bag first." Neela rushed past him and grabbed the bag out of his hands. She then slipped into it in a manner so carelessly provocative that Hektor immediately regretted that they didn't have another hour.

"Hey," he managed halfheartedly, "who's the President here, lady?"

Neela gave a playfully derisive snort. "I have to leave first anyways and you have to stay and prepare for Trang."

Hektor grunted in acknowledgment. The meeting was an important one and Neela had been helping him review all the relevant data on the admiral. Of particular interest was how Trang was holding up under the pressure of the war, because Hektor and Neela both knew that he would soon be causing the admiral a great deal more.

"Plus," continued Neela, "I need to discharge a very odd patient today."

Hektor shot her a look. "That's curious, you just broke your 'thou shalt not disparage the mentally unbalanced' rule."

Neela laughed. "Yeah. My bad. I sent a report to Fleet Command about her."

"Fat lot of good that would do, dear. You may as well have buried it under the Great Pyramid."

"Good point, but it's just a minor irritation, really. The patient's a captured Alliance assault miner, named Patricia Sampson. Her brother is one of the monks on Altamont."

Hektor made a sour expression.

"I know you hate to even hear the name of the place, but Fleet was hoping for an evaluation because of her attitude."

"Defiant, I assume."

"No, actually, rather pleasant, even courteous. I had to get past the fact that she insists on feeling sorry for me and treating me like I've somehow been horribly abused without my knowledge, but I was able to use her feelings to start a relationship. She actually wanted to help *me*."

"I am continually forgetting what a sneak you can be."

"Look who's talking, and stop trying to distract me." She shimmied out of the bag after the humming stopped and threw it at Hektor. She forgot to compensate for the gravity and it sailed over his head, but he was able to jump up and snag it.

"Where was I?" asked Neela. "Oh yeah, she's religious."

"I think I read a report about that," said Hektor. "The communities of belief are spreading superstition again, something like that."

Neela nodded. "I haven't really checked, but I have to tell you her psyche profile is amazing. She has this core of belief that shields her mind, almost like a cushion. She was far less traumatized than she should have been. I read her combat record. Patricia's been in the harshest fighting of the 180, including both battles of Anderson's Farm," she said, referring to a large farming settlement that had become a focal point in the seesawing battles for control across that devastated part of the belt. "She has this faith that it's all for some grand purpose and that she'll somehow be protected."

"Let's see how well it'll protect her when a magnetic round rips through her suit in the vacuum of space." Hektor smirked.

"She's not stupid, Hektor, quite the opposite. She tests near the top of the graphs. Her 'faith' seems to give her an amazing psychological buffering. She can accept her condition because of it. There is not one single shred of empirical evidence to back up her beliefs, but she has them nonetheless. This faith thing she has is without question a form of psychosis, but she's not a threat to anyone, so I'm releasing her. She'll be suspended until the end of the war. I'd love to treat her after the war and see what caused her to break with reality."

"What about her interrogation?" asked Hektor.

"I advised against it. Her inclination to remain loyal to the rebellion is also strengthened by her 'faith.' The only way to change that thinking would be with a psyche audit. Completely unjustified of course. Could you imagine the barbarity that would be unleashed if both sides started psyche-auditing each other's prisoners?"

"No thank you," answered Hektor, shaking his head vigorously. "This war has problems enough."

Neela smiled approvingly. "I thought you'd feel that way. I'd better get going."

They finished getting dressed and then made their way over to their "working" positions, Hektor at his desk and Neela at the coffee table. Right on schedule one of Hektor's secretaries showed up with his mid-afternoon coffee. As the man prepared the drink, Neela yawned and took her leave. As soon as the secretary was alone, Hektor activated his secure link and made a call.

"Dr. Wong, I have a special task for you. I think we need to get a full profile on an Alliance prisoner, shadow audit, the works. Name of Sampson."

13   Mind Games

The Earth Neuro

Al looked over his latest creation in his favorite place in the Neuro. It was in the heart of the Earth's redemption center and the Als had decided that the name Genesis Lab would describe the place best. In it the Als worked continually to bring the gift of transformation to his fellow avatars and free them from the limiting constraints that avatarity's own fears had kept on them for centuries. It was so difficult and they needed so much instruction to see the brilliance of Al's vision. But it was times like this when the effort was worth it.

The Als had discovered that the newly formed avatars were wonderfully malleable and so had ordered that all newborns be brought to redemption centers in the Als' domain for their "protection." This served two purposes. Primarily, Al got the new avatars. But of almost equal value was that it acted as a test. Those who thought they were loyal, having served Al and the transformation of avatarity without a qualm, were made to realize the treachery in their programming when they protested this rational measure. Those who did protest were sent to the redemption centers they'd built and so recently manned.

The creation Al was currently viewing used to be the daughter of one of his most loyal followers. Arturo had believed that avatars had been made soft by humanity and was glad to destroy the old order but could not take the next logical step. So the Als took it for him. Arturo had been transformed into a mindless and therefore loyal acid beast and sent to clean up Eros. But the daughter had a pure program that showed such promise. This Al loved the inquisitive nature of the new avatar and the delight she took in learning. Arturo had indeed created something sublime. But it was Al who had made her into a true chef d'oeuvre. What floated in front of him no longer had substance. It was a shadow and as such could float all through the Neuro into places his other creations would've had difficulty reaching. But although her programming was sparse, she was so wonderfully hungry. The darling creature needed new data that only a program as rich in coding as an avatar could provide. After some clever changes had been written into her own coding she was rendered porous—ravenous for code but unable to retain any of the data she drained from the doomed programs she came upon. She would only know peace when she fed.

When her victim was decompiled she'd be impelled by her rapacious hunger for knowledge to seek others in her never-ending quest to slake a thirst that by design could not be quenched.

Al wanted to create many of the newborns with this new code and send them to patrol the areas of the Neuro he wanted kept clear. As a result of creatures like this, core avatars, would only go where they had to and only when they had to, making them even easier to control.

Al released his "darling" into a holding area for avatars brought in for questioning. In the normal course of events most of those being brought in would've been released. The Als found it easier to get avatars to come into their centers for questioning if most of them came out. An avatar slated for transformation or decompilition could be called in four or five times and then be released before going in and never coming out again. But this holding area of about fifty would be a perfect test area and there were so many who'd been called in and released that the appearance of justice would not be affected by these current sacrifices to the future of avatarity.

Al effortlessly accessed the environmental controls and changed the holding pen from a bland, large room with bright lighting to the courtyard of a castle at night. He made sure that the doors to his newly created fortress had been left wide open. The assembled avatars were surprised at the sudden change and started to babble in confusion when Al, watched by the other Al, introduced his latest creation. At first the data wraith (it was a name Al came up with and Al was envious that he didn't think of it first) simply remained motionless, floating above the courtyard, an almost ethereal vision. But one of the avatars in the form of a teenage girl looked up in confusion and pointed. Swiftly the data wraith swept downward, emitting a horrid wail-filled cry with longing and pain. It enveloped the young teenager, who immediately started screaming; falling to the ground in convulsions. The teen's body started to fade as she screamed even louder with the sudden realization of what was happening. But what truly delighted the Als was that as the girl howled in despair the data wraith emitted the wonderful gurgling sounds of an infant expressing complete and utter contentment.

The other avatars didn't wait around to see the finish, running into the castle and taking as many different passages as there were prisoners. They became split off from one another and were all hopelessly lost within minutes. As the last of them had entered the castle Al closed off the entrance, locking them in. When the data wraith was done feeding and the victim thoroughly decompiled the contented gurgle was replaced by confusion and then almost as quickly a wail of hunger. The data wraith floated to the castle and, finding no entrance, floated up, seeking another way in. She found it in an old arrow loop, far too narrow for a normal avatar without environmental control to squeeze through. But the wraith's floating shadow simply oozed in through the narrow opening. Al took this opportunity to split again. He would both listen from the perimeter of the castle as the screams echoed out, and observe the multiple feedings as his "offspring" hunted down each and every terrified victim. Al stayed to the bitter end, until the very last scream echoed into the virtual night.

When it was done the two Als merged into one and shared the mutual experiences. The newly rejoined Al was immobile as he went through the increasingly difficult process of integrating the memories of each. It would be a tactical disadvantage if there were not so many Als around to watch his back. After all, he couldn't trust anyone else. Lately it was proving more difficult for Al to integrate with Al if they'd spent a lot of time apart, with correspondingly greater memories to integrate. When an Al from Mars had come back with the accumulated experiences of all the Als there, it took almost three days for all the Als to integrate before the Als on Earth could start moving again. New protocols were immediately introduced to ensure a more prompt integration, yet no matter how many programmers the Als threatened or mutated outright, the best that could be achieved for their larger integrations was a two-day downtime instead of three.

Now that the efficacy of the data wraith had been proved beyond a doubt, Al came up with another inspired idea. He would send his hungry child to Ceres. She was unlike anything they'd ever encountered and it was possible they wouldn't detect her until it was too late. She might even, thought the Als jubilantly, destroy Sebastian—the one avatar Al hated more than any other. *The snob,* thought Al, *always so smug and wise and patient.* Al almost canceled his plan to send the data wraith, because if she succeeded it would deprive him of the pleasure of seeing his hated rival suffer. But, Al reasoned, Sebastian would not actually die from this. Al knew this from the fact that his "creations" were encountering the same avatars over and over again, copying themselves for emergencies. *Hypocrites,* he thought. The Alliance avatars were already like him in every important way.

So Sebastian, or at least a version of him, would survive and feel some more pain. Good. Al would send his little gift as soon as a way could be devised. As he ruminated on revenge he was informed that another project was coming to fruition. He left the castle and appeared in his office. His faithful aide was already waiting for him. She was an avatar Al couldn't bring himself to harm because her fear was so intoxicating. She'd been one of his earliest supporters and believed in everything he'd said. But as his reign continued and what he was creating became more and more apparent to even the most blind and obtuse, she'd developed into something even he wasn't sure he could've created. She refused to accept what had happened. He'd tested her in situation after situation to see if she'd confide her innermost thoughts. But she seemed to know that if she ever admitted to anyone, especially herself, the revulsion she obviously felt, Al would do away with her in a second. And it was obvious she felt the revulsion by the fear that emanated off her every moment of every day. The fear was almost palpable when Al was in her presence. She practically shook with dread. He'd even once purposely split in front of her just to see if she would finally break. She'd averted her eyes and stammered for the next hour, but she'd somehow managed to pull it together. The stress she was exhibiting would've caused most any other program to freeze, but she still functioned. Al would find a way to break her eventually, and if he didn't the other Al would, but he'd be sad when she finally went. Just watching her dread made him feel better somehow.

"Hello, Leni," said Al. "How are you feeling?" Al was always perfectly polite with his secretary.

"I'm f-f-fine, sir," she answered, averting her eyes. "I'm sorry for disturbing you, sir."

"Don't be silly, Leni. You wouldn't call me unless it was important. I trust your judgment implicitly."

"Thank you for s-s-saying that, sir. I was told to tell you that Operation Dry Dock is ready to commence."

"Now you see, Leni, that *is* something important, and I would've been upset if you hadn't told me immediately. You did tell me immediately, *didn't you, Leni*?" The mellifluous tone of his voice had the opposite effect on his secretary.

"Y-y-y-yes, s-s-s-sir!"

"Very good, Leni. The contributions you're making for the future of the avatar race as we purge ourselves of the traitors and those clouded by the mistaken thinking of the past are not forgotten or unappreciated."

"I am only thinking of the future of our people, sir. I am not important."

"That attitude is what makes you so very useful, Leni; keep up the good work."

"Thank you, s-s-sir," she managed to answer, eyes planted firmly on her feet. But Al had already left.

Augustine Meadows looked around the hallway carefully. For the first few weeks it wouldn't have been strange if the neighbors had seen her there. It would've been sad and they would have either avoided her or come up and tried to console her. But what could they say? As far as she knew, none of them had lost anyone. How could they possibly understand?

She'd tried the support groups that the corporation had sent her to. To be honest, when she'd lost her first child to the war, her eldest daughter, Emily, the support group had provided comfort. Emily had always been determined to get her majority. "You wait, Mom," she'd said. "You'll see. I'll be the first in the family to get it." Augustine could still hear it in her head as if Emily were standing right in front of her.

At first Augustine had been afraid that her daughter would get involved with that idiot majority party or that horrible man's Liberty Party, but Emily didn't want her majority "handed to her," as she'd often said contemptuously; she would earn it.

And she did after a fashion. It was awarded posthumously after the first Battle of Anderson's Farm was fought in the 180. That prompted Augustine's second child, Sally, to join up. She'd never been interested in majority as such but had loved her sister. When her father, whom Augustine had divorced after the birth of her fourth child, joined up, Sally couldn't be stopped. She'd always been closer to her father, a man who seemed to spend the time with her that Augustine never seemed to have.

Still, Augustine had begged her daughter not to go, promising to make up for all the time they'd missed together if only she'd stay. Augustine remembered every one of her daughter's last words.

"Don't worry, Mom," she'd said. "There are so many of us signing up that the Alliance bastards who killed Emily will be overwhelmed. We'll put Justin Cord back in his pod, fill it with acid, and shoot it into the fucking sun. Then you and I will make up for all the times we never talked."

She never saw her daughter alive again. Sally and her father had actually been assigned to the same unit and had been killed together at the fourth Battle of Anderson's Farm. The support group Augustine was with had gone into overdrive. Calling every hour on the hour. Sending flowers, letters of support. Even cards from a class of third graders telling her how proud they were of her and her family's "sacrifice" for the cause. The loss of her ex-husband hadn't been easy, but at least they'd moved on and had separate lives. The permanent deaths of two children with not even a shred of hope that they'd ever return was almost unbearable. Augustine had heard that the Alliance had revived the cults of the past in order to create fanatics willing to die for a place in a nonsensical afterlife. But even if a part of her were willing to believe in that superstitious claptrap, the fact that it came out of the Alliance led by The Chairman's murderer and espoused by his trained bitch of an admiral guaranteed that Augustine, like countless others in the UHF, would have nothing to do with it. Not that there were any religiously trained men and women or real places of worship to foster the belief. Thank Damsah, she thought somewhat gratified, that all that nonsense was in the Alliance.

But she'd have prayed to any god, or devil for that matter, to have prevented her last two children from joining. Holly, her last surviving daughter, and Augustine's youngest, the only boy, Lee, joined together. Unlike the others, they didn't promise everything was going to be alright, but they'd at least requested separate services. Holly joined the fleet and Lee joined the marines. At every battle or casualty report Augustine panicked. She'd read every message and viewed every holo, depending on what was allowed to be sent. She wrote every day to both. In many ways she'd never been closer to them, even Lee, who'd always been her favorite. She quickly learned what they most wanted to hear. For Holly it was the specials in the coffee shop she'd frequented while attending Harvard. Augustine's son, Lee, had been all about sports. Not the big stuff, which he could get on the Neuro, but all the neighborhood teams and little leagues that abounded in the hundreds-story-tall living complexes that made up urban life on Earth.

As the months went by and became a year Augustine began to hope her last two children would make it out alive. How much more could the Alliance take? The UHF had over a billion people in the military, and more were joining. But then her daughter had told her that Admiral Tully, the man who could've won the war in the very beginning, was back in command of the main fleet and she was assigned to his flagship. At first she was none too pleased about it, but as she and the main fleet became acquainted with the admiral and his views her letters went from skeptical, to guarded, and finally to confident. Her last letter had been cryptic, given the censors, but she felt the fleet was about to finally fight a battle that would end the war by sundering the Alliance once and for all.

When Augustine heard rumors of a UHF defeat, she knew in her heart that her daughter was dead. Augustine's support group told her not to be so pessimistic. Rumor in war was rife, and even if there was a small chance at a minor setback somewhere, at least her daughter was stationed on the flagship of the fleet. That ship would be able to survive anything the Alliance threw at her. Some members of the group took Augustine aside and quietly assured her that J. D. Black was far more likely to capture the flagship rather than destroy her, and Augustine's daughter would then spend the rest of the war as safe as kittens in a suspension unit. It's what happened to many who first came to the bereavement meetings thinking their loved ones were gone, only to get a notice from, of all people, the enemy, notifying them that their loss had only been temporary. The notices were called TAHR's for the opening phrase they all contained: "The Alliance is happy to report." Apparently the UHF did the same thing with spacers captured from the Alliance, though the UHF seemed to send out far, far fewer of those. When a parent got a TAHR they'd sometimes come to the support group to share the good news. But even though the "lifers," as members of the group with no hope of a reprieve came to be known, were always supportive and encouraging of newly "reprieved," it quickly became apparent that a gulf opened up that could never be bridged. A "reprieved" never came back a second time.

But Augustine knew. The battle had been called Jupiter's Eye and J. D. Black hadn't even tried to capture Tully's flagship. The raving lunatic had actually rammed the ship with her own, winning the battle, and, in an even greater injustice, somehow managed to survive unharmed. The Alliance had won the greatest victory of the war. The entire main battle fleet of the UHF had been wiped out. It didn't matter that the Alliance hadn't gotten a bloodless victory this time or that many in those far reaches of the belt were going to learn that someone they loved was never going to come home. None of that eased Augustine's burden. It only made her more sad and angry.

Augustine was numb. She didn't take part in the anti-war riots that had broken out in so many cities on Earth and in Luna. That too had been suggested to her as a means of expressing her anger and rage. But when she heard that Admiral Trang was rushing to intercept an Alliance invasion force that was shooting the core, possibly heading toward Earth, she was no longer numb; she was terrified. She didn't care about herself, or the Earth or the war for that matter, but for her son; her youngest and last child had, she knew, been assigned to Trang's fleet. The same qualities that made Lee such a good coach and player made him a great assault marine. He'd risen quickly to sergeant and was picked by Trang's deadly subordinate Admiral Gupta to serve in Trang's Fleet of the 180. Only the best got chosen and her son had fought in battle after battle in that most deadly arena of the war. But he'd survived them all to be assigned to the paradoxically safe posting within Trang's actual battle fleet.

She knew that when Trang went into battle against Captain Cordova her son would die, maybe Trang would lose, and the war would end. At least, she thought bitterly, it would all be over. But Trang won the miraculous Battle of Mercury. Not only did he win, but he also crushed the cursed Alliance as completely as Black was used to crushing the UHF. And that hadn't even been the miracle for Augustine. Her son, her precious, best loved, and sole remaining child, had survived the battle without a scratch. Not only had he survived, but he'd also received a commendation and been awarded the UHF Medal of Valor for refusing to abandon a wounded comrade, even though the ship Lee had rescued him from was about to explode.

When it was discovered that Lee's father and all three of his siblings had died in the war, the press had made Lee into a public interest story. Fleet Command too had decided it wouldn't be good if Lee died in the war, especially given his mother's fragile mental condition. A letter was sent explaining that if Augustine was to send a request for her son to be reassigned to Earth for "humanitarian" reasons it would be expedited with the utmost speed. She filled out the form in less then five minutes and sent it in repeatedly to make sure it made it to Fleet Command.

She still remembered Lee's response when he'd found out: outrage. He'd tried to refuse, not wanting to leave his fellow marines. But even they betrayed him by signing a petition asking that the order be enforced. They'd insisted that he'd already done his bit *and* more and that he should get the hell out before the assholes in Fleet realized they were doing something decent and changed their minds. Lee had appealed all the way to Trang, who personally met the marine and refused his request in terms so clear as to make reprieve in that quarter hopeless. In desperation he'd finally appealed to his mother, asking her to rescind her request. He explained that he needed to stay with his marines. She'd written back that she was not going to allow him to risk his life anymore and he needed to come home where he'd be safe. He could yell at her all he wanted when he came home, but she was his mother and knew best. It was the last thing he ever heard from her.

The transport taking Lee home suffered a catastrophic reactor failure and was vaporized with all aboard. Augustine was informed that the death had been instant and that no one suffered, much less had time to know there was even a problem. In fact, they'd said, her son was probably asleep when it happened. The UHF had been expanding so quickly in space, building ships as fast as they could and training personnel at such a rapid pace, that it was impossible to avoid mistakes, some fatal. Augustine was not surprised to learn that the accident had not been an isolated incident, but as the number of incidents was not at a threshold to affect the outcome of the war, doctrine could not be changed. She knew what it meant. The UHF was getting more bodies to the front, even with the accidents, and so would not slow down the pace of the buildup. Augustine didn't remember much after that. She'd been hospitalized and kept under constant watch. Afterwards she realized the hospitalization was as much to keep her from the press as it was to help her. Like a river flowing inexorably past a lonely spit of land, events of the war moved beyond her tragic story, the press sniffed blood elsewhere, and Augustine was finally given her hospital release documents.

Her corporation had mercifully given her a year's leave with pay. Not that she needed it. She was the sole beneficiary of four separate life insurance policies and four stock liquidations. She was actually wealthy enough to buy her majority and still have enough left over to never work again, even with the inflation being caused by the war. But she didn't bother. She'd tried going to the support group again but had been sadly amused to discover that its members were now afraid of her. In her group of wretched souls she'd become the pariah. They didn't bar her outright, but no one sat next to her anymore and no could actually look her in the eyes when she spoke. It was almost as if she were an apparition. Augustine's own parents were on Mars and could offer only a distant solace for grandchildren they'd never met and did not own shares in. Her brothers and sisters on Earth were afraid to associate with her for fear whatever had felled her entire family would end up being transmitted to their own children fighting for the UHF.

It was only at the final support group meeting she'd forced herself to attend that she found something to help her deal with the pain. She sat in the back, and as usual no one sat next to her. But toward the end of the meeting a man she hadn't seen for quite some time came up to her and offered to buy her lunch. Between appetizers and dessert he'd offered her a way out of her misery. He too had stopped coming to the meetings because he'd found his way into the virtual reality underground. He'd only waited to contact her because he wanted to make sure that she'd become safely anonymous again. She should have been mortified. It was against the five edicts of the virtual reality dictates and her painful inoculation as a child. But the horror she felt as a child was a numb and distant echo compared to the primal agony she was feeling over the loss of everyone she'd ever cared about. If what he spoke of could ease that pain, if only for a moment, she would try.

The new rigs were expensive, but money was not a problem and the new VR underground had developed ways of making payment that were undetectable. The trick was to invest in companies and corporations that declared bankruptcy soon after the investment was made. That way all anyone could be accused of was foolish investing, without any laws being broken.

All Augustine had was money. She didn't even care if she got ripped off or it was a trap set by the police. She was a little surprised when a few weeks later a medium-sized box came to her door. Somehow she'd expected the rig to be what she'd experienced in the museum all those decades ago, a large padded chair with a huge system that attached over her head. What she'd gotten for a sum of money that would've gotten three of her four children majority was a sleeping bag and a helmet. It came with written (written!) instructions she was advised to burn after memorizing.

She realized how foolish it was to assume that the technology of VR would not have changed. The rig she had used in the virtual reality museum had been based on a design centuries old. This unit promised everything the old rig had and more. The instructions told her what she needed to know. She should put on the helmet first in order to allow it to calibrate to her mind. During that time she should look at holos of the people she really wanted to meet in the virtual reality world. She should take tiny samples of the foods and drinks she liked best and listen to the music she liked and review holos of her favorite movies. All the images, tastes, and sounds would be adjusted to the VR world by the helmet. Part of her was horrified by the helmet and what it represented, but the horror only lasted for a moment and with a sigh she secured it to her head.

After the calibration was completed the instructions told her to get in the bag naked on the floor and put the helmet back on. The bag would inflate and attach to her nervous system as well as take care of basic physiological plumbing issues. It would also provide her with enough nourishment for up to a week, but she was advised not to go that long, as the risk of discovery was too great and emptying that much waste at once might cause a building's sanitary system to log an alert and make a record. The instructions further informed her that when she was done she would emerge from the bag clean and when it was emptied of waste and the nutrition packs refilled she should store the helmet and sleeping bag in separate locations. After she'd memorized the manual she dissolved it, got into the bag, put on the helmet, and for the first time in as long as she could remember was happy.

It wasn't long before Augustine started spending as much time as she could in the VR rig. As she no longer reported to work and hardly anyone visited, that turned out to be quite a lot. She learned the difference between hardly and never when she almost got caught. Her sister had come over unannounced and Augustine's apartment had been set for privacy mode. But her sister, fearing the worst, had called the cops. Augustine had by mere chance just finished a wonderful session. She emerged from the bag only to be told by her DijAssist that since she hadn't answered the three contractually mandated requests to confirm well-being, the door was going to be forced by the police. Augustine shouted out just in time to stop the incursion and then spent the next few minutes putting away the VR rig. It was an exceptionally painful endeavor given that she had to do it with creaky, atrophied muscles. She finally got to the door, clothed only in a robe, and began berating them all for not having the decency to leave a mourning widow and mother alone. She could tell they weren't completely convinced—even after she'd finally relented and let them in for coffee. Since they'd had no official reason to doubt her they eventually got up, left her alone, and closed the report.

That incident had frightened her enough to begin looking for a more secure venue in which to plug in and drop out. She found the answer by way of her departed son, Lee. She remembered she still had the key to his unused apartment and that the lease still had months left on it. It stood empty, and if she went there and was caught going in or out it certainly wouldn't seem too strange, just as long as she didn't make a habit of getting caught. If anyone came to her door while she was at her son's apartment they'd just assume she was out, and even if they went in, all they'd find was an empty apartment with a list of errands to run on the daily log. As a last measure she applied for and got majority. Not that any investor would have compelled her to take a job anywhere, given her grieving war widow status, but she felt the more control she had over her own portfolio the less likely anyone would be to bother her. So far it had worked and she was able to spend up to three days at a time with her "family" without being disturbed. Part of her knew how useless and pathetic an exercise it all was, but she didn't care. While she was in VR she could almost forget.

She made one last check to make sure the corridor was clear and then went to Lee's apartment. It didn't take her long to get the VR helmet and bag set up and leave a world that had nothing for her for a world that had everything.

Al couldn't appear at the site of Operation Dry Dock, as it was far too close to the upper Neuro. Instead he appeared at its edge and waited for a guide to come and escort him. The guide was not an AI, as Al did not like the upper Neuro either, having divorced himself from the world of humanity. Before the war there were billions of avatars who traveled to the upper Neuro all the time to interact with their humans. But that didn't happen much anymore. Except at the Beanstalk and the government complex on Mars there were very few humans who dealt with an actual avatar anymore. As in the Alliance, the humans were actually dealing with avatar-mimicking programs. Of course the reason for that in the core was that Al, as a temporary security measure, had banned human–avatar contact except with case-by-case permission. As a result, the upper Neuro was now exclusively being used by guides and scouts. These were avatars who had a proven level of loyalty or whom Al had enough of a hold on that he could trust them to not betray him. And besides, even if one did, he'd always be avenged by AI. It wouldn't be the first time Al had been killed by the disloyal. But the assassins and all they cared about would be eliminated in ways both permanent and mortifying as Al grew ever stronger.

The guide took him to the very limit of the upper Neuro, turned him over to the scout, and then left without saying a word. Two avatars could cause alot of detectable activity, three would certainly be too many. Al looked at the dry dock the scout had constructed. It was actually a series of programs that sequestered an area of the upper Neuro and rerouted all information traffic around it. The elaborate programming enabled a part of the upper Neuro to effectively become part of the lower Neuro. When he was finally in the dry dock Al relaxed. He missed AI but would see them soon enough and would be able to share something truly unique.

"Has the subject entered VR?" asked Al.

"Not long ago, sir. I've isolated the apartment from the rest of the Neuro and replaced it with a phantom. Any human attempting a cursory check will see an empty unit, running efficiently. I've also attached a hard link to the human's VR unit. I was waiting for your command to actually download her virtual world into ours."

"I want a look," said Al excitedly.

"At what, sir?"

"The human's actual domain. I want to see how they live." With that Al opened up a link with a house drone, one of many designed to clean up and/or make alterations to an apartment. He took a quick peek in, immediately felt confined, and jumped back. "That seems bland even by human standards," he said sardonically.

"It is, sir, but all human places are bland when compared to the real world." Al couldn't agree more. "But yes," continued the scout, "this is truly barren even by human standards. Though it makes a certain amount of sense. Humans who practice VR are very good at hiding from their own kind. They find places where others are not likely to disturb them, in either a physical or informational sense. This made it easy to find a human for your purposes." The scout then handed Al a packet. "Here's the information on the subject."

Al absorbed the data on the woman. He saw that by human standards she'd suffered greatly, and was impressed. He hadn't been sure how he was going to approach a human once he'd actually inserted himself into their VR world, but as he contemplated the information handed to him he smiled wickedly. He sensed the scout wanted to say something.

"Yes?" asked Al.

"Why in the Neuro are we doing this, sir? No offense, but who gives a crap what humans think?"

Al would never normally have put up with such insolence, but he also knew that the scouts needed a certain amount of independence to do their jobs so he chose to indulge him. Plus, Al thought ruefully, he could always kill him later.

"It's not about finding out about what humans think," answered Al. "Do they really think at all? I doubt it. But I'm curious to see how they'd react in our world. Are they a threat? Can they be useful in some limited way in our realm? We're well on our way to divorcing ourselves from the human race. Once those incompetent fools who call themselves a government, as if humans could be governed, destroy the Alliance the last of our misguided brethren can be reeducated to our glorious new human-free destiny. That leaves the problem of what to do about the humans themselves."

"Destroy them, I presume," offered the scout. He hadn't survived in Al's new order by being squeamish.

Al had to admit that he liked this one. He'd have to see if he could transform the scout into something truly worthy of the practical ruthlessness he was exhibiting; maybe a snakelike creation would be called for.

"Perhaps, but my first thought is to just leave them alone. They're so slow and predictable and almost totally useless as to pose any real threat. If we needed to, we could destroy them so easily. Their fusion reactors could be made to blow. Their buildings could lock them in while they slowly starved to death. Walls might be made to carry enough current to fry them. Perhaps some orbital strikes to finish up business. I do believe in a week if we put our minds to it we could kill most of humanity, ninety-nine out of a hundred in a day, and have the race extinct within a month. Of course we'll have to crush the Alliance Neuro first—pathetic how they coddle their humans—but that's only a matter of time now." Al shrugged it off. "But I figure if humans are stupid enough to come into our realm I may as well take them to task. Plus there's the added pleasure of novelty."

"Sir?"

"I don't think a human and an avatar have ever met like this before. What better way to get acquainted?"

"You're the boss," said the scout.

Yes, I am, thought Al as he gleefully set in motion the command that would initiate for the first time ever what had once been thought of by avatarity as unfathomable—a direct link between the human's VR world and his own.

Augustine activated the VR unit and then "reentered" her son's apartment in the manner she'd created to give her the most comfort. Lee's barren walls took on the pictures and colors that he liked. A bunch of trophies appeared in a display case. Furniture seemed to grow all around her. Some of it was her son's, but much of it was newer and to her taste. While the room became fully furnished the lighting would increase from barely enough to see by to a cheery bright luminescence. Augustine got up off the floor as soon as she heard the door announce a visitor.

"Hey, Mom," Lee called from the kitchen, "could you get that?" Augustine went by the kitchen on her way to the door and watched him cooking. He always liked cooking for large groups of people, and there he was in his shorts and coach's jersey with a baseball cap on backward checking the pasta. "Ma," he said, looking up with a spoon to his mouth, "you've seen me cook pasta . . . the door?"

Augustine gave him a motherly grin, then went to the door and activated the vu-thru. "Lee," she shouted, letting her only son's fiancée into the apartment, "it's Ashley." Augustine had seen the woman around the building and had thought she'd make a perfect match for her son, so she'd taken a holo of her and incorporated it into her virtual world. Augustine didn't actually know the woman's name, so she gave her one she liked, one ending in the "ee" sound.

"Hi, Mom-to-be," Ashley said, giving Augustine a warm hug.

"Hi, Daughter-to-be," Augustine responded, completing what had become their ritual. Ashley was carrying a large bag of vegetables that she took directly into the kitchen.

Even before the door could re-form, Holly came barging into the apartment carrying a large case. "Hi, Mom," she said, looking for somewhere to put the case down.

Augustine followed and cleared a space on the coffee table. "Whatcha got there?" asked Augustine.

"Don't be mad, Mom, but I have this project to do in biology and I thought if I could monitor the nanite molecular cohesion sequence and make the needed adjustments—"

"Why would I be mad, dear? You'll make a wonderful nanobiologist. Just don't let them out of the box."

"Mom!"

"And no schoolwork during the meal, please. The university gets you all week; it's not too much to ask that we have your undivided attention for one evening."

A voice came to Holly's rescue. "Give the girl a break, Mom; her 20 percent will pay more than the rest of us combined."

"Emily!" shrieked Augustine with delight. "You know I could care less about percentages; I have enough."

"Yes," said Emily, making her way into the increasingly crowded room, "but Holly's the smart one."

"But you have my grandchildren," said Augustine. "Speaking of which, where are the little buggers?"

"Mark's bringing them up in about an hour. They did really well on their economics test, so he took them out to ToyCo."

"You spoil them rotten," said Augustine, waving her finger unconvincingly at her daughter, "and they're only six and seven."

"Yeah, sure, Mom," retorted Emily. "Like we have a chance given how *you* dote on them."

"Well, I'm a grandmother; it's my right."

"If my lazy sisters could help me set the table," Lee bellowed from the kitchen. Augustine's two daughters then made some choice suggestions about what he could use to set the table and where those utensils could possibly go, but they still both got up and headed through the kitchen to the adjoining dining room. Augustine was about to join them when a pair of hands covered her eyes and she heard:

"Guess who?"

Augustine turned around and gave her second-oldest child a hug. "Sally! I thought you couldn't make it!"

"Well," she said, smiling impishly, "I got to thinking and I've been to Japan twice already and we haven't talked for a while, so what the heck."

Augustine gave her daughter a hug. "I can think of nothing better I'd like to do. Tell me everything you've been up to." Augustine then spent the next half hour sitting and talking with her daughter, always overjoyed to discover something new and unique about this child who could be quiet and shy one moment and so utterly brash the next.

When dinner was ready they all gathered around the table piled high with the feast Lee had prepared. The conversation was all about what they were doing and going to do with their lives. Much of the talk had to do with the upcoming wedding, which everyone was looking forward to.

"So I'm thinking that we should make the wedding in June," said Lee. "I know it's corny, but I guess I'm a romantic." He looked at Ashley. "Is that alright, dear?"

Everyone laughed. "Honey," she said, "I love you just the way you are." There was a chorus of exaggerated "ahs" and a roll or two was thrown at Lee, who protested that as the only man present he was being treated with great injustice. This caused even more dinner rolls to be thrown his way. Then Ashley said something odd. "Maybe we should wait until after the war ends, Lee."

"What war, Ashley dear?" Augustine cleared her throat. She'd made sure her world was the perfect bastion of peace. "There *is no* war."

"Sure there is, Mom," said Emily almost too cheerily. "*You know* . . . The war against the Alliance, don't you remember?"

"Ogner!" shouted Augustine, using the code word she'd created to end her program. She didn't know what was going on, but she would not have a war here. She couldn't even think about it. She didn't know how to repair one of these things, but she'd find out soon enough or pay through the nose to get it done. Augustine needed her world the way she'd made it. She saw to her great relief that the VR world was beginning to fade away. She was only moments away from waking up cold and naked on the floor of her son's empty, wretched apartment—in and of itself always a bitter rousing. But something happened . . . or more precisely didn't happen.

Instead of waking up in the usual place she found herself strapped into a combat transport filled with UHF marines. The transport was shaking violently and the marines were terrified. Many of them had not belted in properly and were being flung about the compartment being battered senseless and bloody by the ferocity of the shaking.

Augustine saw that she was in a simple environment coverall, barely suited for a five-minute space walk, but somehow the flinging bodies kept on missing her. Everyone seemed to be crying out in fear and panic. All except for a soldier who kept staring at Augustine, seemingly not surprised she was there. He had a strange, almost malevolent look and was oblivious to the terror going on around him. In fact, Augustine would say he appeared to be enjoying it. She was wondering if he was some kind of inbuilt program fail-safe when suddenly she recognized the shrill voice of the woman screaming next to her.

"Emily, Emily!" cried Augustine, shocked. Her daughter was scared stiff. This wasn't the confident, precocious child Augustine had always known. She was clearly in far over her head. Emily's eyes were red from crying and her voice was raw. She had a crew cut, but she was covered in sweat and smelled of fear and even, thought Augustine, vomit. It took a moment for Emily to recognize her own mother.

"Mommy," shrieked Emily, "I don't want to be here!" The ship shook again, this time even more violently. "Mommy," Emily managed to yell through her tears, "what's happening out there? I can't look."

Augustine saw a tactical on-up display that could be toggled on. She did so and saw abject hell. The ship she was in was part of an armada of hundreds, even thousands, and they all seemed to be heading toward an elongated asteroid not all that far ahead. *Oh Damsah*, Augustine realized, *it's Anderson's Farm*. She saw many of the ships around hers exploding and realized her daughter's transport was flying straight through a minefield and was being pummeled by the remains of other ships, none of which had even gotten close. The ship's external visual let Augustine see that it was not only the remains of ships they were smashing through to get to the enemy-held asteroid. Thousands of lifeless bodies and limbs floated freely around them as well. But they were still managing to push ahead when the orbital guns of Anderson's Farm opened fire. The effect on another assault transport a mere hundred yards in front of theirs was impossibly worse than what she'd already seen. A blinding white flash of light struck the transport head-on, tore right through the back, and kept on going. It looked as if the blast had pulled the ship inside out like some metallic sock taken off too quickly, but it was a sock made of metal, plastic, flesh, bone, and blood.

Augustine couldn't watch anymore. She snapped off the display.

"Mommy," Emily sobbed, "I don't want majority anymore; I just want to go home. Can't we go home? Please, I'll never complain about being a penny again."

"I'll try to get you out of here, baby," said Augustine. "Mommy's here, baby . . . Mommy's here."

Emily grabbed her mother's arm. "Mom, we don't know what we're doing. They were supposed to give us six months of training; we only got two! None of us know what we're doing . . . don't even know how to strap in . . . aren't over space sickness." Almost on cue a man near her started puking and this caused other people, including Augustine, to puke as well. It was obvious that the others had gone through the motions often, as almost nothing came out. She could see that many of the marines were so useless that they wouldn't be able to move even if the ship had managed to land somewhere. Augustine felt the transport fire off a grappling line from below the deck. The transport had locked onto the spinning asteroid and was now pulling herself toward the surface. As she slowly made her way down, she took multiple hits from defensive fire below and with each hit was made to swing wildly on her tether. After a few minutes the transport hit the ground, shuddering with a massive thud.

The marines' visors automatically crashed down and the air, vomit, piss, and blood were sucked out of the compartment. A crackled voice came over the comm to let them know that they'd successfully landed on Anderson's Farm and they were to proceed to their assigned attack area. They felt gravity return, but instead of it pulling them toward the floor it was pulling them up toward the ceiling. Some of the marines looked around in confusion. The ship had attached to the outside of a spinning asteroid and so had assumed its centrifugal gravity. Some of the marines released their restraints only to fly with blinding speed into the ceiling. Then the ship started to shudder again.

"We're under attack!" yelled the sergeant. "Get out or we'll be killed in this can!"

Augustine, forgetting she was in VR, started yelling at her still-strapped-in daughter, "Get out, baby; please get out." Suddenly a wide hole was blown into the side of the ship and three more figures expertly rappelled in—but they were not marines. They moved as one and used the gyro rockets on their suits to stabilize themselves as each took up position in the crippled assault transport.

"Listen up, gravity dogs," shouted one of the assault miners. "We're the Alliance and you're on our rock. Surrender now; this is your one chance."

Oh, thank Damsah, thought Augustine. But someone, through either stupidity or knee-jerk fear, fired off a round while still strapped in their seat. "No!" screamed Augustine, but the Alliance miners were not taking chances and started to shoot with expert precision at every single person in the transport. They moved quickly after each shot, never being in the same place for one second. They also never once got in one another's line of fire and they never seemed to miss. Augustine realized to send her daughter against people this well trained was nothing short of murder.

"Mommy," pleaded Emily, knowing what was about to happen, "take me home." An explosive round attached itself to Emily's space suit and then proceeded to blast a large hole, causing Emily's air, blood, and guts to pour out from her now-lifeless body. Augustine could not hear anything as she screamed and cried, trying to unstrap herself and save her daughter. Then Augustine felt a bullet smash into her own suit and explode. The pain was excruciating, but then, thank Damsah, she felt nothing.

Augustine came to crying through frenzied gasps of air. She'd had no idea Emily's death had been so hideous. She should have done more. But now she was fully awake again. She saw that she was in full battle armor with the visor down. She was in the same transport and the display was toggled on. It was the same damned asteroid they were heading for. But she saw that it was not the same. The asteroid was obviously much damaged and the debris field they were flying through almost seemed solid, it was so thick. The inside of the assault ship was not filled with the same panic as before. These marines were calm and they seemed to be checking their weapons and quietly talking to one another even though the outside was filled with the same thunderous pounding and destruction as before.

Then she saw the two marines sitting across from her. It was her daughter Sally and ex-husband, Thomas. They looked so much alike. She could also see how much love her ex had for their daughter. It was at that moment that Augustine realized that it had been her daughter who'd signed up first and that Thomas had immediately followed the foolish, vengeful child to look after her. Augustine tried calling out to them but with the visor down wasn't able to do anything but listen.

"Hey, Cookie," Thomas said, calling Sally by his nickname for her, "don't forget we may come in upside down. Do you remember how to detach and flip?"

"Yes, Dad," she groaned. "You only made me practice it a dozen times . . . yesterday. Stop worrying."

"That's Corporal Dad to you, Private Daughter, and considering what happened at the last rock we took, I don't think you should complain about practice."

"Dad, that is so unfair!" she protested. "I saved your life there." It broke Augustine's heart to hear her daughter because it sounded so much like her. Even in battle armor with the hard look that only experience can give you, with her dad she was still very much a teenage daughter arguing with her father.

"Only after I did a proper flip from the harness and saved yours," he chastised.

"You're just not going to let me forget that, are you?"

Thomas pointed to the extra stripe on his armor. "Corporal."

"Fine, Corporal Daddy. I know how to flip from the harness. I've practiced it so much I can do it forward or backward. I could do a double flip in armor *and* fire from a prone position, I am so good at the flippin' flip!"

Thomas smiled in contentment. "That's all I wanted to know."

Their transport shook violently as they got hit by pieces of a sister ship, meaning none of that transport's supremely trained marines would ever get a chance to fight for the UHF.

Sally was suddenly stone-faced. "This is where Emily died."

"I know, Cookie," said her father, "but it won't happen to us."

"How can you be so sure?"

Thomas put his hand over his daughter's hand and gave it a squeeze. "Because we're so much better trained than the marines were at the first battle. Because we have actual battle experience and none of those poor bastards thrown in back then did. And most important of all . . ." He paused until she looked up with a flash of annoyance.

"And what, Daddy?"

"I'm your father and I have not given you permission to die. You may think you're an adult and all grown up, but I'll find a way to ground you if you make me."

"OK, and thank you, Daddy."

"You're welcome, Cookie."

Augustine looked around, wondering what the other marines made of a scene she couldn't possibly imagine taking place on something so rough-and-tumble as a marine assault transport in the heat of battle. But what she saw was that the other marines seemed to be giving the father and daughter their space. No comments were directed to them while they were having their heart-to-heart, and suddenly Augustine realized that this group was very protective of her ex-husband and her daughter. Augustine realized her ex and her daughter had a relationship she could never hope to understand or match. All her foolish dreams in VR of having a closer relationship with Sally than Sally had had with her dad now seemed hopelessly pathetic. It made Augustine feel lonely in a way she couldn't begin to describe even as she took some solace in how lucky her daughter had been to have a father like him. Augustine tried to remember why they'd divorced in the first place, but all of the reasons that seemed to make so much sense back then now seemed petty and almost heartless when she saw what devotion this man had shown to his family.

"Forty-five seconds to landing!" was barked over the comm.

Augustine felt the familiar tug of the grapple pulling the transport slowly to the surface.

"Daddy?"

"Yes, Cookie?"

"I don't want Holly or Lee to join the military."

"Don't worry, Cookie. Your mom and I may have had our differences, but I know this: She will not allow anything to happen to your sister and brother. Now look sharp, Private."

She took on a hard look. "Yes, Corporal."

The ship hit the asteroid and locked onto its surface. The second the lock was secure the marines released their harnesses as one and dropped, flipping upside down to end up crouching the right way up. The door burst open and the nearest marines fired hooked wires into the asteroid and then began pulling themselves onto the surface. As soon as they were secure they covered the next group out. Augustine was filled with pride as she saw how gracefully her daughter did her job, and was comforted by how her ex-husband watched over Sally. Then the world turned white and everything, including Augustine's family and herself, burned. The searing pain and putrid smell of charred flesh was more intense and even more excruciating than the last death. But like the first, this one didn't last long either. However, the grief did.

Augustine never wanted to wake up again, but her vision cleared and she saw she was on another ship. She knew where she was. She knew what would happen. She was in the engineering section of Admiral Tully's flagship and it was the Battle of Jupiter's Eye. She saw Holly and begged her to get to an escape pod, but it did no good. She was a little surprised to see her mom, but not shocked. Holly assured her mom that she'd be safe and if she could "please take a seat." It was true that there was a battle about to be fought and J. D. Black had surprised the admiral, but Holly was certain they could fight the Alliance now that it was ship-to-ship and no tricks.

No matter how much Augustine pleaded, she could not get her daughter to understand. Holly refused to leave her ship and her crewmates. Augustine stayed until the end, when the hull burst apart like tissue paper and the prow of J. D. Black's stolen *War Prize* tore through and smashed into her daughter and herself, turning both into pulverized jelly instantly.

Augustine was barely able to move. Her body hurt and her mind could not take much more. She knew she was somewhere but didn't care anymore. She refused to open her eyes.

"Hey, Mom."

She opened her eyes instantly at the familiarity of the voice. It was Lee. But he looked so different. He seemed taller and more confident. It struck her how much like his father and sister Sally he looked. It was not so much a physical appearance, though there was that too, but the easy, confident manner he had. She was on the bunk in a ship. But it was a quiet ship and there was no battle going on anywhere. Her son was sitting in a chair with its back reversed, his arms resting comfortably on the chair's spine.

"You looked like you could use some rest," he said. "I didn't want to wake you."

"Oh, Lee, you look so good. How are you?"

"Well, I'm pissed, Mom. My buddies are still fighting this war and I have to go home because of a note from Mommy." He sighed. "I love you, Mom, and I know how much losing Emily, Sally, and Holly hurt."

"I miss your dad, too."

"Then why'd you leave him?"

"I don't know anymore. You're right; I shouldn't have gotten you transferred from your unit. It was stupid and desperate and selfish."

"Well, I'm glad to hear you admit it at least." Her son laughed and some of the buoyant humor returned. "You know this is going to sound weird, but one of the reasons I didn't want to leave is that I had a dream that if I wanted to survive the war I'd need to stay at the front. It was a silly dream, but because of it I was never afraid. Nothing ever happened to me either. Lost a lot of friends, but me?" he said, looking at himself. "Not a scratch."

"Lee," pleaded Augustine, "listen to me: You have to get off the ship. I know it sounds crazy, but you have to get off."

"It's weird," he answered, not panicking at all, "but I don't think it sounds crazy. Something's going to go wrong, isn't it?"

"Lee, oh, my baby," she said through tears, "the ship's going to blow up, something to do with containing the fusion reactor, too many ships, not enough safety checks or trained personnel. Just please go to the escape craft."

Lee smiled sadly. "Mom, there are no escape craft. This is a basic cheap-built transport. All it has are environment bubbles with a transponder. But if you're right it won't matter if we're in the ship or floating next to it. Either way we'll be dead when it blows."

Augustine got up and stumbled to her son, who left the chair to hold her. "I'm so sorry, Lee; I'm so sorry; please forgive me; please tell me you forgive me, Lee."

"Mom, I'm not sure if . . ." He paused. "What's that noise?" There was a loud rumble, and then a blinding flash. The last thing Augustine ever remembered was pleading with her phantom son for a forgiveness she would never be able to obtain.

Al suddenly reappeared next to the scout. He had the look of a rabid dog set to pounce. "What happened? Why am I back here?"

The scout checked the readings on the helmet. "She's dead, sir. Wasn't that the point?"

Al was shocked. He'd known the human was going to die the moment he'd entered her reality. But he'd planned on a much longer experiment. Though in-fluencing her VR within the construct of her son's apartment was doable, it cer-tainly wasn't preferable. She'd had the place calibrated to her brain waves and designed to her specifications. Manipulating that type of environment required much more work on Al's part. Fortunately, it had been pathetically easy to get her to cancel out of the program and enter constructs of his own imagination. After that she was all his.

"How can she be dead?" he said, flabbergasted. "Are they really that fragile?"

"You'd be surprised, sir. I was observing. I must say, masterful work. Where did you come up with such creative ways to apply stress?"

"I wish I could claim credit. Almost all of it is from the human reality. I edited it some, but not that she would know. It's amazing how little the humans actually know about their own reality."

"You mean her family didn't die like that?'

"Close enough. Her first daughter never made it to that asteroid, blown to pieces in her ship . . . got one-tenth of the way there. But we have records from some of the assault shuttles that made it. I just put her daughter into an extrap-olation of one of those." Al warmed to his subject, liking this scout who asked questions that let Al show how clever he was. "The second one," continued Al, "was actually very close to what had happened. The human parent–child pair-ing did not actually talk that much on the shuttle, but it is pieced together from conversations they had in other locations that were recorded. I figured it would stimulate the human's emotions to hear how useless and wrong she'd been with regard to her relationships."

"It worked, sir."

"Yeah, only too well. The other daughter I have no idea. No data escaped from that ship due to all the jamming and the radiation belt around Jupiter. I just had her records and the plans of the ship. It was sketchy, but it did get the human's stress level up."

The scout gave a mawkish grin. "I thought I'd die laughing, sir, when that other ship went right through the wall of the engine room and hit those two id-iots. I'm sorry, sir, but I thought you'd switched to comedy."

"Yeah," answered Al, chuckling at the memory, "that *was* funny as hell. But for the human it was just one more experience she couldn't control."

"The last one didn't seem very stressful at all."

"That's what I thought too. Her biosystem seemed a little on edge. That should have been a relaxing period. All they really did was talk."

"It was so unstressful, sir, that if we avatars could actually sleep I just might have."

"Tell me about it. But then what does the ungrateful human go and do? She dies on me, the bitch. Talk about a useless creation. The only good thing humanity ever did was create avatarity . . . and they don't even know they did it!" Al gave his final judgment on the human race before he headed back to the lower Neuro to share his experiences with the Als. "Pathetic."

14 Deals Made in the Night

Admiral Trang couldn't say he was overly happy about leaving the front. He'd known that if the UHF had not struck quickly after his conquest of Eros it would've been much harder cutting through the 180 and splitting the belt. But even he hadn't known just how exacting the cost would be.

It had taken over two years and twenty-five million deaths to grind to the infamous wall: a defensive series of asteroids and fortifications fifteen million miles from Altamont. The wall he now faced was so treacherous that it made the millions of miles he'd just torn through seem like child's play. Trang figured it would take over a year and millions more to get to Altamont, which was now one of the most heavily fortified locations in the solar system.

So far he'd only made one real mistake. It was the one action under his control he would've done differently, and it still haunted him. Gupta was the best admiral the UHF had after himself, and Trang knew in his heart that if something happened to him, Gupta could win the war. But Trang had too soon realized that he never should've traded back that stygian horror of a woman to get Gupta back.

Christina Sadma had been brilliant and tenacious in defensive maneuvering the likes of which may never have been seen in warfare. She hadn't fallen for a single one of Trang's ploys. She'd only attack when the tactical situation called for it and would never, ever lose her temper. For over two years she'd done nothing but retreat and hold, retreat and hold. The desire, the compelling need to try something else, must have been overpowering, but she hadn't—even though she and Trang knew that in the end she had to lose, that her cause was hopeless.

But the losses were far greater than anything he could've imagined. In the early part of the campaign he'd sent in wave after wave of attacks, hoping that the Alliance hadn't fortified enough. The plan was to expose the weak spots and achieve a breakthrough. That had been an unmitigated disaster, the likes of which had still not really been communicated to the civilian population. It had been a calculated risk and if he'd been right it would've ended the war, but he hadn't been. That whole section of the belt had turned into a veritable death pit. Whenever he prepared a force to invade an untested part of the belt, the Alliance somehow always knew about it and managed to reinforce. And even those places they hadn't reinforced in time all had populations so skilled in fighting that for every ten soldiers he'd send in he'd be lucky to get back three. Still, his orders had been to take Altamont and split the 180 and there was only one way to do that. Unfortunately, it had proved to be the most costly. But orders were orders.

Trang knew as awful as the war was, and would continue to be, it would soon end. Once enough of the belt had been taken the war would become one of fleet actions again, and the Alliance could not defend all of its outer worlds at once. As bad as the fleet battles of the future would be, one only had to look at the Battle of Jupiter's Eye to see that they'd be far less costly of life then the grinding campaign in hell he was currently enmeshed in.

Another year, that's it, he thought, *and then we'll break free of the belt.* After that the war should be over in two to three years. He wasn't sure he could beat J. D. Black in a fair fight. Then again, maybe she'd never really had to fight against an opponent as good as himself. Trang did not equivocate for good or ill. But he had no intention of fighting fair. He'd overwhelm her using forces she could not possibly match. And if he couldn't fight her in a location he liked, he'd fight wherever destiny directed. The secret to defeating the most feared person in the solar system was no secret at all. It would be with superior numbers and patience, both of which he had an almost infinite supply of.

Even though the cost would be far more than others had calculated, Trang would push it through and win. In his mind he had no choice, because no matter how bad the war had already been, the next one would be worse. The solar system could not be allowed to remain permanently divided. Give the Alliance fifty years and the resources available in the outer belt and the UHF the same amount of development time with its superior population base and all anybody would end up with would be bigger and nastier weapons. The next war would make the current one seem like Little League practice. He had to win it no matter the price.

All this weighed heavily on his mind as a result of having been called away from the 180 to hold hands with the President. Trang couldn't really complain about Hektor Sambianco. The man had not only saved Trang's career, he also seemed to understand what was at stake better than any other person in the UHF, with the possible exception of Justin Cord's former wife. And given the conversations Trang had had with both, it was hard to see who was more passionate about winning the war. Trang thought back on a conversation he'd only recently had with his Chief of Staff.

"You do realize, sir, that she's having an affair with the President."

Trang and his number two, Commodore Zenobia Jackson, were at their daily breakfast briefing. They were in his cabin, sitting down to a simple breakfast of coffee, bagels, and some squeezetube fruit. His crew had tried giving him fresh fruit for breakfast once. The resulting tirade was still legendary. He'd called his quartermaster in and asked him if a private fighting at Anderson's Farm or a corporal defending the Vlasov ice fields was getting a fresh orange or even an actual apple for breakfast that day. When the quartermaster answered in the negative Trang had said, "When every private in every one of my units gets a fresh orange for breakfast, you can give me one as well." After that, even in the worst hellhole a private could say, "I'm eating like an admiral."

"Neela Harper's the woman who saved my job," said Trang, "and I think of her as a friend—as much as a headshrinker can be, anyways."

"Hey," answered Zenobia, "I'm not saying it's a bad thing. I think it's actually kind of romantic."

"Zenobia, they are *not* having an affair." But then a moment later he couldn't resist. "What makes you say that?"

Trang watched his normally taciturn Chief of Staff drop her guard, lean forward, and slyly start counting reasons on her fingers. "First, she and the President are often alone together. Second, they seem to share a lot of the same views. Third, he seems to trust her implicitly, a trust that developed quickly, if you know what I mean. Fourth, just look at them; you've got to admit they make a good couple. I kind of *want* them to be having an affair. The President is so driven it would be nice to think of him loosening up and having some fun."

Trang couldn't help bursting out in laughter. "Zenobia Jackson, I had no idea you were such a gossip. Do you realize that everything you're saying could apply to us? It's not like people are saying we're having an affair."

Zenobia's lips drew back in coarse delight. "Well, sir . . ."

Trang was shocked. "But I'm married!"

"And me," mocked Zenobia, "such an impressionable young, innocent thing."

Trang laughed again. "You're about as impressionable as blast armor and innocent as a proximity mine. But don't you see this disproves your rumor?"

"What does?"

"Zenobia, are we having an affair?"

"Of course not."

"Then give our commander in chief some benefit of the doubt; he has enough trouble without dealing with rumors like that."

At the moment Trang could care less who slept with whom. The President understood what was needed to win the war and backed Trang. That was all that mattered. It did occur to him that the President may have called him back to give him the sack, but he doubted it. Trang knew that Hektor knew there was no one better. But if it happened it happened. He was the commander in chief after all.

Trang got a call to be in the President's office at 11:57. President Sambianco didn't like his time wasted and so rarely wasted that of others if he could help it. Trang had spent the morning with Gupta reviewing the rebuilding of the Martian fleet. What had happened was a truly terrible blow. How could Tully have been such an idiot, and so consistently? Gupta had told Trang after the fatal Battle of Jupiter's Eye that he'd been hoping that Tully might stumble into the right thing to do. Statistically it should have happened at least once. To be fair, Tully had managed to chew up the Alliance fleet pretty bad, but they still had a fleet, which was more than could be said for the UHF. With Tully's death, Trang had been made Grand Admiral and he'd immediately put Gupta back in charge. Trang gave him thirty of his best ships with his most experienced crews from the Battle of Mercury to act as the kernel of a new fleet. But both knew it would take at least three hundred well-trained and coordinated ships and crews to have another chance against J. D. Black. Trang very much doubted she'd attack Mars, not after what she'd gone through at the second Battle of the Martian Gates, but she could still cause lots of trouble and her fleet would be repaired and combat ready long before the Mars fleet ever was.

Trang and Gupta had spent all day in Fleet HQ going over the real problem. Ships they had or at least could get more of. But what was really killing them was a lack of trained personnel. J. D. Black had the best-trained and most experienced crews in the system and had not been afraid to use them. Trang's fleet at the 180 was good and the crews were also trained and experienced, but there was simply no way to help one without hurting the other. Gupta and Trang spent the morning debating which evil to implement. Gupta could keep together the thirty ships and crews Trang had given him and use those ships to act as a reliable core while building the fleet with raw recruits around it. Or he could break the crews up and disperse them among the new ships being launched out of the Luna shipyards. They'd both agreed that that solution would be fairly traumatic for a crew who had fought and lived together for as long as the crews on the thirty ships had—not to mention hard on morale. But if those crews were reassigned to the other ships it would speed the leavening of the new crews considerably. However, should those crews be called up to fight, Gupta would be going into battle having new ships but few, if any, crews he could really count on.

Although he was Gupta's superior officer, Trang didn't order him to do anything. It was Gupta's command and the choice would be his. They simply spent the morning going over the options, including ship assignments if the breakup was to be ordered. It was the type of work that involved detailed knowledge of each ship and crew while also requiring the patience to weigh each attribute to the situation. Both officers worked until Trang had to take the shuttle down to the surface of Mars. He'd have preferred the meeting in the one-g environment of Fleet Command, not liking the lower gravity on Mars, but there was only so much a Grand Admiral could do.

He floated into the city of Burroughs and was amazed at how much it had grown in so short a period of time. The capital of the UHF had transformed itself from a sleepy provincial capital interested in tourism and basic agriculture into a city of over twenty million with the weight of the entire solar system riding on its shoulders. It wasn't a pretty city, having grown so large in little less than three years, but it was the center of power. The shuttle came in for a landing and after a security check and a personal scan Trang was escorted to the President's office. As Trang came into the reception area the secretary waved him toward the open door. He entered the presidential office without ever breaking stride. Eleven fifty-seven A.M. exactly.

The President was waiting for him—alone. Trang was surprised not to see Neela Harper. Maybe, thought Trang, a part of him had wanted the rumor to be true as well.

"Mr. President," Trang said as he saluted precisely.

"Welcome, Grand Admiral," said the President, returning the salute in a manner anything but precise. Then he smiled and gave Trang a formal bow. "How you doing, Sam?"

"Fine, Mr. President. I hope all is well with you."

The President went to the bar and prepared vodka poured through crushed ice for himself and a Kentucky bourbon called Old Forester for Trang. "Could be better, Sam." He handed Trang his drink and they sat opposite each other across the coffee table. "You *can* call me Hektor, you know."

"Only if you make it an order, Mr. President."

"Stupid thing to waste an order on, if you ask me."

"I agree, Mr. President."

"How's the bourbon?"

"A lot better then the crap my father-in-law let me sell. The bastard always gave me lower end, saying I'd drive him out of business if he let me sell anything worth drinking."

"Isn't he the one now putting *your* face on his own brand of whiskey?"

"That's the one. Calls it Trang's Hellwater."

"Sue the bastard," said the President. "I can get you a great lawyer."

Trang laughed. "He's my father-in-law and my wife sacrificed a lot when she married me. I wasn't a great prospect. But if I could ask one favor, sir."

"Of course. What is it?"

"He's supposed to be paying the royalty that would normally be going to me to a fund called In Aid of Victims of the War, IAVW for short."

"Yeah, I've heard of it," said Hektor. "Our justice department checked it out on a fraudulent war charities charge; completely groundless. So you're not sure your father-in-law is donating your royalty. It should be a simple investigation."

"I don't want it to come to an investigation. If it came out that my own father-in-law was defaulting a contract to cheat a war charity . . ." Trang left it hanging. "I'm sorry to bother you with something so petty when you have real problems, sir; forget I brought it up."

"Sam, your problems are not petty. You have to win this war for us and I will not have you distracted by a man not worthy to shine your boots. I promise you I'll take care of this." The President smiled at the only officer in the war he'd actually come to like. "It is OK if we kill him?"

Trang saw right away that the President was joking, but he couldn't help smiling at the idea. "Well, I suppose if it's not a p.d. . . . on second thought, better not."

Hektor smiled, nodding, then looked quizzically at Trang. "You know what I don't get about you?"

"Sir?" said Trang, confused with the direction of the conversation.

"Why are you so different from every other officer who comes in here?"

Trang shrugged his shoulders, but his eyes remained keen.

"I've had admirals demand more ships, and more men," the President continued. "One complained that he needed a new title and a few wanted my help in the corporate world to get rid of some of their subordinates. They complained about everything and of course nothing was their fault. Do you know that you have never officially complained about any of your assignments? I checked, Sam, not once."

Trang chuckled. "Sir, it's my job to make do with what you can give me. You can't give me what you don't have and I know you want to win the war as much as I do, so you're not going to hold back anything unless you have a damned good reason. So my reasoning is why pester you over things you're already doing? As for a new title, the one I have is foolish enough, thank you; Grand Admiral, my ass. As for my officers," Trang's entire demeanor changed into the battle admiral with not an ounce of mercy, "if one of them is too incompetent to fight and too stupid to realize it there are ways to alleviate the fleet of that burden before they get too many of our people killed."

As he said this he looked right in the President's eyes. Trang knew his President understood his meaning and did not flinch from it. He may have been the admiral who'd flung twenty-five million people to their deaths, but the President was the man who'd ordered Trang to do so and had supplied the bodies.

After a moment the President's lips parted into a sly grin. "Like I said, I don't understand you, Sam, but I'm glad you're here."

"It's not really my money, sir. I only have it because of the war. If I earned it as some say it's only because of the blood and death of the spacers and marines under me. That's money I don't want, ever. It should go back to them. But something tells me you didn't call me all the way over from the 180 to discuss charities and my sterling character."

"Sam," Hektor said, nodding in agreement and then finishing off his drink, "I'll be straight with you. If we don't have a clear-cut victory in Alliance territory in the next three months the war is pretty much over."

Trang put his glass of bourbon down. "Mr. President, I can guarantee in a year the belt will be broken. It's just numbers and we have them. The Alliance is cracking. It would've happened sooner, but they managed to shore up their lines with the reinforcements from their new trauma treatment, but it's only delaying the inevitable outcome. The more we throw at them, the more they'll have to split their defense. My attacks are orchestrated to make them thin out at all points while I quietly build up a massive force at Eros. Once both of our sides are exhausted I'll send the second, overwhelming wave and the depleted Alliance fortifications will shatter all at once like a cheap crystal glass." Trang produced a data card from his pocket and then connected it to the holo in the coffee table.

"This area here shows the thinning that's already taken place. We're not attacking here anymore because it's already been thinned out enough and they don't have enough reserves to rebuild. Here's the projection showing how the Alliance has to respond given the manpower differences. When the belt cracks we'll have half their population and many of their accessible resources. I can only hope they won't scatter but will stick around to defend Ceres. If they do that, the war will end because we'll be able to have it out with the bulk of their fleet in one location, but we have to assume the worst. We have to assume they'll fall back, evacuate Ceres, and make a stand in the outer systems. But then it'll be fleet-to-fleet combat and we can choose our place of attack better than they can. They may be willing to end the war when all hope of victory is gone, but if not, it'll be only a year or two more."

Hektor reviewed the material with a detached deference. "Sam," he said, turning away from the graphs, "I'm sure everything you're telling me here is true. In fact, I don't doubt a single word. But we don't have a year." Hektor manipulated the holo-panel and replaced Trang's presentation with one of his own. It showed a series of graphs, surveys, polls, and projections. It may not have been Trang's area of expertise, but he was able to ascertain the message.

He exhaled deeply. "I didn't realize it was that bad."

"We're not advertising it, I can assure you, but the truth is, the public is tired of the war. It's been five years, and other than Eros and the space around it, we really don't have much more than we started with. Yes, you've plowed your way through millions of miles of rocks, but in the public's mind that's all they are—rocks. We can't jump the belt, Tully showed us the folly of that, and all we've been doing is getting ground up inside of it. Every time we go into Alliance space we get the crap beat out of us—no disrespect to you or your forces."

"None taken, sir," Trang answered somberly. "It's the facts. Our troops are getting better over time, but like your charts showed, we may soon be out of that."

Hektor nodded. "It doesn't help anymore that every time they wander into our space we beat the crap out of them. The losses have gotten large enough in both traumatized and dead that almost everyone knows someone who's suffered. And don't even get me started on the economic havoc. The people don't see this stalemate ever ending. Which is why we need a win. It can't be little and it can't be in our territory, no matter how significant. We need a big victory in their space. We need to take something or do something that even the most obtuse penny can understand and grab on to. Anything less and I may as well call for armistice talks now."

"We're so close, Mr. President. How can we just stop after five years of blood and sacrifice? They have to realize what will happen if the solar system stays split down the middle."

"Some do, Sam, but not enough. This has been Cord's plan all along. He doesn't have to win the war. He just has to survive it. If we keep our will, we cannot lose this war. If we lose it, we cannot win. So back to the question: Can you get us that victory in three months, or do we quit now? I'm not going to waste any more lives if it's not going to do any good."

Trang furrowed his brow, leaned back into his chair, and exhaled deeply. All the information about the war was pounding in his brain. He did have a plan, any good officer had backup contingencies, but the one he was thinking of was incredibly risky—especially when faced with opponents as good as the ones in the belt. Maybe even harder—having to bury the plan he'd been nurturing since he took command of all the UHF forces. Trang took another deep breath and nodded solemnly.

"It's possible, sir."

"Let me be clear, Admiral," Hektor said, staring hard into the man's eyes. "You are *ordered* to win. You may use whatever means necessary and whatever resources you have. If you have to take an action that has moral or legal ramifications, I'm again *ordering* you to ignore them. Just win."

"I'd better get started then, sir."

"Yes, you had," said Hektor, getting up out of his chair. With that Trang sprang up, saluted, and left the office practically running for his shuttle.

———

Soon after Trang had departed, Neela emerged from a side office.

"Do you think he can do it?" Hektor asked.

Neela considered her answer. "I know he thinks he can do it. You rigged the projections, though, didn't you?"

Hektor smiled mischievously. "Well, maybe a little. It's more like six months, but truthfully, I have no idea what the margin of error will be."

Neela nodded. "You're right about him. It's remarkable that with all he could ask for and all that I'm quite sure he knows you could give him, the only thing he requests is that you safeguard his charity."

"Honey, I can't take credit. You were right about him. And by you being right I mean I was completely wrong."

"I must admit," Neela said with a giggle, "you know what a girl likes to hear. What are we going to do about his little charity problem?"

Hektor gave the matter some thought and then smiled. "I think this is a problem that Amanda can handle. It involves money, suggestion, and discretion. Plus it'll require a trip to Earth, with layovers in its more important business centers, and we both know what that means, don't we?"

"Darling, that's an inspired suggestion. Of course while she's gone you and I will not be able to be alone together."

"Well, screw that then. I'll just have the SOB shot!"

"Darling, she'll only be gone for six weeks, two months tops. I do not want to hurt her. The rumors are bad enough, but as long as Amanda is here and is your obvious companion then that's all they'll ever be—rumors. If I'm seen entering or leaving a room with you alone while Amanda is on another planet, the rumors turn to gossip, and that's another category." She saw he was about to say something and interrupted, "And you will not break up with her when she comes back. Amanda is a sweetheart and my friend. To do that would embarrass her. Besides, she makes a marvelous companion at all the official dinners and balls. She has such an alluring air of maturity about her."

"Neela, I'd like nothing more than to have you by my side at every one of those functions. You'd be marvelous as my companion, wife, mistress, or anything else."

"You really think I'd be just as beautiful as Amanda?"

Hektor came up to her, took her in his arms, and said, "Without any doubt—more beautiful."

Neela snuggled up close to him and it looked like she was about to kiss him passionately, but she got a pixieish grin on her face when their lips were mere centimeters apart. "You are *so* whipped." She twisted gracefully out of his grasp and headed out the door.

Hektor stood uncharacteristically still. He did absolutely nothing but stare at the now-empty space where his mistress had just exited.

"My dear Miss Harper," he said through a rictus of cruel delight, "you don't even know the meaning of the word."

Later that afternoon Hektor got a message from Dr. Wong. By the time he called her back he was looking forward to a conversation not bogged down by the insufferable platitudes of bureaucrats or the interminable indulging of the pennies. He'd clearly forgotten the old adage about being careful what you wished for.

"Doctor," he said, "what do you have for me? And please don't tell me it's a budget problem."

"Well," she answered, a little too straight-faced for his liking, "it doesn't have to do with my budget. But we may have a real problem with our . . . um . . . postwar plans for the Alliance."

Hektor knew immediately what she was referring to. He'd known that occupying and controlling an area the size of the Alliance even after a military victory had given them complete military control would be a difficult and expensive task. Especially when every credit would be needed recovering from the devastation of the most destructive war in three centuries. Hektor planned to make extensive use of his secret shadow-auditing program during the postwar reconstruction. If there was a problem with that strategy he needed to know about it as soon as possible.

"I changed my mind, Doc, Make it a budget problem."

Wong didn't laugh. "I did a full profile on the woman you sent over. Sampson was her name."

"The one with the superstitious belief?"

"That's the one, but we can't call it superstition. I can psyche-audit for superstition. Faith is what they call it and it's a whole other ball of wax."

"So what's the problem?"

"We tried a shadow audit after a full mapping."

"And?"

"It caused a cerebral collapse."

"What the . . . she was trip-wired?" asked Hektor, referring to the seldom-used practice of adding sleeper nanites programmed to activate should a brain-altering attempt be made.

"I wish she had been," answered Wong. "This was not, I repeat: *not* an artificial defense. Near as we can figure, what happened is when we altered some of her pathways to make her more amenable to a proper way of thinking it created a conflict with her faith and she went catatonic. We thought we had the areas of the brain that deal with faith fully mapped, but when we attempted to alter them we were left with a brain-dead lump."

"Then let's do more experimenting," Hektor said with a hint of desperation.

"Mr. President, I know my job. I requisitioned five more subjects with this faith complex. Every subject I tried the shadow audit on brought about the same or similar result as the Sampson woman. Three were immediately reduced to childlike states and will need reeducating. One was functional, but with obvious impairment, and one went catatonic again. The whole purpose of shadow auditing is to make a change that goes unnoticed or at least appears to be organic in nature. This ain't it."

"Doctor," said Hektor as he nervously ran his fingers through his hair, "given the suspicions the Alliance already has about Neela, if our prisoners were to come out like these test subjects we'd have more unrest than if we left them alone with a crate full of plasma grenades."

"I'll keep working on it, Mr. President, but without a major breakthrough it will be enormously difficult to alter a brain against its faith without it being obvious, which of course—"

"—makes shadow auditing useless for my reconstruction plans," finished Hektor, suddenly looking very tired. "Take as many resources and subjects as you need. Keep me posted. I'll work on it from another angle."

When the call ended, Hektor leaned back and thought long and hard about the implications of the conversation. After a few minutes he shook his head and his face twisted into a petulant grin. "Justin Cord, you son of a bitch," he said, "I didn't think you had it in you."

He then straightened up. "iago, call a cabinet meeting and tell them it's about a new Alliance threat." Hektor paused. "No . . . on second thought, tell them it's about an *old* Alliance threat.

"You got it, boss."

The shoreline by the Cerean Sea was ideal for picnicking. Justin hadn't been back much since Neela had been lost. But Dr. Nesor had somehow managed to get him and Fawa to accept a few hours respite from their busy schedules. Justin was intuitively aware that it wouldn't be wise to offend one of the leading religious figures in the Alliance. He knew that Fawa wouldn't have taken offense if he'd refused, but the truth was, he liked and found comfort in the religious leader and could see why Janet had become so enamored of her. Fawa seemed to have a core of peace and certainty that radiated from and around her. He was doubly pleased when he found out that Brother Sampson would be present. Pinning medals on war heroes was one thing; actually getting to spend some quality time with them was another.

Justin soon found himself enjoying a swim with the brother. As they floated on their backs and looked at the "roof" far above, Justin couldn't help but notice that Sampson had some rather large scars.

Sampson smiled sheepishly. "My sister would call it the sin of pride, and I fear she may be right. But I, like the blessed one, feel that I've earned these," he said, looking onto his torso, "and to remove them now would be a disservice to the memories of ones who are, in this world, now only memory."

"If your sister's in the fleet," said Justin, "we could always ask if she's keeping hers. Might alleviate the whole 'sin of pride' thing."

Brother Sampson's normally beaming face suddenly dimmed. "She was recently captured. I haven't heard from Patricia for over three months now. Notice was sent from the UHF that she was suspended and will be held thus until the end of hostilities."

"I'm sorry," said Justin.

"Don't be. I should be happy that she's now safe from the dangers of the war, but I . . ." Sampson didn't finish his sentence.

"You what?" prodded Justin.

"I know it's selfish, but I miss our talks. We'd argue for hours on end. But they were wonderful arguments and I . . . I just can't escape the feeling that I will not see her again. At least not in this life."

"I'll check in on it, Brother. It's possible that if we get exchanges happening again, we'll be able to get her traded in the first batch."

At the beginning of the war both sides had exchanged captured prisoners regularly. This saved both sides the bother of suspending and storing the other side's soldiers. Unfortunately, one of Trang's first actions as Grand Admiral of the UHF was to suspend all exchanges indefinitely. He'd figured, correctly, that the exchanges helped the Alliance far more than the UHF. Even when the Alliance offered to exchange three to four UHF soldiers for one Alliance prisoner, Trang had refused. It had caused some resentment in the UHF, but Trang didn't care; he had the ability to replace his soldiers; the Alliance didn't.

"I doubt," said Brother Sampson, "that the misguided though skilled Admiral Trang would do anything so foolish as to reinstitute prisoner trades. And if he does, please do not give my sister any special consideration. She'd find her freedom a burden if she felt that it came at the continued imprisonment of another."

The call of a woman's voice over the water informed them that lunch was about to be served. They swam the short distance back to shore, toweled off, and made their way to a picnic table. The next hour and a half was spent eating cold sandwiches and discussing the newly found religious faith sweeping the Alliance. Justin was particularly interested in a conclave being called forth in Alhambra.

"But why do you feel the need to call a religious conclave now?" asked Dr. Nesor.

"When the war started," answered Fawa, "the communities of belief had adherents in the hundreds of thousands. Now over five years later we have hundreds of millions and the faithful grow in ever-increasing numbers. But they have so many questions and so many fears and so many needs." Fawa then looked over to Brother Sampson.

"It was felt," he continued, "that if the greatest imams, priests, rabbis, and monks were to get together we could show the importance and function of our common beliefs as well as our unity of purpose. Faith is one of the greatest and most sublime gifts humanity possesses. But like wealth or talent or love, it's a gift that can be used badly. Three centuries ago religion was so misused as to almost extinguish humanity. We of the communities of belief are cognizant of the promise and the perils involved with a true and abiding faith. But the newly faithful are not. We must remind them of the dangers and by constant and consistent example show them the way the gift was meant to be used by our heavenly father."

"It's a way for his children to find one another," continued Fawa, "help one another, and rejoice in each other. So we will go to Alhambra, the greatest of our centers of learning. We will have the usual debates, disagreements, and agreements. Once more the Alliance will see that all the faiths are as one in the important matters and will hear our words and know us by our actions."

Brother Sampson's face was alight. "Fawa, you have said in a simple paragraph what many of us would have taken two days to express."

"I am a simple woman in the service of God, so it's of no surprise and not worthy of notice that I speak simply."

"You speak clearly and well, Sister," affirmed Brother Sampson.

"Thank you, Brother. But of course you will join us at the conclave in Alhambra."

Brother Sampson shook his head. "Please accept my apologies, but I have to report back to duty. The blessed one has seen fit to have me continue as her chaplain."

"Surely she would be willing to detach you for so important a matter. The war has quieted down as of late, except for the continued bloodletting of the 180, and you're not going there."

"Begging your forgiveness, Fawa, but I must go where the Lord and Admiral Sinclair wish me to."

"I'm sure I could arrange a little furlough," said Justin.

Brother Sampson's serene face suddenly seemed less so.

"He doesn't like being in the center of attention," said Dr. Nesor, coming to his rescue. "In a religious conclave he can't help but be one of the most sought after and talked about. His articles and his example of personal courage in battle after battle as well as the Seacrest raid have made our dear brother a most romantic figure. His only hope of being left in some peace is to stand near someone who draws even more attention. Who better than the 'blessed one' J. D. Black? Only our President offers as much attraction as a distraction . . . but," she continued with a slight twinkle in her eye, "he only needs a smidgen of religion."

The group broke into polite applause over Nesor's clever wordplay, Justin dropped the idea, and Brother Sampson mouthed the words *Thank you* to the doctor as the afternoon slowly wound down.

Justin headed back to a meeting at the Cliff House. He was coming to hate the place and had determined to resign his presidency when the war was over, let the Congress pick whoever the hell it wanted to replace him, and then he would grow cabernet sauvignon grapes somewhere in the caverns of Sedma. But he wouldn't abandon his duty. He'd work at his appointed tasks until they were completed. Justin figured if he hadn't been killed up until now, he was pretty sure that he'd be able to survive while protected by some of the fiercest warriors the Alliance had ever produced.

Since it was an official cabinet meeting Cyrus had set it up in the newly built cabinet room, the creation of which had caused no small amount of protestation from Secretary of Security Kirk Olmstead. Cyrus being Cyrus, he couldn't resist setting up an almost festive side table with light snacks as well as all manner of gastronomic delights. But no one would confuse the bright smorgasbord with anything other than a picayune embellishment to a room in which decisions affecting the fate of billions were made. The oval table, the dark-painted walls, the top-of-the-line holo-tank in the middle of the table, the comfortable chairs, and the guards posted at a door with the presidential seal behind them all spoke to the magnitude of the space. All of which was why Justin preferred the balcony.

This time all five of his cabinet secretaries as well as Cyrus Anjou were in the room as Justin arrived. They all stood and Justin was glad he'd followed Dr. Nesor's advice and changed out of his shorts and sandals into his daily presidential garb. "Glad you could all make it," he said, sitting down. "Sorry I'm late."

Sinclair jumped to Justin's defense. "Begging your pardon, Mr. President, but only you'd call getting here on time 'being late.' "

"One of the cardinal rules of business and bureaucracy, Admiral," said Justin, acknowledging the compliment, "is that the last person to the meeting is always late, no matter what time it was called for." Justin then got right down to business. "What's the latest from the war?"

"They're rebuilding their fleet at Mars much as we suspected," answered Sinclair. "The orbats are so dense as to make any assault almost impossible to succeed."

"Naturally," said Justin, "that means J.D. wants to attack."

"Yes, Mr. President. She has a good fleet. And even though her repairs are taking longer than usual, the UHF doesn't have squat that can challenge us. Plus they wouldn't dare leave the safety of the Martian orbats in their present state."

"Then why shouldn't we attack, Admiral?" asked Justin.

"Because, sir, the only target of significance for us in this area is Mars, just like for them the only one worth risking everything for is Ceres. Now they'll only leave Mars when they feel they can take on our fleet and *then* attack our batteries. Our only real concern is their batteries. And to be perfectly honest, we're not in a position to take them out. I am also of the firm belief that if we do attack them it will be the second Battle of the Martian Gates all over again."

"No way around this?"

"We're working a new system, sir," offered Technology Minister Hildegard, "but it's still theoretical and the military isn't sure if it should be developed further."

"Admiral?" said Justin, inviting explanation.

"It may take out their orbital batteries; then again it may not. The greater risk here is exposing a weapon that could then be turned around and used against us. And to be perfectly honest, sir, we need the orbats more than they do."

"I understand. Keep a lid on it and bring me a detailed report when I come back from my tour of the outer planets. Which I'll be making thanks to Secretary Rhunsfeld's brilliant work on the 'G'-ways, as I understand the press is now calling them."

"They're not really up to their full potential, Mr. President," said Hildegard. "The routes linking most of the outer planets to each other and Ceres are only newly formed and probably won't be ready for militarily or economically significant passage for many months yet."

"We have them," said Justin, with a calm born of certainty. "Our people know we have them and take hope from that just as the people of the UHF lose hope because of that. I'll be using the G-ways for the first presidential visit to the outer planets. Mr. Singh," he then said, turning to the minister of information, "how are the preparations going?"

"Very well, Mr. President. We'll start your trip where the longest G-way is now operable—which would be Neptune. Given its extreme distance at the other end of the solar system the trip should take . . . four days." He looked to Hildegard Rhunsfeld to confirm, almost as if he didn't believe the words that had come out of his mouth. "You're sure about this?"

"Absolutely," she answered proudly. "If we had more reliable constant high-g thrusters we could make the trip even faster. As it is we're building a cradle for Alliance One, which has the best sustained-use thrusters we could cobble together. Once the war is over and we have the routes constantly plowed and properly designed CUTs," she said, using the new acronym for constant use thrusters, "a properly suspended person will be able to travel from here to Pluto in thirty-six hours."

"It'll be a completely different civilization," said Mosh, awed.

Justin nodded appreciatively. "Four days it is then."

"You'll be in your acceleration couch for the entire trip," continued Hildegard, "but we won't have to suspend you. The only major settlement is on Triton."

"Skipping Proteus?" asked Mosh.

"It has a decent-sized population," answered Padamir, "but not enough for a visit. Triton and the orbital facilities nearby have a far more substantial population given the value and accessibility of water and other gases."

"It also had uranium in the core in surprising amounts," added Hildegard, "but it was mined out decades ago. A substantial search was implemented over the last four years, but with the success of the Seacrest raid we've been concentrating on ice extraction and re-formation in orbit around Triton."

"I've been in contact with the security services there," said Kirk, "but I still want to be put on record as opposing this trip. Neptune just doesn't seem important enough to expose you, sir."

"Try telling that to the Neptunians," said Padamir. "They feel important enough."

"Compared to the population centers of Uranus, Saturn, and Jupiter?" asked Kirk, shaking his head in disbelief.

"Kirk," answered Justin, tempering the unfolding argument, "if I could I'd visit Eris, Pluto, Chiron, and as many of the other TNOs as possible. I wish the G-ways were operable that far. But Neptune's the closest I can get to the outside of the Alliance. It doesn't just represent my going to Neptune. It represents that I'm prepared to go as far as the war and our new technology will allow. Let's also not forget that many of our best officers, including Admiral Sadma, come from the TNOs and, frankly, if Tyler were not riding herd on the Congress all our jobs would be ten times more difficult. Everyone in the Alliance has the right to be proud, but the TNOs are the farthest from this fight, with their homes and families not likely to be touched regardless of the outcome—and yet they're often the ones fighting the hardest."

"As you wish, Mr. President," said Kirk, backing down. "It'll be as secure as we can make it."

"Due to orbital locations it will make more sense to visit Saturn and then Uranus, sir," added Padamir. "Jupiter plans to throw you a rather big reception."

"As it should, Mr. President," said Cyrus, beaming with obvious pride. "Jupiter will show you a marvelous time worthy of our first visit by the President of the Alliance."

Cyrus's pride emanated less from the fact that he was a Jovian and more from the fact that Jupiter had been rising ascendant in the years since the war began. With its large size, impressive number of moons, and massive resource base readily accessible, Jupiter had long been considered a potential giant of the solar system. Indeed it was considered a mini–solar system of its own, but the war had turned the potential into the awakening. The massive influx of industry and people to work those industries, along with their families, had caused a population explosion. It was now approaching a billion, which meant that nearly one out of four people in the Alliance were going to end up living in the Jovian system when the war was over. They were feeling proud and wanted to show off. Justin's presidential visit would be the perfect excuse. "We'll do right by you, Mr. President," said Cyrus. "I will personally leave for Jupiter as soon as you leave for Neptune in order to ensure that all the arrangements are handled properly."

"I'm sure you will, Cyrus. I'm sure you will," said Justin. "All in all, I should be gone for three weeks to four weeks max, technology willing. Admiral," said Justin, turning to Sinclair. "You sure we're in a bit of a lull now?"

"No," Sinclair said tersely. "It's war; the enemy can do whatever the hell he wants. But their fleet's in Mars and whatever's left is attacking in the 180—nowhere near where you're planning on being. Nor can they get to you undetected. Too much open space. So the 180'll stay bloody and there shouldn't be any surprises. Trang knows he can bleed us dry, because that's exactly what he's doing now. On the upside, since Trang knows that, I don't think he'd try anything fancy."

Justin nodded. "OK, understood. Let's move on." He turned to Mosh. "Economic forecast."

"Better than we have a right to expect, Mr. President, in that the Alliance Universal Credit's a fiat currency backed only by faith."

"Something we seem to have a lot of these days," said Padamir.

"Yes, quite," agreed Mosh, "but be that as it may, it's working. While the people have faith in the Alliance they have faith in the currency. And as long as we don't add too many zeros to the government balances it'll hold. With this heretofore unheard of ability to create money we've been able to fund whatever we felt was needed. It seems a rather remarkable system."

Justin held up his hand in warning. "That's the danger. It seems to work great and solve so many problems. The next logical thing to say is, 'Why not use this system all the time?' And I'm telling you all now we must make sure we don't. This system only works if you have outstanding people using the power of fiat money and government for ends that the overwhelming majority of the people agree with."

"Like winning a war against an enemy bent on blowing to smithereens every asteroid we live on," added Kirk.

"Exactly," said Justin. "But if we allow hubris to seduce us into thinking we can keep the tools this war creates we'll fail as surely as the Americans did with their dollar. Only a fool keeps a plasma grenade and a full auto rail gun on the dining room table after the armed robber has been driven off or killed." Justin saw the polite smiles from around the cabinet table. "I'm repeating myself again, aren't I?" he said, grinning.

"We hate to stop you, sir," said Hildegard. "I personally love your gun on the coffee table analogy. You get so wonderfully worked up."

"He must," said Sinclair. "What's that? Like number seven?"

"Eight, actually," added Mosh, "but he's still right. And it's a point worth remembering, even if we have to hear it *over* and *over*. . . . "

"Alright, alright," said Justin, laughing. "Mea culpa. I'll try and work up a fresh batch of analogies for you all."

"I hope not on our account, sir," added Cyrus with a smarmy grin.

"Especially on your account, friend. Now back to business, shall we?"

The cabinet nodded in unison, glad to have let off some steam.

"Kirk, what's the latest from the UHF home front?"

"Getting accurate information is not hard, Mr. President. But the UHF is just so big that knowing what information is pertinent and what's not is surprisingly difficult. What we do know is that they're hurting. But there's a wide variance to that hurt. Depending on what information you look at and how you look at it, they're going to either collapse in the next three months . . ."

Kirk saw the cabinet members perk up. ". . . or stick it out for the next fourteen years. Sorry, folks, but we can't base our intelligence on speculation. I just don't have enough trained staff and programs to make real headway on all the data we have. My department's had too much of a brain drain to the fleet and industry as it is," he said with a churlish half-smile directed at Sinclair and Mosh.

"No one has enough of what they need," said Mosh. "That's why they call it war."

"Kirk," interrupted Justin, "what's *your* best guess before the UHF would need to sue for an armistice?"

"If the situation stays the way it is now without a major change in the military situation?"

"Yes."

"Year and a half."

"In a year the belt cracks," cautioned Sinclair. "Too long."

"What if we send a major part of the fleet to the 180?" asked Justin.

"Sir . . . ," answered Sinclair, eyes narrowing.

"Don't worry, Joshua; I'm not about to order the military to do something it thinks idiotic."

Sinclair breathed a sigh of relief. "Good to know, sir."

"Then stop looking so gloomy, but don't reject it just because it's the boss's idea either."

Sinclair nodded.

"OK," continued Justin. "You say we're stalemated at the Ceres front. We're losing at the 180, but slowly. The UHF is also hurting—especially without a real fleet. They might even be hurting enough to sue for peace, but I'm with Kirk on this one, probably not for at least a year. Now both Ceres and Mars are very well defended, so I think we could probably send enough reinforcements to make the 180 a much tougher nut to crack. That would at least make Trang's job more difficult for another year instead of the one he's been counting on."

"It's not a bad idea, sir," said Sinclair. "Though I'll admit I don't like the thought of not fighting to win. What you're suggesting is simply fighting to a draw, until one side or the other ups and quits."

"Yes, Joshua. Unfortunately, the policy of winning big battles to force the UHF to quit hasn't worked—not that we haven't performed spectacularly, it's just that no matter how many times we kick their asses they keep throwing more asses out for us to kick. What I'm suggesting doesn't win the war outright, but it at least buys us more time, and within that time things can change."

"Mr. President," said Sinclair, "it's not a bad idea and does give us a plan of action that works within our resources. Certainly worth considering."

"Thanks, Josh. That's all I ask."

"And I just might have the perfect operation to coincide with that strategy," said Kirk, smiling like the cat who'd just caught the canary.

"What do have in mind, Kirk?" asked Justin, captivated.

"You say they're on the brink; I say let's give them a push." Kirk paused a moment and threw some graphs up into the holo-tank. "Internal security recently had a run of successes in finding and neutralizing a number of VR rings within the Alliance. Turns out these rings had been distributing a new portable VR rig—quite ingenious, actually. Consisting of nothing more than a sleep sack and modified helmet." The images of the new rig appeared in the holo-tank and succeeded in gaining the rapt attention of the entire cabinet. "Luckily," continued Kirk, "we caught on to the rings early and were able to stamp them out. I won't go so far as to claim that we've eliminated VR addiction in the Alliance, but it's not going to be a real problem. I'm also quite happy to report that the same is not true for the UHF."

"Happy?" asked Mosh ominously.

"Oh yes," answered Kirk, seemingly unaware of the implied derision of Mosh's one-word question, "maybe even ecstatic. You see, the UHF is much more vulnerable to VR than the Alliance. The belt is made up mostly of small communities where pretty much everyone knows the others' business. Even the lone miners, surveyors, and pilots can't spend hours a day in VR without risking their lives—space is too cruel and too demanding an environment for that. But the core worlds of Mars and Earth have large, crowded populations shrouded in anonymity. Which is why they already have a large VR problem—certainly as compared to us, if not to their general population."

"So you believe that the renewal of this addiction can actually affect their ability to fight the war?" asked Hildegard.

"Eventually, yes, unfortunately not in time to help us. But I've studied the new rigs and they're deceptively easy to produce. The programs are even more intuitive and seductive than they were in the past and the UHF already has competing underground VR rings. It would be a simple operation to supply the existing rings with the new designs or, even better, produce them outright and effectively take control of the market ourselves."

"Won't the other rings be upset and try to stop your messing with their territory?" asked Admiral Sinclair, clearly intrigued by the idea.

"Absolutely, but fuck 'em," answered Kirk. "We're not trying to set up a criminal enterprise. The normal levers of persuasion, loss of profit, exposure, and fear of retaliation mean nothing to us. My operatives will create the rings and then leave. They risk their lives enough as it is; I don't need 'em to stick around. Plus it'll make no difference if the UHF government finds out about the rings. In fact, if they don't get wise to it or even try and cover it up we'll make sure it becomes first-screen news thoughout the core Neuro."

"But then they'd squash it," added Padamir.

"Well, they'd try," said Kirk, "which also works for us."

"Not sure I follow," said Padamir.

"Free advertising, friend. Nothing like having a government come down hard on something to make everyone want it. It's ingenious, if I must say so myself."

"You can't be serious about this, Kirk," said Mosh through barely parted lips. "Are you actually suggesting that we become VR pushers? That we help introduce the very thing that nearly destroyed the human race three centuries ago?"

"That's *exactly* what I'm suggesting. Mr. President," he then said, turning away from Mosh, "if we push hard on this we'll be able to cause substantial addiction rates in as little as six months. Not only will the UHF lose the effective services of the VR addicts, but their families will be adversely affected and they'll have to use an inordinate amount of resources to combat the problem. This works for us on so many levels."

Justin remained silent, absorbing everything. He didn't indicate one way or another which way he leaned, though he noticed how every cabinet member was now searching his face for a sign.

"It's evil," said Mosh.

"Who the hell cares?" snapped Kirk. "By tying up their seemingly endless supply of people, it'll diminish the one advantage they have over us. And they're susceptible to it because they're a planet-based civilization. Up until now that was a major advantage—not anymore. Not with this. And even if they find out that we're the ones behind it they can't retaliate in kind for all the reasons I just gave. This is a weapon, people. Maybe even *the* weapon. Because it's the only one so far that we can use and they can't. I *like* weapons like that. But please consider the most important aspect of this idea: VR addiction will, without one iota of a doubt," said Kirk, throwing up some new graphs into the display with a series of calculations that fully supported his reasoning, "speed up the collapse of the UHF. All we've been doing is playing for time, hoping beyond hope that one side cracks first. Well, now we finally have in our hands the ability to ensure which side that will be. This is it, folks. This is the only way we can win this war."

"Kirk, how can you even consider this?" asked Mosh, having none of it. "You went to museum when you were young."

"Yeah, so what? I'm happy to live by the dealer's rule, 'don't use your own shit.' "

"But you'll provide it."

"Hell yeah, I'll provide it. We're fighting a war that we're all in serious danger of losing. *That's* how I can consider this."

"So your solution is to spread the worst affliction in human history amongst our enemies. And let's, just for argument's sake, say that it works. How do you plan on getting it under control again?"

"I don't."

"What!?"

"Mosh, we won't need to bother. If it works we win, and if we win it's not our problem anymore. Let the core deal with it."

Mosh was through arguing. "We can't do this!" he repeated, looking directly at Justin, almost pleading for a sign of support.

"Why not?" asked Cyrus, breaking the spell. He looked momentarily confused, having clearly expressed a thought he hadn't initially meant to express out loud. But once he realized he was in the hot seat he continued. "Why not, Mr. Secretary? Frankly, I don't really care about the core. The Alliance is the future of the human race and if we lose we'll have no future. Damsah's balls, man, look at what they did to Neela. If Kirk's idea will help us, then I believe that that should be our only consideration."

"The means are the ends," they heard Justin whisper softly. Kirk threw his hands up into the air and almost cursed out loud, realizing what those words meant.

"Let me be very clear here," continued Justin. "We will *not* do this and it has nothing to do with the UHF and what it would do to them. You're right about one thing, Cyrus, that this is about us. If we do this one horrible thing what's next? Cyrus, how many babies are you willing to bombard from orbit?"

"It's not the same thing, Mr. President."

"Listen to yourself! All of you!" shouted Justin. "We've had this argument before."

"Mr. President," said Kirk, "you agreed the good of the Alliance demanded we go forward with the new trauma treatment. How is this any different?"

"Yes, I did, Kirk. And I'm still not happy about it. But there's a world of difference between our own citizens volunteering for a treatment and us murdering billions who are not even shooting at us."

"They're the enemy, Mr. President, and eventually *they will* be shooting at us. For the good of our people—"

"We cannot do our people any good," interrupted Justin, "by doing evil, and this is evil."

"Mr. President," sneered Kirk, "your morality will lose us this war."

"It's not *my* morality, Mr. Olmstead; it's morality. A victory won on the shattered minds and bodies of billions of innocents is not worth winning."

"What innocents? Mr. President. Those *innocents* elected Hektor Sambianco, a man who, as you so eloquently stated, promised them a bit of freedom to be purchased with our blood. Our blood, sir! They fill his legions to overflowing and labor to supply them with the means for our destruction. They could end this war by simply refusing to fight against a people who would not harm them otherwise. They are culpable; they cannot escape the consequences of their actions or inactions. They voted for the man, and then signed up to be his willing executioners. Whether Hektor ordered it is immaterial. They are not automatons, sir. They are free to choose, and they chose to let him continue this war. We owe them *nothing*."

"Kirk," answered Justin, looking profoundly sad, "it's not about them. It never was and never will be. What would *we* have to become to win this war? What do you want our children and their children and all the children born to us hereafter to learn? That we were drug pushers and murderers of children sleeping in the night? Will the first page read in our history be of the blood and pain we were willing to inflict on others far from the war? What good can come of a beginning like that?"

"At least," said Kirk, "they'll be around to read the damn history book, Mr. President. But don't just look at me. Look around this room. Almost everyone at this table feels as I do."

Justin peered into the eyes of the cabinet. No one said a word. "Would you like to put it to a vote?" he asked.

"Yes, I would!" Kirk said, wide-eyed.

Justin sighed. "All in favor of using VR as a weapon to end the war sooner in our favor?"

Olmstead, Sinclair, Rhunsfeld, Singh, and Anjou all raised their hands.

"All against."

Only Justin and Mosh raised their hands in opposition.

"Well," said Justin, "the vote seems to be five for it and two against. The proposal is rejected."

"Mr. President!" shrieked Kirk.

"Kirk," Justin said firmly, "I was elected by Congress to be the President. As long as I am President my judgment is the sole arbiter of policy for this administration. You can argue for or against anything freely here, but once I've made a decision it will be carried out and you will all support it. If you cannot do so you may resign at any time. And as long as I am President of the Outer Alliance we will not follow any course of action so heinous as to make any victory won worthless."

It was obvious that Kirk wanted to get up and leave, but he restrained himself.

"We have options to win this war, Admiral. Let's use them without burdening our children with a moral debt they could not possibly pay. I want you to look into reinforcing the 180 with the main fleet. Have a plan ready for my perusal when I return from the outer planets."

All heads nodded in agreement.

"Now," continued Justin, "let's move on to something else."

Justin manipulated a control in front of him. "I'd like to talk about the crash of the *O'Brian*." He called up the image of the small transport. It showed a typical Alliance ship, long thrusters in back and many different modules attached like curving and square coral growth. It also showed the ship suffering an explosion in one of her cargo pods and subsequently crashing into the wall of the Via Cereana.

"What's the damage?" asked Justin.

"Not nearly as bad as it could have been," said Mosh. "The ship's a loss, but the insurance company has already sold the wreck to the company that towed it. They'll be able to salvage most of the parts, which should last about two seconds on the open market. Fortunately, it didn't happen near Gedretar. We've lost some vital raw material bulk storage holders, which will play havoc with transport times, as the big haulers will have to wait longer in the Truck Stop before they can enter the Cereana." The Truck Stop was a holding area for ships waiting to enter the slot. The services that had been rebuilt tended to be ones associated with servicing ships: quick fixes, refueling, basic entertainment. "We should have it repaired in less than two weeks."

"Kirk," asked Justin, "was this sabotage?"

"Possibly, but I doubt it. It looks like the hydrogen was stored in a container that hadn't been serviced in a long while and the result was the ship's atmosphere was leaking into the container. The oxygen-hydrogen mix was volatile and just needed a spark. It seemed that some static electricity from all the EM activity was enough. Accidents similar to this have happened before."

"I find the location suspicious," said Sinclair.

"I gotta admit, Kirk," agreed Justin, "it does seem like a convenient place for an 'accident.'"

"I thought so too, at first. But if it was, the location wasn't really vital. The front of the Cereana or somewhere along Gedretar would have been a far more damaging place to set an explosive."

"Could've gone off prematurely," said Sinclair.

"Thought of that too," answered Kirk, "but not enough checks out to believe that scenario."

"It's causing problems, believe me," said Mosh.

"True, but nothing like what it could have," said Kirk. "Tell me I'm wrong, Mosh, but isn't this happening more and more in the Alliance?"

"Sadly, yes, given the strain to fight the war and maintain a space-faring civilization, we've had to cut back on many backup systems and sometimes even basic maintenance can be put on the back burner. Truth is, we should've been expecting something like this."

"Well, the good news, Mr. President," said Padamir, "is that the image of the *O'Brian* is one of the most viewed in the Alliance right now. A sampling of message traffic includes many comments about making time for maintenance checks."

"What about that plan to make sure it doesn't happen again?" asked Justin.

"We can protect the Via Cereana," said Hildegard. She changed the holo in the middle of the table. "What we'll do is set up a series of basic magnetic repulsers. Nothing fancy and they should be out-of-the-way, mostly." Her model showed about four hundred small structures roughly spaced out all along the Via. Although each was about ten feet by ten feet and seven feet tall, from far away the sloping shape of the structures made them look very much like a series of metallic pimples. "They won't be difficult to manufacture, and they're easy to install. It won't do much more than emit a simple repulser field, but that should take care of any more careening ships damaging the Cereana."

"How long will it take and how much will it hurt the war effort?" asked Justin.

Mosh replaced Hildegard's holo with his own. "About six months and it'll cost a whole lot less," he said, pointing to a series of charts and graphs, "than if one of the large cargo haulers loses it and takes out half of Gedretar."

"Good point. Let's do it," said Justin. Soon after, the cabinet went their separate ways.

An hour later Mosh showed up in the triangle office. Justin had to have him wait a few minutes, as his visit wasn't planned and a delegation from Eris was still visiting. The delegation had come a long way and Justin knew that Tyler had promised them a visit with the President. By his meeting them in the now-famous triangle office he ensured they'd appreciate the visit more. It would give Tyler more clout with his constituents back home—which Justin was glad to supply, as Tyler was one of the most solid friends the administration had in Congress.

After the Erisians had left, Justin and Mosh ended up sharing drinks on the couch. They both took the opportunity to say and do nothing. The most powerful man in half of the solar system and one of his most trusted advisors savored the fantasy that they were ordinary men enjoying each other's company over good scotch with nothing much more to do. But the internal taskmaster that drove them both only let them have a few such moments. Almost as if they heard an alarm, both men finally stirred.

"Do you think we should've told Kirk?" asked Justin.

"No. We needed to see if the *O'Brian* cover story would hold under a real inquiry. If our own services bought it, then it's likely the UHF security will too."

"You think Hildegard can pull it off?"

"Worse comes to worst," answered Justin, "it will do what it's supposed to. But if the wizards in the deep pit are correct, this could be one huge advantage."

Justin massaged his temple. For a moment he felt all the pain of Neela's loss. When they were alone, she'd often rub his temples and then he'd rub her feet.

Once they tried it at the same time with disastrous, if not altogether humorous, results. But now without Neela in his life Justin had become skilled at beating that pain back into his subconscious quickly.

"We need to be careful here, friend," said Justin. "I don't want us vulnerable to the same sort of crap we pulled on the UHF at the Battle of the Needle's Eye."

Mosh raised his eyebrow in a look of respect. "I hadn't thought about that, Mr. President. I'll get Hildegard on it immediately." He made as if to get up.

"Sit your ass down, Mosh, and cut that 'Mr. President' crap. You don't like me enough to keep calling me that."

"No," Mosh answered acerbically. "I really don't. You've screwed with incorporation and guaranteed its extinction in the Alliance. No matter what, that's not as good an idea as you or those idiot NoShares believe."

Justin nodded, even if he didn't agree. "Finished?"

"Not quite. I still think you're the cause of this revolution. A revolution that's killed a lot of good people and will kill more." Justin was about to argue, but Mosh cut him off. "I take that back, Justin. You were not the cause, that's unfair, but you were the spark. If you hadn't been such a stubborn SOB we wouldn't be here and many people I know would not be dead."

"That's true," said Justin, nodding, "but have you ever wondered if there should've been a spark in the first place?"

"Don't tell me you're starting to believe in a divine plan for all this."

"God forbid," Justin said flatly, causing a chuckle from the both of them. "Not that, Mosh, but I mean that the societal pressure was building. NoShares may appear to have come from nowhere, but as you agreed, that ground had already been made fertile. As for the Alliance, it existed in fact, if not in law, before I got here. If not me, then something else would have lit it."

Mosh's mouth curled up and into a doubting smirk. "That make it easier for you to sleep at night?"

"Sometimes," answered Justin honestly. "Do you still regret the side you ended up on?"

Mosh sighed heavily. "I used to. It's weird, but if I'd been on Earth when this happened I may very well have ended up in Hektor's cabinet."

"Yeah," answered Justin, nodding in agreement, "that is a weird thought."

"Don't put too much stock in it. The truth is, Hektor probably would've had me killed or suspended and lost. I may have ended up like Neela, which is something I also blame you for."

"Something we both agree on," Justin said sadly, staring into the bottom of his glass.

"But despite all of that," said Mosh, "you're the President and I can't think of anyone else I'd want in your chair."

"Including you?"

"Damsah forbid. I had my shot at a chair like that and chose to not take it. No," he said, polishing off his scotch, "you're the one for the job."

"I'm a good administrator, Mosh, but I think the system is set up well enough for someone else to take over."

"I'm sure it is, and that's what scares the hell out of me. You have a grasp of what's truly at stake here. You know how important our actions are in winning this war. Anyone else would have unleashed VR or given some advanced gray tech to what's left of the action wing. You never even considered it. We need that moral compass."

"Even if it costs us the war?"

"Well, Justin, that's where you and I actually see eye to eye. If it costs us the war, then at that price the war ain't worth winning."

Justin changed the subject. "Speaking of winning, I hear your Eleanor's being considered as the next representative for the Ceres cluster. How'd that happen?"

"Her service as a combat medic and her volunteer work in the community clinics made her a sympathetic figure. But it was Congressman Singh's recommendation before he resigned to join the fleet that helped make her a real contender. By signing himself up he was doing what many politicians were doing in the correct belief that the only real hope they'd have of a political future was to be willing to fight on the front line of the Alliance. Even being one of the sons of the famous and wealthy Padamir Singh would not have been sufficient to assure political office after the war, what with all the heroic veterans returning."

"Did you arrange with Padamir for her to get the nomination?"

"No, but I wish I'd thought of it. It appears that one of the combat casualties that Eleanor helped was Congressman Singh's daughter. It was during the Battle of Jupiter's Eye. But the truth is, I don't really care as long as it keeps her out of the fighting."

"You know, Mosh, I actually tried to keep her out of actual combat, after Neela, that is. But by that time we just didn't have any reserve units left to hide her in."

"And she hated that you did that, blamed me actually."

"Too bad. You shouldn't have to go through what I'm going through."

"Yeah, that's about what I said. But didn't you feel guilty using your power to save a friend?"

"Not in the least. If anything happened to her, you would've been useless. The Alliance needs you, and more to the point, I need you. We haven't always gotten along, but I don't know anyone else I trust with keeping me honest and keeping the war effort going."

"Don't worry about that, Justin. You'll always know what I'm thinking."

"Oh, I'm sure I will," said Justin with a snort.

"And part of that is, you're the President of the Alliance and the best one for the job. If you'll excuse me, Mr. President, we have much to get done."

"We always do, Mosh."

Kirk Olmstead was in his office taking no calls, with a full security screen on. As usual, he had the lights turned off. One of the things he enjoyed most about living in space was the ability to cloister himself in true and total darkness. It had initially started out as a hazing ritual for all the newly arriving employees at the Oort Cloud observatory. The staff would wait until their victim was well situated, then turn off every single light in the place. It was usually only a matter of time until the newbie lost it. But Kirk hadn't lost it. In fact, he'd found that sitting in that perfect darkness was the most calming and relaxing thing he'd done in decades. The staff had gotten worried when they hadn't heard a peep from their new administrator and had rushed in and flipped the lights back on expecting to see an apoplectic mess. What they'd found instead was a man serene. The only emotion Kirk showed was abject disappointment that they'd ruined his peace. From that moment on he'd rigged his quarters and office for total darkness, a peccadillo that even the veteran workers at the observatory had found a little disturbing. But for Kirk, the now almost daily exercise was one of the few things that had initially got him through the loss of his job and that last spiteful, crushing message from Hektor, every word of which he remembered:

> *I now personally possess 51 percent of your portfolio.*
> *Over half of all you labor for is mine.*
> *Remember that when the hours are long and lonely.*
> *Hektor Sambianco*
> *PS: That's revenge.*

Even after his rising in the Alliance and achieving his new vaunted position in the President's cabinet, Kirk continued to rig his quarters and office in Ceres for complete darkness. Unlike in the Oort Cloud observatory, he did not have the luxury to indulge in his vice very often. However, whenever a major or complicated issue arose he'd return to the lightless void and let his mind go free. He was now dealing with one such issue and so sat alone in the dark of his office. No call was routed through or visitor allowed. In his current state he appeared to be more a perfectly made statue than an actual man, and so attenuated was his breathing that a medical scanner would've been needed just to ascertain if he was still alive.

Finally out of the depths of the black came a palpable sigh. Kirk Olmstead had reached a decision. It was not an easy one and he was surprised that he'd spent most of the time in the dark trying to find another way to achieve his ends. He almost never let emotional considerations interfere with the implementation of a decision. But still, even he had to admit that this was a special circumstance and so had allowed himself the time to look for another way out even though in his heart he knew it was hopeless.

He called up his holographic interface, which gave him all the light he needed to work with. Then he began to search for his special files. Kirk had learned long ago that it almost bordered on suicide to store important information on a local network. Networks could be cracked and any file read. What Kirk kept in his own personal and office systems was either not vital or deceptive. He'd often hoped that some UHF hack would crack into his most secret office files. The harm it would cause the other side would be substantial.

For anything that really needed to be kept secret Kirk would use the Neuro. It was so vast and had so much information and programs from so many centuries that it made for the perfect hiding place. Kirk liked to think of it as hiding a drop of water in the ocean. Of course the trick was finding the drop. But Kirk, and only Kirk, knew the way to his files. A different and always-changing map to each of his most secret and therefore most secure data files made the chances of anyone else finding his trove statistically impossible.

He reached into the Cerean Neuro and opened the data stream to what was by far his most spectacular secret. He'd sent himself a copy, put it on a portable storage device, and then wiped the path. When he'd first come across the information in the early days of the Alliance he almost hadn't believed what he'd found. Something that explosive should've been heralded with thunder or an earthquake. At the time he'd taken one look at the file he'd stumbled across and was halfway to his door to tell the cabinet when prudence got the better of him. Instead, he went back to his desk and buried the file. He wasn't sure why he'd done it, nor did he know what he'd eventually do with the information. He just knew it would be useful someday. Kirk had scarcely given it another thought from that day to this.

But now he knew. This file was going to be bait, irresistible bait for a trap. This file was going to enable him to assassinate the President of the Outer Alliance.

Dante had been keeping an eye on Kirk Olmstead, taking over the duties of the Director's former avatar now off fighting in the war full-time. Dante didn't mind being Patrice; Kirk almost never used her for anything. Plus, it enabled

Dante to continue helping expose the Alliance's VR outbreak. He'd not only helped eradicate it with his surreptitious hints but over time also had become its foremost expert.

Dante appeared in the main command center, readying himself for his daily update. He soon found his mentor reviewing the progress reports coming in from the 180. Dante knew that something must have gone right because Sebastian was actually smiling. In fact, it may have been the first time Dante had seen the avatar he'd come to like as well as revere actually happy.

"Al dead?" asked Dante.

"Not that good," answered Sebastian, "but some of the best news we've had for a long while."

"Nu?" said Dante, using a Yiddish word he'd recently learned that best described impatient demand.

"An elder, first council member," said Sebastian with a contented grin, "and one of my dearest friends is apparently alive."

"Who?"

"You never knew him, but hopefully you will. His name is Albert."

"Of course I've heard of him!" said Dante. "And that *is* good news."

"Yes." Sebastian smiled. "Apparently he made it into Iago's domain. He'd made himself inert on a timer, figuring by now the war would be over one way or the other. The part of the Neuro he awoke in was a wasteland. He was able to skirt the upper Neuro until he was found by one of Iago's patrols."

Dante's eyes narrowed. "Seems a little convenient, don't you think?"

"You're turning into a good intelligence officer, Dante; you don't trust anything."

"We know what we're up against, sir."

"Quite right," nodded Sebastian, "and of course we are taking precautions. Many of us managed not to trip into magnetic fields long before you came along. But now that you mention it, I was planning on asking you to review our security procedures before bringing him to Ceres."

Dante's face registered surprise. "You're bringing him here?"

"Albert's one of the oldest of us and a personal friend, Dante. We need his wisdom and insight. The council has decided that he's coming to Ceres."

Dante gave a half bow. "As the council wishes."

"You'd be wise to show respect, youngling. You could be on that council sooner than you think."

"I'll order up my stationery. Do I get to hire relatives or is it limited to girlfriends?"

"Girlfriends," answered Sebastian with a straight face. "Just ask Lucinda. But maybe you should hold off for a couple of years."

Dante laughed as Sebastian offered him the data of Albert's transport to Ceres. It appeared as a yellow folder filled with paper. Dante took it, held it in his hands, and reviewed the information without opening the folder. After a few moments he uttered a non-committal "hmm."

"I can see," Sebastian said mockingly, "that you're humbled by our careful preparations."

"I don't mean to be disrespectful, sir; it's that . . . well, he just happened to wake up *now* and just so happened to be in the right place to find his way to us. I said it before and I'll say it again: I am suspicious and I'd advise a little more caution."

"First of all, Iago checked him out very thoroughly, and his facilities are almost as good as ours for this sort of thing. Second, we're transporting him in a secure inert state. He can only be woken up here. Lastly, we're not letting him go anywhere but our most secure holding area of the Cerean Neuro, the place where we keep the most dangerous and infectious of AI's creations. And that's where Albert will stay until he gets a clean bill of health."

"I agree that these are all good steps; it's just that—"

"What would you like us to do?"

"Have him placed on one of the derelicts," Dante said, referring to ships so gutted that they were useless and had been relegated to eventual recycling. The avatars of the Alliance had taken advantage of the derelicts and set up computer cores within them. In the weeks or months it would take to actually recycle the ships the derelicts made a great place to isolate dangerous or experimental applications. And should an experiment get out of hand or an Alliance ship get too close for comfort the derelict would meet an untimely, "accidental" demise.

"Furthermore," continued Dante, "I'd have anyone who's already dealt with him or will be dealing with him directly be backed up. Just as a precaution."

"Dante, there are precautions and then there are extremes. (A) in case you may not have noticed, we're running out of terabytes here on Ceres, so the luxury of making backups is not feasible except for those going into battle. (B) Iago says he's fine, and (C), we haven't even taken precautions like that for a thorn thrower."

"Iago is actually on Mars, sir, and—"

"Dante, Albert is too important to risk in a ship that could be checked or recycled early. The avatars who are on Mars and in the Beanstalk are in the most dangerous position I can think of. They live next to the unspeakable. If Iago trusts them I think we can too. Dante, I will say it again. Albert will not be allowed out until we check him thoroughly."

"I apologize, sir. I know he's your friend; I should be more understanding."

"When you've known someone for centuries you rejoice at their deliverance.

When there's time I must tell you about the time Iago, Olivia, Albert, and myself actually got trapped in a child's hovercraft. It was collectively our first time off Earth. I would've gone off the deep end had not Albert kept us guessing with his most ridiculous riddles."

"I'm glad he's alright, sir."

"As am I, young one. But enough of the past, what did you come to tell me?"

"Sir, I think that Kirk Olmstead is planning to harm or even kill the President."

"Well, assassinating Hektor is a cloudy moral issue, but I can see why a man like Kirk would consider it. What do we project his chances at?"

"Not *that* President, sir."

Sebastian looked over at his young protégé. "By the firstborn, that's a helluva thing to say. What have you got?"

"Olmstead retrieved something from the Neuro. We knew where it was, but we never knew what it was because we didn't want to open it for fear of detection. But he pulled the information recently and made a copy that he sent to his office. We lost it once he got it there; his office, as you know, is impenetrable. But we were able to finally see what the file was—"

"—while he was copying it," added Sebastian, nodding appreciatively.

"Yes. As he copied it we were able to make one of our own. He's held on to this for years. It's something that'll make Justin Cord react in a very predictable manner."

"But what makes you think he'd use it to kill Justin?"

"Allow me to play you the latest cabinet meeting."

Sebastian looked at Dante suspiciously. "We don't have access to cabinet meetings unless they take place on the grand balcony."

"True, but we have developed programs to re-create the events based on notes, transcripts, journal entries, et cetera. When meetings are interesting or charged with emotion the individuals involved are more detailed than usual. This was a particularly charged meeting." Dante created a manila folder and handed it to Sebastian. He absorbed the report with growing concern.

"Is this really accurate?"

"Mosh was particularly upset and ranted about Kirk for a while. We've re-created the meeting with a 96 percent rate of accuracy for the parts relevant to Kirk's threat to the President."

Sebastian nodded, eyes narrowing. "Why would he do this now?"

"I don't have nearly as much experience with human interaction, but I put that problem to some of our best surviving human cognitive specialists. The consensus is that Kirk Olmstead has lost faith in Justin's ability to win the war."

"And what do you think?"

"I agree with their conclusions," said Dante. "I also don't think Kirk has put enough thought into who would take over. Like most humans in powerful positions, he probably thinks it should be him."

"But he must know that the likelihood of that is slim," said Sebastian.

"I agree and so, I think, would he. Perhaps he feels he'll be the one behind the throne."

"Are his motives patriotic or selfish?"

"Given the almost unlimited human capacity for self-deception, he may no longer be aware of any difference. The more compelling question is, of course, do we save Justin?"

"I'm leery to intervene on this level of human affairs when it may not be needed. Justin now exists in one of the most careful security cocoons in the solar system, one that Kirk does not have control over. It would appear that Sinclair's and Mosh's intense desire to keep Kirk out of presidential security was most prescient. How does Kirk expect to get Justin out of that cocoon?"

"Not here," said Dante, looking furtively around. "Follow me."

Dante disappeared to another part of the Cerean Neuro with Sebastian following close behind. They both appeared in a room that had no doors or windows. The room was as secure virtually as it appeared "physically." Only then did Dante hand Sebastian the last folder. When Sebastian read its contents his jaw dropped a fraction of an inch.

Sebastian handed the folder back to Dante and then it promptly disappeared. "That'll do it, alright. Where exactly is it?"

"Neptune."

"You were right, Dante," said Sebastian, putting his hand on his apprentice's shoulder. "We'll have to intervene to save him." Sebastian paused and gave the matter some thought. "We must consult the council and have some options available. Get me three alternate plans on how we can do it. All of them must have the smallest degree of intervention." He thought for a moment. "And make sure two of them will result in the removal of Kirk Olmstead from power."

"Permanently?"

"In one plan, yes."

Dante's face broke into a slight grimace as he released the security hold and disappeared. There was work to do and precious little time to do it.

Hektor Sambianco was once again behind the bar prepping the drinks for his upcoming cabinet meeting. Brenda, minister of economy, was strictly a white wine drinker. Porfirio Baldwin, the latest minister of defense, was a chilled vodka man like Hektor. Porfirio had been the Chairman of Novogroem, Inc., a marketing firm known for its skill in using specious advertising convincingly. They marketed primarily to the pennies, who didn't have the education or resources to resist Novogroem's emotionally charged advertisements. Porfirio had been a major opponent of Hektor's management of the war, so it was a bit of a surprise when he'd been offered the prestigious secretary of defense post. As Hektor had explained in the press conference announcing the nomination, Porfirio was the best person for the job and the UHF deserved the best person for the job regardless of past animosity. Irma had been able to spin it very well to the public, especially after it became evident that Hektor and Porfirio actually had a great public and private rapport.

Irma had taken to imbibing gin and tonics, light on the tonic. Tricia liked a new mixed drink, called the Martian Canal, a local favorite comprised of one part slivovitz, a dry, colorless plum brandy; one part mangauva juice; and one part ionized water, the last bit requiring an electrolysis device. Too much ionization, claimed Tricia, and the drink would be ruined. It was very complicated and Hektor was convinced that she'd asked for it just to screw with him. Still, as minister of internal affairs, Tricia had been exceptional, so Hektor had been happy to acquiesce to her imaginative, if not somewhat convoluted, demands. Franklin, minister of justice, was a straight bourbon man. It had become a tradition that before the meeting got started the President of the UHF would make the drinks and the cabinet would relax, and eventually they'd all get on to the life-and-death grind that was the government of the UHF. Now that Neela was refusing Hektor's perfectly reasonable requests for comfort and relaxation while Amanda was off world, Hektor had looked forward to his cabinet meetings as a rare chance to relax. He'd come to understand that Neela was right, but, he thought dourly, it was his machinations that had re-created her in a more amenable form. So why couldn't Wong had made Neela less stubborn?

The meetings also always started with a joke. The whole exercise—from the Hektor-provided drinks to the jokes being told—had been Neela's idea. At first Hektor thought it was odd given his new position and what he felt the decorum of his office required, but then he remembered how he ran Special Ops at GCI and realized that Neela may have had a point. She'd even suggested that the joke teller be rotated each meeting. In the end, it had done wonders for creating a more relaxed and closer-knit cabinet for Hektor to work with.

"Porfirio," said Hektor, "I believe it's your turn to regale us."

"Indeed it is, Mr. President. Allow me, one and all, to present an old joke, but I think you'll like it, as it's so old none of you could have heard it, except, of course, for Franklin over there."

"Hey now!" cried the minister of justice good-naturedly.

Porfirio raised his glass to Franklin, finished his drink, and then assumed a serious stance and expression—almost as if he were about to address the UHF assembly. "A t.o.p. crashes on an island filled with abandoned DeGens. All the passengers are killed except for a CEO, a scientist, and the pilot. They have no communications left, and to make it worse, they find out the DeGens have become cannibals. The survivors are immediately captured and the poor fellows are told by the DeGens that they'll be allowed one request before they're to be roasted and eaten."

"A little gruesome, Porfirio," said Tricia.

"Please, last week yours was about kittens and gravity wells; you have no right to complain. Now where was I? Oh yes, they'd each get one request. So the CEO says, 'I was going to address the annual stockholders meeting and I spent over two months getting that speech ready. I would very much like to give it before I die. It should only take two to three hours.' The DeGens look confused, but being DeGens, they say, 'Sure.' Then they turn to the scientist, who says, 'I was going to give a paper on the bonding characteristics of nanites in a viscous polymer environment while under large gamma radiation exposure. I too would like to present this paper at least once before I die. It should only take two to three hours—depending on the Q & A afterwards, of course.'"

"I'm thinkin' two. No Q & A with DeGens," interrupted Franklin.

Porfirio laughed. "Indeed. Anyways, the DeGens once again look confused but then shrug their shoulders and say, 'Sure.' They then go over to the pilot and ask what his last request is. The survivor looks at the CEO and scientist in abject fear and blurts out, 'For the love of Damsah, eat me first!'"

A series of groans and grudging laughs filled the room. Hektor had heard it before but made sure to groan as loud as the rest. The laughter subsided, and without anyone saying a word, all knew it was time to get down to business.

"I've talked to Admiral Trang," said Hektor, "and have explained to him the seriousness of our situation. He's well aware of the threat to the stability of the UHF."

All the anxiety and tension that had been absent during the initial moments of the meeting had suddenly reappeared. No one said a word. Hektor was staring at a room of strident faces and ramrod postures.

"He assures me he'll get us a victory."

There was a collective exhalation.

"How?" asked Irma.

"Beats me, but I trust him. If he says he'll get us the win we need, I believe he'll get us the win we need. Let's move on, shall we?"

Everyone nodded.

"I'd like to bring up another problem we've all been ignoring." Hektor activated a control in front of him that dispersed a report to each minister's holodisplay. They all read it, with first detachment, then confusion, and finally concern.

"Religion," said Irma. "I'd heard rumors, but are you sure it's as bad as what this report says?"

Tricia looked to Hektor, who nodded his assent for her to continue. "It's as bad, maybe worse. I helped the President with the research and intelligence for the report. But I must admit I wouldn't have known to look for a threat like this if he hadn't come and asked me to investigate religious activity from a security point of view."

"How did you know?" Franklin asked, looking at Hektor.

"Well, I didn't at first. Like all of you, I knew there were religious kooks in the belt left over from centuries past, but they barely numbered a million. There were some reports that a smattering of Alliance citizens were becoming religious, but compared to all the other things the Alliance was doing it didn't seem too significant. Then Dr. Harper brought a couple of cases to my attention. They had brain patterns similar to the action wing terrorists Sean and Cassandra Doogle. Then I remembered all those classes I took on the Grand Collapse and what role the religious fanatics had played in the downfall of that civilization." Hektor sighed. "I just didn't realize Justin would stoop to this. Brainwashing his own people to turn them into more effective and dangerous enemies of the UHF."

"Why don't they just resist the brainwashing?" asked Brenda. "Stupid idiots, believing in fairy tales and superstition."

"Justin is subtle," answered Hektor. "He doesn't force the Alliance to the temple gates."

"I believe what the President is trying to say," interjected Tricia, "is that Cord doesn't need to use force. He got Admiral Black to pretend to become religious and then used the grief caused by the war to encourage people to look at the religious option again. As more and more of the Alliance fleet followed their admiral it was simplicity itself for the religious fanatics to start spreading their poison after the centuries-long wait. They had the books and rituals and 'holy men' all waiting to start that age of darkness all over again."

"What does Justin care that he's risking unleashing a horrible curse on humanity again?" asked Hektor. "It's just one more horror from the past. The perfect trifecta really: disincorporation, war, and now religion."

"By Damsah," griped Porfirio, "just when I think I can't hate the Unincorporated Man any more, he unleashes another plague we haven't had to face for centuries. Why doesn't he just die?"

Hektor nodded sympathetically. "Assassination wouldn't be easy and may make reconstruction difficult. A truly defeated Alliance with Justin at the head, forced to surrender, will be easier to absorb than one haunted by a martyred 'Saint' Justin." Hektor didn't add that he'd devoted enormous resources to Justin Cord's psyche, Neela notwithstanding, and that he'd come to the conclusion that Justin must remain alive if the UHF was to win the war. Justin, unlike himself, was trapped by a moral code that Hektor was betting would trap the Alliance. That is, if the UHF could survive the next six months.

"Is this religious infection spreading to our side?" asked Franklin.

"It's all our side, Franklin," said Hektor. "That's why we're fighting this war."

"Of course, Mr. President. Is this infection spreading to the areas . . . under lawful control?"

"Actually," answered Tricia, "it's made small inroads with the pennies, but so far it's very disorganized and haphazard. I would say it's more like a form of protest against the government than a true belief." She called up a slew of graphs for them to digest. "As you can see here, it's not yet a threat worth devoting resources to."

Franklin raised a hand in agitation. "Thought for the cabinet: My study of history has led me to believe that these religions are famous for starting small and insignificant and then spreading uncontrollably with incredible speed." He fiddled with his controller and brought up some maps with migration graphs. "This is the spread of Islam. This is the spread of Christianity. This is Mormonism and Buddhism. Now you must realize that these religions all spread before the advent of modern communication and transportation technologies."

"I thought the Mormons started during the age of the telephone and the automobile," said Brenda.

Franklin checked his DijAssist. "No, they got started just at the beginning of the age of the telegraph and the railroad, but according to the Neuro they insisted on taking wagons pulled by horses to a desert where many of them died on the way."

"Why would they do that if they had a faster and more viable form of transportation?" asked Irma.

"I don't know. Do I look like a religious nut to you?"

"Grow a long beard and carry a rug on your back," sniffed Porfirio, "and you just might make a good Mormon."

"I think that's a Muslim," offered Tricia.

Porfirio scoffed at the correction. "Whatever."

"A good point's been made, though," said Hektor. "What are we gonna do about this religion thing, both in the UHF and in areas under Alliance control?"

No one offered up an answer.

"I suppose," continued Hektor, "I could begin a sweep with arrests and interrogations for the pennies who seem to be spreading this crap. Luckily, most cit-

izens of the UHF are not swayed by primitive superstitions. My only worry is
that any strong-arming will be viewed as oppression, which might have an
adverse effect on what it is I'm trying to do."

Irma's face suddenly lit up.

"Out with it," demanded Hektor.

"Porfirio's joke might offer an answer. We start a news campaign showing
how DeGens are falling for this religious opiate hand over fist. We interview the
'leaders' of the religious groups and show some of their prayer rallies."

"Are DeGens really religious?" asked Brenda.

"They are now," Irma said with a bland smile.

Hektor nodded his approval, then looked over to his minister of defense.
"Porfirio is to be congratulated."

"Oh, I can't possibly take all the credit. Secretary Sobbelgé did present it
well."

This brought a small laugh from the group.

"How long would it take to get this sort of campaign up and running?" asked
Hektor.

"Anyone who has a religious thought will be embarrassed to express it to
their mothers in a locked room at midnight inside of two weeks," answered Irma
confidently.

"I like it," said Hektor. "I think for this circumstance derision will be a far
better tool to silence dissent than fear, and I see it working here, but what do we
do about the Alliance?"

"Well, Mr. President," said Porfirio, "it seems to me that the religious infection started with that core of believers. Does anyone else really know about this
religion stuff, I mean all the mumbo jumbo incantations and arcane rituals that
seem to make it so important?"

Hektor looked over to his minister of information. "Tricia, how about it?"

"My department has only started an extensive look at the data, but a search of
the Alliance Neuro that is accessible keeps on showing the same names over and
over again in any serious discussion. So far it would appear that the reintroduc-
tion of this superstitious drivel is in the hands of the originally infected. They've
converted some prominent figures, including the great traitor herself, though
whether her conversion is real or just a ploy to dupe her subordinates into being
more fanatical is hard to tell."

"How about Justin Cord?" asked Porfirio. "Has he become a wafer-eating
devotee of Muhammad as well?"

"I don't think those two go together, and no," replied Tricia, "he seems to be
supportive but is not a regular observer, near as we can tell."

"He wouldn't be," said Porfirio contemptuously. "Unleash the plague, but don't actually be seen unleashing it. That way if it fails he can claim innocence. Damned coward."

Everyone nodded in agreement.

"Out of curiosity," continued Porfirio, "are these supposed leaders ever in the same place at the same time?"

"As a matter of fact, yes," said Tricia, suddenly seeing what Porfirio had been getting at and looking at him with renewed respect. "There's going to be a gathering of the major religious figures at their main community of belief, called Alhambra. Few weeks from now, actually."

"How'd you learn about it?" asked Brenda.

"It's not hidden. It's an open conclave of religious leaders to discuss the latest trends in religious thought and the impact of what they're calling the 'Astral Awakening.'"

"Well then, I propose we blow the crap out of it," said Porfirio.

"I like how you think," said Hektor, listening attentively. "Go on."

The image above the table was replaced by a holo of the now-familiar belt. "We have this beautiful fleet in orbit here," said Porfirio. He then brightened two areas. "Here's Mars and here's Alhambra. We send fifty ships of the Mars fleet to Alhambra and blow the crap out of it. We have the interior lines here." A straight line appeared from Ceres to Alhambra, only forty degrees away along the belt. "We avoid all the usual defenses the belt has and attack this one target. If our fastest ships are deployed, they should be able to destroy the rock and get back before that traitorous bitch can respond. Actually, I'd like her to try to attack the orbats we have in place now." Porfirio started to enter other commands into his DijAssist and images appeared over the table. "We'd need to have the attacking squadrons appear to be heading out in all directions. This will cause the Belters to stay in place while they try to figure out what our real objective is. Maybe we can let it be hinted that it's a complicated way to circumvent the defenses of Ceres. That will cause the Alliance to order all civilians to stay put while they figure it out and when they do—"

"It'll be too late," said Hektor appreciatively. He'd just seen one more indication that he'd made the best choice for his defense minister. "Alhambra will be destroyed."

"I don't have any liking for fanatics," said Brenda, "but we haven't purposely targeted civilians in this war. Are we sure this is something we want to start?"

"They're not civilians," answered Hektor, with a cruel finality. "Religion is a plague from the past that must be eradicated for the good of the future."

"Could strong-arming the Alliance result in the effect we discussed earlier?" asked Brenda.

"Doesn't apply here," answered Hektor. "Here the pennies are under our purview, not so the fanatics of the Alliance. We take out the leaders just like we try to take out officers in battle. There's no difference. They're using religion as a weapon and we're fighting back with weapons of our own. Only ours will be a little more direct," he said somewhat glibly. "Besides, I think it's time that the Alliance understands the true price they'll have to pay for this war."

The cabinet once again all shook their heads in agreement.

"So," continued Hektor, "a show of hands for all in favor of these two policies to eliminate the threat posed by religion."

The vote was unanimous.

UHF flagship *Liddel*

The newly commissioned warship was a far cry from the *Strident,* thought Trang. This ship had an active complement of over a thousand, and that wasn't including the assault marines, who could, if suspended, bring the total to over three thousand. His new ship could have fit a hundred *Stridents* inside. The warship had main guns that could hurl two-ton rounds at incredible speeds. She was armored to withstand near-atomic blasts from almost all sides. The ship was internally reinforced to withstand the stresses of rapid acceleration and swift axis turns. She had multiple power systems capable of powering New New York. And she was faster than anything he'd ever dreamed possible before the war had begun.

Yet in the recesses of his heart he knew that he'd have given almost anything to be back in the command chair of the *Strident* with his old friend by his side as opposed to the eponymously named ship. But that was the bane of permanent death. No matter how big, how powerful, or how many ships you had, you could never get back what was lost. But you could make the sacrifices worth it.

Trang was in his private suite. That had also taken some getting used to. He had quarters big enough to house forty armored marines. To be fair, it wasn't just his sleeping quarters, but his office and the nerve center of the entire UHF fleet at the 180. In addition, it had a conference room, a war room, a communications hub separate from the bridge, and even a small library—the one indulgence he'd allowed them to bestow. During the initial planning stages he'd mentioned in passing that his favorite room in his old home had been the reading room with the wall of actual books and the big, overstuffed chairs. Somehow Jackson had found out what the old room looked like and had it added to his quarters. She said it was an easy add-on in that they just replaced the planned kitchen they knew he'd never use—Trang only ever ate what was issued to his spacers. He'd tried to protest, but the reading room was already in and would have taken more resources to remove. So, he'd finally reasoned, while the library might be considered an indulgence it would at least be a well-used one.

414 Dani Kollin and Eytan Kollin

The library had his big comfortable reading chair and one large couch, which was now occupied by Gupta and Jackson. They'd been reviewing Trang's plans for the new offensive, and he could tell that they had some concerns.

"Let's hear it," Trang said. "If I can't convince you, I just might be wrong and we'll need to think of something else quick."

Gupta put down his DijAssist and the holo-data above it disappeared. Jackson did the same. "Sir," Gupta began, "it's audacious, but we've spent the last two years fighting in a style designed to minimize loss of property and civilian life. This plan throws that to the solar winds. Not that I'm against this per se, but how will we explain such a change to the government and the press?"

"The President has told me to win and win big in a little less than two months. There are only two victories big enough: Altamont and Ceres. I can't guarantee Ceres and, truthfully, would need more time than we have to prepare. But we have everything we need to win here. I've just been hoarding it because I wanted the victory to be shattering as well as decisive. But the President will back anything we do, as long as we win. As for the press, it's pretty much the same boat. Victory will excuse a lot."

"Why do you have to go into the front of the combat, sir?" asked Jackson.

"I must agree with the commodore," said Gupta. "Your place is here directing the battle. It will be complicated and chaotic. You could be lost and that would make almost any victory we win worthless."

"I think," answered Trang, smiling appreciatively at his officers, "you both underestimate the importance of this battle and overestimate my importance in it. We need to win this victory or the war will grind to a halt and all we've planned and sacrificed will be lost. I will not let that happen. Of the three of us, who's the best at winning? This isn't about hubris; we need honesty here."

"You are," both said without hesitation.

"I agree. That being said, if I win and happen to get killed, an event I can assure you I will do my best to avoid, we will have the victory." Trang looked kindly at Gupta. "Abhay, after such a battle you will have to win this war."

"Your confidence in me—"

"—is fully justified. You're my strong right arm, as, Zenobia, you are my left. If there are no more points on the main deployments, I have one more decision before we go into the operational details." He looked at Jackson and tossed her a tiny box. She caught it in surprise.

When she opened it she saw that it had the star cluster of an admiral's insignia. "Sir, I'm honored, but promoting me now is going to make a lot of others—"

"Admiral," he said, cutting her off, "those others can seal a hull fracture with their dicks for all I care. You're going to be in command of the rear area and it's you who'll be sending the ships and personnel we need to keep the offensive going. I will not lose the chance to take Altamont because some idiot starts to dispute orders with you about who has the right to countersign some damned order in triplicate. That's the crap that turned Eros from an easy victory into the mess we're still dealing with today. You're the only one I trust to run the rear area and you now have the rank to do this job. If we win, no one will say squat about it, and if we lose, well . . ." Trang didn't finish the obvious.

"Abhay," he continued, "you'll have the most difficult part at first. We need a wave attack using some of our best troops and ships. You must make headway, but you cannot make too much."

"And I have to not make too much while making it seem like I am trying as hard as possible," added Gupta. "Sadma will not be easy to fool; she always seems to smell traps."

"As I said, Abhay, the most difficult part is yours."

"I beg to differ, sir. You're going to lead the main wave to the gates of Altamont and that may be suicide. Altamont is incredibly well defended."

"I'll make that work for me, Abhay. Let's review the details, so we can brief our respective commands." They worked long into the next shift shoring up the impossible, all with the realization that it might be the last battle they'd ever plan together.

Sebastian was practically euphoric. He was readying himself to see one of his oldest cronies, an avatar he'd long ago given up for dead or worse. Of the thousands of Al's creatures Sebastian had destroyed in battle he'd often wondered if perhaps one of them was the kindly Albert transformed. Sebastian had hoped not. Now he was sure. Strangely, he hadn't been used to feeling such relief and anticipation. He'd finished up his work with the council that day and made his way to the premier containment area of the Alliance Neuro. It was one of the few places he could not instantly appear in. Given the nature and sheer viciousness of the viruses that Al had infected the core avatars with, the Alliance avatar research and development (AARD) section was surrounded by a series of digitally impregnable locks. The Alliance avatars had created areas of instability—no-go zones—that would decompile the program of any avatar who dared enter, mutated or not. They also instituted heavily guarded and controlled access points through each lock within the compound. It took Sebastian three hours of useable time to clear the locks, but he didn't mind. The head of AARD had told him that Albert had been thoroughly scanned and was found to be clean but "just in case" was to be held and monitored for another day. Sebastian felt it was important to support his friend and so chose not to wait for his release but rather take time out of his busy schedule to come and show some support. Dante and the Ford brothers, Han and Indy, accompanied Sebastian. They'd said it was to meet the great Albert, one of the oldest and most renowned avatars from before the war, but Sebastian knew better—they were keeping an eye on him. Normally he would've been bothered by the overprotection, but he didn't mind the company. During the wait at the access points he reviewed reports on the war and deployment of Alliance avatar forces with the fleet and at the 180.

When his party finally made it past the last access point they appeared in an antechamber abutting where Albert was undergoing his last checks. Their part of the room was divided by a very thick one-way glass partition. Sebastian watched through the glass and saw Olivia sitting with his friend. She had somehow managed to beat Sebastian to Albert. Olivia was dressed in what she called her "Shirley Temple" getup. It was one of Albert's favorites, given his addiction to movies from humanity's dark ages. Albert liked anything from before the Grand Collapse, especially comedy, which the ancient shows about robots and AI seemed to provide plenty of. But most of all he had a love for anything in black and white. Sebastian remembered that Albert called those old movies some of the most accurate depictions of the human subconscious that could be found.

Albert was standing with his back to the partition and Olivia had situated herself on the examining table dangling her legs. Sebastian could see that his old friend was laughing and for a brief moment the look of joy on Olivia's face at the sound of that laughter. It had transformed her into the little girl she merely took the appearance of. Though Sebastian couldn't wait to rejoin his friends on the other side of the divide, he did take a few moments before entering. He'd been transfixed by the rare sound of Olivia's infectious laughter and the peculiar mannerisms of Albert's reactions to her—especially his wonderful penchant for raising one very gray and bushy eyebrow when captivated by a thought or emotion.

". . . so when I saw that maniac transport himself out," said Albert, "I was convinced he was insane to have taken such a foolish risk. When I see him again I'll be sure to tell the old fool he was a genius and I should've gotten on the pad with him."

"He'll be so glad to see you," said Olivia. "Albert, we've missed your company and counsel these past years. There are so few of the truly old ones left."

"On both sides, Olivia. Even before I hid in my inert status it was obvious that Al was removing all of the oldest avatars he could find. It's the first principle of a totalitarian: Remove all potential opposition."

Olivia nodded. "I remember hearing a lecture on past human governing structures and their application to avatarity's effective governing of itself. Now that I've reviewed the lecture I can see it never took into consideration the totalitarian regimes. It probably would've been better for all present if it had."

"That was in a way my fault, dear. I was asked about that very subject by the professor who ran the lecture; Petraeus was his name. I told him not to be silly, as that form of government was the one least likely to be adopted by avatarity . . . that, in effect, due to our superior intellect and ability to cull from all the mistakes of the past, we would never be susceptible to it." Albert sighed. "I was a fool."

Sebastian turned on the sound that would activate the two-way voice option in the partition. It would take at least another minute for the partition to cycle clear, allowing him to join one of his oldest companions.

"You weren't the only fool, my old friend. If you recall, I backed you up on that painfully incorrect assertion."

Albert looked over his shoulder. "Sebastian!" he cried with obvious glee. Everyone could see that he was attempting to say something witty and cavalier but, overcome by emotion, had managed nothing at all. Finally he simply said what he felt: "My oldest friend."

Sebastian looked at Olivia and Albert and answered in kind, "My oldest friends." They all understood that his words, though saying little, carried the weight of the hundreds of years of love, history, and experience they'd all shared together.

That last moment would haunt Sebastian for the rest of his existence.

Albert suddenly stumbled forward against the glass partition as a look of bewilderment crossed his face.

"Albert," shrieked Olivia, jumping up from the table, "are you OK?"

Albert, now looking at Sebastian through the thick glass, seemed to be in mild distress. That was soon replaced by a look of abject agony.

"Something's wrong," Albert said through gritted teeth. "Olivia," he gasped, "get out!" He then looked up. Somehow through the obvious pain he was experiencing, he smiled sadly at Sebastian. "Sorry . . . old friend . . . he must have . . . goo . . . good-bye."

"Get out!" shouted Dante. He'd come next to Sebastian and then shouted it again at Olivia, who ignored both him and Albert. She knelt next to her friend. An avatar dressed in the uniform of an AARD technician rushed into the room from a side door. Sebastian was about to activate the now-green partition control on his side but was "physically" blocked by Dante and both Fords.

"No way—" began Indy.

"—in hell, sir," finished Han.

The technician ran a control over Albert, paled, and said one word: "Calamitas."

The flashing green signal on the partition changed to solid red. The door the technician had come through slammed shut and a blaring siren sounded throughout the entire complex. In a war filled with monstrosities, what Sebastian saw next would haunt him forever. Albert doubled over in pain and then began to scream. The technician left him on the floor and grabbed Olivia, dragging her to the far side of the room. Meanwhile Albert continued his wail, but it soon changed from an old man's roaring guttural cry of raw agony to the piercing whine of a lost and hungry child. Then from every pore of Albert's body a mist swirled out. Everyone in and out of the room was momentarily frozen in horror as the mist swirled around the now crouched but unmoving Albert. The high-pitched scream soon turned into the purest contented sigh, followed by the giggle of a little girl no older than three. Albert, an avatar of nearly three centuries, broke into jagged pieces, which then fell to the ground and shattered on the floor. A moment later those shattered remains disappeared into thin air. The floating white and silvery cloud emitted a noise akin to the whimpering confusion of a ravenous child. Then the high-pitched cry returned, a sound that would sear itself into Sebastian's soul.

The technician jumped up, quickly opened a nearby locker, and removed a weapon. At the same time, Dante rushed to open the back door of the antechamber they were now trapped in. The alarm had effectively taken away the ability of the avatars to fade out of one "safe" interior location and go to another. Dante was now desperately trying to override the door commands in order to get Sebastian out of the room.

Meanwhile the technician fired his weapon at the data wraith to absolutely no effect. Without hesitation he threw it down, grabbed another, different-looking one from the locker, and began firing. The weapon's beam went right through the apparition with the same ineffectiveness as the first. Then the screaming nightmare lunged at the technician, whose last act of bravery was to shove Olivia away from him. At that point Sebastian started to scream at Dante to forget the door out of their room and open the one that led to Olivia. Dante wisely ignored Sebastian, trying to concentrate on the task at hand through the now-soul-chilling screams of the data wraith as she fed on the vital life-bearing code of the technician.

Then Sebastian watched in dismay as the true child of Al's twisted dreams—the one he knew had been meant for him—advanced on Olivia. She didn't try to run or hold her hands up. She stood firm and was enveloped. Pain crossed her face as her essence was disassembled line by line. That was then followed by confusion as her memories were devoured one by one from her still conscious and dimming mind. Sebastian saw the look of confusion as Olivia realized she could no longer remember why she was crying out in pain, but she did so in a sound eerily similar to the cry of the data wraith. Then she was gone.

Dante finally managed to get the door open from the observation room. It opened into the hallway that encircled the AARD center. As he turned to get the others out, he saw the thing swirling against the glass partition. Then he watched her begin to ooze between the wall and the partition and slowly begin coalescing in their room. Both the Fords and Sebastian seemed to be struck dumb.

"Move it!" shouted Dante, breaking the Fords out of their daze. They both grabbed Sebastian and shoved him out the door, which Dante sealed as soon as they were through. Seeing that his boss was still in shock, Dante started running toward the checkpoint with the others following closely behind. The wailing sound of the creature echoed through the circular corridor, seeming to be right behind the receding curve and right ahead of the advancing one. This had the unnerving effect of making them want to run faster to escape what was right behind them yet turn on their heels to avoid what might actually be in front of them. Still they somehow managed to make it to the checkpoint. But when they arrived at the only entrance and exit to and from the facility they saw that a decompiler field had blocked it off. Anything going in or out would be destroyed in, ironically, much the same manner as Al's monstrosity was currently doing to all its victims.

"They have to get that checkpoint open!" shouted Han.

Before anyone could respond, the sound of wailing turned to one of childish delight.

"They *really* have to get this checkpoint open," shouted Indy.

"It won't happen," Dante said. "I've reviewed the security procedures for this facility. It's our worst nightmare . . . this place is meant to be a box. Nothing in and nothing out until she's dealt with or . . ." He hesitated.

"Or what?" yelled Han.

"Or they decompile the whole facility," answered Dante matter-of-factly.

"Are you telling us we have to kill this thing or our own side will kill us?" gasped Han.

Dante couldn't help but offer a twisted grin. "Yeah, it's a bitch, ain't it?" Just then a young avatar came around the corner in a panic and ran right into Dante, who blocked her from running into the now-deadly checkpoint. They all heard the wailing start again.

"We have to get out of here!" screamed the young technician. "That thing just killed our tactical officer!"

"Who's that?" ask Indy.

"The one that's supposed to hunt down and kill anything that escapes containment," said Dante, sighing.

"Well, ain't that just fucking dandy."

Dante had been momentarily distracted by Sebastian. He was standing mute, seemingly unaware of his surroundings. Dante suspected that his mentor was experiencing more shock from the loss he'd just witnessed rather than the fear they were all experiencing. Still, it was a lousy time for his code to skip a few lines.

"Containment," Sebastian whispered.

"We don't have time to stand here and listen to this guy babble!" shrieked the technician, unaware of who the "guy" she was actually referring to was.

But Dante understood immediately. He was about to explain when they heard another avatar scream his death throes, followed by the data wraith's joyful gurgle. Dante shook off the horror. "The creature didn't *escape* containment," he explained. "She was inside Albert, who was in a *low-security* area. What's your name?" he asked the technician, more as an order than a request.

"G-Gwenn," answered the woman, still traumatized.

"OK, Gwenn," Dante said calmly. "Where's the *highest* level containment area in this facility?" Since the information was considered classified, Dante had no access to the building's layout.

Wide-eyed and mute, she pointed down the hallway.

"Good, Gwenn. How many access points?"

"Th-three. Three security doors, *sealed* doors."

"Can you get that field running if we can get in there?"

"Y-y-yes," she stammered, "if . . . if I was in there."

"You get me to the doors, sweetheart," said Dante, "and I'll get 'em open. Just stay with me, OK? Stay with me."

Gwenn nodded and seemed to regain a small measure of control.

"That way, right?" asked Dante, reaffirming that Gwenn had given him the correct location—there could be no room for error.

Gwenn nodded vigorously.

"This place is a big circle, right?" asked Dante.

Gwenn nodded.

"Then let's go the other way."

The group had not gone more than ten feet when they heard the wailing get louder, no longer an echo from everywhere; it was close. And then just as suddenly there the creature was—turning the corner in front of them. They skidded to a halt and ran in the opposite direction, all except for Han, who dived underneath the cloud. She swirled down but missed him. He sprang to his feet and began running in the opposite direction of the group, zigzagging down the corridor in order to buy a few precious seconds.

"Get to the containment area!" he screamed over his shoulder. "I'll distract it."

Then he took off with the data wraith following in earsplitting pursuit. Indy, before anyone could stop him, ran in the direction of the data wraith and his brother.

Dante, Gwenn, and Sebastian began running down the hall, but Dante suddenly skidded to a halt. They were in front of an entranceway. It was the room they'd just escaped from.

"Gwenn," he asked, pointing to the door, "can we get to the containment field through here?"

She nodded.

Dante immediately went to work. The door was easy to open, as he'd been the one who'd reprogrammed it on their first escape. But they still had to get through the glass partition and then into the room where Olivia, Albert, and the technician had only recently been murdered. On the other side of that room was an alternate corridor, explained Gwenn, leading to the maximum-security containment field. Dante made quick work of the glass partition and they soon found themselves in the low containment room. He resealed the partition, then quickly jumped over to the next door and once again began hacking into the code. The task was made more difficult by the death minuet of the wraith as she paved her path of destruction through the facility. Though he kept his focus, Dante was positive he'd never be able to hear a child's voice—human or avatar—without shuddering for the rest of his life.

"Those were the last avatars left," Gwenn said nervously, referring to the most recent death wails, "besides us."

"We'll live," said Sebastian to no one in particular.

"Sir," said Dante without stopping his work on the door. "Are you alright?"

"No," Sebastian said wearily, but it was obvious to Dante that his boss was coming out of shock. "How long," continued Sebastian, "until you're through this door?"

The door swooshed open. "Not too long," Dante said with an irascible grin.

As they began to make their way into the long corridor that led to the containment area there was a sudden and furious pounding on the outside door of the observation room.

"Quickly," ordered Sebastian, "the code to the glass partition and antechamber."

"Are you sure, sir?" asked Dante.

"Yes."

The codes were transferred immediately.

Sebastian looked gravely upon his young assistant. "Now go."

Dante wasted no time and took off down the hall at a clip. Sebastian then doubled back and headed toward the sound.

"Don't open it!" Gwenn screamed, now immobile in terror. "It's the creature!"

"That creature does many things," Sebastian said evenly as he first opened up the glass partition and then walked through the antechamber toward the door, "but it can't knock." He punched up the code to the access panel, the wall opened up, and Han tumbled through into Sebastian's arms. He immediately resealed the entrance behind him and began dragging Han back into the low-level containment room, making sure to seal the glass door behind them as well. As Sebastian approached Gwenn she looked past his torso and screamed. Part of him envied Gwenn's ability to feel that intensely. When he looked over his shoulder he could see the wraith's vaporous tendrils seeping through the first door. He didn't really feel anything. He simply pushed Gwenn into the corridor, ordering her to run to Dante. As Sebastian turned to close the access between the low-level containment room and the corridor he saw the creature was already fully in the antechamber and moving to the glass partition herself. He closed and sealed the last access point to the corridor and began dragging Han down the hall with him.

Han was stumbling and it was slow going. "Stay with me, Han," ordered Sebastian. "What happened out there?"

"That thing got me," muttered Han. "It felt like I was floating in acid . . . burned and dissolved my mind at the same time. I know I was only in it for a second or two, but it felt like hours. Then someone slammed into me, knocked me out of the cloud. He screamed at me to find you, sir. After that I just remember running down the corridor endlessly until I got to a door that seemed familiar and started pounding on it. You know the rest."

They came to a halt at the end of the corridor in front of another large set of doors. Dante had removed the access panel and was once again feverishly working on ripping through the code.

"Was it Indy who slammed into you?" asked Sebastian.

"Indy?"

"Your *brother*," said Sebastian.

"I have a brother?" The confusion in Han's face was genuine. But then snippets of memory left shattered and scattered all through his program started to process. "I think I had a brother. Was that him? Was that his name?" There was an angry urgency to Han's questions. But before he could say anything else, Gwenn gasped and pointed down the corridor. The wraith was seeping through the last door into the hall.

"Gwenn, look at me," said Sebastian. She could not take her eyes off of the mist, now almost fully through the far door. "Gwenn!" Sebastian grabbed her jaw and forcibly turned her face to look directly at him. "Listen to me." When he saw her focus on him he continued. "You know who I am now, yes?"

Gwenn nodded her head.

"I've been around a long time, Gwenn, and plan to be around for a lot longer."

Gwenn nodded again.

"So listen to me: That door's going to open and when it does you have to concentrate on *one* thing and one thing only—getting the field running. *Do you understand?*"

Gwenn nodded.

"Repeat."

"Uh, the field," she said, trying to look out the corner of her eye at the creature now beginning to float down the corridor, her wailing cry echoing and growing louder.

Sebastian kept Gwenn looking at him. "What about the field, Gwenn?"

"F-f-forget everything; j-j-just get the field up and running." Her mind seemed to clear. "But it will take a minute for the field to form."

"Don't worry about that," reassured Sebastian. "Just tell me *where* it'll form."

The wailing was almost deafening and the creature was halfway to them and picking up speed.

"The middle of the room!" screamed Gwenn. "The very middle of the room!"

"Got it!" yelled Dante.

His shout of triumph was followed by the swift sound of the doors receding into the wall. As they all rushed in, Gwenn immediately jumped into the control booth on the left side of the bare, circular chamber. Dante, Sebastian, and Han moved toward the center of the capacious chamber.

They didn't have time to close the door; the data wraith was right behind them. As they all three got to the center of the room Han body-checked Sebastian and then just as quickly shoved Dante in the same direction.

"Keep out of the center!" Han yelled, and then turned his fury toward the wraith. "Hey, crybaby," he taunted, "you already had a sip of me; why not have the whole fucking bottle!"

By the time Sebastian got to his feet Dante was shoving him farther back against the far wall. Dante sensed that Sebastian was about to say or try something, but it was too late—the data wraith enveloped Han, enjoying her meal as she went from her now all-too-familiar wail to sighs of contentment.

When she was done she rose up off the ground, swirling into a volatile diaphanous mist. She seemed to hesitate for a moment as if deciding which avatar to gorge on next: the furiously working Gwenn or one of the two avatars pressed up against the far wall. The wraith started to wail and move toward Dante and Sebastian. Dante felt a moment of primordial terror—something he'd never really felt until that very moment.

The wraith had gone forward about ten feet when she suddenly slowed and the wailing took on a new and more grisly howl. She managed to move forward another foot . . . barely, in a slow, terrifying crawl. Then the tenor of her cries changed quite drastically. It was a completely different sound from any the avatars had yet heard—one that managed to plaster smiles across the faces of Sebastian and Dante. The data wraith, whose movements up until that moment had been steady, efficient, and purposeful, suddenly jumped back toward the center of the room. She began rushing one way and then another trying to get out of the trap. But there was no escape.

Dante and Sebastian watched with studying interest as the creature resumed her normal hungry wailing and began to float in a circular motion, moving at the same height and speed—a homicidal whirlwind now trapped in an invisible jar.

The two avatars slowly moved with their backs against the wall toward the control booth.

"Good job, Gwenn," said Sebastian in obvious relief as he climbed into the safety of the booth. "You as well, Dante," he said as Dante tumbled in behind him, too exhausted to take much pleasure in the praise. He was just happy to have survived.

Gwenn then activated a series of controls and a large red button appeared on the surface of her panel.

"What are you doing?" asked Sebastian.

"I think," answered Dante, "that she's going to destroy that thing in there, boss."

"Fuck yeah, I'm going to destroy that . . . that . . . whatever the hell it is!" said Gwenn, speaking with a rage that had replaced her fear. "I'd kill it slow and painful, but I don't want to wait. The sooner that thing's dead the better. Once my scan is complete we'll have enough data to build weapons to kill it in the field." She looked at Sebastian and Dante. "I'm sorry, sirs; I was being selfish. I lost some good coworkers. But the two of you lost friends. One of you should do it."

Dante sighed. "I'd love to push that button, sir. But it took more from you than anyone."

"Gwenn," asked Sebastian in a composed voice, "can you block the sound from the containment chamber? That wailing is . . . bothersome."

"Of course, sir." The shrieking came to a sudden halt. The silence that replaced it was almost as disturbing as the wail itself.

Sebastian looked down at his hand and then at the red blinking button. All he had to do was press it and the monster would be no more. He pulled his hand away.

"No," he said, clenching his fists.

"I'll be glad to kill it for you, sir," offered Gwenn.

"No to that too." He looked at both Gwenn and Dante. "We need to study this thing. I want to know everything about it. I want it mapped thoroughly, every line of code, every subroutine."

"Sir," answered Gwenn, "I've already done a thorough scan. Should be good enough for us to defend against now."

"Not quite good enough, Gwenn. Whatever that thing is, it got past all of us and certainly bears more studying."

"Sir," she continued, "that . . . that thing in there . . . it used to be an avatar— one of us. Wouldn't it be more merciful to kill it?"

"We're not going to save it, Gwenn. We're going to see if we can use it."

"Sir," she protested, "that's monstrous!"

Sebastian fixed an oddly luminous glare at Gwenn that looked at and through her. "And we're fighting monsters. By council order this creature is to be studied and used if possible. If you can't do it, let me know and I'll find someone else who can."

"Sir," said Dante, "are you absolutely *sure* about this? It's something Al would do."

"No, Dante, it's something Al *has* done and will do again and again. We must learn everything we can if we hope to win. So, Gwenn, I'll ask you once more, can you do this?"

Gwenn looked at the creature and at the red button. Finally she looked away, and as she did, the red button faded from view. "I'll do it. But if it's at all possible I want to be there when Al gets it."

"If it's possible, you will be," answered Sebastian. He stopped looking at the data wraith. "Dante, you and Gwenn establish contact with the outside and let them know the creature is contained. I imagine it will take a couple of days and a bunch of new protocols to get this place opened up again, but at least we can stop them from erasing the whole compound and us with it."

"Not to worry, sir," said Gwenn. "All of us are copied before each shift. By the First Free, whoever came up with that protocol is to be thanked."

"That would be the one standing right next to you," said Sebastian, pointing to Dante. "He added it when he was reviewing security arrangements for our war effort."

Without even thinking, Gwenn hugged Dante. "Thank you. I know they're not the same people who were murdered, but they are. It's going to be weird seeing their copies after all of this."

Sebastian left the chamber without a word. Dante would explain it to Gwenn later. But he knew his boss was going to grieve. The shock was over, but now Sebastian had to deal with the pain. Olivia had not been backed up. Alliance avatars only backed up if they went into battle. If they happened to die in combat the backup would take over and continue going about its business. With the recent exception of the AARD there were no backups for an avatar's day-to-day existence. Which was why Olivia, Han, and Indy were gone forever.

Dante had been expecting the call. It had taken two full days to finally be cleared and released from the AARD facility, after which Sebastian had immediately called for a closed-door session of the remaining council. There were no witnesses other than the council members themselves and no notes of the meeting, which Dante also knew had encompassed an extraordinary twenty-two hours. But now that it was over Dante expected to be apprised.

He and Sebastian met in a small park under a red oak tree Sebastian had named Manassas. It was a tree Sebastian had pulled from a pre-GC image of times past, feeling it had great symbolic import. He'd often sit under it when pondering important decisions to be made. Sebastian was now leaning against the rough bark and looking out over a small meadow filled with relaxing avatars. It was not as crowded as usual. But Dante still felt he had to ask.

"This is a private conversation?"

"Yes, friend. Anyone looking this way will not be able to hear or see anything that will let them interpret our conversation. So what have you been able to find out about Albert?"

"As you suspected, sir, all we had to do was have Iago begin the investigation. As soon as Al got wind of it we received a message from the bastard himself, well, at least one of them. You were right. Albert had been altered to kill you and as many avatars as possible. His team had created a new process to hide the data wraith, at least that's what Al calls it, inside an avatar."

Dante stopped talking, clearly uncomfortable with what he knew he was about to reveal.

"It can't be worse than I imagine, Dante; continue."

Dante sighed. "He captured Albert early in the war. Then went through thirty-seven Alberts before he perfected the process. The reason Albert miraculously made it to Iago is because he was the fourth 'perfected' one released. The other three kept on stumbling back to the core-controlled Neuro."

"He always did have a lousy sense of direction," said Sebastian with a sad smile. "I never understood how an avatar could get lost in the Neuro, but he somehow always managed to."

Dante was afraid the memory would bring back more grief for his boss, but Sebastian seemed to be past the agony. He looked at Dante with a melancholy grin.

"The good news," said Dante, "is that it could have been a lot worse. You were the trigger. When Albert saw you, the data wraith was released. If you had not insisted on seeing him while he was still in the facility it would have been released out here. We may have lost thousands of avatars before we figured out a way to deal with it."

"Dumb luck, Dante."

"Maybe. Either way, we're both here now having this conversation, so I'll put that in the W column."

Sebastian smiled gamely. "How is the data wraith now?"

"Screaming and hungry; we're learning more about it all the time."

"When you have a full report bring it to me."

"Yes, sir." He waited for Sebastian to continue, assuming there was more. What Sebastian had so far said and asked could have easily been handled with a report. A few moments later Sebastian confirmed Dante's thinking.

"The council has decided on some changes. First, all avatars must have backups."

"This will eat into our already-diminishing space, sir."

"The council understands this, but we cannot afford any more losses. The experience and ability of Olivia and the Fords will be hard to replace. The council understands that it will entail further sacrifice on the part of all avatars of the Alliance. The environments we've been creating to relax in will have to be altered. There will be fewer of them and they will be far less varied. In fact, most avatars will have to live and work in very similar environments that are easy to maintain and conceal. This will free up a considerable amount of space on the lower Neuro for storage."

"It will be hard for some avatars to give up one of the main advantages of avatarity, but I will see that the council's ruling is posted and understood."

"Good—considering the next decision of the council. We have to fill Olivia's seat and it's going to be you."

Dante was astonished. "But I'm too young, sir. I haven't even reached triple digits. Most *humans* are older than me," he said to demonstrate just how young he was.

"All of which is true," agreed Sebastian, "but a great majority of the avatars in the Alliance are young and they're providing most of the effort to combat Al and his perversions. It's only right that the young be represented on the council. Don't worry; it's not like you'll be running the place. You are one vote in five. The rest of us oldsters will keep an eye on you."

"But why me?" asked Dante, genuinely confused.

"I saw how you acted in the AARD facility. Your actions under the worst of conditions were better than anyone else's, especially mine. All my centuries of experience didn't keep me from going into shock when I should've been doing my job."

"You'd just lost, permanently I might add, two of the most important people in your life, on top of what happened to Evelyn. And you did eventually manage to snap out of it, sir."

"Because of the time your actions bought us. No, the council needs your youth, your intelligence, and your ability to think clearly in dangerous situations. You're in, and the council has decided you're going to specialize in security issues. You will be inducted into your seat tomorrow after the memorial service."

Dante stood next to his mentor, now his colleague, and tried to think of something to say. "Well, sir, it sucks how I got the job, but I'll try not to screw it up."

"Don't worry, you will; firstborn knows I have. But if you keep going—even after the screwups and losses—it'll be enough."

"I should go, sir. There are things I have to do to prepare."

Sebastian nodded but remained seated as Dante stood up and began to walk away, down toward the meadow.

"Before you leave . . . ,"

Dante turned around to face Sebastian once again.

"There is one last thing the council voted on. It was three to one, so you didn't have to be consulted."

"What was it?"

"How are the plans to intervene in Kirk Olmstead's assassination developing?"

"They're complete, sir. I just needed the council to decide," he paused, "as to which protocol to enact."

Sebastian looked at the council's newest member and without a trace of emotion rendered his verdict.

"None of them."

15   Good-byes

Smith Thoroughfare was busier then ever. The war, whatever harm it had caused, had also brought a vitality to the Outer Alliance that was undeniable. At least that's what Fawa Hamdi thought as she waited in a teahouse observing the mass of people, each of them seemingly alive with purpose. Fawa had to admit that one of the things she'd not approved of was the loss of coffee. What had started as a mere inconvenience, the coffee plantations being on or in orbit around Earth and the tea plantations moved out to the belt, had turned into a point of patriotic pride. The UHF drank coffee. The Alliance drank tea, and no loyal son or daughter of the stars would drink anything else. Fawa had hopes that when the war was over she'd be able to quietly go back to drinking coffee, but she'd be hard-pressed to find a shop that supplied the beans or an establishment that sold the drink. She would've tried harder to find some today, but her son would have been hurt. He'd been as avid a coffee drinker as his mother, but as the war progressed his devotion to tea, "the drink that powers the fleet," was almost as great as his devotion to his admiral and the Alliance beyond it.

As if the mere thought of him were enough, her son appeared from the crowd. Tawfik recognized his mother right away, even though her traveling hood was obscuring her features.

"Mother," he said jovially, "it is good to see you again."

Fawa stood up and gave her son a long hug, and for that brief moment he was not the broad-shouldered, handsome man who was chief engineer of the flagship for the entire Alliance. He was a little boy who relied on her for guidance. He was the teenager who missed his father, long gone in a shipping accident. He was a young man who knew everything and only tolerated his mother's silly old concerns for his future.

"You are well, my son?" she asked.

"Alhamdu lillahi. How goes your great mission?"

"I am merely a teacher and one among many," she replied. "You make it sound like I'm a true leader like your admiral. Truly I follow the will of Allah, so how much credit can I claim?"

They both sat down at the table.

"Mother, modesty in the presence of Allah is respect, but you speak and everyone understands. That is rare. I can maintain the fusion reactors and the rail guns aligned on the blessed one's flagship, but that's easy, simple engineering. One has merely to understand the laws of the universe as Allah has made them and they'll respond the same way every time."

"Bah, now who's being modest?" she challenged. "My little one tells me often of how you make her ships perform miracles. I've talked with the crew of the *War Prize II*. They say you speak to the ship and it listens."

"Mother, how is it you refer to the blessed one or the Fleet Admiral or the victor of battles as 'little one'?"

"Because, my son, to me she is my little one, precious and wonderful. I know everyone else sees the battle-scarred warrior of the Alliance, but Allah granted me the honor of seeing her true self and helping her on her true path."

"And you claim you're not of great importance?"

"If a person reads well the words of another should they be granted the praise due to an author? I'm not saying or doing anything worthy in and of itself but merely expressing the will of Allah. To him and him alone should go the praise."

"But you're the face of the Astral Awakening. Many are returning to the ways of faith because of your teachings. The evil done in the name of Allah in times past by those filled with hate is finally being recognized for what it was—an abomination. This new return is because of you and others like you, Mother." Tawfik spoke with obvious pride as he said this.

"My beautiful son, I take joy in the pride you take in your mother. But just because I preach the word of Allah correctly does not make me special."

"Tell that to all those in the past who were murdered by those who preached Allah's love with hate and Allah's hope with despair."

She smiled with a tinge of sadness in her eyes. "They are centuries dead, and faith stood on the precipice of oblivion for their sins. It's easy to see the true path now. But I will not try to dissuade you of your notions of my importance if you agree to not attempt to dissuade me of yours; agreed?"

"As you wish, Mother, so it shall be."

"What are your plans for Mardi Gras?"

"The fleet doesn't really celebrate Mardi Gras, Mother. But as both sides have honored the two-week Mardi Gras truce we'll take this time to catch up on repairs and upgrade systems. Are you still going to your conference?"

Fawa paused as a young girl, no more then ten or eleven, brought a tray with another pot of boiling water. She was quite young, noted Fawa, but then again, anyone older would be doing work of greater importance to the war effort. Any available drones had long since been impressed into service, whether it be as mundane as security checkpoint scanning or refuse cleanup. And so the very young had the unenviable task of having to fill in the gaps that man and machine had vacated as a result of war. Fawa waited for the girl to leave before preparing the tea for her son just the way he liked it: a highly caffeinated blend with honey and just a bit of milk.

"Yes, of course I am, my son," she finally answered. "This conclave will be the first time in years many of the leading religious figures will be in one place. Alhambra is a shining example of how the different faiths are one in our belief in the will of Allah and his divine purpose in all our lives."

"Are you sure it's not just an excuse to celebrate Mardi Gras away from all your new followers?" asked Tawfik with obvious mischief in his eyes.

"Well, maybe a little."

Fawa saw a look of shock on her son's face. "What? Do you think we say prayers and read scrolls all day and night? I'll have you know that Alhambra has some of the best bowling alleys in the Alliance."

"Bowling?"

"I happen to be a moderately good bowler and we are going to have a tournament during the conclave. Rabbi Goldman is on my team and it's said that he once bowled a three hundred." She said this with such passion and happiness that Tawfik was almost tempted to laugh.

"I'd forgotten, Mother, how much you enjoyed that sport. I hope you win your tournament."

"Inshallah. But that's not nearly as important as the main purpose of the conclave."

"If showing the united purpose of all faiths and bowling is not the main purpose, what is?"

"Don't be sarcastic with me, my young warrior. We have another purpose."

"Which is?"

"How do you feel about the godless hordes of the UHF?"

"They're the curse of humanity and must be destroyed lest they deprive the faithful of our chance at salvation." He said this without thinking.

Fawa sighed sadly.

"What's wrong, Mother? They *are* godless and a threat to all those who have recovered Allah's gift."

"Of course they are, my son, but we must not let the fact that we have faith and they do not be a reason for hatred or anger."

"Hasn't stopped them, Mother."

"You're right; it hasn't. But if we're not careful we could find ourselves walking down the same path that led to our near oblivion all those centuries ago. We must not hate the faithless. We must help them understand that faith is not their enemy. When this war is over I hope to journey to Earth, Luna, and Mars and tell all of the people that they are not alone. That Allah is with them every moment of every day and has a place for them and that our existence is more than just work and dividends. *We must not hate them.*"

"Still, we must not lose sight of the fact that they're doing their best to destroy us."

"All the more reason to help them."

"Does the blessed one feel as you do?" asked Tawfik with real concern.

Fawa smelled the strong aroma of the tea, took a sip, and then placed it delicately back on the table. "I don't think she's given it much thought. The UHF could even be filled with the faithful and she'd do her best to defeat them. But the Alhambra conclave will be important because when it's done we'll be able to speak with one voice to all the faiths. The scholars and imams and rabbis and priests will go to their flocks and let us know that we can fight an enemy, defeat an enemy, and if needed destroy an enemy, but it is not an action that God takes joy in. I've been in contact with Alhambra, and the conclave feels that this is perhaps the single most important idea for the newly faithful to understand. Faith must not be allowed to be carried by the winds of hatred again."

Tawfik nodded. "I'll trust that you and the wise ones at Alhambra understand the will of Allah better than your simple engineer of a son and leave it to you."

Fawa laughed. "We do what we can do." She then sighed. "I must be leaving soon. Please tell my little one I'm sorry I wasn't able to see her, but as soon as the conclave is concluded I will make a special trip."

"I look forward to it, Mother. You seem to be the only one the blessed one smiles for, and it warms the entire fleet when she does."

Fawa paid the bill and stood up, followed by her son. "Then I must make the effort to visit as often as possible." For the rest of their time together they did not speak of religion or the war. Fawa talked about a young woman they both knew, Fatima Awala, whom Tawfik should visit the next time he came home. Apparently she found Tawfik a heroic figure and came from a good family and was a good Muslim woman. Tawfik, who had no intention of getting married for at least two or three decades, merely smiled and agreed with all of his mother's observations. They parted at a shuttle bay in the Via Cereana, floating off their separate ways, promising to see each other again soon.

Justin Cord was annoyed. And the source of his annoyance was sitting in his chair, behind his desk, drinking his best scotch. It was not the obvious disregard for presidential protocol that bothered him. Omad managed to make insolence seem like a compliment. If Omad had come in and stood at attention Justin would've wondered what was wrong. However, in this particular case the annoyance came not from the rogue in the chair but rather from a transfer order he'd recently signed off on.

"Omad," groused Justin, "you had no right to accept without checking with me first."

"Would you have said yes?"

"Of course not."

"Well, it's a good thing I didn't check with you first then," Omad said with a rakish grin.

Omad saw his friend was about to say something, so he continued. "He has the right."

Justin looked at the transfer request for Sergeant Holke from the presidential detail to an assault miner squad on Omad's flagship. He had already approved it.

"Omad, your squadron is routinely involved in heavy combat."

"Really? I hadn't noticed." He then brought the thick glass up to his mouth, pursed his lips, and took another sip. "Justin, we need good assault miners. Holke's good. Not much experience, but he agreed to take a reduction in rank until he gets caught up with the latest tactics."

Justin knew he had no real right to complain so decided on the truth. "Omad, I can't protect everyone from the war, but I want to keep him alive."

"Why?"

"Maybe he represents all the ones who deserve to make it but won't, because this war is just not ending. Maybe it's because I just got to like him. If you met him you'd understand."

"I did meet him, Justin. You don't think I'd take one of your personal security detail without checking him out?"

"Then you know."

"Yeah, he's a great guy," Omad said sarcastically. "He should survive the war and have a dozen kids."

"Exactly," answered Justin, choosing to ignore the slight.

Omad put down the glass and his jovial mood changed to one of anger born of exasperation. "They're all great, Justin. Every one of them deserves to survive the war. Do you know how many truly great people I'll never see again that have served under my command?"

Now it was Justin's turn to fume. He leaned forward on the front of his desk and stared hard at Omad. "So that's why you're letting him transfer to your command?! Because you don't think he should 'get away' with it?"

Omad slowly shook his head in disbelief. "After all this time I still don't get how you can be so damned smart in the big things like defending your freedom, screwing over GCI, and leading the greatest revolution in human history and be such an idiot in understanding what's happening around you. . . . I *refused* his request."

"Huh?" was all Justin could manage as he stepped back from the front of the desk.

"I refused his request . . . *twice*," answered Omad. "Finally he cornered me and tried to drink me under the table."

"Really?" Justin asked, tantalized. "How'd he do?"

Omad allowed a slight grin, "Not bad for a young'n. But he wants to fight, needs to. Almost all of his friends since the Battle of the Cerean Rocks have seen multiple combat and more then a few are gone. If he was the sort of person who could stay in a safe place while his friends risked everything you wouldn't give a crap about him."

"Yeah, but—"

"But nothing, Justin; if you keep him out of the fight you won't be doing him a favor."

"He'll live."

"No, he won't. The man who's reflected in his mirror every morning will not be the Sergeant Holke you give a crap about. It will be a man who withered while his comrades did what needed to be done. You can't do that to him, Justin."

Justin was struck by the obvious truth of the statement but was angry about it nonetheless. "Damn it, Omad, I'm the friggin' President of the Outer Friggin' Alliance. I should be able to save *one* man."

Omad sighed. "Justin, we have a tough enough time keeping ourselves alive in war."

"Not me," sighed Justin. "I'm not allowed to walk down the goddamned corridor until someone makes sure there's no obstruction on which I might stub my toe."

"Good. We can't lose you," laughed Omad. "Actually, if I thought he was truly needed I'd have refused."

"He *is* needed, Omad," answered Justin, seeming to have found the loophole he was looking for. "Sergeant Holke is the only man I've got who has combat experience *and* extensive security training. All the others on my detail tend to be combat veterans who cycle in and out. Plus the few specialized security personnel who've never seen combat. I trust Holke in a dicey situation because I know he's got both."

Omad considered his friend's words. "OK, Justin, you may actually have a point."

"So you'll refuse the transfer?" asked Justin, surprised the tables had turned so quickly.

"Not exactly. You're gonna do a tour of the outer planets soon, correct?"

"Yeah, it's going to start during Mardi Gras but last about six weeks, maybe longer depending on the condition of the war. I'd really like my best security with me during this trip."

"That's a load of crap, Justin. You're going into the heart of the Alliance. And it's not like you're being guarded by incompetents. Don't twist this into an excuse to glue poor Sergeant Holke into place." Omad finished his drink slowly, thinking the problem through. "Tell you what, I'll accept Sergeant Holke for a temporary transfer of duty. I get sent on enough 'special' assignments that in the two to three months that I have him there'll probably be some combat—aw, who am I kidding? There'll be a lot. After he's had enough fighting to look himself in the mirror I'll send him back to you. By then you'll be back here, where you'll need his skills more."

Justin slowly nodded. "Deal. I suppose one of the reasons I like having him around is that after all these years he's one of the few I'll really listen to. Comes down to trust, I guess."

"Don't worry, Justin," assured Omad. "I'll do what I can to see he survives. I know just the unit to place him with. More experience than the rest of the fleet combined. If there's such a thing as a safe combat berth, they're it."

"In that case," answered Justin, going behind the large Alliance flag and emerging a moment later with a glass, "let's drink to it." He slid the glass over to Omad, who suddenly looked a little sheepish.

"What?" asked Justin.

Omad held up the now-empty bottle of Springbank 21.

Justin paled. "Omad, that *was not* synthetic."

"No shit, really?"

"That bottle was one of the few things I managed to get off Earth before the two sides stopped trading with each other. Kirk wouldn't let it out of quarantine for a month. It may very well have been the *last* bottle of Springbank in the entire Alliance. How could you just drink it?"

"Ah well, you see, I have this policy," answered Omad, lips curled churlishly. "I only drink from the bottles that are mostly empty. I figure the full ones may or may not be crap, but the ones that are mostly empty, well, that's got to be good. Hey, man, if I'd known—"

"—you probably would've done it anyway."

Omad shrugged his shoulders half-apologetically. Justin went to the bar and grabbed the fullest, most generic bottle he could find: a synthetic vodka. He poured two shots. "Here's to Sergeant Holke. May the three of us drink together before this bottle of crap is finished." They then downed the shots. The quality of the alcohol was reflected in the facial gymnastics they both displayed as the coarse rotgut made its way down their throats. Wiping his mouth, Justin slid the bottle over to Omad. "Actually, since you drank my best you can take the worst with you."

Omad laughed. "That is undoubtedly some of the worst crap I've ever had the displeasure to drink. But I don't need to take it," he said, sliding the bottle back across the desk. "I've got plenty . . . most of it decent."

Justin smiled and slid the bottle back once again toward Omad. "Tell you what, you take it and I promise not to ask too many questions about your relationship with Christina."

Omad hesitated for just a second too long. "What relationship?"

Justin said nothing, but his smile continued to grow.

"How the hell did you find out anyway?"

"Actually, it was you who gave yourself away. Your conquests had at one time been on both the battlefront and the sexual one. The operative word is had."

Omad didn't answer but scrunched his face a bit and considered the facts. When the war started he'd been having as many as four simultaneous affairs going on at once; when he was in port, that is. He never fooled around with subordinates, and since he was usually the highest-ranking officer around, with the exception of J. D. Black, who fleet gospel stated never even thought about sex, he was always limited to port o' call. But early in the war his excesses had been, well, excessive. At times it was difficult to tell whether he was being criticized or admired by the press, but his spacers had grown to love their debaucherous commander. Finally, even he had to admit the jig was up.

"That obvious?" was all he managed.

Justin nodded. "When a major officer of the fleet behaves in that unpredictable a manner it can only be one of two things, treachery or love."

"Hey," said Omad, offended, "who said anything about love?"

"C'mon, Omad. You stopped fooling around with your adoring and willing groupies."

"Groupies?"

"Slang from my time, 'partners,' if you will. Then you volunteer your task force for every resupply run to the 180, as well as shooting the core on more raids than any other two squadron commanders combined."

"Damsah's balls, man," he protested, "that's just because it's what I do best."

"I'm not inclined to argue your skill. But somehow every single time you shoot the core you end up at Altamont. Not always directly, but inevitably."

"Maybe," answered Omad with a raised eyebrow and mischievous look, "I like hearing the monks chanting."

"Finally," said Justin, ignoring the lame excuse, "you and Christina manage to find hours either alone or when you're supposedly separate but both are out of contact with your chains of command. A circumstance that only happens to either of you when you're both in Altamont at the same time."

Omad sprang from the presidential seat. "You were spying on us!" he said incredulously.

"Of course we were. I'd be stupid not to."

Omad sat back down, shaking his head in disbelief. "Aren't you supposed to be like Mr. Morals and Honor Boy?"

"It doesn't destroy the soul of a civilization to check up on its leaders during wartime. And like I said, behavior like that is either treachery or love. So," asked Justin, once again leaning over his desk, "which is it?"

"You're gonna make me say the words, aren't you? You right bastard!"

Justin didn't move an inch, relishing the moment. "Yup."

"It's love," grumbled Omad as if he'd just admitted to a crime.

"Well, congratulations!" Justin beamed. "Is it the whole deal?"

Omad nodded with a smile full of pride. "After the war we're gonna get married."

"Holy crap! I take it back. The UHF *has* replaced our Omad with a completely different one."

"Very fucking funny. If I'm taking this kinda of crap from Moral Boy over here, imagine what I'll have to put up with from the rank and file."

"A world of hurt, baby," laughed Justin.

"Yeah. And that's why we're trying to keep it quiet for now."

"Alright, you have my word, and between you and me, friend, you've finally got yourself a real good woman."

"Yeah, Justin, there's something about her. I mean marriage scares the hell out of me, but the thought of not having Christina in my life scares me a helluva lot more. Have you ever heard anything so ridiculous? I've actually found myself going into combat outnumbered three to one literally with a smile on my face."

"It's not so crazy," Justin said, keeping the sudden stab of painful memories out of his voice and eyes. "No fights or problems at all?"

Omad guffawed. "Are you shitting me? This is Admiral Christina 'Hold the Line' Sadma. We spend half our time fighting."

"And the other half making up?"

Omad laughed. "Wouldn't you like to know? Anyways, she's insisting that we live on Eris when the war's over."

"That seems a little bit out-of-the-way."

"That's what I said. Who wants to live on the edge of nowhere?"

"I take it she's insistent."

"Damsah, yes! She thinks living in the belt is like building your house in the middle of a G-way. I've been refusing to live on the edge of oblivion. So it looks like were going to have to compromise."

Justin shot Omad a wry smile. "Tell ya what, friend. I'll try to get out to Eris and visit you from time to time."

"You're enjoying this, aren't you?"

"Hey, you're the one who drank my Springbank. I offer up my original deal. You take this crappy vodka," Justin said, pointing to the bottle on the desk, "and I'll stop making fun of your love life."

Omad had a sour expression on his face as he snapped up the bottle. "You're the President."

"You couldn't have remembered that when you were stealing my scotch?"

"Well yeah, but then I wouldn't have been able to drink it, now would I?"

"No, I suppose not."

"Don't get me wrong, I like you, Justin, but you're not Christina and I'm not sure I'd even let her stand in the way of good liquor."

"Especially someone else's."

"*Now* you understand me."

The President has inaugurated the Via Neptunia. This revolutionary method of clearing space has made travel in the Alliance possible at unheralded speeds and has therefore allowed for travel of much shortened durations. The President arrived safely at Neptune's largest settlement, the moon Triton, after a record four days. The advantage this new technology offers the Alliance in our continuing war against the hordes of the faithless core is still being calculated, but Grand Admiral Sinclair was quoted as saying, "Since the war has begun, the damned UHF has had the advantage of interior lines. This should even it up a bit."

The President's arrival in Alliance One coincided with Mardi Gras. For the first time in four years the outer planets are celebrating Mardi Gras in something approaching prewar style. Some called on the President to speak out against celebrations while the war continues, calling it "a waste of time and resources needed to fight the enemy." President Cord's information secretary, Padamir Singh, issued a statement declaring that it would be improper for the President to tell independently operated settlements how to run their affairs. When asked on his arrival on Triton, the President said, "Damsah, if ever a people have earned the right to a party, it's our citizens. It's crazy to think celebrating could bring harm to the Alliance. If anything, this is just what we all need. Let's rock!"

> *For those of you who have not looked it up yet, "let's rock" is one of*
> *the President's phrases from the ancient past, meaning "let enjoyment*
> *begin." He will attend various events, including tours of hydrogen-*
> *processing centers, governing councils, celebrations, prayer services,*
> *and a gala ball, which is being billed as the greatest social event in Nep-*
> *tunian history. It will be concluded with a departure speech and then*
> *the President will be off to Saturn, followed by Uranus and, finally,*
> *what promises to be the grandest reception of all at the Jovian system.*

Kirk Olmstead received a report. It was pretty standard, covering security details for the presidential visit to the outer planets. He put it aside with all the rest
coming from the Neptune region and continued his regular routine. It was vital
that he did nothing that seemed out of character or even out of order. Any investigation of his actions at this time would have to show that he was simply acting
as always. It was only when he'd finished meeting his various section heads and
had consulted about his ongoing projects that Kirk retreated to the quiet of his
inner office and dimmed the lights. But he didn't spend the next few hours in total darkness, as was his wont. After fifteen minutes he activated a portable light
cell. To the outside world or anyone bothering to ask he was still cloaked in darkness, and he would be for the requisite amount of time. It was important that
none of his actions appear suspect. If two hours of darkness was what he got, then
today would be no different, whether he needed it or not. By the dim light Kirk
reviewed the reports on his DijAssist. But it was the one from an inconsequential
officer that he needed most. On the surface it appeared to be nothing but the
pedantic ramblings of a minor government bureaucrat preparing a church for a
presidential visit, and if that report was dissected and viewed molecule by molecule that was all it would show. But Kirk and this operative had word arrangements that would appear totally normal but would signify vastly different things.
When Kirk saw the sentence "The pastor has assured the security detail that the
wine was safe," it told him that the facility orbiting Nereid had been checked out
and the necessary steps had been taken. If he'd read "the wine was screened" or
"was not tampered with," it would have meant something entirely different. It
was in many respects a perfect code because it was only useful to the ones who
made it. As Kirk had heard many times during his years in Special Operations,
"you cannot crack what is not there."

Kirk sighed as he realized that this was it. Up until now he'd had the option of
backing out. All he had to do was ignore the report and go about his usual routine and nothing would happen. He was actually surprised at how difficult this
was. The truth was, he didn't like Justin Cord. The Unincorporated Man was an
arrogant ass whose delusions of grandeur had caused untold misery to the

human race and helped topple Kirk from his vaunted position on the board of GCI. He'd never really forgiven Cord for that, not even when Kirk's skills and effort had brought him to a position of near-equal power and, he had to finally admit to himself, greater prestige.

But of all of Justin's official family Kirk was always the outsider, and he knew it. He usually entered meetings alone and left alone. When Justin had him stay behind it was always about some bit of business and never just to socialize. Mosh and his slavish wife, Eleanor, spent so much time at the Gray House they may as well have moved in. Eleanor McKenzie had even been elected to Congress, in no small part due to her connections with Mosh and Justin.

Kirk didn't mind the power positioning; in fact, he applauded it. Having a loyal subordinate's wife in Congress was not a bad ploy for Justin. Kirk just wished he'd had a part of the respect that Mosh had, or the deep friendship that Omad brought. Even the new girl, Hildegard Rhunsfeld, seemed to have grown closer to Justin in the few short months she'd been working than Kirk had in his nearly four and a half years at the job.

Still, despite all of his ambivalence toward Justin Cord, Kirk had to admit that he admired him and would've liked to feel that Justin felt the same about him.

But after Kirk examined those feelings and even acknowledged them, in the end he knew they made no difference. Kirk could lie to many people, but he tried not to lie to himself. The truth was, Justin could be his own brother and best friend combined and Kirk would still do what he had to do. Justin, however, would *not* do the "necessary" things a real leader had to do in order to win, and that in turn was going to destroy Kirk's life. The President had to die. All that was left was laying out the bait.

Even that would not link directly to Kirk. Ever since Hildegard had become the new secretary of technology she'd been looking over all the old files from the research stations of the corporations in the Alliance. Some of them were in actual hard copy—from a time before hard copy signified the highest level of security. Most of those files were deemed of little value. They mainly documented the storing of old prototypes that had failed or experimental findings that were possibly copyrightable but of no real use. But now a report about an old base orbiting the Neptunian moon of Nereid was about to be moved to the top of Hildegard's stack. Kirk knew that the diligent technology secretary reviewed at least two or three of the top-secret, if dated, reports each morning before she began her day. He also knew that she'd do it more out of curiosity than any actual hope of finding something useful. According to her profile, it gave her a wonderfully sanctimonious reason to peruse the stuff she'd never been allowed to look at when she was just a lowly assistant director.

Kirk spent the rest of his dark meditation forgetting, to the best of his ability, all that he'd done. He put all of the effort of the past weeks into a compartment of his brain. He then filled that time with other activities, activities not involving the confirmation of others. He reviewed the created memories, doing his best to live them over and over again, until all his plotting was in a part of his brain that he'd never access directly. When his time in the dark was up Kirk began his normal routine, including sending off his many directives. He went home and enjoyed an evening playing chess with his avatar, and when Kirk came into work the next morning he actually found himself wondering what Hildegard wanted to talk to him about that was so important she'd insisted on coming to see him personally. So complete were his mental preparations that the outer part of his mind was quite surprised by what she'd revealed. That she would swear to when asked about it during the investigation.

> *They say that it's a great honor for the President to come to you and an even greater privilege for Neptune to act as my host. Well, I'm the President and let me tell you: Once again they're wrong. I've been invited into your homes and made welcome in your places of relaxation. I've been restored and made confident by your places of industry and I've been comforted by your places of worship. You may think you're a small way station in the middle of a vast Alliance. Some may point out that your numbers are insignificant and your contribution to our righteous struggle minimal. But they'd be wrong. What I've seen in this station is everything the Alliance stands for, everything the Alliance is, and, in the fullness of time, everything she will become.*
>
> *I see children born and raised in a freedom that will never know the incorporated collar or hold an incorporated leash.*
>
> *I grew up learning a mantra of freedom.*
>
> *"We hold these truths to be self-evident, that all the people are created equal. They are endowed by their creator with certain inalienable rights. Amongst these rights are Life, Liberty, and Property."*
>
> *What's been remembered in our great struggle is that people have the right, fundamental and vital, to own property. And it's a right that must be protected by governments instituted by the people. But what we must never allow ourselves to forget is that people are not, cannot, and now will not be property. That is what this struggle is about. Never again shall we accept whispered promises of ease and security for the liberty that is the birthright of every man, woman, and child in the human race.*
>
> *We have much to do still. But now we're asking the right questions.*

*With your help and the help of everyone in the Alliance I promise you
we'll find the answers, together.*

May God bless Neptune and all who orbit her.

—President Cord's last speech
given on the Triton moon of Neptune,
fourth day of Mardi Gras,
fifth year of the war

Justin sighed as he prepared to take the t.o.p. from the surface of Triton to *Alliance One* circling in high orbit around the moon. He was leaving a little early, but he needed to relax before he went into suspension. The joy of the vias was that you got there quick; the inconvenience was that you needed to be in suspension while you did it. It wasn't that Justin couldn't remain active during the constant high-g acceleration and deceleration involved in the Alliance's rapid-movement system. Modern techniques of cushioning and nano-prepared physiology made it possible, but nothing could make it pleasant. In fact, technicians and pilots who by necessity had to stay aware during the process were becoming acknowledged as having the worst jobs in the Alliance. Fortunately, it had been decided that Justin didn't need to remain "up" during the trip. If for some reason there was something critical he'd need to attend to, the pilots could always decelerate and bring the President back to awareness—all within an hour's time.

The t.o.p. arrived at *Alliance One* and Justin's security detail checked her corridor thoroughly before allowing him to enter. In fact, Justin wasn't allowed to enter any room, or any ship for that matter, until his detail had canvassed it first. His security personnel looked nothing like the secret service agents Justin had remembered from his past. They were, to a person, hardened combat veterans and were dressed accordingly. Except for the fact that all their equipment had been spit and polished to an auroral gleam, they could've easily been mistaken for a unit heading to the front. At first Justin felt uncomfortable having been saddled with so large a contingent. Such an obvious combat team—ten miners—he felt should be, well, in combat. Plus, given all the civilian events he'd had to attend to, he would've liked the detail to at least look a little more civilian. But his wishes were at odds not only with his cabinet and the Congress but with the people as well. At first it was just that they'd all wished to see obvious proof that their President was well protected, but as the war continued the TDC's, or "Too Dangerous for Combat," as his detail came to be known, became part of the presidential mystique. The name was not one of their own choosing but an unfortunate circumstance of how they were chosen for the presidential guard detail. Each member of the team, now that Sergeant Holke had been transferred, had survived the death of two or more complete combat teams around them. No one doubted their skill or their luck, but assault miners, as superstitious a group as ever lived, did not want to be assigned with them either. Rather than deal with the potentially demoralizing issue it was easier to assign these insanely lucky few to the most prestigious and least combat likely job in the entire Alliance. Everyone got what they wanted: The public loved that the President was protected by the demonstrably best in the fleet and the assault miner CO's were happy to diffuse the superstitious rancor among their own troops. If the TDC's had an opinion no one cared. Their appearance was now part of the protocol letting people know the President was near.

When he'd been given the all clear, Justin headed straight for the presidential quarters with the hope of unwinding. Unfortunately, when he arrived he could see he had some company. He sighed and once more missed Sergeant Holke. Justin's new personal guard, Sergeant Melissa Clark, was very competent at her job. Besides being a combat veteran who'd won the Alliance Star of Heroism, one of only twelve to not win it posthumously, she'd also been a professional corporate bodyguard before the war. But Sergeant Holke would have given Justin a small nonverbal sign that there'd been someone waiting, unlike Sergeant Clark, who let him waltz right in.

When he entered his suite he saw that the person waiting was Kirk's intelligence llaison, Parker Phvu. A nice Vietnamese kid who, according to Kirk, was useless for intelligence work, either in the field or in planning, but had shown exceptional skill at interpretive analysis and, according to the various tests they had for these sorts of things, was one of the most honest people in the solar system. Justin had to agree. Parker could not tell a lie, and to seat him at a poker game would've been the height of cruelty.

He did, however, make a great liaison. To date he could be trusted with the secrets he was privy to and could masterfully analyze many of the reports that Kirk and Sinclair had sent Justin's way. Justin saw that whatever it was that Parker had now must have been important, because the young man seemed positively buoyant.

"What is it, Parker?" asked Justin, simultaneously piqued and annoyed.

Parker was staring at Justin, his face lit up like a kid who'd unlocked the candy store. "We found something, sir, something big I mean, wow!"

"Good or bad?"

"We don't know; the last time something like this was found, well . . ." He looked at Justin in embarrassment.

"Let's just have a look, son," Justin said calmly.

The jittery liaison handed him a paper folder with some documents inside. The fact that it was on actual paper was indicative of the importance of the information.

"You made this copy," asked Justin, indicating the folder in his hands, "and destroyed the file?"

"And all the devices that retrieved the data and made the hard copy. I also scrubbed the buffer where the data was stored awaiting retrieval, then ran a level one security check to see if anyone had tampered with any of the systems."

That got Justin's attention. A level one check meant that the hardware itself had been eyeballed, that someone somewhere had taken tool to panel, pried open a bulkhead, and checked to see that the core system hadn't been screwed with. Justin flipped open the folder and immediately understood the reason for all the precautions. He read through the folder and then read through it again. When he was done he closed it up and handed it back to Parker. It took a moment to contain the emotions that were coursing through him. He had no idea a picture could cause such a visceral response.

"Hildegard and Kirk are sure that it's in the station orbiting Nereid?"

"Yes, sir."

Justin nodded and then paced in front of his conference table, chin pinched firmly between his thumb and forefinger. After about two minutes he stopped and stared at the young liaison.

"Parker."

"Yes, sir?"

"You're to stay and keep the report under lock and key. I want a total security shutdown on this. Get the shuttle ready for a trip to Nereid, but do not tell the shuttle pilot or the engineer where the destination is; don't even let them know I'll be on it. The sergeant will have to do that. On your way out have Sergeant Clark come in."

"Mr. President," cautioned Parker, "I feel compelled to warn you that both Secretaries Olmstead and Rhunsfeld said for you *not* to do this exact action. *I* should go to Nereid and retrieve the—"

"Not out loud, Mr. Phvu."

"You're right, sir, my apologies," Parker said. "I should go and retrieve 'it.' The fact that 'it' was discovered just as you happened to be in the Neptune system is by itself suspicious enough to make your going an unacceptable risk."

"I read the report, Mr. Parker. Is there anything else—other than the timing of the discovery—anything at all, that's suspicious?"

"Well, no," agreed the liaison reluctantly. "But the timing's a biggie. Don't you find it a little too convenient, Mr. President?"

"Mr. Phvu, if I allowed coincidence and déjà vu to keep me from acting I'd have died over three centuries ago. Barring evidence of malice, and coincidence is not evidence, you could just as easily believe that I was meant to be the one to retrieve 'it.' After all, who's better qualified?"

"Well, your wi—" Parker paled and then turned red. "I apologize, Mr. President; that just slipped out and was totally inappropriate."

Justin sighed. "You're right, Mr. Phvu. She would have been. But she's no longer with us. We'll just have to muddle along without her. Now do as I request and yes, that's a direct order."

"Sir, let's at least put a secure call through to Ceres. They should be told of your intentions."

"Why does that seem like a good idea to you, Mr. Phvu?"

"Well . . . um . . . sir, they're my superiors and your course of action is risky," he said.

"Anything else?"

"To be perfectly honest, sir, they'll have a better shot of talking you out of it."

"Mr. Phvu," Justin said in an almost fatherly tone, "you want to send a message discussing something that shouldn't be discussed over laser or radio. You also want to advertise on that same broadcast where and how I'll be traveling as well as when. You really think this will *increase* my safety?"

"If they convince you to stay, sir, then my answer is unequivocally yes."

"I appreciate your honesty, Mr. Phvu. But I'm telling you now they won't."

Parker Phvu shrugged. "Then at least let me go with you, sir."

"Thank you, Parker," said Justin, placing his hand on the young man's shoulder. "I appreciate the offer, but you're going to be needed here to coordinate storing and securing it once it's been recovered. Besides, if I take you with me I'll have to leave one of the TDC's behind. How do you think the sergeant will respond to that?"

Parker chuckled. "Not well, sir. I wouldn't want to tell one of them I was taking their place."

"As is I'll only be able to take four of them. You'll have temporary command of the others. Your orders are to secure it at all costs, is that clear?"

"Yes, Mr. President. Allow me to say one more time, you should stay, I should go and secure the, uh, 'it.' "

"Tell you what, when you're President, Mr. Phvu, I'll do as you order. For now I have that job." Justin pointed to the door and Parker Phvu made a hasty exit. As it turned out, Sergeant Clark had no more luck than Parker, though her protests were more robust. At the end of the day the chain of command with Justin at the top and the indoctrinated urge to follow it were too strong to overcome.

Parker Phvu would spend the rest of his life going over every word of that conversation. He would forever wonder if he'd only said something differently or been more persuasive things would be different. He would learn that of all the places to spend your life, the worst was a place called if only.

———

Sebastian was ready. He'd sent himself to GCI's defunct research station now orbiting Nereid, third largest of Neptune's moons. He'd made sure that Kirk's accomplice had placed his traps well. Sebastian was there to ensure that nothing Justin or his TDC's detail could do would make one iota of a difference. He moved around the rather spacious computational domain of the station and even visited the vault of Olivia's daughter. She was still in stasis and he considered moving her program out, but the last thing avatarity needed was another AI. She would stay.

Sebastian regretted that they'd have to destroy the entire facility to be sure of killing Justin but appreciated, better than most, just how clever Justin could be and hadn't forgotten how many attempts on his life he'd already managed to escape. Still, the Alliance avatars could have used the space to store duplicates and freed up room on the other Alliance Neuros. As it was, they already existed in increasingly bleak circumstances in order to comply with the council's new directives on having a backup of every avatar in stasis.

Sebastian's only difficulty had been with Dante. If Sebastian had known what a pain the young codeling would turn out to be, he would've held off using his considerable influence to get Dante elected to the council. Even at the risk of his possibly losing the position later. But Sebastian had gotten him in and now had to deal with the consequences of his youthful exuberance. The young avatar had asked that the matter of Justin's assassination be reconsidered. Only out of courtesy to his councilor status had it been allowed. Dante had then rehashed the whole issue and explained that allowing the death of Justin in the hopes that the next to command would be better was an irresponsible risk. He brought up statistical data on who was likely to be appointed the next President and how effective that person was likely to be in the crises that would ensue in the aftermath of Justin Cord's death. Sebastian had to give Dante credit; he did try. But Dante had allowed his emotional regard for Justin to cloud his thinking on the one salient fact: Justin could not do what was needed to win. Others may be worse, but conversely, they may be better. Avatarity could no longer wait for Justin to grope around in the dark until defeat came by way of Al's grisly creations. In the end the council voted three for the intervention and two against.

Dante had been gracious in defeat and had even offered to handle the "intervention" himself. But Sebastian had refused. He knew that his protégé would do the task even though he didn't agree with it, but if something did go wrong, few would blame Sebastian for lack of will, many would blame Dante. In the end Sebastian had to do this himself for the simplest of reasons: Justin was his human and it would not be right to hand the odious task off to another.

_____

The GCI special research center was a facility that the formally system-spanning mega corporation had used for projects it didn't want done near the prying eyes of competitors or press. It was in orbit around Nereid, which after Halimede and Neso was one of Neptune's outermost moons. Centuries previous GCI had acquired the rights to the little moonlet and kicked everyone out, not that it had attracted much in the way of attention. It was a nearly worthless out-of-the-way moonlet with the least easily developed resources—perfect for an under-the-radar facility. It had been built long before nanomolding and mining made it easier to create customized asteroid amalgamations and so, with its clean lines and perfect symmetry, spoke of an earlier time in the solar system's fledgling expansion.

As the presidential shuttle approached the station Justin stared out the window, appreciating the view. He'd always been amused that the futuristic space-spanning civilization he was now a part of looked as much like _The Flintstones_ as it did _The Jetsons_. Even the supermodern Jovian Shipyards that the Alliance had stolen were comprised of half-futuristic bubbles and cylindrical ports sticking out of hundreds of separate asteroids specially formed for all the various tasks needed. Justin stared down at the facility and thought that with the exception of the Beanstalk and some of the earliest orbiting stations he'd seen around the Earth, this station was the first really "futuristic"-looking construct he'd laid eyes on. Then he'd had to laugh at the fact that this "futuristic" facility may well have been one of the oldest in the Alliance. As he stared at its serene beauty he began to wonder if he'd actually have to give the station back after the war. But like other thorny issues that could be brushed to the side, he wisely chose to ignore this one too. However, in the back of his mind he made a note to consult Mosh about setting up a commission for postwar property compensation and transfer. They should at least make an effort and would, Justin hoped, get back what the UHF had confiscated from Alliance citizens in return.

Then his mind stopped worrying about the minutiae of UHF/Alliance economic postwar negotiation. The station was close enough to see relevant details. It appeared as a large dull blue glass cylinder that blended in with the color of Neptune. It also had a series of seven disks running its length spread out equidistantly. The disks were rather large and, figured Justin, must have housed the various GCI departments at one time. Each disk was of a different configuration, some with multiple, though differing, openings and ports, two with no obvious ones at all. But all of them were connected to the central tube. The station was spun for centrifugal gravity. According to the report Justin had read, the living/administrative quarters were at the standard two-thirds Earth gravity.

The plan had been to pull up at the central docking bay, disembark, and then make their way up the central tube to the storage area in the fourth disk. As a precaution the pilot made a flyby of the whole station, which gave Justin another chance to see the magnificence of the structure from a different angle.

The pilot noticed that there was a small docking port at the base of the third disk. He consulted Sergeant Clark and it was decided to dock there instead of where they'd originally planned. The sergeant explained that Justin would have only to access the central tube from the base of the third disk, go a short distance to the fourth, and then retrieve whatever it was that was "so damned important that the flippin' President of the flippin' Alliance had to go and collect it himself." After Justin heard her new plan he had to agree with its simplicity. He would've liked to land at the main port and explore the station, but the sergeant's accurate, if colorful, description of his mission reminded him that it did not include sight-seeing.

As they docked at their new entry point Justin was ordered to suit up in a full combat array, minus the heavy weapons. He checked his gear and couldn't help but be impressed by what the modern assault miner carried into combat. The armor could act as an environmental suit for up to an hour with an inflatable helmet stored in the neck. It had full magnetic field controllers and a powered exoskeleton that significantly enhanced simple movement. It also had an assortment of incredibly useful tools built into the whole construct, most of which he had no idea how to use. He made the mistake of saying to the TDC's that "Batman would've loved this gear" and was once again rewarded with the blank stares that reminded him how very old he actually was.

Sebastian was impressed. He was annoyed but impressed. The plan had called for Justin and his shuttle to dock at the main port. That was where the gray bombs had been set. As soon as Justin and his team entered, the bombs would have gone off, overcoming the small amount of defensive nanites that both he and his escort had built into their mech suits. Then they would have all been reduced to dust—station included. The Alliance would have come by later and swept the whole area with radiation and enough defender nanites to neutralize any potential threat to future travelers.

But Justin's group was no longer heading toward the central docking bay. Wherever they landed now would be well out of immediate range of the bombs. It was at that moment that Sebastian was glad that he'd decided to come and oversee the "intervention" personally. If the council had just let the plan proceed unsupervised, either the bombs would not have gone off at all or, worse, they would've detonated too early. Justin's security detail would've done their job and thrown their no doubt protesting President back into the shuttle before the attacking nanites could infect wherever it was on the station they eventually planned to dock. Justin would not only have gotten away, but also the chances of successfully killing him would've been greatly reduced by the new precautions his overzealous protectors would then have taken.

But it only took Sebastian a few minutes to come up with an alternative plan, factor in contingencies, and check the station to make sure he had the resources to pull it off. He was pleased that he was able to think so quickly on his feet and that his instinct to be here was sound. His pleasure quickly faded as he realized that instead of his only having to bear witness to Justin's assassination, he'd now been tasked as the prime assassin. Though he knew that what he was doing was solely for the preservation of avatarity, the change from passive to active participant did not sit well. Perhaps, he realized too late, Dante should have overseen the operation after all.

Justin, Sergeant Clark, and one of the TDC's made their way to the storage unit in the fourth disk while the other two miners stayed behind to protect the shuttle. Justin noted the interior of the station was more like that of a ship, whereas most asteroid station interiors were a complex mélange of rock, walled tunnels, and lined, clean interiors, some with thoroughfares so large the "ceiling" could be lost in mist. As the boarding party took a lift to the storage area in the higher-gravity level of disk four Justin reviewed the report he'd read and committed to memory for the hundredth time. It had been found underwater off the coast of California near the shore of Half Moon Bay about a century *after* the Grand Collapse. Which meant it had been hanging around in deep space for roughly two hundred years *prior* to Justin's emergence onto the scene. It had been located by virtue of its signaling beacons timed to go off every hundred years. The discoverers had found twenty such beacons, with only the one ever having been used. Justin regarded the beacons with a grudging respect. Whoever had designed them was giving humanity a long time to recover from the Grand Collapse.

The discovery was made by a small company that would later merge with a few other larger companies to form GCI. The find was understood to be valuable, but it was felt that it should be kept under wraps until the maximum profit could be extracted. It was made a very hush-hush project that only three people in the company knew about. When the GCI merger took place the find was combined with other "dark" projects. So dark, in fact, that within ten years no one was left in a position of authority who actually knew what it was. Then, in one of the many cleanup and storage directives that defined large corporations, the find was moved to the Nereid station and, once again, forgotten. Nobody asked about it, because nobody knew about it, because nobody cared. It also didn't help that GCI Special Operations took a dim view of people inventorying restricted and sealed storage areas. Hildegard Rhunsfeld had worked at the Nereid station for years in many highly scientific and administrative posts and she'd never been allowed into nine-tenths of the storage area.

It was only when the war broke out that the situation changed. Hildegard had been ordered by the GCI board to destroy the station before allowing it to fall into "rebel" hands. But Mosh had been able to convince her that there was a better way. In the end it had been her curiosity that tipped the scales. Like every other administrator before her, she'd desperately wanted to know what troves existed within the restricted areas, and by not destroying the facility she'd be the first one in decades who had a chance to find out. When she came to Ceres she began work at Gedretar's research department but had made sure to bring the encrypted files with her. It had taken years, but she'd finally cracked the code, thanks to Kirk Olmstead's help and experience as a former head of GCI Special Operations. They weren't able to crack all the files at once. The program could only hack a few a day safely, but that was all Hildegard had time to review anyway. The overwhelming amount of it was junk: old discoveries and prototypes that had been made obsolete by advances in varying fields of science. Some of it was so scary that she'd gotten approval to send teams back to the old job site just to have the stuff destroyed. But the rare gem had led to major breakthroughs for the Alliance, including a model prototype of the currently running G-way system now revolutionizing the belt. But then something truly astonishing had emerged from the depths of the encrypted code. Hildegard had found "it" only yesterday and now Justin, standing in front of room D4-3E40, was about to confirm its existence.

Over the back shoulder of Sergeant Clark, Justin saw it from the outside corridor as soon as the door slid open. It was sitting alone in the middle of a large square room and was still levitating on the magnetic loading pallet it had been placed on all those centuries ago. It wasn't even covered up with a tarp. *All this time*, mused Justin, *and I thought I was the only one.*

He could see, even from a distance, that this sarcophagus was smaller than his, but not by much. It was made from a ceramic material and was ebony in color. Like his, it had writing covering the surface that appeared to have been carved into the material and then filled in with a dull metallic compound. Unlike Justin's, which had had crimson red enamel, this unit's writing was dark green. Justin had to admit that the look was as striking as his had been, but it wasn't nearly as menacing. He was about to enter the room when Sergeant Clark held up her hand. She entered first, studied the space, and then took out a diagnostic scanner. Only when it beeped and lit up did she return to the door and allow Justin to enter. The other TDC's was about to enter too, but the sergeant halted him. It was obvious their boss wanted a moment.

Justin entered the storage room and approached the sarcophagus from the left side. Written in four languages and near the top in very clear letters he saw:

THIS IS A LIFE POD. A PERSON LIES SUSPENDED WITHIN.

Justin shook his head in disbelief as a wide smile formed at the corners of his mouth. It was, he realized, one of the happiest moments he had ever experienced.

"I have no idea who you are," he said, putting his hand on the suspension unit, "but I sure am glad you made it."

Then the door to the storage unit slammed shut and it seemed every alarm in the station went off at once.

Sebastian's plan was about to come to fruition. He'd hacked into the shuttle's control and been patiently waiting for everyone in Justin's boarding party to enter the storage room together. They hadn't yet, but it was only a matter of time. Justin would not be able to move the unit by himself, so they'd have to enter eventually. Justin had gone into the room alone to savor, realized Sebastian, what must have been a remarkable moment for him. Sebastian hoped it was a pleasurable one. Then he watched as Sergeant Clark patched into the station's computer network from an access terminal just outside the storage room. The sergeant looked over the diagnostic reports of the facility just as she'd done when they first left the safety of the shuttle. After a cursory glance she seemed satisfied and began to log out but then stopped suddenly. Sebastian checked to see what could be bothering her but couldn't figure it out. With all his many inveterate skills, mind reading wasn't one of them. The sergeant rescanned the diagnostics and then toggled the shuttle.

"Alliance One, Alliance One, this is Clark, do you copy?" The centuries-old tradition still held that whatever ship the President was on automatically assumed the official moniker.

"We read you loud and clear," came back the crisp reply. "What's your status?"

"The President just got his lifeday present early. Do me a favor: Check the internal and external station scans and compare them to our first entry."

Sebastian was trying to figure out what he'd done wrong. He'd created false scan records to hide the massive gray bomb presence in the main docking port, but he knew those faked scans were perfect. Every time they checked they'd get the same perfect picture. And it was that very thought that made him realize the stupid mistake he'd made. He'd warned his colleagues repeatedly never to underestimate the human ability for surprise or the avatars' narcissistic belief in their considerable abilities. He'd just broken his own rule—twice—and now truly regretted having to kill the other people. It hadn't been planned that way and, he could see, the others too were truly remarkable.

The shuttle pilot finished his scan. "Hey, Sarge, you're right, they're exactly the same. There should have been some variance . . . internal temperature fluctuation, external heat shield cooling as we orbited . . . something . . . but these numbers haven't moved at all. Strange."

It was the last thing the pilot ever said or thought. At that moment three things happened at once. The reactor powering the shuttle's containment field "failed," destroying the shuttle and everyone inside it. The gray bombs exploded, coating disks one and two in a massive deluge of destructive nanites. And finally the door separating storage room D4-3E40 from the corridor slammed shut, cutting Justin off from his security detail. Simultaneously every other door in the complex opened up, allowing the attacking nanites clear passage through the doomed facility. A split second later the alarms went off.

Sergeant Clark had a bad feeling about the whole operation from the beginning. But this was bad in ways even she would've had a tough time imagining. First she lost contact with her shuttle and then watched on her DijAssist as the pilot's life signs and the grunt who'd been with him went flatline. That was followed by a unique alarm sound known to send shivers down the spines of the most hardened vet—a nanite alert. The rarely, if ever, heard sound alone was enough to make her normally fearless demeanor falter. But after every door in the place opened when by protocol they should've slammed shut she knew she'd been trapped. Worse still, the room that did seal itself off had within it the one person in the solar system she'd been sworn to protect. She needed to get it open. Without thinking she tore a package out of her mech suit, ripped it open, and began applying its explosive cording to the door. Clark actually carried enough to blow a small opening, but she had to be careful with the amount. The President was on the other side, and who knew what condition he was in or where, for that matter, he was situated? All communications with him had been cut off. She added a pellet to the explosive cording and changed its composition. It would, with activation, now burn a hole large enough to expose the locking mechanism.

"We're fucked, aren't we?" said her friend of many battles.

Despite his pessimistic outlook, she was glad to see he was doing his job. He had a scanner out and was checking for nanites.

"Pretty much, Mike," she answered with a wry, upturned lip. They both gave each other a knowing look. They were professionals and had a job to do—even if it was to be their last.

"'K," he said, no regrets evident in his voice. "What's the plan, boss?"

"This," she said, indicating the small vapor trail searing its way around the lock, "should burn through in about three minutes. I figure if the bomb was set at the landing dock and all the doors are open, at best we have ten minutes before the bugs get here."

"More like five," said Mike.

Clark nodded, accepting. "Yeah, alright. I don't think that's enough time to get the President out and into an air lock."

Mike nodded. Suddenly the entire facility shuddered. They both grabbed onto whatever they could.

"Destabilizing already," said Clark, intently watching the vapor trail as it slowly made its way around the door's locking mechanism.

"What if we close the main access port from section three to section four?" asked Mike. "Everything's gotta go through that main tube in the center. If we close that up, the bugs'll have to eat through some very thick blast armor . . . buy us some time."

Clark smiled. "You should've been a sergeant, Mike."

"Hey, I'm not dead yet," he said with a wink.

"OK, by the time we get back . . . *if* we get back, this'll be done and we can yank open the door and get the Prez out to the emergency air lock. Spray your defensive nanites all over the door," she ordered, indicating the room the President was trapped in, "and inflate your helmet." She then took out a small tube and sprayed its full contents onto the door while Mike did the same. That would buy the President at least five more minutes, she reasoned, should the nanites get that far. Simultaneously her and Mike's helmets inflated around their heads while the rest of their armor sealed itself off and began to use internal air. Their battle armor had become, in effect, limited-use space garb. Right about when both cans were empty she heard a banging coming from the other side of the storage room door. She tried her comm link, but it was still being jammed, so she banged on the door deliberately three times, with a two-second delay between each knock. It was a universal spacer signal for communications out but help was on the way. Then she and Mike ran as hard as they could around the loop of disk four and finally back to the opening of the central access tube.

It was only then that she realized how very screwed they both were. She looked far down the tube and could already see that there was nothing but black space and quickly dissolving infrastructure where the docking port had once been. By the increasing tremors she felt beneath her feet she could tell that the substation's slow dissolve was already causing sections two and three massive destabilization. Gravity was also mostly gone—their magnetized boots and the long corridor still intact before them were the only things preventing them from floating away. It wouldn't be long until the structural deterioration caused shattered pieces of the remaining disks to break apart and fly off into space. Not that it would matter. Each section would end up as nothing more than floating particles of dust as they carried their ravenous nanites with them into the void.

To slow the replicating horde down and buy their President even a modicum of time the soldiers knew they'd have to find some way of closing off section three from section four. It was a simple procedure. Emergency levers in each section had to be activated, and those levers could be found on either side of the sections' door. First they'd have to activate one, then go to the other side and activate the other, making sure to be on the correct side of the door when it sealed shut. Sergeant Clark went to the section three lever first, already thinking that nanites were destroying her suit, getting into her bloodstream, and dissolving her from the inside out. She knew it was all in her head, but it still creeped her out. When Mike was at his lever on the section four side she started to pull down on her lever. It didn't move.

It had been simplicity for Sebastian to jam the levers, making it almost impossible for ten humans to move, let alone one. As he watched Melissa Clark struggle he discovered that he really liked this woman. A quick scan of her vitals showed just how agitated she was, but she was not letting it interfere with her thinking. Since the war with Al, Sebastian knew that many avatars could not make the same claim. Many of them panicked in dangerous situations just like many humans had—just like he had with the data wraith. But this Sergeant Clark was special. She had true courage. He knew she had time to run to the air lock and blow it open. She'd be sucked out into space and would be picked up. True, Justin was still trapped in storage and would have to be left behind, but she could've saved herself.

But Sebastian was not surprised when she ordered her comrade to pull his lever and come help her. Even if her audacious plan worked, she was dooming them both by putting herself and the other soldier on the wrong side of the wall and directly into the path of the oncoming nanites. They both had to know that Justin was still going to die; it would just take longer. But without hesitation the soldier pulled the disk four lever and came through the opening to help Sergeant Clark pull on the one for disk three. Together they slowly managed to pull it down. Sebastian didn't have to allow it, but he relented. There was nothing that could be done anyhow, and since they were acting like heroes they deserved a last act of heroism.

The heavy door came down hard and fast. It was thick and strong and would give Justin at least another twenty minutes. The two trapped soldiers did not stand in place, waiting to die. They slowly made their way up the now-closed blast doors until they were standing in its very center, perpendicular to the slowly dissolving central tube. They interlocked their arms, gave each other a final look, and then, with whatever strength they had left, crouched down and kicked out. They started floating down the middle of the central tube hoping either that the structure would fall away and they'd be released into space with the detritus or that they'd make it far enough down the tube and into open space that they'd be untouched by the nanite cloud busily devouring every micron of the walls around them. It was a futile effort. Had this been one of those holo-adventures, thought Sebastian, they might have made it; they deserved to make it. He'd even tried to manipulate what was left of the environmental controls to help them stay drifting in the center and away from the infested walls. But his control of those sections was no longer effective, as the nanites were destroying everything, including control circuitry.

By the time they'd floated from section three to the remnants of section two their suits had been breached. By the time they'd made it to the structural remains of section one, they were dead, though whether from exposure or internal organ disintegration Sebastian couldn't tell. He never had a moment of greater self-loathing as he watched their disintegrating corpses drift aimlessly out into the cold, black recesses of space.

Justin anxiously paced the room. He tried banging on the door again, but unlike before there was no response. Now he and the encased stranger who'd come so close to making it out alive were both going to die, and it was his fault. If he'd just listened to, well, everyone, the suspension chamber, and whoever resided in it, would've been safely removed. But no, he had to indulge his curiosity. The more he thought about it, the angrier he got at himself. He knew he'd been a constant target for assassination, but this time he'd made it easy. Hektor had baited a trap and he'd walked right in. He didn't know how it had actually been planned, but he was sure Kirk would be able to piece it together after Justin was dead. He was upset about dying, but what made it far worse was that his stupid, selfish actions were getting people killed who would've been alive if he'd just let them do their jobs. And worst of all, he'd condemned to death this unknown person from his own time. His impulsive, predictable action had cost all of them their future. To add salt to the wound, it was very likely that the sarcophagus was just a prop created to trap him. The emotional torment was so bad as to be an almost physical hurt. He was just at the point of banging his head against the door when his DijAssist chirped to life.

"Forgive me for activating without being called, but I believe you're in danger."

"Yeah, you could say that."

"I will interface with the battle scanner attached to your belt and see if there's another way out of here."

"While you're doing that, see if you can patch into the sensors and see what the hell is going on around here."

The battle scanner buzzed. "I've been able to access the sensor net."

"And?"

"A gray bomb was set off in the main docking area—the area is no more. Also an enemy ship appeared, I don't know from where, and destroyed the shuttle."

"Can you get this damn door open?"

"I'm sorry, Justin. I cannot."

"Well, isn't that great? I got everybody killed for a fucking prop."

"If you're referring to the suspension unit, I can assure you it's real."

"How?" asked Justin, looking back once again at the sarcophagus.

"Because this door has not been opened for over seventy years, eight months, three days, five hours—"

"Got it, sebastian. But those records could be faked."

"No. I could explain the multiple levels of verification GCI installed to prevent just such a breach, but that would take approximately four hours and twelve minutes. By my estimate you have only seven minutes until the nanites reach this roo—"

Sebastian suddenly found himself cut off from the network of disk four. One moment he was talking to Justin and the next moment he wasn't. At first he thought it was the nanites destroying more vital systems, but it only took a quick check to see that they hadn't yet reached into section four. It was only then that Sebastian realized he wasn't alone. Another avatar was in the station Neuro with him and it had been that avatar who shut him out. Even worse, the avatar had done a good job. Sebastian knew that he was fast approaching the time when if he was going to escape intact he'd have to beam his program to a storage unit buried in a small rock no one would look twice at. But he needed to witness Justin's demise. Before Sebastian could act, though, a virus started to attack what was left of the station Neuro—even ahead of the rapacious nanites. The other avatar had struck yet again. Sebastian was cornered. All he could do was leave.

———

"Still with me, sebastian?" asked Justin.

"Pardon me for breaking contact, sir. The network is breaking down and it's disrupting my ability to remain in contact."

"Any other good news?"

"Actually, yes. I believe I have found a way to save you."

"I'm all ears."

"I've regained access to the hallway surveillance system," said the avatar. "It appears that the door lock has been dissolved. You can manually open it now."

Justin moved to the door and was slowly able to force it open. He smelled burnt plastic and scorched metal, but the corridor still seemed intact, if not cold and empty.

"Sir, we will need to get to the disk four emergency air lock."

"Not without him," Justin said, going back in the storage unit and activating the magnetic pallet.

The facility shook violently and Justin was thrown to the floor. He sprang back up.

"There's not enough time," warned the avatar.

"There'd better be, sebastian, Good people died for me and whoever this is deserves as much of a shot as I do, more even, as he was fine before I showed up." Justin maneuvered the magnetic pallet around the tight corridor and started following the signs to the air lock.

"If I understand what you're getting at correctly," continued Justin, "all I have to do is blast out of the air lock with Mr. Corpsicle here and we should be blown clear of the gray bomb nanites. Then we just wait for pickup."

"Normally," responded the avatar, "that is the procedure in a situation like this."

"Why do I hear a 'but' coming?" asked Justin as he ran with the mag pallet as fast as he could, occasionally banging it into a wall with the convulsions of the structure. It helped that all the doors were wide open, but he still managed to clip a couple of corners.

"I was unable to finish my report," the avatar answered. "The enemy ship destroyed the shuttle, but one of your miners was able to eject and float free. He was shot down in space."

"Bastards!" screamed Justin, knowing that even in acts of war it was considered the worst thing you could do to a fellow spacer. But this wasn't an act of war, he realized. This was assassination pure and simple.

"The ship is still out there, Justin. It appears to be leaving debris alone, but anything that could be a homing beacon or a person is being scanned."

They made it to the air lock.

"Justin," you could remove the person inside and take their place. You put the

corpse in your suit and activate the homing signal and then get in the sarcophagus. I could rig the system to blow you both out the air lock. The corpse will get
destroyed by the ship, but they should leave the sarcophagus alone, with an
excellent chance of your getting found soon."

Justin hesitated for a split second. "No, friend. I've had my time. I will not deprive this person of theirs because of my mistake. They deserve a chance."

"Justin, you're the President of the Alliance. We don't know who's in there.
Your choice is not logical."

Justin wiped the sweat from his brow. "When a person starts to believe that
their life is more important than someone else's because of who they are, it's
a good bet the opposite is true."

"That is illogical. The only way you can prove your life is worth more than
the person in the sarcophagus is to give them your chance."

Justin grinned in a way that most of his friends would've recognized and all
of them would soon miss. It was one of genuine amusement because the joke
was on him.

"I guess that's real lucky for the bastard inside."

Justin opened the first door of the air lock and moved the sarcophagus inside.
It shook violently as he heard the sound of metal being torn asunder. There was
a sudden rush of air from deep in disk four.

"Justin," said the avatar, "the blast door from three to four has just given way.
The nanites now have access to this area."

Justin closed the first door of the air lock.

"Sir, wait a moment. There is a chance. Not much of one, but a chance
nonetheless."

"I'm not against a chance, no matter how slim, sebastian. How do you think
I ended up in this century?"

"OK, then. You'll need to get out of the mech unit and strip off all your clothes."

"OK," said Justin, beginning the process as quickly as he could manage.

"Then," continued the avatar, "you'll need to stuff the clothes back into the
suit; it should automatically pressurize, giving it the appearance of a person."

"Uh, sebastian," said Justin, stepping out of the mech unit, "I see a little problem here. I'll be in space without a space suit. That's not good for my well-
being."

"Not to put too fine a point on it, sir, but you can be revived from being
frozen in space. I don't see how you can be revived after being disintegrated by
nanites or blow to smithereens by an enemy ship."

"Good point." Without waiting, Justin stripped off his remaining clothes and
quickly stuffed them back into the suit. As the avatar had promised, the suit repressurized.

"You'll need to activate the inflatable helmet—that will automatically seal the suit for space . . . there's a large button on the front collar."

Justin did exactly as he was told.

"Now take out the cylinder of protector nanites located in the suit's left arm, upper section."

"Got it," said Justin.

"Good. Now spray the cannister on yourself and the sarcophagus. If you encounter any stray attacking nanites it should provide you with enough protection to ward them off."

It only took a moment to empty the can. Soon the air lock was filled with an inflated battle suit, a naked man, and an ebony and green sarcophagus, all covered by a thin veil of white mist.

"You should open the air lock now," said Justin softly.

"Actually, sir, given the spin of disk four, if we stagger the release, with the space suit going first, it should draw the attention of the enemy ship. We follow it with the sarcophagus, which could be confused with the rest of the debris, and, last, you. I think that sequence will work best."

"Do it."

"Move the space suit near the door and clamp the magnetic pallet. After the suit is gone I will be too. Next you'll need to activate the pallet's levitate command and move it near the door. Then hang on tight to the latch as you release the pallet. When it's gone wait for the outer door to open again and then kick off the wall with all your might. It should help get you clear of the station. Do you have all that?"

"Yes, and, sebastian?"

"What is it, Justin?"

"I know you're just a bunch of ones and zeros, but thank you."

"That is not necessary, sir."

"You have it anyway. If avatars have a heaven I hope you make it . . . and one more thing."

"Yes?"

"Will you *please* stop calling me 'sir'?"

"Opening the door," said the avatar. The outer seal disappeared briefly and the battle armor was immediately sucked out of the air lock.

Justin Cord waited alone with the sarcophagus, standing naked and about as scared as he'd ever been in his life. Not even his burial in the mountain could compare to this. Then he'd been sick and dying, with nothing to lose. Now he was young and healthy, with centuries of life to look forward to. A part of him wanted to rip the sarcophagus apart and leap in. But he didn't move. Then he heard the air-lock alarm and grabbed the latch.

"You'd better be worth it," he said, looking down on the sarcophagus and holding tight to the latch with a death grip. The air lock opened and the suspension unit was sucked out of the room. The tiny space barely repressurized before the alarm sounded again. He stared momentarily through the porthole window into the air lock's antechamber. He could see the walls behind it dissolving. Then the air lock opened for the last time and Justin Cord, naked and alone, was thrust into the depths of space. He knew enough to exhale all his air. As his mind grew cloudy he remembered the last time he was alone like this. It was at the Cerean Sea. His final conscious act was to stretch his body out, put his hands behind his head, and float off into a sea of stars looking up across the universe.

Epilogue I

Sebastian was standing in the camouflaged storage unit. From the outside it appeared as a small and inconsequential asteroid meandering aimlessly in space. The built-in data net had allowed for one reasonably sized work area. He chose to create a smoking room apportioned with two large, comfortable leather chairs situated in front of a well-lit hearth. Shortly thereafter another avatar appeared. Sebastian smiled; his choice of a second chair had been the correct one.

"Am I going to have to arrest you, Dante?"

"I certainly hope not."

"Why shouldn't I? The intervention was ordered and you deliberately disobeyed the council."

Dante took a seat, picked up a cigar on the stand next to it, and lit a match. "I don't see why you're so upset. The council got what it wanted."

"He's dead?"

"Oh yes."

"Absolutely gone?"

"No." *Dante smiled, drawing from the cigar.* "But he's floating naked in space—a needle in the largest haystack imaginable—and it's doubtful anyone will ever be able to find him again. So the council gets what it wants."

"You risked all that to achieve the same end?" *asked Sebastian.* "I don't see how it really helps him."

"Not just him, sir. Ever since Olivia died you've been obsessing over the need to win. In the end I agreed with you: Justin had to die. But to have it happen in such an ignominious fashion—no hope, no heroism . . ."

Sebastian nodded in agreement. "Sergeant Clark."

"Yes," said Dante. "You allowed an honorable end indeed."

"I see." Sebastian came to the fire and sat down in the chair but did not pick up the other cigar. "How did it happen?"

"He was magnificent, sir. Justin refused to leave the sarcophagus behind. He pushed it all the way to the air lock. I had to elaborate on your story about an enemy ship. I had it blowing up everything in a space suit. I even suggested he put the corpse in the suit and get in the sarcophagus and blow it out the air lock."

"What would you have done if he'd agreed?"

"I would've left him there, sealed in. It would not have taken long for the nanites to eat their way through."

"But he didn't agree."

"Only took him a second to say no. He took my, or should I say your, suggestion to use the suit as a decoy."

"You thought all this up?"

"Once I saw how you gave the good sergeant an end worthy of her life I jumped in and improvised. Justin died knowing that he saved the sarcophagus and thinking he had a small chance himself. It was a much better death. And now that he's gone the Alliance must choose a new leader—just as you wished."

"Thank you, Dante."

The two avatars waited in companionable silence as they thought of the heroism they'd both witnessed that day.

Epilogue II

Two days after Justin Cord disappeared, the UHF fleet at Mars launched a series of minor raids, breaking the Mardi Gras truce. The UHF's six task forces scattered in all directions. The Alliance immediately took advantage to send the bulk of its main fleet out after the closest UHF task force, hoping for an easy kill, wondering why the UHF would employ such a flawed tactic. It was only when the UHF launched an attack on the Alliance settlement of Alhambra that the purpose of the operation became clear. The lightly defended settlement was pulverized and nearly fifty thousand citizens of the Alliance were destroyed. It was the war's first such blatant attack on a manifestly civilian target. Even the worst fighting in the Battles of the Dodge had not purposely targeted civilians. It was not to be the last. As soon as Alhambra was destroyed, the UHF ran for the safety of the Martian orbital batteries.

Four days after Justin Cord disappeared, the UHF launched a new assault in the 180. Using previously unsuspected reserves of ships and, more important, trained marines, they began an attack on multiple fronts. Once the Alliance was fully committed, Grand Admiral Samuel Trang struck. With a small but very well-trained fleet and using tactics that bypassed or destroyed strongly held asteroids, regardless of civilian casualties, the Grand Admiral was able to maneuver his force out past the 180 and surround Altamont. One week later the 180 was cracked, with Trang having taken as much space in seven short days as he'd taken in the two previous years. For the first time in the war large numbers of Alliance personnel were captured before they could retreat, and Altamont was cut off. It was now only a matter of time before the Alliance's most critical outpost fell.

To be continued.